Song of *Erin*

BJ HOFF

HARVEST HOUSE PUBLISHERS

EUGENE, OREGON

Cover by Koechel Peterson & Associates, Inc., Minneapolis, Minnesota

Cover photos © Keith Nolan / Fotolia.com; Koechel Peterson & Associates

BJ Hoff: Published in assoication with the Books & Such Literary Agency, 52 Mission Circle, Suite 122, PMB 170, Santa Rosa, CA 95409-5370, www.booksandsuch.biz.

SONG OF ERIN
Copyright © 1997/1999 by BJ Hoff
Published by Harvest House Publishers
Eugene, Oregon 97402
www.harvesthousepublishers.com

Library of Congress Cataloging-in-Publication Data

Hoff, B. J.
    [Cloth of heaven]
    Song of Erin / B.J. Hoff.
        p. cm.
    ISBN-13: 978-0-7369-2352-1
    ISBN-10: 0-7369-2352-7
    1. Irish Americans—Fiction. 2. New York (N.Y.)—Fiction. I. Hoff, B. J., Ashes and lace. II. Title. III. Title: Ashes and lace.
    PS3558.O34395C57 2008
    813'.54—dc22

                                                                                2007044409

Printed in the United States of America

        08 09 10 11 12 13 14 15 16 / LB-NI / 10 9 8 7 6 5 4 3 2 1

Book One

Cloth of *Heaven*

PART ONE
THE BIG WIND

❧

And a mighty windstorm hit the mountain. It was such a terrible blast that the rocks were torn loose, but the Lord was not in the wind. After the wind there was an earthquake, but the Lord was not in the earthquake. And after the earthquake there was a fire, but the Lord was not in the fire. And after the fire there was the sound of a gentle whisper.

1 Kings 19:11-12

THE SILENCE

Deadly still was the heavy air,
Horrible silence was everywhere...

THOMAS D'ARCY MCGEE

IRELAND, JANUARY 6, 1839

On this day in Ireland there were those who searched the sky with anxious frowns, as if they half expected to see an omen or perhaps a hint of some dark, unnatural force lurking behind the clouds. The warm stillness of the winter day was unnerving, no matter how welcome a change from the bitter cold.

Epiphany Sunday had dawned upon a hushed world of white, blanketed by the heavy snowfall of the night before. By afternoon, the day had warmed to unthinkably mild temperatures. Men stood at the crossroads in their shirtsleeves, making conjectures about the odd weather and what, if anything, it might forebode.

The women across the island had no time for such speculation. Instead, they busied themselves throughout the afternoon preparing what few savory dishes they could manage, given their meager budgets. Cottages grew steamy from hours of baking, and children turned more restive by the hour in anticipation of the coming evening. If entire villages seemed to hum with excitement, it was to be expected, for festive occasions were all too rare in the Irish countryside. Of late, the sound of the funeral dirge had become far more familiar than the lively tunes of merrymaking.

On this day, even in the most remote and primitive counties, every warm moment seemed a gift, a respite from winter's gloom and the general climate of dread that had long clutched at the very heart of Ireland. For a few hours this evening, those families fortunate enough to still have a roof above their heads would gather around the hearth fire and enjoy their blessings, blessings all the more precious for their scarcity. Tonight, at least, Irishmen would lay aside their worries about rising rents and unnerving tales of eviction while their women donned brave smiles and bright colors as they, too, attempted to forget their fears. There would be laughter and songs and prayers for God's keeping, and at the heart of it all, the deep music of living—a music created from centuries of sorrow, a longing for freedom—and hope.

Yet there were some whose hope rested not in the evening's lighthearted festivities nor in the ancient land of their birth—nor even in the God of their fathers or in the faith that had sustained their families for ages past. Instead, their hope clung solely to the idea of escape.

These were not always the ones who spoke most often of leaving the "poor old island" behind. They did not necessarily shudder by the fire at the thought of forsaking home and country for a harrowing voyage across the sea in search of a better life. More often they *had* no homes or at least knew the threat of eviction upon the daily horizon, and they shuddered more from the reality of winter's cold and encroaching starvation than from any fear of crossing the great Atlantic.

For these, escape had become their hope. For many, it was their *only* hope.

I

TERESE

But the haunted air of twilight is very strange and still,
And the little winds of twilight are dearer to my mind.

EVA GORE-BOOTH

INISHMORE, ONE OF THE ARAN ISLANDS IN WESTERN IRELAND

Terese Sheridan stood in the hulking shadow of Dun Aengus, watching night gather over the ocean. The day had been warm, unnaturally warm, and so close that the flame of a candle wouldn't have flickered. But now a light breeze had picked up and was playing along the stones, while in the distance a random flare of lightning illumined the sky.

The huge stone fort towering overhead had been there forever—since long before the coming of Patrick, according to the Old Ones in the village. With its vast rings of stone walls and what must surely have been thousands of jagged stones placed upright to ward off ancient attacks, it loomed over Inishmore and the island's people like some colossal, magnificent creature risen from the sea, turned to stone by its long centuries of vigil.

In its permanence and hovering immensity, the fort had somehow become to Terese not only a sentry to the entire island but a kind of personal guardian as well. Dun Aengus was the only thing of any real stability in her life. But tonight she was bidding it farewell. She had walked out from her aunt's cottage in the village to say good-bye to the fort and to Inishmore; before first light dawned tomorrow, she would be gone.

She and her best chum, Peggy O'Grady, had been planning their departure from the island for months. Tomorrow they would go. Yet, despite her eagerness to get away, Terese could not entirely ignore the heaviness of heart that had settled over her throughout the evening. There had been many partings in her life—too many by far—and for all the bitterness and sorrow she had known in this place, there were memories here, whispers of her life, of the family she had lost, the all-too-rare times of love and warmth they had known together.

At seventeen, Terese was the only one of her entire family left on this side of the Atlantic. Both her father and her brother, Cavan, had made the crossing to America more than six years ago, leaving behind nothing more than a promise that within a year they would send for the rest of the family to join them.

The streets in America, however, had turned out to be paved not with gold, as was rumored, but with animal droppings instead. The fine jobs that were to have ensured ship passages for the family—and perhaps even a house in the new land—had never materialized. Their father had died less than a year after leaving Ireland, and Cavan had ended up in a place called Pennsylvania, digging coal below the ground with their uncle Tibbot and his sons.

Within a year of her father and brother's leaving, Terese and the rest of the family, unable to keep up the rent, had been evicted. Forced to spend most of the winter living in a rock cave by the shore, baby Mada and Terese's older sister, Honor, had both died of exposure and pneumonia. Within a week of their passing, their mother was also dead, leaving Terese, not quite twelve years old at the time, completely alone.

Ill from the cold and nearly dead from starvation, Terese had gone to beg a bed with her aunt Una in the Field of the Horses, a tired little village close to the sea. The first time she went, her aunt had turned a deaf ear to her plea for shelter. "And how would I be making room for one more mouth to feed?" Aunt Una had asked. "There's no room and no food. You're a fine big girl now. You'll have no trouble finding work to keep yourself."

There had been no work on the starving island, of course. More desperate than ever, Terese had finally swallowed her pride and gone to Aunt Una again. This time, whether out of guilt or some newly remembered trace of family feeling, her aunt had relented, allowing her niece a smelly pallet in the corner where the pig sometimes slept and a cramped place at the table among her five cousins.

Not a day had since passed that her aunt had not reminded Terese of what a burden she was and her incredibly good fortune in having Christian kin willing to give her a roof over her head, and at such a sacrifice to themselves. And not a day passed in the ensuing years that Terese did not burn with resentment as she counted the money that had finally begun to arrive from Cavan, carefully hiding it away with the intention of amassing enough to escape Inishmore and her aunt's "Christian charity."

There had been times during the worst of her loneliness when she wondered if she might have been better off to have died in the cave with her mother and sisters. But she could always rouse herself from the temptation of self-pity with the reminder that there was something better in store—something out there, across the Atlantic, just waiting for her to claim it. She had only to endure her aunt's spitefulness, her uncle's indifference, her cousins' ridicule for a time, not forever. Repeatedly she told herself that she could endure *anything* so long as there was hope for something better.

In truth, Terese had kept herself alive through hope. It was all she had, this fierce hope of hers, the anticipation of a time when she would finally escape the squalid poverty of her existence for that "something better."

Now that time had come. By this hour tomorrow she and Peggy would be in Galway City. From the money Cavan had sent her over the years and her earnings in the kitchen at Corcoran's Inn, Terese had managed to squirrel away almost twice again the amount she customarily handed over for her keeping. At last she had enough for her passage to America. Enough for a new life.

Suddenly, the melancholy that had been pressing in on her throughout the evening lifted, almost as if hope itself had come swooping down and borne it away on the wings of the wind. Terese felt a sense of release, of deliverance, that made her want to shout her impending freedom to the entire island.

At that moment, an unexpected squall of wind came wailing across the shore, followed by a crash of thunder and a stunning display of lightning. The air turned sharply chill, and Terese wished she had worn her coat instead of her cousin Nancy's thin sweater.

She realized it was growing late—surely past eight by now—and with a last glance at the stone fort, she turned to start back toward the village. Without warning, another gust of wind, this one stronger, roared in on her, howling like a banshee over the treacherous stone walls of the fort.

Terese looked to the sky, ink dark and heavy with the threat of rain, then back to the shore, where the tide had risen. Farther out, waves surged and rolled with mounting fury. A storm was blowing in, and with incredible swiftness, it seemed. The wind slapped at her face and shoulders, and she hugged her arms to herself against the cold as she turned to run toward home.

2

BRADY

"I am of Ireland..."

W. B. YEATS

❧

GALWAY CITY, WESTERN IRELAND

After a long day in Galway City, Brady Kane wandered into the district called the Claddagh. He had read about the place, had heard Jack speak of it through the years, but nothing could have prepared him for its strangeness.

He felt as if he had stepped into another world, another age. Here, in this southernmost quarter of the town at the mouth of the harbor, lived a colony of fishermen and their families that time and the world seemed to have forgotten. Everything about the area and its inhabitants spoke of the past. Winding lanes and squares of thatched-roof dwellings, the quaint, colorful clothing of the inhabitants, and their language—Brady had heard more of the Irish spoken today than he had heard during his entire month in Dublin—gave the observer a sense of a people and a culture unchanged for centuries.

He stopped and looked over the bay. A few small boats were in the water—the small, primitive curraghs mostly, and a couple of brown-sailed rigs—but for the most part the harbor was deserted.

The sudden puff of wind blowing in off the water felt good. The day had been surprisingly mild until an hour or so ago, but now the waves were beginning to churn as the breeze picked up, and Brady welcomed the cooler air.

This was his first trip to Ireland, and he had had to fight Jack all the way for it. Brady wasn't sure why his brother was so set against the idea, but he had his suspicions. Somehow he didn't think Jack's opposition had anything to do with the flimsy excuses he'd been mouthing for months—*We're too busy at the paper; I can't possibly spare you, not now...Don't forget I'm going to be in Boston for two or three weeks soon,*

and you'll have to take over for me at the paper and at the publishing house as well...We
have manuscripts coming in, authors to meet with...Then there's all the work at the
Committee...

In the end, it was the Committee that had won it for Brady. He had finally managed to convince Jack that he would be far more effective in helping to raise money
on behalf of Ireland if he could see for himself what the conditions in their homeland
really were, if they had been exaggerated or not. How could he possibly be effective
with the Committee, he had argued to Jack, unless he was acquainted firsthand with
Ireland and its people?

"If the conditions there are really as intolerable as we're told, I'll come back with
the proof to support our work—sketches, paintings, and a full account of the truth.
Come on, Jack," he had pressed. "I need to go, and you know it."

"You *want* to go is more like it," his brother had countered.

"You said yourself we need to establish some European reporters, Jack. Why can't
this be the first step?"

The black scowl eased slightly, and the long Irish sigh that followed told Brady
he had won.

"Two months," Jack finally agreed. "Two months, and not a day longer, mind!"

Brady suspected that Jack's reluctance to grant him leave to Ireland had something
to do with concern that he might end up wanting to *stay* in Ireland. He had to admit
that his brother's instincts were sound. They always were. It had been over a month
now, and Brady seldom thought of home.

It was true that he had squandered much of the time indulging his fascination with
Dublin City, rather than exploring the Irish countryside as Jack expected. The old city
had drawn him in almost immediately, with its gypsylike charm, its heady, almost
intoxicating, variety of sights and sounds, its buildings, and its fine bridges—and its
even finer women.

Ah, the women!

Still, when he hadn't been playing the rake or cultivating all things Irish in
a fevered attempt to rid himself of his more obvious "Americanisms," Brady had
sketched and painted like a madman, often working until dawn. He had also managed to rationalize his preoccupation with Dublin by telling himself that it was
Ireland's principal city, after all, and so it was only reasonable to make a thorough
study of it.

Indeed.

Finally, however, when he had lingered as long as he dared without sabotaging the
rest of his expedition, he left Dublin and headed for Galway, in the west of Ireland. He
had arrived in the city of his birth yesterday but after settling in had been too fatigued
to do any real exploring. Today, though, he had wandered much of the town, making
some interesting sketches of its different quarters and its people in the process.

The wind was whipping up harder now, the spray off the water stinging his face.
Brady turned away and stood studying the small, rough-hewn houses about him,

many already darkened for the night. Every now and then a man would go in or out, occasionally a woman as well. The men seemed a reticent lot, for the most part: dark and taciturn in their old-fashioned breeches and jackets—and those surprising light blue stockings. As for the women—well, he had seen a beauty or two, barefoot, decked in their peculiar short cloaks with red petticoats swirling about bare legs as they darted in and out of the lanes.

He stretched, breathing in the tangy sea air that was laced with the strong, acrid odor of a quayside fish market. It was a curious feeling, standing in this place knowing that his parents or even Jack might have ventured among these peculiar people at one time or another in the past. Perhaps he even had relatives in one of those small thatched houses.

He doubted it. He hadn't seen many Spanish-looking faces since he entered the Claddagh—faces like his own and Jack's, common enough in Galway City. His gaze went to one of the aged Spanish archways off to the left, then back to the nearest dwellings. No, Brady thought it unlikely that there would have been much intermarriage here. These people had remained independent over the centuries, an isolated, exclusive settlement. Why, they were said to even have their own king, who governed them, claimed dominion over the bay for the community, and flew his own personal sail and colors from the masthead of his boat!

Outside the Claddagh, Brady had seen abundant evidence that Galway had once been a busy trading port with Spain. The black Irish—like his own family—could be seen everywhere. He spied more than one black-haired, dark-eyed lovely so exquisitely formed and graceful that she could have served as the ideal artist's model.

Their mother had been raven haired, according to Jack. Brady hadn't known her, of course, nor his father. His mother had died giving birth to him, and his father hadn't lived much longer before being hanged as the result of a midnight raid on a British post, apparently by one of those secret societies. Whiteboys, Thrashers, Ribbonmen—the Irish had boasted countless numbers of them over the years.

Jack had done his best to keep their parents' memory alive as Brady and his sister, Rose, were growing up, and perhaps he had been more successful than he realized. Brady had come to feel an uncommon closeness to the young mother who died giving him life, and to Sean Kane, his doomed father.

Jack had instructed him not to "waste time" in Galway, claiming that there was nothing of any real interest to be found in the "city of the tribes." But for Brady, it was enough that his parents had once lived here, worked here...died here. In some bizarre fashion, that tragic duo had continued, even in death, to play a significant role in what he had become. His fierce, ongoing desire to see the country of his birth; the elemental streak of rebellion that seemed to fire his spirit, no matter how vigorously Jack tried to dampen it; and the unaccountable attachment he held for this small, struggling island and its people—somehow those two shadowy figures of the past were a part of his passion.

Perhaps what accounted for the difference in the way he and Jack felt about the country was the fact that Jack at least had his memories of Ireland—he had been almost fourteen when they emigrated—whereas Brady remembered nothing.

But he was here now, and he intended to see it all. He had gotten himself lost several times during the day, wandering along the narrow, winding streets of the city before ending up here in the Claddagh. He supposed he should be getting back to his room instead of standing here staring out at the sea. The wind had begun to churn up in earnest, and it held the distinct threat of a rainstorm on the way.

Shifting his sketchbook to the other arm, he started off. He had just turned onto one of the narrow lanes leading away from the harbor when a small girl with a merry laugh darted out from between two crude huts, nearly colliding with Brady.

"Whoa!" he cautioned the child, putting out a hand to steady her. She was a wee thing, no more than four or five, surely: barefoot, reed thin, and none too clean. But her eyes danced with lively mischief, and when Brady smiled at her, she laughed in pure delight.

At that instant, another girl—no, not a girl, but more a young woman, he realized after taking a closer glance—emerged from the same dirt path. She, too, wore no shoes, but a bright blue cloak flew about her in the wind, and her kerchief had slipped to reveal a wild mane of black hair.

She turned on the child, firing a stream of what Brady took to be Gaelic invective as she wagged a scolding finger at her charge. It took her another second or two to notice Brady. When she did, her impatience seemed to give way to alarm. Grabbing the little girl's hand, she tugged her close and began to pull her down the lane alongside her.

The wind blew her kerchief free with the movement, and Brady flung out a hand to catch it, returning it to her with a small flourish. Her eyes narrowed—wonderful eyes, enormous in her thin, delicate-featured face—but she gave a grudging nod of thanks.

A blast of wind swept down the lane at that instant, surprising Brady with its force.

The child squealed, but obviously not in alarm—the odd little creature was laughing again!

Her guardian, however, was not amused. Her gaze went to the harbor, and Brady turned to look. There was thunder now, and the peculiar closeness of the day was gone, broken by the wind and an accompanying drop in temperature. Lightning streaked over the water, and the child cried out in glee. The older girl seemed not to notice. Her finely sculpted features had gone taut, and although she spoke not a word, Brady could sense the tension gripping her.

Was she the child's mother? he wondered. She appeared awfully young herself and, like the little one, somewhat peculiar.

As he watched, the older girl ducked and hauled the child up in her arms, though she was obviously too slight for such a burden.

Strangely reluctant to see her leave, Brady put a hand to her arm. "Wait, please."

She looked at his hand, then raised her gaze to his face. Brady actually flinched at the anxious look she turned on him. "Sorry," he said, releasing her. "But I thought you might be able to help me with some directions. Do you speak English?"

The girl made no attempt at a reply, but instead stared at Brady as if he had suddenly grown horns.

He tried again. "English?" he repeated. "Do you understand?"

The wind slammed against his back, nearly knocking him into her. The girl froze, her gaze going to something over Brady's shoulder, and the raw fear he saw in her eyes caused a sudden burst of panic to spiral up in him. He whipped around and saw for himself the dizzying charge of lightning hurtling across the bay, as if a heavy arm from heaven had unleashed an assault of fiery arrows.

At that instant, Brady realized that there was something far more treacherous on the wind than a rainstorm.

3

IN SEARCH OF SHELTER

Oh! thou, who comest, like a midnight thief,
Uncounted, seeking whom thou may'st destroy...

JOHN KEEGAN

A shrieking gale caught Terese up, nearly tossing her off her feet. For the first time she realized that this was more than a winter rainstorm, that something unthinkable was happening and she might actually be in danger. Instinctively, she threw herself to the ground, crouching behind the stones and shivering as much from fear as from the suddenly frigid air.

For a moment she could do nothing but lie, dazed and shaking, against the rocks. A rumbling deeper than thunder rushed in off the sea to sweep the cliffs and the fort like a fury. Never had Terese heard such a sound, as if the wind would tear the earth itself asunder. Lightning streaked wildly, arcing over and around her.

The sky released a deluge of hail and rain, slashing her head and arms like a storm of needles. Terese screamed in pain, throwing her arms up to shield her head as she scrambled to her feet and began to run.

She felt the savage wind slapping at her, shoving her, as if to lift her from the ground and into the deadly maelstrom. Panicked, her heart thundering so violently she could no longer distinguish the pounding of her blood from the roar of the wind, Terese practically threw herself at one of the taller stones, wrapping her arms around it and clinging desperately as the downpour of rain continued to pummel her without mercy.

She screamed into the night, but the storm stole her voice, dashing her cry against the rocks before finally carrying it out to sea.

Every muscle in Brady's body went rigid as yet another blast of wind slammed

15

against him. On instinct, he threw himself in front of the two girls, trying to shield them. "Over there!" he yelled, pointing at the low ditch running between two of the houses.

The black-haired girl stared at him, clutching the child in her arms even closer. It occurred to Brady in a split second that she might be slow-witted, for she seemed not to understand, even when he grabbed her arm and began tugging her toward the ditch.

She fought him, shaking her head violently, hugging the child to her as she twisted free of Brady's grasp. At the same time, she made a sharp motion that they should run in the opposite direction. Not waiting for Brady to follow, she bolted off.

At that instant, another furious gust of wind hurtled over them. There was a crash, then the sickening sound of something tearing and splitting as the roof on one of the houses just ahead lifted completely free and blew apart, sending clumps of thatch flying wildly into the night.

Before, Brady had merely felt dazed by the unexpected onslaught of the storm. Now he knew his first stab of real fear. This was no ordinary wind, and he knew that there was no time to lose in finding shelter.

There were others now, spilling out from the houses in a flurry of panic and bewilderment, sending up a chorus of wailing and screaming as they poured into the streets. Many seemed in a state of shock. Others, nearly naked and marked with bruises and lacerations, stumbled through the crowds calling for family members and loved ones.

As Brady reached the girl, he could hear her muttering something in the Irish, repeating it like a litany. It struck him then how slight she was. He slowed her with a restraining arm and, without giving her a chance to protest, moved to take the child from her. Those enormous dark eyes challenged him for a split second as she retained her hold on the small girl in her arms. Even when she finally relented and handed the child over to him, she eyed him closely, as if to make certain he was not an abductor.

"Where?" Brady shouted above the wind as he bundled the child to his chest. "Show me!"

Again the girl pointed, and they started off at a hard run. The night had become a tempest. The wind caught them up from behind, threatening to drive them to the ground as a sudden deluge of cold rain burst from the sky. Lightning rent the darkness, stabbing wildly at houses, piercing everything in its path in a dizzying assault.

Brady looked for some sign of shelter, but the small houses were clearly more hazard than haven in this kind of storm. Besides, the girl seemed to know exactly where she was going. At least he hoped she did.

He glanced down at the child in his arms, surprised to see that her expression was more bemused than frightened. As if sensing Brady's gaze, she looked up—and actually smiled at him!

She was odd, no doubt about it!

Nearly blinded by the rain and pummeled by the merciless wind, Brady had all he could do to keep up with the dark-haired girl racing down the quay ahead of him. She was as fleet as a deer, and he had the feeling that if she hadn't been so intent upon keeping the child well within range she would have easily left him behind and fled into the night.

They charged on, the baleful wind shrieking at their backs, in their faces, all about them now—for it was moving inland at incredible speed, like a horde of demons unleashed from the very pit of hell. Brady cried out a warning as a wooden pail came flying at them, barely missing the girl's head before banging against a yard pump and splitting into pieces.

Slates and stones flew in all directions, creating even more danger. Brady thought himself to be as fit as any man, but now he became keenly aware that the exertion of the hard run and the burden of the child were beginning to tell on him. When a particularly vicious gust of wind seized him, shaking him and sweeping him forward, he came treacherously close to sprawling headfirst in the street.

Brady saw that the girl was heading toward a small, thatched-roof cottage at the other side of the street. When he realized her intention, he stopped her with a firm hand while bracing the child tightly against himself with his free arm. "That'll do us no good!" he shouted, suddenly angry that she had led him past stone buildings and harbor businesses to what looked to be a worthless refuge.

There was fire in her eyes when she whipped around to face him. She jabbed a finger rapidly in the direction of the cottage, then opened her hand and beckoned furiously for Brady to follow with the child.

Brady snapped another look at the small dwelling, with its crumbling chimney and thatched roof. He wouldn't have been surprised to see it lifted from its very foundation and flung aloft. He gave a violent shake of his head. "Are you daft, girl? We'd be better off in the streets!"

But she had already started off and was leaping over the debris in the street, making her way toward the hut. Brady swallowed a cry of disgust, then followed, tripping over stones and jagged pieces of metal as he pressed the child to himself, all the while wondering why he hadn't simply left both of them standing in the street and saved himself.

4

TERROR ON THE WIND

A great storm from the ocean goes shouting o'er the hill,
And there is glory in it and terror on the wind...

EVA GORE-BOOTH

Terese knew her very life depended on the stone wall withstanding the wind. The shock of the storm and the cold, slashing rain had temporarily paralyzed her and dulled her senses. But on the threshold of her foundering consciousness lurked the awareness that the walls of Dun Aengus were her only hope.

So she lay, drenched and freezing, clinging to the jagged piece of rock as if by the very force of her own weight she could anchor it and herself to the earth. For a time, anger displaced her terror. The bile of bitterness rose in her throat at both her father and her brother for their abandonment. But when she tried to scream her rage into the wind, she found her voice locked inside her, her teeth clenched in a vise that shot searing flashes of pain through her jaws and up her temples. Too dazed to think, she could only lie, stricken, in the darkness, engulfed by the fury and horror of the storm.

Once, she tried to pray, but the effort was futile. In the mind-numbing terror of the storm and the sheer misery to which her body was fast succumbing, she could think only of surviving.

Besides, if her aunt Una was right, God was in the midst of this tempest, in control of the madness that had been unleashed upon the island this night. Terese felt only outrage at a God who would wreak such savagery upon the very land and people he had created.

She could not fathom a God of such wanton devastation. She could not plead with such a God. Certainly, she could not *trust* such a God.

She could only resist him. Her arms tightened about the cold, slippery rock. No doubt her aunt would say that God was the only anchor in the storm, even in a storm such as this. But to Terese, God had somehow *become* the storm…He was in it, over it, all around it, a part of it. Her anchor, her *only* anchor, was this ancient, rugged piece of rock. The rock, at least, she could touch and embrace and cling to.

A low groan now tore from her, a bold, primitive cry in the face of this God of destruction. If she survived this night of horror—and in that moment Terese vowed that survive it she would—then she would know herself capable of surviving anything, and surviving it on her own, without any help from God or anyone else.

Suddenly, the wind hurled what seemed the full force of its fury at her. The gale hammered at her, whipping and slashing, pelting her with hail, pressing her into the earth, yet threatening to sweep her up and over the rocks. Terese shook with such violence she thought all the bones in her body would surely shatter. Blinded by hail and bruised by the merciless wind, she could do nothing but cling to the rock.

At last, she began to scream…terrible, wild cries, not of fear, but more of rage—rage, and a desperate, almost savage, shout of defiance. And with each bitter cry, she seemed to absorb the force of the storm, claiming it and making it her own.

———

Brady felt as if his clothes were being ripped from his back, so fierce was this wind that seemed to have come out of nowhere. He knew about hurricanes only from books, except for what he'd been told by Ransom, the black carriage driver Jack employed, who claimed to have survived such a tempest somewhere in the Caribbean. As he blundered up the path toward the miserable little dwelling that was clearly his guide's destination, he reasoned that this storm could be nothing less than one of those terrifying gales.

As he recalled, a hurricane could supposedly lift a church right off its stone foundation and send it hurtling across town. Yet this wild-eyed young woman thought they would be safe inside that pitiful cottage just ahead.

She was daft, no doubt about it!

Disgusted with himself for following the simpleminded girl to his own destruction, Brady could see nothing for it but to change course and look for more suitable shelter somewhere else. He stopped, digging his heels into the ground against the force of the wind as he looked this way and that. To his dismay, none of the other thatched houses nearby appeared any more substantial than the one in front of him.

He felt a rough yank at his sleeve and looked to find the girl tugging at him, her dark eyes snapping. She began to jabber something at him in the Irish. The word *amadon* was the only thing that registered, and that was because he'd heard Jack apply it to any number of his business acquaintances in New York.

If he wasn't badly mistaken, the word meant "fool."

Brady stood his ground, refusing to follow her into that thatched death trap. The next thing he knew, the wild girl was trying to wrest the child out of his arms, all the while scalding him with her Gaelic diatribe, most of which was immediately swallowed up by the wind.

They were nearly at the house, but they had to struggle mightily now just to keep their footing. Brady still had the child anchored securely in his arms, but his chest felt as if it were about to explode, and fatigue and the battering wind were threatening to bring him down at any moment. He knew they had no time to lose, so when the girl would not be deterred, he gave in and followed her.

At that instant, a towering hulk of a man, lantern in hand, appeared in the doorway of the cottage. He looked to be hewn from stone, a colossus with hard, craggy features and a rugged frame, a full head of jet black hair laced with silver, and a riot of black beard. It struck Brady that all the behemoth needed was a pike in his hand and he could have easily been taken for one of the ancient warrior-chiefs who had once gone roaring into battle sporting little more than a kilt and brandishing a rough-hewn spear.

Without warning, the fierce-looking creature rushed at them, whipping the child out of Brady's arms as if she were no more than a twig and at the same time hauling the older girl to his side. Before Brady could even react, the big fellow hissed something in the Irish at the little girl locked against his chest. She chirped a response, and the man turned a blistering scowl on Brady.

The giant gave the dark-haired girl a tug and moved to turn away, clearly intent on leaving Brady to his own resources. But the girl snapped a quick look over her shoulder, then grabbed the big man's arm, gesturing insistently in Brady's direction.

The man's look dripped suspicion, but with a hard jerk of his head he indicated that Brady should follow. Brady hesitated. There was no telling what might lie in wait inside this great oaf's dwelling.

But then another wall of wind slammed him in the back, shaking him like a rag doll and propelling him forward. He followed the three inside, reasoning blackly that if this was his day to die, he might just as well have a bit of company in the passing.

❧

Only once did Terese dare raise her head to look about her. Wicked bolts of lightning still pierced the night with abandon, but even with the intermittent light she could scarcely make out her surroundings through the wind-tossed sheets of ice and rain.

The stones and ground were glazed with sleet, as were her own face and hands. Even her hair felt stiff and weighted with a thin layer of ice. Still clinging to the stone, she pulled herself up just enough to look toward town. A hail of icy rain struck her like a whipsaw, slashing her skin. She cried out in pain, then screamed again at the sight of a table, all four legs intact, scudding across the fort only to be dashed to pieces against one of the taller stones.

Lightning knifed the sea, the fort, the cliff, revealing momentary glimpses of things Terese would have expected to see only in nightmares. Boats had been smashed to pieces, their debris now bobbing wildly in the water. A poor, terrified hen, feathers plucked from its body, went screeching into the sea, carried by the wind. Torn remnants of clothing whipped across the shoreline like a macabre parade of boneless corpses. Other objects flew by: crockery, bits of wood, clumps of sod and thatch, shrubbery ripped free of its roots—even animals, pathetic, broken creatures swept up from the earth and flung out upon the night.

Terese knew she was weeping, but her tears were lost in the downpour of sleet and rain cascading over her upturned face. When a vicious blast of wind seized her, her hands slipped free of her stone anchor. Panic barreled through her, but she clambered to regain her hold, fastening herself once more to the ancient rock of Dun Aengus.

Still the baleful wind continued to shriek and hurl its wrath, as if hell itself had been loosed and would this night claim not only its own but whatever innocent might chance upon the march of its deadly destruction.

❧

As Brady passed through the open door into the small dwelling, he was surprised—and vastly relieved—to note the thickness of the walls, far sturdier than they had seemed upon first glance. Inside, the cottage was not quite as wretched as he might have imagined—but it didn't miss by far.

There looked to be no more than two rooms, partitioned by a curtain that hung between them. He saw only one window, and this too narrow to allow much light. No doubt the place would be gloomy both night and day. A beeswax candle burned weakly in the middle of a deal table, and the wild flickering of the flame revealed the force of the draft blowing through cracks in the walls.

Brady took in the furnishings in one quick sweep. The turf fire, flanked by stone benches, had been allowed to go out; no doubt this break in tradition was in deference to the dangerous wind. There was a painted dresser of surprisingly good craftsmanship, two three-legged stools, a wicker basket half-filled with potatoes, and a good-sized but badly sagging bed pushed against one wall. The floor was dirt, but well swept. In one corner was a pool of water, apparently the result of a leak in the thatched roof above.

He had seen enough of the cottages of the poor to imagine that beyond the curtain probably lay little more than a straw pallet or two, covered with thin blankets for the girls. He heard a scurry in the corner nearest the hearth and saw three or four chickens scratching in the dirt. It had taken him a long time to grow accustomed to the sight of fowl or pigs inside even some of the better Irish dwellings, but now he found the sight strangely comforting, as if this sign of domesticity meant the inhabitants might not be quite so peculiar after all. It was clearly the home of poor but ordinary people, not a charnel house where unsuspecting sojourners might disappear.

He was allowed little time to appraise his surroundings, however, for once inside, the big fellow shoved the table out of the way and drew up a large, wooden slab door from the dirt. He said nothing but merely made a sharp gesture to the girl and the child, then to Brady, that they should all descend.

A huge wave of relief washed over Brady. They were going below ground! It seemed that his guardian angel had not abandoned him entirely!

Thick walls aside, the little house was shaking like a creature caught up in the grip of a violent palsy. Brady hurried to join the others. When he would have stopped long enough to offer a word of gratitude to the man holding the door, the unfriendly giant froze him with a dark glare and an impatient snap of his head. Those cold blue eyes left no doubt whatsoever that he thought Brady a fool—an unwelcome one, at that—and that Brady's bid to share their underground shelter was granted grudgingly.

Despite the man's churlishness, Brady gave a quick nod of thanks as he prepared to descend a hemp ladder leading below. At the instant he turned to lower himself into the pit, a screaming blast of wind roared in on the small dwelling. There was a deafening shriek, then a groaning overhead, followed by the terrible sound of something splitting.

Brady hesitated, shooting a glance upward only to see the thatched roof begin to rock, then whip madly up and down just before it lifted completely free and went flying off into the furious night. For a split second he locked gazes with the big man holding the slab door open and saw his own terror reflected in that hard blue stare.

He watched the giant reel and stagger, losing his balance in the furious gust of wind that now came howling through the house. The door fell away from those large, rough hands, and in one lightning flash of clarity Brady realized what was about to happen just before the heavy slab came crashing down on his head.

5

THE WEARY AND THE WOUNDED

Solomon! where is thy throne? It is gone in the wind.
Babylon! where is thy might? It is gone in the wind.
Like the swift shadows of Noon, like the dreams of the Blind, Vanish
the glories and pomps of the earth in the wind.

JAMES CLARENCE MANGAN

The madness had gone on until nearly dawn. Even after the storm finally subsided, Terese had remained sealed to her rock of anchor, half-frozen and numb from the relentless battering of the wind and icy rain.

Now she stood on the shore, watching the sea. After the deafening, seemingly endless roar of the storm, the present silence was somehow unnerving. The waves were still turbulent but not so violent now, mostly roiling crests keeping harmony with the morning wind.

The harbor teemed with floating debris: broken boats, dead animals, pieces of furniture, and clumps of shrubbery and other vegetation. All around her, the smell of smoke mixed with the acrid odors of salt water and dead fish.

Exhausted from her night's ordeal and still dazed by the unthinkable devastation she had found upon returning to the village, Terese could do nothing but stand and stare, letting the spray off the ocean bathe her face. The nightmare of the past few hours had totally depleted her, drained her last vestige of strength. Her skin still tingled from the long exposure to the elements, and she felt the onset of a head cold. More than anything else, however, there was merely the somber awareness that the storm had passed, that she had survived it only to find herself more alone than she had ever been in her life.

Behind her, the small village had been nearly decimated. What few houses remained were without roofs. Most had either been burned or leveled or swept away altogether. Many villagers had already declared their intention to go on the road, to make their way to Galway City and seek refuge with relatives. Terese suspected that by the end of the day the town would be virtually deserted, except for those who had vowed to stay and rebuild. As to whether these few were brave or merely foolish, she couldn't say. She knew only that she did not intend to remain with them.

She turned slowly away from the sea and stood staring at the village. There was nothing there for her. Her aunt's house had been razed, crushed to random heaps of thatch and rubble. Like countless others, the entire family was now homeless.

Aunt Una had wasted no time in announcing, with an unmistakable hint of spite in her tone, that Terese need not expect to accompany the rest of the family to Galway, where they would shelter for a time with Uncle Felim's aging parents. No doubt by now they had already started off, and without so much as a final farewell.

Earlier, her mild, subservient uncle had made a halfhearted attempt to assuage his conscience by seeking out Terese to explain. "You understand, lass? The old man and woman, they haven't the room for us as it is, much less yourself. Your aunt is fearful lest they turn us all away."

Terese had never found it in her to either like or dislike her uncle. Even though he was the only member of the household to favor her with a kind word now and then, he was so cowed by his wife that he always seemed a mere shadow of a man. She could not respect him, and so she could not feel any real affection for him. Most of the time, she held no more than a faint contempt for him, tempered only slightly by the awareness that Uncle Felim was not a bad man, really, nor an unfeeling man. He was simply a weak man.

Terese had no use for weakness.

So even though she was trembling inside at the time, she had brushed off his feigned concern, telling him she would manage well enough, that he was not to worry. "I'm seventeen years old, after all. 'Tis time for me to be on my own."

"You won't be holding it against us, then?" he said, glancing around as if to make certain his wife was well out of earshot.

Terese assured him that, far from holding it against them, she thought things would work out perfectly fine for her. She carefully refrained from divulging her plans to go to America, however; if they suspected that she had money put aside, they would be after her like starving dogs at a kill.

Now, as she watched the procession of the displaced that had already begun to file out of the village, their few remaining worldly goods tied upon their backs, she wondered if Galway might also have been struck by the past night's storm. Was there any cause to believe that the evil wind had confined its destruction to Inishmore?

Well, then, and what of it? America was her destination, and the sooner the better. So long as there was a harbor where she could board a ship, she was not long for this wretched island.

If she felt a prickling of fear at the thought of launching into such an adventure alone, she suppressed it. In the aftermath of the storm, her friend Peggy had decided she could not leave her family now. Her father had hurt his back, and her mother, she said, could do nothing but stand and weep; she must stay and help however she could.

At first, Terese had been angry, and they had exchanged bitter words. But not for long. She had no strength left to waste on anger. Besides, Peggy was only doing what she thought she must do, after all. And it would be *her* loss, would it not? She would be the one left to Ireland's mean poverty while Terese went on to prosper in America.

She could fend for herself well enough. She had her wits, the dress on her back—a dry one, thanks to Peggy, whose personal belongings had fared somewhat better than Terese's—and the money she had buried in the ground behind the henhouse. She needed nothing more, at least not for now. Once she reached Galway, she would try to purchase a better dress for the crossing. But for the present, she looked as respectable as anyone else she was likely to encounter this day.

Stooping, she retrieved her weathered *pampootas*—her shoes—and slipped them on. Earlier she had found a piece of a shawl, which she now knotted about her shoulders, savoring the warmth against the chill air. Finally, she cinched the *crios*—the bright sash she had made for herself—at her waist and lifted her face for one final look at the towering eminence of her old friend and protector, Dun Aengus.

Then, squaring her shoulders, she turned her back on her past and went in search of a shovel.

❦

Pain.

Hard, red explosions of it in his head, down his neck…

Brady had been dreaming that he was standing on a bleak shore, alone and shivering as he suffered the attack of dark-featured sailors who hurled massive stones at him from a ship that bobbed up and down in the bay.

Behind him and all around, there was nothing but barren land. No houses, no shops, no trees, and no people. The unknown waters were silent, as were the sailors on their battleship. Nothing broke the stillness except for the splitting of his skull beneath the onslaught of the stones…

He felt nothing but the pain as the sound of whispering crept in on him, prodding him awake—short, harsh whispers and utterances he couldn't make out. Meaning to ease the pain, he tried to turn but stopped, gasping as a white-hot bolt of agony shot through his skull.

Someone was holding his hand. He felt the warmth, the slight pressure. He forced his eyes open, groaning as the dim, flickering light set off another sharp wrench of pain in his head.

On a stool close beside him sat a dark-eyed little girl, gripping his hand. When she saw him turn toward her, she smiled.

Brady stared at her, recognition gradually dawning. The fey child squeezed his hand as if to encourage him.

He blinked several times against the pain as his eyes finally began to focus. He was in a cold, dark hole of a room, the air thick with dust and mildew. He could make out a slight, womanly figure in the corner, bent low as she rolled what looked to be a piece of cloth. She glanced up at the tall, dark form hovering over her and murmured something in the Irish.

Brady tried to speak, but when he opened his mouth nothing came, only a blinding slam of pain at his temples and the back of his head.

Again, the child pumped his hand a little, then turned to the others and chirped something at them. The hulking form emerged out of the shadows and stood scowling down at Brady. Memory rushed in on him, driving through his confusion: the storm, the violent wind, the rickety little house—the heavy door crashing down on his head.

His ears rang, and nausea surged in him, then ebbed. He touched his head and became very still. Bandages swathed his forehead and a portion of his skull. He wondered how bad his injuries were. He tried to sit up, but a hand the size of a bound book thrust him back.

He stared up into the dark-skinned face looming over him, realizing now that the granite-visaged man was younger than he had thought upon first sight of him. Younger, but a hard man all the same, he sensed, harder even than Jack, who had his soft spots once you knew him. He doubted that this towering stranger in his garb of homespun had many soft spots.

Brady wanted to ask what time it was, if it was night or day, then remembered that these people spoke the Irish. Though he might recognize bits and pieces of the old language from Jack, he didn't know enough of it to communicate.

He glanced over at the older girl and saw her watching him, but she made no move to rise from her place in the corner. The child finally released Brady's hand but stayed seated at his side, her curious gaze following his slightest movement.

"'Tis a bad blow. The door fell square on top of your head. You will need to lie still for now."

Startled by the deep, resonant voice and even more by the English, Brady gaped at the man. "You speak English?"

The man merely lifted one dark brow at Brady's surprise. "Who are you?" he bit out. Something in that drumroll of a voice seemed to carry a hint of a threat.

Still taken aback, it took Brady a moment to recover. "Kane," he finally replied. "Brady Kane."

The other's eyes narrowed slightly. "American."

In one clipped word, the black-bearded giant had managed to convey a monumental contempt.

"*Irish* American," Brady shot back, his head throbbing with the effort.

The man's expression didn't change, and Brady had all he could do not to squirm under the full force of that burning stare. "The girl says you helped with the wee wane," he said, giving a small jerk of his head in the child's direction.

"They were more help to me than I to them," Brady offered. "I might have been blown out to sea if they hadn't come along and led me here."

"What would you be doing in the Claddagh, Yank?" Something about the way the giant flung the words at him made Brady feel as if he had committed some sort of heinous offense simply by showing up in Galway.

Weak as he was, he refused to be intimidated by this bad-tempered Irishman. "Business," he said, grimacing at the furry thickness of his tongue. "I'm here on business."

His interrogator crossed his massive arms over the broad expanse of his chest. "And what sort of business would it be that brings a rich Yank to Galway City? It's a poor, backward people we are, after all."

Brady found himself wondering if that mocking brogue might not be somewhat affected. He had caught a glint behind that hostile stare of what appeared to be a keen wit, perhaps even a formidable intelligence. Was the man deliberately goading him? But if so, why?

"Newspaper business," Brady answered. "An assignment of sorts." He paused, deliberating as to how much he ought to tell this stone-faced stranger.

The man's gaze held steady for a moment more. Finally, he lifted one large hand and gave a tug to the kerchief about his neck, twisting his mouth as if Brady merited no further interest. "Are you seeing me clearly, Yank?" he snapped with a sudden change of subject. "Any blurring of your vision at all?"

Brady shook his head, instantly regretting the movement. Pain struck his skull like a well-sharpened ax, and he couldn't stop a groan of protest.

"Be easy," said the other. "There was no real damage done, I'm thinking. You'll be fit enough in a day or so. But for now, you'd best lie abed." His tone left no doubt that he found the situation less than desirable.

"Where—what is this?" Brady asked, glancing around the dark room.

"You've never seen a cellar before, Yank?"

Brady twisted his lip, again irked by the man's seeming dismissal of him as a fool. "What time is it?" he hurried to ask before the other could turn away.

"'Tis morning. Well past first light. The storm has gone, but we will stay below for a time, all the same."

"Your house—"

"It still stands, except for the roof."

Brady glanced at the girl in the corner, who had turned back to her occupation with the bolt of cloth on her lap. "I'd like to thank her," he told the man hovering over him. "I don't even know her name." He paused. "Nor yours."

The giant's eyes went hard as stone. "Don't be making more of it than it is," he said, his tone harsh. "The girl is soft. She would bring a wolf into the house if the beast followed her home."

His dark look seemed to imply that perhaps this was exactly what had happened. Caught off guard by this unexpected rudeness, Brady could manage no response.

The man started to turn, then stopped. "She can't hear you when you speak," he said, the words hard as driven nails. "The girl is deaf."

The giant walked away without another word, leaving Brady to stare at his back. After another moment, he again felt a small hand close about his own and looked to find the child watching him. She squeezed his hand, then mouthed a word he didn't catch.

He frowned at her, and she spoke again. "Gabriel," she said clearly, giving a jerk of her head toward the big man who had planted himself on a stool near the older girl. "His name is Gabriel." She pronounced it *Gah-brul*.

"I'm Evie. Eveleen," she added smartly. "And that—" she nodded toward the older girl in the corner—"is Roweena."

So the child also spoke English. He wouldn't have expected as much. The books had led him to believe that most of the Claddagh's fishermen and their families spoke only the Irish, and he had already heard much of the old tongue in the streets of Galway.

"Roweena," Brady repeated, studying the child. "She's your sister, is she?"

The little girl shook her head. "Gabriel found her. Her was lost, like me."

The child's speech was remarkably clear for one so young. "I don't understand," he said. "What do you mean, lost?"

She pursed her lips. "Lost, don't you know? I was put out, but Roweena, her was in a fire when she was a babe. Most everyone died, except Roweena."

Brady dragged his gaze from the dark-haired girl in the shadows back to the child. "So, then—this man, Gabriel, he's not your father?"

Again the child shook her head. "We don't have a da, Roweena and me. We have Gabriel."

The man snapped something at the child just then, his words cracking like a whiplash. The little girl pressed her rosy lips into a tight line but couldn't seem to resist explaining. "Gabriel says I'm not to blather, that I must leave you to your rest," she whispered hurriedly, leaning closer to Brady. "I will thank Roweena for you."

Brady reached out to stop her. "Wait. He said the girl's deaf, yet she speaks."

The child—Evie—regarded him as if he were dim-witted. "Her's clever, Roweena is," she said with a trace of childish indignation. "Gabriel taught her to talk. Like this." She framed the small column of her throat with both hands and worked her jaw up and down.

Still confused about the relationship of the two girls and the grim-faced giant, Brady glanced across the room, where Gabriel was now holding the bolt of cloth while the girl wrapped it over and over again.

After a moment he turned back to the child. "You live here with him, then?" he asked. "You and…Roweena?"

She nodded. A quick grin revealed a noticeable gap where both front teeth should have been. "Gabriel is our angel," she said matter-of-factly.

Brady stared at her. "Your angel?"

She nodded vigorously. "Roweena says Gabriel is like God's angel who looks after us and keeps us safe."

While he knew very little about angels, Brady could not imagine a less likely example of one than the dour colossus who sat scowling at him from his shadowy corner across the room.

⟡

Near the remains of Aunt Una's house, Terese found a shovel, its handle broken down almost to a nub. Gripping what was left of it with both hands, she went at her task with a vengeance, lifting the dirt away.

By the time she reached the pouch that contained her secret savings, she was in a fever. Her ordeal of the night before had left her more shaken than she cared to consider. She was intent only on retrieving her money so she could be on her way while the morning was still calm—in the event that the wind should come back.

She drew in a ragged breath. The pouch was intact, still neatly tied, just as she'd left it. She gave the shovel a toss and with shaking hands lifted her treasure from its nest in the ground.

The moment she touched it, she knew. Her hands began to tremble so violently that she could scarcely untie the string.

She upended the pouch, then sat staring at what was left of her years of saving. Not quite two dollars. There had been nearly twenty when last she counted it only three nights past. Twenty American dollars.

Every hope of her heart drained slowly out of her. She felt as empty as if her lifeblood had been sucked from her body.

Aunt Una.

She knew immediately who had stolen from her. No doubt her aunt had watched her at some time in the middle of the night, when she had gone to check the pouch or to add the latest sum from Cavan.

Two dollars would not take her to America.

She didn't know how long she sat there, hunched over the hole in the ground, rubbing her fingers over the pouch as if it were something that had once lived but was now cold and lifeless. Anything could have transpired about her, and she wouldn't have known. She heard no sound save the beating of her own heavy heart, felt nothing but a sick disgust at her own carelessness.

After a long time, she blinked and looked about at her desolate surroundings. Gone. Everything was gone. And she should have been gone, too, gone from Inishmore.

She should have known her aunt would snoop. She should have taken more precautions, hidden the money farther away from the house, even taken it to Dun Aengus—

No! This wasn't her fault. *She* wasn't the thief. *She* hadn't robbed her own kin, hadn't spied on her own blood in order to commit so vile a deed.

Slowly, she came to her feet, propelled by a fierce surge of rage rushing up within her. What—or *who*—was responsible for the misery, the injustice of her life, the trouble that had plagued her ever since she was a wee wane?

Her mother would have claimed it was the will of God, that Terese must "persevere" and "endure the Lord's chastening." Aunt Una, no doubt, would blame the devil, would say that old Satan himself was behind life's mischief and torments, working to discourage and destroy "the innocent."

Aye, and if that be the case, then, sure, her deceitful aunt was one of the devil's own helpmates.

Terese didn't know who to blame, but she desperately needed to blame *someone*. Someone should answer for the wretchedness of her life, shouldn't he? And for the lives of so many others. Someone had to be responsible.

With a sudden cry of fury, she lifted the near-empty pouch toward heaven. "You won't stop me!" she screamed. Without knowing the real object of her rage, she went on screaming into the hushed morning. "Whoever you are...wherever you are, I'm going, do you hear? I am leaving this wretched island, and I am never coming back! I'm going, and there is nothing you can do to stop me!"

She fell silent as quickly as she had given vent to her rage, gasping for breath and clutching the pouch close to her heart. "I'm going," she announced again, this time in a whisper. Then she turned from the empty hole in the ground and walked away.

6

JACK

Brother, son, beloved one, Your absence mocks my heart.

ANONYMOUS

NEW YORK CITY, MID-FEBRUARY

The sun had yet to rise as Jack Kane sat in his study, outlining ideas for his editorial. Most of his time was spent on the business end of the newspaper, but he had refused to relinquish the editorial page. If there was one thing an Irishman enjoyed more than politics and pretty women, he was fond of saying, it was spouting his opinions. If he happened to be in a position where he could inflict those opinions on an entire city, so much the better.

These early hours before dawn had always been Jack's favorite time of the day. He relished the quiet, the stillness of the house before Addy set the kitchen help to stirring and started her morning forays in search of offending dust mites. Normally, Ransom would be showing up in another hour or so. Although he knew full well Jack never left for the office before seven-thirty, the crafty old stableman always came early with the sole intent of enjoying a biscuit or two and a slice of ham. No doubt he would be thoroughly put out by Jack's instructions not to arrive before noon today.

Jack was having a hard time concentrating this morning. His feelings about the city being "overrun with filthy, debauched immigrants"—as asserted in an anonymous letter received by the paper earlier in the week—were somewhat difficult to express, given the fact that "filthy, debauched immigrants" referred almost exclusively to the Irish.

Even though there were twenty-five years and an ocean between Jack and old Ireland, he tried never to deceive himself: He was as Irish as any of those poor souls who made up the city's plague of poverty. So even though he had tried for balance in his current editorial, he'd ended up scratching most of it out, recognizing that the tone was far too defensive, even petulant. No doubt he sounded a bit like an irascible drunk.

Perhaps he should simply ignore the diatribe this anonymous writer had directed at the refugees pouring into New York Harbor. Nothing chafed a small, self-important man more than being ignored, after all.

He got up and went to stand at the window. The street lamps were still flickering, casting only enough light to reveal shadows from the large old trees and ornamental fences that fronted Thirty-fourth Street's gracious mansions. A trace of snow from the night frosted the street, while tree limbs swaying in the wind promised another bitterly cold day.

The stirring of the wind took his thoughts to Brady. Ever since word had come of the devastating storm that struck Ireland in early January, Jack had tried to convince himself that his precocious brother, always resourceful, would fare perfectly well, even in a hurricane. Even so, if he didn't hear from the young jackanapes soon, he was going to send one of the lads from the paper across to look him up.

His brother's infuriating recklessness, his inclination to think only of the moment—and only of *himself*, Jack reflected with a sour twist of his mouth—was nothing new. It never seemed to occur to Brady that people worried. Under normal circumstances, Jack wouldn't have been alarmed if no word arrived for weeks at a time. But surely Brady realized that news of the storm would have reached the States by now. The least the irresponsible whelp could do was drop a post as to his whereabouts and his circumstances.

He turned away from the window and crossed the room to stoke the fire. The study was one of the smallest rooms in the drafty old house and as such should have been one of the warmest. But the ceiling was high enough to clear an oak tree, and the windows were anything but tight; consequently, there was always a chill.

Poker in hand, he straightened and turned his back to the fire. Of late, he had given an occasional thought to selling the place. He had bought the rambling old horror a few years past on a whim. At the time, he had still been young enough—and crass enough—to enjoy flaunting his success. An Irish upstart with a bank account large enough to stake his claim on Thirty-fourth Street was a scandal and an affront, and he had thoroughly enjoyed outraging the gentry nearby with his "vulgarity."

But now the sprawling old mansion, by the very fact of its immensity and flamboyance, was almost an embarrassment. Certainly, it was an annoyance, and an expensive, inconvenient one, at that. Yet he was loath to give it up because it was the first home he had ever owned. Besides, he still rather fancied the idea of offending the carriage trade.

Black Jack Kane: a pig plopped down in a palace, he thought with a grin.

Still grinning, he glanced at his pocket watch when Addy appeared in the doorway. As usual, she had given him no more than thirty minutes alone. The woman couldn't seem to endure a man having himself a bit of peace and quiet.

Jack feigned a scowl at her. Unmoved, she stood, hands on angular hips, square jaw thrust forward, black eyes snapping.

"A pity you won't stay abed like most respectable men," the Irish housekeeper challenged. "No doubt we're the only household above the Bowery that serves breakfast before sunup."

"Don't start on me, woman. Even if I slept until noon, you'd still come prowling about before dawn, just so you'd have something to harp on."

As was always the case, his contrived crossness didn't faze her. "Didn't you say you weren't going to the office this morning?" she reminded him, the perfect point of her slate gray widow's peak puckering with disapproval.

"I did."

"Well, now, had you told me you'd changed your mind, I'd have seen that your breakfast was ready earlier."

"Did I say I had changed my mind?"

She glared at him. "And why else would you be all slicked up at this hour of the day?"

"As it happens, you sour old woman, I am *not* going to the office this morning. But I do have appointments *here,* beginning at ten."

The dark brows arched, and the hatchet jaw lifted a notch more. "Appointments, is it? Here at the house?"

Jack nodded, replaced the poker, and went back to his desk. "I'm seeing applicants for the driver's position. You can show them in here one at a time as they arrive. I thought I'd see them here so if I find a likely candidate he can have a look at the stables."

She tightened her mouth. "No telling what sort will show up, I expect."

Jack bent over the desk and began stacking his papers to the side. "Don't worry a bit, Addy," he said straight-faced. "There's a gun right here in the top drawer. Naturally, I'll protect your virtue with my life."

He glanced up and saw her narrow her eyes. The dear invariably narrowed her eyes when she was bent on baiting him. Addy was nothing if not predictable.

"And what's to become of old Ransom, the poor man? You'll be sending him out on his keeping with the ragpickers, I suppose."

Jack bared his teeth at her. "You know perfectly well that Ransom has asked for a position here in the house. Faith, woman, he must be at least a century or more by now, wouldn't you say? He's only a step short of being crippled by rheumatism, and he's all but deaf. We could be run down in the street by a stampede of horses, and he'd never hear them until they'd flattened us." He paused. "He will work as a handyman about the house from now on."

The housekeeper made a short sound of disgust. "Handyman, indeed! The old fool is about as handy as a drunken sailor."

"You'd know more about drunken sailors than I, you outrageous woman," Jack said evenly as he went to the door. "I believe I will have my breakfast now, Addy. If you please."

She sniffed and started off ahead of him. The tight little bun at the back of her neck didn't budge—Jack half suspected that she anchored it with chicken wire in the mornings—as she took off down the hall toward the kitchen, muttering to herself all the way.

Jack smiled as he followed, knowing full well that she was smiling, too—rather like a she-wolf at the thought of its next kill.

Addy O'Meara had been with Jack since he and Martha rented their first flat, after their marriage. Formerly a part of Martha's household, Addy had come to assist the newlyweds—and never left. She had nursed Martha through the long months of illness that ended in death two years later, all the while helping Jack to raise "the wee brother"—Brady, who in truth was more son to Jack than brother—with an eagle eye, a firm hand, and an Irish mother's heart.

Addy had been mother, friend, and confidant for so many years that Jack no longer thought of her in any other way except as family, and he quite simply could not imagine life without her.

Unfortunately for him, the cantankerous old woman was well aware of the fact.

7

An Encounter between the Strong and the Strong

And because I am of the people, I understand the people,
I am sorrowful with their sorrow,
I am hungry with their desire…

Padraic Pearse

Cavan Sheridan stood, cap in hand, studying the fine room into which the prickly housekeeper had directed him. "The *Study*," she had called it, her Irish tongue lingering on the word as if the study were a holy place. "Mr. Kane will see you in the *Study*."

The room was spacious but not immense. The quiet decor was a surprising contrast to the somewhat gilded furnishings he had glimpsed beyond the open doors flanking the great marble corridor. The windows were shrouded in velvet, but the draperies had been drawn to admit the weak morning light. Green damask covered the walls in those places where there were no bookshelves, and Cavan had a sense of a forest retreat, dense and calm and sheltered. The man who had chosen the sturdy furniture of leather and rosewood, the fine paneling that gleamed like aged honey, and the thick, richly textured carpet that silenced each footfall would be a man who favored comfort over luxury, he mused—contentment and warmth over opulence.

The room didn't fit the stories he had heard about Black Jack Kane. Although he'd been in New York City for only six weeks, Cavan had already heard numerous tales—some conflicting—about the "Irish black bear" who allegedly showed no restraint in flaunting the wealth and power of his newspaper empire. Depending on who happened to be giving the account, Kane might be depicted as a rogue, a scoundrel, an upstart, an infidel—or a genius. Some described him as ruthless, others as arrogant, wily, and cold-blooded. Most, however, tended to agree that, whatever else he might happen to be, Kane was brilliant.

At the sound of a soft whistling outside the door, Cavan turned. His curiosity had heightened to the point that he had all he could do not to gape at the man who entered the room. Kane's acknowledging nod was neither condescending nor rude, but strangely cavalier—as if he had more important things on his mind than this interview but intended to be good-natured about it all the same.

For a moment he stood behind the desk, fixing Cavan with a gaze too dark to register any hint of emotion. Kane was younger than Cavan had expected, given the man's colorful reputation and the influence he apparently wielded; he might have been forty, but scarcely more. And if he was indeed the rascal he was reputed to be, his appearance was deceiving. Where Cavan had anticipated a middle-aged, overweight swell with the florid face of one accustomed to excess, Jack Kane was tall and trim—a dark, lean man with an air of hard elegance and the arrogant good looks of the black Irish.

Cavan, who at an inch or two over six feet seldom found himself at eye level with other men, noted that Kane probably topped him by another inch or so. Below the coal black mustache, Kane had the long lip of the Irish. His not-quite-swarthy skin and raven hair bespoke a trace of Spanish descent seen mostly in the west of Ireland.

Cavan had done his homework on his prospective employer. He knew that Kane, an orphan, had come across while still a boy, along with a younger brother and sister. According to rumor, he had attained his present level of success by a combination of hard work, an almost legendary shrewdness, and a brassy kind of courage that took chances most men would run from. In less than two decades, Jack Kane had risen from sweeping floors at an upstairs print shop on Chatham Street to an apprentice position, eventually going on to become the owner and publisher of one of the country's largest, most influential newspapers. There was also speculation about a political career in the making. Despite his youthful appearance, the man was practically a legend.

Cavan meant to be "the legend's" newest employee. He had been without funds for nearly a week now, had not eaten more than a few stale crusts of bread in all that time, and was virtually reeling on his feet. The latest in a series of temporary odd jobs had ended nearly two weeks past; since then he'd been sleeping in alleys among the newsboys and ragpickers, using discarded papers to ward off the wind.

He was desperate, indeed had never wanted or needed anything quite so much as this job with Kane's newspaper. At the moment, it represented the difference between starvation and survival.

Yet, as his eyes met and held the black gaze of Jack Kane, it was something more than desperation that fueled his resolve to work for Kane's paper, the *Vanguard*. In a way he couldn't have begun to define, Cavan sensed that the man across the desk from him held the power to change his life, to offer him something more than a respite from hunger and humiliation.

He had been hoping, searching, praying for this moment—his crossroads, as he had come to think of it—since he was a small boy. He had always known he would recognize it when he came upon it.

Now that it was here, he knew he must hurry to claim it before it slipped away.

———

Jack was curious and even a little amused to feel himself scrutinized as thoroughly as if he were the applicant rather than the employer.

The lad had brass, that much was plain.

The boy had caught his interest immediately. He was almost as tall as Jack himself, with shoulders broad enough to balance his height, even though his frame was all angles and sharp turns. In truth, he looked as if he had not sat down to a full meal in a very long time, if ever. But it was the fiery glint of intelligence behind that startling blue gaze that intrigued Jack.

"The name's Sheridan, sir," the youth volunteered. "Cavan Sheridan."

"And where are you from, Cavan Sheridan?" Jack asked him, at the same time glancing down at the surprisingly legible handwriting on the paper the youth had thrust at him.

"Pennsylvania, sir."

Jack glanced up. "What in the world are you doing in New York?"

The boy shrugged but made no reply.

"On the lam, are you?" Jack pressed.

The other bristled visibly. "No, sir! Nothing like that."

The accent was right out of the west: western Ireland. One of the islands, more than likely. "Then why did you leave Pennsylvania?"

"To get out of the mines." The brogue thickened perceptibly. "I couldn't stay in the mines."

Jack felt an unexpected softening within. He knew a fair amount about the conditions the country's coal miners worked under—abominable conditions, for the most part. His eyes went to the thin scar that traced the right side of Sheridan's face, from eyebrow to long, lean jaw. "Got yourself banged up a bit, did you?"

The youth hesitated, then nodded. "There was a cave-in. Broke my shoulder and my collarbone. But I would have left the mines in any event."

"How old are you, lad?"

"Nearly twenty, sir."

Older than Jack would have thought. Perhaps because of the lanky frame or the light band of freckles running across his nose, Sheridan looked scarcely more than a boy. Or was it something in those unsettling blue eyes? Some hint of vulnerability that didn't quite go with the hard line of the mouth or the scar.

Jack studied the youth for another moment, then motioned him to a chair. "How long did you work the mines?" he said, sitting down at the desk.

The wide mouth tightened. "Since I was fifteen, sir."

"That's a bit young for such a place."

"Not really, sir," Sheridan said, hesitating another second or two before lowering his long frame into the chair across from Jack. "Lots of boys go down before they're ten."

Jack leaned back, locking his hands behind his head. "Can't imagine that's much of a life."

Sheridan's gaze darkened, and the earlier hint of youthfulness and vulnerability seemed to fade. "No, sir. It's not. In truth, it's no life at all."

Jack studied him. "You're from the islands," he said, making it more statement than question.

Sheridan looked surprised. "Aye, sir. The Big Island."

"Inishmore?"

The lad nodded.

"How long since you left?"

"I was thirteen when I came across, sir."

Jack had been fourteen. At the time he had believed himself to be a man. Now he realized how very young he had been. "So—you've been here in New York for how long?"

Sheridan sat on the edge of the chair, large hands knotted on his knees. He looked stiff and uncomfortable with his surroundings, Jack noted.

"Not long, sir. A few weeks is all."

"Where are you staying?" Jack could almost anticipate the answer. He knew all too well where penniless immigrants kept themselves when they had no place to go. New York could be brutal to its poor, relegating them to the worst of its slums or the mean streets themselves.

The boy glanced away, looking more awkward than ever. Something pricked at Jack's heart. "I've been down that road myself, lad," he said gruffly. "There's no shame in it."

Sheridan expelled a long breath. "I'll have me a place, once I hire on some-where."

Jack lowered his arms, took a cheroot from its box, and lighted it. "I'd be interested in knowing what qualifies you to be my driver."

Sheridan wiped his hands over his knees, first one, then the other. "I drove the coal wagons at the mines for the past two years, sir. I'm a good driver. I'm strong and do well with the horses."

Jack's eyes flicked to the youth's hands, large and chapped, with a faint residue of coal dust under the nails. In spite of his leanness, the lad did give the appearance of strength, even a kind of restrained power.

"Not exactly the same thing as driving a buggy," Jack pointed out.

Sheridan leaned forward still more. "More than likely, you'll be seeing a fair number of applicants for this job, Mr. Kane. But you won't be finding one better suited, and that's the truth." He paused. "I'd also be good to have around in the event of trouble."

"Well, now, I'm not hiring a bodyguard, lad. It's a driver I'm needing." Jack heard his own brogue slip out but made no effort to curb it. It came and went, and nothing evoked it so much as a fit of temper or a boy, like this one, fresh off the boat.

"Still, I'm the best man."

"Sure of yourself, eh? That's all right. No harm in it, unless there's nothing but air behind the starch." Jack considered him for a long moment. "Tell me the truth now, lad: Are you running from the law? I'll find out soon enough, so don't lie to me. I don't hire trouble. It finds me easily enough as it is."

Sheridan shook his head with convincing vehemence. "I'm in no trouble, and I'll be bringing you none, Mr. Kane. All I'm wanting is an honest job and a fair wage."

"Are you a drinker?"

Again the youth shook his head. "No, sir. I can find better ways to spend my wages."

"Curse of our people," Jack muttered, as much to himself as to young Sheridan. He held a bitter resentment toward the gross exaggerations of his countrymen's drinking habits, yet he was forced to acknowledge that the caricatures were not without some substance. Many of the Irish *did* drink to excess, there was no denying it. They drank to drown their troubles and their sorrows, seemingly blind to the fact that they were only borrowing even more grief for themselves and their loved ones.

To Jack, the whiskey was a beast—a beast that fed upon the soul as much as the body. For that reason, he had not lifted a glass of the stuff in over twenty years. Nor would he knowingly hire a man who couldn't stay out of his cups. It was his contention that if a fellow couldn't control his appetites, whatever they happened to be, he could not be relied upon as an employee.

He looked at Sheridan. "The job pays four dollars a week."

Actually, he had been prepared to offer only three, but something in the rangy youth sitting across from him prompted a more generous figure. "You would be required to either live here, on the premises, or remain as late as you're needed each night—which wouldn't usually be very late at all, but on occasion could run past midnight. You could take your meals here, in the kitchen, so long as you're on time and don't inconvenience the cook."

"I could stay here?"

Jack noted the quickening of interest and nodded. "There's a comfortable room above the stables. You could have that, if you like. My present stableman, who'll still be coming in to help out some about the house, has his own quarters elsewhere."

"Are you offering me the job, then, sir?"

There was no mistaking the eagerness in his eyes, the hunger. Not only hunger for a decent meal—though that, too, no doubt—but hunger for opportunity. Perhaps in a way, Jack thought, it was a hunger for hope itself.

"You be straight with me, lad," he said sternly, deftly shifting his cigar from one side of his mouth to the other. "Is there anything else I ought to know about you? Any reason at all I shouldn't hire you?"

Sheridan seemed to consider the question carefully. His reply was a surprise. "I left the church," he finally said.

Whatever Jack might have expected, it certainly wasn't this. "Indeed," he said evenly.

The boy nodded. "I couldn't stomach the way the priests treated the miners. Some of the men tried to protest the terrible conditions in the mines, the way the owners took advantage. Working us like mules from before dawn to long past dark, threatening our jobs if we so much as made a complaint, attaching our wages—why, by the time many a man picked up his pay, there was often so much held out for 'payment of accounts' that *he* owed the *company*. After all that backbreaking work, he would go home to his family empty-handed!"

There was no mistaking the anger, the outrage in the youth as he went on. "But when the men began to protest, the priests would have none of it. Labeled those who spoke out as 'troublemakers'; gave them a thorough tongue-lashing in front of the entire parish."

"Would I be right in assuming that not all of these protests were of a peaceful nature?" Jack put in.

Sheridan delayed his answer, but when it came Jack felt it was truthful. "Well, some of the men did get a bit more…physical with their objections, pulling rough stuff on the property, the mine offices. No one got hurt, mind, but it made the priests wild. They called the men out at Mass, made spectacles of them, thoroughly denounced them."

"You could hardly expect a priest to condone violence," Jack pointed out.

"Aye, that's true. Nor do I. But it wasn't right, the way the priests went after those men. They did their best to demoralize their own people." He paused. "At least, that's how it seemed to me."

"So you broke with the church," Jack prompted.

"I did. As I said, I'm not for violence, Mr. Kane; truly I'm not. But I was in the mines long enough to see why the men are desperate, why they feel forced to fight for their rights. You can't imagine what it's like, breaking your back underground day in, day out, the dank air, the dust, never seeing the light of day—I think that must be what hell is like."

He stopped, releasing a shaky breath as if the memory had choked off his words. When he finally went on, his voice was so low that Jack had to lean forward to hear him. "I didn't leave *God*, you understand, sir, though sure the priests would say I did just that. But it seems to me that God is not the one to blame for the deplorable conditions of the mines and the suffering of the men and their families. 'Tis men, not God, who must bear the shame of that injustice. But I simply couldn't continue to sit and listen to the priests blathering about the slavery of sin while turning a blind eye to another kind of slavery. Most of the miners did what they did in hopes of gaining better conditions for their wives and children. It did seem to me that the priests should have been trying to help the men, not humiliating them or condemning them."

Jack continued to study the boy for a moment more, then pushed away from the desk. When he stood, Sheridan also drew quickly to his feet. "There's nothing else, then?" Jack said. "Just this business with the church?"

"There's nothing else, sir, and that's the truth."

"Well, what you do with your religion is your own business, Sheridan. As I'm sure anyone would tell you, I'd be a most unlikely man to give you spiritual counsel." He came around the desk. "We'll try you for a month to see how it works out. I warn you, my schedule is often erratic—I'll expect you to be ready at a moment's notice and with no complaining."

"You'll hear no grumbling from me, I promise you, sir." The lad seemed to be debating with himself over something. Finally, he said, "Mr. Kane? There is one other thing perhaps I ought to mention."

So the boy was in trouble after all. The disappointment that rose in Jack was probably unreasonable, but he had responded to Sheridan's unmistakable intelligence, his eagerness, and his straightforwardness. Clenching his jaw, he waited.

"I feel I ought to be honest with you, sir." The youth stood wadding his cap between his big hands. "Grateful as I am for the job, it's not the sort of position I'll be wanting forever."

"And what exactly does that mean?" Jack growled around the cheroot.

"It means, sir, that in time I hope to gain a place for myself at the newspaper. *Your* paper, that is," he added quickly. "Once I'm better prepared, of course."

Jack frowned. "I think you'd best explain yourself. If you wanted a job on the paper, why didn't you apply at the *Vanguard*'s office to begin with?"

Sheridan's features tightened. "I did, sir. But I was told there was no place for the likes of me, my not having the book learning or experience required. Your manager wouldn't even let me into his office, you see. Said I was too young, too shabby, and too ignorant."

Jack suppressed a smile. Walter Goff had never been a man to mince words. "No doubt he was right," he quipped. "So, you thought you'd work your way into my good graces by hiring on as my driver and then wangle a place for yourself on the newspaper?" Though he deliberately roughened his voice, he regarded the youth with growing interest. "And what makes you think you'd want to work on a newspaper in any event?"

"Not just any newspaper, sir," Sheridan corrected. "Your newspaper. The *Vanguard*. 'Tis the best of the lot."

"Well, thank you very much for the vote of confidence, Mr. Sheridan," Jack said, his tone dry. "But that doesn't quite answer my question."

The young man—for by now Jack found it strangely difficult to think of Sheridan as a boy—appeared to frame his reply with great care. Once again, his answer was surprising—and obviously fired by a deep-seated conviction.

"Most men seem to believe there's power in guns or in great wealth—or in politics," Sheridan said. His tone was studied, his expression thoughtful, yet Jack could sense the passion behind his words. "It seems to me, though, that the real power of a people—of an entire country, if you will—is in what they read. Books. The press. These are the things that change people's minds...even their lives. You of all people must know what I mean, Mr. Kane. You and your newspaper, you can make people look at things the way you want them to, make them believe what you want them to believe—even move them to act the way you think they should act. *That's* real power, it seems to me, and the only kind worth having."

Jack expelled a long breath. What Sheridan said was the truth, and he couldn't have stated it better himself, though he had never thought of it in quite that way. For some reason, Sheridan's insight made him both curious and somewhat uncomfortable. "And that's what you want, then, is it, Cavan Sheridan? Power? For what purpose do you want this power, if you don't mind my asking?"

The level blue gaze never wavered. "I don't actually want it for myself, sir. At least, not entirely."

No, he wouldn't, Jack thought. There was more to this one than a narrow selfish streak. Much more, he'd warrant.

"What, then?" He couldn't resist probing a bit further.

For the first time since their meeting, young Sheridan smiled. It was a peculiar smile, and though it eased the good-looking, taut features somewhat, it neverthe-less seemed far too grim for a youth of Sheridan's years. It was a smile that failed to conceal the haunted look in the eyes, the hint of old, unhealed sorrows—and unless Jack was badly mistaken, a low-burning but ever present anger.

"For our people," Sheridan said quietly.

"Ah, for our people," Jack repeated, unable to keep the sarcasm from his voice as he extinguished his cigar. "On which side of the ocean in particular?"

Cavan Sheridan regarded him with a steady, oddly unsettling stare. "It seems to me," he said slowly, "that things are pretty much the same for the Irish on both sides. Wouldn't you say so, Mr. Kane?"

Jack said nothing, other than to indicate to Cavan Sheridan that he was hired and could assume his duties at once.

He reached to seal their agreement with a handshake, strangely moved when his new employee, as if out of long habit, wiped his hand quickly down the side of his leg before responding.

8

TOO LONG APART

Bitter is your trouble—and I am far from you.

DORA SIGERSON SHORTER

A week later, Cavan sat in the kitchen of the Kane mansion, having his breakfast and taking in the morning prattle of Mrs. Flynn, the cook, and Nancy Lynch, the young Irish day maid.

The latter was a bold sort, plump and pretty enough with her laughing eyes, high color, and shiny chestnut curls that invariably resisted the confines of a dust cap. From Cavan's first day on the job, the girl had made it clear that she would not be averse to his attentions. Cavan, however, was not interested. Even if the girl hadn't been a bit too coarse for his liking, he had more important things on his docket than dallying with the maids.

Besides, Jack Kane made it known to all his employees that he would not tolerate such goings-on among members of the staff, and Cavan had no intention of getting off to a bad start with his employer. This job was too important to him. So while he endured the maid's coquetry with good humor, he made no pretense of encouraging her. Despite his indifference, though, the girl did not seem easily daunted. Already this morning she had been eyeing him, taking what seemed an excessive length of time to collect the previous day's soiled tea towels and napkins for the laundry.

Aware of her scrutiny, Cavan made a determined effort to avoid her gaze as he ate his oatmeal and picked at the plate of bacon Mrs. Flynn had set before him. A fine cook, Mrs. Flynn, and she seemed to have taken a liking to Cavan right away. Every morning when he entered the house he found a generous breakfast waiting for him.

"So, then, Mr. Sheridan, how are you faring in your new job with Black Jack?" Nancy Lynch asked, watching Cavan as she pressed the linens down into the basket.

"Ach, girl, hush with such talk!" Mrs. Flynn swept the kitchen with a furtive

43

glance, as if she expected their employer to suddenly appear from one of the dim corners. "Don't be repeating that vulgar nickname. He is 'Mr. Kane' to you and all the rest of us."

"As if he doesn't know what he's called behind his back," the girl countered with a shrug. She shot Cavan a smile as she snapped another towel into the laundry basket.

"His knowing it and liking it aren't the same thing, now are they? You'd do well to keep a civil tongue, miss, if you value your position here."

The maid wrinkled her nose. "Well, I wasn't talking to you, now was I?" She angled another look at Cavan. "So, what does *Mr. Kane* have you doing when you're not squiring him about town or cleaning out the stables?"

Cavan set his spoon carefully beside his bowl. "I keep busy," he replied, "looking after the horses and doing odd jobs about the newspaper."

"From the looks of that woodpile out back," put in Mrs. Flynn, "you've been busy with the ax as well. And, sure, aren't we going to need it this day? 'Tis bitter cold out. With snow on the way again by evening, I'll wager."

"I'll bring in more wood if you like," Cavan offered, pushing away from the table. "There's time before we leave for the office."

The good-natured cook waved a hand, then reached to tuck a strand of gray hair back under her cap. Her face was flushed from the heat of the cookstove, her crisp apron beginning to wilt, even at this early hour. "No, there'll be more than enough until later this evening. See here, Cavan Sheridan, you've scarcely eaten anything. You don't take in enough to keep a wee boy fit, much less a big strapping lad like yourself." Ignoring Cavan's protests, she scooted a plate of buttered scones closer to him.

Cavan's lack of appetite was nothing new. He supposed the idea of sitting down twice a day to the bountiful fare of the Kane household should have seemed like a gift from heaven itself after so long a time of going without. Yet Cavan could never quite bring himself to enjoy the variety of dishes from Mrs. Flynn's kitchen. Too often the savory morsels brought a bitter image of his mother and sisters, turned out in the cold and dying hungry and homeless by the sea. Those times the food sat on his tongue like so many dry, tasteless kernels of grain.

From the hallway just then, a tuneful whistle heralded the approach of their employer. As Jack Kane entered the kitchen, it seemed to Cavan that the man didn't so much walk into a room as *appear* in it. Kane moved with the silent, lithe grace of a mountain cat, often creeping up on a body with no warning except his soft, melodic whistling.

He had already donned his well-tailored black overcoat and, as always, appeared jaunty and brisk. "As soon as you've finished your breakfast, lad, we'll be leaving. I need to go in a bit early this morning."

Cavan was already on his feet. "The carriage is ready, sir."

Nancy Lynch slipped out the door behind Kane, darting one last look at Cavan.

Mrs. Flynn turned around from the sink, wiping her hands on her apron. "Has there been any word from Mr. Brady yet, sir?"

Kane's features darkened. "I'm afraid not. I expect I'll be sending a man across to see what's become of him, once the weather eases."

Mrs. Flynn wrung her apron with hands red and work roughened. "Sure, he'll be perfectly fine, sir. It would take more than an old windstorm to foil Mr. Brady."

Kane's smile appeared slightly forced. "No doubt you're right, Mary. But I'd feel better if I knew where he was."

In the entryway, Cavan waited while Kane snapped a white carnation from a vase and slipped it into his lapel. On the way outside, his employer seemed inclined to conversation, which wasn't always the case; most mornings, Kane had little to say until they reached the *Vanguard*'s offices.

Today, though, he peppered Cavan with questions. "You told me you still had family in Ireland. A sister, I believe?"

Cavan nodded, his throat tightening. "Aye, sir. My sister, Terese."

"There are just the two of you?"

"That's right, sir. Terese has been staying with our aunt, but I hope to bring her across soon."

They took the walkway with care. A light coating of freezing rain had fallen during the night, leaving the grounds glazed and slippery. Cavan shrugged his aching shoulder a couple of times against the chill; the pain from the injury always seemed to worsen as temperatures dropped.

He felt his employer's eyes on him, as if the other were expecting more in the way of information. After a moment, Kane again took up the conversation. "I don't suppose you've heard how your sister fared in the storm yet?" he said, slowing his pace as they approached the carriage.

Cavan stopped, looking at him.

Kane frowned. "Sorry, I thought you knew or I'd have said something before now. There was a bad windstorm, it seems. From all accounts, I'd say it must have been nothing less than a hurricane."

"When—when exactly was this, sir?"

Kane smoothed his gloves. "Right after the first of the year, on Epiphany Sunday. Swept over most of Ireland, apparently—just about blew the country to pieces. Terrible destruction. Trees uprooted, houses leveled, fires—" He paused, then added, "I'm afraid the reports indicate great numbers of people dead or missing." He stopped. "You've had no word at all from your sister?"

Cavan shook his head. He felt suddenly chilled, and the ache in his shoulder escalated. "I wrote her with my whereabouts, but that was only a few days ago. The last letter I had from her was before I left Pennsylvania."

"How old is she, your sister?"

Cavan had to think. "She must be close on seventeen by now, I expect." He swallowed. Terese had not even been eleven years old when he and Da left Ireland.

"Do you know, sir—did this storm strike the islands as well? Inishmore and the others?"

Kane nodded, his expression sympathetic. "I'm afraid so." He climbed into the carriage then, saying, "As I told Mrs. Flynn, I'll be sending a man over to see about my brother when the weather breaks. We'll have him stop at the islands to ask after your sister as well, if you like."

"That's very kind of you, sir," said Cavan. "Sure, I'd appreciate it."

"Yes, well, that may be a few weeks yet. Perhaps in the meantime you'll hear something from her."

Kane ducked his head back inside the carriage then, and Cavan climbed up to the driver's bench, trying not to think about Terese on her own in the terrible storm. He knew she was no longer a child, yet he could not think of her as anything else. The image of the way she had looked that last day in the harbor, the day he and Da had left for America, was frozen on the frame of his memory. She had not aged in his mind since then but had remained a thin, awkward little girl with slightly wild hair and eyes red and swollen from crying after himself and their father.

She had clung to him, her arms locked about him as if to physically bind him to her. "Take us with you! Please, Cavan! You mustn't leave us here! Take us, too!"

They had made promises that day, he and Da. They would send for the others soon, they vowed. In no time at all, they would all be together again. "As soon as we find jobs for us both, we'll arrange for a flat. Or perhaps even a house. The time will pass before you know it; you'll see."

Their mother had stood by, oddly silent, holding Baby Mada, while Honor, the oldest of the girls, hovered near. Terese would not let go of Cavan but instead begged him not to leave without her and the others. At the end, Cavan had practically shoved her away and run for the ship, hiding his own sobs from his father.

Even now when he thought of that day, his eyes stung with unshed tears of grief—and guilt. They had failed, he and Da. Failed his mother and the little sisters…and the babe. They were all dead, and so was Da. No one was left except for Terese and himself.

And now, with word of this storm, who could say that he hadn't lost her as well?

He tried to console himself with the reminder that Terese had always been strong. From the time she was small, she had possessed an uncommon nerve and a will of iron. Indeed, she had always been the boldest and most resourceful of them all. Fiery, clever, and stubborn to the point of their mother's despair at times. Terese would be fine. She could take care of herself. Besides, she wasn't entirely alone after all. She had Aunt Una and Uncle Felim.

Small comfort, that. Those two had been more children themselves than a man and woman grown, he thought uneasily.

But Terese would manage, he assured himself. She would be all right.

All the same, he spent the rest of the drive praying for his sister, beseeching God to guard her until the day he could finally bring her across. Just as fervently, he implored—and not for the first time—divine forgiveness for having left her behind in the first place.

❧

As was his custom, Jack Kane perused a number of rival newspapers during the morning ride to his office. The *Herald* presently lay open on his lap, but his attempt to read Bennett's latest splash of sensationalism was halfhearted at best. For some reason, he couldn't keep his mind off Cavan Sheridan.

Jack had seen guilt often enough in his life to recognize the signs of it in his young driver. The look on Sheridan's face when he'd learned about the storm had been one of unmistakable shock mixed with fear—and guilt.

No doubt the boy had left Ireland, like thousands of other Irish males, with the intention and expectation of bringing the rest of his family across within a few months at most. As was often the case, months had turned into years, with still no means of sending for the others.

Young Sheridan talked sparingly of himself. He had spoken but once of his parents and two younger sisters, all deceased. This morning's conversation had been only the second allusion to the surviving sister. Jack thought it highly possible that the lad blamed himself for not being able to save his family.

He put the *Herald* aside, slid his feet closer to the warming bricks, and gave the lap robe a tug against the early-morning chill. He didn't know the facts, of course, but something told him that his new driver was the sort who tended to be excessively hard on himself. He appeared to own a keen conscience and an equally keen sensitivity.

If Sheridan had a sense of humor—and Jack suspected that he did—he kept it under wraps in the presence of his employer. He seemed to look at all things soberly and seriously, which made Jack speculate as to just how much the lad might be blaming himself for something completely beyond his control.

Odd, the difference in men when they lost control of their circumstances. He had seen it more than once. Some seemed to take on a kind of fierce resolve, a strength of purpose that eventually turned out to be either the making or the breaking of them. Others allowed guilt to oppress them to the point that it completely distorted their sense of reality. The latter very often ended up believing themselves to be less than the men they actually were. Some managed to shake off the guilt completely, either through their religion or by sheer force of will. Others, however, let it eventually destroy them.

He didn't know young Sheridan well enough yet to speculate on what sort of man he might become. New York would make it difficult for him, of course; the city was no friend to the immigrant, especially the Irish immigrant. The battles he was almost certain to face would challenge him mightily. Given the predictable difficulties, combined with whatever was obviously gnawing at him, who could say whether the boy would succeed or fail in his aspirations?

Jack found himself hoping that his solemn young driver with the wounded eyes would prevail over his demons, whatever they happened to be. Cavan Sheridan had been in his employ only a week, but Jack was already coming to like the youth, even to gain a measure of respect for him. He wanted better for the lad than a life of guilt and regret.

He knew only too well what that kind of life could do to a man.

9

TO CATCH A THIEF

The end of ages is drawing near;
As the world grows withered and old,
Charity will grow icy cold.

FROM *SAINT BRENDAN'S PROPHECY*,
EARLY SEVENTEENTH CENTURY

THE CLADDAGH, WESTERN IRELAND, MARCH

An oppressive fog shrouded the Claddagh in the early-morning hours. The mist hovered low over the district's narrow streets, its talonlike fingers creeping between the houses as if to beckon the unsuspecting to a deadly tryst.

Terese Sheridan stood shivering in a doorway, clutching a basket of stolen bread as she assessed her chances to break and run without being caught. Her stomach pitched at the smells from the river and the fish market. Her heart pounded crazily as she scanned the marketplace near the old gates.

She could not be caught! Under English law, she could swing for stealing. Somehow, she must get away!

Terese held her breath, watching for the right moment. At another time, she might have berated herself for the act she had just committed. She was no thief. Time had been, and not so long ago, that she would not have stolen a crumb from another's table, much less bread from a stranger. But the rules that once governed her behavior had succumbed to the burning misery in her belly. If she was to survive, she must eat. Her two dollars were long since gone, and she had not been able to locate even the most menial employment in the whole of Galway City. So for the past few days she had lifted a fish here, a crust there, until by the time she came upon the two housewives gossiping in the marketplace, a basket of bread resting nearby, she did not stop to consider the deed but merely acted upon instinct.

Even when the women had begun to screech at her and give chase as she dashed across the quay, Terese had felt no real guilt. There had been only a scalding flash of anger—anger at landing in the kind of circumstances that would bring her to such a thing. Another day or more without food would find her too weak to search for work, too weak to withstand the raw March wind as it came gusting in on the abandoned door stoops or alleyways where she sought shelter at night. It had come down to stealing or begging, and Terese would die before she would beg.

The damp chill steamed her breath and stung her skin, and she reached with her free hand to tug the ends of her shawl more tightly about her. If she had any real regret at all, it was for having drifted into the Claddagh earlier that morning. She had not intended to come this far, but in the fog she had lost her bearings.

If the old city of Galway had unnerved her when she'd first arrived, the Claddagh discomfited her altogether. The people in the Claddagh were known to be reclusive and somewhat peculiar. The colony was made up mostly of fishermen and their families, who had not changed their ways for centuries. Here, the inhabitants married among themselves and lived their lives along the narrow lanes of small but well-built houses of mud walls and thatched roofs. Outsiders were not encouraged to enter.

It was said that the people of the Claddagh were so religious—or so superstitious, depending on who happened to be giving the account—that the men would not go out in their boats to fish except at certain prescribed times blessed by the priest. They believed that the presence of God was always among them and tried to live accordingly, even refusing to greet one another without first invoking the name of God.

She wondered bitterly if these peculiar folk still felt so piously inclined toward their God after the monster wind he had unleashed upon them. For here in the Claddagh, as well as in Galway City, the storm's devastation was evident everywhere. Many of the small, sad houses lacked a wall or a roof, while others had been reduced to no more than a heap of thatch and mud.

As Terese's attention returned to her surroundings, she recalled with uneasiness that the Claddagh fishermen claimed complete rights and control over the bay and the entire district. It was rumored that if those rights happened to be violated, the people had been known to become so violent that there was no withstanding them.

Perhaps she might have chosen a better place in which to commit her thievery, but now was no time for such speculation. She could hear the voices of her pursuers, their shouts strangely muted by the dense fog overlying the entire district. Fear gripped her. At the same time, the heavenly aroma wafting up from the bread basket filled her senses, causing her stomach to wrench in a fiery spasm.

The angry voices were closer now. Terese knew she had no time left if she was to avoid capture, but fear and weakness threatened to buckle her legs. Only the thought of the precious, sweet bread so near at hand—and her resolve to survive—gave her the courage to bolt from the doorway and go charging down the street, intent on ducking into the nearest alley.

With her long legs and lean form, Terese was uncommonly fleet. But hunger and the bitter elements had taken their toll. Her lungs felt ablaze, her heart banging against her chest so fiercely she thought it would surely explode. Her ears roared with the thunder of her own pulse as she ran.

Behind her, the angry shouts began to close in. She felt like a fox with a pack of slavering hounds at her back. Dizziness washed over her, threatening to bring her down. An alley opened before her, and she lurched into it, gasping for breath as she sprinted over the cobbled street.

She heard the heavy tread of boots scraping the stones and knew others had joined in pursuit, turning into the alley behind her. Suddenly, at the exact instant when Terese feared she would go sprawling facedown into the street, she saw a man appear at the exit of the alley, blocking her escape.

She was trapped!

She stopped, pivoted about to see the mob of enraged pursuers closing in from behind, then whipped around to see the man at the other end of the alley coming toward her. She lowered her head and butted forward, hoping to push by him and gain her freedom. But he was upon her in two easy strides, a hand shooting out to break her flight.

Terese twisted, attempting to wrench free. The bread basket went flying out of her hand onto the street, its precious contents spilling onto the wet stones.

She threw her head back, a long wail of despair tearing from her throat. The man eased his grip on her but only for an instant before catching her by the arm and pinning her in place.

Terese's eyes burned, and she squeezed them shut, refusing to weep in front of her captor and the others. Even now, though she knew she had lost all hope of escape, she tried to shake free. But the man's grip was like an iron band about her arm.

She opened her eyes, surprised to encounter a gaze more curious than hostile. Indeed, the dark, deep-set eyes sparkled with something that almost hinted of amusement. Fury welled up inside her, and Terese found herself wanting to slap his smug face. Wasn't it enough to be starving and on the run from her own foolishness? Must she be an object of this *amadon*'s entertainment as well?

She tried again to break free of his grasp, a vain attempt, for he was strong, his hold on her unyielding. She caught an expression of impatience in the dark eyes, but nothing more. "Stop it, you little alley cat!" he grated out. "I'm only trying to save your hide."

Terese stared at him in surprise. He wasn't Irish, and he was no Britisher either, not with that accent. She thought he might be American. He was young and nice looking, his clothes casual but obviously of good quality. He had the look of a man who wanted for nothing. Who else but an American could sport such a well-fed appearance and the clothing to go with it? But what under the sky would an American be doing in the Claddagh?

A few renegade tears had spilled over in spite of her best efforts, and Terese lifted her free hand to brush them away. The man's expression seemed to change slightly as his eyes followed her movement.

Shamed as much by the tears as by her capture, Terese twisted to avoid his gaze. To her surprise, he turned to face her pursuers, bringing her gently, but firmly, around to stand at his side.

He raised a hand as if to ward off their complaints. Then, without waiting for the angry accusations and outcries to abate, he called for their attention. He spoke to them in English, his voice deep and well controlled, but with a distinct note of authority.

Terese had no choice but to face the crowd, and when she did she saw that, although their tempers were obviously still inflamed, they were at least paying heed to the man who stood before them.

To her astonishment, the American—if that's what he was—seemed to be defending her!

"Will you look at yourselves? Running down a defenseless girl like a pack of wild dogs! Why, you ought to be ashamed!"

"Defenseless in a pig's eye! She's a thief!" someone shouted from the crowd.

"Is she now? And what did she steal, this dangerous felon?"

One of the red-faced housewives who had been standing near the bread basket stepped out and jabbed a finger at Terese. "Didn't she steal me bread? The entire basket!"

Someone in the crowd muttered a dire admonition Terese took to be from Scripture, something to the effect that "bread gained by deceit tastes sweet but leaves the mouth full of gravel."

Terese was surprised that they were speaking in English. Even though many in the west knew the language of the Crown, most preferred their native tongue, especially on the islands and here in Galway. She wondered if some of these people knew the American and were speaking English out of deference to him. Yet they did not seem in the least deferential.

The American glanced at the basket in the street and its spilled contents, then turned back to Terese's accuser. "Two loaves, mother," he said, his tone laced with contempt. "What were you going to do, tear the girl to pieces for two loaves of bread?"

"We'll see her in gaol!" shouted another woman.

A collective cry swelled from the crowd. Terese's dark-haired rescuer dug his free hand into the pocket of his trousers, tossing a few coins at the housewife. "This will pay for your bread! Now go home and leave the girl alone."

From the back of the mob, a lantern-jawed man pushed forward, his eyes blazing as he confronted the American. "Who do you think you are, to be telling us our business? *You're* the one who had best be going home, Yank, if you value your neck!"

Again the crowd began to grumble among themselves, but the American shouted over them. "You've been paid for your bread! Now back off, and leave this girl alone!"

"Or you'll do what, Yank?" his challenger bellowed.

Now the grousing among the mob grew louder and more agitated. Terese saw two other men wedge their way to the front. One of them, wearing a broad-brimmed hat and a red kerchief around his neck, came to stand directly in front of her and the American.

"Claddagh men don't take kindly to meddlers, Yank," he grated out.

"Nor to desperate young girls either, it seems," countered the American.

He didn't look a bit frightened, Terese decided, wondering if he was fearless or merely foolish. At the same time, she caught a glimpse of movement, and as she watched, a dark colossus of a man stepped into the alley.

He was an intimidating giant with a head of curly black hair, an inky beard, and shoulders wide enough to block the light. Involuntarily, Terese flinched, again reviling herself for the folly that had brought the wrath of these savage people against her.

The American was standing his ground, but she felt his grasp on her arm tighten as he began to draw her slowly behind him. The man in the wide-brimmed hat took a step forward, his expression ugly. The crowd too began to press closer. The American muttered something under his breath and suddenly dropped Terese's arm.

"Run!" he cried, shoving her toward the exit of the alley.

At that moment, a shout exploded from the back of the mob. Terese whirled around. The towering figure who had entered the alley only a moment before was now parting the crowd, shoving his way through to the front.

The American uttered something that sounded like "Gabriel," then, "Just in time!"

The giant reached them, locked gazes for an instant with the American, then, ignoring Terese entirely, turned to the crowd. "Go back to your homes and your work, the lot of you!" he commanded them in the Irish.

His voice was like a low rumbling of thunder as he raised a fist the size of a dinner plate and jabbed it at them. "The girl is hungry! She's one of the islanders, can't you see? No doubt the big wind drove her out. Haven't you seen more of the same these past weeks, roaming the streets half-starved?"

At last the pandemonium subsided, and the crowd's anger and hostility began to ebb. There were a few additional murmurings, but these, too, soon faded as the giant went on. Terese could scarcely take in the fact that he seemed to be rebuking the others instead of her. More amazing still was the effect of his words. Watching the facial expressions in the crowd, it seemed to Terese that this was a man they respected, a man of great influence among them.

He called to the owner of the bread basket, whose face was still flushed. "The American paid you for your bread, Bridget O'Brien!" he roared. "Go home now, woman! Go home, and say a prayer of thanks for your blessings and one for mercy on those less fortunate."

Relief washed over Terese as the crowd began to disperse.

Not waiting until they were gone, the giant turned to face her and the American. This time he spoke in English, his tone dry as he faced the younger man. "That was a foolish thing to do, Brady Kane. The blow to your head must have been worse than I thought."

The American grinned. "You may be right, Gabriel. In any event, you are a welcome sight, I can tell you!"

So they knew each other, then! Dazed by this sudden turn of events, Terese shrank back as the giant turned a piercing blue glare upon her. "Are you slow-witted, girl, or daft entirely, to try such a stunt? You're from the islands; you must know about Claddagh law. It might have gone much harder for you."

Terese refused to let the man think he could intimidate her, though in truth he did.

Despite her own height—she was taller than most women—he was an oak, towering more than a head above her, and he looked somewhat wild, with that unruly hair and black beard.

He continued to impale her with his fierce, hard stare until Terese had to look away. "'Twas steal or die," she muttered.

His dark brows lifted. "Some would say the one deserves the other."

Terese lifted her head to meet his gaze straight on. "I would have gotten away," she said stubbornly, "if it hadn't been for *him.*" She jerked a finger at the American.

Anger flared in her when she saw the younger man's impudent grin break even wider.

"I saved the girl from jail, and she's angry with me," he said, shaking his head as if to bemoan Terese's mental state.

"It seems to me that the both of you need to be locked away," the big man said sourly, "if for no other reason than to let you collect your wits. 'Tis obvious you've lost them somewhere along the way."

The two men proceeded to ignore Terese, speaking over her head as if she were no longer there. The giant did a great deal of mumbling and glaring, but it seemed to Terese that in truth he wasn't all that vexed.

Even so, she had had quite enough of their boorishness. Her legs were trembling, her entire body shaking from cold and exertion. Even her head seemed to be swimming, making it difficult to see, much less think.

Somehow she managed to draw herself up and stand without swaying as she looked first one, then the other, in the eye. "If the two of you will allow me a word," she said, mustering what was surely her last shred of dignity, "I will thank you both for 'rescuing' me, and then I must be on my way."

10

ANGELS UNAWARES

The luck of God is in two strangers meeting,
But the gates of Hell are in the city street
For him whose soul is not in his own keeping
And love a silver string upon his feet.

T. D. O'BOLGER

Brady had all he could do not to applaud the girl. She was absolutely *magnificent!* Even with the smudges on her face and the shadows beneath those great smoke blue eyes, she was nothing less than splendid: all fire and passion and bravado.

Nearly as tall as most men and willow slim—she stopped short of actual gauntness—she reminded him for all the world of a high-strung mare. He half expected her to toss that wild mane of russet hair over her shoulder and go bolting down the alley.

Despite her fiery pride, however, she was obviously about to fall where she stood—no doubt from hunger, given the fact that she had been caught stealing bread. If that was the case, if the girl was actually hungry, what were they to do with her? They couldn't very well set her off on her own to steal again. As Gabriel had pointed out, she could bring real trouble down on her head.

"Where will you go?" Brady blurted out.

The girl whipped around, eyes narrowed. "Wherever I please, I should think."

"But...do you have a place to stay?"

Her nostrils flared, and again Brady thought of a restless young mare.

A thoroughbred.

"I expect that is my affair."

She was a scrapper, this one. But somehow her brass didn't irritate him as much as it might have coming from another, perhaps because of the fear he saw lurking in those enormous eyes. He was beginning to suspect that her sauciness was mostly show—a defense. The girl was obviously hungry, more than likely homeless and on her own. She had to be frightened.

Gabriel had been silent throughout this exchange, had merely stood, quietly watching the unlikely thief as if taking her measure. Now he spoke, his voice giving no hint of what he might be thinking. "It was bad on the islands, they say."

The girl looked at him.

"The big wind," he explained.

"How would you be knowing I'm from the islands?" she challenged, her tone defiant.

The big man shrugged, his gaze flicking over her as if her clothing were explanation enough. Brady realized that he had seen similar apparel on some of the other women wandering around Galway City: the long scarlet skirt against bare legs, a tattered shawl, and that strange multicolored sash at the waist.

"The Big Island, I expect?" Gabriel said.

After a slight hesitation, the girl nodded. "Aye. Inishmore."

Unwilling to be excluded, Brady posed a question of his own. "What about your family?"

She shot a look of impatience at him, making no reply. Clearly, she found him of less importance than the mighty Gabriel.

Understandable, certainly. Even so, he couldn't resist vying for her attention one more time. "If you need a place to stay, there are rooms to let at my flat. Mrs. Hannafin's rents are fair."

The girl's look would have quenched a live coal. "And would she be letting out rooms for *free,* then?"

Out of the corner of his eye, Brady saw Gabriel begin to dig down in his pockets. But apparently he came up empty-handed, for he remained silent.

Brady had a little cash on him, but he sensed that to offer it would invite yet another rebuke. Besides, Gabriel had already succeeded in engaging her in a brusque dialogue—one that again excluded Brady.

"Are you on your own keeping, girl?"

"I am," she said, the strong chin lifting a bit.

"The storm took your home, did it?"

She looked at him, a hard look that dramatically altered her appearance, adding years to her features. "Aye," she said, the word sounding as if she'd forced it out between clenched teeth. "The storm took it all."

Brady saw with some interest that the Big Fella's expression had gentled considerably as he went on questioning the girl. "And what has brought you to Galway, then?"

"I mean to find work to pay my passage to America."

Gabriel crossed his sturdy arms over his chest. "But you have found no work, so you resort to stealing, is that so?"

Her mouth curled downward, her eyes betraying a great depth of bitterness.

There was a long silence, during which Gabriel continued to study the girl closely, as if gauging her mettle. When he finally spoke again, his words were a surprise.

"You will come home with me for a bite to eat," he said.

It was not an invitation but a command. Brady had known the cryptic giant long enough by now to have learned that the Big Fella did not ask. He spoke, and others obliged.

The girl was a stranger, however, and either she did not realize she had just been given a direct command or, if she did, she chose not to acknowledge Gabriel's authority.

"I will not, but my thanks to you all the same."

Gabriel scowled at her. Not for the first time, it occurred to Brady that nobody could scowl quite as fiercely as Gabriel, except possibly his brother, Jack.

"Then you will starve," the big fisherman said flatly, as if he cared little one way or the other.

"Perhaps I will; perhaps I won't."

"Pride goes before a fall," Gabriel said in the same even tone of voice.

She glared at him. "I do not go off with strange men to their houses."

Brady almost strangled. Good heavens, did the girl actually think Gabriel was propositioning her?

He glanced at the Big Fella, somehow finding it impossible to imagine the dour giant with a woman. Why that should be the case, he wasn't sure. Gabriel wasn't an old man, by any means—he was probably no more than forty, if that—and though some might find his size intimidating, he wasn't a homely man, not even a plain one. In fact, he might actually be considered good-looking by the women, especially if he were to smile every now and then.

Perhaps it was the presence, the bearing of the man, that seemed to place him above the needs or weaknesses of mere mortals, Brady thought, intrigued. Somehow Gabriel seemed to exist and move within his own sphere of power, drawing, even trapping, those around him in its force. So compelling was the giant's persona that Brady had seen others actually shrink back when the giant came near. At the same time, there seemed to be a fundamental decency about the man—a sense of goodness and an innate morality to which others, even Brady, invariably responded.

But even if Gabriel had been inclined to lasciviousness, Brady doubted that this half-starved runaway would entice him. She was all angles and planes, for one thing—too thin by far. The riotous mane of hair was badly tangled, her face smudged, her clothing shabby, and, splendid as she was with that fiery temper and brave show of dignity, at the moment she wasn't exactly a sight to turn a man's head. Besides, Brady sensed that she was also very young. Perhaps younger than she would want them to know.

Gabriel appeared to dismiss the girl's shaded insult. "You are to be commended for your virtue, lass," he said dryly. "But I do not fancy scrawny little girls."

Her face flamed, and she was clearly about to spit out some venomous retort, but

Gabriel ignored her indignation. "I do not live alone," he said. "There are others at my house—a girl older than yourself and a wee wane—and we will take this strapping young Yank along for your protection, if you like."

The girl cut Brady a scathing glance before turning back to Gabriel. "Why would you do such a thing?" she challenged.

"Our Lord bids us feed the hungry," said the big fisherman, his tone mild. "You are hungry, I think. So come along now, before you faint here in the street. I have no wish to carry you the rest of the way." With that, he started off.

The girl watched him, and Brady watched her. He could almost see that monumental pride warring with her body's obvious privation. Then, as if conceding defeat, she gave a short nod and started off, scurrying to keep pace with Gabriel's long stride.

Brady, having received an invitation of sorts, followed after. As he hurried along behind the two, a portion of Scripture came to mind. Of course, the only Scriptures Brady knew were those his sister, Rose, a nun, was fond of quoting. This particular verse was one of her favorites—Jack accused her of pulling it out every time a stray beggar came to the door, so as to justify the lack of good sense in taking a stranger into their midst.

It had something to do with "entertaining angels unawares."

Brady grinned to himself as he watched the haughty girl with the thoroughly disreputable appearance take off after the Big Fella. No angel, that one, he would warrant. But wasn't she fascinating all the same?

II

IN THE HOUSE OF THE FISHERMAN

What change has put my thoughts astray
And eyes that had so keen a sight?

W. B. YEATS

Terese Sheridan was her name. She pronounced it *T'reece,* her tongue merely grazing the first syllable before lingering on the second. She was seventeen years old, she said, and the only surviving member of her family, other than an older brother who had emigrated to America years before.

Brady listened to the girl recite the basic facts about herself as they ate their midday meal of potatoes and buttermilk. The room was dim, for there was only one window, too narrow to admit much light. Both the Sheridan girl and Gabriel sat on stools pulled up to the rough-hewn plank that served as a table, while across from them Brady perched on a *boss*—a low seat made of straw. The child, Evie, sat beside him, wide-eyed and for the most part ignoring her food as she took in the conversation.

As was frequently the case, Roweena declined to share the table. Instead, she busied herself at the fire, watching over a fresh pot of boiling potatoes, then tossing them into the *kish*—a wicker basket—for straining. Brady knew from experience that when she eventually got around to eating, she would seat herself on one of the stone benches by the hearth, her milk and potatoes set out neatly beside her as she watched the exchange taking place around the table.

It still puzzled him—to some extent *annoyed* him—that Roweena so seldom participated in a meal but instead behaved as if she were a servant, compelled to wait table for others. He had carefully broached the subject of her odd behavior with Gabriel on one occasion, but the big man had simply shrugged and replied, "That is her way."

By now, this small, humble cottage had become comfortably familiar to Brady. After his recovery from the head injury, he had returned to help restore the roof, as a way of thanking Gabriel for taking him in. During that time, he and the Big Fella had become *almost* friendly, at least tolerant of each other. While Brady was no longer intimidated by the taciturn giant, he still had a tendency to tread with care when his host fell into one of his tight-lipped moods.

He hadn't expected that he would actually come to like, even admire, the big fisherman, especially in so brief a time. Incredibly, he found himself coveting the man's approval; the fact that that approval didn't seem to be forthcoming puzzled, even irritated, Brady more than he cared to admit.

Roweena puzzled him even more. At first he'd suspected that her subservient behavior must be Gabriel's doing, had wondered if the man had deliberately consigned her to a housemaid's role, perhaps as a way of payment for providing her a home.

It hadn't taken him long to realize that wasn't the case. Although the big fisherman made a show of sternness with both girls, he was much more a father figure to them than a master. With Evie, especially, he could be surprisingly gentle, in spite of his occasional feigned severity.

When it came to Roweena, Gabriel's conduct was somewhat more complicated. Although he was kind to her and openly protective, at the same time he seemed to maintain a certain distance between them. Whereas he would tease Evie, and even rough and tumble with the child, with Roweena he became more a patriarchal figure: watchful, often stern, though never bullying or impatient.

Now he seemed to have adopted a similar stance with the Sheridan girl. At the moment, he was studying her with that fixed gaze of his that seemed to discern everything while revealing nothing. For her part, Terese Sheridan appeared to have steeled herself against the giant's scrutiny and brusque demeanor, answering his questions succinctly, and once or twice a little sharply.

Mostly, she ate. Brady hadn't missed the eager way she eyed the food when they first pulled up to the table. But instead of digging in, as he suspected she was longing to do, she partook of the meal with an admirable measure of restraint, as if she were too proud to call attention to her hunger.

Gabriel didn't seem in the least offended by the shortness of her replies but went right on questioning her. He added little to the conversation but mostly sat listening to her replies with the poker-faced expression Brady had come to know well by now.

Although the two frequently lapsed into the Irish as they spoke, Gabriel would occasionally glance at Brady and steer the conversation back to English. Brady was able to catch the gist of their exchange well enough. Apparently, Terese Sheridan was on her own, had lost her entire family except for the brother in America, and had survived the killing windstorm with no more than the clothes on her back. It sounded to Brady as if she had made her way here from her island home by sheer spunk and her own wits.

When she calmly declared her intention to join her brother in the States, there seemed no reason to doubt that she would do just that. Despite her disheveled, half-starved appearance, the girl's iron will and strength of purpose were blazingly evident.

Even so, Brady suspected she would find her course a difficult one, for by her own admission, she was penniless.

"I had my own money, you see." The reply to Gabriel's question about her circumstances was given without hesitation, though her tone was not without an edge of bitterness. "Money I'd saved from what my brother sent. But didn't my aunt Una steal it away from me? All but two dollars, which are now gone. That's why I must find work, and find it soon. Not only for my keep, but to earn my passage."

"Your *aunt* stole your money?" Brady put in. "What kind of woman steals from a member of her own family?"

The girl shot him a look that clearly questioned his knowledge of human nature. "A spiteful, greedy woman, it seems to me." Her lips curved slightly in a cold mockery of a smile. "But a *Christian* woman, you understand."

Brady stared at her. There was the same hard edge he had seen earlier. It was gone as quickly as it came, but not before the thought occurred to him that while Terese Sheridan might be only seventeen, she seemed to be more woman than girl—and one with a marked streak of cynicism, at that.

"So...what do you mean to do now?" he asked casually.

She looked at him but offered no reply. Instead, she turned back to Gabriel. "Is there work to be had in the Claddagh?"

He shrugged. "The work of the Claddagh is fishing. We go out in our boats, and we fish." He studied her. "Still, there might be something for a strong girl who is willing to work."

The girl leaned forward slightly on the stool. "I *am* strong, though you may not see it in me today. I am strong, and I am not afraid of hard work."

The big man rubbed his chin. For a moment he lapsed into the Irish, but with a quick glance at Brady, reverted to English. "There is a woman. Not wealthy, mind, but not poor either. She's not an old woman, but her man is dead—died at sea, God rest his soul. The daughter married outside the Claddagh and moved away to Australia."

He paused and sat stroking his heavy black beard in a reflective gesture. "Jane has a sickness in her bones," he continued, "that grows worse by the day. Her hands are drawn and knotted like old tree limbs, her legs, too—she can scarcely walk at all but must use a chair most days. She can no longer tend the house or do her own marketing. She suffers in a bad way, Jane does."

He shook his head, then went on. "Roweena goes and helps sometimes, but I can't be sparing her every day. She has work enough to do here, and there's the little one to look after. Besides, it makes it difficult, her not being able to hear. I expect poor Jane would pay if she could find a reliable girl to do for her."

This was by far the longest speech Brady had ever heard from the big fisherman, and he stared at him in surprise.

"This widow woman—do you think she would hire me?" Terese Sheridan watched Gabriel closely for his reply.

He gave a shrug. "She will or she won't. We will take you to her and let Jane speak for herself, if you want." He paused. "But the woman is in a bad way, mind. On her worst days, you would have to do for her almost as you would a babe. And then the house needs care and the cooking done. If you're shy of sickness or lowly work, don't be volunteering yourself."

The girl pressed forward even more, her meal seemingly forgotten. "I'm not too proud to care for a poor sick woman. And there is no work I would not do. Would you be taking me to her, please?"

Gabriel regarded her for a long moment. "First you will finish your food and warm yourself," he said. "Afterward, Roweena will help to make you more presentable."

Brady saw the girl's face flame, but she said nothing, merely glanced down over herself with a rueful look. "And then you will take me to this woman?" she pressed.

Gabriel's steady gaze continued to measure her. Finally, he gave a short nod. "Then I will take you to Jane."

Brady studied the big fisherman, somewhat puzzled by his ready acceptance of the intriguing young thief. But then, Gabriel was a constant enigma to him. One minute the man seemed little more than a sour-tempered hermit, the next, a kindly benefactor. The Big Fella had myriad facets to his nature, all of them unpredictable.

Despite his many peculiarities, however, he had been decent enough to the "bothersome Yank," as he sometimes was wont to call Brady. So long as Brady did not annoy him with too many questions—or pay Roweena excessive attention—the Big Fella seemed tolerant of his presence. In fact, Brady suspected that the only reason he and his sketchbook were allowed to roam at will among the Claddagh community was because Gabriel had first accepted him at his hearth fire.

That the big fisherman wielded that sort of influence among the colony's inhabitants had become obvious to Brady early on. Gabriel might not be the "king," as they referred to their official governor, but he clearly held a great deal of power in his own right.

It hadn't taken long to discover that Gabriel—if the man had a last name, it was his secret—was a man of great importance in the Claddagh. There was his formidable physical presence, of course; it was difficult not to be awed by the giant. But there was much more to this man than mere brawn. For one thing, the people of the settlement seemed to view him as a sort of healer. They brought him their ill children, the occasional accident victim, and even sought his advice on ailing animals. Apparently, the big fisherman had a way with such things, for more often than not his "patients" went away much improved.

Brady had noticed an abundant supply of dried herbs and tins of medicine stored on shelves above the painted dresser. He had also seen the Big Fella, with Roweena's assistance, set a broken arm or foot. Less frequently, Roweena might be summoned to help with a birthing. At those times, Gabriel would sign some hurried instructions, then send her off with a small valise that looked like a physician's case.

Brady was roused from his thoughts when Terese Sheridan stood and made an oddly formal statement of appreciation to her host. "I am grateful for your hospitality, sir. I will repay you as soon as I find a position."

Gabriel took a long sip of tea, then said mildly, "You will not speak of payment for an open door and a plate of potatoes, lass, unless you mean to insult me."

The girl blanched, then tried to stammer a protest, but Gabriel ignored her. Getting to his feet, he summoned Roweena to him and began to instruct her, voicing his words slowly and emphatically as he always did, much like an accompaniment to the fluid hand movements by which he "spoke" to her.

Roweena cast a quick glance at Brady, then made a gesture that the other girl should follow her. Struck by the contrast between the two, Brady could not help staring. The dark-haired Roweena, slight and delicate in appearance—and clearly awed by this stranger in their midst—was like a timid fawn in contrast to the taller, oddly regal Terese Sheridan. The latter, with eyes of blue smoke and a tumultuous, wild beauty, might have been one of the mythic warrior queens readying herself for battle as she accompanied the diminutive Roweena behind the curtain. Queen Maeve on a rout.

Abruptly, Brady tried to force his thoughts away from the two girls—especially from Roweena, who he sensed might, if he did not take care, represent the first serious threat to his emotions in a very long time. Roweena was no mere girl, as he had thought upon their initial encounter during the storm. He had come to realize that she was probably in her early twenties at least—not all that much younger than himself, at twenty-seven.

Even so, he had found her to be nothing like he would have expected from that first encounter during the storm. That night, in her frenzy to get the child, Evie, to safety, she had appeared impetuous, brave—even impassioned. But inside these snug walls, she was scarcely more than a shadow of that fleet-footed sprite. At times, she seemed almost childish, less womanly than the subtle curves of her body might indicate. To Gabriel, she was submissive, scurrying to do his bidding and see to his comforts. With others she maintained a shy, deferential demeanor that almost made her appear slow-witted.

Even with Evie, she seemed more a big sister than a maternal figure. And her pretty blushes each time Brady caught her eye only confirmed his suspicion that Gabriel had kept her thoroughly sheltered from the outside world—particularly from men.

As for the strange relationship between Gabriel and the two girls, Brady had learned nothing more than what Evie had expressed the night of the storm. The child, apparently abandoned when she was little more than an infant, had been rescued and taken in by the big fisherman. Similarly, Gabriel had provided Roweena a home from the time she was a small girl. There had been something about a fire, but he hadn't been able to figure out much else from Evie's chatter.

So far as Brady knew, there was no blood tie between Gabriel and either of the girls, but both were obviously devoted to their guardian. On numerous occasions, he had wanted to ask about the girls' backgrounds, but Gabriel had a way about him that discouraged too many questions.

As for Roweena, the appeal she held for him had come as a total surprise to Brady, and a distinctly unsettling one. He had never been attracted to the shy, "nice girls" at home. No doubt it spoke volumes about his character that his tastes had always run to the more flamboyant sort of women, often older than himself, whose morals—according to Jack, at least—were as questionable as Brady's own. It wasn't typical that a girl like Roweena—lovely as she was—would capture his interest.

Yet he couldn't deny his response to her. She aroused something akin to tenderness in him—an instinct to protect, to cherish—that up until now he hadn't known he possessed. He found himself uncharacteristically considerate of her feelings, careful of his behavior toward her. At the same time, he fervently wished he could somehow breach her defenses, draw her out of her shyness so he might get to know her better.

Not that he would allow himself a serious attachment. He had made a practice of shunning commitment. To even consider some sort of involvement with a backward deaf girl in this remote, primitive place would border on sheer lunacy.

He blamed his temporary fascination on the fact that Roweena was so dramatically different from the other women he'd known. Brady adored women. He had made an art of pursuing them, flirting with them, enjoying them. And *leaving* them, more often than not with little rancor on either side.

He had no interest in the domestic life. There was too much he wanted to do, too many places he wanted to see. Jack sometimes accused him of having "the Gypsy in his soul," and Brady wasn't so sure that his brother might not be right. In truth, he was restless by nature, seldom satisfied for very long at a time. Something inside him continually urged him on to new faces, new experiences, new relationships.

That being the case, he would be the worst kind of fool to let his emotions run out of control. To take up with a girl like Roweena would jeopardize the freedom he prized so highly.

Besides, Gabriel would almost certainly murder him.

Fortunately, it wasn't all that difficult to turn his attention elsewhere. The Claddagh itself had captured his interest. The place and its people had almost immediately seized him and drawn him in. Brady was convinced that some of his best portraits to date would come out of the Claddagh. Among these dusky, narrow lanes and crooked alleyways, he had found the many faces of sorrow, suffering, and despair. Yet he had also seen features chiseled of strength, endurance, and a strange kind of peace—a serenity unlike anything he had ever before encountered. Here the past blurred with the present. An age-old faith and ancient secrets were as much a part of the people's existence as the sea that fed them and the God who they insisted dwelt among them.

The dark mystique that was the Claddagh had staked a claim on his soul. Nowadays he found himself increasingly reluctant to leave the place and return to his flat and even more loath to think of leaving Galway for good.

Later, when Terese Sheridan reappeared from behind the curtain—now scrubbed clean, her riot of russet hair brushed to a blaze of copper—it occurred to Brady that perhaps here was yet another attraction to heighten the Claddagh's appeal.

❧

Gabriel watched the young American rascal—for if his instincts did not serve him false, this Brady Kane was just that, a *rascal*—as Roweena and the island girl returned. At first he thought the spark of interest in the lad's eye was for Roweena, and his jaw tightened.

But upon closer appraisal, he realized that the object of the Yank's scrutiny was the girl from Inishmore.

He almost smiled. That one would be a match for the young *jackeen,* he would warrant. She might be young, but she was no foolish girl. Trouble and hard times had hardened her; that much was plain. In her own way, she seemed years older than Roweena or the American.

He stood, gave a nod of approval to the tall island girl, then another to Roweena for her help. The wee wane was clearly wanting to be included in their midst, so he dipped low to scoop her up. "You may go with us to see Jane. She likes your company well enough, for some unaccountable reason," he teased.

The child beamed at him and chuckled. "I like your company, Gabriel."

"Indeed? And I expect you would like to ride upon my shoulders as well, eh? Come on, then," he said, swinging the child around to piggyback him. "We will be on our way."

He turned to Roweena, then Brady Kane. "It is time for you to be getting along, too, Yank," he said pointedly. "Roweena will go with us to see Jane Connolly."

The young American looked at him, then glanced at Roweena, not quite concealing his disappointment. But he made no protest. Instead, he cracked his roguish grin and, with a courtly bow for the girls and a wide sweep of his hand, made a jaunty exit.

With wee Eveleen still hugging his neck, Gabriel stood watching the American leave. He was disquieted to realize that Roweena's gaze also followed the bothersome Yank until he was completely out of sight.

12

JANE CONNOLLY

For who can say by what strange way
Christ brings His will to light…

OSCAR WILDE

Terese hurried along the cobbled streets, close behind the others. With her belly satisfied for the first time in weeks and the chance for a position as well, she could almost allow herself to feel hopeful. But fast on the heels of this flicker of optimism came the reminder that she must not dare to hope too much, lest the devil should resent her light heart and cast a weight on it.

For all she knew, this Jane Connolly person might turn out to be an evil old shrew who would shriek and squawk and make life wretched altogether. But sure, wouldn't she plug her ears and tend to the woman in spite of her hatefulness if it meant paying her passage to America?

Not to mention a reprieve from the workhouse…

People died in the workhouse, and from the tales Terese had heard, they died from worse things than starvation. For her part, she would rather drop in the street from hunger than die of some filthy disease or at the hands of a raving lunatic.

The little girl—Evie, they called her—glanced back over her shoulder and smiled. An imp, that one. But the child's ingenuous, cheerful nature was somehow heartening after the hostile stares to which Terese had grown accustomed.

These seemed to be good people, if somewhat peculiar. She had always heard that the Claddagh fishermen were a wild lot, but the giant, Gabriel, and the two girls certainly appeared civilized enough. At least they had been kind to her—kinder than she had any right to expect, she conceded grudgingly.

Even the American had seemed genuinely concerned for her safety, although Terese didn't quite know what to make of him. There had been something disturbing in those dark eyes, something too bold, too inquisitive—and something too much like amusement, as if he found her curiously entertaining. Terese didn't trust him, but it was clear that he had some sort of connection to these Claddagh folk—and she *was* inclined to trust them. She had never met an American before, of course. For all she knew, they might all be as insolent and peculiar as this Brady Kane.

Ahead of her, the big man, Gabriel, and the two girls now came to a halt in front of a stoutly built thatched house. The place was set off to itself, not squeezed in among others, as were the majority of dwellings Terese had noticed on the way. Although the house appeared sturdy enough, there was a forlorn air of abandonment about it. Rotted netting and other debris had been strewn across the yard. On one side of the front door was propped an eel spear, on the other, a splintered barrel. The thatch of the roof also showed signs of neglect.

Terese suppressed a shudder at the gloom and pall of dejection that seemed to hover over the place. But when the big fisherman gestured for her to accompany them to the door, she didn't hesitate. She had already decided that a leaking roof over her head would be better than no roof at all.

❧

Inside, the afternoon gloom bathed the room in deep shadows, but here, too, the same sense of neglect was unmistakable. A stale odor of dust and mold hung over the room. Terese took in the unswept floor, the dingy furniture, and the unwashed dishes with the eye of one who had not so long ago labored over such things in her Aunt Una's household.

Despite Gabriel's description of Jane Connolly, Terese had to make a concentrated effort to conceal the blast of pity that shot through her at the sight of the woman. She had expected to be greeted by a hunched, misshapen figure whose temperament would no doubt be as dismal as her physical state. But the widow Connolly was something of a surprise. The woman seated in the wheelchair by the turf fire was so small that she could have easily been mistaken for a child. Her head was bent low, and she appeared to be dozing. But when Gabriel called out a greeting of "God bless all here," she looked up with eyes that were bright and welcoming.

Gabriel had said the woman was neither young nor old, and Terese could see what he meant. Jane Connolly had the kind of pinched and wizened features that might have been drawn by pain just as easily as by the passing of time. Her hands on the wooden arms of the chair were almost deformed; the wrists were swollen and red, and her right hand in particular was painful to look upon, with its thumb bent toward the palm and the other fingers toward the wrist. The body beneath the lap blanket was clearly twisted. But the hair coiled at the back of her neck was more brown than gray, and the hazel eyes were alert and knowing.

Terese didn't miss the way the woman's features softened at the sight of Roweena and the child, who immediately ran to her and, at the instruction of Gabriel, handed over a small pouch. The woman gave the fisherman a nod as if to thank him, then turned a narrowed gaze on Terese.

When Gabriel began to explain in the Irish, Jane Connolly seemed more intent on studying Terese than on hearing what the big fisherman had to say. The woman's scrutiny was bold and somehow unnerving, and Terese found herself wanting to look away from those searching eyes. Instead, Roweena caught her hand to bring her up close to the crippled woman as Gabriel set about making an introduction.

There was no acknowledgment by the widow, no effort to make a civil greeting. Only that sharp-eyed, measuring stare. After another moment, she turned to Gabriel, and a quick, barbed exchange ensued in the Irish.

"What are you thinking, man? I am not a wealthy woman. I can't afford a hired girl."

"We've talked of this before, Jane. You need a girl. You know you do." The big fisherman spoke evenly and quietly but with a firmness that brooked no argument. "This girl will work for a reasonable wage."

"Ha." The small face creased even more as she shot a skeptical glance at Terese.

Ignoring the woman's surliness, Gabriel continued. "The girl needs a place to stay. And you need help. Look at her—she's strong and fit and will be of much use to you."

The widow glared at him. "She's not one of us. She might be a lunatic or a murderer, for all we're knowing."

"Jane, Jane, I thought you trusted me," the fisherman countered reasonably. "Would I bring you a dangerous girl?"

The woman sniffed. "She might steal me blind, a wild girl like that."

Terese clenched her hands at her sides. The big fisherman's eyes sparked with something that might have been amusement, but his tone was offhand and agreeable as he replied. "Now, Jane, you say you are but a poor widow woman, with nothing to steal."

Jane Connolly rolled her eyes toward heaven and gave an exaggerated sigh. " 'Tis true," she said. "But she might murder me in my bed, even so."

The woman was daft entirely, Terese decided. The dread disease that had twisted her body must have also afflicted her brain.

Gabriel shook his head. "Now, Jane, haven't you told me that most nights you cannot get yourself *into* your bed at all but must sleep in your chair?"

Ah, now the eyes *really* narrowed, and the square little chin jutted out a bit more. Terese felt an irrational urge to laugh. This poor crippled woman was such a wee thing, yet she obviously considered herself a force to be reckoned with. Something told her that the widow Connolly was actually warming to the idea of hiring her on, but for some fatuous reason of her own was bent on making the fisherman first prove his case.

The giant was nothing if not even natured—Terese would give him that—allowing this sour-tempered woman to rant at him so.

"You surprise me, man, truly you do, putting me at the mercy of an outsider."

Gabriel crossed his sturdy arms over his chest. "Why don't you just speak with the girl, Jane? Have you no word of welcome for a stranger?"

She curled her lip at him, then turned to rake Terese with a hawkeyed stare. "Well, girl? You're from the Big Island, says Gabriel."

"I am."

The woman curled her lip. "My husband never did trust an islander."

Terese clasped her hands behind her back, drew a long breath, then let it out.

"My man always said the islanders were a bunch of savages."

Only the thought of another cold night in the alleys enabled Terese to hold her tongue.

Jane Connolly lifted a gnarled hand, and Terese couldn't help but notice the way she flinched with the movement. "Well, come here, then, girl," the woman demanded. "Come closer."

Terese stepped up to her, hands still behind her back.

"Show me your hands," the little woman demanded. "Let's see how well acquainted you are with work."

Grinding her teeth, Terese extended both hands palms up and stood unmoving as the woman examined them. The widow's eyes gleamed almost spitefully as she looked up. "Ach, and don't those nails need a good scrubbing? I'll not have a slatternly girl working for me."

With an effort, Terese clamped down on her anger. She was familiar with humiliation, but that did not mean she would tolerate it gladly. Still, the woman was in a pathetic condition. Sure, her pain must be fierce.

"What of your family?" the widow probed. "Why would a young girl like yourself be on your own keeping?"

Terese looked at her. Reluctantly, she gave a brief account of her father and brother's emigration, the subsequent deaths of her family members, and the destruction of her aunt's house in the storm.

She was aware of the widow's scrutiny as she spoke, the knowing expression, the curt nod. "So, then, your menfolk abandoned you," the woman put in, "and now you've run off from your aunt in her time of need, is that it?"

Something in Terese snapped. She yanked her hands back and whipped about as if to go. "You are a batty old woman, do you know that?" she shot over her shoulder as she started for the door. "I will not work for a mad woman."

"Get yourself back here, girl," the big fisherman rumbled. "And mind your manners. Jane isn't through with you yet."

Terese whirled around, facing him. "But I am through with *her!*"

She was amazed when the widow woman cackled. "Didn't I tell you, man? She is a wild island girl."

"And you," Terese repeated through bared teeth, "are a rude old woman!"

Again Jane Connolly laughed. The child, Evie, laughed, too, obviously delighted by the exchange taking place.

These people were more than strange, Terese decided. They were demented.

"Ach, enough now, enough." The widow Connolly attempted to wave a hand, but the twisted, swollen appendage made the gesture seem almost grotesque. In spite of herself, Terese felt another quick stab of pity. Even so, she had no intention of suffering the woman's abuse.

Jane Connolly's next words surprised her, however. "It seems to me that you will do well enough, girl. They do say the island girls aren't afraid of hard work."

Gabriel nodded now in apparent satisfaction, while Roweena smiled at Terese as if to encourage her. And from the corner where she had perched herself on a stool, the peculiar Evie chuckled.

"I will give you a bed and food," said the widow in a brisk, no-nonsense tone. "You don't look as if you eat all that much in any event. You will cook for us and tend to the house, inside and out." Her tone now turned grudging. "And you will tend to me as well. It's little enough I can do for myself these days."

"That sounds to me like a great deal of work," Terese pointed out.

The woman gave her a fierce glare. "Was I looking for you when you came, girl? You can go out the door just as easily as you came in, it seems to me."

"Jane—"

The stern word of rebuke from Gabriel merely earned him a terrible scowl.

"What will you pay me?" Terese broke in before the two could take up again.

"Didn't I just offer you a bed and potatoes?"

"A bed and potatoes are not enough. You are requiring a full-time girl. I will work for wages or not at all."

The woman turned to Gabriel. "Impudent. You see? She's a very lowbred girl."

The fisherman lifted his dark eyebrows. " 'Tis true for her, though, Jane. You are expecting a great deal of work for no wages. I doubt that you'll find another girl as strong and willing to work as this one."

The shrunken widow woman glowered at him, then turned an even blacker look on Terese. "One shilling a week," she finally said, the words sounding as if she might choke on them.

Hands on hips, Terese glared down at her. "Two."

"Ach, girl, do you think I am the goose laying eggs of gold?"

Terese didn't so much as blink an eye. "Two," she repeated.

Jane Connolly muttered something to the effect that she would "die in the workhouse and all for a greedy girl," but after a moment more gave a grudging nod. "You will begin today."

"If you wish," Terese said just as shortly.

The widow woman wheeled around to Gabriel once more and gave a semblance of shaking a finger at him. The finger, Terese noted, was swollen at the knuckle to almost twice the normal size and was badly inflamed. "And you, man, will bear the burden if she steals from me or murders me altogether."

The big fisherman appeared to be suppressing a smile as he dipped his head in a gesture of agreement. "'Tis as you say, Jane." He straightened then and beckoned to Roweena and the child. "We will be away now and let you and your new girl get acquainted."

At their departure, Terese braced herself. As cantankerous as her new employer had been in the presence of others, she hated to think what her temperament might be once they were alone. She consoled herself, however, with the thought that she finally had found a position—a position that included two shillings a week and a roof and hearth fire, not to mention "a bed and potatoes."

With that in mind, she actually managed to force a tight little smile for the woman in the wheelchair. "And what shall I be doing first, Mrs. Connolly?" she asked politely.

Jane Connolly regarded her with the same narrow-eyed scrutiny. "I don't suppose an island girl knows much at all about hanging out a proper wash."

"This island girl does," Terese said evenly. "My people were clean and civilized."

"Ha. We will see about that, now won't we? Well, then, get on with your work, girl. Behind the curtain there's a basket of clothes needing to be laundered. All this blather with you and that thickheaded fisherman has exhausted me entirely. I will need to rest now."

"Would you be wanting me to help you to bed, then?"

Slowly, Jane Connolly shook her head. "I can no longer find any còmfort in my bed," she said, averting her gaze. The woman appeared drawn and deathly pale. "I spend most of my hours in this infernal chair. That great oaf, Gabriel, doesn't he nag at me to get up more, never mind the pain? 'Get up, Jane, and uncoil yourself,'" she said in a sneering imitation, "'or you will surely turn to stone.'"

Her head dropped even lower. "He doesn't know," she said bitterly. "He can't know what it's like for me. I *am* turning to stone, and there is nothing anyone can do about it."

She glanced up at Terese then. "I am not an old woman, you know. You think I am old, and our dear Lord knows I feel it. But in truth I've no more than ten years or so on Gabriel."

Terese evidently failed to conceal her astonishment, for the woman gave a rueful smile and nodded. "'Tis true." As if she suddenly decided she had said too much, she clamped her jaw. "Well, all right, then. Go and see to your work now. Make no mistake about it, miss, you will earn your two shillings a week."

Not doubting for a moment that she would do just that, Terese gave a resigned sigh and went in search of the clothes basket.

13

REGARDING WOMEN

One had a lovely face,
And two or three had charm,
But charm and face were in vain...

W. B. YEATS

❦

NEW YORK CITY

Jack Kane looked idly around the ballroom of the Harrington mansion. It was unlikely that a Russian palace would have boasted more opulence or excess. White fire danced back and forth from the crystal chandeliers to diamond-bedecked socialites, only to be swept up in the flames of what must have been two hundred or more flickering candles placed all about the room. The place was so brightly lit it might have set the entire city ablaze.

Not the typical Irish *ceili,* that was certain. The thought brought a wry grin. For once, being Irish hadn't prevented Jack from receiving an invitation, indeed had actually helped to guarantee it. Had he been shanty Irish, however, that wouldn't have been the case. Only the very rich Irish would be showing their gobs at this affair, a benefit ball put on to aid the work of some of the immigrant societies.

There was never enough money, of course, to keep up with the increasing waves of immigrants flooding the harbors these days. So when Richard Harrington and a select few among the city's elite circle—those who had not lost their fortunes in the crash last year—agreed to host a benefit for "the destitute and the despairing," every Irishman with a bank account and a tailcoat got himself an invitation.

For most of the evening, Jack had been preoccupied with his own thoughts, primarily of his brother's whereabouts. The young rogue's unaccountable silence had gone on long enough. Foul weather or not, Tom West was set to go across and have a look if there was no word from Brady in the next couple of weeks.

At the moment, there was another source of irritation, this one closer at hand: the annoying Miss Patricia Woodstock. It wasn't that his dinner companion lacked appeal. To the contrary, Miss Woodstock was quite fetching. Blonde and elegant, she had the kind of patrician features and form that never failed to turn heads. But to Jack's thinking, her looks were just about all she could boast of. In fact, in one of his more fanciful moments, he had decided that the fair Miss Woodstock rather resembled one of those French cream puffs that Addy was forever bringing home from Cree's Bakery—a kind of powdery confection that made the mouth water but turned out to be little more than sugar-sprinkled air.

All frosting and no filling, as it were.

The girl had been like a leech throughout the entire evening, fixing her attention on his every word, rolling her china-doll eyes and chiding him with a dainty shake of the head at each hint of what she referred to as his "outrageous wit." Even when Jack had deliberately taken up flirting with *Mrs.* Woodstock, Patricia's widowed mother—who was actually far more interesting than her daughter—the vacant young woman had continued to fawn on him in the most foolish fashion, as if she hadn't noticed his boorishness.

Jack had toyed briefly with the idea of deliberately insulting the girl, then decided against it. He supposed she was only trying to help her family, after all. Perhaps she should even be commended for her willingness to sacrifice herself by consorting with an Irishman. As for her dear, departed father, poor old Woodstock would almost certainly turn in his grave at the idea of a Paddy for a son-in-law.

Still, if Miss Patricia was to be successful in her campaign to restore the family fortunes, he thought nastily, she would have to learn not to patronize the candidates. Even an Irishman had his pride, after all.

Jack held no illusions about the girl's interest in him, and he wasn't about to underrate what he suspected might be some very highly developed predatory instincts. She would retract her claws for only so long. She might tolerate him well enough at a banquet table; since she, no doubt, believed him to be filthy rich, perhaps she didn't find him altogether offensive—for an Irishman. But if he were to fall for her ploys and take her to the altar, things would change quickly enough, he'd warrant. Once she got her mitts on his money, she would more than likely bar him from the bedroom and find a way to boot him out of the rest of her life as well.

Too bad for Patricia Woodstock that he wasn't quite the dolt she apparently believed him to be. As a widower for nearly eight years now—and a *wealthy* widower, at that—he had been targeted several times by most of the empty-headed fortune hunters about town. For a time he had actually considered the possibility of making a marriage of convenience. He would have liked children and a home. Although Addy kept his household running as efficiently as any wife would have, perhaps more so, it wasn't the same as having a family.

But he had never given any real credence to the idea. He knew himself too well, knew he could never be satisfied with anything less than a real marriage. He would always end up comparing another woman—a woman he didn't love, at least—to Martha.

She had been no beauty, his Martha, but she had had a certain charm, a quiet graciousness, and a fundamental goodness that, combined with her quick, incisive mind, had not only made her desirable to Jack but won his respect as well. Martha had been his lover, his sweetheart, and his best friend, and every woman he had known since seemed to pale in comparison.

Unfortunately, they had had less than two brief years together before she died from cancer. That had been almost eight years ago, and Jack still missed her.

But not so much that he would make an ill-fated match with a silly little schemer like Patricia Woodstock. He had been nearly thirty when he married Martha, was close on forty now, and he would spend the rest of his life alone if he must. He had the newspaper, enough money to live the way he wished, and, of course, he had Brady and Rose.

His mouth turned sour as he reminded himself that his brother was missing somewhere in Ireland, and his sister, Rose, was *Sister* Rose, a nun in a New Jersey convent.

But even though Rose might never make her home with him, Brady would eventually come back. Though at times he worried himself to desperation about his brother, somehow Jack could not imagine anything really disastrous happening to the careless young rascal. Brady always seemed to come out with a winning hand.

Please, God, let that be the case this time…

A rather insistent tug on his arm reminded Jack that he had been too long disengaged from the philistine ritual taking place around him. He gave a discreet sigh, then turned back to his dinner companion, forcing a show of interest that served to brighten still more the calculating glint in her eye.

❦

Cavan Sheridan was having trouble concentrating on the grammar text in front of him. His difficulty had nothing to do with the lesson itself, however, but rather with the instructor, who at the moment stood beside his desk, watching his progress as he attempted to rearrange the parts of a sentence.

Samantha Harte was like no other woman Cavan had ever met. Certainly, she defied every preconceived idea he might have had about schoolteachers before he enrolled in this night class.

The classroom itself, which was in the basement of the parish hall, had turned out to be predictably gloomy, cold, and musty. Cavan had expected the teacher to be equally drab.

As it turned out, the slender Miss Harte, though quiet and seemingly possessed of great dignity and reserve, was anything but drab. By tonight's session—the fourth so far—Cavan was half in love with the woman. It concerned him not in the least that she might be a few years older than he. Indeed, it only made her that much more intriguing. Nor did it bother him that Samantha Harte was obviously an educated, refined woman whose genteel demeanor and graceful manners clearly marked her as a lady. From the first night, she had dazzled him, until by now he was thoroughly smitten.

Everything about the woman fascinated Cavan: the thick knot of glossy chestnut hair from which one or two pins were invariably escaping; the delicate oval face; the enormous brown eyes in which flecks of amber caught the light; the faint scent of soap and rose water that accompanied her every move; the beautiful, rich voice and the shy smile that seemed strangely at odds with her air of quiet confidence. With such a splendid distraction, he told himself throughout the evening, was it any wonder he had to make an extraordinary effort to keep his mind on his studies?

When he had finally finished the assignment, Cavan deliberately lagged behind the other students, the last to approach the teacher's desk. She gave him that quick little smile he had come to look for, then scanned the paper he handed her.

"This would appear to be very good, Mr. Sheridan," she said, glancing up. "Your usual fine work. You do seem to have an excellent grasp of grammar. I almost think you could have omitted this session and gone on to the more advanced class."

Cavan shook his head, at the same time trying to ignore the skip of his heart at her approval. "I'll be needing all the grammar and such I can get," he said, "for the job I'm wanting."

She folded her hands on top of the desk. "What job would that be?"

"I mean to work for the *Vanguard*—the newspaper—you see. So I'll be needing a great deal more education."

She smiled at him. "You plan to be a printer, do you?"

"No, ma'am," Cavan said firmly. "It's a reporter's job I'm after."

Her dark brows lifted slightly. "A reporter? Well, that's certainly an ambitious goal for—" She broke off, as if embarrassed by what she had almost said.

"For an Irisher?" Cavan finished for her, managing a tight smile. She blushed, and he hurried to ease her awkwardness. "You're right, of course. But I already have one foot in the door, you see, and I'm hoping to get myself the rest of the way in before long. I mean to be ready when the time comes."

At her questioning look, Cavan went on to explain. "I'm presently employed by Mr. Jack Kane as his driver. But that's only temporary. I won't be driving his buggy forever."

"I see." Again she smiled, then stood. "Well, I can see you have ambition, Mr. Sheridan," she said, looking up at him. "And you're a very good student. I should think your chances for success are excellent."

Was he imagining it, or did she seem slightly flustered? Had he said something wrong? Or perhaps he had said too much. Perhaps he'd embarrassed her with his crack about the "Irisher."

"Miss Harte?" he ventured, her name on his lips threatening to choke him.

She gave him another quick smile.

"I—" he had to swallow before finishing—"I want to thank you. You're a fine teacher. You've helped me more than you can know."

"Oh…well, I meant what I said, Mr. Sheridan. You're an excellent student. A pleasure to teach, actually." She put a hand to her throat, where a small black bow was tied, and Cavan couldn't help but admire the long, slender fingers. Her skin was like rich cream, he thought. Wouldn't it be grand to hold that fine-boned hand in his?

He realized with a start that she had apparently said something and he'd missed it. "Ma'am?"

"I…before…I wasn't referring to your…being Irish. I was about to say that you're ambitious for a young man." She paused. "And also, it's…*Mrs.* Harte."

The bottom drained out of Cavan's heart, and he glanced away, unable to meet her gaze. Suddenly, he felt very much the oafish schoolboy.

When he made no reply, she went on, her voice low. "I'm…a widow, actually. My husband passed away four years ago."

May God forgive him, he had all he could do to conceal his relief. Instantly guilt ridden, Cavan mumbled, "I'm—sorry to hear that."

He felt like the most wretchedly selfish lout under the sun, to be grateful that she had suffered such a loss. Yet grateful is what he was, or at the least relieved, and there was no denying it.

Abruptly, her mood turned brisk as they started for the door. "Well, it's getting late. The custodian will want to lock up."

Cavan followed her from the room, then up the steps and down the dim, deserted corridor. In the silence between them, he found himself wondering what her life was like. Since she was a widow, would she live alone, or had she gone back to her family after her husband's death? It struck him then that she might even have children. The thought caught him up short. Somehow, he could not imagine Samantha Harte as a mother. She seemed so youthful herself, so delicate and vulnerable.

There were many questions he would have liked to ask, so much he wanted to know about her. But he didn't want to pry, didn't want her thinking he was too bold.

As it happened, she had questions of her own. "What is it like working for Mr. Kane?"

They were at the front of the building now, and Cavan held the door for her, then followed her out before replying. "Jack Kane is a fair man, I suppose. Some might find him demanding, but it seems to me he asks no more of his people than he does of himself. He treats me fine, I'd have to say."

"Really? He has a, ah…rather *questionable* reputation, doesn't he? I would have thought—" She broke off. "I'm sorry. I shouldn't have said that. Mr. Kane is your employer, and his reputation is certainly none of my business, after all."

There was just enough light from the streetlamp across the way that Cavan could see the golden flecks in her eyes, and for a moment he couldn't seem to find his tongue.

"I've heard the stories," he finally managed. "And I expect Jack Kane is no saint. But I've seen nothing to indicate he's the blackguard some claim he is. In fact, I would say I have it pretty good—" he grinned—"for an Irisher."

It was too dark to tell if she was blushing again, but she smiled up at him somewhat ruefully. "Haven't I heard that Mr. Kane is Irish himself?"

Cavan nodded. "He is. And he makes no apology for it."

"I should hope not." She stood there a moment, regarding Cavan as if she couldn't quite decide whether to go on. When she did, her words surprised him. "I must say, I think it's a disgrace, the way the Irish are treated in this city. I want you to know, Mr. Sheridan, that not everyone feels unkindly toward them." She blinked. "That is…toward you…and your people."

She was obviously finding it difficult to express herself. Sensing her hesitancy, her awkwardness, Cavan warmed to her that much more.

"Well," she said, turning to go, "thank you for seeing me out, Mr. Sheridan."

On impulse, Cavan put a hand to her arm. "You're not walking, sure?"

Her glance went to his hand before she again met his gaze. "I always walk. I really don't live that far away."

"Still, you ought not to be walking alone in this neighborhood, Mrs. Harte, a lady like yourself." He dropped his hand away. "I'll be happy to drive you home."

Cavan thought she was about to agree, but instead she shook her head. "No, really, that's not necessary, Mr. Sheridan. It's only a short walk, and I don't mind it at all."

"Please?" he insisted. "It would be my pleasure. I have the small buggy, you see. Mr. Kane lets me use it most nights I have class."

"Well, I don't know—" Still she hesitated. "You're quite certain you wouldn't mind? But what about Mr. Kane? Are you sure he wouldn't object to your using the carriage for someone else?"

Cavan again took her arm, starting toward the street. "Jack Kane would never allow a lady to go home unescorted if he could help it. Why, if he were here, he would insist on driving you home himself."

She raised one eyebrow in a skeptical glance. "I must say, I can't quite see myself getting into a carriage with your notorious employer, Mr. Sheridan."

"Ah, well, I'm a very *un*notorious fellow myself, so you can feel entirely safe with me," Cavan said as he helped her into the carriage, then draped the lap robe over her. She leaned forward, settling herself, and for a moment her face was very close to his, making it nearly impossible for him to catch his breath. "If you'll just tell me where you live?" he finally managed to choke out.

"Oh, it's not far. Bleecker Street, near Thompson. Do you know it?"

Cavan nodded, vaguely aware of the district.

"It's a brick four-story," she said, adding, "I have a flat on the second floor."

Living in such an area of decent but modest brick fronts, she would not be well-to-do, Cavan reasoned as he climbed onto the driver's seat and took up the reins. A comforting thought, that. Her being an educated woman was obstacle enough. He would not have had any chance whatsoever with her had she been a wealthy woman as well.

❦

Later that night, Samantha Harte sat at the small painted table in the kitchen of her apartment. Her intention had been to grade papers. Instead, she found herself drifting back in time, an exercise she would normally have avoided because of the pain that inevitably accompanied it. Tonight, however, she seemed unable to stop the memories.

And all, she thought with a sad smile, because of a carriage ride.

The carriage had felt strange to her, almost unnatural. For a long time now, she had availed herself of that sort of luxury only on rare occasions, for special events— holiday dinners or the rare wedding or funeral. Tonight, it seemed as if each bump of the wheels had jarred her back to another time, a time when she had taken things like carriage rides and fur lap robes and handsome, high-stepping horses for granted.

It wasn't that she minded walking; to the contrary, she thrived on it. During that awful time after Bronson died, the long, solitary walks had helped to bring about a kind of healing in her. She had actually sneaked out of the house numerous times, just to extricate herself from the smothering solicitude of her family, sometimes walking for hours before returning home.

She smiled at the irony, to think that a habit initially born of willful desperation had turned into one of sheer necessity. The reality was that she simply could not afford a carriage, not on the meager wages she earned as a textbook proofreader and a part-time teacher for some of the immigrant societies.

She knew that her family and few remaining friends thought her a little mad. She could almost hear them whispering among themselves, speculating as to whether Bronson's death might have unhinged her mind. What else could possibly account for her decision to leave the fellowship *and* seek independence from her family?

There were times in the dead of night when Samantha wasn't at all sure that they weren't right. Even she would be hard-pressed to cite a sensible reason for the direction she had taken.

Although Samantha *did* feel a sense of purpose in her life these days, if she were to be altogether honest she would have to admit that she had gained far more from her new lifestyle than she had given. There was never any real thought of any kind of "sacrifice."

So even though some might view her behavior as a reaction to grief, others as an act of foolishness, Samantha knew it was more an act of self-preservation. She did hope that the Lord approved. Whether anyone else recognized the truth or not, she could not escape it: Her decision to break with her past, and by doing so reject all the comforts it would have offered, had been an almost desperate attempt to finally make something meaningful and worthwhile of her life.

For a long time after Bronson's death, she had been unable to focus on anything more demanding than getting through one day at a time. It had been months before she was able to grasp the reality that, even if her marriage had produced nothing else of any lasting value, it had at least enabled her to grow to the point where she could no longer return to the shallow, self-centered creature she had once been.

She knew now that if she *had* gone back to her former useless mode of existence, she might well have perished, might never have come to believe that her life could have some real value after all.

Her thoughts went to the awkward young Irishman who had driven her home earlier that evening. Perhaps her prize student wasn't the best example of why her work mattered—Samantha suspected that Cavan Sheridan would attain his goals with or without her help—but she *was* helping him, and others like him, to improve their lives, even as she enriched her own. That was worth something, surely.

With a rueful smile, she admitted it had also been nice to have a handsome young man like Cavan Sheridan pay her a measure of attention. He had been so sweet in his insistence on seeing her safely home. His thoughtfulness had almost made her feel young...even attractive...again.

She had almost forgotten what it was like to feel that way...

Immediately, the memory of Bronson's voice forged a stern rebuke in her spirit for such frivolous, worldly thoughts. With an effort, Samantha shook off both her girlish musings and the echo of her husband's denunciation. Then, straightening, she raised the wick on the lamp and returned to her students' papers.

14

A LETTER OF OPPORTUNITY

All for the good comes an unexpected word,
God opens a window, a door,
And hope comes in.

CAVAN SHERIDAN, FROM *WAYSIDE NOTES*

❦

A week later, a letter from Brady finally arrived. Jack stood by the fire as he read the first few words, breathing a deep sigh of relief once he learned the young pup was safe.

He scanned his brother's account of the devastating windstorm, giving most of it little more than a quick glance, since he had already read much of the same information in some of the city's rival newspapers. Another sore subject, and one he meant to raise with Brady as soon as he returned. The *Vanguard* was usually first to report European news of any significance, not last!

As he continued to read, his initial relief gave way to exasperation, then anger as he realized Brady's intentions:

> I know I agreed to stay no longer than two months, but I'm sure you'll understand that, in the wake of the storm and all that's happened, I can't possibly complete the job in such a short time.
>
> There's so much to tell, Jack! Surely there never was a country like Ireland, so rife with poverty, so oppressed by invaders. Why, what the British Crown has done to our people is nothing short of an abomination!

So, it was "our people" now, was it? And this from the same little brother who was always so quick to rib Jack about his "insufferable Irishness." A grim smile played about his mouth as he went on reading:

> The Irish are magnificent, Jack—so bold and fearless. They may be held

captive to the British, but you won't hear them crying "uncle!" For the first time I'm beginning to understand the "Celtic soul" you used to speak of. I always knew I'd love this land, Jack, and I've not been disappointed a bit. I've already made dozens of wonderful sketches, some from my memories of the storm, others of the landscape and the people. I think you'll be pleased when you see them.

What I want to propose, Jack—and I fervently hope you will agree, for there is a far bigger, more important story here than either of us could have imagined—is this: every two or three weeks, I'll post to you a series of articles, along with the appropriate sketches, for your use in a kind of serialization of the Irish condition. My idea is to first present Ireland as it was before the windstorm—in all her agony and glory—and then cover the storm itself and show what terrible devastation it wrought upon an already desperate land.

Think of it, Jack. There are thousands and thousands of Irish in New York alone, not to mention the countless numbers within the circulation area of the Vanguard. Add to that the benevolent societies springing up all over the place, and the interest in this kind of story should be extraordinary! Just imagine what it can do to generate financial aid for Ireland. And wasn't that one of the primary reasons you sent me across in the first place?

Jack's scowl deepened as he read on. Brady knew him too well, knew exactly how to work him. Any newspaperman worth his salt would not miss a story like this, especially an *Irish* newspaperman. Not only would it make a banner serialization—if he agreed to run it Brady's way—but it might actually help the Irish, both here and across. And while this wasn't exactly the kind of information the Committee was looking for, it was a start. Certainly, it should help to increase the contributions. He dared not hope it would put an end to the rank prejudice and hostility leveled against the Irish, but at the same time it couldn't hurt.

Jack had little faith in the "basic decency of man" some of the do-gooders in the benevolent societies were always blathering about. He was far more familiar with man's basic *depravity*. Even so, he was willing to concede that the first step in gaining acceptance for those who were "different"—*foreign*—might be to foster understanding of them. Perhaps a measure of compassion would eventually follow.

Certainly, he would be the last to underestimate the power of the press. Cavan Sheridan had simply echoed Jack's own conviction with his remark that "the press can change people's minds...even their lives."

He had seen it happen. Look at the way Horace Greeley, though little more than a pawn in the hands of Thurlow Weed and his bunch in Albany, had all but guaranteed their man Seward's election as governor—the first New York governor in forty years who wasn't a Democrat.

Jack shook his head. Ah, yes, his clever little brother knew just how to get his attention—and get his own way in the process.

He almost smiled at the rascal's cunning. As he read on, however, he quickly sobered. Apparently, Brady had rented a flat for himself in Galway City and meant to stay "for a time." He had even taken up with some strange Claddagh fisherman and his brood.

Jack drew a sharp breath. His hands shook as he stared at the letter. Of all the rotten luck! The one place in Ireland he had hoped to keep Brady out of, and he had landed right in the heart of it!

Galway. There was no telling what he might come upon there. Not in the Claddagh; he was unlikely to stumble onto anything of any real importance there. In fact, Jack was surprised to learn that Brady had found his way into the place. Odd folk, the Claddagh people.

But in the Old City itself—in Galway—there was always a chance the lad would unearth something that was best left buried. He thought for a moment, searching his memory. So far as he knew, they had no close kin left in Ireland. Both uncles were gone, along with their father. That left only Aunt Selia, and she had remarried and gone with her new husband to live somewhere near Killaloe. Their mother had been an orphan herself, so there was no immediate family there.

But Jack had spent his boyhood in Galway, and Brady had been born there. Da and his brothers had been well known in the district. Wasn't there a possibility of a distant relative or acquaintance…someone who might remember?

By the time he reached the end of the letter, Jack was grinding his teeth:

> *I hope you approve of my plan, Jack. Now, I know that with my past history, you might be thinking that I'm just loafing around, looking for excuses to avoid any real work. But I swear to you that I am working, and that's the truth! I'm writing and sketching like a madman—I've never been so inspired—and I think you'll be pleased with what you see. So what do you say, Jack—can we try it my way for a couple of months more? Then if you're not satisfied I'll come home at once, my word on it.*
>
> *In the meantime, give my best to everyone. Tell Mrs. Flynn that I miss her cooking in the worst way. As I told you, the food situation here is a disgrace. Once I get back to the states, I doubt that I'll ever want to see another potato again!*
>
> *Write soon, big brother. Just post any letters to the Galway address. I'll be here for at least a few more weeks.*
>
> *My best to Addy, of course, that terrible, fierce woman!*
>
> *God bless us all…Your brother, Brady*

A few more weeks, was it? Slowly, Jack folded the letter and stuck it in his pocket before going to stand at the window. It was a bitterly cold evening, already dark, with nothing to be seen but the shadows cast by barren tree limbs quaking in the wind. Much as he tried to shake off the infernal Irish darkness that sometimes overcame his spirit, on nights like this it was as thick and heavy as a grave shroud.

Brady's letter hadn't helped the melancholy that had plagued Jack for years, even as a boy. In truth, it had been on him that first day off the ship, his first day in America…

❦

He had been fourteen at the time and doing his best to act as both father and mother to his baby brother and little sister, though he was little more than a frightened child himself.

With Brady in his arms and his sister, Rose—no more than seven or eight at the time—clinging to his free hand, Jack had taken his first long look at the city of New York. They trudged along the docks, pressed on all sides by countless other immigrants—all of whom seemed to be carrying babes in their arms and shouting at one another in foreign tongues.

Rose was squeezing his hand hard enough to send pain shooting up his arm. "I don't like it here, Jack! Please, take us home." Her curly black hair was wet from sea water and perspiration, her tiny face streaked with sweat and dust. She looked like a street urchin, and Jack was ashamed he hadn't been able to clean the children up better before they got off the ship. But their bunks had been squalid, their water foul, and their clothing long ruined from weeks in the dark, wet steerage.

Rose began to cry then, and wee Brady took up the chorus, wailing against Jack's shoulder. For one interminable black moment, a flood of fear and despair overwhelmed Jack, and he almost turned and ran.

The noisy, teeming city terrified him, and he wanted nothing so much as to rest his head on his mother's bosom and weep. But his mother was dead, had died in childbirth with Brady, and their father was in the ground as well. The wee ones had no one to look after them, no one but Jack. And the truth was that they could not go home to Ireland. There was nothing to go back to, and even if there had been, there was no money to take them. They were poor—poor as beggars.

But Jack would not beg, nor would he allow his siblings to demean themselves in such a manner. So somehow, instead of giving in to his own terror, he found the courage to calm the children and go on walking. They made their way past the docks and merged onto the stinking, filthy streets of New York, where at some point, Jack realized that he would conquer his fear of the city only by conquering the city itself.

❦

Sometimes Jack deluded himself into thinking he had accomplished that boyish resolve. But a deeper, saner part of him knew that that sort of thinking was only illusion. The truth was that New York would not, could not, be conquered, not by any man. She was a terrible, mean woman who ate princes as easily as paupers and spit them out of her mouth without a thought, showing no pity for those who allowed themselves to be swallowed up. Anyone who believed otherwise was a fool, and he was no fool.

At a light rap just then, he swung around to see Cavan Sheridan standing in the doorway, scrunching his cap against his chest and watching Jack.

"Begging your pardon, sir, but I was wondering if I might leave now?"

For a moment the youth's request didn't register.

"'Tis Thursday, sir. I have the night class—"

"Ah, yes," Jack said, nodding. "Of course. That's fine, lad. Go along to your Miss Harte."

"'Tis *Mrs.* Harte, sir. She is a widow."

Again Jack gave a nod, not really interested in the teacher Sheridan had so obviously enshrined. The lad clearly had himself a case of puppy love, but Jack suspected it would not really take much of a woman to turn the head of a *gorsoon* like his driver. The boy had a strange and uncommon admiration for knowledge and those who owned it. His Mrs. Harte might be squat and middle-aged with a row of warts hanging from her lip, but if she was even half the scholar Sheridan apparently believed her to be, no doubt she had the means to dazzle him.

Jack's mood had brightened somewhat, and he detained young Sheridan long enough to share the news about Brady. "I've heard from my brother at last," he said, patting his coat pocket. "It seems he is alive and well after all."

Sheridan smiled and stepped into the room. "I'm glad for you, sir. You must be relieved."

"Yes, well, I'm relieved, all right, but no less annoyed with him for taking so long to let me know his whereabouts. Still, he's had an idea for the paper that might help him wangle his way back into my good graces." Jack paused. "And I expect he knows it."

Briefly, he explained Brady's suggestion, then added, "Serializations seem to work nicely, if the reader cares enough about the subject."

He was surprised at Sheridan's response. "And you think they will care enough?" he said quietly. "About Ireland?"

Again Jack caught a glimpse of a certain cynicism in the lad that chanced to appear at odd moments, when least expected. "You disagree?" he asked, going to sit down at his desk.

Sheridan shrugged. "I confess I've not seen much sign of any real interest in Ireland." As if he sensed he might have overstepped, he added, "But it's not for me to be saying, of course. You and Mr. Brady would know better what to expect from your readers."

Drumming his fingers on the desk, Jack shook his head. "Not necessarily. There's no predicting human nature, Sheridan, at least not consistently. It's folly for any man to think otherwise."

He studied the tall youth, who had filled out a bit on Mrs. Flynn's cooking.

Sheridan was anything but brawny, but he no longer had the hollow-eyed look of the starving immigrant about him. "What's on your mind? You might just as well spit it out."

Of late, it wasn't unusual for Jack to bounce an occasional idea off the lad. He had caught a glimpse every now and then of a fine mind, with exceptionally keen instincts. "But perhaps you need to be going—"

"No, sir, I have time." Sheridan hesitated only a second or two, and Jack had the impression he hadn't far to search before forming his reply. "I agree with what you said, sir, about giving readers a subject they can care about."

Jack leaned back in his chair, waiting.

"It's just that…I'm not certain you can make them care about an entire country," Sheridan went on. "At least not in a way that would be of any help to our people. To the Irish, that is," he quickly amended, as if perhaps he shouldn't be lumping Jack and himself together. Sheridan's gaze held steady, but the way he continued to knead his wool cap with his hands told Jack the youth was not entirely comfortable with speaking freely.

He moved to reassure him. "I never ask a man his opinion unless I want it, lad. Speak your mind."

Sheridan seemed to relax a little. "I was wondering if it might not be better to single out only a few individual stories, rather than try to give a broad view of the entire country. It might help to make the people seem more…*real*. If your readers could come to know the Irish as real people, on a more…personal basis, they might take the plight of Ireland itself more seriously. I think—"

He stopped, watching Jack as if he might have said too much. But Jack's interest was piqued now, and he gestured that Sheridan should go on.

"What I'm trying to say is that it would seem a difficult job, at best, to interest the readers in something as big and impersonal as a country, but not so difficult perhaps to interest them in a young mother whose husband has died at sea and left her with two or three hungry tykes and no money to buy food or pay the rent."

Sheridan's clear blue eyes began to sparkle as he continued. Something in Jack wrenched at the sight of this youthful enthusiasm, this excitement about something as simple and as fundamental as an idea. Had he ever been that young? he wondered almost sadly. That exuberant, that eager? Somehow it didn't seem as though he had ever been a boy—carefree, idle, with the luxury of carving a whistle or daydreaming in the sun. He had worked from the time he was old enough to run messages and make collections.

As a boy, his existence had been worry and hard work. As a young man, his existence had been less worry and more hard work. And now—well, nothing had changed much.

But as Sheridan went on, Jack felt a quickening of his own senses, the familiar skip of his pulse that almost always signaled a worthwhile idea or, back in his gambling days, an unbeatable hand.

"I'm not saying your brother's idea isn't a sound one, mind. Giving your readers a close-up view of Ireland and all her troubles—well, with Mr. Brady's ability as an artist, no doubt a firsthand account of Ireland as he sees it will be fascinating. My idea is to add a bit more to it—to *personalize* it, if you will, perhaps choose four or five particularly desperate families or individuals, tell their stories—complete with Mr. Brady's sketches, of course." He stopped, his expression, even his tone, less confident as he added, "And then bring the subjects of those stories to America."

Jack's head snapped up. "Bring them across?" he repeated incredulously. *"All* of them?"

"Indeed, sir." Sheridan said nothing more for a moment, but simply stood looking at Jack.

"An expensive venture, I know, sir," he finally said, his voice low, "but perhaps if you have the means it would eventually pay for itself. In terms of increased readership," he hurried to explain, "not to mention the…ah…goodwill that would be sure to accrue to you for your generosity."

Jack looked at him in amazement, then quite suddenly threw back his head and laughed. It took him a moment to recover, and when he did he could still scarcely keep from laughing even harder. "Sheridan, I expect I ought to be grateful entirely that I didn't hire you on as my bookkeeper. Hang it all, but you're generous with my money!"

Sheridan blushed but grinned at Jack. "Sorry, sir. It just seemed a good idea. I didn't mean to presume—"

Jack waved off his apology. "It *is* a good idea," he said, his mind racing. "I must admit, I think you're on to something. But if you'll permit me an observation—this being your idea but my newspaper—it could take a bit of doing. Even if I'm willing to finance the crossing of several good Irish souls—and mind, I'm not committing to that particular madness just yet—but if I do, someone is going to have a bit of work on their hands, seeing to the arrangements and getting them settled after they arrive, wouldn't you agree?"

Sheridan nodded, his mind obviously working. "Mrs. Harte and some of her friends could help with that."

"Who?" Jack said, his own thoughts coursing ahead.

"My teacher—Mrs. Harte. You recall my telling you that she works with the immigrant societies—"

"Right, right," Jack said, eager to spare himself further rhapsodizing on the part of his infatuated driver, who no doubt would have Mrs. Harte, too, spending the *Vanguard's* money with unbridled enthusiasm if not held in check. "Well, perhaps that sort of thing can be taken care of easily enough. But there's the actual reporting—the developing of the stories, if you will. Seems to me it would take a clever fellow to carry off that sort of writing, wouldn't you say?"

Sheridan smiled a little. "Addy—Miss O'Meara—goes on and on about Mr. Brady, how clever and bright he is."

Jack shook his head. "Brady is good enough with getting the facts straight, and he can draw pictures that would make a saint weep. But that's the rub. He's an artist, not a writer. He could sniff out the stories and give us a good enough rough draft, but I'd have to hire a top-notch writer to whip them into shape."

His mind darting from one thing to another, he almost missed young Sheridan's quiet reply.

"I could do it, sir."

15

KEY TO A DREAM

A little love, a little trust,
A soft impulse, a sudden dream,
And life as dry as desert dust
Is fresher than a mountain stream.

STOPFORD A. BROOKE

Kane looked up, clearly distracted. "What's that?"

Cavan expelled the breath he hadn't realized he'd been holding and cleared his throat. "The writing. I could do it. I could write the stories from Mr. Brady's material."

Kane's black eyes raked him so thoroughly that Cavan's skin tightened in self-defense. "I seem to recall your admitting a need for more education, if you're to better yourself," Kane said abruptly. "That's the reason for the night classes, isn't it?"

Without giving Cavan a chance to reply, he added, "There is also the fact that I need you as my driver—which, you might recall, is the reason I hired you." Kane's expression was neutral, but Cavan knew Kane was testing him.

"I would continue as your driver, sir," Cavan hurried to assure him. "I could write the stories at night, after you no longer needed me, don't you see?"

Kane continued to study him. "What makes you think you can write, lad? Do you have some sort of experience you've kept to yourself?"

Cavan ignored his lightly mocking tone. "No experience, sir. I've written only for myself up until now. But it's something...I know I can do it, Mr. Kane. I wouldn't have asked for a chance to try if I didn't believe I could do it."

Kane lit a cigar. As he did so, his features drew into a hard, speculative expression that Cavan had come to recognize by now, a look that meant he was paying an idea careful consideration. There was nothing Cavan could do at the moment except to hold his tongue and wait in silence.

He could almost feel the tension that crackled from his employer. The longer he worked for him, the more he had begun to understand the city's love-hate fascination with Black Jack Kane. The man's meteoric rise from poverty to riches, his outrageous but wildly successful business dealings, his deadly black-Irish charm and even deadlier Irish temper, and his enviable attraction of some of the most beautiful women on the eastern seaboard were the stuff that legends were made of.

But Cavan had begun to question some of the more lurid tales so freely circulated by the gossipmongers. From what he could tell, Kane's spectacular success was due more to the fact that he worked harder than any two men combined than to any sort of incredible luck or corrupt business practices. Though it was true that Kane demanded a great deal from his employees, he gave even more of himself; he appeared to never run out of energy. Yet he did not seem so much a driven man as one who truly enjoyed his work and went at it with a passion.

As for his prowess with women, the tales of Kane's endless love affairs were almost certainly exaggerated. Oh, the women couldn't resist him, that much was true. Some of them made absolute fools of themselves over the man. But to the best of Cavan's knowledge, his employer seldom involved himself in any sort of liaison more entangling than a dinner engagement at one of the city's elegant restaurants or an evening at the theater—most often, the opera. He had never known Kane to bring a woman home, nor had he ever left him at a woman's residence. While Jack Kane might spend a great number of evenings out on the town, he spent his nights at home. Alone.

Cavan was beginning to suspect that at least a part of his employer's charm with the ladies was in the way he managed to elude them.

But as he faced him across the desk, he reminded himself that Kane had not attained the pinnacle on which he stood by being soft or careless. He was a hard man who, as Addy was fond of saying, "brooked no foolishness and suffered no fools."

He was also inclined to be impatient, so Cavan hurried to make his case. "I understand you're probably wondering why you should consider such a suggestion on my part," he said in as steady a voice as he could manage.

Kane stood, crossing his arms over his chest, his dark eyes glinting with mild amusement. "I must admit the question had occurred to me, yes."

Cavan considered going into a long, detailed explanation as to why he thought himself qualified for such an undertaking, but the truth was that he *wasn't* qualified, and both he and Kane knew it. So he took a deep breath and offered the only reply that seemed truthful. "My only experience is the writing I've done for myself. But you can trust me, sir. My grammar may not be expert just yet—" Kane lifted one dark brow in a wry expression as Cavan pressed on—"but Mrs. Harte is helping me a great deal, and she says I'm the best scholar she's ever taught. Besides, wouldn't one of the proofreaders be correcting me if I trip up too badly?"

Kane twisted his mouth downward. "I have only two proofreaders I can trust," he said. "My front-page reader, Hailey, can no longer see well enough to be of any real value. And Jimmy Kidder is set to retire come fall."

Something went off in Cavan's mind, but for the moment he kept his silence.

"You meant what you said that day, didn't you, Sheridan?" Kane asked abruptly.

Cavan frowned. "Sir?"

"The day I hired you on as my driver, you admitted that what you *really* wanted was to work for the newspaper."

Cavan did, of course, remember. "Aye, I meant it, sir." He held Kane's gaze. "I still do."

Jack Kane dropped his arms away from his chest and put his hands in his pockets. For a long time he made no reply but simply stood there, regarding Cavan in an unhurried, speculative manner.

Cavan felt his hands turn clammy with perspiration. Even though Kane kept the study reasonably cool compared to the rest of the house, he could feel the heat rising up the back of his neck.

"All right, then. Why not?" Kane flung out, his tone surprisingly casual. "An old gambler like myself can't resist taking a chance now and then. Here's what we'll do, Sheridan," he went on in a clipped, precise voice. "I will write to my brother and explain your idea, ask him to design his copy in such a way that he focuses on only a few specific people—and on highly interesting ones, at that."

Cavan had all he could do to suppress a shout of excitement. Instead, he balled his hands into such tight fists at his sides that he feared he might draw blood.

"When Brady's first post comes," Kane went on matter-of-factly, "you will make it into a story so compelling it will seize the city by the throat, sizably increasing the *Vanguard*'s subscription list—" he paused, his tone again turning sardonic—"and at the same time making you the most sought-after reporter in the state of New York." The dark eyebrows quirked. "You will, of course, remain wholly loyal to me, in spite of your newfound fame."

As Kane finished, a quick, challenging grin broke over his face.

Cavan didn't quite manage an answering smile. "Of course, sir." He swallowed hard. "You mean it, then—that you will let me try my hand at the stories?"

Below the black mustache, Kane's mouth thinned slightly. "I mean that I will give you a chance, but only if you do not slack off in your responsibilities as my driver. And if your aspirations to be a reporter are genuine, you will familiarize yourself with the *Vanguard*'s operations from the ground up. You will learn the presses and even a bit about keeping books—though only if you vow to control your penchant for spending my money. And you will get to know the newsboys and their trade."

Cavan nodded, scarcely able to contain his excitement. Perhaps Kane thought he was demanding much of Cavan, when in truth the man was handing him the key to a dream.

"One more thing," Kane went on. "You will do your writing on your own time, not mine. And if I decide your effort is lacking and not up to the *Vanguard*'s standards, you will accept my opinion as final in the matter. Oh, and Sheridan—you will lose most of your Irish brogue, at least enough that it doesn't destroy your credibility as a writer. Understood?"

Cavan never wavered as he looked his employer in the eye. "Understood, sir."

Another slow grin broke over Kane's dark features as he chomped on his cigar. "Do you know, Sheridan, you sometimes remind me a bit of myself at your age?"

Now Cavan did manage a smile, but in truth he wasn't at all sure whether he had just been saluted or insulted. He braced himself, wondering how far he dared press. "Mr. Kane? Do I understand that you're thinking of hiring a new proofreader for the paper?"

Kane nodded, his smile giving way to a frown. "I can't think what else to do. I'll not be kicking old Hailey out, of course. He has to eat, and no one else is likely to hire him, the shape he's in. I expect I can find another place for him somewhere downstairs."

"I thought I would mention a possibility as a replacement," Cavan ventured carefully, "if you're interested, that is."

"And that would be...?"

"Mrs. Harte, sir. I'm sure she would do an excellent job for you. She's had experience, you see."

"*Your* Mrs. Harte? The schoolteacher?" Kane's look was altogether dubious.

"Aye, sir. She teaches the night classes, but she also works part-time as a proofreader for a textbook company. The problem is they don't give her enough work that she can earn a fair wage."

"Well, now, lad, it sounds to me as if you and your Mrs. Harte are becoming quite friendly, if she's letting you in on her financial affairs."

Kane's smile was somewhat snide, his tone teasing. But Cavan didn't mind. He had observed that Jack Kane characteristically confined his teasing to those few men he favored.

"Nothing like that, Mr. Kane. But we do talk now and then. Mrs. Harte indicated that the textbook company can't afford to employ her more than a few hours a week, and she's looking for a more lucrative position."

"I could hardly bring a woman into the newsroom. Especially a lady."

"Yes, sir, but she works for the textbook company from her home. Couldn't she do the same for the *Vanguard*?"

Kane flicked the ash from his cigar. "That's a possibility, I suppose. But see here, Sheridan, you've already proposed this paragon of perfect womanhood as a coordinator for our newly conceived immigrant program—if that works out and I allow you to spend my money as freely as you seem to think I should. I want your word that you won't have your lady friend snatching away my position as publisher when my back is turned."

Cavan fought madly to quell the hot blush he could feel rising up his neck. "She's hardly a lady friend, sir—"

Kane laughed good-naturedly and came around the desk. "That's fine, lad. Perhaps I'll just stop by the school one evening to meet this glory of a woman, see how she strikes me. But for now, I expect you'd best be getting along to class. Else you may find yourself in trouble with the teacher. Besides, you've still got a bit to learn before we turn you into the city's most illustrious reporter."

16

POSSIBILITIES

Let nothing pass, for every hand
Must find some work to do,
Lose not a chance to waken love—
Be firm and just and true.

CHARLES DICKENS

Jack wasted no time in getting a reply off to Brady. The next morning in his office he hurriedly penned a brief letter, saying just enough to let the cunning young pup know in no uncertain terms that he wouldn't be duped:

> *I had hoped to see some evidence of maturity from you by now—evidence long overdue, I might add. An effort to relieve our worries about you would have done nicely for starters. In view of the horrendous accounts of the storm—and the unconscionably long silence on your part—perhaps you will concede that I had just cause for concern. At the very least, you might have sent a quick note assuring us of your safety. Your customary thoughtlessness allowed me to endure weeks of not knowing whether you were alive or dead. And then when you finally got around to dropping a line, you set my teeth to grinding with the information that you have taken up with some wild Claddagh fisherman and his pack and now hope to turn what was meant to be a brief reporting stint into an extended tour—and all, I might add, at the paper's expense.*
>
> *I never intended for this to become a holiday, boyo, and I rather resent your taking advantage, especially in view of the fact that I could use you here in the office right now. I am in desperate need of a couple of good reporters—men who can spot a story when it bumps up against them—not to mention a front-page proofreader who isn't half-blind. I could also use*

an extra pair of hands on the presses, not that I would consider asking you
to stain your artist's mitts with news ink, mind.

He went on for a few lines more, bludgeoning his brother with sarcasm—which he knew would merely amuse Brady even as he ignored it. Only at the last did he indicate agreement to his brother's proposal, and then based solely on one condition:

You will not get the sort of stories I want by wasting your time in the
Claddagh. That place is a world of its own, and a strange and backward
world, at that. I can't imagine your finding anything newsworthy there,
nor do I intend to worry myself white-headed that some mad Claddagh
fisherman will go after you one night with a hatchet.

If you're serious about staying in Ireland, and if your reasons are as
genuine as you would have me believe, then get yourself out of infernal
Galway and tend to business. Go where the people better represent the
country and its problems.

Now I mean it, Brady. That is my condition, and I will not be swayed.
You have yourself a bargain, albeit a reluctant one on my part—but only
if I see a change of address in the very near future.

He proceeded to explain what he wanted him to do, then, in the way of finding a select few candidates whose stories would have great appeal for the *Vanguard*'s readers, with the idea of eventually bringing them across. He would have added more—he hadn't as yet told Brady about Cavan Sheridan or given him any news of Rose—but just then Sheridan ducked his head inside the door. "Begging your pardon, Mr. Kane, but you're needed downstairs right away. Some sort of problem with the newsboys."

Jack had taken to giving Sheridan odd jobs about the paper, at which the ambitious young driver busied himself between his other responsibilities. The lad had already proven himself an asset. No job seemed too mean for him; instead, he set himself to any assignment with a cheerful capability Jack could only wish for in Brady. Earlier that morning he had sent Sheridan to Ben Cross in the pressroom, telling him to make himself useful however Ben directed.

"I thought you were downstairs," he said, following Sheridan down the steps.

"Aye, I was, sir, but one of the printers heard a ruckus in the alley and called for Mr. Cross. He took me along."

In the alley behind the pressroom, where the newsboys picked up their papers, Jack found the small, sharp-featured Ben Cross with two raggedy lads. He recognized only one of the boys: Willie Shanahan, a redheaded, eight-year-old little scrapper, who worked harder at his "business" than any other two newsboys combined. His companion looked a bit older—nine or ten, perhaps, but he was as scrawny and narrow faced as Willie, his clothes hanging on him like sails.

"What's the trouble here?" Jack asked outright. The words were no more than out of his mouth when Willie stepped up to him. Jack fumed as he saw the boy's swollen eye and cut lip. Apparently, the older boy had been knocked about as well, for he had a bad mouse around one eye and an angry red scrape near the other.

"What happened, Willie?" But Jack knew the answer even before he asked. "Rynders' thugs again?"

"Captain" Isaiah Rynders was a scoundrel of the roughest sort, who controlled almost every gang in the city. He and his kind had been giving the newsboys a rash of trouble for months now.

Willie shrugged, and his fine red hair lifted out in all directions. Like baby hair, Jack thought. And why not? The boy was little more than a babe, and that was the truth.

"Don't know, Mr. Jack. There was a bunch of 'em, though. They gave us a terrible pounding, and didn't they say they'd do it again tomorrow if we showed up on the corner with our papers? Said next time they'd break our legs, if we don't pay the protection money." The boy stopped, wiped a hand over his nose, and added indignantly, "They even robbed us of our shoes, Mr. Jack."

"They took your *shoes?*" Anger scalded Jack's throat.

He dropped down to one knee in front of the boy. "How bad are you hurt, Willie? Are you all right?"

The thin lower lip trembled slightly, but Willie nodded. "I got off a couple of good punches, Mr. Jack. I think I might have hurt one of 'em."

Beside him, the taller, dark-haired boy gave a nod of agreement. "We put up a fight, Willie and me did."

Jack straightened, his fists knotted hard at his sides. "I'm sure you did, lads. But we can't have you scrapping just to do your jobs. Tomorrow morning, first thing, when you come for your papers, I'll have a couple of men at the door to go with you. You're not to go out alone, mind." He dug down in his trouser pocket. "Here," he said, "take this money, the two of you, and go get yourselves some shoes."

Wide-eyed, the two stammered their thanks, then bounded off. Jack knew this was no real solution. He couldn't afford to send men from the office with the boys every day.

But what else could he do? These assaults on the newsboys were becoming routine, one gang after another harassing the boys with threats and beatings, bullying them into paying a part of their hard-earned wages simply to avoid a bruising and having their papers slashed. The police had been largely ineffective against the rampant gang violence across the city, and the newspaper owners were at a loss. What made Jack even more furious was that many of the gang members were Irishmen who thought nothing of victimizing their own people—including children.

Jack would have wagered his new printing press that Isaiah Rynders was behind it all. Whatever the crime—gambling, policy games, opium dealing, brothels, or just plain petty theft—Rynders was a part of it. The slippery snake seemed beyond the law. He ran the gangs—made up mostly of hard men, the dregs of the city—with iron control and an eerie knack for evading the jail cell he deserved.

Trying to explain the situation to Cavan Sheridan as they headed back upstairs, he was surprised when the youth offered to accompany the boys the next morning. Jack shook his head. "Your heart's in the right place, lad, but I wouldn't be putting you in that position. Besides, the boys pick up their papers well before dawn. I want you available to me in the mornings, not out on a street corner swapping punches with Rynders' bully boys."

"Who is this Rynders fellow?"

Jack gave him an earful about the city's most notorious ruffian, leaving out the fact that he had known Isaiah Rynders personally some years back, when he still visited the gambling dens. He had left the gambling madness behind him after he and Martha were married—she had coaxed a promise from him, and he'd held to his word, even after her death. But there had been a time when he would have rather played blackjack than eat or sleep—and he had made a small fortune at it. That was the source of the nickname still used behind his back, though he suspected most assumed the epithet referred to his character. Or his soul.

In any event, he knew "Captain" Rynders and his toughs well enough to know they were capable of anything, including beating up defenseless little boys.

"I was surprised to learn," Cavan Sheridan said as they reached the landing, "that this sort of ugly business went on in America. Until I ran into the bully boys in the mines, I thought I'd left such trouble behind in Ireland."

Jack lifted an eyebrow. "The barbarians are everywhere, lad, especially in the city."

They stopped outside the pressroom. "Every place has its no-accounts. They're just called by different names. Here in New York we call them Bowery B'hoys and Dead Rabbits and Slaughter-Housers."

Sheridan's smile was thin. "And in Ireland they're called the Sassenach."

"Aye, that's true, the British have given us our share of grief. But don't make the mistake of casting an entire people into one great lump, lad. Some of the blackest scoundrels in New York have names that start with a *Mac* or an *O*. On the other hand, I've known a number of Brits who were decent enough fellows."

At his driver's openly skeptical expression, Jack grinned and added, "Well, perhaps not all *that* many. But two or three, I should think. You take my point."

❧

Jack's day didn't get any better. After the exchange with the newsboys, he went back to his office to resume work on the financial article he'd begun the day before, only to discover that he'd left his notes at home. Later, his meeting with key staff members deteriorated into an argument about the advisability of employing European correspondents.

Their arch rival, the *Herald,* had set the precedent, and Brady's trip to Ireland had been Jack's first move to establish a similar system of his own—a move wildly disputed by Clark, his head bookkeeper, and Kaiser, his general manager. As was often the case, any talk of the *Herald* led to an even more heated discussion about the reasons for its phenomenal success. The paper's owner, James Gordon Bennett, had been the target of a great deal of spiteful speculation ever since he'd launched the *Herald*. Jack had his own ideas about why the *Herald* had been so hugely successful and had, in fact, incorporated some of Bennett's ideas into the *Vanguard*'s operation with almost immediate dividends.

There was no denying that the *Herald* thrived on scandalous crimes and shock effect. Bennett was said to have no morals at all—some of the upstanding citizenry referred to him as a "serpent." But there was also no disputing the fact that the dour, sardonic Scot's revolutionary ideas had worked well. Part of the *Herald*'s success, Jack was convinced, could be directly attributed to the fact that Bennett had found a way to reach directly to the servant girl as well as her master. The shiploads of immigrants landing at the Battery, as well as the business owners who employed them, needed information—and entertainment. Bennett had managed to provide both, and consequently the *Herald* sold like wildfire.

A great deal of jealousy had been stirred up by the squinty-eyed Bennett's penny daily among other newspapermen in the city. Even Jack occasionally winced at the *Herald*'s unprincipled dredging up of scandal for the sake of sheer sensationalism. But at the same time he had made a thorough study of Bennett's success and would be the first to admit that he had learned a great deal from the effort.

There was still a question in his mind, however, about what accounted for the loyalty of the *Herald*'s readers. He had not been able to identify exactly what he was missing until Cavan Sheridan had made his observation the night before about the difficulty in interesting readers in something big and impersonal, as opposed to attracting them with the story of an unfortunate widow unable to pay her rent.

At that instant something had clicked in Jack. Later, he had mulled over Sheridan's idea, finally seizing on the one element he thought he could use to far better advantage than Bennett ever had: the personal-interest story.

And as for young Sheridan, he thought he might just give the lad a raise.

But in the meantime, he was still grinding his teeth from the disgruntled staff meeting as he spread out his copy of the *Vanguard*'s morning edition on his desk. In only seconds, bile hot enough to choke him rose in his throat. His eye went relentlessly down the copy, stopping at every error. Even before he reached the end of the front page, he was seething. Two generalizations that Jack knew to be wholly unsupported, four wrong-font letters, two spelling mistakes, and at least half a dozen style faults.

His stomach knotted hard enough to make him flinch, and when Cavan Sheridan appeared in the open doorway to drive him home, Jack shot him a killer glare that made the lad step back.

"You're not ready...I'll come back later," Sheridan said, turning to leave.

"I'll be ready in a shake!" Jack snapped. "But first you go and fetch Bob Hailey for me."

❦

A few minutes later, on the way out to the carriage, Cavan, mindful of his employer's mood, remained studiously silent. By now he had seen Kane in a temper on occasion. He recognized the unyielding set of his back, the tight line of his mouth, the granite-hard jaw beneath the black mustache. He knew from experience that Kane would most likely not say a word the rest of the way home and on throughout the evening.

But to give the man his due, Jack Kane never inflicted his wrath on the members of his household. His anger was more a rigidly contained heat, boiling just beneath the surface of his composure, perceptible but under control.

Kane surprised Cavan this evening, however, by not keeping his silence. Instead, after muttering a stream of disjointed complaints about certain members of his staff, he stopped beside the carriage and said, "I believe I would like to meet your Mrs. Harte. I'm going to have to find someone rather quickly to help with the proofreading. Have you mentioned the idea to her at all?"

As a matter of fact, Cavan had, after Tuesday evening's class. He had driven Samantha Harte home again that night and had lingered for a few minutes in front of her flat, talking. At that time, he had carefully raised the possibility of an opening at the *Vanguard* for someone with her qualifications.

At first she had seemed flustered, protesting that she wasn't qualified. But she also conceded that her job with the textbook company was tenuous at best and she wouldn't mind finding something more dependable. Cavan was sure she was interested but suspected that her misgivings regarding Kane's reputation were at least in part responsible for her resistance to the idea. Even so, he had determined to pursue the subject with his employer, should the opportunity present itself.

Now it seemed that it had. "I raised the possibility," he admitted.

Kane seemed preoccupied as he climbed into the carriage. "I'm moving Bob Hailey to the pressroom tomorrow. They'll find something for him there. I'll handle the front page myself until I can find someone."

Cavan waited until Kane pulled the lap robe over him, then said, "The class meets again tonight. Would you like me to talk to Mrs. Harte about the proofreading position?"

Kane gave a short nod. "Why don't you? If she's interested, tell her to come round to the paper tomorrow afternoon. I'll see her then."

Cavan hesitated, and Kane noticed. "What, you don't think she'll be interested?"

Cavan shook his head. "'Tis not that, sir. It's just that Mrs. Harte strikes me as being a very…reserved lady. Shy, if you will. I don't know that she would be all that comfortable coming to the offices alone, you see."

Kane frowned and made a dismissing gesture with his hand. "All right, then; if that's the case, tell her you'll come for her with the carriage. Perhaps that would put her more at ease."

"Aye, sir, I think that might be best," Cavan said. He would have gone on with more questions, but Kane had clearly turned his thoughts elsewhere.

Later that evening, Cavan stood at the doorway after class, striving to conceal his disappointment as he heard Samantha Harte's response to the news about the proofreader's position. He had thought she would at least be willing to talk with Kane, despite her apparent skepticism about the man. He hadn't counted on the level of her resistance, however. Her refusal was polite but immediate. And unmistakably firm.

"You understand that I would be driving you to the office?" he said, hoping to convince her. "It's not as if you'd be going on your own."

Again she shook her head. "Cavan, I really do appreciate your confidence in me, but it's as I told you: I don't consider myself qualified for a position of this nature." She paused, then added, "And to be perfectly frank, I don't know that I would be comfortable working...for the *Vanguard.*"

"You mean you wouldn't be comfortable working for Jack Kane," he said, making it a statement rather than a question.

She flushed slightly. "Please. I don't want to offend you. You enjoy your job, and you seem to like Mr. Kane—and that's just fine. And as I told you, I'll be only too happy to help you in any way I can with the articles you're assigned. But as for the job—it simply wouldn't be right for me."

Still reluctant to give up, Cavan pressed. "He's not what they say, you know. He's not anything at all like what they say." He was making a poor effort of this, was botching it badly, and he knew it. The thing was, he really thought she would be improving her situation by accepting a position with Kane, and he wanted to help her.

The rest of it, of course, was that it would be a way to see her more often. He tried once more. "He's not a bad man, Mr. Kane," he said lamely. "You'd see for yourself, once you got to know him a bit. This is going to be an important responsibility, you know, if he actually brings some of the people across. I thought—I'd hoped you'd agree to coordinate things, in addition to the proofreader's position."

She regarded him with a questioning frown. "Cavan...why are you so intent on this? I don't think I understand."

Cavan felt the heat rise up his neck. He tried to look away from those searching brown eyes, but her gaze refused to release him. He swallowed, clenching his hands at his sides. "I only meant to help," he said, hearing the unnatural thinness of his own voice. "You indicated that your job with the textbook company might be phasing out soon, and I thought—" He stopped, shrugged, and looked away from her. "I wouldn't mind seeing you more often," he said miserably. "There's that."

A prolonged silence met his admission, and when he met her eyes again, he saw that she wore a positively stricken look. She put a hand to her crisp white collar. "Oh, Cavan, no. You can't mean...you mustn't...*think* about me...that way! Why, I'm...your teacher, Cavan. I'm years older than you, you must know that..."

He shook his head. "I'm sorry, Mrs. Harte. I don't mean to embarrass you. But I doubt that you're *years* older than me, and even if you were, it wouldn't make a bit of difference, don't you see? I...think you're a wonderful lady, and I enjoy being with you, and I expect I can't apologize for that."

Still pale, she studied him. "How old are you, Cavan?"

He hesitated. "Almost twenty," he finally said, grudgingly.

"I'm twenty-nine years old, Cavan. A widow. You're—"

"A man," Cavan said, his tone hard. "I'm no *gorsoon,* if that's what you're thinking. And I told you, I don't care a whit about your age. Or the fact that you're a widow woman." He stopped, groping for words. "Well, I care about your loss, of course. But as for the years between us—" he looked directly at her, and his impatience fled—"you mustn't mind that at all. It's of no importance."

She moved as if to speak, then stopped and glanced away. After another moment, she murmured something unintelligible, her voice low. Cavan caught only the last few words, delivered more firmly: "Your admiration is very gratifying, but undeserved, I'm afraid. And I must ask you not to raise the subject of this position with the *Vanguard* again. Please."

She had turned cold all of a sudden, had withdrawn from him even as he stood there wanting nothing so much as to take her hand or touch her hair. Cavan felt a door close against him with a finality that sent a cold blast of wind sweeping over his heart.

17

THE WOMAN IS A PUZZLE

There is something here I do not get,
Some menace I do not comprehend.

VALENTIN IREMONGER

Samantha Harte might not have held Jack's interest for more than a moment had she not balked as she did at meeting him. Unaccustomed as he was to rejection from a woman, however, he found the very act of her refusal enough to pique his curiosity.

Further, Cavan Sheridan's somewhat stilted account of the conversation that had transpired between himself and Mrs. Harte on Thursday night only served to intrigue Jack that much more. He was fairly certain his eager young driver was keeping something back, but when Jack pressed him for details, none were forthcoming.

Jack probably would have dismissed the elusive Mrs. Harte from his mind entirely had Monday not been such a devilish day. He had his hands full on any day, but on Monday he added to his normal routine an exhaustive line-by-line proofing of the late edition's front page. Consequently, he didn't leave the office until almost nine, arriving home tired, hungry, and decidedly out of sorts. He gulped down his supper without really tasting it, skipped his nightly walk, and retired to a restless sleep fraught with bizarre dreams.

Tuesday didn't start off much better. He got out of bed with a thunderous headache and a bad temper, neither of which improved as the day went on. To save himself some time, he brought Donny Sullivan up from typesetting and charged him with proofing the front of the daily edition. The end result was another disaster. Jack's own quick check of the front page later that day fired his already throbbing skull with another shot of pain. The entire page was riddled with misspellings and other editorial flaws. When he confronted the perspiring Sullivan, it was painfully clear that the lad was either severely nearsighted or too dull entirely to grasp what he had neglected. And that was the end of the raw young cub's short-lived stint as a proofreader.

A little before five, Jack called Cavan Sheridan up from the pressroom. "Tell me again exactly what your Mrs. Harte had to say last week," he said from behind his desk, "about the proofreading position."

It had occurred to Jack that, as charming and clever a fellow as Cavan Sheridan might be, he was still wet behind the ears—and royally smitten with the schoolteacher. There was always a chance he might have bungled things in his approach.

The lad proceeded to recap the exchange between himself and the schoolteacher, revealing nothing he hadn't already told Jack.

"Didn't you say you thought you detected some interest on her part when you first raised the subject?"

Sheridan stood just inside Jack's office, hovering near the door. "It seems I was mistaken," he said stiffly.

"You're quite certain she understood that she could work from her home?"

Sheridan nodded. "I explained that, sir. I told her what you said about using a messenger to pick up copy and deliver it."

"Well, then, what do you think her reason is for holding out? More money?"

An angry red flush spread over Sheridan's features. "Indeed not, sir! She's not that sort of woman."

"Don't be so sure," Jack muttered, unconvinced. He looked up. Something about Sheridan's demeanor seemed a bit odd, he thought. It was unlike the boy to be evasive, yet at the moment he had an almost furtive look about him. "Too quick to judge, too quick to trust—either is folly," he said, ignoring the spark of defiance that leaped in the other's eyes.

Drumming his fingers on the desk, he tried to think. "The woman is a puzzle. What exactly do you know about her?"

"Sir?" Sheridan's strong chin lifted a fraction more, and Jack saw his hands knot at his sides, as if he were nervous or a bit riled.

Too bad. At the moment, Jack hadn't the patience to smooth the lad's feathers. "Aside from the fact that she's incredibly brilliant and bonny, what do you know about your Mrs. Harte?" Not waiting for a reply, Jack continued to speculate. "Apparently her late husband didn't leave her in such good straits," he said, "or she wouldn't be working two jobs. What was his name, this husband of hers, do you know?"

Sheridan shook his head. "She talks about herself very little. Hardly at all. The only comment I recall her making about her husband had to do with his being a clergyman."

"Ah, then there wouldn't have been much money," said Jack, his thoughts darting ahead, only to skid to a stop as an elusive bit of memory skirted the edge of his mind. *A clergyman...a clergyman named Harte...*

"Good heavens!" he burst out. "She's not Bronson Harte's widow, is she?"

Sheridan looked startled. "I…don't know, sir. I can't recall ever hearing her husband's given name. Why, did you know the man?"

Momentarily distracted, Jack shook his head. No, he hadn't known Bronson Harte, but the man and his wild-eyed followers had captured more than their share of space in the *Vanguard* and the other leading newspapers around the state.

Some called them "Reformists" or "Utopians," among other high-minded epithets. Jack called them "socialists" when he was inclined to be generous, "madmen" when he happened to learn of some new, particularly daft behavior by one or more of the pack.

He'd heard it rumored that Horace Greeley had fallen in with a similar bunch, although Jack couldn't imagine even the gullible Horace being bamboozled by that bunch of pompous fools. Still, Greeley was known to have taken up with stranger company. There was that showman P. T. Barnum, for example, who exhibited such sensations as embalmed mermaids and dancing midgets. No, in truth one never quite knew what to expect of Horace.

In any event, he knew of Bronson Harte, all right, and now found himself fascinated by the possibility that Sheridan's *inamorata* might be Harte's widow.

His need for a competent proofreader suddenly took a backseat to his pillaging curiosity.

He realized that Sheridan was watching him with a puzzled frown, but Jack said nothing more. Instead, he reined in his errant thoughts and went on with his own questions. "You told her about our discussion—that there would be a need for someone to help settle any immigrants we decide to bring across?"

Sheridan nodded.

"And you offered to drive her here, to my office, for an interview?"

Again Sheridan gave a nod, shifting from one foot to the other. He seemed unable to make eye contact with Jack, who wondered anew at the lad's peculiar conduct. "Aye, sir, I did. But it made no difference. She couldn't be swayed."

"And you have no idea why she's being so stubborn?"

Sheridan glared at him. "I don't, sir. And I must say I don't believe it's a case of her being stubborn. I'm sure she has her reasons."

Jack sensed the lad was about to add something else, but after a slight pause Sheridan's features took on the same strange, ill-at-ease expression as before.

It suddenly occurred to Jack that perhaps the almost certainly pious Mrs. Harte objected to the idea of working for a known reprobate like himself.

Ordinarily, he might have been mildly amused at the thought. At the moment, he was simply annoyed. He needed a capable proofreader, but up until now he hadn't been inclined to waste any more time on Samantha Harte. He had to admit that he was intrigued, however, by her unwillingness to even discuss the position—even though it sounded as if she could use the money. But even more intriguing was the possibility that she might have been married to a highly controversial figure, a figure whose death had left a number of still-unanswered questions.

In the midst of his musings, Jack remembered that Sheridan's evening class would be meeting tonight. He glanced at his driver, who was watching him closely. Saying nothing, Jack stood and went to the closet to get his topcoat. With his back turned to Sheridan, Jack shrugged into his coat, still thinking. If he left now, he would have time to stop by the barber for a shave, make himself a bit more presentable. He could have dinner later.

His decision made, he smiled a little to himself. That's what he would do, then: If the cagey Mrs. Harte would not come to him, he would go to *her.*

Still smiling, he turned back to Sheridan. "We'll be leaving early today," he said, ignoring the other's questioning stare. "Bring the carriage round."

❧

That night, after the other students had gone, Cavan lingered near the classroom door, watching Samantha Harte. She was making a great show of straightening her desk, then filing the evening's assignment papers into her case. Clearly, she was avoiding him. Indeed, she had scarcely looked in his direction the entire evening, glancing away whenever her gaze chanced to meet his.

Only when the silence became awkward did she finally look up. Her smile appeared forced, her expression impersonal as she continued to shove papers into her carrying case.

"I wanted to apologize," Cavan said without preamble. "For last week. I—perhaps I shouldn't have spoken as I did."

She seemed to be looking at some nonexistent object past his shoulder. "There's no need to apologize. Let's just…forget it, shall we?"

Cavan shook his head. "I believe I offended you, and I'm deeply sorry for that."

Her gaze darted to the door. She looked as if she wanted to flee the room, Cavan thought miserably. Humiliation, combined with impatience at his own rash behavior the week before, rushed through him. He was tempted to bolt and run himself. Instead, he stood, feeling very much the bumbling schoolboy, watching her as she renewed her absorption in tidying the desk.

"Really, it's all right, Cavan—Mr. Sheridan—we won't speak of it again. That would be best, don't you—?" She broke off, turning sharply toward the doorway at the sound of approaching footsteps. Footsteps accompanied by a soft, melodic whistling.

Cavan recognized the buoyant step and the familiar low whistle at once. Stunned, he stood staring at the doorway as Jack Kane appeared.

18

THE PRINCESS AND THE PIRATE

*The most desperate place for the proud to stand
is upon the scorching coals of need.*

ANONYMOUS

Still bending over the desk, Samantha froze at the sight of the tall man silhouetted in the doorway. A dim light from the lamp in the hall haloed a broad expanse of shoulders, a head of glossy raven hair, and a black topcoat. Around his throat was tucked a snowy white scarf, and a single white carnation rested on his lapel.

"Mr. Kane!"

Even before Cavan Sheridan blurted out his name, Samantha recognized the man who stood watching them. Actually, she had seen Black Jack Kane once before tonight, several months ago at the opera, during one of her rare evenings out with her parents. Her mother had pointed out the notorious newspaper baron between acts, giving his name a distinct edge to identify him as thoroughly *disreputable*. With a stunningly beautiful woman on his arm and others ogling him from the sidelines, Kane had towered above the retinue surrounding him. Even at a distance, everything about him exuded a striking, dark elegance—and an unmistakable arrogance.

He was a man not easily forgotten: imposingly tall and lean but with a powerfully set frame and features that were strangely foreign. Samantha had heard it said that every Irishman considered himself a "son of kings," and for a moment she had the foolish thought that the man framed in the doorway might just lend credence to such a claim. Yet, with his snapping black eyes and bronzed skin, she decided that Jack Kane more closely resembled a Spanish pirate than an Irish prince.

He stepped inside the room, and Samantha was instantly suffused with a sense of menace, almost as if she had been physically threatened. She straightened with a jerk, facing him. Kane smiled, his white teeth flashing beneath that dangerous, dark mustache, and Samantha was seized by the mortifying sensation that the man knew

he had unnerved her. She gave herself a mental shake. Obviously, she was reacting to
what she had heard about Kane rather than to the man himself.

Without ever taking his eyes from her, Kane acknowledged Cavan Sheridan in
short order. Then, with an almost courtly gesture, he inclined his head to Samantha
in a mockery of a bow. "Mrs. Harte, I presume? Allow me to introduce myself: Jack
Kane." His voice, startlingly deep and resonant, held a marked lilt that clearly identified his Irishness.

He straightened, his dark brows lifting a fraction. "I hope you'll forgive me for
intruding like this, Mrs. Harte, but as Cavan may have explained, I'm very anxious
to talk with you."

Samantha looked at him, then at Cavan Sheridan, who was staring at Kane
with an expression of bafflement that she was certain mirrored her own. When she
turned back to Kane, she found him studying her with the same self-assured smile.
"I'm sorry," she said, wincing at the uncommon shrillness of her voice. "I'm afraid I
don't understand—"

"Ah, I apologize," Kane said. "I was referring to the position at the *Vanguard* that
I believe Cavan here discussed with you. I'm in rather desperate need of a qualified
proofreader, you see. Cavan conveyed your reluctance to meet with me—so I took
the liberty of coming to you."

Again the quick gleam of a smile. "Actually, I was hoping I could change your
mind. Perhaps I should explain that, for the right person, the job would be as much
that of a copy editor as a proofreader. I'm needing an individual with some editorial
sense in addition to a keen eye." He paused. "Naturally, I would offer a salary com-
mensurate with the demands of the job. If you'd be kind enough to give me just a
few minutes of your time, I'd like to explain in more detail."

Samantha glanced from Kane to Cavan Sheridan, vaguely aware of the similarity in height between the two. But whereas the latter's was as yet the undeveloped
lankiness of youth, Jack Kane's stature was that of a mature man—and a supremely
confident one.

Cavan was watching her intently, his expression a plea for her to hear Kane out.
But after his awkward confession of the previous week, Samantha was only too well
aware of his reasons for wanting her to accept the position. She had already decided
she would be foolish to even consider the idea.

Turning back to Kane, she said, "I'm sorry you've gone to so much trouble, Mr.
Kane, but as I explained to Cavan—Mr. Sheridan—I'm really not qualified for this
sort of position."

"Nonsense," Kane said dismissively. "Cavan here believes otherwise, and I've come
to trust his judgment." He darted a quick look at his driver, then turned again to
Samantha. "Fifteen minutes?" he said, his brows lifting a fraction in appeal.

Samantha felt herself being drawn into the field of those compelling dark eyes.
With an irrational sense of panic, she stepped back from him. "I—no, I'm sorry, but
I'm…simply not interested."

His gaze narrowed, and Samantha felt herself examined with a bold directness that somehow stopped just short of being offensive. After the slightest hesitation, Kane again turned to Cavan Sheridan. "I summoned Ransom out of retirement to drive me here this evening. Why don't you take the buggy and go on along? I'll see Mrs. Harte safely home after we talk."

Samantha tensed, suddenly angry. Kane was obviously accustomed to bullying his way past anything and anyone, but she was having none of it. There had been a time when she might have been intimidated by his bravado, but after enduring Bronson's tyranny, it would take more than a swaggering Irishman to cow her.

A quick glance at Cavan Sheridan only served to fuel her resolve. The boy was looking from Kane to her with a gaze that held both confusion and disappointment. Samantha thought there might also be a spark of anger in his eyes, anger at his employer.

"Perhaps I didn't make myself clear," she said, speaking directly to Jack Kane. "I have other plans for this evening, so I really need to be leaving. As for seeing me home, that won't be necessary."

Kane was regarding her with a wry expression. *"Five* minutes?" he said. His tone was deceptively meek, not at all in keeping with the intensity of his gaze. "Surely you won't refuse me five minutes, Mrs. Harte?"

Disgusted with herself, Samantha felt her resistance slip a notch. Years of her mother's coaching in "good manners and proper behavior" now threatened to overcome her common sense.

As if he had seen her waver, Kane moved to seize the advantage. Once again he turned to Cavan Sheridan with a word of instruction. "You might as well be getting along now, lad. And mind the streets—you'll find a lot of ice on the way."

Cavan's face flamed, and for a moment Samantha thought he might challenge his employer. But at last, clearly demoralized, he bade them a hasty goodnight and left the room.

Anger surfaced anew in Samantha—anger at Kane for his insufferable arrogance, and at herself for faltering even momentarily in the face of this presumptuous barbarian.

"Why don't you sit down, Mrs. Harte?" Kane said. Samantha didn't miss the fact that, when issued by Jack Kane, even a simple suggestion seemed more a demand.

She hesitated, and he grinned at her, his dark eyes warming with amusement. The man was so infuriatingly *insolent*. "May I?" he asked, shrugging out of his topcoat before Samantha could reply.

Dismayed, she realized that he almost certainly had no intention of limiting himself to the five minutes he'd requested. Her exasperation with the man boiled higher, and in an attempt to make her own statement, she went to the coat closet, retrieved her wrap, and draped it very carefully and deliberately over the back of the chair.

She took her time in lifting her gaze to meet his. When she did, she found him grinning at her as if he found her incredibly entertaining. "Point taken," he said with another low travesty of a bow. "I'll be brief, my word on it. But won't you at least sit down? And if at all possible, Mrs. Harte, stop watching for me to sprout horns. Despite what you may have been told, I'm not all that dangerous—certainly not to a respectable lady like yourself."

Samantha caught her breath. His insight into her thoughts seemed almost uncanny. It had struck her only a moment earlier that Kane *didn't* seem quite as outrageous as the myriad rumors purported him to be. Oh, he was brash, certainly, his bearing impossibly arrogant, even imperial; probably he could be ruthless and autocratic, and she sensed a coarseness in him somewhat at odds with his darkly urbane good looks.

Nevertheless, he was almost certainly not the dragon she would have expected, based on his reputation. Once or twice she even thought she might have glimpsed a hint of something behind those hooded dark eyes—some fleeting glimmer of a lingering sorrow, an old, not yet healed pain—that belied the mocking air of amusement from which he appeared to view his surroundings. She might have been mistaken, of course. She had only just met the man, after all.

In the end, it was that totally unexpected perception of his humanity, that vague sense of a basic decency in the man, that—combined with her own ingrained code of conduct—caused Samantha to relent. Even then she might have hesitated had she not caught a glimpse of his hands when he removed his gloves. There was no explanation for the peculiar feeling that swept over her at the sight of those large, callused hands with the sturdy, blunt fingers—not carefully manicured as she would have expected, but instead stained with traces of news ink.

Why it should move her so, she couldn't say. But something about the possibility that Jack Kane might actually dirty his hands by working at his own trade struck a chord in her that was still resonating when she sank down into the chair behind her desk, waiting for him to begin.

❧

Jack's instincts about Samantha Harte had proved sound. Within minutes of first meeting her, he had sensed a fundamental spirit of fairness and the innate good manners of one who had grown up in a gracious, civilized environment. As he watched her sit down, then lift her face to him with a cool stare, he was struck by the woman's almost regal bearing.

She was a princess in a dusty schoolroom, a patrician in a city of Philistines. Blast it all, he almost felt as if he should bend his knee and call her *milady!*

Confronted by her slender elegance, her quiet composure, Jack felt himself very much the rough-edged lout and infidel she probably believed him to be. For the first time in years, he found himself at a loss in the presence of a woman.

And what a woman she was! She was nothing like what he had expected, that much was certain. Despite the smitten Cavan Sheridan's accolades to her shrine, Jack would have been surprised if Samantha Harte had been anything more than pleasant looking—perhaps even attractive in a mousy sort of way, but hardly memorable.

He realized what he had done, of course. Because she had been married to one of the more recognizable clergymen of the day, and because she apparently gave much of her time and effort to the impoverished immigrants of the city, he had fostered an image of her as virtuous but rather drab.

So much for supposition. The woman was anything but drab. She was absolutely exquisite. Jack suddenly found himself wondering to what length that lustrous chestnut hair would fall if released from the fussy little knot in which it was trapped or how it might feel to have those magnificent amber-flecked eyes turned on him in something other than suspicion or distaste.

He was completely unprepared for the sudden stab of shame that ripped through him, as if by merely speculating about her—however innocently—he might somehow sully the cloak of decency she seemed to wear.

She was sitting on the edge of her chair, regarding him with that same dignified calm that was beginning to rankle Jack for some reason. He had seen her poise slip, ever so slightly, when he'd first come into the room, but it hadn't taken her long to recover it. Now it was his turn to grope for control. What was it about the woman that put him at a disadvantage and made him feel like such a great, ponderous dolt?

But he had started this, hadn't he? He had no choice but to get on with it, though he had been a fool to come here, he knew that now. He felt a sudden sting of resentment at Samantha Harte's ability to evoke such an uncommon defensiveness in him. Peevishly, he reminded himself of why he had come. Wasn't she the one who stood to benefit most from this meeting, after all?

"Let me get right to the point, Mrs. Harte," he said, his tone sharper than he'd intended. "I came here for one reason, that being to offer you a job." When she would have interrupted, he stopped her with an upraised hand, crossed his arms over his chest, and went on. "Our lad Cavan has a great admiration for you—but no doubt you're already aware of that." Jack watched her closely, saw a faint flush creep over her features, and smiled to himself.

"He tells me that in addition to your teaching in the settlements—a most admirable vocation, for which you're to be commended, I'm sure—you also work part-time as a proofreader. You're employed by a local textbook publisher, I believe?"

She nodded, her gaze still fixed steadily upon him.

Jack hesitated only a second or two. "That publisher wouldn't happen to be Josef Stein, would it?"

The change in her expression was dramatic. It had been no lucky guess on his part, of course. Jack had made it his business to learn the place—and the status—of her employment before ever coming down here tonight.

He gave her no chance to reply. "I expect you know they're about to close their doors."

He saw the slender throat tighten as she made an effort to swallow. "How—how would you know that?"

"You haven't heard?"

She frowned, then shook her head. "No, I try to ignore rumors."

"It's no rumor, Mrs. Harte," Jack said, softening his tone.

"You can't—how could you know something like that?"

Jack dropped his arms away from his chest, putting his hands in his pockets. "Stein came to me not long ago with the idea that I might want to buy the company. He knew I'd bought out Perriman and Ware last year and thought he might interest me in acquiring his house as well."

Jack had deliberately given her no warning, meaning to catch her off guard. Clearly, he had. What he hadn't expected was the regret that coiled through him as he watched her composure seem to slip beyond her grasp.

"And…are you—buying him out, that is?" Her voice was so low Jack had to step closer to make out her words. When he did, he saw that she had gone deathly pale.

"No," he said with a shake of his head. "Nor, I suspect, will anyone else. Stein's son has run the company to ruin. They're desperately overextended, thanks to young Joey's excesses. There's nothing for them to do but sell off what they can and close the doors. Quite frankly, there's not enough there to make it worth my while."

Her expression was more than confused. It seemed to border on despair.

Self-disgust whipped through Jack, and he almost wished now he'd let her learn of the situation for herself, rather than from him. "I'm sorry you had to hear this so abruptly," he said, meaning it, even though he knew the situation might work to his favor. "I thought you should know before you summarily turned down my offer."

He pretended not to notice the slight trembling of her hand, which now gripped the leather case on her desk. "You're…quite certain?" she said, her voice sounding strangled. "I don't suppose you could be mistaken?"

"Mrs. Harte," Jack said softly, "it's no mistake." He waited only a second or two, then said, "In light of this situation, am I correct in assuming that you'll be needing a new position?"

He saw her stiffen, watched the play of conflicting emotions dart across her features. The bitter look she turned on him made Jack feel as if he had ripped the job away from her himself. "Mrs. Harte, I don't mean to take advantage—"

"Of course you do," she said icily, the challenge catching Jack completely off guard.

He blinked, not quite managing to stop a smile at this blunt assessment of his motives. "Yes…well, perhaps you're right. But before you sling that book bag at me, won't you at least allow me to tell you a bit about the job I have in mind? I think you might be interested, if you'll just hear me out."

Her expression never wavered, but she inclined her head ever so slightly to indicate that she would listen. *The princess grants an audience to the pirate,* Jack thought with some amusement.

In that moment, he wanted more than anything to convince her to take the job. He liked this woman, he realized—not merely because she was exceedingly attractive, though she was that, all right—but it was more than that. He sensed that Samantha Harte was an admirable woman, probably an exceptional woman—a woman he suddenly wanted to know better, even have her know him, although the very idea would probably send her running from the room.

"May I sit down?" Not waiting for a reply, Jack lowered himself into one of the student chairs closest to her desk. "First off, I want to assure you that you could work from your home. If you have any concern at all about that, let me put your mind at ease."

Pretending not to notice the way her eyes lighted with interest ever so slightly, Jack went on. "I believe I can also promise you that I'd be offering you a considerable increase in wages. And," he added, leaning forward, "a much more interesting variety of duties as well."

Yes, he definitely had her attention now, he thought, watching her. Contempt, at least for the moment, seemed to have given way to curiosity.

Even so, she voiced a protest. "Mr. Kane—what makes you think I'm the right person for this position? Or for any other position with your newspaper, for that matter. You haven't the faintest idea of my qualifications or—"

"You're absolutely right," Jack interrupted, brusquely professional as he acted to convince her of his sincerity. "Would you mind if I asked you a few questions?"

She frowned as if she hadn't expected this. "I…well, I suppose not, but—"

"Good," Jack said, not letting her finish before firing a rapid barrage of questions at her, all very businesslike and timed so as not to give her a chance to do more than catch her breath between replies. He resisted the temptation to toss in a few queries of a more personal nature, knowing instinctively that Samantha Harte would be offended and more than likely driven away by even the slightest attempt to breach that carefully erected bastion of self-defense.

Even so, he was intensely curious about this woman with the steel backbone and soft eyes. For starters, Jack wondered what might account for the apparently precarious state of her finances. Her distress at the prospect of losing her job with Stein had been almost palpable, and unless he was sorely mistaken, she was now leaning toward serious consideration of his offer.

He was also fascinated by a certain duality of nature he thought he perceived in her. The face she presented to him—and to the world, he suspected—was that of a quiet, almost rigidly composed, virtuous widow. Yet in the flinty edge of anger that had earlier sparked in those magnificent eyes, as well as in the sudden, unexpected glint of challenge that had shone out at him for just an instant, Jack had caught a glimpse of something else—an intensity, a vitality, carefully banked but glowing somewhere behind the wall of her control.

Increasingly, he found himself wanting to know more about the woman behind that wall.

He would warrant that Samantha Harte came from a good family, perhaps a privileged family. By her own admission, she had received a better-than-average education for a woman. Clearly, she had been a young bride, for she didn't look as if she could be much past her early or midtwenties.

He wondered how she had ended up needing two jobs to subsist. Even though Bronson Harte had apparently given his life to the ministry, the man shouldn't have been entirely without means. As Jack recalled, Harte had been the only son of a wealthy family—textile-mill wealthy—from somewhere in Massachusetts. A controversial, highly visible clergyman, he had also been widely published and sought after as a public lecturer. Surely he would have managed at least a comfortable living.

He turned his attention back to Bronson Harte's widow. Just as Cavan Sheridan had said, she seemed more than qualified for the proofreader's position—and unless Jack was badly mistaken, Samantha Harte would also be perfect for the additional responsibilities he had in mind.

Indeed, she seemed ideal, exactly what he needed, and Jack offered her the job on the spot.

19

QUEST OR CONQUEST

I have spun the fleecy lint and now my wheel is still...

ETHNA CARBERY

"The job is yours if you want it," Kane said. "You'll want to know what's involved, of course."

"You said it was a proofreading position. I'm probably familiar with most of the requirements—"

"Ah, but I'm thinking it may likely develop into more than that for the right person," he interrupted. "Let me explain."

He leaned back in the chair—which was too small for him—stretched out his long legs, and crossed them neatly at the ankles. Samantha realized anew what a big man he was and was surprised that she no longer felt quite as...overwhelmed by him as she had at first.

Bronson had not been a large man, yet being in the same room with him had often given her a sense of being restricted...confined.

She shook off the thought and returned her full attention to the man across the desk from her. How quickly he had adopted an informal, casual stance with her. She couldn't help wondering if it might be merely a ploy to make her relax and throw her off guard.

Did he really think her that gullible?

Again Bronson came to mind. He had played that sort of game, not with her, but with others, especially those he considered inferior. He would feign a kind of camaraderie to gain their support—or their adulation—then cast them aside after they had served their purpose.

Bronson. Always Bronson. Would she never be free of him? How long would he continue to exert his influence over her—even from the grave?

Samantha looked up, suddenly aware that Jack Kane was watching her with a questioning frown. "I'm sorry," she said quickly. "I'm afraid I'm more tired than I realized. What were you saying?"

His look of concern seemed genuine. "Perhaps I should leave. You've already given me more time than I asked. I can come back later in the week—"

He half rose in the chair, but Samantha gestured that he should remain. Most of her initial aversion to Kane seemed to have passed. And she *was* going to need a job, she reminded herself grimly.

"No, please go on," she told him. "You made the effort to come here, after all. The least I can do is listen. Besides, I...just go on. It's all right."

He looked pleased, which puzzled Samantha. For the life of her, she couldn't imagine why a man like Kane would care one way or the other whether she accepted his offer. But as he went on to give her what seemed to be a carefully thought-out, concise description of the position he had in mind, her bewilderment only increased—as did her interest in the job.

Watching him, listening to him speak in that distinctive, rich rumble of a voice, she realized with some surprise that this was a man who obviously loved his work— thrived on it, perhaps even lived for it. His hard, sardonic features underwent a dramatic transformation as he spoke. The almost black eyes danced with boyish enthusiasm as he told her a little about his plans for the *Vanguard,* in particular his desire to broaden the scope of the paper and heighten its appeal for the entire city—including the immigrant population.

"Actually," Kane said, smiling, "I have young Sheridan to thank for reminding me that readers are far more eager to learn about people than politics, that they're likely to care more about a poor mother in the workhouse than a meeting at the White House." He paused, leaning forward to clasp his large hands on his knees. "I could use your instincts in that regard, Mrs. Harte."

Still uncertain as to what he wanted from her, Samantha reserved her questions for the time being. She was intrigued by Kane's account of his brother's assignment to Ireland and why he thought that assignment would benefit the newspaper. She noticed that he was careful to give Cavan Sheridan full credit for the novel idea of crafting individual stories and even eventually bringing the subjects of those stories to America. Would other men in Kane's position be so generous, she wondered?

"What a splendid idea!" she finally blurted out, unable to mask her own enthusiasm.

Kane nodded. "It is, isn't it? I ragged the lad a bit about spending my money, but in truth I think he's onto something."

He explained then that they would need someone to help the immigrants get settled, should the plan become feasible. "Preferably someone who already has some experience in that area," he said. "I think we could work that in with your other responsibilities nicely. And as I told you," he added, "your wages would reflect the additional work."

In spite of the excitement that seemed to fairly crackle about Kane as he discussed his ideas with her—and her somewhat revised impression of the man—Samantha couldn't help but question where his real motives might lie. *Altruistic* was not a word she had heard used in relation to Black Jack Kane.

"I thought you might have particular interest in this part of the job, Mrs. Harte," he was saying, "assuming that your work with the immigrants stems from a genuine desire to bring about better conditions for them."

"I can't think of any other reason," Samantha said dryly. "Obviously, the financial compensation wouldn't be much of an incentive."

"Yet you don't quite strike me as just another ordinary Polly-Do-Good."

If the remark was meant to provoke her, it didn't. Samantha thought she had a fairly clear idea as to his opinion of her. No doubt in his eyes she was just another bored, discontented widow who used benevolence work as a means of adding purpose to an otherwise uneventful life.

It didn't matter what he thought, of course. Besides, she could hardly expect him to understand her situation when her own family remained baffled by her choices.

She found his silent scrutiny increasingly unsettling, almost…invasive. She deliberately looked away as she framed her reply. "There really aren't that many positions available to women, Mr. Kane. I do what I must to make a living, that's all. My needs are fairly simple. I do what I do, at least so far as my work in the immigrant settlements is concerned, because it supplements my income and because I enjoy it. I like the people."

When she turned back to him, he was regarding her with something akin to approval. He gave a small nod then, almost as if he had made a judgment about her, which only unnerved Samantha even more.

To deflect his discomfiting stare, she decided to ask a question of her own. "I'm curious about *your* interest in the immigrants, Mr. Kane," she ventured. "Oh, I understand that if you can make the *Vanguard* more accessible to the immigrant population—give it more appeal for them—you can expect to sell more newspapers. But mightn't there be a simpler way to add to your readership?" She paused. "Frankly, I can't help but wonder why a man like yourself would be…concerned about these people."

His eyes suddenly hardened to cold black marble, and she saw his hands tighten on his knees. "But I am *one* of those people, Mrs. Harte."

His words came slowly and deliberately, laced with a distinct Irish overtone. Of course, she had known that Kane was an immigrant himself—an Irish immigrant, though hardly a typical one. But, then, she doubted there was much of *anything* typical about the man who sat staring at her with such fierce intensity.

Unexpectedly, his dark brows lifted with a sardonic smile. "To answer your question, Mrs. Harte, I definitely expect to sell more newspapers. Aside from that, however, I doubt that you'd understand the full extent of my interest, even if I tried to explain."

Samantha felt her face heat with embarrassment, but he continued on as smoothly as if he'd already forgotten her blunder. "If you'll indulge me for another moment," he said, "I'll explain that, what with breaking in Cavan Sheridan and perhaps another new reporter or two, I expect I'm going to need a more experienced editorial eye for a time. That being the case, the position will be a higher-salaried one than that of a proofreader. And there's one more thing: I'd be offering you a bit extra if you would be willing to keep a close eye on young Sheridan's education."

Samantha frowned. "I don't understand. I'm already working with Cavan here at the night school twice a week."

With a nod, he drew himself up from the chair and went to stand at the only window in the classroom. "The lad fancies himself a reporter," he said, his back to her, "and I'm inclined to believe he just may have the makings of a good one." He swung around to face her. "I don't actually have enough top-notch reporters, you see, especially with my brother, Brady, out of the country. Now Cavan's instincts are keen, that's certain. And it seems to me the lad has a fine mind, wouldn't you say?"

Samantha nodded. She was intrigued by Kane's intention to test Cavan Sheridan by allowing him to work with some of the copy his brother would be sending from Ireland.

"Depending on how well he does with Brady's material," he went on, "I'll eventually let him try his hand at some local news, see how he manages."

He paused. "No doubt you know better than I that Sheridan's grammar is still a bit too—Irish," Kane said with a grin. "And he also has an excessive amount of idealism for a reporter—he's still very young, after all. But he's sharp—sharp as they come, I'll wager, and he's absolutely desperate for knowledge. The lad gobbles up books like a starving man at a banquet. He doesn't think I know it, of course, but many's the time he drives the carriage with one hand and holds a book in the other."

Samantha couldn't help but smile at the image. She could almost see Cavan Sheridan doing just that.

"He really can't afford anything more in the way of schooling-—the lad has no extra funds, as you may have gathered," Kane continued. "I pay him a decent enough wage, but I think he socks away every penny in hopes of bringing his younger sister across."

Samantha wasn't aware that Cavan Sheridan even *had* a sister, but she could easily imagine him being that conscientious.

"Sheridan needn't know that I'm paying the bills," Kane said. "What I want you to do is give him the finest education you can manage in as short a time as possible—without making him suspicious as to what—or who—is behind it."

Had Samantha not been so intrigued by Kane's obvious desire to help Cavan Sheridan, she might have taken offense at the way he seemed to be ordering her around, as if she had already accepted the position. As it was, she dismissed a prickle of irritation at his presumption.

"The lad is quick," Kane said. "He'll soak up your teaching in a flash. I doubt that it will require all that much extra effort on your part, but whatever it takes—within reason, of course—I'll see that you're compensated." He paused, then added, almost defensively, Samantha thought, "I happen to believe Sheridan is worth it."

It was all too much for Samantha to take in—Kane's showing up as he had, completely without warning, not to mention the fact that he was nothing—*nothing*—like what she would have expected him to be. She had imagined a dragon but had instead encountered a rogue knight. Instead of flaunting his wealth and power, he seemed more concerned about an immigrant employee's future. And as to the job he was offering her, she thought she could not have custom designed a more suitable position—or a more desirable one—for herself.

Her head was already spinning with confusion and a host of conflicting emotions when Kane named a salary figure that literally stunned her. "Oh…no, I couldn't possibly—"

"I wouldn't hire you for less," he said, his tone making it clear he meant it.

"But you don't even know me—"

"And you don't know *me,* Mrs. Harte. Obviously, I'd be taking a risk. But I'm sure your family and friends would feel that you're taking a much bigger one."

Samantha squirmed a little at the meaning implicit in his statement. Obviously, he had recognized her suspicions, her initial hostility. But how could he know that she was already speculating on the reaction of her few friends—Bronson's friends, really—and her family? What would they make of her working for the infamous Jack Kane? Oh, dear heavens, her mother would be *livid!*

"However, you wouldn't regret the risk, Mrs. Harte. I think I can promise you that."

Samantha was struck by an irrational urge to laugh. The idea of placing any value at all in a promise from a man like Kane should have seemed outrageous. Yet as she stood, debating over whether or not she was mad to even consider his proposition, something told her she could trust his word.

But wouldn't it only make things worse for Cavan Sheridan, what with his infatuation with her?

"Even if I were inclined to accept—and I'm not saying I am—I'm not sure I ought to spend any…additional time with Cavan—Mr. Sheridan."

Kane made a dismissing motion with one hand. "Young men often fancy themselves in love with the schoolteacher. Especially such an attractive one," he said lightly with a smile. "It will pass in time, I expect. He'll recover."

Samantha was fairly certain that Kane was right, though she felt a trifle miffed at the offhanded way he relegated the problem to a place of no importance. She was also determined not to respond too hastily.

"I won't deny that I find your offer…appealing, Mr. Kane. But I would have to take a few days to think it over."

"No," he said, astonishing her with his abruptness. "If you wait, you'll talk yourself out of it. I'll need your answer tonight."

"Really—" Even as Samantha drew herself up in protest, she recognized the

possible truth behind his statement. The longer she delayed, the more likely it was that she would reject his offer, if for no other reason than Kane himself. But how could *he* possibly know that?

"You can think it over while I drive you home," he said smoothly, shrugging into his coat, then reaching for hers.

"Oh, no, I told you, that won't be necessary—"

"I gave young Sheridan my word," he said, holding her coat, waiting for her to slip into it. "Surely you'll not be responsible for my disappointing your protégé, now will you?"

Once into her coat, Samantha turned to face him, intending to meet his barb with a firm objection that Cavan Sheridan was not—at least as yet—her "protégé."

The quick smile that broke over his dark features made it clear he had anticipated her. "And if you're concerned about my seeing you home," he said with mocking gravity, "you'll be quite safe, I assure you. My driver, Ransom, is very respectable." He paused. "Even if I am not."

❧

To Samantha's great surprise, Kane remained silent during the entire drive to her flat. Even so, she found it nearly impossible to think. She stared out the window of the carriage into the night, trying to ignore his dark presence at her side. More than once she was aware of his gaze on her, but she kept her face turned resolutely toward the window, making at least a pretense of concentration.

Finally, she did manage to think through Kane's offer in some detail, weighing the merits of the job with the possible pitfalls—the most obvious of which was, of course, Kane himself. Yet despite his dubious reputation and her own conflicting emotions about the man, Samantha thought she would be wise to base her decision not on her prospective employer but on the opportunities presented by the position.

If she really were to lose the part-time job with Stein—and she had no reason to doubt Kane's story—she would be reduced to living on her teaching salary until she could locate something else. That or accept help from her parents, an option she didn't even like to consider.

The increase in wages would afford her more security. It might mean a few extras in her life—perhaps even her own buggy eventually, the only real convenience she could honestly say she missed. Oddly enough, though, the money wasn't the greater appeal. It was the work itself, as Kane envisioned it, that excited her.

The two things she thought she could accept unequivocally from Kane's discourse were his desire to help Cavan Sheridan attain his goals and his interest in appealing to a wider segment of the immigrant population. While she understood how she might be helpful in the former, Samantha wasn't at all certain she would be of any real assistance in the latter—though Kane obviously thought otherwise.

It disturbed her to think that by working more closely with Cavan she might only make things more difficult for him. Yet here, too, she suspected that Jack Kane was right. Cavan was a bright, good-looking young man. Whatever appeal she held for him would likely pass with the first pretty girl who came along to turn his head.

All things considered, it seemed to Samantha that the positives greatly outweighed the negatives. Except for the most obvious hindrance of all—the man for whom she would be working. There was no getting around the fact that she would have a most difficult time of it, convincing her parents and acquaintances that she had not sold her soul to the devil himself by accepting a salary from such a notorious infidel.

She reminded herself that after Bronson's death, once she had resolved to establish a life of her own independent of her family's standards and strangleholds, she had faced an overwhelming amount of criticism, even censure, from all sides. Even now she endured her share of subtle—and some not-so-subtle—allusions to the sins of pride and willfulness. But she had weathered the denunciation and reproach, had managed to care less about the disapproval than about finding God's place for her, and she had never been sorry. It occurred to her now that if she must, she could do the same thing all over again. The realization surprised her and at the same time strangely comforted her.

In the end, she was able to retreat into the quiet place where even Jack Kane's probing gaze could not intrude. Silently, she closed her eyes and offered up the entire decision to the only One whose opinion really mattered.

By the time the carriage pulled up to her apartment building, Samantha had her answer.

Kane was watching her, his dark features taut with speculation, when Samantha turned to him. "Here is what I will do, Mr. Kane," she said quietly, "and I will commit to nothing else. I will try the position for three months, with the understanding that if I'm not comfortable with it by the end of that time—for any reason—you will pay me one month's severance pay and make no protest to my resignation."

He regarded her with a steady, measuring stare, his black eyes snapping in the faint light from the street lamp. He had removed his gloves and now sat tapping one against the palm of his hand. His tone was as solemn as Samantha's as he stated his reply. "Agreed. So long as your work is satisfactory, of course," he added wryly.

One of his gloves slipped out of his hands, and he bent to retrieve it. When his dark head snapped up, he was wearing a wickedly smug smile, much like that of a pirate raising his colors aboard a conquered vessel.

PART TWO

IN THE CRUCIBLE

❧

The crucible for silver and the furnace for gold,

but the Lord tests the heart.

PROVERBS 17:3, NIV

20

DIFFERENT KINDS OF MEN

I turned my back on the dream I had shaped,
And to this road before me
My face I turned.

PADRAIC PEARSE

THE CLADDAGH, IRELAND, LATE APRIL

It was springtime in Ireland, and Brady Kane was half in love. Half in love with one girl, and half in love with another. With a rueful smile, he wondered if that made him in love entirely.

As he hoofed it down the Claddagh lane toward Gabriel's house, his sketch pad under one arm, a bag of sweets dangling from the fingers of his free hand, he acknowledged that his affection for the one girl could hardly be counted, since she bolted like a frightened rabbit every time he came near her.

He slowed his pace a little at the thought of Roweena, giving a sigh completely out of keeping with his jaunty mood. He had begun to despair of ever winning more than a furtive smile from the girl. If he so much as tried to coax her out for a walk—hoping to escape Gabriel's ever watchful glare—she would quickly shake her head and scurry off to her corner near the hearth, as if he had suggested running off to the North with him. And even though, in spite of her deafness, she could speak, the only words she ever directed to Brady in that strange, strangled-sounding voice were a simple greeting of welcome or a shy farewell. Even these weren't always spoken but just as often indicated by a few quick movements of her hands and a dip of her head.

At first he'd blamed Gabriel—an unspoken accusation, of course—for the way the girl continued to dodge his attentions. The Big Fella directed a singular scowl at Brady whenever he chanced to eke out a few moments alone with Roweena in the yard before she darted back inside. And if he happened to follow her into the cottage, he was sure to be met with the sort of murderous look that only a man of Gabriel's impressive size and fierce features could affect. Except for Jack, of course; Jack had a look that could set titans to trembling.

But Brady had finally come to accept, however grudgingly, that Roweena's reluctance to walk out with him apparently had nothing to do with Gabriel.

"'Tis her way," the child, Evie, had informed him with a look that clearly said he ought to know as much by now. "Her's shy, Roweena is."

It was more than shyness, Brady was convinced. Other than Gabriel and Evie, Roweena appeared to be almost frightened of anyone who came round. Even Terese seemed to intimidate her.

But then Terese could intimidate most anyone, he thought, grinning. She could be a real banshee, his Terese. The fire in her would scald even the toughest fellow. Only Gabriel and that harridan Jane Connolly seemed capable of dousing her smoke.

As he approached the walk to Gabriel's house, Brady reminded himself that he would have to watch it with this "his Terese" stuff. He fancied the girl, that was true, and he had no doubt but what she was sweet on him as well. But he had no intention of leading her to expect anything from him in the way of love everlasting. He wasn't about to fall into *that* trap.

As keen as Terese was for him, she was even wilder to go to America, he knew. Lately, she'd begun to drop thinly veiled hints that perhaps Brady could help advance her aspirations. He had said nothing to encourage her hopes, but she continued to hint.

He had deliberately kept his silence regarding Jack's idea to introduce a few specific individuals—or even entire families—to the *Vanguard*'s readers, with the possibility of later sponsoring their passage to America. It still amazed him that his brother had dreamed up such a scheme. Jack had never been tightfisted with his money. In fact, Brady would have to say that he had always been generous, at least with himself and Rose. But neither had Jack ever been unnecessarily extravagant, and Brady couldn't help but wonder if there was something more behind this sudden idea than his big brother was letting on.

In any event, he wasn't ready to let Terese in on the plan. She would hound him to death if she thought there was any possibility he could help her get to the States. Actually, he had every intention of making sure she got onto the list of prospective candidates, but later.

Terese's story was just what Jack was after, a real tearjerker, complete with suffering, deprivation, and struggle. But Brady wasn't ready to make a break with her, not yet. Even though he would soon be leaving Galway for a time, he planned on coming back. And when he did, he wanted Terese here, waiting for him.

At the thought of leaving, he gave another sigh and slowed his pace a bit. He had delayed his departure as long as he dared, had even deceived Jack into thinking he *had* moved on, paying a coach driver to post his letters outside the county. In one of those letters, he had given Jack a spiel about having to look around a bit for prospective subjects, then interview them and make some sketches before putting together the accompanying stories. The truth was he hadn't even begun looking as yet, but at least he'd bought himself a longer stay in Galway.

On Wednesday of next week, though, he was leaving for Limerick. He hadn't told Terese yet. He had a hunch she might take on, even though she liked to feign indifference to him. He smiled at the thought. She wasn't indifferent, and he knew it. Over the past few weeks, they'd gotten pretty cozy. He even thought it wouldn't take much at this point to coax her up to his flat, if she could just sneak away from old Jane long enough. It was a tempting possibility, but he wasn't at all certain he wanted to deepen the relationship just yet.

Sometimes he thought he was crackers about the girl, but other times she worried him a little. Terese had this...*intensity* about her that was almost threatening. She had grit, that much was certain, a kind of dogged determination and stubbornness he hadn't encountered in any of his other girls. She could be downright fierce sometimes.

Brady was used to being the one in control of a relationship, never the one being controlled. And he had no intention of changing roles, not with Terese or any other girl. He was in no hurry to get further involved with her, not until he knew just what he wanted from such a liaison.

In any event, he would have to say his good-byes over the next few days. When he came back from Limerick, he would let her in on the business with the *Vanguard* and the rest of it. For now, though, he would tell her nothing.

Actually, he hadn't told Terese much of anything about himself. The only thing she really knew about him was that he worked for a New York newspaper and had a brother named Jack.

As it happened, it was Jack who had cautioned him never to reveal too much about himself, especially to women: *"A woman may take up with you for your dandy looks and your devilish charm, boyo. But make no mistake about it, if she learns you've got a bit of money, she'll be harder to shake than a bad case of the grippe. She may adore you as a pauper, but won't she love you to death if she learns that you're a prince?"*

Was that what he was—a prince? He supposed that's how it looked: Brady Kane, heir apparent to the Kane dynasty, pretender to the throne. Brady laughed aloud at the thought, but the sound had an empty ring to it. He could never fill Jack's shoes, should it ever become necessary for him to try. He had no illusions about that. He was a different kind of man altogether than his brother—perhaps no less a man, but certainly not so *big* a man either. Jack had the stuff of greatness, whatever it was, and Brady not only didn't aspire to those heights but he found the whole idea somewhat distasteful. He was more than content with his life as it was. He had the traveling, his painting, and almost always a pretty girl nearby wherever he went. What else could a man want?

He looked around the yard—the best kept of any in the Claddagh—and saw no sign of Gabriel or the girls. But the front door was standing open, so after rapping

on the door frame once, he walked inside, where he was greeted by a smile from
Roweena, a childish trill from the precocious Evie, and a look that clearly said, "You
again, Yank?" from Gabriel.

Brady sought Roweena's smile again, and in that instant it struck him that he was
going to be saying good-bye to her soon as well. The awareness was like a knife in his
heart, much more painful than the thought of leaving Terese.

But he wouldn't think about that at the moment.

❧

Gabriel turned, though he didn't need to look; he recognized the brisk tapping
on the door frame.

Brady Kane. For as often as the Yank visited, Gabriel wondered that he still
bothered to knock.

The American was a welcome enough guest, for the most part, though Gabriel
had full measure of mixed feelings about the young rascal. The lad was clever with
words, well read, and amusing in a brash sort of way. He was generous natured as
well, though Gabriel sometimes wondered where the money came from to finance
his generosity.

He watched as the child, spotting the bag of sweets in the American's hand,
sprinted across the room toward him. Rare was the day that the Yank appeared on
their threshold without something for the wee girl, and Roweena as well. Today it
was candy, enough for them all, though Gabriel had no taste for sweets.

Kane did spoil Evie, but Gabriel considered the occasional indulgence harmless
enough. It was Roweena who worried him most when it came to the American. He
had seen the way she looked for him those days he did not come, had also seen the
way her eyes lighted when he did.

So far, he didn't think Kane had noticed. Roweena was too timid to pay a man
any obvious interest, too shy to encourage his. But Brady Kane wasn't shy, not in
the least. And Gabriel had seen the way those deep-set eyes followed the girl's every
movement about the room.

He went on with the net he was mending, keeping an eye out as the child
coaxed the Yank and Roweena to the hearth for a game of jackstraws. Watching
them, he decided it wasn't a lascivious kind of interest he sensed from the young
monkey. Had Kane shown designs of that nature, Gabriel would have banished
him long ago. In truth, the lad appeared to be more taken with Roweena's shy
sweetness, her fragility, than her looks—lovely though she was. Yet, only the fact
that the American had exhibited no salacious intentions—so far, at least—gave
sanction to his presence. One wrong move—one wrong *look*—and he would
find himself a stranger in this part of Galway. And a mortally unwelcome one,
at that.

Gabriel suspected that Kane's intentions toward the Sheridan girl might not be
quite so innocent. He had seen the two of them any number of times on the quay,

so close together that daylight couldn't squeeze between them, the girl hanging onto the Yank's arm as if she owned him.

The lass would do better to set her sights elsewhere, Gabriel suspected. He couldn't imagine anyone staking a claim to the young *jackeen* across the room. Brady Kane had the look about him of a wild stallion roaming the hills, kicking up dust, then shaking it from his feet as he ran into the wind.

But better the island girl for him than Roweena. That one could take care of herself, no doubt, though at times Gabriel suspected she wasn't nearly as hard as she would have others believe. Even so, she would be immensely stronger than Roweena, less likely to be the victim of an unprincipled rogue—if that's what Brady Kane turned out to be.

Roweena had already endured more than her share of pain in her young life. Inasmuch as he had it in his power to protect her, Gabriel vowed that she would suffer no more.

He was realistic enough to know, however, that there was only so much he could do to shield her, only so much hurt he could spare her. Knowing this sometimes made his spirit writhe in helplessness.

But at least he could protect her from careless young Corinthians like Brady Kane. The very possibility that Roweena was fascinated with the American was enough to evoke caution on Gabriel's part. Although he sensed nothing inherently malicious or brutal about Kane, he *had* perceived a certain callousness in him that might point to an intemperate, self-indulgent nature, the sort disposed to using others, then going on his way with never so much as a backward glance.

Even so, it was not the Brady Kanes of the world that troubled Gabriel most but those who were more beast than man. The predators among them. There would always be those who, possessing neither conscience nor compassion—perhaps not even a soul—took some sort of deranged satisfaction from tormenting, even destroying, the innocent.

Didn't the Scriptures themselves warn of them, those who prowled about like dogs, filth and curses spewing from their mouths as they sought unsuspecting victims on whom to inflict their evil? These were the deadly ones, the ones who struck at random, with no thought of consequence, no concern for the lives they might devastate.

Roweena herself had been born of such mindless savagery.

And her mother had died of it.

❧

Gabriel had been only a boy when he had first heard the story of Ena MacHugh. He hadn't always lived in the Claddagh but had grown up in Galway City until such time as his Uncle Nessan—a well-to-do bachelor who had hoarded his earnings for years—decided that young Gabriel should go to France to be educated, and offered to sponsor him.

While there, a letter from his mother arrived that related, in terms too delicate to convey the real tragedy of the situation, the "MacHugh family's ordeal." Later his uncle had also written, in more explicit terms, of the brutal rape that had been perpetrated, not only on the young MacHugh girl, but upon two others as well. In three separate but related acts of terror, three Galway women had been humiliated, violated, and tortured. Apparently, the victims had all been wives or daughters of men deeply involved with one of the countless secret societies forever springing up across the country, covert organizations bent on ridding Ireland of her English oppressors. These were violent men, riding about the countryside inflicting their own cruel form of justice on landlords, magistrates, even the police. After one particularly vicious incident wherein a dozen or more officials were terrorized and injured, three men considered to be leaders in the movement were captured and jailed.

But imprisonment didn't satisfy their captors. A few nights after the men were apprehended, a gaggle of British soldiers—drunk as lords and afire with bloodlust—visited the homes of the prisoners and inflicted their own manner of "justice" on their womenfolk.

Ena MacHugh, the daughter of Seamus MacHugh, a widower and one of the imprisoned felons, was a girl of no more than fifteen years at the time. Excessively sheltered and innocent of the world's cruelties, she was both mentally and physically devastated by the savagery wreaked upon her. After the birth of the child conceived during that attack, Ena began a spiraling descent into madness.

By the time Gabriel returned from France, Ena and her child were living with the sisters at a convent in the country. Occasionally, Gabriel would catch a glimpse of Ena and the raven-haired little girl in the garden behind the convent. Though Ena herself was clearly demented by now, ranting and shrieking at all who happened by, the little girl—Roweena—had even then been a delicate, achingly lovely child.

Gabriel went away once more, and when he returned the convent was gone, burned to the ground during yet another nighttime raid by unknown marauders. Ena had died in the fire. Her child, Roweena, was living with Gabriel's parents. An elderly couple who had been unable to have any other children after Gabriel, they had volunteered to take in the orphaned MacHugh child after the fire.

Gabriel was immediately drawn to the silent, sad-eyed Roweena, doting on her and caring for her as if she were his very own little sister. In spite of his and his family's affection for her, however, Roweena's situation was a pitiful one. She was looked upon by the townspeople as "that strange, wild girl," born in shame to a mother who was mad as a brush. Her deafness—the result of a severe blow the night of the convent fire—only made things worse, for such a thing was viewed with suspicion and, by some, with outright fear.

Gabriel's parents died within a few months of each other while Roweena was still a child, leaving him to make the decision as to her fate. He went away only long enough to settle his affairs, leaving Roweena with his Uncle Nessan and a kindhearted housekeeper. Incredibly, there was another fire. No one perished this time, but Gabriel was summoned back to Galway, where he found Roweena, numb with shock and frozen in terror, hiding in an abandoned building on the quay.

She was like a wild animal when he finally found her. He had to coax her to him as he would have a badly mistreated pup. He took her home, to the house where he had grown up, but by now a number of the townspeople were in a frenzy about the "little witch on the hill," accusing Roweena of everything from setting the fires to conjuring sea storms and crop failures. A neighbor accosted Gabriel at his own front door, demanding that he "get rid of the witch" before she brought a curse down upon them all.

Finally, desperate to protect Roweena, Gabriel made the decision that was to change his life. Under cover of night, he took her from his boyhood home to a place where he thought they would be safe, a place where few ever entered unless they were born to it. He was known there, and they accepted him and the frightened little girl without questions or condemnation. In the Claddagh, Roweena was not viewed as a wild thing, as mad or accursed. A deaf child was simply "special," touched by God.

Gabriel promised her he would never leave her again, and he kept his word. Over the years, he took in others, mostly children, who had been wounded or abandoned, providing them food and shelter—and as much attention as he could manage—until he could find a home for them. Wee Evie was the most recent. She had been but a babe, put out by a mother who didn't want her. Gabriel had not even tried to find another place for Evie. From the beginning, Roweena had developed such a fierce love and devotion for the babe, he could not think of separating them.

He had made the best home he could for all those who chanced to shelter under his roof. His life was far different than the one he had planned for himself, but it was not without its satisfaction and small rewards. They were good folk, the Claddagh people—primitive and pious, yet with a wisdom the outside world could never comprehend.

And they did not even seem to find it curious that a man who had once come within a handbreadth of a foreign mission field would give up everything to live among them as a fisherman—and a surrogate father and brother to those in need.

21

A Cloak in Which to Wrap the Fire

I gave a whistle and a lie,
And you were deaf to both...

Anonymous

By four o'clock, Terese was planning a scalding speech for Brady Kane—who was late, as usual—when she finally saw him coming up the path.

Closing the door quietly behind her, she hurried out to meet him. "Jane is sleeping," she warned, putting a finger to her lips.

He grinned, pulling her up close for a hug. "Good. That's how I like Jane best."

"Will you stop now? The neighbors will be watching."

"Let them watch," he said, dipping his head for a kiss. "Won't they just think what a lucky man that worthless American is to have such a gorgeous lass after him?"

Terese gave him the elbow and pulled away. "There's no one after you except the devil himself, you conceited Yank."

He laughed at her. "Ah, now, T'reesie, why can't you just admit that you find me irresistible entirely?"

She glared at him. "Aren't you even beginning to sound like a pigheaded Irishman, you fool? And will you stop calling me that silly name? My name is *Terese.*"

Brady lifted an eyebrow. "Aren't we in a state today? I thought you'd be all excited about the play tonight, not carrying on like a bad-tempered fishwife."

Terese mellowed a bit at the thought of the play. She had never in her life seen the sort of thing Brady had been telling her about, where people in bright-colored costumes got up on a stage and acted out stories. She *was* excited, and that was the truth, but it wouldn't do to have him taking her for granted. Besides, he seemed to like it when she showed a bit of spirit.

"Jane hasn't agreed as yet that I can go," she cautioned glumly.

His dark eyebrows drew together in a frown of impatience. "You shouldn't even have to ask. The old crone isn't entitled to your soul, Terese, not for a measly two shillings a week. Stand up for yourself."

Terese squared off with him in the middle of the yard. "Two shillings a week might be nothing to a rich American like yourself, Brady Kane, but 'tis the hedge between myself and the poorhouse. I have to keep my position." She paused. "And don't be calling Jane a *crone.*"

"Your *position,*" he said, his mouth turning down. "The woman treats you like a slave."

"That's not true a bit!" Terese glanced back toward the house. "Didn't she tell me right from the start what she expected? She asks nothing more than what I agreed to." She saw the tight set of his mouth, his stubborn frown, and added, "The only reason you don't like poor Jane is that you know she doesn't like *you.* She doesn't trust you."

He pulled a face, as if surprised to find her defending Jane. In truth, Terese surprised herself. Without question, the woman could still set her teeth to grinding with her cantankerous ways. But even though Jane liked to goad her at every chance, for the most part they lived together peaceably enough.

"'Poor Jane,'" Brady mimicked, "doesn't like *anyone.* The woman's disposition would curdle new milk." He shifted his sketch pad to his other arm and withdrew an envelope from his pocket, bringing it close to Terese's face. "The tickets," he said. "Give us a smile and a kiss now, or I'll go and find myself a girl who's not so cruel."

Hands on her hips, Terese stared him down. "You didn't tell me I had to *pay* for my ticket, Brady Kane. Didn't you say it was to be a treat on you?"

He inched closer to her. "The play is your treat. The kiss is mine."

"You're a fool," Terese said, trying to keep a straight face.

He grinned at her. "Ah, but you're a lovely girl."

"Light in the head, that's what you are."

He dangled the tickets in front of her.

"And late again as well," she reminded him. "What kept you *this* time? I suppose you stopped by Gabriel's house on the way."

He shrugged. "I'm not all that late."

Terese bristled. She had nothing against Gabriel—the man had been kind to her, in his fashion—but she'd seen how Brady's eyes turned all soft when he looked at Roweena. She didn't want him looking at anyone that way except herself. Too much depended on it.

"Did I tell you how pretty you look?" he said. "Dressed up just for me, did you?" Again he tried to steal a kiss, and this time Terese allowed it but quickly turned her face so he managed only a light peck on the cheek. "I'm not dressed up, you great *amadon.* I have nothing to dress up *in.*"

"Still, you're gorgeous. Go and tell Jane good-bye now. And get a wrap. It's already turning cool."

"If she's still sleeping, I'd hate to wake her. She'll be cross."

"Fine," he said, catching her hand as if to start back down the path. "We'll go without waking her."

"Indeed we will not," Terese warned. "But you'll come in."

He grimaced but let her lead him to the door. "I don't see why I can't just wait outside."

"'Tis not proper. You'll come in and make a greeting and tell Jane you'll be very careful of my safety and have me home immediately after the play."

He bared his teeth. "She thinks I'm the wolf at the door."

"Jane is known for her discernment of character," Terese said archly, pulling him toward the front door as she went to check on her employer.

❧

Inside, they found Jane sitting in the shadows by the window, no longer dozing. Her flint-edged stare darted from one to the other as they approached.

With only a slight hesitation, Brady started in on the exchange that had become a kind of ritual between him and Terese's employer. "Good evening, Mrs. Connolly. And how are you this fine day?"

The look she turned on him would have withered a snake. "I am exactly as I was when you last inquired, which was not all that long ago, it seems to me." She glanced at Terese. "You're walking out with him again?"

"Do you mind terribly?" Terese held her breath. She would defy her, if it came down to it, but she would rather not. Jane was a fright when she got upset, those poor gnarled hands shaking and crimson splotches breaking over her skin.

Jane cast a disdainful look at Brady Kane. "Sure, and you must have something better to do, girl."

Brady merely smiled—a thoroughly unpleasant smile.

Terese hurried to take an edge off the tension between the two. Brady was convinced that Jane didn't like him, and there was no denying that's how it seemed. Terese was fairly certain, however, that her employer's behavior toward Brady wasn't born so much of dislike as simple contrariness. Jane had seen early on that she could rile Brady and from then on took pleasure in doing just that. She did the same thing with *her*, but Terese had toughened herself to the constant barbs, could actually ignore them—most of the time.

"Please, Jane," she said in a tone as ingratiating as she could manage. "Tonight's the play—you remember, don't you? I've been counting on going, if you can make do without me."

Terese couldn't understand for the life of her why she wanted this eccentric old woman's approval, yet more and more often of late she found herself striving for at least a measure of it. At the moment, she was deliberately shining up to her, of course, but even so she really did want Jane's favor.

Jane lifted a hand in a weak motion of dismissal. "Go on, then. I'll not keep you from your folly." As if she'd only then thought of something else, she turned to Brady.

"What do you know about this—*play* business, Brady Kane? Is it a decent event, where you're taking the girl?"

Brady gave another tight smile. "Entirely respectable, I assure you, Mrs. Connolly. It's a play based on the legend of Grania and Dermot. One of the traveling guild wagons is performing it in Galway, just for tonight."

"There's very little respectable about that legend," Jane said, her eyes narrowing as if to challenge his opinion. "Grania was a stubborn, selfish girl bent only on having her own way. Got her man killed in the process, as I recall. But then he was a fool for taking up with such a wild, heathen girl and no doubt deserved what he got."

Terese saw the way Brady was staring at Jane, as if some unidentifiable object had just sprouted from her head.

Jane's eyes flared, and she cracked a decidedly nasty smile before turning back to Terese. "Didn't I say to go on, then? 'Tis not for me to keep you from squandering your time."

❧

Outside, Terese linked her arm through Brady's as they started down the path. "I don't know how you put up with her; I swear I don't," he said. "That woman would drive a saint to murder."

"She's not so bad, once you get used to her," Terese insisted. "In truth, she's decent enough to me, in her own way."

He shot her a look of disbelief. "I'd be interested in knowing what 'her own way' might be. I've never heard her give you a kind word yet."

Terese shrugged, then smiled a little. "I didn't say she was kind. But she hardly ever calls me a 'wild island girl' anymore. And she now allows me two cups of tea a day, instead of only one."

They turned into the lane leading away from the house. "Oh, well, of course that makes all the difference," he quipped. "Next thing you know, she'll be offering you a raise in wages."

"And wouldn't I be glad to take it?" Terese muttered.

"You could probably find something better in the city, Terese," he remarked, as he did at least once every time they were together. "Perhaps something in one of the shops."

Terese pulled her shawl more tightly about her, already chilled from the wind off the bay.

Brady noticed. "Don't you have a coat or something heavier?" he asked.

"Wouldn't I be wearing a coat if I had one?"

"We're going to get you a coat," he said firmly.

"You're going to stir your own stew," Terese fired back at him. "I'll be buying a coat for myself when I'm inclined, you insufferable rich Yank."

"Why do you keep calling me rich? I'm not rich."

"All Americans are rich," Terese said. "Everyone knows that."

He looked at her, slowing his pace to match hers. "Is that what your brother told you in his letters?"

Terese didn't answer right away. "No," she admitted. "He told me jobs were often hard to come by. Especially for the Irish."

Brady nodded. "I'm afraid he's right. Have you heard from him yet, by the way?"

Terese shook her head, not wanting to spoil her earlier mood.

"How long has it been since you wrote to tell him where you are?"

She tensed. "I've written twice. Jane loaned me the paper, and I posted the last letter three weeks past."

"Well, Pennsylvania's a long way off," he said somewhat lamely. "But you're sure to hear something soon."

Terese knew he was only trying to reassure her, but with every passing day she grew more anxious. If something had happened to Cavan, she didn't know what she would do. He was all the family she had now.

For years she had counted on joining him in America, where the two of them would build a better life for themselves. He was her big brother, but he was little more than an obscure shadow in her memory. She could hardly recall what he looked like. Of course, he would no doubt be greatly changed by now. Even so, she wished she could remember his face more clearly.

But tonight she didn't want to think about Cavan. She wanted to make the most of every minute of this special evening, wanted to enjoy hanging onto the arm of a handsome lad, going out for an evening to a play, just like the girls in America undoubtedly did. Just for tonight, she didn't want to think of anything unpleasant, anything worrisome. She didn't want to imagine Cavan meeting with some terrible misfortune or accident, and she certainly didn't want to think about what she would do if she never heard from him again.

Tonight, she wanted to savor each moment, make the most of it, make it last as long as possible. Tonight, she didn't even want to think about America.

❦

They had plenty of time before the play, and on impulse Brady led her onto one of the streets fronted with small shops. True to form, Terese's mind focused solely on the event to come—the play—and the detour only made her impatient with him. When Brady tried to lead her into one of the shops, she resisted.

"We've gone too far already. Didn't you say the performance was just off the quay? We need to be turning back—"

"We're far too early. Let's have a look around," he said, tugging her along beside him.

"I'd not want to be late. You said we should watch from the front, so we can see everything that's going on."

"And so we shall. But we've plenty of time. Come on now."

"I think we should be going back," she said, glancing over her shoulder.

"Terese," Brady said, at the same time pulling her the rest of the way into the shop.

Her eyes widened as she saw where he was leading her. A row of cloaks hung against one wall, while tables neatly stacked with woolens took up most of the floor space. On the opposite wall, bolts of material filled the shelves.

With the sharp eyes of the generously whiskered owner following their every move, Brady led Terese down the row of cloaks, until one caught his eye. It was a brilliant, regal green, velvet soft and meticulously sewn.

"Here," he said, "put this on."

Terese stared at him as if he'd taken leave of his senses.

"Come on, try it on," he insisted, holding out the folds for her inspection.

Still, she hesitated. The owner wedged his way between the cloaks and one of the tables and began to comment—in the Irish. At a loss, Brady asked Terese, "What's he saying?"

She looked from the owner to Brady. "He says he'll make us a generous offer, since the weather is warming. But, Brady—"

Brady whipped the cloak free and draped it about her slender shoulders, then stood back just enough to have a look. With sudden mischief in her eyes, Terese spun around, and Brady caught his breath. He had never seen her in anything but her old frayed dress and one other, equally as worn, that Jane had collected for her somewhere. At this moment, with the splendid green wrap drawn close about her throat and the fiery riot of hair haloing her face, she might have been the daughter of the High King himself.

He let out his breath in a low whistle as he studied her. "I wish I could paint you right now, at this moment," he said softly. But even as he spoke, he knew he could never capture the passion, the mercurial spirit or formidable will that lent the fire to her beauty. She was beyond depiction. She was magnificent, and so fiercely alive she almost frightened him.

"Tell him we'll take it," he said, his voice gruff.

Her smoke blue eyes grew enormous. "Brady, you can't mean to—"

"Ask him the price."

She did, then relayed what she obviously thought to be a monumental amount. "'Tis outrageous!" she blurted out.

"We will take it," Brady interrupted. "Tell him you'll wear it from here, not to wrap it."

"Brady! No, I can't—"

Brady turned to the owner himself, gesturing his intent, and soon they were on their way out of the shop.

The entire distance to the quay, he relished the sight of her touching the soft wool, eyes shining with a smile for him at every stroke. She was light on her feet at any time, but now she virtually danced, a vision in emerald, a glory to rival the Galway sunset and the jeweled mountains. She was enough to make a man's heart go wild.

Clearly, she was overwhelmed...delighted. Never before tonight had Brady enjoyed giving a gift quite so much.

And never before tonight had he wanted something so much, yet hesitated to take it, for fear it might consume him.

22

STAR OF DESTINY

The ceremony of innocence is drowned;
The best lack all conviction, while the worst
Are full of passionate intensity.

W. B. YEATS

Brady tried to see the performance through Terese's eyes, for it was a new experience, an exciting one for her, and she was obviously enthralled with it. But he had to stretch his imagination to the limits, for he had seen a number of stage plays in New York and Dublin, and tonight's production was without a doubt the poorest he'd ever witnessed.

The performance was given inside a rickety auditorium by a small traveling group, most of whose members looked too old for life on the road. They also looked hungry, and probably were. The costumes were shabby; the sets were inferior—and for the most part, so were the performers. The actress who played the lead was too clumsy on her feet and too jaded in appearance to make a convincing Grania, but even so, at moments she became a spirited, if not inspiring, rebel. And of course the legend itself was intriguing enough that it held even an indifferent audience captive.

Terese was anything but indifferent. It seemed to Brady that she scarcely caught a deep breath until the last line was spoken. Throughout the entire performance, her face was radiant, her eyes shining, so much so that the height of Brady's own enjoyment came from watching hers.

She was a sight in that emerald cloak, statuesque and vibrant, her hair aflame in the light from the lanterns—a vision that would steal any man's senses. He was feeling especially fond of her tonight, even tender, in light of their approaching separation—of which she as yet knew nothing. He held her hand throughout the performance, and when she reached to clutch his arm at a particularly moving scene, he found that he rued the assignment that was about to take him away from her.

Tonight, for the first time, he realized how foolish he had been, what a mistake he had made, to think he could leave her behind, even for a brief time, with no regrets.

Terese did not weep easily. She had struggled through too much pain, too much anguish in her life, to indulge her sorrows with tears. But when the last line of the play was spoken, the curtain drawn, she wept. Overcome by a sense of loss that the experience must come to an end, overwhelmed even more by a dawning awareness that there was something in this night more significant than the play itself...something waiting for her discovery...she found herself unable to control the storm of emotion sweeping through her.

For almost two magical hours she had stepped into a different world, drawn the breath of another person, lived in a time and place so far removed from her own life that it would have been previously unimaginable. She had *become* Grania, daughter of the High King, condemned to marry the aging hero, Finn Mac Cool...the princess who defied her destiny by eloping with the handsome young Dermot...a fugitive pursued by the Fianna warriors for sixteen years...a widow and mother who trained her sons to avenge the death of her husband—only to end up, years later, as the bride of the man she once fled, the elderly war chief, Finn Mac Cool.

Terese knew the ancient epic, of course—had known it since she was a child. She had always loved the story of Grania and Dermot best of all the old legends. But to see it come to life in front of her eyes—a *wonder!*

In their lively colored costumes, the stage paint bright on their faces, their voices resonating out across the crowd, the actors seemed to take on the very life and essence of the fierce, rebellious Grania and the poor, doomed Dermot, the aged and bitter Finn Mac Cool and his noble Fianna warriors.

Tonight she had walked with giants and kings, moved among chieftains and warrior queens. Tonight her heart had burned with love for a handsome hero, only to break in sorrow at his death. Tonight she had known the thunderous rage of revenge and the unexpected grace of forgiveness. Tonight she had escaped, for two precious hours, the bitter reality of her life for the excitement and drama of another.

And tonight, in the depths of her spirit, she had glimpsed, for the first time ever, the faint and distant star of her destiny.

They stood side by side, looking out over the water, watching the curraghs and other small craft bob up and down in the gentle night wind. It was a heavy night, with lowering clouds and thick shadows hovering over the quay.

Brady put an arm around her shoulder and coaxed her closer to him, brushing his face over the softness of the emerald cloak. "Warm enough?" he asked.

She looked at him and smiled. "In my fine new cloak? Of course I am."

"You enjoyed the play," he said. "I'm glad."

"It was wondrous!" She paused, biting at her lower lip. "How does a person go about such a thing—becoming a stage actress?"

He shrugged. "I don't know. I suppose you're born with the ability, though I expect you'd have to take a few lessons all the same."

"You mean at a school? Where would I be finding such a school? Are there such places in America?"

"Sure," Brady said, assuming there were, though he really didn't know.

"In your city?" she pressed. "In New York?"

He laughed a little. "If it's not in New York, it doesn't exist, T'reesie."

She frowned at him.

"Sorry. *Terese,*" he amended. "What's this all about? One play, and you've decided to go on the stage?"

"Don't laugh at me, Brady!" she warned, tossing her hair. "Perhaps that's exactly what I will do, once I get to America. It's something I *can* do. I know I can."

Brady didn't laugh. He was struck by the realization that she was probably right. She had a certain...presence. An inner fire that sometimes seemed to set her ablaze. Tonight had been such a time, right now, at this moment. She was so...intense, so vibrant. Her eyes were enormous in the night, glistening with excitement and purpose. She had pulled the hood of the cloak about her face, but now the wind played at it until it slipped away, leaving her wild russet hair to blow free.

Brady smoothed a strand of hair away from her face, his hand lingering on the cool softness of her cheek. She looked at him, and he caught his breath. She was so incredibly *beautiful!* He actually tried to look away from her, to drag his gaze from hers. He told himself he couldn't afford this kind of entanglement, not now...he was leaving. It would be madness to become any more involved with her than he already had. There would be time enough later, when he came back to Galway. But not now.

Her face was close, and she was watching him, her expression puzzled but rapt, as if the magic of the evening still enveloped her. He reminded himself of how young she was, though in truth he had never felt the difference in the years between them. Still, he had a responsibility...she was innocent; he was sure of it.

Something warred inside him...tried to force its way past the temptation, past the need—something not quite strong enough to overcome either. Heat scorched his face, and he lifted her hands, brushing a light kiss over the knuckles of each, making a weak attempt to cool the fire flaming up within him.

He looked at her, saw how her eyes had grown heavy, her lips full and willing. The blood thundered to his head. One last time he tried to count the cost of what he was about to do. She was no bored cosmopolitan looking for an idle, meaningless evening of pleasure. She was a seventeen-year-old girl who cared about him, even trusted him in her fashion...at least he thought she did. She had already known more than she ought of cruelty and loss and deprivation. She could be hurt even further if he treated her lightly. But he *did* care about her. She had become important to him, perhaps *too* important.

He released her hands, cupped her chin, and lifted her face to his. His eyes searched hers, probing, trying to see some sign of fear or hesitation or even rejection—something to make him stop, because he knew by now that he wouldn't stop himself. What he saw was something he hadn't seen before, something he couldn't comprehend, and for a moment his desire slaked.

Then the moment passed, and he knew he had only imagined it. She was too young to calculate, too naive to speculate. Besides, she was wild for him, just as he was for her. The yielding warmth of her body was proof of it, despite whatever he thought he had seen lurking behind her gaze.

"Terese…"

She locked her arms about his neck, and for an instant he had an unbidden thought of the foolish Dermot, beguiled—*used*—by the ruthless, cunning Grania.

Then she was in his arms, and he was leading her back the way they had come, through the night, back to the town, to his flat.

❦

Terese knew it was wrong, knew she could have stopped it, could *still* stop it if she would. Even at the door to his flat, when he put both arms around her and coaxed her inside, she could have stopped things from going any farther.

At first she told herself it wasn't so wrong, after all, because it was Brady, and she loved him…of course she loved him. But in an instant of brutal clarity she knew that was a lie, because in truth she didn't know what love was, didn't know if she wanted any part of it, not if it meant being weak or dependent or foolish. Besides, at times she didn't even *like* Brady, so how could she love him?

Even as he led her inside the flat, her mind was flinging out questions and warnings, telling her she was doing not only a wrong thing but a foolish thing. But she shook off the caution, shook off the shrieking questions for what she *did* know—that she must get to America, must get out of Ireland, or she would wither up like poor Jane Connolly and simply die of defeat and despair. She had to get out if she was to survive, had to follow that faint beckoning star she had glimpsed for the first time tonight, had to find what was out there waiting for her.

She must not let it matter whether she loved him or that it was wrong, a terrible sin. What mattered was to make him love *her,* at least make him *need* her to the point of desperation. So she went with him, went up the steps into his flat with him. She would let him believe what he obviously wanted to believe, that she was mad for him and must be with him now, tonight.

Eventually, she knew, he would leave—leave Ireland and go back to America. Before that day, she must make absolutely certain that he would not go back without her.

23

REVEREND RUTHLESS

Thank God for one dear friend,
With face still radiant with the light of truth.

John Boyle O'Reilly

❧

NEW YORK CITY

Jack's lunch was already sitting heavy on his stomach when he came back to his office and found the Reverend Rufus G. Carver waiting for him.

"I'm warning you, Rufus, I've just come from Wissen's—beef and dumplings and a cherry torte. Don't you be stirring up my digestion."

With a thunderous laugh, Reverend Ruthless, as Jack had dubbed him years ago, hauled his considerable girth out of the chair and extended a mammoth hand in greeting.

"Jack, God bless you, brother!" he boomed. "How long has it been?"

"A week, as I recall," Jack said dryly. His treacherous insides clamped in protest as Rufus yanked his hand up and down several times. It was a bit, Jack imagined, like being mauled by a bear. A large, extremely well-fed bear.

When Rufus finally released him, Jack sank down in the chair at his desk to recover. "Well, Rufus—how much this time, and what for?"

Still standing, the burly black preacher feigned a hurt look. "Jack...Jack," he said, shaking his glistening bald head sadly, "I surely hope you don't think I only come around when I'm looking for money for the Work."

The *Work* covered a vast array of projects, mostly in the slums and tenement settlements of the city, spearheaded by Rufus and two or three other members of the clergy. Jack bared his teeth in a semblance of a smile. "Not at all, Rufus. I recollect a few times that you settled for the shirt off my back and a pint of blood."

Rufus folded his hands over his ample midsection and rolled his eyes toward

141

heaven. The black preacher had a number of standard postures; having seen them all, Jack tended to think of this one as *The Divine Messenger Pleads for Patience*.

"Before you make your pitch, Rufus, how's Amelia? And the family?"

The other's dark, good-natured face now broke into a smile. "Why, the children are as well as can be, and my Amelia, the good Lord love her, is just fine, Jack, just fine!"

Jack nodded. "I'm glad to hear it. The woman is a saint."

"Now that's the truth, if ever the truth was told, Jack! She is a beautiful, pure-hearted, God-fearing woman, if I do say so myself."

"You forgot *long-suffering,*" Jack pointed out.

"That, too," Rufus said cheerfully, ignoring the jibe. "She sends her best, by the way. And she said I shouldn't come home without a definite date from you as to when we can expect you for supper again."

Jack put a hand to his stomach, trying to ignore the fact that the dumplings had seemingly turned to lead. "I will be only too happy to plop myself down at Amelia's table any night of the week, and she knows it. Best cook in New York."

"Now that's a fact. It just so happens that the reason I came by today was to invite you to a special supper. This one's not at our house, though Amelia will be doing some of the cooking. She sent me special to ask you, and she said I shouldn't take no for an answer."

Lowering himself into the chair across from the desk, Rufus unbuttoned his black suit coat to reveal a multicolored vest, no doubt tailored by his wife. Rufus always wore a plain white shirt and a black suit—shiny enough that Jack sometimes wondered if it was the *same* black suit—but he had the finest collection of good-looking vests in New York, and today's was no exception.

Knowing he was expected to comment on it, Jack did so. "Amelia's latest creation, I suppose?" he said, inclining his head toward Rufus's middle.

Rufus smiled and opened his coat a bit wider. "You like this? I never did care for those worn-out drapes in the front room, but I do believe they made a right nice vest, don't you? Amelia said she had to patch several pieces together to get enough cloth to stretch around me, but isn't that woman a wonder?"

Jack shook his head, unable to stop a smile. "What's this supper you're inviting me to? What are you up to now?"

"Ah, this Saturday. It's going to be a fine evening, Jack. A fine evening. The church is hosting a meal as a way of thanking some of the good folks who helped build the new schoolhouse. You being the one who made the school possible in the first place, we're counting on you to be there, maybe even say a few words to the people."

Jack leaned back in his chair and locked his arms behind his head. "The building's all done, is it?"

Rufus nodded. "It is indeed. And it's a fine, sturdy building, thanks to you, brother."

"Thank the men in your church. They did all the work."

"Wouldn't have been any money to buy the lumber without you, Jack. They're setting in the stove first thing Monday, by the way—more thanks to you. 'Course they won't be needing it much longer now, with warm weather coming, but in the fall those children will be glad for it." He paused, then gave Jack a wide, beatific smile. "You're a good man, brother. A mighty good man."

Jack scowled at him and dropped his arms. "What do you want, Rufus?"

"Now, Jack, I already told you. I'm here to invite you to the supper. It'll be held in the church basement, by the way. We realize you might have other things to do, you being such a busy, important man and all, but it would mean a lot to Amelia and me if you would honor us."

"Oh, *stop* it, Rufus!" Jack growled impatiently. "All right, all right; I'll come. But I won't be making any speeches, and don't you dare try to trick me into it once I'm there, do you hear?"

Rufus put a hand to his heart. "Whatever you say, brother. Far be it from me to interfere with a man's humility before the Lord. I consider it highly commendable, Jack, your insisting on giving your alms in secret. That's the Good Book's way, after all."

Rufus was forever trying to put a religious connotation on everything Jack did. He ignored the remark and sat silently studying the man across the desk with concealed fondness.

Rufus G. Carver was the *blackest* black man Jack had ever known— a big, jovial man of indeterminate age, with a polished dome of a head and a fastidiously trimmed beard. It didn't take much stretching of the imagination to picture Rufus as an ancient African chieftain. It never failed to baffle Jack how the smiling dark monolith sitting across from him could wind him around his little finger with such a minimum of effort. After all these years, Rufus could still squeeze more money from Jack than any two con men combined and talk him into doing just about anything he or his incredible wife, Amelia, asked.

No two men could have been farther apart in terms of personality, philosophy, or perspective. Rufus, though hardworking and energetic, tended to let things roll off his solid back, never fretting about whether or not a job would get done, but simply "trusting the Good Lord" to take care of things. Jack, on the other hand, would drive himself until he was ready to drop. Something in him resisted any kind of dependence. Even today, after years in business, he still found it almost impossible to delegate responsibility. He thrived on the demanding pace he set for himself, in truth found his enjoyment far more in the work itself than in the financial gains or influence that went along with it.

In matters of the spirit, he and Rufus were drastically removed from each other. He was fairly sure that popular opinion had him at best a lapsed Catholic; at worst, a hopeless infidel. At the opposite end of the pole was Rufus, a washed-in-the-blood, filled-with-the-Holy-Ghost, pulpit-thumping PREACHER—Rufus invariably spoke the word *preacher* in capital letters

—who delighted in telling Jack he was a good man at the same time he was nipping at his heels to save his soul.

They traded insults like sworn adversaries, lived in two different worlds, associated with none of the same people, and viewed life from radically diverse platforms. But when it came right down to it, Jack loved Rufus Carver like a brother, and he never doubted that the feeling was mutual.

He could hardly fail to appreciate the irony in the fact that the one man he could honestly count a friend was a zealous black evangelist who viewed money as nothing more than a tool to feed the hungry and build churches and schoolhouses—and who thought the only thing wrong with Jack Kane was that he'd never had a "face-to-face meeting with the Lord."

Jack wasn't even sure what Rufus meant by that, but he had a suspicion there was a lot more wrong with him than his friend would like to think. Even so, he appreciated Rufus's giving him the benefit of the doubt.

Their friendship had begun years ago, before Martha had taken ill. Against Jack's better judgment, she had spent a considerable amount of time helping out at some of the orphanages—perhaps because even then she was longing for the child they would never have. In any event, one of the homes had been for black children, and during that time she had struck up an acquaintance with Rufus and Amelia. One thing had led to another until Jack—despite his fierce resistance to the very idea of befriending a preacher—found himself doing just that.

During Martha's illness and the agonizing days leading up to her death, Rufus had continually stood by Jack, ignoring his embittered tirades against the God who had allowed Martha's suffering.

Perhaps it was Rufus's total lack of pretense, the fact that he made no attempt to give Jack pat answers that would have meant nothing, that had allowed their friendship to come through the ordeal intact and even stronger than ever. To this day, Jack couldn't think of that terrible time at the end without also thinking of Rufus standing by, silently weeping, quietly praying for the friend he could not help. And to this day, there was no man Jack trusted quite as completely as Rufus Carver.

He sighed now and made a resigned gesture with one hand. "What time should I be there?"

Rufus beamed. "Amelia said you should come at six-thirty." He paused, his dark gaze wandering to some unseen object across the room. "She also said that you should feel free to bring a lady friend, if you like."

Jack laughed, and Rufus looked back at him, smiling. "Amelia still thinks all I need is a good woman, eh?" Jack said, shaking his head.

"Well, now, Jack, you've said it yourself—Amelia, she is one smart woman. Could be you ought to take her more seriously."

"Oh, I take her seriously, all right. I just don't agree with her." He shot Rufus a wicked grin. "Besides," he said, "I'm not at all sure I even *know* any good women."

Ah, now it was the *Father Admonishing the Prodigal Son* stance. Rufus wagged a finger at Jack and tried to twist his features into a disapproving frown—not entirely successfully, Jack noted, probably because Rufus's face didn't lend itself to frowning. "Now I'm going to pray that's not so, brother. And I don't believe it is."

Still grinning, Jack stretched and yawned. "If you're through making a nuisance of yourself, Rufus, I have a newspaper to get out."

"Far be it from me to keep an important man from his work, brother. We each have our jobs to do, don't we?" Rufus brought himself to his feet, with some groaning at the effort. "I'm getting to be an old man, Jack. I really am."

Jack watched him. "How old are you anyway, Rufus?"

"Well, now, I don't rightly know," the other said, adjusting his suit coat. "When Dr. Sandleton took me and my mama in, I was just a little fella. Couldn't have been much more than five or six, I don't suppose. That was a lot of years ago. I must be an old man by now, sure enough."

"You're not a day over forty-five, if that, and don't give me that poor-little-slave-boy routine," Jack countered. "You were probably as much of a slyboots when you were five years old as you are now."

Rufus grinned back at him. They both knew the truth, that Rufus Carver *had* in fact been a little slave boy but had never once considered himself *poor*. By his own account, his mother had been an amazing woman—"a little crazy, maybe, but a truly remarkable woman all the same"—who, after his father had been killed by a water moccasin, still managed to escape the slave hunters and get herself and her son to safety in the North. Along the way she had almost drowned pulling another slave child out of the water. In Cincinnati she had narrowly avoided being trampled by a runaway wagon. Finally, a kindhearted Christian doctor and his blind wife had taken in the two runaways, given Rufus's mother a job, and provided both of them with a home for the ensuing years. Rufus was fond of telling anyone who would listen that "if the Good Lord can get a poor little slave boy out of Mississippi with his head still fastened on his shoulders, then he can surely get the devil out of any man's soul."

He left Jack with a hearty reminder not to be late come Saturday, that "the family" was counting on him.

An evening with the Carvers was always a grand time for Jack. Rufus and Amelia's six children, who ranged in age from four to sixteen, were a fine, lively set. Jack was fond of each of them. Yet at times the experience turned bittersweet for him, when, after a noisy, rambunctious evening at the Carvers', he went back to his spacious, silent house, feeling his own lack of family even more keenly.

The thought of family jerked him out of his self-absorption with a reminder of something he needed to take care of, and before he started anything else he sent one of the messenger boys downstairs to fetch Cavan Sheridan.

❦

"Two things," Jack said shortly when young Sheridan stepped into the office. "First off, I wanted to tell you that I wrote my brother a couple of days ago, and I mentioned your sister's name and last known whereabouts to him. I told him to do some checking around and see if he could locate some word of her."

The boy smiled, his ink-smudged features creasing in pleasure. "I can't thank you enough, sir!"

Jack waved off his thanks. "Yes, well, with all this business about bringing others across, it occurred to me we ought to see to your sister first off. I told Brady, if he can find her, to arrange for her passage as soon as possible."

Sheridan wiped his hands down the sides of his trousers. "I—not that I don't appreciate it, sir, you understand—but I haven't quite saved up enough to pay her way—"

Again Jack made a dismissing motion with his hand. "You needn't fret yourself about the cost. I'll take care of it."

"No, sir, I can't let you do that."

Blast, the boy was stubborn. "And why *can't* you let me do that?" Jack said with forced patience.

Sheridan looked uncomfortable—but then, he usually did. "I'd rather not be beholden, sir. As I said, I'm extremely grateful to you, but I'd really like to pay Terese's passage myself, you see."

"No, I *don't* see," Jack snapped. "It seems to me that you shouldn't be splitting hairs about your own sister's well-being. But if you're bound to be pigheaded about the issue, we'll make it a loan, which you can repay when you have the money. Will that satisfy your pride?"

Sheridan regarded him with a solemn expression. Suddenly, he smiled a little—a wonder in itself, Jack thought, gratified that the boy was actually learning to smile in his presence.

"Yes, sir. Thank you, sir. I—you'll let me know if Mr. Brady learns anything?"

"You'll be the first," Jack assured him. "But remember, it will take some time. Now, then, I wanted to see how you're doing with the story on Willie."

As yet, there had been no posts from Brady regarding the new assignment. In the meantime, to let Sheridan try his hand at some writing until the stories from Ireland began to come through, Jack had given him the job of coming up with an article about the newsboys: where and how they lived, their family situations, and especially some of the dangers and dilemmas they faced in their work. He'd suggested to Sheridan that he use little Willie Shanahan as an example—unnamed, of course, for the boy's own protection.

It had been Jack's observation that most of the boys took their jobs very seriously—and why wouldn't they, since to most of them it meant their survival? He had the idea of exposing the worthless scum who were beating them up and stealing from them. Perhaps if he could get some of the decent citizens sufficiently aroused, they'd apply a bit of pressure to the police and the politicians to clean some of the human rubbish off the streets.

"I talked with Willie and two of his friends just yesterday," Sheridan said. "It took some explaining, but I finally convinced them they weren't in trouble. I tried to speak with Willie's mother later on, but the woman acted as if I had a tail and horns. She told me to go away and practically slammed the door in my face." He paused, then added, "Mrs. Harte offered to approach her. She knows some of the other women who live in the same building."

At the mention of Samantha Harte, Jack's interest quickened. "How would that be?"

"From her work with the society, I expect."

"Where does Willie live?"

"Well, Willie lives on the street with the other boys, sir. But his family lives in one of those belowground flats in the Bowery."

"Good heavens, you can't ask Mrs. Harte to go into the Bowery!" Jack exclaimed.

Sheridan gave him a puzzled look. "Mrs. Harte goes to the Bowery all the time, sir. And the Five Points as well."

"Five Points? Samantha Harte goes into the Five Points?"

"Well, not alone, naturally. The police provide protection for some of the members of the benevolent society when they need to visit the Points."

Five Points—so named because of the five streets that converged in the center of a squalid square in the infamous Sixth Ward—was the worst slum in New York City. In fact, from what Jack had been told by some who had traveled extensively, the mean streets of Five Points just might comprise the worst slum in the world. It was a vile, nightmare of a place, the terror of decent people, and a veritable blight on the city. Reeking with human waste, animal filth, and all manner of corruption, the area provided a perfect hideaway for hardened criminals and a breeding ground for unbridled evil.

It was also populated by what was probably the largest Irish settlement outside of Dublin and a fast-growing community of Negroes—two groups continually at odds with each other, which only added more friction to a place already teeming with trouble.

Even the police avoided going into the foul sinkhole unless it was absolutely necessary, and then entered only in pairs and with their weapons at the ready. The thought of Samantha Harte so much as allowing her skirts to brush the filthy stones of the streets was almost beyond Jack's comprehension.

"A remarkable woman," he muttered. "If a bit foolish."

"She *is* a remarkable woman, that's true," Sheridan agreed, his tone somewhat defiant. "But I'd hardly call her foolish."

"Neither she nor any other decent woman has any business going into Five Points. Or the Bowery either, for that matter. And I'd suggest you not encourage her to take such preposterous risks."

Giving Sheridan no time to object, Jack went on. "Mrs. Harte studiously avoids me, so perhaps you would give her a message?"

"Sir?"

"Just tell her I couldn't be more pleased with her work," Jack said, meaning it. "I haven't seen a typo since she took over the proofreading. I'd like her to know I'm impressed."

Sheridan broke into one of the brightest smiles Jack had ever seen on that thoroughly Irish face. So that's what it took, then, to lighten the boy's typically severe countenance—a bit of praise for Mrs. Harte.

"I'll be happy to tell her, sir. I'm sure she'll appreciate hearing it."

After Sheridan left, Jack pulled in a long breath and sat for a moment thinking about Samantha Harte. She really was doing an exceptional job with the editing and proofreading responsibilities. And based on what he could learn from Sheridan, she was working him like an army mule at the books—with progress already evident. Clearly, the remarkable Mrs. Harte was more than meeting the terms of their agreement.

In fact, Jack's only disappointment with his newest employee was the fact that he never caught so much as a glimpse of her. Sheridan or one of the other boys delivered the daily copy to her flat and went back to pick it up. It was a smooth, efficient system, and he could hardly complain about it, since he'd approved it at the start.

Still, he wouldn't mind seeing her again.

Indeed, he wouldn't mind at all.

24

A MOMENT BETWEEN MEMORIES

They never knew the carefree dust of gladness,
but only ashes scattered in the wind.

ANONYMOUS

Samantha left her apartment earlier than she'd planned Saturday afternoon. Since the Shanahan residence wasn't all that far from the church, she decided to make the visit Cavan Sheridan had asked of her before going on to the dinner.

Even though she didn't especially like walking alone on Houston Street, she'd grown used to it by now. She couldn't stop a rueful smile at the thought of her mother; Angela Pilcher would almost certainly fall over with a stroke if she knew her daughter was on foot in such a neighborhood.

But it was a lovely spring day, so warm she scarcely needed a wrap, and she'd been traipsing this area long enough that for the most part even the more disreputable types left her alone. Besides, if she wanted to get anywhere these days, she had to walk. And despite the ever present stench of New York's notorious garbage problem, she usually enjoyed the experience.

The streets were bustling, as usual, with a continual press of people. Young girls in bright-colored dresses giggled as they strolled along with their beaus. Children laughed and shouted as they whipped in and out among the pedestrians. Hard-looking women and even harder-looking men, their voices often raised in anger and in a variety of languages—mostly Irish and German—shot suspicious looks at Samantha in passing. Others, recognizing the schoolteacher, eked out a smile. Dogs were everywhere, sniffing out their choices from the rubbish piled along the streets. As she rounded the corner onto Mott Street, Samantha met a signboard man with his advertising signs slung over his shoulders. He gave Samantha a toothless grin in greeting and went on by.

In front of the tenement house that was her destination, Samantha had to step

back to avoid being run down by a pack of ragged children playing ball. The Shanahans lived in the rear of the building, and Samantha's sense of well-being fled
as she took a long look at the front before going around to the back. It was a dark,
leprous-looking place, three stories and a basement. Some of the windows were
broken, others missing altogether. Rust-covered barrels of waste stood near the
stoop, ringed by a group of poorly clad, hungry-looking men who huddled together,
talking and laughing loudly.

Samantha was familiar with the neighborhood, having visited numerous families
here from time to time. Even so, she felt increasingly uneasy, especially when she
caught a glimpse of flasks being passed among the loiterers. It was a corner lot, so she
could reach the rear of the building from the outside rather than having to navigate
one of the dark hallways typical of these old structures. Keeping her gaze averted, she
ignored the catcalls and smirks as she started around the building.

An almost palpable stench met her in back, and she hesitated before going any
farther. Not for the first time, she questioned the wisdom of coming into such a
neighborhood alone. But she was here now, and she thought it would be even more
foolish to come this far and turn back.

She took in a deep, steadying breath and started down the rickety steps, surprised
to note that the steps and the stoop were completely free of litter and grime, as if they'd
recently been swept. At the unpainted door, she rapped and waited. When she heard
no stirring from within, she knocked again, a little more firmly this time.

Finally, the door creaked on its hinges and cracked open, but only enough for
someone to look out. Samantha could scarcely make out the appearance of a thin
female face with frightened eyes. Shadowed as she was in the late-afternoon gloom,
she might have been either woman or child, Samantha couldn't tell which.

"What d'you want?" she said, her voice hushed, as though to avoid being heard.

"Mrs. Shanahan?" Samantha ventured, for a closer study revealed that the door-
keeper was indeed a woman and not a child. "My name is Samantha Harte. I was
wondering if I might speak with you for a moment."

Immediately, the door began to close. On impulse, Samantha put her hand
between the door and the frame to keep it from shutting in her face. "Please, Mrs.
Shanahan—I won't take much of your time. I'd just like to talk with you, if I may.
It's about Willie."

The woman's face, already pale, turned ashen. "What about Willie? Is he hurt?"

"Oh, no," Samantha hurried to reassure her. "It's nothing like that. Willie is fine.
I'm employed by the *Vanguard,* you see, and the paper is doing a story on newsboys.
I'd like to ask you some questions to help our reporter write the article. Please, can't
you just spare me a few minutes?"

"Willie's all right, then?" The woman seemed less than convinced, but she did
finally crack the door a little wider.

"He's perfectly all right," Samantha said again. "I'm so sorry if I frightened you.
I—may I come in, Mrs. Shanahan?"

Something Samantha recognized as fear leaped in the woman's gaze. "No! I mean, not now...the baby is sleeping..."

Her accent was Irish, of course, but not terribly pronounced. Apparently, the Shanahans weren't new to the city. "I'm sorry," Samantha said, disappointed. "I suppose I *have* come at a bad time. Perhaps I can stop by one day next week."

The woman glanced over her shoulder, then opened the door just enough to step outside onto the stoop. She was a young woman, small, not quite as tall as Samantha, who wasn't much more than three or four inches over five feet herself. Mrs. Shanahan was also painfully thin, almost to the point of emaciation. Studying her, Samantha thought she might have been pretty once, but now she simply looked worn-out and ill. Her red-blonde hair needed combing and fell idly over one side of her face. But her dress, though well worn, was clean and neat.

There was something else about her, something strangely...familiar that Samantha couldn't identify. She suddenly realized that she must have been staring, for the woman was eyeing her suspiciously.

"Mrs. Shanahan, let me explain about the article—"

"I don't have time for that," the other said, not rudely, but more as if she was intent on getting rid of Samantha. "There's three besides Willie, don't you know." She glanced behind her at the door. "They keep me busy. Right now I have the supper to cook and—"

"*Maura!*"

Without warning, a man lumbered into the open doorway. He wasn't a big man, probably only a few inches taller than his diminutive wife. But his wiry frame looked muscular, and there was a hard, mean look about him that didn't stop at his eyes. At the moment, he was scowling at his wife with undisguised anger. Then his gaze cut to Samantha, who felt his malice like a blow.

She saw two things at once: first, that the woman was trembling, shrinking from him as if she expected him to lash out at her, and second, that the man's pale gray eyes didn't quite conceal a spark of wildness that might have been either rage or lunacy.

The recognition was so unexpected, so sharp, that Samantha nearly doubled over. She actually had to wrap her arms around herself to hide her own trembling. Immediately, she took a step back, almost stumbling with the effort. She knew too well what she was witnessing, and she felt sick with the awareness.

"Who's this?" the man growled, his eyes raking first Samantha, then his wife.

"'Tis only a lady from the newspaper, Heber, asking after Willie—"

"Willie?" He glared at Samantha. "What about Willie? What's the worthless little jacksnipe done now?"

The need to defend the boy was all it took for Samantha to recover her composure. "Willie hasn't done anything wrong, Mr. Shanahan! Nothing at all. Please don't misunderstand—as I explained to your wife, the *Vanguard* is considering an article about the newsboys, and I'm just trying to gather some information for the reporter."

The man drew himself up to full height, fixing Samantha with a look that was clearly meant to be intimidating. "If Willie's in no trouble, then it seems to me you got no business coming around here, bothering us with your questions. You leave us alone now."

Obviously, he felt no urgency to see that his dismissal was carried out but turned sharply and started back inside. "Get yourself in here, woman!" he shouted over his shoulder. "You've enough to do without standing out there blathering to some busybody."

The woman darted a look at Samantha, who realized for the first time that Maura Shanahan seemed to have either an injured or perhaps a withered left arm; the entire time she'd been standing there, she had kept the arm drawn up against her side, slightly crooked at the elbow but motionless. Her mouth trembled as she started to back up toward the door. "I'm sorry," she stammered, again glancing behind her. "You'd better go now. I—have you seen my Willie?"

"No, I haven't, Mrs. Shanahan. But I'll be glad to see that he gets a message from you, if you like."

The woman lifted a hand to her hair. "Just tell him…that his mother said to take care of himself." She brushed the hair away from her face, and Samantha saw it then, the ugly bruise mottling her temple. Her stomach knotted, and she fought against the nausea welling up in her. There would be similar bruises on her arms, concealed by the long sleeves of her dress, and perhaps others as well over her body. And that arm, that poor thin arm the woman had been favoring throughout their exchange, was no doubt stiff or injured from being wrenched…

"I'll tell him," Samantha choked out. She swayed slightly, fighting off the weakness that threatened to seize her. She had to get away from here before she was ill. On impulse, she dug down inside her bag for a pencil and paper. "Mrs. Shanahan," she said, trying to stop the shaking of her hand as she scrawled on the paper, "here's my name and an address where you can reach me if you should—" she glanced up, then handed the paper to Maura Shanahan—"if you should want to talk with me about Willie…or anything else. I teach a class there every Tuesday and Thursday evening until eight. And on Friday afternoons I'm at the new Negro school on Mercer Street. Please, feel free to come and see me."

Samantha gave the woman a quick, forced smile, then turned and practically ran up the steps. She knew she had to get out of there, had to get away from Maura Shanahan before she lost the last remnant of her self-control. She could not endure the woman's obvious pain, her humiliation, a moment more.

When she reached the front of the building, she scarcely noticed the same group of men who had jeered at her only minutes before. She had all she could do not to take off running. The entire distance to the church, she felt as if the dogs of her past were hot on her heels in pursuit.

❧

The first person Jack saw when he entered the church basement was Samantha

Harte. She was standing with Amelia, near one of the serving tables at the far end of the room, looking absolutely splendid in a simple frock of a dusky rose hue, her only adornment a bit of frothy lace at the throat. She was just as lovely, her bearing as coolly elegant, as he remembered.

Just inside the door, he caught Rufus by the arm to stop him from going any farther. "What's Samantha Harte doing here?"

Rufus glanced across the room, then at Jack. "You know Mrs. Harte? Isn't she a *fine* woman, though?"

Jack nodded, not taking his eyes off Samantha Harte. Three rows of long banquet-length tables stood between them, and he took advantage of the distance to study her.

"How is it that you know her, Jack?"

Jack turned to look at him. "Actually, I don't know her—at least not very well. She's an employee." At Rufus's look of surprise, he went on to explain. "Mrs. Harte proofreads for me on a part-time basis. I met her through Sheridan, my driver. She's the instructor at the night school he attends." Jack returned his attention to the woman across the room. "You didn't say what she's doing here."

"Why, Mrs. Harte is one of our volunteer teachers," Rufus said. "She donates her Friday afternoons to the school. Yes, indeed, she is a fine woman. A *good* woman," Rufus said pointedly. "Amelia thinks the world and all of her."

"Yes, I'm sure," Jack said, his attention still diverted as he watched Samantha Harte now turn to survey the room. Her gaze locked with his, and Jack smiled and gave a small bow when he saw her look of surprise.

"Rufus," he said, not taking his eyes off Samantha Harte. "A favor?"

"Why, anything for you, Jack. Anything at all."

"Seat me beside Mrs. Harte at the table, would you?"

Jack wasn't so distracted that he missed the smile in Rufus's voice when he replied. "I surely will, Jack. I surely will."

With a quick check of the carnation in his lapel, Jack started to make his way across the room.

❦

Samantha was just beginning to put the visit to Maura Shanahan behind her and relax when she saw Jack Kane standing next to Rufus, looking directly at her. There was no accounting for the sense of panic that slammed into her at the sight of him.

He caught her eye, gave her a roguish smile, and bowed. As Samantha saw him start toward her, she whipped around to Amelia. "What is *he* doing here?"

Amelia followed the direction of Samantha's gaze. "Jack? Why, land, he and Rufus have been friends forever."

Samantha stared at her. "Jack Kane...and Rufus? You aren't serious?"

Amelia smiled as if she understood Samantha's surprise and was completely unoffended by it. "Not exactly what you'd expect, I reckon, but they do get on. Always have." She looked at Samantha with a puzzled frown. "I didn't realize you knew Jack."

Samantha shook her head. She could almost feel Kane closing in on her and tried to ignore the frantic clamoring of her heart, the sudden dryness of her mouth. "I—I've been working part-time for Mr. Kane from my home, proofreading. His driver—one of my night-school students—introduced us."

"You're working for Jack?" Amelia beamed. "Well, now, isn't that nice, Samantha! He is such a *fine* man!"

Samantha stared at her. "Jack Kane?"

Amelia laughed and ran a hand over her perspiring brow before bending over the table to rearrange a few of the dishes that had been moved too close to the edge. "Oh, I know all the stories about Jack, but I don't pay them any heed. This town don't know all there is to know about Jack Kane—nor half of what it owes him, and that's the truth!"

Samantha's eyes widened still more in disbelief. "Are you *serious,* Amelia?"

"I reckon no one knows Jack Kane any better than Rufus and me, and I can tell you that man is not the devil he's made out to be. No, sir," Amelia said emphatically, straightening. "Not at all. He's just a man who made some mistakes when he was young. Don't we all?" She shook her head. "Some folks can't seem to get past the man he *used* to be long enough to get to know the man he is today. Jack, he's just a lonely man who's got nothing much in his life except money—and maybe too much of that."

"Lonely?" Samantha parroted. Out of the corner of her eye she saw Kane and Rufus stop to speak to one of the deacons in the church. "Are you sure we're talking about the same man, Amelia?"

Amelia nodded, the satin sheen of her black hair catching the light from the lamps flickering around the room. She, too, was watching Rufus and Kane as they stood talking. "Oh, Jack's lonely, all right—not that he'd admit it." She looked at Samantha. "He was married once, you know."

Samantha hadn't known.

Amelia gave a long sigh. "They weren't married all that long before Martha took sick and passed away. Jack did love that woman. I think he still misses her, though she's been gone a long time now."

Samantha swallowed against the thickness in her throat. Somehow the thought of Jack Kane as a loving husband or a lonely widower was almost impossible to grasp. "But what is he doing *here?"* she asked again.

A head taller than Samantha, Amelia smiled down at her. "Why, Samantha, honey," she said, "if it weren't for Jack Kane, we wouldn't be *havin'* this supper tonight! There wouldn't be a *school.* Jack, he put up almost all the money for it, don't you know?"

She stopped, eyeing Samantha with a peculiar expression before slowly turning to Jack Kane with a big smile as he reached the two of them.

"Jack! I knew you'd show up!" Amelia said, laughing. "And won't you be glad you did, once you see the dessert table!"

Stunned, Samantha watched Jack Kane draw Amelia's ample frame into a brisk hug and kiss her lightly on the cheek. "How are you, my beauty?" he said, grinning as he set her at arm's length to admire her. "How did an old dog like Rufus ever win such a woman?"

Then he turned to Samantha. "Mrs. Harte," he said, his voice low as he gave that quick, mocking bow again. "My elusive employee. I'm delighted to see you again."

Samantha swallowed with difficulty. For one insane moment she half feared he was going to embrace her as he had Amelia, and she took an involuntary step backward.

One corner of his mouth quirked, and his dark eyes danced as if he knew exactly what she was thinking. Embarrassed, Samantha felt the heat rise to her face and, for the second time that day, knew the urge to run.

25

A MEETING ON MERCER STREET

And I knew what it meant
Not to be at all.

RHODA COGHILL

Seated at the table to Jack Kane's left, directly across from Rufus and Amelia, Samantha struggled to swallow another bite of chicken. She knew her anger toward the man at her side was irrational, but at the moment she didn't much care. Had it not been for Kane, she would have been able to enjoy Amelia's succulent chicken and dumplings. As it was, every morsel she took into her mouth tasted as bitter as old coffee grounds and seemed to bond with her throat all the way down.

It was evident that Jack Kane was having no such problem. Out of the corner of her eye, Samantha saw Kane attack his third helping of dumplings as eagerly as if it were his first. Between mouthfuls, he and Rufus had been trading stories about some of the more colorful city officials, regaling each other like a couple of schoolboys. Obviously, they found themselves highly amusing.

It was a noisy gathering, partly because most of the families were large, with several children, a number of whom had finished eating and were scampering in and out among the tables, laughing and poking at each other. Rufus had more than once ordered them back to their places, but they obviously knew their good-natured preacher too well. For the most part, they simply waved and went on.

Samantha had actually been looking forward to this evening, and she resented Jack Kane's showing up to spoil it. She thought she might even resent Rufus for inviting him—and that *was* irrational. Most of all, she resented herself for letting a man like Kane get under her skin to the point that she couldn't even enjoy a church supper. She might have found him easier to ignore if Amelia hadn't confused her with all that talk about Kane's reputation not being entirely deserved, planting just enough doubt in Samantha's mind that she now found it somewhat more difficult to dislike him.

But why was she so set on disliking Kane in the first place?

The question unsettled Samantha more than she cared to admit. Up until now, she had found it fairly easy to rationalize her feelings about her employer. He represented everything she had been taught to abhor, everything any decent Christian woman would find anathema. Jack Kane was a known libertine. A gambler, a mercenary, a womanizer. A *shark*. Before tonight, aversion would have been a perfectly natural response—indeed the only acceptable response—to a man of his reputation.

But now, if the rumors *had* been exaggerated as Amelia seemed to believe, Samantha supposed she had to consider the possibility that her own judgment of him might have been unfair. After all, she *had* formed her opinion of Kane on little more than hearsay. Even so, she wasn't entirely convinced of Amelia's defense of the man. Wasn't it just possible that Rufus's friendship with Kane might have clouded the Carvers' perception?

On the other hand, she had always known Amelia to be remarkably objective about everything and everyone, even Rufus and the children. That made it difficult to simply disregard her remarks about Jack Kane.

In light of that, why was she still so set on disliking him?

The unsettling reply came roaring in on her like a tidal wave. The truth was that her dislike of Kane amounted to little more than self-deception—because in some perverse way she was actually *attracted* to him.

The admission stunned her. Samantha had never thought to feel even a vague attraction to any man after Bronson. In fact, she would have thought the very idea impossible. The realization that she had deceived herself, that a man like Jack Kane could actually hold some sort of appeal for her, shook her to the point that she froze with a momentary sense of panic.

Suddenly, Samantha was keenly aware of the shoulders that were too wide to comfortably fit the space between her and Dr. Younger without brushing against her, as well as the faint scent of cinnamon and tobacco she'd noticed the night she had met Jack Kane for the first time. She couldn't seem to drag her gaze away from the movement of those large, sturdy hands every time he lifted his water glass or his silverware. And when he laughed, the deep, rich rumble struck a chord that resonated somewhere inside her.

Instinctively, she edged to the other side of her chair as much as possible. As if sensing her movement, Kane turned to her, his dark eyes glinting with something unreadable. *Amusement,* Samantha thought, resenting him anew for the fact that he seemed to find her so entertaining.

"You're not enjoying your supper, Mrs. Harte?" he said. "I hope you're not unwell."

"I'm fine, thank you," she replied formally, keeping her eyes focused on her plate. Her food was virtually untouched, and she made a quick, almost involuntary stab at a piece of chicken. She could feel him watching her as she lifted the fork to her mouth. Her hand jerked with the motion, causing her to gouge her lower lip. She suppressed a wince and resolutely began to chew the chicken, trying not to choke as she swallowed it.

"I hope Cavan Sheridan gave you my message," Kane said, matching the formality of her tone.

Samantha glanced at him, not comprehending.

"I asked him to convey to you how impressed I am with your work."

"Oh—yes, he told me. I—yes, thank you. I'm glad you're pleased. I'm...enjoying the work, actually."

"Good, I was hoping you would."

This line of banal chatter seemed harmless enough, and Samantha tried to cooperate. "Cavan is doing extraordinarily well in his studies," she volunteered.

He took a sip of water before replying. "I should hope so. I seldom see the lad without a grammar or a dictionary, and I notice the midnight oil is often burning in his room."

"He's very dedicated."

Kane seemed intent on finding at least one more bite of chicken. He managed and, after finishing it off, said offhandedly, "Still sweet on you, is he?"

"I beg your pardon," Samantha fairly snapped at him. She glanced across the table to see if Rufus or Amelia had heard, but the two of them were engrossed in conversation with their oldest son, Gideon.

"I asked if Sheridan is still sweet on you, or has he recovered?"

"You needn't make it sound like a *disease,*" Samantha said caustically. While she wouldn't want him to think she had encouraged Cavan—she would never have done so—she didn't particularly like the idea that he considered her something to "recover" from. He grinned at her but, to Samantha's annoyance, made no apology.

❧

Dessert was a fairly lengthy process, involving a long stroll down the aisle to choose one's favorites from among the countless varieties lining the table. Jack followed Samantha back to their places, holding her chair for her as she sat down. As he seated himself, he glanced from his own plate, with its two samplings of cake and generous slice of apple pie, to her dainty serving of custard.

"Do you always eat so little?" he said, so absorbed in the way her dark lashes brushed the delicate curve of her cheek that he suddenly lost interest in his own food.

She looked at him, blinked, then turned her gaze back to the custard in front of her. "I...must have eaten too much dinner. I'm really not all that hungry."

In truth she had eaten hardly any dinner at all, but Jack let the remark pass. "I confess that I'd make room for Amelia's apple pie, no matter what," he said amiably. "That woman is the best cook in New York City."

Samantha smiled and nodded. "Rufus says that's why he's always outgrowing those wonderful vests she sews for him."

Jack looked around, saw Amelia gathering her choir members together on the other side of the room, and smiled. "I believe we are to be treated to some music."

"Have you heard them? They're a superb choir."

Jack nodded. "A performance by the Mercer Street Tabernacle Choir is quite an event, even for a sinner like myself."

Samantha Harte turned and looked directly at him. Much to his surprise, Jack found himself slightly unnerved by that searching, amber-flecked gaze.

"According to Amelia," she said gravely, "you're really not such a sinner at all. Should I believe her...or you?"

The instant the words were out, she flushed slightly. No doubt Samantha Harte was not one given to impulsive remarks. Jack studied her, intrigued and at the same time somewhat amused. "Ah, well, I'd advise you not to pay any heed to Amelia," he said lightly. "She knows very well I'm a terrible man, but, softhearted soul that she is, she pities me all the same."

Not quite comfortable with the way she was studying him, he moved to change the subject. "I wanted to tell you that I've seen a great deal of improvement in young Sheridan already. Your tutoring is obviously successful."

She regarded him for another moment, then returned her attention to the custard in front of her. "He's extremely bright, you already know that. I don't so much tutor Cavan as make the material available to him and monitor his progress. If you don't mind my saying so, it's almost a waste to employ him as a driver. He's far too capable for that sort of position."

Jack pushed a morsel of cake around idly on his plate. "I couldn't agree with you more, but don't concern yourself. I'll be replacing him soon in any event, I expect."

"You *wouldn't!*"

Jack lifted an eyebrow. She had misunderstood him completely, but her indignation only heightened her attractiveness. "Eat your custard, why don't you?" he said, gesturing toward her plate. "I didn't mean that I'm going to *fire* him," he explained. "To the contrary, if he comes through on this story about the newsboys the way I suspect he will, I plan to put him on the *Vanguard*'s payroll. I'm fairly certain I can find an adequate driver. Finding a capable reporter is another matter entirely."

"Oh," she said softly. "I see."

"Sheridan says you're helping him with the article," Jack said. He'd lost interest in stuffing himself any further and put down his fork. "He told me about Willie's mother shutting the door on him, said you were going to try your hand at speaking with her."

She paled slightly. "I—yes, as a matter of fact, I stopped by this afternoon, before I came here."

"Ah. And how did it go?"

She replaced her silverware, not looking at him. Jack saw that her hand was trembling slightly. As though sensing his scrutiny, she kept her back straight, her gaze fixed on the table in front of her. "Not very well, I'm afraid."

"She wouldn't talk with you either?"

She shook her head, still avoiding his gaze. "Only for a moment. Not long enough to really learn anything helpful." She paused, then added, "Willie doesn't live at home, you know."

Jack nodded. "A number of the boys don't. They band together, stay on the streets or in one of the shelters. Usually, they're either not wanted at home, or things are so hard for them there that they prefer the streets."

She offered nothing further. Jack sensed that mention of the visit had disturbed her in some way and wondered why that should be. As far as he knew, she had never even met the boy. "What's she like, Willie's mother?"

She turned to look at him, but her reply was slow in coming. It was almost as though she found it painful to answer. "She's...a very sad woman, I think."

"Sad?"

Samantha nodded. "Sad. And frightened." Her hands went to her lap, and Jack didn't miss the way she began to twist her napkin.

"Frightened of what?" he probed. He leaned toward her, for her voice had become so soft he could scarcely make out her words. But when he saw her flinch, he quickly withdrew. There was no accounting for the hurt that shot through him at this evidence of her dislike, though he forced himself to pretend he hadn't noticed.

"Frightened of *what?*" he asked again.

Still avoiding his gaze, she continued to wring the napkin. "Her husband," she said, her voice sounding strained and unnatural.

"Oh, *that* type," Jack said, making no effort to conceal his disgust. "Small wonder Willie prefers the streets, then. Well, don't worry about getting any more information. Sheridan will just have to manage on his own."

He was puzzled by the peculiar tension that seemed to have gripped her all of a sudden and wondered at the reason for it. But just then chairs began to scrape the floor as people pushed away from the tables, their hands clapping in rhythm with the choir, which now broke into its first number.

Amelia was the primary soloist for the group, and there was nothing Jack enjoyed so much as that strong, soulful voice and the lively, swaying rhythms of the huge choir as together they filled the room and shook the walls with their songs of praise.

Jack loved music, always had. It probably would have surprised even those who thought they knew him reasonably well to learn that he attended the opera regularly, not with any thought of elevating his social status, but rather because he simply could not resist the music. No doubt it would have astonished his contemporaries even more to discover that the music of this wholly unprofessional black church choir affected him in much the same way. Sitting here tonight beside the lovely Samantha Harte, tapping his foot along with the rest of the people in the room, he would have found it difficult, if not impossible, to name his preference—*Don Giovanni* or the rousing rhythms of the Mercer Street Tabernacle Choir.

As it happened, his enjoyment was short-lived. When they were almost at the end of the evening, Amelia stepped forward. As soon as she began singing, Jack recognized the selection and felt a familiar, uneasy stirring deep within, followed by a creeping heaviness, like a stone slowly being rolled over his spirit. It was so intense he wanted to bolt from the room, but it would have been decidedly awkward to do so at that particular moment.

This had happened to him before. On each occasion his mood had been one of contentment, even lightheartedness, so no preexisting melancholy could be blamed for the experience. He had simply been assailed without warning, without reason. It took only the first few words, the first notes of that plaintive, wrenching hymn, and suddenly it was as if a kind of bleak bereavement had seized his soul and held him captive…

> *Amazing grace! how sweet the sound,*
> *That saved a wretch like me!*

Wretched was an apt enough description for the enormous emptiness that now engulfed him. Chilled, Jack crossed his arms over his chest and hugged them to himself to prevent any outward show of his inner trembling. His surroundings seemed to recede and fade from view. The longer the song went on, the greater his feeling of utter desolation. As was usually the case, he heard few of the words past the first line or two, for he was pressed into immobility by the weight of this wintry isolation and despair.

When the music ended and the assault on his emotions had lifted, the sense of loneliness remained. Jack looked about the room, almost painfully aware of a separation that had nothing to do with his surroundings or skin color or social station. It was a far more profound schism between himself and these people. No matter that he sat among them, had been invited into their midst, was even held in a certain measure of respect and, at least by Rufus and Amelia, affection. He was not a part of them and what Rufus referred to as their "holy joy." The faith they professed somehow made them what they were and at the same time served to separate Jack from them as effectively as a towering wall. He was an alien, a stranger among them, and somehow he knew that at the heart of the enervating oppression from which he had just emerged lurked a yearning, an agonizing to be like them.

He shook it off, this inexplicable strangeness that always left him feeling restless and somehow deprived, as if he lacked something in the very essence of his being. He reminded himself that within the hour, the gloom would likely pass and he would undoubtedly be mocking the infernal black Irish depression that could enshroud even a church supper in crepe.

❧

At the end of the evening, as the fellowship hall began to empty, Amelia cornered Samantha and insisted that since Samantha had been foolish enough to walk to the church alone, she and Gideon would see her safely back to her apartment. Samantha saw Jack Kane watching this exchange and half feared he would insist on taking her home, as he had the first night they met. That would have been unthinkably awkward for her, what with Cavan Sheridan being Kane's driver.

She need not have worried, however. Kane made no offer of his carriage, even though once outside Samantha saw that he had come alone, without a driver. In parting, he merely gave her a distracted nod and indicated that it was nice to have seen her again. Then, springing up to the driver's bench of his carriage, he drove away as if in a terrible rush.

Samantha stood watching him for a moment. When she realized that the relief she would have expected to feel at his departure was minimized somewhat by a faint sense of disappointment, she turned and hurried back inside in search of Amelia and Gideon.

⋙—

When Jack heard Amelia scolding Samantha Harte about walking to the church alone, his first instinct was to interrupt and insist on driving her home. He had given Cavan Sheridan the evening off, driving himself to the supper with the intention of spending some time with Rufus and Amelia afterward. He could just as easily have used the opportunity to spend some time alone with the elusive Mrs. Harte. In fact, he had even considered asking her if he might take her to the theater or to supper one night soon.

By the end of the evening, however, he was feeling too raw, too edgy and restless, to be with anyone—especially Samantha Harte, who so clearly did not want to be anywhere near *him*. He was still smarting from the way she had drawn back from him at the table, as if she had somehow caught the stench of corruption about his person.

Well, perhaps she had, he thought angrily. *And what of it?*

Feeling as he did, he could not get away fast enough. Without giving Rufus or Amelia time to question him—and with little more than a curt acknowledgment to Samantha Harte—he took his leave. He was aware of Rufus's searching look and Amelia's surprise at his hasty departure but made no explanation.

As for Samantha Harte, no doubt she was relieved to see him go.

Again came the sting of wounded pride. That and a sudden breach of self-assurance—an uncommon ailment for him, to say the least—had quickly escalated to an impatience with himself that now threatened to burst out of control and turn to rage.

As he pulled away from the church, his eyes were smarting, his skin virtually crawling with agitation. Had he not given up the whiskey years ago, he would have gone straight home and gotten blind drunk, just to dull his senses. As it was, he drove the carriage like a madman through the streets for close to an hour, slowing the horses and turning toward home only after the night air had finally cooled his fevered skin and quelled his fury.

26

A DAY OF SURPRISES

And the gray, chill day
Slips away with a frown.

JAMES STEPHENS

Samantha's mother showed up at her door at half past ten on Monday morning. It occurred to Samantha that a visit from one's mother, even so early on a Monday morning, was probably not all that unusual among ordinary families. But her family had never been ordinary, and since this marked only the second time her mother had deigned to visit since Samantha had taken the apartment, it was practically a historic event.

"Mother!" Samantha blurted out, unable to mask her surprise.

"Well, you might invite me in, Samantha," her mother said with unconcealed impatience. No word of greeting, no "How have you been, dear? I've missed you," not even a smile.

"Oh, of course! I'm sorry!" Samantha stammered, moving aside as her mother made a sweeping entrance into the narrow hallway.

It had been raining since dawn, and even in the short walk from the carriage to Samantha's second-floor apartment, Angela Pilcher had gotten her hat feathers doused and her skirts stained with mud.

"Here, Mother, let me help you with your wrap." But her mother had already removed her rain cloak. Pressing it into Samantha's arms, she started off to the kitchen.

"I'll fix us a cup of tea," Samantha said, hurriedly hanging up the wrap before following her mother into the kitchen. "You must be chilled through from the rain. It's such a miserable morning."

In the kitchen, her mother stood surveying the room with obvious distaste.

"Really, Samantha, this apartment is deplorable. If you insist on living like a pauper, couldn't you at least brighten the place up a bit?"

Samantha suddenly saw the tiny room through her mother's eyes, and a heaviness settled over her. It was no longer the cozy haven of a quiet, reasonably contented life. Instead, she now saw the walls that needed new paper, the small cookstove that would have been more appropriate for a child's playhouse, the ironing board propped in the corner, and the towels she had just folded and stacked at one side of the table.

"I've been planning to redecorate soon," she said, irritated at the note of defensiveness she heard in her voice. "Please, sit down, Mother, while I start the kettle."

"I don't want tea, Samantha. I didn't come here to visit."

She made no move to sit down but simply stood, statuesque and thoroughly aristocratic in her elegant gray morning dress trimmed in rose. Samantha realized anew what a striking figure of a woman her mother really was. Even in the midst of their worst disagreements, it was impossible not to admire her.

Samantha had never been able to find a trace of her mother in her own appearance; she had taken the dark hair and deeper skin tones of her father rather than the Saxon fairness and blue eyes of her mother. Angela Pilcher possessed an almost Junoesque figure—rigidly corseted, of course—and the clear, virtually unlined skin of a much younger woman. With her imposing height and extraordinary good looks, she still turned heads when she walked into a room.

And she could still make Samantha want to run from the room when she turned that chilling blue stare on her in disapproval. Samantha hated herself for the way she suddenly felt like a child—like a nasty little girl who has once again disappointed her mama. It took a concentrated effort not to squirm where she stood, for she was fairly certain she knew why her mother had come.

"I have heard a most disturbing rumor, Samantha, and I felt the only thing to do was to confront you with it. I can only hope you will have a reasonable explanation."

Samantha said nothing. She had to look up to meet her mother's gaze, but she steeled herself not to glance away.

"I hope you can tell me it's all a mistake, that you're not really associated in any way with that *disgusting* man!"

Samantha swallowed. "What man is that, Mother?"

"Jack Kane!" Her mother sounded as if she might strangle on the very words. "I have been told that you are—*working* for him." She stopped. "Well?"

Samantha drew a deep breath. "As a matter of fact, I am, Mother. But only part-time."

Her mother actually paled. Her mouth thinned and pulled downward. "Why in heaven's name would you do such an outrageous thing? Have you taken complete leave of your senses?"

Samantha braced one hand on the back of a chair. "My job with Stein was about to end, Mother. They're closing their doors. Mr. Kane offered me a position, and I accepted. I might add that it's a much better-paying position."

"Oh, Samantha, how could you degrade yourself like this? Have you no pride?"

Samantha tensed. She actually considered telling her mother that this was none of her business. She was a grown woman, had not lived at home for years, was self-supporting, and did not need to submit her actions to anyone for approval.

Instead, she swallowed down her anger and said, "Mother, it's a perfectly honest position, and it pays well. I don't see what possible difference it could make who pays my salary."

"Oh, *really,* Samantha! Of course, it makes a difference! That man, Kane, is so disreputable that decent women won't even mention his name in public. And you think it doesn't matter that you're *employed* by him?"

Samantha recalled some of the "decent women" she'd seen fawning over Kane in the theater some months ago and had to suppress a rueful smile. "No, Mother, I don't think it matters in the least. But if you don't mind telling me, how did you learn of this?"

Angela's eyes could have sharpened knives. "From your friend Marjorie Fletcher. And I might add that she and Gordon are as appalled by your behavior as your father and I are."

"The Fletchers were never *my* friends, Mother. They were Bronson's friends."

"Yes, well, perhaps that's why they're concerned that you might degrade Bronson's memory with your behavior." She paused, raking Samantha with a look of abject disapproval. "There's something I feel I should say in that regard, Samantha. I'll confess that your father and I had misgivings about your marrying Bronson Harte. There was the matter of his being so much older than you, and all those…religious fanatics that flocked around the man. But I think you'll admit that, once we got to know your husband, we accepted the marriage and made the best of it."

From experience, Samantha knew where this was going, and she had to fight the surge of nausea that boiled up in her. "Mother, please, I'd rather not discuss Bronson."

"Samantha, I simply do not understand you." Finally, her mother sat down. She sat the way she stood—straight backed, rigid, and uncompromising, her hands clasped tightly together at her waist. "How could you possibly be married as long as you were to a decent, God-fearing man like Bronson and then do something so foolish as to involve yourself with a total reprobate like Jack Kane?"

Something in Samantha threatened to snap. She clenched her teeth together with such force that a sharp stab of pain shot up her jaw. "Mother, for goodness' sake, I'm *working* for the man, not having an affair with him!"

"Samantha!"

She had genuinely shocked her mother. Unrepentant, Samantha reminded herself that her mother was easily shocked. Or at least pretended to be.

"I'm sorry, Mother, but you really are making altogether too much of this. I needed a job. This one came to my attention through one of the students in my night classes—" she ignored the look of contempt that creased Angela's features at the mention of the night school—"and I accepted it. I work right here, at my own kitchen table. The copy is delivered and picked up by a messenger. I've never even been inside the *Vanguard*'s offices. I have virtually no contact whatsoever with Mr. Kane."

"*Mister* Kane." Angela spat the words out of her mouth as if they were tainted. "Really, Samantha, what will people think? What would *Bronson* think? That poor man—even your father and I came to realize he was a saint—cared so deeply for you. Your behavior would horrify him; I really believe it would. Moving into a dismal little pesthole, in this awful neighborhood—and now...*this*."

Everything in Samantha screamed to lash out at her, to finally tell her the truth about Bronson, the *God-fearing* man, the...*saint* she had married. Tears, not of sadness but of rage, scalded her eyes, and she actually had to turn away from her mother, else she knew she would lose the last thin shred of control left to her.

With her back still turned, she choked out, "Bronson is dead, Mother. I can't live my life based on what he might think."

"Well, your father and I *aren't* dead, though heaven knows your willfulness may well drive us to early graves!"

Samantha heard the chair scrape the floor and turned to see her mother draw to her feet. Her face was no longer attractive but rather waxen and taut with anger. Samantha knew, however, that her mother would not lose any more of her composure than she already had. Angela Pilcher was far too genteel for vulgar displays of emotion. No, she would simply issue a final pronouncement and take her leave.

"I can see that I've made a mistake by coming here, Samantha. You obviously have no self-respect, no shame. I suppose that comes from associating with those immigrant people in the slums, not to mention your new employer. I would simply remind you that, ultimately, you are known by the company you keep."

She rejected Samantha's attempt to help her into her cloak. "You ought to know, Samantha, that you have broken your father's heart. All he ever wanted for you was a good marriage to a decent man, with a home and children. It isn't as if you couldn't have married again, after all."

Samantha cringed at the thought, but she kept her silence. At this point, it was best to let her mother believe what she wanted, have her final say, and leave the apartment.

At the door, her mother turned and said, "I cannot for the life of me understand why you've chosen to live your life among the dregs of the city. Your father and I don't deserve this from you, Samantha. You do have a responsibility, whether you realize it or not—to your family and friends and to the members of Bronson's congregation. Those people looked to you to continue in his work after he passed away, and instead, you not only abandon their fellowship but you defile your husband's memory as well." She paused, then fired her parting shot. "You should be ashamed, Samantha. Truly ashamed."

Samantha waited until her mother had reached her waiting carriage. She suddenly felt feverish and closed the door, leaning against it with her cheek pressed to the cool wood.

After a moment, she went to the window and looked out on the street below. She stood, one hand against the windowpane, watching her mother leave. *I am ashamed, Mother,* she cried out in her spirit as she watched the carriage clatter off down the street. *You'll never know how ashamed. But not for the reason you think. Not because I've defiled Bronson's memory…but because I allowed him to defile me…*

❧

Bronson Harte had been forty-seven when Samantha, then twenty-three, married him. At first her parents had attempted to dissuade her, in part because of the difference in their ages, but even more because they hadn't realized right away that Bronson was from a "fine old family"—indeed, a very wealthy family. Later, after learning that his background was impeccable and that he wasn't quite the zealot that some of his followers were, both Angela and Samuel Pilcher affected a real fondness for their renowned son-in-law, treating him with parental pride and affection even though Bronson was more nearly *their* age than Samantha's.

The difference in years between her and her husband, though considerable, was of no importance whatsoever to Samantha. Nor did she care about the Harte family's reputation or fortune. She loved Bronson for what he was, loved him deeply when she married him—at least she thought she did.

He had come into her life unexpectedly—and suddenly. One day Bronson Harte had been a cloud on the horizon, a name with increasing recognition about the city, but to Samantha still only a name. In a heartbeat, he became real to her, sweeping into her life…and sweeping her off her feet.

She met him through some friends, young adults who, like herself, had grown disenchanted with the lukewarm formality of their own congregation and, unlike Samantha, had left their home church to go seeking after something more dynamic, something more "spiritually challenging." At first Samantha stayed put, unwilling to disappoint her parents, outwardly resigned but inwardly resentful. As time passed and her friends began to rhapsodize over the exciting new "fellowship" they had discovered—and its compelling, visionary leader—she finally gave in to their coaxing and accompanied them to a midweek meeting.

Although she went more out of curiosity than from any real intention to effect a change, after that night Samantha never went back to her former congregation.

The fast-growing new fellowship was made up of a wide spectrum of individuals. Many were members of the academic community—educators and intellectuals—but there were also a significant number from among the laboring classes. They were an outgoing, energetic group: friendly, warm, and seemingly hungry for a deeper experience with God.

As for Bronson Harte, he seemed unimpressed by his personal magnetism, if not entirely unaware of it. A vigorous, attractive man whose silvering hair marked him more with dignity than with aging, Harte had never married but instead had apparently led a life of quiet devotion and self-sacrifice, dedicating himself to his God, to the members of the fellowship, and to the work of the movement.

He was a man with great presence, yet a man who seemed possessed of a genuine humility and gentle nature. At the podium, he was nothing short of mesmerizing. Unlike the soft-spoken Pastor Chapman at Samantha's family church, Bronson Harte wore no stately robes, used no notes when he spoke. In his rich, well-modulated voice, he addressed his listeners as if he were speaking to each one on an individual basis.

His messages were universal ones; he spoke about suffering and peace, death and eternity, the slavery of sin—and the enslavement of men. He neither thundered nor raved, yet his words about the depravity of man and the wrath of God caused many to squirm where they sat. For the first time, Samantha was convicted of a sense of her own worthlessness, a degradation of spirit so intense that she, who had never once breathed even the most frivolous of confidences to anyone else, was soon seeking out the counsel of Bronson Harte for her soul's miasma.

He was not easy on her that day but instead instructed her about the weakness and corruption of the flesh to the point that she might have given in to total despair, had he not placed a firm but gentle hand upon her head as if to administer the healing of forgiveness. Through a veil of tears, Samantha looked up into his face, and from that moment she was never the same again.

Soon, despite the protests of her parents, she was spending more and more time with the fellowship—and with Bronson Harte. She devoted her days and most of her strength to following the example of other members, teaching and working among the immigrant settlements, even going into the vile streets of the Bowery and the hideous tenements of Five Points.

She was young and idealistic, and the beliefs of the fellowship appealed to that part of her that had always yearned to change the conditions of those less fortunate— indeed, to help change the world. Bronson Harte taught, and his congregation eagerly accepted, a doctrine of social reform—a type of "social Christianity" that began with self-examination and criticism, a continual purging of individual sin.

As the movement grew, it was often likened to the Utopians and other similar reformation groups, but in reality it shared little in common with any of them. It was, Samantha came to realize later, first and foremost Bronson Harte's movement. Yet, in spite of the adulation of his followers and the phenomenal growth of the fellowship—they never referred to themselves as a "church"—Bronson never seemed to hold himself above the other members. He worked as tirelessly as anyone else, giving away most of his personal wealth to fund the work they carried on.

It was a fact that Bronson had a great deal to do with the reputation and effectiveness of the fellowship. The Hartes were an extremely wealthy New England family, known for the fair labor practices in their textile mills and their charitable efforts among the underprivileged. Bronson had shortened an intellectual tour of Europe, during which he had studied under some of the great reform leaders of other countries, to return to the States and begin his own organization. His unceasing efforts, his compelling personality and riveting appeal as a speaker—combined with his family's money—had brought a rapid, exceptional growth to the fellowship, which he soon moved from New England to upstate New York, then to the city.

The movement wasn't without controversy and criticism. Some of the more traditional churches in the city had branded Harte's followers as extremists, dangerous radicals, or socialists. Their reformist doctrine seemed threatening to many among the more conservative congregations, while other advocates of class equality and equal rights considered the fellowship's work a distraction from the more critical problems facing the country. For the most part, however, the fellowship enjoyed a healthy measure of respectability, even admiration. It didn't hurt that they counted among their members several esteemed leaders of the city: politicians, businessmen, and academics.

Samantha married Bronson six months after becoming a member of the fellowship. Her parents fought her, as she had known they would. But she had the support of her friends in the fellowship and Bronson's dizzying devotion to buoy her resolve. Besides, by then she was so much in love—and so in awe of Bronson Harte—that she would have braved the gates of hell if he had demanded it of her.

To her near destruction, he did just that.

27

AMONG THE SHADOWS

A pity beyond all telling
Is hid in the heart of love.

W. B. YEATS

Samantha's second surprise of the day arrived with Cavan Sheridan, only minutes after her mother had left.

As was his practice, Cavan took the news copy to the kitchen for her and laid it out on the table. Today, however, he also handed Samantha an envelope. "From Mr. Kane," he said.

Samantha looked at him as she took the envelope and placed it, unopened, with the news copy. They had fallen into a daily routine by now, she and Cavan, whereby he would bring the copy in and exchange pleasantries for a moment or two, then leave until it was time to return for the work. Samantha always offered him a drink of water or a cup of tea—which he always refused.

He never seemed quite as comfortable around her during these brief daily encounters as he did in class. Samantha thought she understood. Even though they were often alone in the school building on those evenings when they stayed over to drill on a particular assignment, it was a more impersonal setting than her apartment.

He had been the soul of propriety ever since that night when he had blurted out his interest in her. Samantha had hoped the infatuation would have ebbed by now, but she was sometimes aware of him watching her at odd moments, his gaze following her about the schoolroom. Occasionally, if by chance their eyes met, he would flush slightly and look away.

Cavan Sheridan was by far the most exceptional student she had ever taught. Samantha admired his intellect, his energy, and his eagerness to learn. Because she also liked him as a person, she hated the awkwardness between them. However, nothing she did seemed to ease the tension.

On his way out, Cavan turned. "I almost forgot—Mr. Kane said you could send your reply by me if you would," he said, gesturing toward the envelope. "This morning or when I come back this afternoon would be fine." He seemed to delay for a moment, but when Samantha merely nodded and smiled, he turned and started for the door.

After he left, Samantha raised the wick on the lamp. She was still shaken from her mother's unpleasant visit, and her hand trembled as she slit the envelope and withdrew a thin sheet of paper. As she deciphered the broad scrawl of Jack Kane's handwriting, she could feel the hammering of her pulse in her throat:

> *Dear Mrs. Harte,*
>
> *It occurs to me that I might have appeared rude Saturday night when I left the church so abruptly. My only defense is that I was somewhat pre-occupied that evening and needed to get away. I would very much like to apologize in person if you would extend me the opportunity. Moreover, I'd like to further discuss your ideas on our young Cavan Sheridan's proposition regarding the stories and possible resettlement of some selected Irish immigrants.*
>
> *I was wondering if you might allow me to take you to dinner one evening this week. Let me be very direct—since I sense that you would be too kind to address the subject: I understand if you're reluctant to be seen in my company. That being the case, I have in mind a small, out-of-the-way—but perfectly respectable—club where we would be well chaperoned but afforded the sort of privacy I imagine you'd prefer.*
>
> *I confess that I am most eager to see you again, not only to make amends for my boorishness Saturday night, but in hopes of getting to know you better. You've only to name your choice of evenings and can do so by sending a reply with Cavan Sheridan today.*
>
> *I am most sincerely yours,*
> *Jack Kane*

Samantha stared at the note in her hand as if it were a snake. Heat rushed to her face. Her emotions began to riot, anger and indignation colliding with an unbidden tingling of excitement, which she instantly shook off.

As the full impact of the note struck her, she expelled a sharp breath. Her first thought was that he had an outrageous nerve, a man of his notoriety asking her out for an evening. Did it demean her somehow in his eyes that she had to work to make a living? Or did he think that just because he employed her she would feel an obligation to accept an invitation from him? Did he seriously believe she was that weak?

Her heart raced so crazily that she had to sit down at the table to steady herself. Her feelings were still warring against each other as she sat there, staring at the note, trying to fathom the intent behind it. A man like Jack Kane would hardly care if he'd been rude to an employee, would he? Certainly not enough to feel the need for an apology. And even if, by some stretch of the imagination, he *did* care, it wouldn't require a dinner invitation to set things right. A simple note like the one he'd sent today would be more than adequate.

Could Kane have possibly sensed the pull she had felt toward him, the reluctant—but undeniable—attraction? Did he think she was the same as all the other women who reputedly threw themselves at him?

Samantha closed her eyes and fought down a wave of humiliation as she tried not to consider too closely the initial flush of excitement she had felt upon reading the note. Unexpectedly, it occurred to her that her feelings of "righteous indignation" might be just as misplaced as the forbidden sense of attraction. Surely it was insufferable snobbery on her part to consider his dinner invitation a kind of insult.

As Samantha reread his blunt assessment of her supposed unwillingness to be seen with him, something tugged at her heart. Even though she couldn't deny the truth of his statement, she found herself mortified that he would have anticipated her so well.

The truth was that, for an instant, she had known a genuine desire to accept his invitation. She wouldn't, of course, but not entirely because of his questionable character. There was the fact that whatever else Jack Kane might or might not be, depending on whose account she believed, he was by his own admission a "sinner"—an unbeliever. The very fact that he rejected everything on which Samantha had staked her life and her future made him forbidden.

She refused to delude herself for a moment that she could influence a man like Kane or change him. Her attraction to him had nothing to do with wanting to "win him for the Lord," although she would certainly be willing to try just that if the opportunity presented itself. But her feelings were not godly, and she would not compound the sin by pretending they were.

For too long she had existed in the shadows of deception, and the darkness had almost sucked the very life from her. The worst of it had been *self*-deception. She had deceived herself—or attempted to—as well as her family and friends. It had taken her months—no, years—to grope her way out of those shadows and find the truth. Once she found it, she promised herself that she would never live in darkness again.

She began each day by praying for the light of discernment, that she might recognize truth and find the strength to live by it. But she sensed that Jack Kane, and the conflicting feelings he evoked in her, held the potential to draw her back into the shadows.

She wasn't at all certain she could escape the darkness a second time.

Finally, Samantha drew in a deep breath, then very deliberately and precisely shredded the note, as if by tearing it into pieces she could remove the temptation from her path.

It took her only a moment to pen a polite, but unmistakably firm, refusal.

❧

Jack wasn't surprised when he read Samantha Harte's reply to his note later that afternoon. Her rejection, while courteous, could not have been more final. Whatever had possessed him anyway, to think she might have accepted? He had acted on impulse, and this was the humiliating result.

And it *was* humiliating, he realized. He wasn't used to women turning him down. Some of them might be interested in him for their own mercenary reasons, that was true—but at least they were *interested!*

Samantha Harte was a cool one, all right. Not the sort he usually went for, as it happened. For the most part, he had little use for the "ice maidens," those paragons of virtue and good breeding. If they weren't altogether boring, they were often the worst sort of snobs.

So why couldn't he get Samantha Harte out of his head? Oh, she was attractive, all right, an uncommonly lovely woman, and with an understated elegance about her that both intrigued and annoyed him. She was smart, too—not just book smart, but sensible as well, he'd wager. And he was almost certain she wasn't entirely indifferent to him. He had sensed...something...at the church the other night—a look in her eyes, some pull between them that hadn't really surprised him. He had felt it the first time he met her, and again the other night at the church. He suspected she had felt it too, though she would probably never admit it, not even to herself.

But what of it? It wasn't the first time he'd been attracted to a pretty woman, hang it all! He wasn't looking for anything special, no lifetime commitment, just a pleasant evening. He hadn't asked the woman to *marry* him, after all, just to have dinner with him!

He couldn't stop the image of her that suddenly filled his mind, any more than he could deny the fact that he was lying to himself—a practice he rarely indulged in. He might just as well face the truth: He had seen something extraordinary in Samantha Harte, had seen it right from the beginning—something rare and fine and unsullied. He already knew that she was no ordinary woman, knew that he would eventually want something more of her than a casual evening or a brief, tawdry affair. But apparently she thought having anything at all to do with him would be just that—*tawdry.*

He crushed her terse note in his hand, as if by doing so he could destroy the reality of her rejection. He had wanted to somehow touch the goodness in her, that unspoiled, unstained part of her that put him to shame even as it seemed to hold out to him some hope of redemption. He had thought if he could know her, be with her, perhaps—

Perhaps *what?*

Suddenly furious with himself, he shoved away from the desk. He tore out of his office, slamming the door with such force that those employees nearby froze.

Outside, Jack charged down the alley. He walked for an hour in the rain, going almost at a run, taking the slick streets like a dark bull in a rage, seeing nothing and hearing only the sound of his own blood pounding in his ears and the driving roar of his own self-disgust.

28

SAD AND UNEXPECTED NEWS

The Lord God judges "crime" above,
But not as man has weighed it.

MARY KELLY

Samantha met the newsboy Willie Shanahan for the first time on the day Willie's mother shot and killed his father.

The night before it happened, Samantha had stayed late after the evening class to help Cavan Sheridan with the article he was writing about the city's newsboys. He was doing a splendid job, indeed had required little editorial guidance from her, other than in some of the finer points of grammar. Another day or so and he would have the copy completed.

On Wednesday afternoon, when Cavan returned for the day's proofing, he arrived out of breath and visibly distraught. His face was crimson, and although the day wasn't particularly warm, he was perspiring.

The instant he was inside the apartment, he burst out, "Mrs. Harte—have you heard? Mrs. Shanahan has shot her husband! She's killed Willie's father!"

Stunned, Samantha struggled to take in what he was saying. Even as he spoke, the image of Maura Shanahan's forlorn countenance flashed across her mind. She saw again the ugly bruise, the frightened eyes. She shivered in apprehension as all the warmth seemed to leave the room.

"What happened?" she choked out.

Cavan shook his head. "I don't think anyone knows yet. One of Willie's sisters came to the office, looking for him. They hadn't found him yet when I left."

Samantha was already regretting that she had not gone back to the Shanahans' after Saturday's failed visit. She had known even then, seeing that poor, careworn woman, her fear and despair so starkly evident…she had *known*. And she had done nothing.

She reminded herself that there was nothing she *could* have done, at least not then. And there had been no time since to go back. But would she have gone in any event? She recalled with disgust how she had practically run away from Maura Shanahan, her own emotions rioting in sick turmoil at the memories the woman's distress had called to mind.

Cavan Sheridan's rush of words jerked her back to the present. "Mr. Kane has sent two of the other newsboys out to fetch Willie. He'll be needed to help with the younger children now, with his mother in jail."

Samantha stared at him in horror. "Maura Shanahan is in *jail?*"

He looked at her strangely. "Why...yes, of course she is. The police took her away right after it happened."

"Dear heavens," Samantha murmured. "What will become of her?"

"Are you all right, Mrs. Harte? Wouldn't you like to sit down?"

He was watching her closely, his expression fraught with concern. Samantha made an attempt to shake off the sick weakness that had seized her. "No, I'm all right." She looked at him. "Cavan, I wonder...would you take me to the jail on your way back to the office?"

He frowned. "The jail?"

Samantha was already heading toward the closet to get a wrap, although she knew the chill that had gripped her had little to do with the weather. "Perhaps I can help," she said. "Would you bring the copy off the table, please?"

Cavan hesitated only a moment before going to the kitchen, but when he returned he stopped in the foyer. "Mrs. Harte, if you'll excuse my saying so, I don't think it's a good idea for you to be going to the jail. From all accounts, it's a terrible place, even for the criminals who end up there. 'Tis not a fit place for a woman."

Samantha looked up as she shrugged into her wrap. "Maura Shanahan is a woman, too, Cavan. Besides, I've been there before."

He stared at her. "You've been to the jail?"

Samantha nodded and gave a grim smile as she locked the door behind them. "Several times."

It occurred to her that he would be altogether dismayed to learn of the places her work among the immigrants had taken her over the years. She wasn't the fragile hothouse flower Cavan seemed to think her. Most of what her mother called her "delicate sensibilities" had been stripped away long before now. She had grown all too familiar with the more squalid features of the city—she knew the slums, most of the hospitals, the foundling homes—and the jails. She had witnessed more than her share of filth, disease, and debauchery.

The city of the poor was an entirely different place from the city of the privileged. By now Samantha was well acquainted with both worlds, enough to know that each bred its own share of secrets and horrors.

Cavan was reluctant to leave her at the jail, but Samantha Harte insisted. "You have to get the copy back to the office," she told him. "I'll be fine. I know most of the guards and the policemen. I'll be well protected; you needn't worry."

Even so, he insisted on escorting her into the building. Just inside, a young, red-faced policeman was haranguing a small boy hunkered down near the door. Cavan hadn't seen Willie Shanahan since the swelling had gone from around his eye, but he recognized him immediately.

"Willie? Whatever are you doing here? Your sister has been looking for you."

"You know this boy?" said the policeman.

Cavan nodded.

"Then make him understand that he's to leave. He's been skulking about since early morning. If he doesn't go along, I'm going to lock him up!"

"You will do no such thing, Officer Malloy."

Cavan stared as Samantha Harte stepped up to the policeman. He wouldn't have guessed that those delicate features could turn so severe. Crossing his arms over his chest, he watched the exchange with interest.

Only then did the policeman seem to notice her presence, stammering out her name and muttering an apology. "Sorry, Mrs. Harte—I didn't see you. But this boy here is making a nuisance of himself, hanging about as he is. This is no place for the lad."

"I can't disagree with that, but I hardly think you need to threaten him."

"Yes, ma'am—I mean, no ma'am. But—"

"You're Willie Shanahan?" Samantha Harte said kindly as she turned to the boy.

Willie unwound himself and stood up, crushing his tattered cap to his chest as he nodded. "Yes'm."

"Well, I'm afraid Officer Malloy is right. This is not a good place for you. Wouldn't you be better off at home with your brothers and sisters?"

"Buster—that's me brother—is looking out for them," the boy said. "I mean to stay nearby, should Mum need anything."

"And that's just the thing, Mrs. Harte," Officer Malloy put in. "He'll not be allowed to see his mother anyway. He's only in the way here."

Samantha Harte studied Willie for another second or two, then turned back to the policeman. "I find it hard to believe that one small boy would be that much in the way," she said. "Surely he could see his mother for just a moment?"

The policeman shook off the suggestion like a dog throwing off cold water. "The sergeant said absolutely not, ma'am!"

"That would be Sergeant Garvey?" she said coolly.

"That's right, ma'am."

"Would you tell the sergeant that I'd like to speak with him, please?"

Officer Malloy looked at her for only an instant before hoofing it down the hall. In the meantime, Samantha Harte turned back to the boy. "Willie, if they let *me* speak with your mother, will you do the right thing and go home until I can arrange for you to visit?"

The boy studied her, his thin face utterly solemn. "You can do that? You'll get me in to see Mum?"

"I'll do my best, Willie. I believe I can arrange something for you by tomorrow. But you must cooperate. Do you understand?"

Finally, Willie ducked his head and, with obvious reluctance, nodded agreement.

"Good," Mrs. Harte said softly. "You're obviously a very good boy, Willie."

Willie Shanahan brightened considerably. It occurred to Cavan that the boy was probably not accustomed to that sort of kindness or affirmation.

Officer Malloy reappeared just then, followed by a big hulk of a fellow with small, watchful eyes and an astoundingly large belly—Sergeant Garvey, he presumed.

It was clear from their greetings that he and Samantha Harte knew each other. She wasted no time in stating her request. "I realize you don't have to allow it, Sergeant, but I'd like to ask that you let Willie here visit his mother, just for a moment."

The sergeant frowned. "You know the Shanahan woman, Mrs. Harte?"

Samantha Harte nodded. "I do."

The sergeant glanced from Willie to Mrs. Harte. "Then you know she's a murderer," he said, dropping his voice. "I can't be letting the boy into a cell with a murderer."

"She's his *mother,* Sergeant Garvey." Samantha Harte's voice was like a splash of icy water.

"Even so," the policeman muttered. "Sorry, Mrs. Harte. But if the captain found out, wouldn't he have my badge? No visitors for the felons. That includes family. Besides, Mrs. Harte, you know what it's like in the back. You wouldn't want the boy to see his mother like that."

Cavan looked at Samantha Harte. Her face could have been sculpted of marble, so taut were her features. "You may have a point, Sergeant. In that case, I must insist that you let *me* see Mrs. Shanahan. And afterward, I will speak to Captain Ryan about arranging some sort of a visit for Willie, perhaps outside the...cell."

The sergeant was visibly flustered. "Now, Mrs. Harte—no visitors means just that—*no visitors.*"

"You've been kind enough to bend the rules for me before, Sergeant," she said quietly. "Besides, I'm here not as a visitor but as a representative for Immigrant Aid. In that regard, may I ask you if Maura Shanahan has been charged yet?"

"She's to be charged with murder." This came from Officer Malloy, who received a sour look from his sergeant.

"If I let you see her—just for a moment, mind—will you send the boy home?" asked Sergeant Garvey.

Samantha Harte looked from him to Willie. "Willie? You remember our agreement?"

Willie Shanahan hesitated only a moment before replying. "Yes, ma'am." He plopped his cap down over his ears, and, after a slight delay, during which he made eye contact with Samantha Harte one last time, he turned and went out the door.

"All right, Mrs. Harte," said the sergeant. "Officer Malloy will take you back. But he's to stay with you. And you'll have to leave in ten minutes." He paused. "You won't be telling the captain about this, will you?"

"Of course not, Sergeant." Samantha Harte smiled sweetly at him, then turned to Cavan. "You really should get that copy back to the office now, Cavan."

He nodded. "I'll do that. But I'll be back to drive you home."

She hesitated, but only for a second. "That would be very kind of you. I am feeling a little tired."

Cavan dropped his arms away from his chest, waiting until Samantha Harte and the police officer had disappeared at the end of the corridor before he opened the door and stepped outside. On the way to the buggy, he shook his head, almost smiling as he made a mental note to tell Mr. Kane about the way Mrs. Harte had handled the policemen.

29

THE FAMILIAR FACE OF DESPAIR

A prison wall was round us both.

OSCAR WILDE

"You took her *where?*"

Kane's look was murderous. Cavan tensed but didn't cower in the face of his employer's fury. He had only done what Samantha Harte had asked of him, after all. Besides, he couldn't see that it was any of Kane's affair *where* he had taken her, other than the fact that he had used the office wagon.

"To the jail, sir," he repeated evenly, hands clasped behind his back. "She insisted on seeing Mrs. Shanahan, once she learned of the shooting."

Kane stared at him, cigar clamped between his teeth, his face a thundercloud. "Which jail?"

Cavan didn't relish the idea of his employer's wrath. Although he had never as yet felt the brunt of Kane's temper, he had worked for the man long enough to know that he could get ugly when riled. "Eldridge Street, sir."

"What in blazes were you thinking, Sheridan? I haven't been inside the place, but no doubt it's as bad as all the other city jails. Do you have any idea what those places are like?"

Irked at being treated like a recalcitrant child, Cavan forced himself to maintain an even tone of voice. "'Tis what she wanted, sir. As I said, she insisted."

Kane bared his teeth, his cigar wedged between them. He got up from his desk with such force that the chair banged against the wall. "And if the woman is fool-headed enough to stand in front of a runaway coach, will you oblige her by driving the team?" He shook his head, muttering something Cavan couldn't make out but assumed to be an oath.

"Mrs. Harte assured me that she's familiar with the jail, sir," he said in his own defense.

Kane's head snapped up. "What? How would that be?"

"Because of her work with the Immigrant Aid Society, I believe. She seemed well acquainted with two of the policemen."

"So you did go in with her, then?" Kane still looked like a storm rolling in, but his voice had dropped a bit, and he was no longer chomping down on the cigar quite as fiercely.

"Aye, I did, sir. She talked with a Sergeant Garvey and an Officer Malloy, and I can tell you, neither was any match for Mrs. Harte."

Kane frowned, his dark eyes hard as marble. "What do you mean?"

"'Tis my impression that once Mrs. Harte sets her head to something, she won't be easily dissuaded. She may not look the part, but I suspect she is a very strong-willed woman."

Kane regarded him with a studying expression, then muttered a grudging sound of agreement. "You may be right. Even so, she's got no business inside a jailhouse—" He broke off, glancing sharply at Cavan. "Well—I suppose it could have been worse, if she was that set on the idea. At least you were there to drive her. Otherwise she might have walked, and that's hardly a neighborhood for a lady."

"Exactly, sir. That's why I told her I'd come back to drive her home." Cavan paused. "If you've no objection, that is."

Kane looked at him as he stubbed his cigar out in the copper bowl he used as an ashtray. "That won't be necessary," he said.

"Oh, but, sir, I as much as told Mrs. Harte I'd be back."

Kane cracked a testy smile. "I admire the way you volunteer yourself on my time, Sheridan—as well as the office wagon."

Heat burned Cavan's face, and he started to explain, but Kane waved him off.

"No harm done. I only meant that you needn't bother. I'll see to Mrs. Harte myself."

Cavan stared at him in bewilderment. "Sir?"

Kane was already shrugging into his suit jacket. "You take the wagon home, and I'll drive the carriage. We can drive in separately tomorrow."

"Yes, sir, but—"

Kane didn't give him time to finish. With a wave of his hand, he swept out the door. "Lock up the office for me, if you would."

Cavan watched him leave, his first sting of disappointment giving way to apprehension and even a kind of resentment. He told himself he was surely wrong. What interest could Kane possibly have in a fine lady like Mrs. Harte? She was a good Christian woman, virtuous entirely. And while she was exceedingly lovely, she wasn't any of the things he would have expected to interest Jack Kane.

On the other hand, he hadn't actually seen Kane with a woman often enough to *know* his interests. But wouldn't he be more likely to favor the flamboyant, perhaps even vulgar, sort of woman, rather than the subtle, refined beauty of Samantha Harte?

Uneasily, he realized he might be deluding himself. In all fairness to the man, Kane's tastes seemed anything but ostentatious. His few excesses appeared limited to expensive cigars, fine food, and quality tailoring. No, he might as well admit it—there was every possibility that Kane would find Samantha Harte highly appealing.

What man wouldn't?

Anxiety rose up in Cavan, an acid bile that threatened to steal his breath. Most of the time, he liked his employer, even admired him. But there was a darkness, a ruthlessness about Kane—and at times, an almost feral shrewdness—that was unsettling, even somewhat frightening. He found even the thought that Kane might actually pursue Samantha Harte nothing less than revolting.

His hands shook as he locked the office door and started down the steps. He wished he had protested, but what possible good would it have done? Kane might treat him decently enough most of the time, but he was still the man's lackey. Any objection on his part would have been futile. He would have either angered Kane or amused him; it was hard to say which.

Black Jack Kane did what he wanted and, from all accounts, almost always *got* what he wanted.

That being the case, Cavan could only hope Kane wouldn't decide he wanted Samantha Harte.

Inside the cell, Samantha sat looking into the face of utter hopelessness and despair.

It was a dank, cold, squalid place. Several women—some raucous, others bitterly silent—milled about, but for the most part, they took no notice of Samantha and Maura Shanahan.

Although she wouldn't have expected the other to welcome her visit, Samantha was still taken aback at Maura Shanahan's air of remoteness. Her eyes, glazed and seemingly without focus, had not met Samantha's once. Her white, taut face registered no emotion—only a number of dark, ugly bruises. One eye was red and crusted—probably not from tears, Samantha speculated, but with blood.

It took every shred of self-control she possessed to sit there, confronting the wretchedness of the woman across from her. Every glance at the other's face made Samantha wince in pain, and the awareness of the woman's misery caused her insides to virtually writhe in anguish. Upon entering the cell and seeing Maura Shanahan, she had wanted to turn and run. Even after the initial rush of panic, it still took a deliberate act of will to stay.

"Mrs. Shanahan? Do you remember me?" she asked softly. "I'm Samantha Harte. I came to see you last Saturday about Willie."

Maura Shanahan made no response but simply looked at Samantha, her eyes dull and clouded.

Samantha drew in a steadying breath and tried again. "Maura—may I call you Maura? I…came to see if there's anything I can do for you. Any way I can help you."

Something flickered in the lusterless eyes, then quickly died.

"I wanted to tell you how sorry I am…about everything." Samantha cringed at the inanity of her own words. "This is awful for you, I know. Would it help to talk about it?"

Finally, there was a flicker of recognition. "I shot him." She might just as well have stated the time of day, for all the emotion the words held.

"So…you did it, then?" Samantha asked gently. "You shot your husband?"

Maura Shanahan nodded, a gesture that appeared fraught with numb exhaustion. "He's dead."

Samantha swallowed. She was almost certain she knew the answer to her next question, yet she felt compelled to ask. "Why, Maura? Why would you do such a thing?"

The other looked at her with an expression so devoid of feeling that Samantha felt suddenly chilled. "Because he was going to kill me," she said flatly. "This time he meant to murder me entirely."

Samantha gripped her hands in her lap to still their trembling. She swallowed, her throat so swollen she almost choked. "This time?" she said thickly.

Maura Shanahan's hair had fallen over the encrusted eye, giving her the forlorn appearance of a battered child. " 'Twas different this time. He beat me with the gun. He hadn't never done that before."

She lifted a thin, unsteady hand to brush the hair out of her eye. Her gaze was level, but Samantha suspected she wasn't really seeing her, was instead recalling the terror—and the pain.

"This time he said he would murder us all. Me and the children as well." As she spoke, Maura began to rub a hand up and down her injured arm, which she hugged tightly to her side.

The words came as little more than a whisper, but they struck horror into Samantha's heart. "Oh, Maura…I'm so sorry…so sorry." It was all she could say. She didn't trust her own emotions.

"I might not have tried to take the gun away from him if he hadn't threatened to hurt the children," Maura Shanahan went on in the same wooden tone of voice, almost as if retelling the incident by rote. "But I could see he meant it, and something came over me." She glanced at Samantha. "A terrible feeling, like my head would explode. A devilish rage, it was. I got the gun away from him, and when he came at me I just—I shot him. I shot Heber."

Samantha had not known she could feel another's misery as keenly as she felt Maura Shanahan's right now, at this moment. It was almost as if she had taken upon herself the pain and the rage and the desperation of the tiny, worn woman sitting across from her.

"You did what you had to do, Maura, to save your own life—and perhaps the lives of your children as well."

"He wasn't always like that," the other went on, her voice a low drone. "When we was first married and came across, he had such dreams. We both did. We was going to have us a house and a bit of land somewhere. But he couldn't get a job, you see—no one wanted him. There was no work for the Irish."

There still wasn't, Samantha thought. She had seen the signs. They were legion. On storefronts, factory warehouses—all over the city: No Irish Need Apply.

"After a time," Maura continued, "he got on doing jobs for Captain Rynders. That's when he took to the drink—Heber had never been one for the drink back home, don't you know, not until we came across—and he got mean when he drank. He just kept getting meaner and meaner, and when he was in a state, it was as if he blamed me for it all. For not being able to get a decent job, for not having money to feed the children or buy a house—"

Yes, he would have...He would have had to blame someone for his own misery and twisted mind...

Maura lifted her eyes to Samantha's, and there was so much pain, so much regret and hopelessness in that look that Samantha felt as if she had been physically struck.

"I can't help thinking it might have been different had he found a proper job," said Maura Shanahan. It seemed to Samantha that there was an entire world of desolation in those few words.

"Maura," she said, reaching across the rickety table for the other's hand, "I must go—they've allowed me only a few minutes with you. But I'll be back. In the meantime, I'm going to try to find someone to help you. Do you understand? You're not alone in this. I know some people—perhaps I can locate an attorney for you, someone who will know what to do."

Maura Shanahan looked at her with unmistakable distrust and confusion. "Why would you do that? Why would you be wanting to help *me?*"

Samantha held her gaze as she again pressed the woman's hand. "Because...I think I understand why you did it. Perhaps I understand more than you could imagine. I only want to help you, Maura."

Maura Shanahan stared at her with an expression of incredulity, and what Samantha recognized to be no small measure of bitterness. "Begging your pardon, Mrs. Harte—you're a good woman, I'm sure, but you couldn't possibly understand."

"Oh, but I do, Maura," Samantha said quietly, ignoring the tremor in her voice. "Believe me, I do."

❧

When she left Maura Shanahan, Samantha refused Officer Malloy's offer to accompany her to the door. Instead she walked halfway down the long corridor alone, then stopped. Badly shaken and depleted, she leaned against the wall to support herself. In spite of her efforts to restrain them, the tears now came. She turned her face toward the wall as if to hide—from her surroundings and from Maura Shanahan's despair.

And from her own.

When she finally regained control and turned to leave, she uttered a gasp of surprise. Jack Kane was standing little more than a handbreadth away, so close he could have reached out and touched her. Indeed, he did lift a hand as if to do just that, but after an instant dropped it away.

His face was a dark mask that revealed nothing. But when he spoke, the deep rumble of his voice was incredibly low and gentle. "I've come to take you home, Mrs. Harte. If you'll allow me, that is."

Samantha began to shake her head slowly, uncertainly. Her legs were unsteady, and she even felt somewhat faint, but she knew it was because of the emotional drain she had just experienced. When Kane offered his arm she was tempted to take it. "I thought—Cavan said he would come back—"

Kane smiled at her, and there was as much kindness in his smile as in his voice. "I confess to usurping my driver's job. I wanted to see if there was anything I could do to help. I'm fond of Willie." He paused. "Mrs. Harte—Samantha—please, let me drive you home."

Watching him closely, Samantha could detect no sign of insincerity. She hesitated only a moment more before drawing in a deep breath and taking his arm. It was all she could do not to lean on his strength as they started down the corridor and toward the door.

30

A Parting Without Good-Byes

For the vision of hope is decayed,
Though the shadows still linger behind.

Thomas Dermody

❧

GALWAY, IRELAND

Terese's heart pounded with a mixture of excitement and apprehension as she mounted the steps to Brady's flat. He had warned her about his landlady—the "starched and stuffy" Mrs. Hannafin—who without exception forbade any of her gentleman tenants to have "lasses above the stairs." If she should happen to catch Terese sneaking in, there would be the very devil to pay.

But later today, Brady would be leaving. And although it galled Terese something fierce to swallow her pride, she knew she couldn't let him go with things as they were. The bad feelings from last night's quarrel still stood like a pool of tainted water between them. Pride to the wind, she had known since early dawn what she must do.

She had spent most of the night trying to convince herself that she hated him, that she never wanted to see him again, and that she certainly did not need his help to get to America. Even if she *never* got out of Ireland, she assured herself, she would not look to Brady Kane for assistance.

Her bitter resolve had lasted only so long. In truth, she would have let herself be keelhauled all the way across the Atlantic if it meant getting to the States, and getting there with Brady at her side. Her feelings for him had deepened far beyond what she had intended in the beginning. All her sensible plans to go her own way and avoid any attachment that would not advance her goals suddenly seemed unimportant. Ever since the night of the play, she had found it more and more difficult to think of Brady as simply a means to an end, an instrument by which she might further her dreams. To her great consternation, he seemed to have become a part of those dreams.

It was the last thing she would have wanted, to become so involved with him—with anyone—that she would consider subjugating her own needs and desires to his. Yet by allowing herself to care for Brady so deeply, she had done exactly that.

Even in his embrace, she had deluded herself, trying to pretend that she was simply using him to achieve her own ends. Perhaps that had been her design in the beginning, but everything had changed. If she had thought that by giving in to his passion she would somehow gain greater control over him, she had been sorely mistaken. To the contrary, she was beginning to fear that she was losing whatever advantage she might have held. Last night she had realized that there was as much need on her part as on his—and the realization had shaken her to the core.

As she stole down the hallway to his flat, her mind was awash with confusion and impatience—impatience with her own foolishness. She should never have allowed herself to become so entangled with any man, but especially with one like Brady, who made no pretense of being anything but what he was—a sweet-talking rover with no apparent purpose or ambitions. More than likely he would be content to spend the rest of his days trekking from one place to another, his infernal sketch pad tucked under one arm and a pretty girl on the other. He would never put down roots or own more than a pocketful of change to pay the fiddler.

Yet even knowing that, here she was, creeping down the hall like a common slattern, intent on making amends and setting things right between them.

Madness.

The argument had been folly itself, but it had taken Terese most of the night to grudgingly acknowledge that the fault was entirely her own. She was altogether careless to push Brady as she did. It was too soon—much too soon—to make any sort of demands. They had been together the night before, and the night before that, and on impulse she had suggested they could be together every night if he would but take her with him on his travels.

He was clearly taken aback by her boldness, but once into it, Terese didn't know how to extricate herself. "If you've meant all the things you've been saying to me, I can't think why you'd want to leave me behind. You said yourself there's no telling how long you'll be away."

"Terese, I can't take you with me," he said, holding her at arm's length. He looked uncomfortable but not actually dismissive. "I'm not here on holiday—I've work to do." He smiled teasingly at her. "And you, my beauty, make it nearly impossible for me to concentrate on work."

Unable to conceal her disappointment, Terese tried again. "It doesn't seem to me that you've been all that concerned about your work of late."

"That's my point exactly," he said, still smiling. He tried to pull her into his arms, but Terese resisted. "Oh, come on now," he urged. "I'll be back before you've even had time to miss me. It's not like I'm leaving forever. I'm only going to Limerick."

"And who knows where else?" Terese said petulantly. "Didn't you tell me yourself that you've all number of places to visit before you go back to New York?"

"And didn't I also tell you I'd be coming back to Galway in a few weeks, before going on?"

"You've been playing loose with me entirely, haven't you? I'm nothing at all to you, no more than any of your other women."

Gripping her shoulders, he forced her to look at him. "That's not so, and you know it. I've never been with any girl I care for as much as you. Come on now, T'reesie, let's go upstairs. Don't you want to be alone with me on our last night?"

Aching with disillusionment and at the same time infuriated that he could treat her so casually, Terese wrenched away from him. "I don't want to be *anywhere* with you tonight! You've been dallying with me all along, and I'll not cheapen myself for you again! And you needn't think I'll be here waiting for you when you get around to looking me up again."

"You knew I was leaving, Terese," he fired back at her. "I never told you anything else but what I'd be going, come tomorrow. I also told you I'd be back, didn't I?"

"And wouldn't you promise me anything I wanted to hear, to get what you wanted?"

She was completely unprepared for his sudden transformation. His eyes went hard, his mouth even harder, as he stepped back from her. "I don't recall taking anything you weren't eager to give," he bit out. "Now do you want to be with me tonight or not? I'm not going to coax you. If you'd rather go back to Crazy Jane, then go on. It's getting late."

Oh, he was cold! Those dark eyes of his were like polished marbles, registering not a hint of feeling as he made his challenge.

Dumbstruck by this uncharacteristic display of indifference, Terese whipped around as if to go. But he caught her, yanking her around and forcing a hard, bruising kiss on her as if she were nothing more to him than a common strumpet.

Furious, Terese drew back a hand as if to slap his insolent face, but he caught her, trapping her against him. "That temper of yours is going to be your downfall one day, you little alley cat. I swear, sometimes I think you might be a bit mad. What do you expect of a man, Terese? You spend the entire evening playing the cozy kitten, stringing me along—and then you fly into a rage just because I won't destroy your reputation by making a scandal of you. You can't just go rambling around the country with me, you foolish girl—you'd be ruined!"

"Not if I were your wife!"

Her comeback was born strictly of impulse. The instant the words were out of her mouth, Terese knew she had made a mistake. And the worst part was that she didn't even mean them.

Did she?

He stared at her, then drew back. "Whoa, my beauty. I never said anything about marriage. That is one subject I religiously avoid, as you might have noticed."

"I'm good enough to bed, just not good enough to wed, is that it?"

His jaw tightened, and his eyes again went cold. "Don't do this, Terese," he said, his tone a warning in itself.

Regret surged through Terese. Miserable in the growing awareness of her mistake, stung by his coldness, she allowed anger to cover her distress. Turning her back on him, she tried to think what to say, what to do.

"Did I ever once mention marriage to you, Terese?" he asked quietly behind her. Not trusting herself to speak, she shook her head.

"That's not what I'm about, Terese. It has nothing to do with you—I'm wild for you, surely you know that by now. But marriage isn't for me. Not now, maybe not ever." He paused. "It's up to you, Terese. What's it to be?"

In the end her humiliation and self-disgust fueled her earlier rage, and she turned on him. "It's to be *nothing* with you, Brady Kane! Go on to Limerick, then. Go tonight for all I care! You'll not be seeing me again before you go—and I'll not be caring if you ever come back!"

She hurled the words at him blindly, scarcely spitting the last of them out before taking off down the lane at a near run without looking back.

It had been a lie, of course. She *did* care. He *had* to come back! It was no good trying to convince herself that he was important to her only inasmuch as he could make a difference in her future. Even as her mind insisted, her heart cried out in denial.

Perhaps the real truth was hidden somewhere between what she needed to believe and what was actually so. In any event, here she was, skulking down the hall toward his flat like any cheap girl of the streets, set on making things right, whatever it took.

But not for a moment would she allow him to think that she needed him. She realized now that her only hope of binding Brady to her was to make him believe that none of the need was hers—but his alone.

The door to his room was ajar. Terese rapped softly once. When there was no response, she walked in.

"Brady?"

There was still no reply. Terese's gaze swept the small sitting room, and the first prickle of apprehension skated down her spine. The room looked dusty and unexpectedly vacant. No books or papers lay strewn about; there was not so much as a teacup on the table, and the drapes had not been opened.

Her mouth dry, she went on to the bedroom. "Brady?" she said again, her voice echoing in the silence of the flat.

Her earlier uneasiness intensified to a wave of dismay as she saw the evidence of his departure. The bedding had been randomly tossed, and the clothes press stood gaping and empty. No luggage rested near the door, no toiletries lined the dressing table.

There was no sign of him, no indication that he had ever inhabited the premises.

The room had suddenly turned into a hollow shell, devoid of anything to give it warmth and life. The light that issued from the window was weak and gray, for in here, too, the drapes remained closed.

The morning suddenly seemed to take on a chill. Dazed, Terese tried to swallow against the tightness of her throat, but instead nearly gagged on a knot of despair.

She should have come earlier. She shouldn't have left him last night, should never have flung the angry words at him. Now he was gone, and even though he had insisted he would return in mere weeks, that had been before the bitterness of their parting. She couldn't count on his promise now, couldn't count on anything.

Devastated, she stood there in the gloom, scarcely breathing. After a moment, a violent torrent of shivering gripped her, and she began to quake as if a giant claw had plucked her off her feet and was shaking her in a rage.

When the seizure had finally passed, she stood there, looking about the bedroom where only two nights past she had lain with him. Loneliness fell over her like a shroud. Once again she knew herself to be left behind. Not for the first time, someone who was supposed to care about her had instead forsaken her. It made no difference at all that she had brought this latest abandonment on herself. All she could think of was that Brady had left her, and she was alone.

Again.

PART THREE

THE STORM'S EDGE

He calmed the storm to a whisper

and stilled the waves.

What a blessing was that stillness

as he brought them safely into harbor!

PSALM 107:29-30

31

PRICE OF DREAMS, PENANCE OF FOLLY

I am worn out with dreams.

W. B. YEATS

IRELAND, JULY 1839

Brady Kane stood looking east, across the river, to the turrets and towers of King John's Castle. The setting was both splendid and bleak. Limerick itself was laid out on an extensive plain, watered by the majestic Shannon—the "King" of Ireland's rivers. The old city was divided into an "English Town" and an "Irish Town," with a more recent third division called Newton Pery. Brady preferred the old districts and had grown especially fond of the castle that stood frowning down on the main approach to "English Town."

This warm summer's evening would be his last in Limerick, at least for a time, as well as his last opportunity to finish his painting of the castle.

He had quickly come to appreciate Limerick's charm and particular advantages. He had purchased several pairs—some for gifts—of fine Limerick gloves, supposedly unrivaled in quality anywhere in the world. He had also studied and sketched a variety of Limerick laces, famed even in the States for their delicate perfection. And, of course, he had given careful attention to Limerick's lasses. The women of Limerick, after all, were said to be among the most beautiful in Ireland, if not the world. Comely as they were, however, Brady had been frustrated to find that they couldn't seem to distract his thoughts from Terese's fire or Roweena's gentle loveliness—at least not for long.

There he went again. He shook his head, as if by the mere physical gesture he could dismiss the two sylphs who had staked a claim on far too many of his waking hours—and more than a few of his dreams.

As his return to Galway neared, he found himself often brooding over what sort of reception he might expect from Terese. Surely she would have gotten over her pique by now, although the fact that she hadn't answered his letter did not bode well.

He had written to her a month ago. His intention had been not to take back anything he'd said that last night they were together, but to try to explain that his resistance to a permanent sort of commitment had nothing to do with the way he felt about her.

He *did* care about Terese, Brady told himself as he put the finishing touches on the painting. She was beautiful, passionate, sharp-witted, and, although she could be something of a shrew when in a temper, most of the time she was great fun to be with.

But he also cared about Roweena, though in a different way. Whereas Terese was fire and fury, Roweena was like a fine piece of Limerick lace—exquisitely lovely, but perhaps dangerously fragile. His feelings toward her were puzzling, ranging from protectiveness to a sweet, aching kind of desire—not the tempestuous, raging need he felt for Terese, but more a tender yearning for something as elusive as the morning mist.

Of course, he thought ruefully, there was also the fact that the mighty Gabriel stood as solidly as a mountain between Roweena and any man who dared approach. No insignificant barrier, that, by any means. Brady couldn't stop himself from conjecturing what it would mean if by some unimaginable circumstance the Big Fella were to step aside, leaving Roweena more…accessible. Would he still be so averse to a permanent commitment?

Brush suspended in midair, he paused, then shook his head again. Best not to go down that road. As appealing as the prospect might be, it was about as likely as the fall of the British Empire.

In any event, he had a few other things to do yet tonight besides indulging in boyish fantasies. For one thing, he had to finish packing. But before that he needed to make a last brief visit to the orphanage, just to make certain all the details regarding the Madden children were in order.

As he packed away his brushes and paints, his thoughts went to young Shona and Tully Madden. Finally, he had set in motion Jack's plan. After receiving his brother's scrawl of approval for the first story, Brady had moved quickly to draft what he deemed a passably adequate article on the two Madden orphans, at the same time initiating preliminary arrangements for their passage to the States.

As per Jack's instructions, he had gone in search of only those stories with "irresistible" appeal—stories that would "wring tears out of the Cliffs of Moher," as Jack so colorfully put it. Thanks to the local Orphan Friends Society, Brady was fairly certain he had found just the story for his first effort.

Shona and Tully Madden had been orphaned three years ago in an occurrence that was apparently all too common in Ireland. A landlord had set a consumptive widow and her two children out of the house in the dead of winter—for rent in arrears or some such offense. Within a month the mother was dead, leaving the children entirely on their own.

By the grace of God and the intervention of the Orphan Friends Society, the two had managed to stay alive. Shona was now a frail ten-year-old with the sorrows of the world looking out from behind her haunted eyes. Her brother, Tully, was a surprisingly good-natured child with a quick, ingenuous smile that inspired thoughts of the angels.

Poor little tykes, Brady thought, closing his paint case. Tully had lost most of his toes to frostbite and would always be lame, while Shona seemed to live in constant fear of the cold, quaking like a palsied old woman every time a door was opened and she felt a draft. Still, they had survived—no small feat, given all they had endured.

The two made Brady ashamed of every luxury he had ever enjoyed, every indulgence he had granted himself, and he sincerely longed to better their circumstances. Thanks to Jack, it would seem that he could do just that. As it stood now, Shona and Tully Madden would be the first two beneficiaries of his brother's recent, and to Brady's thinking, somewhat uncharacteristic, magnanimity.

He left the bridge, mentally ticking off the tasks remaining before he could grab some sleep. It was going to be a long night, but he felt no hint of fatigue. To the contrary, the thought that he would soon see Terese—and Roweena—infused him with energy and a rush of eagerness to be on his way. He quickened his step, not even taking the time to enjoy one last glorious sunset over the Shannon.

❧

Gabriel waited until the Sheridan girl left the cottage to feed the chickens before turning back to Jane Connolly, who sat in her chair by the window, looking out. He drew an arm over his forehead to blot the perspiration. The day had been uncommonly warm, even for July, and there was still no breeze to relieve the sultry evening.

Jane seemed more uncomfortable than usual. Hot, humid days like this always aggravated her painful joints. Gabriel deliberated over whether or not to even ask the question on his mind, but he wouldn't want Jane unaware of what he suspected.

"Does she know, do you think?" he said bluntly, watching Jane closely to gauge her reaction.

She turned to look at him. He took in the exaggerated puffiness about her eyes, the angry red flush across her cheeks. As he had countless times before, he wished he could find a way to relieve her misery.

"Know *what?*" she said irritably.

Gabriel drew a long breath. So she hadn't noticed.

"I believe the girl is with child, Jane. Has she said nothing about it, then?"

For a moment she simply stared at him, her hands like claws on the chair arms. She glanced once to the door, still standing open. When she turned back to Gabriel, her features were drawn in a taut mask, as if she was making an effort to conceal her pain. "Are you sure?"

"I can't be certain, of course. But she's not nearly so lean, and she has the look about her."

Jane's shoulders slumped, and she looked away. "Aye, you would know," she said simply. "And since you mention it, I've seen it, too." She paused. "I doubt that she's even aware, though she's clever enough about everything else."

Again she raised her eyes to Gabriel. "Will you speak to her, then?"

Gabriel shook his head. "'Tis for you to do that, it seems to me."

Jane's face creased to a sour look. "She'll not be thanking me for it."

Gabriel lifted an eyebrow. "Nor will she be thanking Brady Kane, I expect. But she needs to know her condition, if she doesn't as yet."

"You believe it's him, then?"

"Who else would it be? Of course it's him. We should have seen it coming." He paused. "And so should she."

"She's very young. And raised without a mother, for the most part."

The softness of her tone surprised Gabriel. "All the more reason for you to speak to her," he said carefully. "She will hear it better from you than from anyone else, I'm thinking."

He started for the door, then turned back. "It would be best not to wait too long, Jane."

She gave a nod, a weary gesture. "I'll see to it."

Gabriel studied her for another moment. She looked sad, he realized. Like a mother who has been given sorrowful news and can't quite take it in.

He turned then and left the cottage. Poor Jane. For some time now, he had seen her growing fondness for the girl, had seen as well her attempts to conceal it. This would be a hard thing for Jane, and the Lord knew she had already endured more than her share of troubles. She had cared deeply for her husband, but he had died. She had doted on her only daughter, who had gone to live in a far country.

No doubt she had tried to guard her heart against caring for yet another, but Jane's heart was not the stone she would have others believe it to be. Still, she had to have known that Terese Sheridan would not stay. The island girl had made no secret of her intentions, telling anyone who would listen that she was bound for America as soon as she could pay her passage.

And where would she be bound for now? Gabriel wondered. Brady Kane had left Galway insisting that he would return in only a few weeks, but two months had come and gone, and there was still no sign of him. There had been a letter, Jane said. But only one.

Gabriel sighed, and a heaviness settled over his heart like lowering clouds. It seemed that a part of Jane's sadness had attached itself to him. His own dolor was not for Jane alone, however, not even for the foolish, impetuous girl, although his concern for both was deep. Somewhere in his spirit he also grieved for the child—the unborn, unwanted child who would almost certainly prove to be a burden.

The thought brought wee Evie and Roweena to mind, and his heart wrenched in silent protest. In such cases as this, it was always the child who suffered most. The innocent paid the price for the sins of others, and more often than not it was a dear price indeed.

As he reached the lane that turned home, the Galway sun slipped down behind the horizon, leaving the Claddagh in near total darkness. But in the window of his cottage, a light flickered. Roweena and the little one had instituted the custom, which by now Gabriel had come to count on. No matter where he went, or how late the hour of his return, he knew a candle would be burning in the window until he reached home safe.

He started up the walk, smiling a little as the glow reached out to light his spirit even as it rent the shadows of the night.

❧

Alone with Jane in the dimly lighted cottage later that night, Terese silently massaged her employer's hands with the new supply of oil that Gabriel had brought. Next she would do Jane's ankles and feet, a task that some might find demeaning. Terese, however, didn't really mind; she viewed it as merely a part of her job.

Of late, she thought she had seen some slight improvement in Jane and wondered if the massage sessions might be providing a bit of relief, albeit temporary, from the pain. Terese had even suggested that they increase the frequency of the ministrations, but Jane insisted she could not afford the additional purchases of oil.

She glanced at the older woman and saw that her eyes were closed, the lines of her face smoothed in a rare look of peace. Terese was caught off guard by the quick warmth that poured over her. That she could help to ease her pain-ridden employer's distress gave her an unaccountable feeling of satisfaction.

She had been with Jane some months now, long enough to witness firsthand the extent of the woman's misery. So far as Terese could tell, Jane Connolly was never without pain or, even at her better moments, acute discomfort.

There seemed to be little in the way of any real relief for her suffering. Gabriel often brought herbs in addition to the oil Jane sent for, but many times he left the cottage with a look of utter frustration on his face. His desire to help was obvious; his disappointment that he could not, just as evident.

Terese hadn't realized that she had ceased her movements until Jane's sharp rebuke jerked her out of her thoughts. "You might just as well stop mooning about the Yank. He will be back when he's good and ready and not a day before."

Terese looked at her. "What? Oh—I wasn't thinking about Brady at all, as it happens."

Jane sniffed and rolled her eyes.

"I wasn't, I tell you."

Terese refused to let herself be goaded. Jane dearly loved a match of wits, and Terese was usually quick to oblige. But it was getting late, and she was bone tired. "Here, now," she said briskly, standing to adjust the wheelchair. "Let's have your feet."

She snapped the footrest up too sharply, and Jane cried out.

"I'm sorry, Jane! The rod slipped! I *am* sorry. Are you all right, then?"

Jane glared at her but said nothing.

"I need to be greasing your chair, I'm thinking," Terese offered. "Your right wheel is sticking, and so is that pesky rod. I'll see to it tomorrow."

"You'll have to be getting some grease first. Gabriel used the last of it a week ago when he fixed the gate."

Terese was careful to keep her touch firm but not too heavy as she began to knead the swollen ankles. "Gabriel's very good to you, isn't he? Were he and your husband friends?"

Jane nodded. "As much as Gabriel would be a friend to any man, I suppose."

Terese glanced up. It was an uncommon thing for Jane to respond to even a casual question without a sharp-tongued remark or an attempt at mocking humor. "He's a peculiar sort of man, Gabriel is. Wouldn't you say?"

"Some might think so. But there's not much strangeness about Gabriel except his habit of minding his own business. There are those who don't understand the practice and so might think him odd." She fixed Terese with a pointed look.

Terese still refused to rise to the bait. "I'm not meaning to pry," she said lightly. "'Tis just that he seems such a...different sort of man. He's obviously had a grand education—he speaks like a scholar at times. And doesn't he seem to know something about almost everything—even doctoring?" She glanced up. "And why is it I've never heard his last name? He does *have* a family name, now doesn't he?"

Jane lifted an eyebrow. "You've an itchy nose this evening, it seems. But since you've asked, of course he has a family name, and a fine one, at that. He is a Vaughan. Gabriel Vaughan, son of Martin. An old family and a much esteemed one."

"Are you related, the two of you?" Terese asked.

Jane looked down her nose and frowned. "Related? No, not a bit. Why would you ask?"

Terese shrugged. "He's very kind to you," she said, continuing the massage.

"Gabriel is kind to everyone," Jane said tightly. "'Tis his way. Though the Lord knows there are those who take advantage."

Terese looked at her. "You don't mean Roweena and wee Evie, do you?"

Jane waved a hand. "No, not them. Sweet Roweena would die for the man, she's that devoted. And the little one—Gabriel is the only father she has known, and hasn't he been a fine one, at that? No, those two are blessed to have such a home as he provides, and sure, they seem to be grateful entirely."

She leaned back then, eyes closed. Thinking that all the talk might be tiring her, Terese grew silent. She had learned to let Jane doze whenever and wherever she could, for the woman managed little enough sleep as it was.

For a few minutes more, she went on with the massage, her thoughts drifting past the hushed room to Brady. She wondered if she would hear from him again soon. Miffed because he had taken a good month to write, she deliberately hadn't answered his letter. Of late, though, she was beginning to think she might be cutting off her nose to spite her face and decided that tomorrow she would pen a note to the address in Limerick.

Terese had found herself missing him more than she would have expected. She didn't like to admit that just possibly she was in love with Brady Kane. She found the very idea almost frightening. Love was not for her, at least not yet. There was too much she had to do, too much ahead of her. She had a future. She must not allow anything to divert her from that.

Besides, if this was love, she wasn't at all sure she wanted any part of it. So far she had seen nothing of the lightheartedness, the giddy happiness others seemed to associate with the condition. More often these days, she felt glum and weary, dragging through her work almost like an old woman. And there were her moods—they seemed to swing from testiness to out-and-out rage, though she could seldom single out the object of her resentment. At times she simply did not feel well at all, and these were the times she almost wished she had never set eyes on Brady Kane's insolent face. Perhaps he wasn't directly responsible for her malaise, but if not him, then who?

Still, she *did* have feelings for him, feelings she couldn't simply dismiss. And there remained the possibility that Brady would eventually take her with him to America, even though he seemed to be in no hurry at all about going back—and even though he had made it clear enough that he wasn't even remotely interested in anything permanent between them.

She gave a long sigh, suddenly angry with this ongoing war between her thoughts and her emotions.

"What are you going to do about the child?"

The sharpness of Jane's words startled Terese out of her introspection. When she looked up, Jane's eyes were wide open and probing.

"What?"

"Ach, girl, surely you've realized by now that you're carrying his child! And what are you going to do about it?"

Terese gaped at Jane, too stunned to reply, suddenly numbed by a sense of her own stupidity. Had she known all along but denied what was too devastating to admit? Quickly her mind calculated the time, the way she had been feeling—the fatigue, her treacherous stomach. And hadn't her mother been the same when she carried baby Mada?

Terese froze. *No. No, it can't be true...it mustn't be true...*

But it *was* true. She knew it instinctively, felt the certainty of it closing in on her, could almost hear the sound of the lock turning in the gaolhouse door.

32

LAMENT OF THE LONELY

None care why the colour from my wan cheek has fled—Lonely and bitter are the tears I shed.

LADY WILDE (SPERANZA)

"I don't suppose you know how far along you are?"

Terese blinked, then shook her head. Without warning, a searing blade of shame ripped through her. She scrambled to her feet and turned away from Jane, unable to bear the gaze of those astute hazel eyes.

Instinctively, her hands went to her belly, and she stood in the middle of the room, hunched over, clasping herself as if she might fly apart.

"Two months?" Jane prompted sharply. "Three? You must have an idea, girl!"

Terese tried to think. "I—a little more than two, perhaps," she choked out. "No more."

"Will he marry you, do you think?"

Terese whipped around, her hands dropping to her sides. "Marry me?"

Jane was watching her, her expression unreadable. "When he learns about the babe—do you think he'll marry you?"

In spite of the humid closeness of the room, a wintry cold began to seep into Terese's bones as she remembered her last night with Brady, the argument, the things he had said to her…"*Marriage isn't for me…Not now, maybe not ever…*"

But surely a child—*his* child—would change his feelings…would change everything…

"No," she heard herself saying before she had time to build any false hope. "I think not. He's not the man for marriage."

Jane's eyes glinted with anger. "And knowing that, you lay with him anyway? How could you be so reckless, girl? Didn't you once think where it might lead?"

Terese made no reply. She hated the way Jane was looking at her, with a mixture of pity and something akin to contempt, as if she might as well try to reason with a fool.

And at that moment, a fool is what Terese felt herself to be.

"No doubt you're right," Jane rambled on. "The Yank does not seem inclined to tie himself down to home and hearth fire. So, then—how will you manage?"

Terese thought she would surely scream if Jane hurled another question at her. She shook her head. "I don't know yet. I will have to think."

Even as she said the words, a part of her recoiled at the very idea of her circumstances. She would have to make plans, of course—but what sort of plans?

"Perhaps you should speak to Gabriel," Jane offered. "He might be able to advise you."

Terese twisted her mouth. "You mean *condemn* me."

Jane was immediately defensive. "Gabriel would never condemn you, nor anyone else. He lives his life and allows others to live theirs."

"He makes no secret of the fact that he doesn't approve of me," Terese pointed out. "His face turns to stone every time I walk into a room."

She found herself squirming under Jane's studying gaze.

"Perhaps your conscience makes you see things that are not there. If you're not comfortable in Gabriel's presence, I submit the fault is yours and not his. He is not a man to be deceived."

"And what does *that* mean?" Terese spat out. "Faith, Jane, if you think me such a terrible person, why do you keep me on?"

Jane made no reply but instead regarded Terese with an expression that was not unkind, in spite of her brusque words. "I keep you on because I need a girl, as Gabriel himself was so quick to point out. Don't forget that it's him you have to thank for having a roof over your head at all, no matter how much you may begrudge the fact. Gabriel seemed to think I should take you in, and I did so because I trust his judgment. You might consider doing the same."

Resentment built in Terese, and she tried to hold a steady gaze. At last, though, she had to look away. She could not shake off the humiliation, the burden of shame. As difficult as she found Jane's obvious censure, she could not imagine having to endure the big fisherman's. And no matter what Jane said, Terese was certain he would be openly disapproving.

Jane's next suggestion absolutely appalled Terese. "I expect Gabriel could convince your worthless Yank to marry you, if that's what you want." Her expression was strangely conspiratorial as she added, "In any event, you'd best be sending a letter off to Limerick to tell him of your condition."

The idea of Gabriel strong-arming Brady to the altar made Terese cringe in shame, but Jane was probably right about the letter. She nodded and began to gather up the towels and oil to put them away. That done, she then helped Jane into her nightclothes and braided her hair. Neither of them spoke until they had finished with the nightly routine.

"Will you be wanting the chair tonight," Terese asked, "or shall I help you into bed?"

Jane waved her off. "Just leave me here for now."

Terese was reaching to set a cup of water on the table next to her when Jane caught her arm. "Listen, girl," she said, not quite meeting Terese's gaze, "you can stay here as long as you want. You needn't worry that I'll be putting you out because of the child."

Surprised, Terese had to blink back the quick tears that filled her eyes. Immediately, Jane withdrew her hand and looked away. "You'll have to tend to your work all the same, mind. I can't afford to feed an idle girl, and won't you be eating more than ever now?"

It suddenly dawned on Terese, and she could have wept at the realization, that Jane's gruffness was all a sham. That hard-edged exterior hid a heart that was far more tender than she would allow the world to know.

Overwhelmed for a moment, Terese fought to keep her voice level as she replied. "Thank you, Jane. I'm...obliged. And you needn't fret about the work. I'll not be slacking off on you."

***

Later that night Terese lay in her bed wide awake, trying to decide what to do. Thoughts swarmed in her mind like angry bees, yet she could focus on none of them. From time to time she put a hand to her middle as if to give substance to the fact that she was indeed carrying a child. Brady's child.

But Brady wasn't here, and only God knew when he would be. For a moment Terese nearly crumpled under the fear and shame sweeping through her. She choked on the unshed tears burning her throat, but instead of weeping—or screaming—she bit down on her pillow until she could finally breathe again without sobbing.

She had to think, make plans. But first she must write to Brady.

Why? She did not dare to hope that a baby would really make a difference. Brady was a wanderer by nature, a sweet-talking love whisperer. She knew that by now. He seemed to fancy himself without roots, without responsibilities—and perhaps without a conscience as well, came the bitter thought.

No, that wasn't true. Brady was simply...Brady. Terese even allowed herself the tenuous hope that once he learned of her dilemma he wouldn't merely cast her aside. First thing in the morning—no, yet tonight, for who could sleep?—she would write to him. He would come as soon as he learned, she was sure of it. He would come back, and together they would decide what to do. He would not leave her to face this alone.

It occurred to her that he might even be happy about the child. Proud, perhaps. The idea of fatherhood changed some men, didn't it? Perhaps this was the very thing that would give Brady roots, give him purpose and make him stop his foolish roaming.

And perhaps the bay will turn to wine before sunup, came the hateful whisper at the edge of her mind as she pressed her mouth against the pillow and wept.

❦

That night, for the first time in a very long time, Terese dreamed of Cavan. They were standing on opposite sides of what seemed to be an immense, yawning canyon. Far below, a great waterfall roared over yet another cliff, its raging current flinging uprooted trees and pitiful, bleating animals into a dark abyss where its waters could no longer be seen.

Behind her, snarling and pawing the ground, a pack of slavering wild dogs circled, waiting to close in on Terese. Cavan was shouting at her, motioning that she should jump across the chasm to him, while Terese shrieked that she would surely fall to her death, that she couldn't possibly make such a leap.

"But you *must* jump!" Cavan pleaded with her. "The dogs will be on you any minute! Jump, Terese! *Jump!*"

Whether he was deafened by the thunder of the water or simply chose to ignore her protests, he continued to urge her to jump. Terrified, her heart hammering savagely, Terese shot a look over her shoulder to see the dogs leering and drooling, inching their way toward her. When she looked back to Cavan, he had moved as close to the edge of the cliff as he dared, arms outstretched as if to catch her.

Behind her she could hear the dogs snapping their teeth and growling, edging in on her. They were so close now that she could smell their wildness, hear their excited panting. She stepped dangerously close to the edge of the cliff, and Cavan cried out to warn her. She looked over her shoulder to see the leader of the pack—a great, red-eyed beast—charging toward her at a full run. She screamed, over and over again, but still could not find the courage to jump—

"Are you all right, girl?"

Jane's voice cut across the room, startling Terese out of the nightmare. She sat bolt upright, her body drenched in perspiration. In the clammy darkness, she heard only her own labored breathing and the squeak of Jane's chair as she stirred in it.

"I'm fine, Jane, thank you. 'Twas only a bad dream. I'll be all right now."

The other made a small sound of acknowledgment but said nothing else.

Terese lay awake the rest of the night, unable to sleep, thinking about the dream—thinking about Cavan, wishing he were with her. What would it be like to have someone—an older brother, someone who cared—to look after her, advise her, help her make the hard decisions? At the same time, she supposed she ought to be grateful that Cavan *wasn't* here to see her disgrace.

By dawn she was thoroughly exhausted, yet too tense and anxious to even doze. At last she forced herself to consider the one possibility she had been avoiding throughout the long night. She had heard that there were women in the city who would rid one of an unwanted child, for a price. She had the money she had been saving from her wages—money for her passage to America—though she doubted it would be enough.

And there would be no time to save more. Even with the little she knew about such things, she was certain that the sort of procedure she was contemplating would have to be done soon.

Without warning, Terese began to tremble almost violently. The blood pounded in her head as she stared into the darkness. Such a thing was surely evil. *The devil's doing,* her mother would say. *A thought from the pit of hell itself.* How could she allow the dread idea to even enter her mind? Yet how could she allow herself to be chained to this desolate place by a child she had never thought of—a child she didn't want? And chained she would be as she grew large and unwieldy. Then, when the child was finally born, there would be no escape for her. She might just as well be in prison. She would raise a child of shame, both of them shunned, viewed with disgust and condemnation by their neighbors. By then, her only escape would be death itself.

Jane had been kind to allow that she could stay as long as need be. But bile rose up in Terese's throat as she tried to imagine living out her life in the Claddagh, with its suffocating rules and strange customs, while she went on working for the poor, twisted Jane—who had more than enough of her own troubles.

She stopped trembling and drew a ragged breath. She could not, would not, consign herself to such a life! And what about the babe growing inside her? Would it thank her for giving it life under such circumstances? Better for it to never see the light of day than to be chained to a life of utter hopelessness.

But the question remained, could she do such a thing? Could she actually do away with her own child?

Over and over she argued the same thoughts until she finally convinced herself that she had found the solution, the best solution—the *only* solution—both for herself and for the child. She would go into Galway day after tomorrow. Tomorrow Jane would give her her week's wages, and she would have a bit extra to take with her. The thought of using her hard-earned money for anything besides passage to America made her stomach wrench, but there would *never* be a passage to America if she did not take care of the unborn child.

Terese went on planning. It occurred to her that if she could find a place in the city where women entertained men for money, she would almost certainly be able to find someone who knew how to take care of such things.

Best to get it over and done with right away, before anyone else learned of her situation and tongues began to wag. Before Brady came back…if indeed he *did* come back. Somehow Terese knew he would not take such news cheerfully. It might change everything between them. He might even think she had done it deliberately, in hopes of binding him to her.

She almost managed a bitter smile at the thought. Small chance of that. If anything, a babe might serve to drive him away forever!

Then she thought of Jane and wondered if she could possibly accomplish the act without her knowing. Later, she could pretend that she had lost the child, and Jane would never need to know the truth.

For a moment, Terese realized the route her thoughts had taken, the web of deception that was already drawing her in, deeper and deeper. Scalding rage and self-disgust at her own stupidity almost choked her. She felt sick and even a little frightened. Sick of herself, of the folly—her mother would have called it *sin,* but it was not Terese's word—that had led her to the untenable place in which she found herself. And she was frightened that whatever she did, she would have to go through it alone.

But then she remembered her choices, the life she would lead if she did *not* get rid of the child—and she made her decision.

It *was* her decision to make, after all. It was her life, and no one else could tell her what was wrong or right. No one.

She squeezed her eyes closed, as if to shut out the image of her mother's hollow-eyed, mournful face.

"I'm sorry," she whispered into the darkness, thinking of her mother but bringing a hand to her belly.

I'm sorry...

33

STORM IN THE HEART

The conscience still speaks,
But the heart has grown deaf.

AUTHOR UNKNOWN

The next day, a horrendous rainstorm broke the heat wave's stranglehold on the countryside. Thunder, lightning, and torrential rain hounded Brady all across Limerick, on through Clare, and the rest of the way into Galway. The coach got stuck in mud outside Athenry, and Brady—the only passenger left after two merchants got off at Ennis—had to help the driver dislodge the wheels so they could continue.

He spent the rest of the journey huddled inside the coach, chilled and growing increasingly irritable. He had hoped to reach Galway while it was still early enough to visit the Claddagh, but that seemed unlikely now. At least he had thought to arrange rooms with Mrs. Hannafin in advance. He could go right to his lodgings, have a hot bath, and then have some supper. If not this evening, then tomorrow he would get up early and go straight to the Claddagh, first thing.

He was looking forward to seeing Terese, though he hoped her welcome would be warmer than her farewell. He thought of Roweena. His pulse quickened, and he realized that he was even more anxious to see her than to see Terese.

Best not to analyze the implications of *that*, he decided.

He almost wished the intimacy with Terese had never happened. He suspected that if the relationship continued, she would begin to press him more and more for some sort of commitment—a commitment he was unwilling to give, especially in light of his conflicting feelings for both her and Roweena.

He had also begun to feel increasingly guilty that he hadn't told Terese the whole truth about himself and what he was doing in Ireland. Knowing what he did about her almost obsessive desire to go to America, he supposed he ought to be thoroughly ashamed of himself. Her dream of leaving Ireland for a new life in the States was the most important thing in the world to her, yet by her own admission, she still had a ways to go before she'd be able to pay her passage. He had the power to make her dream a reality but had deliberately withheld any hint of that fact.

By doing so, he might just as well have been lying to her all along. His deception had been deliberate, calculated for the most selfish of reasons.

He was using her.

Brady shivered inside his wet clothes, then leaned his head against the seat in an attempt to doze. But if he thought that by closing his eyes he could shut out the wave of self-reproach rising in him, he was wrong. Lately he found himself unable to think of Terese without an accompanying slam of shame. He was beginning to wonder if he should just come clean with her. Tell her the whole truth, and let her choose—stay in Ireland *with* him, or go to the States *without* him.

Brady was of no mind to go back to New York. Certainly not yet, possibly not for a long time. In a few short months, Ireland had become home to him. He had never expected to fall in love with an entire land and its people, but that was exactly what had happened. Every time he seriously contemplated his return to the States, he ended up rejecting the idea altogether.

He thought he could drag out Jack's assignment for quite an extended period yet. Eventually, of course, it would end, and at that point Jack would insist that he come home. But that was a distant tomorrow, and he refused to worry about it now.

He *did* worry about Terese, though. He had no illusions about the future of their relationship. With her uncommon beauty, her passion, and her mercurial spirit, Terese was more desirable than many of the more mature women he had known. Certainly, she was never boring. He found her fascinating, exciting, and he held a deep affection for her. But he wasn't in love with her, at least not in the way he thought he would have to be before he could consider a more serious commitment—like marriage.

The truth was that Brady didn't always trust his own emotions. As Jack was fond of pointing out, he could be deplorably irresponsible where women were concerned. Try as he might, he couldn't imagine himself married. Even if his wanderlust—and his other lusts—should one day wane, he still couldn't envision himself loving any one woman enough to spend the rest of his life with her.

A fleeting, luminous thought of Roweena suddenly impressed itself on his mind, and he started, catching his breath. Just then an explosion of thunder rocked the coach, and the storm renewed itself with a furious downpour and a frenzied dance of lightning. The noise was deafening, the wild display outside the coach almost frightening, but Brady was virtually numb to everything except the memory of another wild storm and the dark-haired fawn of a girl he had met that night.

Roweena...

In that moment, he decided that he *could* let Terese go, that indeed it would probably be best to do just that, for both their sakes. He drew in a long breath, almost smiling as he felt his guilt start to break up and give way to a more familiar, comfortable sense of well-being.

That behind him, he dug down in his leather satchel for the most recent letter from Jack. It had arrived yesterday, but in the flurry of activity before leaving, he hadn't taken time to read it. He slit it open now with his pocketknife, squinting in the dim light to make out his brother's scrawl.

There was mention of the Madden children and a reminder to Brady that he should advise Jack as to the date of their departure. Apparently, a Mrs. Samantha Harte would be directing the children's settlement once they arrived in the States. It seemed that Mrs. Harte, in addition to being employed as a part-time proofreader with the *Vanguard,* also worked with one of the city's immigrant societies. Jack went on about the woman for two or three more lines, and Brady smiled at the thought of Jack combining forces with some long-nosed charity worker. Not exactly his brother's usual taste in women.

He went on reading, bringing the pages closer to his face as the road wound through a stretch of low-hanging trees, blocking even more light from the coach's interior. Jack had penned his usual admonishments regarding "responsibilities," "extravagance," and "self-discipline," but Brady gave these only a cursory glance along with the next few lines, which had to do with circulation figures and news about the city.

He was on the last page, scanning it quickly, when a name suddenly seemed to leap out at him. He stared at the words, frowned, then went back to the beginning of the paragraph.

> *I can't recall whether I've told you about my new driver, Cavan Sheri-dan, or not. Actually, he's not going to be my driver for long. I've found him to have a nose for the news and more than his share of good writing instincts—as well as ambition. That being the case, I will probably be putting him on the paper as a cub reporter soon.*

Cavan Sheridan. For a long moment, Brady's gaze locked on the words, his frown deepening. It couldn't be. It would be too much of a coincidence by far. But he distinctly remembered Terese calling her brother...*Cavan.*

He dragged his gaze away from the name and, holding his breath, went on, his eyes racing over the words that followed.

> *Sheridan is actually the bright young fellow who thought up the idea of "personalizing" the stories by featuring a number of individuals and bringing them to the States. He's as clever as a loan shark, though of vastly higher principles, I'm happy to say. Given the lad's natural ability and ambition, you'd best not stay too long over there, little brother, or I may end up giving Sheridan your job as well.*

Brady was not amused as he read on:

> *Sheridan has a sister over there, by the way, and I promised him I would*

mention her to you. He thinks the girl might have been caught up in the big windstorm back in January and is greatly concerned about her. They're island people—Inishmore, to be exact—so it's not likely you'd be running across her now, traveling as you are in a different direction. But I did tell him I would write you about her. The girl's name is Terese, and she would be about seventeen. Sheridan hasn't seen her since he left for the States several years ago, so anything could have happened to her by now. It would be grand if by some stroke of luck we could locate her, though, for the lad's lost his entire family except for the girl.

Brady went no farther, other than to retrace what he had already read. *Terese's brother—working for Jack?* How such a thing could be was beyond all understanding, but there it was, in black and white, so to speak. He sagged back against the seat, the letter still dangling from his hand. His mind was spinning. He felt almost as if a stone had grazed his head and stunned him badly.

Terese would be wild once she heard. He would have all he could do to stop her from jumping onto the next ship bound for the States.

Not that she need learn of this right away, of course. Certainly, he would tell her, but first there were a few other things that must be taken into account.

It occurred to him that if he *were* to make Terese the subject of one of his articles and arrange for her passage to the States, it wouldn't do for her brother to know of their relationship—just in case he happened to be the vengeful sort.

And under no circumstances should Jack know. Jack was no saint, that much was certain, but he could be surprisingly old-world when it came to women. Given the fact that Terese was only seventeen—and the sister of one of his employees—he would be absolutely livid at the thought that Brady had been involved with her. No doubt he would accuse Brady of taking advantage.

No, he would have to give this considerable thought before breaking it to Terese. He wanted to make absolutely certain that he had his own plans clearly in mind before making any plans for her.

❦

When Jane handed her her weekly wages, Terese drew a deep breath and said, "Could you be doing without me for the afternoon tomorrow, Jane? I'll be going into the city, if you can spare me."

Jane's eyes were sharp and searching, her reply a long time in coming. "I suppose you've earned an afternoon for yourself. Though sure you won't be wanting to go if this storm doesn't let up, I expect."

Terese had half expected a fuss, for Jane was not inclined to grant her time away. Her employer's easy assent caught her off guard and only increased her nagging guilt. "No...no, I'll not be going in such weather as this. But I'm needing some things…some items for myself…and I thought I might…see a performance or the like, if any of the players are about." She paused, then added, "I might be gone until late evening, you see. You're certain you don't mind?"

She shrank inwardly as Jane went on regarding her with that peculiar look, her eyes like glistening stones in the dim afternoon light.

Again, Jane delayed her reply. At last she looked away, toward the window. Her tone was dull and neutral when she finally spoke. "Do what you must, girl."

Still, Terese hesitated. Something inside her seemed to be waiting for Jane to voice an objection, a more typically sour refusal. When it did not happen, she could think of nothing else to say and went to stand in the open doorway to watch the storm.

The rain blowing in felt cool and welcome after the closeness of the past few days. Water overran the ditch beyond the cottage, splashing and gurgling as it flowed into the lane. The wind was coming heavier now, the thunder stronger, too, and the ground seemed to shake beneath the cottage. The noise was fierce, blasting at Terese like an angry assault.

She hugged her arms tightly to her as she stood staring outside. Her sense of approaching doom had not dissipated since last night. To the contrary, she felt more anxious and apprehensive now than ever. Yet, when a jagged bolt of lightning slashed the front yard as if to set the grounds ablaze, she scarcely flinched, for the storm taking place around her was no more violent than the tempest raging within.

34

AN UNEXPECTED WELCOME

I looked for the lamp which, she told me,
Should shine when her pilgrim returned,
But though darkness began to enfold me,
No lamp from the battlements burned!

THOMAS MOORE

Brady had never been a particularly late sleeper, but, exhausted from his journey, he slept until after ten the next morning. By the time he'd shaved and had breakfast, it was nearly noon.

He took the cobbled streets at a brisk pace, reaching the quay in minutes. The rainstorm had cleared and freshened the air, and the morning was bright and sharp, if somewhat cool for this time of day.

The unmistakable smell of the fisheries permeated the quay, along with the pungent aromas of salt and burning kelp. Some fishermen—large men for the most part—in their work shirts and coarse trousers, milled about the boats moored at the quay. They were a quiet lot, their cavernous eyes watchful as they worked and talked in low voices.

Two black-cassocked priests invoked the name of God in greeting and smiled as they passed, and Brady responded. A number of women in the familiar blue mantles and red skirts, bright kerchiefs bound around their heads, hurried to and from the markets. He saw half a dozen or more boys casting stones from rough-hewn slings—a sport for boys and men, but, in this remote quarter, also a mode of warfare known to be particularly treacherous.

Brady never entered the Claddagh without feeling as if he had stepped back into the Middle Ages. In most ways it was a pleasant, even an oddly comforting, sensation. The isolated colony was a place of bright colors and dark mysteries, a place steeped in superstition and religious ceremony. He had grown fond of it all, including the hand-some, taciturn people. In the beginning they had eyed him with suspicious glances, but eventually some had begun to offer an occasional gesture of friendship.

Brady never forgot that he was an outsider here. Yet there had been times when he felt an inexplicable sense of belonging. There was an almost mystical quality that seemed to permeate the narrow lanes of the Claddagh, giving him the sensation of being able to step in and out of an entirely different way of life as if it were the most natural thing in the world.

He hesitated for a moment when he realized that he had turned not onto the lane leading to Jane Connolly's house and Terese but instead onto Gabriel's street. He thought about it, then went on, promising himself that he would stay only a few minutes. Just long enough to say hello and let them know he was back. Then he would go on to see Terese.

The decision made, his steps quickened even more in anticipation.

❦

Gabriel saw him first. The door was standing open, and he had just finished his bowl of potatoes and was pushing away from the table when he looked out to see Brady Kane at the far end of the yard, turning onto the walk.

He darted a glance at Roweena, but she was washing dishes from the midday meal and had her back to him. Quickly, Gabriel started for the door, meaning to stop the American before he reached the house.

But wee Evie had spotted Brady, too. She came scurrying around the table, flapping her arms and crying his name. Roweena, apparently sensing the little one's movement, turned with a questioning look.

Gabriel blocked the child with his body and a stern word of warning, at the same time rapidly signing his words to Roweena. "I must speak with him alone today. I want the two of you to stay inside."

The child's face crumpled in disappointment. Roweena, too, who had already taken a step toward the door, stared at Gabriel in unconcealed bewilderment.

But Gabriel merely shook his head and lifted a restraining hand. "Stay inside, I said. I will explain later."

With that, he stepped outside into the yard, closing the door firmly behind him. The girls' disappointment weighed heavily upon him, but he would not relent. Better that they should be disappointed now than later, he told himself.

❦

At the look on Gabriel's face, Brady lost his smile of anticipation. The big fisher-man stood in the middle of the yard, legs astride, his brawny arms crossed over his chest.

Puzzled, Brady looked beyond the big man's rigid posture to the house. But the door was closed, with no sign of either Roweena or Evie anywhere.

By now, Brady suspected that something was going on, and whatever it might be, it wasn't good. The big man's eyes were chips of blue ice, his expression stony and unreadable. Brady suddenly felt about as welcome as a leper.

"Gabriel..." he said uncertainly, extending his hand.

If the other noticed the outstretched hand, he ignored it.

"So, you are back." It sounded less a statement than an accusation.

Thoroughly baffled, Brady slowly dropped his hand back to his side. "I am. And I couldn't be happier about it. I've missed...everyone." He made a weak attempt at small talk, but Gabriel seemed not in the least inclined to reciprocate.

"And Roweena and Evie—how are they?" Brady finally asked.

"They are both well. Have you been to Jane's yet?" Gabriel was watching him as if he already knew the answer.

"Jane's? No, not yet," Brady said, hating the fact that he felt like a schoolboy caught in some offense. "I was on my way there, as it happens, but I thought I'd just stop by and say hello." He paused long enough to take a breath. "Something wrong, Gabriel?"

The big fisherman's expression remained fixed. "I'll not be keeping you, then," he said, as if he hadn't heard the question. "You will want to be on your way."

Brady's puzzlement gave way to irritation. "You're not even going to ask me in, Gabriel? I had hoped to say hello to the girls."

"Not today, I think. You should go on to Jane's first."

It struck Brady then that something had happened to Terese. "What is it? Terese—"

Gabriel's eyes sparked blue fire. "You need to go to her. Your place is there with her, not here." He turned and started walking back to the house.

For a moment, Brady could only stand and stare at the broad expanse of Gabriel's back as he walked away. Then, heart pounding, he swung around and took off down the yard, now intent on finding out for himself what exactly was going on.

❧

"Are you sure?" he asked her again, feeling sicker by the minute. "You couldn't be mistaken?"

"It's been over two months now." Terese's tone was laced with accusation, as though he knew as well as she that her condition was indisputable.

She was watching him with a keen closeness, a kind of urgency, as if the entire direction of her life would be determined by his next words.

Had he not been so overwhelmed by the shock she had just handed him, Brady might have laughed at the idea that he could possibly utter anything even remotely meaningful at a time like this. He had all he could do not to turn and run.

He couldn't do that, of course. Instead he stood there, in the middle of Jane Connolly's yard, his mind reeling, his pulse pounding, as he tried to think of what to say. He had to say *something*, after all. Terese was clearly waiting.

He had begun to perspire, though the day was comfortably cool. His shirt clung to his back, and his collar felt wet and sticky around his neck. "Well—" he said, and then again, "well—this is quite…a surprise, isn't it?"

She stared at him, still waiting.

"I—I may need some time to take this in, T'reesie." He laughed, a harsh, dry sound that even to him sounded like the croak of an injured blackbird. "A man doesn't hear this sort of thing every day, you know. Why didn't you write? You might have warned me."

He suddenly felt defensive, meeting her accusing gaze with one of his own.

" 'Tis not the sort of thing you put in a letter," she countered. "Besides…I wasn't certain…until recently."

Brady looked away, trying to think. He had known from the moment he walked into the house and saw Jane watching him like an ill-tempered gnome that trouble was afoot. And when Terese made no gesture of welcome but insisted that they go outside "to talk," the stone of dread sitting on his chest had grown heavier still.

She had provided him with no hint of what was to come, but once outside, simply turned to face him with the blunt pronouncement that she was going to have a child. *His* child. Had she pulled a gun on him and squeezed the trigger, she could not have shocked Brady more effectively.

He was still dazed, still fumbling to collect his wits. Somehow he had to deal with this. Not only for himself, but for Terese as well. She was looking to him for a solution. But where was he to find it?

"I—ah, you won't like my asking this, but I think I must," he ventured, his disgust with himself building even as he formed the words. "You're quite sure that it—that the child is mine? I mean—"

She hesitated only a second before rearing back and slapping him hard across the face. Stunned, Brady touched his hand to his burning cheek, suddenly wanting to strike back at her—to hurt her for the way she had complicated his life. Why couldn't she have been sensible and taken precautions?

His resentment cooled as quickly as it had flamed. He was being unfair, and he knew it. Terese was seventeen years old. She had spent her entire life on a remote island that, to hear her tell of it, must surely be even more primitive and backward than the Claddagh. He could hardly expect her to be sophisticated in such matters. The responsibility had been his, and he had been careless.

And this, then, was the consequence.

"I'm sorry," he said, meaning it. "That was uncalled for. I know you haven't been with anyone else." He went on, ignoring the murderous look she had turned on him. "Terese…I *am* sorry. Don't let's quarrel. That's not going to accomplish anything. We have to go somewhere private."

"Why?" she spat out. "So you can accuse me of being a harlot?"

Groping for patience, Brady reached for her hand. She backed away, her eyes still blazing.

"This won't accomplish anything," he repeated firmly. "Go inside and tell Jane that you're going with me to have a bite to eat. Make her understand that you are coming with me and she needn't argue matters."

He saw her uncertainty, saw the anger and pain she was obviously trying so hard to hide, and he felt like the worst kind of bounder. How had he forgotten how young she was? In the midst of his self-disgust, he suddenly wondered if she was well. The high color so common to her complexion had faded to an unhealthy pallor, and her eyes were deeply shadowed. She had gained a bit of weight—he supposed that was only to be expected—but the extra pounds did nothing to soften the sharpness of her features. Indeed, she seemed even more tightly strung than he remembered, with a look in her eyes that appeared almost feverish.

Finally she spoke. "I already have the afternoon off," she said grudgingly.

At his questioning look, she said, her tone still sullen, "I was going into the city anyway to make some purchases." She paused, studying him. "You're right. We must talk. I will go and tell Jane we are leaving."

Brady stood where he was, waiting for her to return. He rubbed a hand over the back of his neck, feeling for all the world as if he had stepped into someone else's bad dream. He hadn't the vaguest idea what he was going to say to her. Somehow he had to reassure her without making any sort of foolish commitment. No doubt she was hoping for marriage, but as far as he was concerned, marriage wasn't even an option. He would help her, even support her and the child if it came to that. But he wouldn't marry her, and he wasn't about to give her any false hopes to that effect.

He remembered then what he had been planning to do before Terese had stunned him with the news of the child. It struck him now that her condition needn't change anything. In fact, it might even prove the deciding factor in her decision. The *Vanguard* article—and the subsequent offer of immigration—would give her a chance at a whole new life. Surely she would see it for the opportunity it was.

The more he thought about it, the more sense it made. He would arrange her passage and set up a bank account for her in the States. Once there, no doubt this Mrs. Harte that Jack had mentioned would make any arrangements necessary to get her settled. She might even see to having the baby adopted, if that's what Terese wanted—and he had no doubt that she would. She could then get on with her life. As could he.

It would all work out, he told himself. She would listen to him—he would make her listen—and she would do the sensible thing.

35

A PLAN FOR THE FUTURE

One heart,
wounded and weary,
searches for the remnant of a dream.

CAVAN SHERIDAN, FROM *WAYSIDE NOTES*

❦

The small, out-of-the-way tavern where Brady had taken Terese was empty except for two elderly men seated at a corner table. The midday trade was gone by now, and it was too early as yet for the shopkeepers to be filing in.

Brady had ordered meat pies and tea for both of them, but Terese had scarcely touched hers. Although they had been talking for over an hour, she was only now beginning to grasp the full significance of what she'd heard. "Why didn't you tell me the truth about yourself before now?" she asked him, not for the first time.

He sighed and swiped a hand through his hair. Terese knew him well enough by now to know he was growing impatient with her. She didn't care in the least. He had deceived her from the beginning. He owed her an explanation, no matter how long it took, and she meant to have it.

"I've already explained that, Terese. Jack has drilled it into me over the years that I shouldn't tell anyone *anything*. Especially women. You have to understand that my brother is the consummate cynic," he said with a thin smile. "Jack is convinced that every woman who gives him a second look—or gives *me* a second look, for that matter—is only interested in his money. And to tell you the truth, he's had a few experiences that would seem to prove his point." He paused. "Let's just say that he's impressed it upon me to keep my mouth shut about who I am—and who *he* is. Jack…is a very wealthy, powerful man, and it's probably not in my best interest to go around boasting that I'm his brother."

Terese twisted her mouth. "So that's the way of it, then? You think if a woman knows about your family's money, she'll try to trap you into marriage?"

He gave her a dark look, and she knew she had made him angry. Again, she didn't care.

"It's not as if I actually *lied* to you," he said, his tone defensive.

Terese laughed, a harsh, ugly sound even to her. "Oh, indeed not. You simply neglected to tell me the truth. How could you have deceived me like that, Brady? Knowing as you do how desperate I am to get out of Ireland, to go across—yet you kept your brother's entire scheme to yourself? How *could* you?"

He leaned back, watching her. "I really was going to tell you everything when I came back from Limerick, Terese. If you don't believe me, I'll show you the notes I've already made for the next article—the article about *you*. And I had every intention of arranging for your passage to the States as soon as possible—if that's what you want, that is. Now that's the truth, whether you believe me or not."

"Why *should* I believe you?" Terese shot back, forgetting herself and raising her voice to the point that the men in the corner slanted curious looks in their direction. She leaned toward Brady, still fiercely angry but lowering her voice. "How do I know you're not lying to me *now?*"

He frowned. "What would be the point, Terese? Be reasonable. I'm trying to help you—in case you haven't noticed."

"So you're going to post my shame in a newspaper for an entire city to read? Ship me to America like a useless piece of baggage and pass me off to some…immigrant society as a charity case so *you* can get on with your life?"

The quick look he gave her told Terese she'd hit a nerve. She realized then that he had worked all this out in his mind before he'd even talked with her. She wanted to slap him again. Had they been alone, she probably would have.

"You are *despicable!*" She hurled the words at him, pushing away from the table so violently that she almost knocked the chair to the floor.

He reached across the table and caught her wrist. "Terese, listen to me!"

She tried to pull free of him, but he held her. *"Listen* to me, I said! Neither of us counted on this happening, but it *did*. I'm trying to take responsibility for it, but you're going to have to meet me halfway. Just don't expect me to act as if I'm happy about it—that would only be more pretense."

Again Terese tried to yank her hand away, but he refused to let her go. Finally, grudgingly, she sank back into the chair.

"Terese," he said, still holding onto her wrist, "I didn't mislead you about my feelings for you—I *do* care about you. And if you want to stay in Ireland, I'll look after you—and the child. You won't lack for anything. But I'm not going to marry you." He stopped, regarding her with a speculative look. "Besides, I was under the impression that the most important thing to you was getting to the States. If that's still what you want, I can make it possible. The baby is…a complication," he said, not meeting her eyes. "But it's not the end of the world."

"A *complication?*" she hissed, incredulity surging within her. Again she half rose from her chair. Inflamed now, she began to harangue him in the Irish, not caring that he would understand nothing of what she said.

"*Stop it!*" His voice rang in the room. The tavern keeper and the two men across the way paused to stare.

Terese, trembling with anger and disillusionment, was too upset to be embarrassed. Brady glanced around, as if only then mindful of his outburst. A shock of hair had fallen over one eye, and his face had turned a deep, dark crimson, but this time when he spoke he dropped the tone of his voice so that only Terese could hear him.

"*Sit down and listen to me.*" He groped at her forearm, and the strength of his grasp burned her skin. "I haven't told you everything yet. There's more, and it's something you need to know. Now stop acting like a spoiled child—I think you'll want to hear this."

Terese glared at him, wanting to strike out at him again, hard—hard enough to make his head ring. She wanted to scream at him, punish him.

More than anything else, she wanted to weep.

Refusing to look at him, she slid dejectedly down onto the chair, wondering what more he could possibly tell her. She felt the pain of his deceit—his betrayal—bitterly, like a knife in her heart. She did not think he could hurt her any more than he already had. Certainly, he could not help her.

Finally, he released her arm, gesturing with one hand that she should wait. As Terese watched, he withdrew an envelope from his shirt pocket, unfolded what appeared to be a letter, and, after a slight hesitation, slid it across the table to her.

❧

"I didn't know about this, Terese," he said. "I swear to you, I only learned about it yesterday."

She looked at him, then at the letter, but made no move to touch it.

Brady inclined his head toward the letter. "It's from Jack—my brother. It seems that *your* brother, Cavan, has been working for him—for some time now, apparently. Read it."

Her head snapped up, and Brady could see that his words hadn't registered. She stared at him in bewilderment.

"Read it," he repeated, again gesturing toward the letter. "Apparently, Jack hired your brother some time ago as his driver. Now he's talking about putting him on staff at the newspaper."

She frowned. "What are you talking about? Cavan is in Pennsylvania with our uncle Tibbot. He's not in New York."

Brady shook his head. "I don't know how long it's been since you've heard from him, but if you'll just read the letter, you'll see what I'm talking about."

He watched her closely as she picked up the letter and began to read. After a moment, she uttered a choked sound of astonishment, bringing one hand to her mouth. She looked at Brady, her eyes wide, before returning to the letter.

He could tell that she was reading the same words over and over again. Once she opened her mouth as if to cry out, but no sound escaped her. She must have spent a good five minutes or more going over the same page before finally meeting Brady's eyes across the table. "It *is* Cavan," she said. Her voice sounded as if she were strangling. "It *must* be! Your brother—how else could he know my name? You never told him...about us?"

Brady shook his head. "No. Jack could have learned your name only from your brother." He saw the pages of the letter trembling in her hand, the tears glistening in her eyes. His heart wrenched, and self-loathing poured through him like a poison.

"Cavan." The name was like a prayer on her lips, and Brady feared she might dissolve into a fit of weeping.

Her hand, still shaking, went to her throat. "You truly didn't know?"

"I didn't, Terese—honestly, I didn't. Jack has never mentioned your brother's name until now. I would have told you if he had. I wouldn't have kept something like that from you."

They stared at each other in silence. Her look was openly skeptical, her eyes smoking, and Brady could almost see the war of emotions going on in her.

She swallowed with obvious difficulty. When she finally spoke, her voice was thick and unnatural. "To think that all this time, Cavan has been...there, with your brother. And I didn't even know..." She shook her head slowly, as if to clear her mind. "He wouldn't know where I am...or what has happened...he doesn't know anything about me—"

She broke off, looking positively stricken. Brady reached across the table to take her hand, and she made no attempt to pull away. "Terese...do you see what this means? If you want to go—if you want to leave Ireland and go to New York, your brother will be there. You'll have family waiting."

Slowly, deliberately, she withdrew her hand from his, staring at her fingers as if they might have become diseased. When she looked up at Brady, her eyes appeared almost feverish. "Do you think I could face him now? That I could allow him to find out—what I've done?" Her hand dropped to her stomach. "Cavan will still remember me as a child! A little girl running after him. I couldn't face him after what I've—"

She stopped, an anguished cry exploding from her as she hurled the letter across the table at Brady. She stumbled to her feet, wild-eyed, her face splotched with color.

Brady jumped up, reaching for her. She turned on him, shrieking, "Leave me alone!"

Indifferent now to the curious looks of the others in the room, Brady lurched around the table and caught her by the shoulders. "He's your brother, Terese! He's not going to condemn you—"

She brought her arm up in an arc, violently shoving him away. "Shut up! You don't know! You don't know *anything!* And you don't care!" She put her face in her hands. "Oh, God in heaven, how could I have been so blind, so foolish? I've let you ruin me! You've ruined everything! Now I'll never get away from this infernal place! I'll never be able to face Cavan, not after this! I'll rot here on this ugly old island, me and the child—*your* child!"

Brady finally managed to grasp her shoulders and bring her about to face him. She was on the edge of hysteria, and he shook her, trying to bring her to her senses. "Terese! Stop it! Listen to me! Sit down and just *listen* to me. I have a plan. Everything is going to be all right, but you have to do what I tell you."

She had gone pale, staring at him mutely, as limp and lifeless under his hands as a rag doll. Brady coaxed her back to the chair and pulled up beside her. "All right," he said, careful to keep his tone soothing, "here's what you'll do."

Over an hour later, they parted, Brady promising to arrange her passage the next day. "You'll need to go soon, if you're going," he said, not quite meeting her eyes. "While you're able to travel."

Terese merely nodded.

"You're sure you don't want me to walk you back to Jane's?" he asked.

Terese shook her head. The familiar tenderness in his gaze no longer moved her. She was exhausted, drained. She wanted nothing more than to be alone, so she could think. She had decisions to make, no matter how loath she was to make them.

She had listened to him, had agreed with him because there seemed to be no alternative. But as she watched him walk away, toward the bridge, she wondered if she could really go through with this. Brady had been insistent that it would work, that indeed it was the best way, perhaps the only way.

She had to hand it to him—he was clever. Smart. Quick-witted. A great schemer, Brady was. He had made it all sound so reasonable, so easy, back there in the tavern...

"Your brother needn't know about us. In fact, he *can't* know," he had insisted. "If Cavan finds out, then he'll be sure to tell Jack. And I'm afraid my brother won't take it too kindly. Jack's a hard man. He can be as mean as a snake when he's riled. Oddly enough, he tends to be a bit old-fashioned about things like this. If he were to find out that you and I—that the child is mine—"

He broke off, searching her face. "Promise me you won't tell anyone that the child is mine, Terese. For both our sakes. Jack may be my brother, but he also pays my salary. I can't afford to have him cutting me loose in a fit of temper, especially if I'm going to help you and the child."

Disgust washed over Terese in that moment as she realized what she was seeing in his eyes. He was *afraid*. If not actually afraid of his brother, then afraid of the power the man held over him—afraid that he might sever the purse strings. And Brady, she thought grimly, would not enjoy being poor. Not at all.

"He might even fire your brother as well," Brady went on to warn her. "You must understand the importance of this."

Terese thought she understood much more than Brady would have guessed.

He laid it out before her then, the plan he'd concocted. She would say she had been attacked, he explained, and that her pregnancy was the result of that attack. He would set everything in place with the news article. The attack, he assured her, would evoke even more sympathy from Jack and the *Vanguard*'s readers.

Terese sat there, saying nothing as she listened to him arranging her life for her—fashioning her *lies* for her. The peculiar thing was that she felt nothing the entire time he was coaching her.

Strange, in light of what he had meant to her—and not so long ago—that she could feel so little for him now. Only contempt.

At the end, he tried to encourage her. "You know, you've come through an unbelievable succession of tragedies, Terese. Most people, if they'd gone through everything that you have, would be sitting around whining and feeling sorry for themselves. But not you. You're a survivor." He paused. "Whether you believe this or not, Terese, I've always admired you for your pluck. You're stronger than you know."

His flattering words had given Terese no sense of satisfaction. Perhaps when the shock of this day had worn thin, she would again come to care about what he thought of her. But at this moment, it meant nothing.

Moreover, in spite of the neatly arranged plan he had devised for her, Terese wasn't convinced that she ought to go through with it. There might be an alternative.

The thoughts she'd had during the night now resurfaced. The prospect of going to America had seemed far more desirable when there had been no child to consider. She could have gone unencumbered. There would have been no need for subterfuge and secrets. She wouldn't have had to lie to Cavan just to face him. Now everything was so complicated.

She shuddered, remembering how angry she had been with Brady for calling the baby a *complication*. But how could she possibly make such a drastic change in her life while carrying a child? And she must not forget that she would have to raise that child. Brady might make all sorts of promises to help, but she knew she couldn't trust him. And as for his rich and powerful brother, if Jack Kane was truly the hard man Brady made him out to be, it would be folly itself to rely on *him*.

Was she really willing to gamble her entire future on a wastrel like Brady or, more foolish still, a complete stranger like his brother? Hadn't she learned by now that she dared not trust anyone but herself?

Even Cavan, once he learned of her condition, might turn his back on her. He had abandoned her once, when she had been only a child. Who was to say he wouldn't do it again?

Without realizing it, she had begun to walk. She glanced around once, then quickened her pace. An urgency had begun to build in her, a need to act now, before she lost her nerve.

She had already decided that she would let the Kanes pay her passage to America. That seemed only fair, after the way Brady had deceived her. That meant she would be able to keep her meager savings either to give her a start in the States…or to do something about the child.

Surely the latter made more sense. Without the burden of the child, she would be free to live life *her* way. She would not have to depend on the Kanes or anyone else—not even Cavan. She would be responsible only for herself. She could make her own way.

Just as she always had.

36

CONFRONTATION WITH EVIL

I see black dragons mount the sky,
I see earth yawn beneath my feet—

JAMES CLARENCE MANGAN

❦

Terese had taken care to make herself as inconspicuous as possible for her excursion into this shameful, secret district of Galway, knotting her hair at the nape of her neck and then tying a kerchief over her head. Even though she was not known in the city, she would hate to have anyone recognize her in this infamous place.

The afternoon had turned gloomy, with lowering clouds threatening another downpour like that of the previous day; consequently, the narrow streets were not as crowded as they might have been otherwise. She found the area she was looking for with little difficulty, but it was another matter entirely to locate the specific place she needed to go. Once inside the district, she began to ask questions, which only invited the attentions of some of the rough sailors and other men lurking about. One great, filthy ape put his hands on her, but Terese turned on him with such viciousness that he backed off with a sneer and a shrug. Slatternly women stared at her with open resentment. Some jeered or hurled coarse epithets as she passed by, and one even stopped her with the abhorrent suggestion that she should join their ranks.

Finally, she gained a civil answer without mockery, this from a weary-looking harlot who appeared to be well past the years when a man would be likely to pay for her favors. The woman—who called herself Letty—appeared brittle and even fragile beneath the layers of face paint and tinted hair. She looked at Terese with a knowing sadness and told her of a place on the fringes of this sinful sector where she might find the solution to her problem.

"Ask for Gypsy Sorcha," she said, giving a reassuring pat to the stained red bodice of her dress. "Be sure to tell her Letty sent you. And never mind her face, love. Most get used to it after a time." Her faded blue eyes studied Terese for a moment. "You know you'll need money."

Terese nodded. She had her money pouch with her, as she always did, ever since her aunt had robbed her of her meager savings.

"Use your wits next time, love," Letty warned her, her powdered face cracking with weblike wrinkles as she sent Terese on her way. "You'll not be wanting to do this more than once, I'll wager."

It had begun to sprinkle rain by the time Terese came upon the garishly painted wagon squatting in the rear of a V-shaped pocket of dilapidated buildings.

She was shaking all over. As she approached, she felt the hair at the back of her neck rising. The street reeked with the smell of animal dung and garbage. From the front of the buildings came the sound of bottles breaking and loud, raucous laughter. But here in the back, there was no one to be seen.

The door to the wagon was standing open, but she knocked on the frame anyway, then stepped back. After a moment, the ugliest old woman Terese had ever seen appeared in the doorway. She was encased in what appeared to be several layers of multicolored fabrics, the topmost soiled and faded in several places. Some sort of headdress—a kind of turban—framed her jowly face. Strands of wet-looking gray hair tangled across her forehead. Terese tried not to stare at the sizable warts protruding from the old woman's chin or the angry red scar that trailed the right side of her face, from her forehead to her jawbone.

"Well, what is it, then?"

Terese was shaking even more treacherously now and felt almost lightheaded. "I—I am here to see Gypsy Sorcha."

"And now that you've seen me?" snapped the hideous old woman. "What d'you want, girl?"

Before Terese could answer, the other twisted her lip, saying, "So it's *that* business, is it? Have you money?"

Terese's mouth tasted like seawater. "I—yes, I have money."

"Get yourself in here, then, and let's get on with it." The woman turned and went back inside without waiting to see if Terese would follow.

The first thing Terese saw when she stepped into the gloom-veiled interior was the soiled bed on the opposite wall of the wagon. She did not want to think what the dark stains might be or how the randomly tossed blanket might smell.

"Get out of your clothes and lie down over there," ordered the old crone, pointing to the bed and taking several sharp-looking utensils out of a basket.

Terese turned her gaze to the sagging bed, taking in the table nearby, which held an assortment of empty liquor bottles and a stack of unfolded rags. Again she looked at the old woman, who was still bent over the basket, muttering to herself as she rifled through its contents and came up empty-handed.

The stink of waste and the squalor of her surroundings suddenly struck Terese like a wall of floodwater. She felt the floor of the wagon tilt beneath her. Her legs threatened to buckle. She uttered a moan of despair, then went stumbling from the wagon into the street, looking for a place to be sick.

Behind her, the old gypsy woman shrieked an oath, then after a moment went back inside.

Terese fell to her knees on the cobbled street, heaving. It was raining hard by now, and as she huddled there, sick, her body racked with violent weeping, she welcomed the drenching rain like a blessing. She was desperate to rid herself of the sights and smells of this sordid place. She felt as if the stench of evil was all over her, and she willed the rain to wash away the filth from her body…and from her soul.

After a long time, she finally raised her head. Still on her knees, hunched over the street, she found herself looking down into a pool of water. She stared for a long time at the reflection of her face. She still felt dirty…contaminated…as if the filth, the wickedness of this place and the old gypsy woman had somehow mired her. In that instant, the terrible reality of where she was…and what she had been about to do…stared back at her, and she saw with dreadful clarity her own debasement.

She had no idea how long she stayed there, hunched and soaking, looking into the pool of rainwater as if it were the mirror of her soul, until at last she found the strength to get to her feet and start toward home. She staggered, stumbling over the rain-slicked streets, fighting her way past the gauntlet of questions pressing in on her, driving herself to leave the horror and the pain of the past behind her.

For the first time in what seemed an *endless* time, she prayed. She prayed to a God who, for all she knew, might not condescend to hear the prayers of a sinful girl like herself. She prayed out of the depths of fear and desperation and disbelief. She prayed for a forgiveness she was no longer sure she even believed in, a mercy that would wash away the stains from her soul even as the drenching rain washed away the reek of corruption still clinging to her body.

And for the first time since she had learned of the child she carried, she sensed— even in the frenzied confusion of her thoughts and the black uncertainty of her future—a purpose, a reason to look forward and not turn back.

37

OF LAWYERS AND LAWSUITS

The Pharisee's cant goes up for peace,
But the cries of his victims never cease.

JOHN BOYLE O'REILLY

NEW YORK CITY

New York City sweltered in August. No air moved between the buildings. No rain fell to ease the blistering heat. The days ended with no relief from the same hot stickiness with which they had begun.

Jack Kane, on his way to the first of two calls, slung his suit coat over his shoulder, making a face at the vicious stench given off by the garbage heaped in the streets and gutters. Even the dogs seemed loath to forage on a day like this. The rubbish piles in the street didn't bother Jack so much in the winter; frozen, they didn't stink. But in the summer he felt that the stuff was a veritable affront to a city that considered itself one of the leading commerce centers of the world.

Some commerce center, that couldn't even manage its own garbage removal.

Jack had decided against taking a cab, thinking the heat would be more tolerable if he walked. But after only a few minutes of winding his way between clattering carriages, brewery drays, and freight wagons—and the foul clods of droppings deposited by the countless horses drawing these vehicles—he was already questioning his judgment. He was drenched with perspiration, his shirt glued to his back and his hair as wet as if he'd just stepped out of the bath. By the time he reached the offices of Foxworth & McCann, he would have traded his gold watch for a jug of cold water. But at least he'd arrived free of horse dung on his shoes and had managed to avoid being run over—neither of which came easily in New York these days.

There was nothing pretentious about the painted sign in front of the building where Foxworth & McCann maintained one of the most profitable law offices in the city. They occupied only the ground floor of a four-story building in one of the seedier parts of Broadway. Supposedly, a couple of rooms on the second floor were used for storage, but Jack suspected that this "storage area" offered refuge to some of the firm's more unsavory clients until their attorneys could persuade them to turn themselves in to the authorities.

Jack stopped inside the vestibule to mop his face and hair with a handkerchief before entering the waiting room. It was late enough that there were no other clients around, and Harry Ogg, the firm's fussy, pompous clerk, wasn't at his usual place of command at the front desk.

Of course, this wasn't exactly the type of office in which respectable clients sat around waiting to keep appointments. In reality, *respectable* clients were probably at a minimum at Foxworth & McCann. The firm was known to deal with any number of individuals whom the more prestigious law firms declined to represent—the criminal underworld, crooked politicos, husbands of straying wives, and the occasional "gentleman" who compromised his reputation by the inability to control his passions.

No doubt it was this flourishing, corrupt clientele that largely accounted for the firm's prosperity. Not that Foxworth & McCann limited themselves entirely to the disreputable element. They also looked out for the interests of selected theater performers, artists, and other members of the less illustrious professions.

Since journalists were usually considered suspect—if not actually vulgar, at least common—by the old guard, Foxworth & McCann also attracted more than their share of newspapermen, Jack Kane among them.

It never failed to amuse Jack that some of the wealthiest, most influential men in the city—in the state, for that matter—were summarily rejected by the upper classes. Without a distinguished genealogy, either through his own family or his wife's, a man could acquire one fortune after another and still be held in contempt.

To be descended from an affluent, upper-crust family—an *old* family—automatically stamped a man as a person of breeding, character, and unquestionable morality. That was another source of amusement for Jack, since he had unearthed substantial evidence to the contrary. He knew for a fact that some of the most sordid and outright criminal establishments in New York were owned by a number of the city's more eminent natives.

Being Irish, of course—even if obscenely wealthy—automatically disqualified one from any sort of estimable position in society. Unlike some, however, Jack had never coveted such standing, nor did he resent the inequity. To the contrary, he took a certain perverse satisfaction in the knowledge that he could rankle most of the uptown swells simply by being what he was: an Irishman who had a great deal more money than they did—and considerably more power in city and state affairs. When the occasion warranted, he didn't hesitate to flaunt his Irishness or his influence. He was equally comfortable with both and rather enjoyed the awareness that others weren't.

The door to Avery Foxworth's office was open, and Jack wasn't surprised to find the attorney waiting for him. Foxworth stood when Jack entered, not from any sense of deference, certainly—Avery Foxworth deferred to no man—but more from the courtesy that so often seemed at odds with the rest of his character.

"I got your message, Jack. It's good to see you." Foxworth came halfway round his desk, smiling, hand extended. There was still a trace of Britain in the attorney's speech, though he claimed to be twenty years removed from his native land. As always, the man was impeccably barbered and impressively tailored. Jack had never seen Foxworth in anything but solemn gray or sober black, yet he invariably managed to give his somber apparel a certain enviable elegance.

Jack took the chair offered to him, settling himself across the desk from Foxworth, who reached to adjust an iron paperweight until it was exactly square with the edge of the desk. Jack watched him, as always curious about the enigmatic attorney. Everything about Avery Foxworth reeked of breeding. He wasn't tall but somehow managed to give a sense of height. Slender and fine-boned, he nevertheless appeared anything but delicate. His hair was the color of dark sand and showed very little gray. Overall, Foxworth projected a quiet dignity that stopped just short of being severe. Only those deep-set, slate eyes gave away the man's intensity and keen intelligence.

How Foxworth had ever ended up in his present situation was anyone's guess. His partner, Charlie McCann, was one of the most flamboyant, ostentatious Irishmen around town—and one of the most corrupt. Charlie was as ample in girth and as jolly in nature as Avery was slight and serious. Yet here in the heart of one of the city's shadiest districts, these two, wildly opposite in every respect, had made a veritable fortune defending all manner of degenerates and reprobates—at the same time disproving the almost universal assumption that an Irishman and an Englishman could not possibly coexist in any atmosphere other than that of murderous loathing.

Jack got along with both men but tended to trust Foxworth more and dealt with him almost exclusively. This puzzled him to some extent, because at times he had a sense that Avery could be brutally ruthless and utterly lacking in compassion.

But then, perhaps that was what made him such a formidable foe in the courtroom.

"You've roused my interest, Jack. Your message sounded almost urgent. Now, you're much too smart for a breach-of-promise suit, and no one in his right mind would try to cheat a mad Irishman. So what's the problem?"

"Problems," Jack corrected with a rueful smile. "I think I'm about to be sued, for starters."

Foxworth merely nodded. "I can't believe it hasn't happened long before now. And?"

"There's a woman I want you to help. You can start by getting her out of jail."

It was Foxworth's turn to smile. "If the woman is suing you, why would you want her released?"

Jack waved a hand. "Two different cases, Avery. The woman first. She killed her husband, and I'm hoping you'll defend her."

Foxworth lifted an eyebrow. "Perhaps I was wrong about you after all. I thought you had more sense than to play around when there's a jealous husband on the scene."

"Shut up and listen, Avery," Jack said with no real asperity. "I don't even know the woman. There's a…friend who's concerned enough to want to help, that's all. Apparently this woman's husband was a drunk, a mean one. You know the sort, forever beating up his wife and terrorizing his children."

"Irish, was he?" Foxworth's expression was perfectly bland.

"As it happens, he was," Jack said agreeably.

"So uncivilized, your people."

"Don't start. I know a bit about British history, as it happens."

The attorney's expression sobered. "So you think the wife acted in self-defense?"

Jack shrugged. "I can't see how a woman could tolerate such abuse indefinitely. It seems to me that sooner or later she would fly apart—perhaps do something desperate."

Foxworth nodded. "Would you care to enlighten me as to your interest in this particular case?"

Again Jack gave a wave of his hand. "I promised an employee—a friend—I'd look into it, see if I could help." He studied Foxworth. "There's not much I can do, but you've managed to free a lot worse rascals than a poor battered woman."

"A poor battered woman who by the law's definition is also a murderess," Foxworth pointed out.

"I still think it sounds more like self-defense, Avery."

Foxworth gave another nod. "I won't dispute the point. But the court might."

"You'll take her case, then? Her name is Shanahan, by the way. Maura Shanahan."

Foxworth regarded Jack with a thin smile. "Who will be paying my bill, if I might ask?"

"Mrs. Harte seems to think the immigrant society will help as much as they can."

Again Foxworth arched an eyebrow. "Mrs. Harte?"

"She works for me," Jack explained. "Part-time. She's also associated with one of the immigrant organizations. She's taken an interest in helping this Maura Shanahan."

"Are you talking about Samantha Harte? Bronson Harte's widow?"

Jack's head snapped up. "You know her?"

Foxworth gave a nod. "Yes, I know the lady. Not well, of course. I've represented a few clients for Immigrant Aid, in which Mrs. Harte is apparently very active. She would seem to be an…interesting woman."

Jack said nothing.

"And an uncommonly attractive one as well," Foxworth added, watching Jack closely. "So, Samantha Harte works for you?"

"For the paper." Although the Irish had never been known for being tight-lipped, Jack was determined to reveal no hint of his interest in Samantha Harte. He had the unsettling sensation, however, that Avery Foxworth missed very little.

"Odd that she would be working at all," said the attorney. "Her family is quite well-to-do, I believe."

"She's actually very efficient at her job," Jack said. "I haven't caught an error on the front page or in any of my editorials since she started proofing the copy." Not altogether comfortable with the conversation, he deftly moved to change the subject. "As to your fee, Avery—" The attorney laced his fingers together under his chin, waiting.

"You'll be paid, never fear," Jack assured him. "I'll pick up whatever the immigrant association doesn't pay. I rather doubt that they'll pay anything at all, though Sa—Mrs. Harte seems to think otherwise."

"Good of you, I must say." Foxworth continued to study Jack with an increasingly annoying smirk. "You know, Jack, you occasionally display an alarming tendency toward being a Christian gentleman."

"For an Irisher, you mean."

Foxworth shrugged. Then, opening an elaborately engraved wooden box, he passed it across the desk to Jack.

"Now I remember why I admire you, Avery," Jack said, "in spite of the fact that you're a lawyer. You're one of the few men I know who can tell a good cigar from a bad one."

He helped himself to a slim cheroot, then, at Foxworth's insistence, another, before passing the chest back across the desk. They lit up almost simultaneously.

"What's this about a lawsuit?" the attorney prompted after a moment.

"My series on prostitution hasn't been all that popular in some quarters, it seems."

Foxworth made a grimace of distaste and nodded slowly. "Ah, yes, the 'Harlots and Hypocrites' piece. Not one of your more sensible efforts, Jack. I must admit, I've wondered why you couldn't simply be content with antagonizing City Hall. Heaven knows you'd have a virtual storehouse of scandals to choose from, and lawsuits shouldn't be a problem with that gang." He paused, then added, "Death threats, perhaps, but not lawsuits."

"I've had a few of those, too," Jack said before he thought.

Foxworth's expression sobered. "Death threats? You're not serious?"

"It happens," Jack said, not willing to pursue the subject. "A man makes a lot of enemies in my business. I can't afford to pay much heed to every crackpot with an ax to grind."

The attorney leaned back in his chair. "If you make someone angry enough to threaten your life, Jack, you might do well to take that threat seriously." When Jack made no reply, he went on. "What form did these threats take? Are you saying there's been something recent?"

Jack shrugged. He truly did consider this sort of thing little more than a pesky aggravation. "A couple of random notes," he replied. "Nothing of any importance."

The truth was that one of those notes, received at the office only the past week, had been rabid enough that at first reading he'd actually felt a slight chill. The insults had been particularly vicious, with an unmistakable depth of hatred lacing the entire letter. The writer had left nothing to the imagination about how he viewed the Irish in general and Jack in particular. He was clearly of the popular persuasion that all Irish were subhuman and blights on the land.

But Jack hadn't come here to discuss lunatics. "So, then—you'll take the Shanahan woman's case, I hope?"

Foxworth shrugged. "If you want. Where are they holding her; do you know?"

"Eldridge Street."

Foxworth nodded, adding something to the notes he had been making throughout their meeting. "Now," he said, looking up, "are you going to tell me about this lawsuit or not?"

"Turner Julian," Jack said without preamble. "He seems to think that I've defamed his sterling reputation, caused him unwarranted embarrassment, and maligned his family name. Come to think of it, if you believe the people he's been talking to, I'm responsible for just about every unpleasant thing that's ever happened to him. Why, more than likely he even blames me for his ugly daughters."

"He'd best look to his wife for that," said Foxworth, straight-faced. "Does he have grounds for these accusations?"

Jack gave him a level look. "Some, I expect. Though I'll not take the blame for his poor daughters."

"Julian wasn't the only individual you identified by name, was he?"

"Indeed not. Although I may have paid him special attention. I did apply a few appropriate epithets."

Avery Foxworth gave a dark smile and nodded. "Such as the 'crown prince of physicians'?"

"'Scion of the arts and charitable endeavors,'" Jack added. "And, ah, 'Fifth Avenue medicine man.'"

Foxworth expelled a long breath. "You questioned his professional competency, among other things, if I remember correctly. In fact, I seem to recall your calling him a 'charlatan.'"

"He is," Jack bit out. "He overdoses most of his patients with laudanum so they'll not catch on to how incompetent he really is. As for his 'charitable endeavors,' he owns no less than three high-class bawdy houses and an entire block of some of the most squalid tenement buildings—death traps is what they are—in Five Points." He paused. "The pesthole that burned down on Mulberry last month, the one in which the Negro children died? Julian owned it."

Foxworth regarded Jack with a curious look. "And because Julian thinks your series defamed him, he is now threatening to sue the pants off you, is that it?"

"I expect he would phrase it in rather more high-minded terms than that."

"No doubt." Foxworth let out another long breath. "You don't think Julian has anything to do with these threats you've received?"

Jack shook his head. "Not his style. Too crude for a man of his situation."

"Mm. You're probably right. I assume you have proof of your allegations against him and the others, seeing that you emblazoned them all over the front page for a week."

"I'm not a fool, Avery. Of course I have proof."

"What kind of proof?"

Jack shrugged. "A couple of the newsboys also work as bagmen for Julian and the rabble he employs."

Foxworth frowned and gave a short shake of his head. "No one is going to pay any attention to your newsboys. You'll have to do better than that."

"I have signed statements from two of his former landlords." Jack twisted his mouth. "And a fourteen-year-old prostitute who not only worked in one of his more prosperous establishments but was also one of the good doctor's favorites." Jack paused. "Until he all but beat her to death on his last visit."

Foxworth studied Jack, his expression speculative. "All right, Jack. The truth: Why are you so intent on exposing Turner Julian? I sense something a little more personal in all this than a right-minded desire for reform."

Jack met the attorney's scrutiny with a direct look. "Part of it's personal, part of it's news. I'll not be discussing the personal aspects of it. Not even with you."

"I don't like nasty surprises, Jack. I can't provide you with the best representation if you're not forthright with me."

"I'm no more inclined to air my personal linen than you are, Avery. You'll just have to accept that."

After a long silence, Foxworth inclined his head in a gesture of agreement.

The truth was that the esteemed Dr. Turner Julian had made Martha's last days of life a virtual hell, and Jack simply could not bring himself to rake all that up again. After all these years, he still found the memories of her final two weeks almost unbearable. He had never told anyone but Rufus what he suspected—no, what he *knew*—and he saw no reason to do so now.

Turner Julian's disdain for Martha's Irishness—and for Jack's, of course—had been almost palpable throughout the course of her treatment. Julian made no secret of his contempt for Jack or his resentment of the fact that a vulgar Irishman could afford his high-priced medical "skills." He was unforgivably callous to Martha's pain, seemingly indifferent to the savagery with which the cancer had stripped every last vestige of dignity from her.

Finally, Jack, enraged and half out of his mind with grief, confronted the physician about his failure to act. "There must be *something* you can do! I'm not asking for a cure—I know she's almost gone. But surely there's a way to ease her suffering."

Julian's Nordic features grew taut. "I told you days ago, I've done everything I can. If you want miracles, call a priest."

It occurred to Jack that a priest might know more medicine than the arrogant Julian, but lest he make things worse for Martha, he held his tongue.

The next day, Julian attempted—and botched—a hasty surgical procedure that only added to Martha's agony and final humiliation. Unable to control his fury any longer, Jack stalked the hospital corridor for nearly a full day before finally managing to confront Julian.

"You made her worse! She's in more agony than ever!"

When Julian tried to push past him, Jack caught his skinny neck with one hand, tightening his grip until the physician's eyes bulged. "You worthless piece of garbage! You call yourself a doctor? You're nothing but a quack!"

He completely snapped then, choking off Julian's air with one hand while pushing him hard against the corridor wall with the other. Had Rufus not come out of Martha's room and physically pulled Jack off the terrified physician, he probably would have killed the man.

He never saw Turner Julian again. By the next morning, he had retained another doctor, but early that afternoon Martha died, screaming in mindless anguish right up to the end. Jack thought he would go mad before it was over for her.

He would never believe anything else but that Julian's refusal to prescribe some sort of opiate or other painkiller for Martha during those torturous last days had been deliberate, born out of the physician's contempt for Martha—and Jack himself—because of who they were.

To the British aristocracy, the Irish weren't quite human, and so they let them die, cold and hungry. To New York's aristocracy, they were also not quite human, and so they let them die in despair and agony.

Nothing much had really changed for the Irish here in America. They still lived in squalid dwellings, still lived with hunger and deprivation, still faced the contempt and oppression of the upper classes. They were good enough to sweep the streets and haul the manure wagons, build the canals and mine the coal, shoe the horses and work the factories. But they were not to dirty the linens of the better boarding houses or marry the daughters of decent men or even presume to die with the same dignity as their betters.

Simply because they were Irish.

Jack had wondered then, and still wondered, how long it would take—*what* it would take—before the Irish were accepted instead of despised, respected instead of condemned.

Sometimes he thought it would take an eternity to right the wrongs that had been done to his people.

As for Turner Julian, at the time, Jack hadn't yet accumulated enough money or enough power to touch the fraudulent physician. But that was no longer the case. He had waited for years to expose the man for the charlatan he was. Information on the shameful financial dealings and shadowy, secret lives of Julian and his pharisaical counterparts had fallen into his hands during an exhaustive investigation he'd conducted on the slum areas of the city. Once he'd been able to substantiate the facts, he hadn't hesitated to print them.

———— ❧ ————

Avery Foxworth's low voice brought him back to the present. "You have a right to keep your silence, Jack. But I warn you, if a man like Turner Julian takes you to court, you'll have few champions. His family pedigree is bloated with famous ancestors, and between his wife's and his own resources, Julian has enough money to take ten newspapermen to trial, if he should so choose. Now tell me, has he made an actual charge against you? How do you know he's considering litigation?"

"Rumor," Jack said, giving another casual wave. "Apparently, Julian is given to rash talk when he's in his cups—which is rather often, I'm told. He's been bandying about all manner of wild threats, mostly to do with 'hauling my hide into court.' Horace Greeley, for one, let me in on some of his blather."

Jack got up. "Look, Avery, the only thing I've done is to expose Julian and his kind for what they are. I can support my story, and the lot of them know it. But if they sue, I'm going to need representation. I wanted to make certain you'll handle it for me."

Foxworth stood and came around his desk, his eyes glinting with something akin to anticipation. "Let's just say it will be my pleasure. Get in touch when you need me."

"And Maura Shanahan?"

"I'll see what I can do about getting her released yet today. You'll make bail, I assume."

Jack nodded. "Whatever it takes."

Foxworth followed him to the door. "Samantha Harte must be a very good friend indeed."

Jack kept his expression carefully impassive. "She's a fine woman. I'm happy to do her a favor."

Foxworth searched his gaze for a moment but said nothing. They shook hands once again, and after flicking his cigar into a nearby cuspidor, Jack stepped outside to head toward his second destination. A glance at his watch showed that it was nearly five. Rufus was probably home by now, so he would go directly there.

He smiled a little. Amelia would almost certainly invite him to supper, of course.

And he would almost certainly accept.

One of Amelia's delicious meals might even help take the bad taste of Turner Julian out of his mouth.

38

CLOTH OF HEAVEN

Had I the heavens' embroidered cloths,
Enwrought with golden and silver light,
The blue and the dim and the dark cloths
Of night and light and the half-light,
I would spread the cloths under your feet.
But I, being poor, have only my dreams;
I have spread my dreams under your feet;
Tread softly because you tread on my dreams.

W. B. YEATS

Jack had quite a walk from Broadway to Rufus's house, behind the church on Mercer. It was nearly six-thirty by the time he arrived, and it was still as hot as it had been at two. The sky was darkening, however, and off in the distance a faint, low rumbling of thunder could be heard, signifying the possibility of a rainstorm.

He'd been utterly foolish to hoof it on a day like this, but at least he wouldn't be walking home. He had instructed Sheridan to pick him up at Rufus's house by eight-thirty. Mopping his brow, he walked up onto the porch of the Carvers' white-frame house, opened the screen door, and called out. When no reply came, he stepped inside. Rufus and Amelia were used to his unexpected visits and had given him to understand that the door was open to him anytime, day or night.

The rooms were uncommonly still as he made his way down the hall. At any other time the twins would have ambushed him before he got this far, hoping he might have a licorice or some gum balls tucked away in his coat pocket. But there was no sign of them, or the older children, either.

What did assail him on his way toward the back of the house were the tempting aromas from the kitchen. If he wasn't mistaken, he detected the smell of apple dumplings. Jack smiled in anticipation. Amelia's apple dumplings were worth a trek across town, even on a hot August day.

He found Amelia at the back of the house in the small alcove off the dining room that served as her sewing nook. She was sitting by the window, her head bent over what looked to be yet another colorful vest in progress for Rufus.

He rapped lightly on the door frame to warn her of his presence.

"Jack! Land, you gave me a start!"

He walked in, motioning to the vest on her lap. "Whether he deserves it or not, that husband of yours has to be the best-dressed man about town."

"I told him just the other night that if he don't shed a few pounds around his middle before long, I'm goin' to have to stop making these vests and start workin' on a tent. So, how've you been, Jack? And what in the world are you doing down here this time of day? I'd have thought you'd be off to one of those fancy restaurants on a Friday night."

"Not when there's a chance I can wangle an invitation to your table," said Jack.

"You know very well you don't have to ask," she chided him. "I do believe you must have smelled those apple dumplings across town. Well, sit down," she said, gesturing to the only other chair in the room, a slightly sagging, overstuffed armchair. "Don't tell me you walked in this heat? Where's that nice Sheridan boy with your buggy?"

"He'll be by later," Jack said, loosening his tie and tossing his suit coat over the back of the chair before sitting down. "Where is everyone? I don't think I've ever heard this house so quiet before."

"Gideon took them over to the cake social at his girlfriend Helen's church, all except for Mary. She had to beg her daddy for two days, but he finally agreed to let her go to the band concert in the park with that nice Henry Johnson." She gave a long sigh and looked up. "They're all of them growing up, Jack. Rufus and me, we're startin' to feel old."

Jack laughed at her. "Before you know it, you'll have yourselves a houseful of grandchildren, Amelia. You and Rufus won't have time to get old."

She seemed to consider the thought, then smiled. "I expect you're right. But what about you, Jack Kane? That's what I'd like to know. A man your age ought to be thinking seriously about a good woman and a houseful of his own children. What are you doing about that?"

"A man my age doesn't have the patience for a lot of noisy children. That's why I come to visit you so often. Anytime I get the mad notion that I ought to start a family, I just stop by the Carvers' and take the cure."

"Oh, you," she said, feigning a frown and shaking her head. "I don't pay a bit of attention to you, Jack. You're full of that Irish blarney, that's what I think."

"Ah, Amelia, you know me too well. So, where's Rufus? I would have stopped by the church, but I didn't think I'd find him there this late."

"He's over at the schoolhouse, helping Samantha clean up a bit. There was a window that needed to be reset, too. She teaches at the school on Friday afternoons, you know."

Jack nodded, trying to ignore the peculiar squeeze of his heart at the sound of Samantha's name.

They sat in silence for a time, Jack watching Amelia work the thread in and out of the material, a contented smile on her face. A thought occurred to him, and he voiced it. "I don't expect you've ever thought of yourself as an artist, have you?"

She glanced up. "I reckon not," she said dryly. "Mostly I think of myself as the old woman who lived in the shoe."

Jack smiled but shook his head. "Those vests—" he motioned toward the one in her hands—"they're like Brady's paintings. The colors, the design—no two are alike. Each one is unique. And I suspect there's a lot of Amelia Carver that goes into the making of them. If that's not the work of an artist, I don't know what is."

The idea seemed to please Amelia, and she studied the vest in her lap for a moment. "I never thought of it like that. Tell you what I *do* think about sometimes when I'm sewing on something new, though. I can't help but wonder if it might not be a little bit like what the good Lord does in our lives."

Although he was curious as to her meaning, Jack deliberately refrained from asking, lest he invite some sort of religious application. Amelia wasn't usually given to sermonizing like her effusive husband, but she had been known to make a point when the situation allowed.

He suspected this might be one of those times. She held up the unfinished garment, multicolored with a satin sheen and finely stitched in dark gold. "It seems to me," she said, her tone thoughtful, "that the Lord, he takes a piece of drab old fabric—a life—and fashions it however he wants. He plans it just so, gives it its own special shape and size and color. Some people's lives seem to be all bright and glittery—and mighty flimsy, too, just like some of the fabrics I've tried to work with. Others might not be quite as showy—maybe not as elegant or fine looking. But they last longer, and they'll take a sight more launderings and rough treatment than those frilly, useless little scraps." She paused, smiled, then went on. "Even the buttons are different. Some are shiny and tarnish easy—and even break off after a while. Others have buttons that don't show up as well, but they're a whole lot sturdier and last longer."

Still smiling, she traced a finger down one seam. "Now the stitching, that's the most important part of all. That's what holds it all together, what gives the fabric its own special shape and makes it wear real good for a long time."

Again she paused, long enough to run a gentle hand over the fabric with unmistakable care and love. "Seems to me the stitching is like the Spirit's work, taking every part of our life—all the good times and the bad, the joyful times and the hurting times—and weaving them all together to make a perfect, finished garment."

On impulse, Jack voiced a question that had only then occurred to him. "But what really decides the finished product, Amelia? The one who does the sewing or the fabric itself?"

He hadn't meant it as a challenge, but as was so often the case when it came to matters of faith, he heard the faint, sardonic twist to his own words.

If Amelia noticed, however, she didn't let on but simply regarded him with a searching look for a long moment. "Well, I expect that's where the similarity ends, Jack," she said, still caressing the material in her hands. "This piece of cloth doesn't have any say-so over what I do to it. But when it comes to my life, I *do*. It's up to me whether I want my life's 'stitching' to be done by the Lord or by my own stubborn, clumsy hands. Everybody's got a choice about *that*. As for me, I decided a long time ago I didn't want my life to be some old throwaway rag. No, sir, I want my life fashioned right out of the cloth of heaven."

Her reference to the "old throwaway rag" was like a boot in the stomach to Jack. On those rare occasions when a quiet moment or two managed to squeeze between the overly busy, cluttered hours of his days and nights, when he allowed himself a singular clear thought about his existence, he might have described it just like that: an "old throwaway rag."

Jack stared at her, his emotions vacillating between admiration and disquiet. He respected Amelia Carver—and her husband—as much as, if not more than, anyone he'd ever known. For years he had been aware that there was something very special about their lives, something to which he couldn't even hope to relate, could not begin to understand. And yet if he was completely honest, he envied them whatever it was.

But at some deeper, darker level, there was a part of him—a discontented, inexplicably angry part of him—that resented Amelia's simplistic analogy. It had been his experience that nothing was that basic, that fundamental—that *simple*—in life, except possibly life's pain.

He was no fool. At the core of his being, he knew that his obsessive drive for success, for more money, for more power, had nothing to do with need. Whatever he might have felt compelled to prove years ago, as a boy and as a young man, he had proven many times over. The last thing he needed was more money, and he didn't delude himself about the value of success or power—both were as fleeting as a midnight wind.

No, the demon that rode his back, driving him to cram his every waking hour with more and more work—more busyness—wasn't so much born of need, but desperation—a desperation to fill the black, grasping hunger within him. The sick beast called misery in the pit of his soul threatened daily to swallow him whole if he allowed himself time to think...really *think*. About life. About the *meaning* of life. About...something *more* than life.

Rufus had once remarked that he found it next to impossible to comprehend what exactly Jack believed in. Understandable, since Jack himself didn't know. He believed in *something*, that much he would concede. At least he wanted to believe there was something better, something higher, something that might ultimately give value to all the suffering and despair and injustice the game of life was forever dealing its players.

Every year he seemed to sense old age—and death—hurtling faster and faster toward him. It accomplished nothing to throw his hands over his eyes in hopes of warding off the inevitable. He would give much to believe, really believe, in some divine righting of all life's wrongs—some justice for all the innocent who had been slaughtered, some eventual healing for all those who had suffered, some final peace for those who had known nothing but fear or trouble or affliction.

There had been a time, when he was a lad—he barely remembered it now—when his mother had taught him about a baby born in a stable and a Savior suffering on a cross for man's sins. She had made it all so easy to understand, so utterly real and believable—even the part about their "blessed hope," the risen Christ, who would be waiting at the gate of heaven, arms open wide, to welcome his children home.

But then he had been a boy, and he had known nothing of life. Now he was a man and knew too much.

"Jack?"

Amelia's soft, questioning voice brought him back. "Sorry, Amelia. I think the heat caught up with me there for a minute."

She was watching him with undisguised concern. "Why don't I get you a nice cold glass of milk?" she said, putting her sewing down and pushing herself up from the chair. "Gideon went for ice just before he left with the children, so the milk ought to be chilled real good by now."

"Don't go to any trouble, Amelia—"

"No trouble," she assured him. "I need to be setting the table anyhow. Rufus and Samantha will be along any minute now."

Jack had started to get up but froze at her words. "Samantha? She's coming home with Rufus?"

Amelia turned and smiled. "Why, yes. Samantha usually has supper with us on Friday nights, after Rufus helps her tidy up the schoolroom. I'm so glad you're here, too. It'll be nice, with the children gone. Just us grown-ups, for a change."

Jack got to his feet. Suddenly, he felt exceedingly rumpled. Wilted, actually. He needed a shave by this time of day, and his hair was still damp from perspiration. This wasn't the way he wanted Samantha Harte to find him. "I...don't believe I can stay after all, Amelia. I've remembered something I need to do—"

What was wrong with him? Only a few days ago he would have clicked his heels in the air at a chance to sit down to supper with Samantha again. Now here was an incredible opportunity, and he was acting like a backward schoolboy.

"Besides," he added, "you hadn't planned on another mouth to feed. I don't think I ought to impose." He felt as if he were babbling, and Amelia's expression indicated as much.

"Whatever's gotten into you, Jack Kane? Weren't you just hintin' strong a few minutes ago for some of my apple dumplings? And if Rufus comes home and finds that you left without having your supper, he'll fret about it all evening."

Jack glanced down over himself. "The thing is, Amelia, I didn't realize Mrs. Harte was going to be here. I'm not exactly fit company for you ladies."

She looked at him as if he'd lost his mind. "What kind of shape do you think Rufus is going to be in after working all day in this heat? Land, if I didn't know better, I'd think you were trying to avoid Samantha. I thought you *liked* her."

"Well, of course I like her," Jack said peevishly, feeling increasingly foolish. "I hired her, didn't I?"

"That's not what I meant, and you know it," Amelia drawled, her gaze sizing up his appearance—and no doubt registering his discomfort. "You look just fine, it seems to me, but if it'll make you feel any better, go on upstairs and wash up a bit. You can even tighten your necktie, if you think you must. Your shoes aren't so bad, and I don't see any gravy on your shirt, so you'll do. Go on now, and stop with this foolishness. I declare, there's no woman in the world so vain as a man, and that's the truth."

Jack felt a little better at her encouragement, but he had no chance to act on it, for at that moment they heard the sound of Rufus's booming voice in the hall. Jack only had time for a quick swipe of a hand through his hair before Rufus appeared in the doorway...with Samantha Harte.

Her startled expression, Jack noted, indicated that she was every bit as flustered by this unexpected encounter as he was.

39

SAMANTHA'S SMILE

She smiled and that transfigured me
And left me but a lout.

W. B. YEATS

Samantha's first thought upon seeing Jack Kane in the doorway of the sewing room was that she probably could not have looked worse.

The heat in the schoolroom had been almost intolerable throughout the afternoon. By the time she sent the children home, she was already feeling wilted and cross. But that wasn't the end of her day. Rufus had come to work on the window, then stayed to help her clean the supply pantry. In the meantime, Samantha had dusted, swept, cleaned the chalkboard, and tidied up the classroom.

Her hair was damp, and a few strands had slipped free to frizz about her face. The front of her white bodice was dusty, and for all she knew, her face might even be dirty. Instinctively, she put a hand to her hair, brushing away an incorrigible strand that had fallen over one eye. She was disconcerted to see the way Kane's gaze followed her movement. Why hadn't she taken the time to freshen up before leaving the schoolhouse?

Once she recovered from the surprise encounter, however, she observed that her employer's appearance hadn't been left entirely unscathed by the heat of the day. Kane wasn't quite his usual natty self.

So the titan is mortal after all, she thought with a faint touch of grim satisfaction. Unfortunately, the man's slightly rumpled mien seemed to take nothing away from his appeal. The thought brought a stab of annoyance, and Samantha tensed, the familiar walls of self-protection closing in on her.

Jack thought she had never looked lovelier, an observation that only heightened his own sense of dishevelment. Somehow he managed a civil greeting, to which Samantha Harte responded with cool composure.

Rufus saved the moment by slapping Jack soundly on the back and immediately launching into a cheerful prediction of the coming storm. "We'd better enjoy the peace and quiet while we can," he said. Already in his shirtsleeves, he whipped his necktie free and let it dangle around his neck. "Anytime now those children are gonna burst through the door. From the looks of the sky, this is going to be a bad one. Once it hits, the cake social will be over."

When Jack moved to retrieve his suit coat, Rufus stopped him. "Don't you dare put that coat on, Jack! I'm uncomfortable enough as it is. I don't reckon the ladies will mind on a night like this."

They went on to exchange meaningless small talk about the heat and the storm on the way. Jack half wished he hadn't let Amelia talk him out of leaving. For some reason, he felt uncommonly discomfited by the presence of Samantha Harte, and after a muttered remark about "getting some air," he crossed to an open window and stood looking out.

Rufus had been right about the sky. A great mass of sullen dark thunderheads had begun to boil over the city, and for the first time in days there was enough wind to stir the dry leaves. Thunder rumbled in the distance, and as he watched, quick, short bolts of lightning shot from the clouds.

The air was hot and smelled scorched, offering no real relief. Even so, he stayed by the window until he heard Amelia and Samantha Harte leave the room.

Thankfully, Rufus seemed unaware of his tension. They talked about nothing of any importance until Amelia called them to supper. By then, Jack had managed to regain at least a vestige of his composure.

❦

The Carvers' kitchen was a large, high-ceilinged room that also served as the family's dining room. Between two long windows on one wall stood the cookstove and a sink. A rough-bricked fireplace and a large cupboard lined the opposite wall. The room was spacious enough to accommodate the entire family when they were all together, as well as any guests who might drop by. It was a friendly, comfortable room that invited laughter and conversation.

Jack normally thought of the kitchen as a kind of haven. The day's tension would usually begin to leave him almost as soon as he entered, even when the entire noisy Carver clan was gathered round the table. Tonight, however, he felt slightly less at ease. A part of his restlessness might have been due to the approaching storm or even to the unfamiliar stillness in the house without the children. More likely, though, it resulted from his futile fascination with Samantha Harte.

He was like a schoolboy with a crush. Why, he was as bad as Cavan Sheridan, though the boy seemed more or less cured of *his* infatuation these days.

Jack was seething at his own foolishness before he ever sat down to the table. Amelia's dumplings were superb, as always, but his appetite had virtually failed him. He had deliberately taken the chair directly across from Samantha, rather than pulling up alongside her—his first inclination—thinking to avoid a disturbing closeness. It turned out to be a royal mistake because he couldn't take his eyes off her.

The woman was not easy to ignore, after all.

He was, however, a bit curious as to the difference he detected in her tonight. For one thing, she seemed noticeably more relaxed around him than on previous occasions. Not that she had lost all of her reticence. She still confined her answers to his questions to quiet, succinct replies. And if she happened to catch him watching her, her eyes took on the same startled, uncertain expression he had seen all too often before. But for the most part, she appeared to find him less odious than usual, even meeting his eyes across the table once or twice instead of glancing about as if she were looking for a route of escape. And she actually smiled at him. More than once.

He blamed her smile for his undoing.

By the time they were halfway through the meal, Jack had all but forgotten his earlier chagrin about his own appearance, instead allowing himself the luxury of enjoying *her* appearance. She was absolutely delightful with that small, dusty smudge in the hollow of her cheek—of which she was almost certainly unaware—and the delicate tendrils of hair that had come undone to curl damply about her face.

Not for the first time, Jack found himself charmed by her voice. She had a wonderful voice, soft but with an unexpected intensity and an occasional winsome catch in it that somehow made him want to reach across the table and clasp her hand. With Rufus and Amelia, Samantha laughed easily, and Jack caught himself wishing he could evoke the same spontaneous mirth from her instead of the annoying gravity with which she seemed to regard him.

Still, her sober demeanor was a decided improvement. At least she no longer seemed to suspect that he might be the devil incarnate.

❧

The storm that had delayed itself during the meal was now building in strength and rushing in on them. The room had darkened considerably, and both Amelia and Rufus made a hurried exit to close the windows and shutters throughout the house and draw in the awnings.

Samantha got up to raise the wicks on the oil lamps placed around the room. Through the one window that remained open, the wind whipped with a sharpness that felt wonderfully cool.

When she returned to her chair, she glanced across the table to find Jack Kane watching her with the same steady intensity that never failed to unnerve her. He had seemed different somehow this evening. Perhaps because of his slightly less than perfect appearance, a marked departure for him.

But his appearance accounted for only a part of the difference. Earlier, Samantha had detected something she hadn't seen before in Kane's eyes, in the set of his shoulders—even in his speech. Oh, he was in control, as always, with the same faint arrogance she had come to associate with him. And his gaze on her held the same hint of interest and regard she found so puzzling—and so disturbing. The hard, sardonic set of his mouth, the grim amusement with which he seemed to view life in general, the easy, rumbling voice that she suspected could turn to steel in a heartbeat—all seemed as usual.

But there was something else, something less confident, some hint of vulnerability she would never have expected to see in a man like Kane.

And it drew her to him as nothing else had before tonight.

❧

During Rufus and Amelia's absence, Jack told Samantha Harte about Avery Foxworth's agreement to defend Maura Shanahan.

The surprised—but pleased—look in her eyes warmed him, and in that instant he was shaken to realize how much he wanted her good opinion.

"I can't thank you enough for doing this!" she said, her eyes shining. Just as quickly, her expression sobered. "But is he terribly expensive? The Society has a fund for legal aid, as I told you, but I'm not sure how much we can expect from them."

Jack waved off her concern. "Don't worry about the expense for now. Foxworth knows he'll get paid. And by the way, he was going to see if he could arrange bail for Mrs. Shanahan yet this evening. Perhaps you can see her tomorrow at home, if you like."

She tried to press him for more details about the financial arrangements, but Jack dismissed her questions, going on instead to tell her a little about Avery Foxworth himself. He was anxious that she understand that Maura Shanahan would be getting the best of legal defenses. At the same time, he didn't dissemble about Foxworth's somewhat unsavory reputation.

All the while, he was riveted by those incredible dark eyes watching him. The lamplight danced over her face, heightening the glow of her skin and casting golden highlights through her hair. Jack was seized by a sudden, fierce desire to reach across the table and pull her to him. He had never wanted a woman the way he wanted Samantha Harte, but it was a different kind of wanting than that to which he was accustomed. It was more than mere physical longing, more than the primitive urge to take and possess.

His blood pounded in his ears, and his pulse raced as he realized that no matter how desperately he desired this woman, what he wanted more than anything else was her approval—her respect. He wanted her to trust him.

He wanted her to need him.

Was he losing his mind? The woman was obviously more afraid of him than attracted to him. Even worse, he thought she might actually be *repelled* by him. Hardly the kind of responses he would like to kindle in her.

Just then, thunder exploded, and a powerful gust of wind came roaring through the open window. The curtains flapped, and the flames from the oil lamps flickered madly. A sudden onslaught of rain dashed against the house.

Samantha jerked and cried out. They both scrambled away from the table at the same time, rushing toward the window to close it. Jack hesitated a moment, fascinated, unable to resist the wildness of the storm. He could see nothing beyond the small patch of yard separating the Carvers' house from that of the neighbors. The huge old maple trees were writhing, bending almost double in the wind.

Another crash of thunder shook the house, and a fierce blaze of lightning froze the scene outside in eerie incandescence. Jack reached to lower the window, but before he could, a bolt of lightning streaked in front of it, startling them both. Rain blasted through the open window, and instinctively Jack caught Samantha against him with one arm as he slammed the window down with the other.

She was trembling, and it seemed the most natural thing in the world to pull her closer to steady her. The din of the wind and rain from outside was almost deafening, but it was nothing compared to the roar in his head as he stared down at her.

"Samantha?"

Her eyes were enormous, and she paled. Jack tightened his grip on her, suddenly unable to bear the thought that she might pull away.

His mind...his heart...everything in him was screaming as wildly as the night around them. He thought he would suffocate in the sudden closeness of the room and in her nearness. He could not drag his gaze away from her face, from her eyes glistening in the flickering light, holding him captive. For one mad moment, he thought he saw something in those eyes besides the usual aloofness. He felt a quickening of his heart, and without warning, all his former caution and resolve dropped away. He lowered his head, brought his face close to hers, his lips—

And then he saw the change that came over her features.

What he saw was a stark, chilling terror. Not merely revulsion, which would have wounded him badly enough, but a dreadful, stricken fear—a shrinking from him that made him want to moan with despair.

No woman had ever looked at him that way. He drew back, his desire instantly gone as shame and confusion set in. He released her, but she didn't move. It was as if she were frozen where she stood. Jack took in the blank stare, the white, waxen texture of her skin, and for a moment he thought she might be ill or about to fall into some sort of seizure.

Finally her gaze cleared. As Jack watched, her shoulders sagged, and she seemed to go limp. He reached out to steady her, then dropped his hand away, remembering how she had looked at him.

Furious with himself and thrown badly off balance by the vehemence of her rejection, he could only stand and mock himself for being such a fool. He wanted to bolt from the room.

"Samantha...I'm sorry!" he said, his voice rough. "I...don't know what to say. I'm so sorry."

She stared up at him as if he had awakened her from a deep sleep. And then a wash of emotions began to play over her features—a slow, dawning awareness, mingled with something else, something akin to dismay or even humiliation. She began to shake her head slowly, over and over again.

Jack wanted to distance himself, wanted to be angry with her...wanted not to care. Instead, he couldn't seem to stop apologizing. "I am sorry, Samantha. I didn't mean anything wrong. I've had...feelings for you, almost since we met. I thought perhaps you knew, that you might even—I don't know what I thought. I didn't realize you felt so strongly...against me..."

She lifted a hand, and for an instant Jack thought she was going to touch him. Instead, she dropped her hand away, shaking her head. "No. You don't understand."

Her voice sounded strangled. Jack frowned down at her, bewildered. He held his breath, wanting to seize her hand, knowing he dare not touch her again.

"It's not you," she said in the same odd-sounding voice. "It's me. It has nothing to do with you. Nothing." There was a strange ferocity in her words, as if she was suddenly, unaccountably angry.

She was hugging her arms to her body as if to keep herself from falling to pieces. She started to turn, but Jack stopped her—not by touching her, but with the plea in his voice.

"Samantha? No, don't turn away from me! Tell me what you mean."

Her eyes were glazed with unshed tears, and Jack ached to kiss them away. Instead, he balled his hands into fists at his sides to keep from touching her. "I meant no harm, Samantha. I—regardless of what you've heard or what you may think—I would never do anything to hurt you."

She looked away. "I—I think I know that. But—" she faltered, then went on. "I'm sorry. I know you don't understand, but I can't explain. I can't...talk about this."

A vicious, ugly suspicion had insinuated itself into Jack's mind, a thought so vile he couldn't give it any real credence. Perhaps he was only trying to rationalize her behavior, her response to him. And yet that response had seemed too violent, too unreasonable, even if she detested him. What he had seen in her face bordered on sheer horror.

What had been done to her that would account for such a violent reaction to him...to any man?

"Samantha...are you quite sure you can't tell me?"

Still she refused to meet his gaze, but instead stood staring down at the floor. "I can't. Please don't ask me."

Jack drew in a long, steadying breath. He had already made a colossal fool of himself, so what did it matter now if he did it again?

"All right. But, Samantha, if I may—let me say just one more thing. I've seen that you're not entirely comfortable with me, and I think I understand why. And now I suppose I've gone and made things worse by my behavior—and for that I'm deeply sorry. I...ah—" Jack ran a hand through his hair, thoroughly annoyed with himself now. "I'm saying this badly, I know. I just want to be sure that you understand that I mean you no harm, no offense. If I've upset you or embarrassed you, I couldn't be more sorry, and that's the truth."

Finally, she looked at him, searching his gaze as if she could somehow weigh his words. "It's all right. It's really not your fault."

What he saw in her eyes made his heart ache. There was so much pain in her. He wanted to hold her, to somehow protect her from whatever secret torment seemed to bind her. He wanted to comfort her. He wanted to heal her.

But heal her of *what?*

"Samantha, is this about your husband?" he blurted out before he could stop himself.

Jack watched her closely as he waited for her reply. She seemed to have gone perfectly rigid. A white line tightened about her mouth, and her features were as hard and cold as marble. So still was she that she didn't appear to be breathing.

Jack sensed that she would withdraw from him, perhaps even run from him if he made the slightest move to touch her. Yet it was all he could do not to pull her into his arms.

Gradually, her features cleared. "Please," she finally said, not meeting his gaze. "No more. I can't...talk about this any more."

Watching her, Jack knew it would be a mistake to press any further. "Samantha?" he said finally. "Would you—please—at least consider letting me be your friend? Just—your friend?"

She looked at him and opened her mouth to reply, but just then Rufus and Amelia came sweeping back into the room, and she turned away without answering.

Almost at the same moment, the children burst through the front door and came charging down the hall. Any further opportunity to speak with her alone was lost.

A few minutes later, Cavan Sheridan arrived with the carriage. When Jack tried to convince her to let them drive her home, Samantha demurred, explaining that Gideon had already planned to do so.

Although Jack was hesitant to insist, he kept his voice firm. "Rufus's wagon is no match for this storm. I wish you'd ride with us."

"Jack's right, Samantha," Amelia put in. "You'll be absolutely drenched. You'd best go with Jack in his carriage."

At last she relented, though with obvious reluctance, and only, Jack suspected, because she might have feared a scene in front of the others.

Outside, Jack caught her arm and said, his voice low enough that Cavan Sheridan couldn't hear, "I'll ride with Sheridan. I expect you'll be more comfortable."

She turned a look of dismay on him. "No! You'll be soaked through."

Jack shrugged. "I like the rain. I often walk in it."

She studied him for a moment but said nothing.

Jack didn't reply but helped her into the carriage and, closing the door, leaned into the window. "You didn't answer me, Samantha. I'm asking you again—could you possibly allow me to be your friend?"

She regarded him with a long, searching look. Her eyes were solemn, measuring. But Jack's hopes soared when she finally answered. "Yes," she said, her voice quiet, her gaze still locked with his. "I think I'd like that, Mr. Kane."

Joy arced through Jack like a shooting star. "That's grand. And, ah, now that we're to be friends, do you think you could possibly manage to call me Jack?"

She blinked, watching him. Finally, a ghost of a smile curved her lips. "Yes, all right...Jack."

Jack's heart suddenly felt lighter than it had for days. Weeks. "Good! And, Samantha? We really should be going over the plans for the new immigrant resettlement program soon. Do you suppose—now that we're friends—we could get together for dinner tomorrow night and discuss some of the arrangements? I could call for you, say, about seven?"

"We just *had* dinner together," she pointed out.

"Doesn't count. It was unplanned."

She lifted an eyebrow, and Jack thought for a fraction of a second that she would shrink away from him again. Instead she nodded slowly, saying, "All right. But if you don't mind, I'll choose the restaurant."

He made a palms-up gesture to indicate his agreement. "Anywhere you say." He paused. "Anything else?"

"Yes, actually, there is," she said, pointing to the cigar in his pocket. "I'm afraid you'll have to promise not to smoke one of those smelly things anywhere near me."

Jack broke into a slow grin, slipped the cheroot from his pocket, and flicked it out into the street, in the rain.

40

OF SILENCE AND SHADOWS

And love can reach
From heaven to earth, and nobler lessons teach
Than those by mortals read.

JOHN BOYLE O'REILLY

❧

The storm seemed to have passed, at least for the moment, leaving behind only a light, steady rain and cooler air. Jack breathed in the clean, wet scent of the night as the horse clopped along the quiet street. He didn't mind in the least sitting in the open, for he welcomed the rain.

Sheridan, however, seemed uncomfortable with the arrangement. "If you don't mind my saying so, sir, you shouldn't be sitting up here in the rain. Won't you let me pull off so you can ride inside the carriage with Mrs. Harte?"

Jack turned up the collar on his coat and hunkered down to enjoy the ride. "Don't fret yourself about me, lad. I'm fine. As I told Mrs. Harte, the rain suits me. Especially after a scorcher like today."

"Yes, sir." Sheridan didn't sound altogether convinced, but he let the subject drop. "I almost forgot, sir—Mrs. O'Meara said I should tell you that there's a letter, quite a thick one, she said, from your brother."

"Ah! About time! I'll be curious to see what Brady has to say."

Silence settled between them. It occurred to Jack that Sheridan's apparent awkwardness might not be entirely due to his employer's presence up front. On impulse, he decided to broach the subject of Samantha Harte with the boy, partly because he felt the need to clear the air between them—and partly, he supposed, simply because he enjoyed talking about Samantha.

"Are the lessons with Mrs. Harte still going well?" Jack asked.

"Oh, yes, sir. She's a fine teacher, as I've told you."

"About Mrs. Harte, lad—are you still taken with her?"

Cavan Sheridan shot him a startled look. "Sir?"

"Oh, you know good and well what I mean, Sheridan! You were positively besotted with the woman some months back. Have you gotten past all that by now or not?"

Jack watched him. Even in the dark, he could see Sheridan color, then swallow with apparent difficulty.

He sighed, thinking he had probably insulted the lad or at least embarrassed him, though neither had been his intention. Jack knew all too well how it felt to make a fool of himself over a woman who wanted nothing to do with him.

Sheridan's reply was a long time coming, but not a surprise. "I think Mrs. Harte is the finest woman I've ever met."

Again Jack sighed.

"But in reply to your question—" Sheridan cleared his throat before going on. "I suppose I've managed to lay any other feelings to rest. Though it was a grievous disappointment."

It struck Jack that his driver's solemn statement sounded almost funereal, and at another time he might have been mildly amused by the young man's flair for the dramatic. But not tonight. He understood the lad's despondency too well to take it lightly.

"You regard her highly, do you, sir?"

Jack stared at him. He would have been perfectly within his rights had he chosen to give the boy a scathing rebuke. A man's driver was in no position to question his employer on personal matters.

Instead, he merely lifted an eyebrow in grim self-mockery. "It's that obvious, is it?"

Sheridan kept his eyes straight ahead. "Well, sir…it seems to me that only a blind man or a fool wouldn't be drawn to a woman like Mrs. Harte. And certainly you're neither…" He let his words drift off, unfinished.

Jack tried for the proper level of indignation but couldn't quite suppress a rueful smile. "I'm not blind; that's true. As for the fool, I'm beginning to wonder." He paused. "Perhaps you wouldn't mind telling me how you managed to bury *your* unrequited affections, Sheridan."

The boy shrugged. "I suppose I finally came to realize how hopeless it was. I knew nothing could come of it. Mrs. Harte was very firm in her rejection. In truth, I think it was a case of her simply not being…attracted to me. She tried to make me believe it was the difference in our ages, that the years between us were too great—"

"There are as many years between her and *me*," Jack grumbled, "as there are between the two of you. Though the difference is turned the other way around."

Sheridan glanced over at him, frowning. Clearly, he'd been about to make a reply but changed his mind.

"What?" Jack said.

A muscle at the corner of the lad's mouth jerked. "'Tis not for me to say, sir."

"It *is* for you to say, if I give you leave to say it!" Jack snapped. "You needn't always be so provokingly correct, Sheridan, at least not at the moment. Now, what were you about to say?"

Sheridan regarded Jack with a long look before turning his attention back to the street. "Only that it seems to me that Mrs. Harte might not mind the years between yourself and her, that's all."

"I don't suppose you'd care to elaborate?" Jack said through clenched teeth.

Sheridan gave a shrug, saying, "I don't know a great deal about such matters, but I'd have to say that Mrs. Harte looks at you very differently than she ever looked at me."

Jack narrowed his eyes, scrutinizing the youth for any evidence of rancor. But Sheridan's expression appeared temperate and totally without guile as he added, "At least that's how it seems to me, sir."

Completely indifferent to the rain by now, Jack crossed his arms over his chest and sat staring straight ahead. "It is, is it?"

"Yes, sir."

"And just how would you describe the way Mrs. Harte looks at me, then?"

Jack deliberately kept his gaze locked on the rain-veiled street ahead as he awaited the reply.

"Well, sir," Sheridan finally said, "I'd say she might be a bit intimidated by you." He paused, then quickly added, "But I think she also finds you...very interesting."

"'Very interesting,'" Jack repeated. There was no question that Sheridan was right about the intimidating part, he thought sourly, remembering the look of horror that had crossed Samantha's features earlier.

"Actually, sir, I think it's fairly obvious that Mrs. Harte likes you."

"Likes me?" As a means of counteracting any false hopes raised by Sheridan's observation, Jack reminded himself of the way Samantha had visibly shrunk from his touch. Still, hadn't he himself commented on more than one occasion about the lad's keen instincts? Even so, it would be folly itself to make too much of this.

He thought for a moment. "Have you ever heard Mrs. Harte speak of her husband?" he said.

Sheridan shook his head. "Strange, isn't it, but I don't recall her ever mentioning him in any way."

It *did* seem strange, Jack thought. "Still, he must have been a good man. I can't imagine Sa—Mrs. Harte married to any other kind."

"I expect you're right," Sheridan agreed. "But I've often wondered. She has such a great sorrow in her eyes."

"Aye, she does," Jack said softly. "Indeed she does."

"Mr. Kane?"

"Hm?" Jack's thoughts had returned to the disturbing scene with Samantha, and he had to force his attention back to his surroundings.

"Did I speak out of turn, about Mrs. Harte's...'interest' in you?"

Jack waved off his concern. "No, it's all right. Though I expect I'd be wise to discount the notion. It's not likely that Mrs. Harte will ever bear me any affection other than friendship. That much, at least, might be a possibility. But as for anything else—" Jack gave a heavy shrug, as if to throw off a burden. "Her kind of woman doesn't take up with a man like me. If she ever decides to marry again, she'll be wanting a *good* man."

"I'm thinking there's no such thing," Sheridan said quietly.

Jack looked at him. "You are far too cynical for your tender age, lad. Best to leave such jaded opinions to someone like myself."

"No, it's true," said Sheridan. "Mrs. Harte gave me a copy of the Scriptures—I had none of my own, you see—and I've been reading them straight through. What I'm coming to realize is that there's no such thing as a truly good man—except for the Savior, of course—God's Son. The rest of us—even the *best* of us—we're not good at all, not really. We don't even have the *hope* of being good unless we put on the new life offered us by the cross of Christ."

Jack was in no mood for a theological discussion. He'd been down that road already tonight, thanks to Amelia. "If you don't mind, lad, I'd just as soon not pursue the subject."

"You don't believe in Christ's redemption, Mr. Kane?"

Jack turned a black look on him. "Do you really consider that any of your affair, Cavan Sheridan?"

The boy didn't look at him, but his reply couldn't have been firmer. "As a matter of fact, I do, sir. I'd be fearful for your soul if I thought you didn't believe."

"Well, I'd prefer that you tend to your own soul, Sheridan. And your driving as well, if you don't mind."

The boy actually smiled! "Sorry, sir. It's just what you said about Mrs. Harte's deserving only a 'good' man. It made me think that you might not even consider yourself in the running."

Jack stared at him. "Sheridan," he finally said, "has it ever occurred to you that you are occasionally downright insolent?"

"I don't mean to be, sir. Would you prefer I not mention Mrs. Harte again?"

"I didn't say that. Although I expect you resent my...interest in her, in any event."

"I do not, sir. Not a bit. Nor hers in you."

"She has no interest in me, Sheridan!"

"Whatever you say, Mr. Kane."

Jack brooded for another moment or two. "What did you mean back there—what you said about 'putting on the new life'? You make it sound like a wardrobe—take off the old suit and put on a new one. Is that really in the Bible?"

Jack had never liked admitting ignorance on any subject, but his knowledge of the Scriptures was sketchy at best. His mother had taught him some of the old stories, and Martha had been a great one for reading the Bible, had read it faithfully each night. But while Jack had always admired her devotion, he hadn't shared it. On those times when she read aloud to him, he hadn't liked the way the words made him feel. Uncomfortable. Uneasy. And, at times, inexplicably lonely.

Oddly enough, that hymn Amelia liked to sing—"Amazing Grace"—invariably seemed to affect him in the same way.

Jack had long ago written off religion as something for women, certainly something that children ought to be taught as well. But it wasn't for him.

Yet Sheridan had sparked his curiosity with his talk about good men and "putting on a new life." It somehow reminded him of what Amelia had said about her vests.

"It's in the Bible, all right, sir. In numerous places."

It took Jack a second or two to realize that Sheridan was answering his question of a moment before.

"Do you know the story of the Prodigal Son, Mr. Kane?"

Jack nodded guardedly.

"So perhaps you recall that after the son had squandered his inheritance, he came crawling back home, and his father put a fine new robe and sandals on him. Well," Sheridan went on, "Mrs. Harte says that the robe is like the new life we put on in Christ. She says all we have to do is turn away from our old life, and God will give us a new robe—the robe of his forgiveness and redemption."

He paused, then added, "In truth, sir, the Bible is filled with passages about that very thing—'putting off the old,' and 'putting on the new.' If you like, I'd be glad to show you sometime, Mr. Kane."

"That's all right," Jack said dryly, trying to stem the tide of unsettling emotions coursing through him. "I'll take your word for it."

"'Tis God's Word, not mine," Sheridan countered.

"Shut up and drive, boy. You're beginning to annoy me."

"Yes, sir. Sorry, sir." A silence. Then, "Mr. Kane?"

"What now, Sheridan?" Jack said wearily.

"I'd like to say that, as men go, I happen to think you're one to admire. I expect Mrs. Harte does, too, given the way she looks at you."

"*Sheridan*—"

"I know you might not see yourself quite in that light, but Mrs. Harte says that we ought not to pay much heed to how we see ourselves, or how others see us." The lad seemed in such a fierce rush to get his words out that they fairly spilled from him as he continued. "She says it's how God sees us that matters, and that he doesn't see us at all the way others do. Everyone else judges us by the way we act or what they've heard about us, but God looks at the heart."

It occurred to Jack that he wouldn't be comfortable with *anyone* seeing his heart—especially the Almighty—for surely by now it was as black as the coal mines in which the youth beside him had once labored.

"Mrs. Harte says," Sheridan went on, "that once we put on the robe of God's redemption, he doesn't see our old life anymore."

Something tightened in Jack. Sheridan's final words settled over him, sinking so far into the recesses of his being that they seemed to touch the very depths of his soul. He turned to study the strong, lean profile of his young driver, but Sheridan's gaze was fixed resolutely on the darkened street.

"It would seem," Jack said, still watching him, "that Mrs. Harte has been teaching you something more than grammar and history."

A slow smile broke over Sheridan's features. "I expect it would be no exaggeration to say that Mrs. Harte has changed my life, sir."

Jack studied him for a moment more, then leaned back a little and lifted his face to the cleansing rain. *And mine as well,* he thought with a touch of heaviness and solemn wonder. *And mine as well...*

❦

Inside the carriage, Samantha's thoughts were troubled.

The memory of what had happened earlier between her and Jack Kane would undoubtedly plague her the rest of the night. It had been a humiliating, shattering experience. Perhaps she should have been prepared for it, given the agonizing memories—and the fears—she still harbored. On the other hand, Jack was the first man with whom she had allowed any sort of closeness since Bronson. She couldn't have known what to expect and had been caught wildly off guard by the encounter.

Yet, the raw, undisguised hurt she had seen in Jack's eyes continued to torment her, even though to her vast relief he had shown no sign of resenting her for the experience. In fact, he had actually assumed a somewhat lighthearted tone with her there at the last.

It had taken all the control Samantha could muster not to tell him what lay behind her behavior. The plea—and the pain—in his eyes had almost been her undoing. For one of the few times since Bronson's death, she had been seized by a yearning to bare her soul, to pour out the entire hideous truth to another human being.

But what would it have accomplished? Did she really think that the simple act of confiding in someone else would free her from the curse of her marriage? Was she so naive as to hope that purging her soul would somehow bring her healing?

There was no reason to think that any purpose would be served by telling Jack about her past. If he cared for her at all...and she believed now that he did...wouldn't the truth only turn his caring to pity—or, worse still, revulsion? Samantha thought she could more easily bear his rejection than his pity or disgust.

How could she possibly reveal to Jack what she could never even bring herself to tell her own mother? How could she tell *anyone* about Bronson—the ways he had humiliated her, degraded her, *brutalized* her? How could she ever make anyone understand what she had endured as his mind became unhinged and sent him spiralling on a terrifying descent into madness?

To this day, Samantha did not understand how he had managed to deceive so many or how she could have been so pathetically naive and trusting.

No, Jack Kane could not heal her. No one could. A part of her—perhaps the very essence of her womanhood—had been defiled and ruined for any man.

And even if that were not the case, there was still the fact that she and Jack lived in two different worlds, that their differences still stood between them like an impenetrable bulwark. She lived her life based upon a faith and a code of values that she was fairly certain Jack neither accepted nor understood, any more than she could hope to accept or understand whatever it was that drove him.

And yet when he had asked if she would let him be her friend, Samantha had found herself unable to refuse, indeed had eagerly reached out for that much, at least, if nothing else. She needed a friend, and there was something in Jack that seemed to promise that she could trust him.

How long had it been since she had trusted a man...since she had trusted *anyone?*

It had shaken her to realize that she thought she could trust Jack even with the truth about her marriage, though it was doubtful that she ever would. Out of deference to Bronson's family and the people who had trusted him and believed the best of him—and perhaps for her own self-protection as well—she would continue to keep her silence.

Besides, even if she did finally reveal the truth, no one would ever believe her. In the eyes of all who knew him, Bronson Harte had been a good man, a *godly* man. There wasn't one among them all who would ever believe anything else.

Finally, lulled by the sound of the light rain splashing against the carriage, the horse's steady clopping along the street, and an almost comforting sense of isolation, Samantha felt the turmoil, if not the pain, inside her begin to ebb.

She was only vaguely aware of the men's voices above her, was even growing slightly drowsy, when suddenly she felt the carriage skid and careen sideways, tossing her hard against the door. Someone shouted. Cavan, she thought. She heard a sharp crack, followed by another, and with a stunning, dreadful clarity Samantha recognized the sound of gunfire!

Clinging to the door, she tried to see out the window. Without warning, the carriage lurched, gathering speed before finally slamming to a stop, throwing her forward.

Samantha cried out Jack's name, but there was no reply.

41

INTO THE NIGHT

*What brings death to one
brings life to another.*

IRISH PROVERB

The carriage had just turned the corner at Houston and Sullivan. The streets were quiet, no doubt because of the rainstorm. Even at this hour, there would normally have been a few peddlers with their pushcarts, hoping to make an extra penny or two before calling it a night. Two or three streetwalkers—the older ones, whose slatternly features fared better in the darkness—lurked in the shadows as a small crew of factory workers trudged past on their way home. But for the most part, the street was deserted.

It was a black, bitter night. Rain was falling heavily again, as if the storm had changed its mind and turned back for yet another go at the city. The wind had taken on a definite chill, and Jack, now thoroughly drenched, shivered beneath his dripping suit coat. Sheridan fared no better in his thin jacket, and Jack made a mental note to have the lad pick up a raincoat for himself.

Not that he would be driving much longer, of course. Jack had every intention of putting him on the paper full-time soon. But even there, he would find need for a raincoat.

He was beginning to tire, his senses dulled, his thoughts rambling over nothing in particular, when he saw a figure emerge from the alley to his right, just ahead. Whoever it was came to a dead stop, as if waiting for the carriage to pass before crossing the street.

The figure was almost completely concealed in a long, flapping coat, with some sort of soft, wide hat pulled well down over his forehead. But something about the stance, the slight bend of the widespread legs and the rigid set to the shoulders, triggered an alarm in Jack.

Fully alert now, he put a warning hand to Sheridan's arm. "What's this?" he said, his voice low. "Have a care."

He felt the muscles tense in Sheridan's forearm, heard him click his tongue to speed up the horse. They were almost upon the figure when Jack saw an arm come up, pistol in hand.

Sheridan had seen it, too. As if by signal, he rose to a crouch, snapping the reins.

The dark figure stepped out into the street, and Jack saw that the gun was trained directly on him.

In that instant, Sheridan thrust himself almost directly in front of Jack with a shout. *"Watch yourself, sir!"*

Stunned, Jack still had the presence of mind to grasp the boy and try to shove him away. But it was too late.

Everything exploded in a rush. Sheridan took the first shot in his right shoulder, the next in his chest. He gave only a soft gasp, then pitched forward.

The mare squealed, and the carriage shot forward with a clatter. Jack caught the reins with his left hand, flinging out his other arm to block Sheridan's fall. The carriage bumped and skidded, and for a second Jack lost his balance. He righted himself, hauling hard on the reins with both hands as the carriage hurtled into the night.

When he looked back over his shoulder, the gunman was gone—just as Jack had known he would be.

He choked down his own swell of fear as he fought to rein in the panicked mare. Finally, with Sheridan slumped silently beside him, he managed to bring the horse under control and stop the carriage.

Samantha scrambled out the door, practically falling into Jack's arms. He caught her, holding her fast.

"What happened?" She searched his face, going weak with relief when she saw that he was unharmed. "Jack?"

"I'm all right. But Sheridan's hurt."

Samantha tried to twist free, to go to Cavan, but Jack held her. "Get back in the carriage, Samantha. You don't want to see this."

She stared up at him. His face was shadowed, but she could see the rigid set of his features, the hard, angry line of his mouth.

"He's been shot, Samantha. He's bad. We need to get him to the hospital just as quickly as possible."

"Shot?" Samantha felt dazed. She couldn't think, couldn't even get her breath for a moment. "Why would anyone shoot Cavan?"

Jack looked at her. "The young fool threw himself in front of me," he said flatly.

Samantha's legs threatened to buckle.

"The bullets were meant for me," Jack said, his voice flat. "More than likely, Sheridan saved my life."

Weakness seeped through Samantha. "Is he...?"

"He's alive." Jack's voice was hard, his eyes harder.

Samantha tried to push past him. "Let me see if I can help—"

"Samantha—there's no time. No time."

Samantha saw reflected in his eyes the same dread that was coursing through her. She no longer hesitated, but simply nodded and let him help her back into the carriage.

They were a long way from Bellevue, but Jack was set on getting the best of care for Sheridan. He raced the carriage through the night as if the legions of darkness were at his back. From time to time, he glanced over at the still form beside him to make sure the breath hadn't left the boy's body. Once or twice he touched him, but there was no response. And all the while, the rain continued to pour down on them without mercy.

When they finally pulled up to the entrance of Bellevue, Sheridan was still alive, but only barely, Jack suspected. Jack started shouting for help even as he leaped from the carriage and flung the hospital doors open.

By the time he returned, with two attendants and a stretcher in tow, Samantha had climbed up onto the driver's seat and was holding the still-unconscious Sheridan's hand, watching him.

She was bent low over him, as if to shield him from the rain with her body. Her lips were moving, and Jack knew that she was praying.

More than two hours passed before someone finally came to talk with them in the waiting room. Other than making frequent trips to the front desk to inquire, Jack and Samantha spent most of the time sitting on uncomfortable wooden chairs, side by side, mostly in silence.

Even after Jack finally managed to put down the worst of his murderous rage, his thoughts remained stormy. He forced himself not to jump to conclusions about the shooting. More than likely, the assailant had been only a hired gun. The only thing he could be certain of at this point was that the bullets had been meant for him, not Cavan Sheridan.

He knew he had enemies, knew some of them by name. But doubtless there were others who despised him in secret and harbored no end of malice toward him. Whoever was behind this, Jack vowed he would find him and make him pay.

He had already talked with the police, but tomorrow, as soon as he had the chance, he would have Avery Foxworth set his best investigator to the case. He considered offering a sizable reward but was reluctant to advertise the fact that someone had tried to shoot him; there was no telling how many additional cranks that kind of sensationalism might bring out of the woodwork. Still, if that was what it would take to find the snake behind this, that was what he would do.

His thoughts swung back to Sheridan. He still couldn't take in the enormity of what the boy had done. To risk his own life—Jack refused to think that by now Sheridan might have actually *given up* his life—what in the world had possessed him?

An unexpected chill trailed down his spine as he recalled something Sheridan had said during their first meeting, the day Jack had interviewed him for the driver's job. After assuring Jack that he was strong and "did well with the horses," the boy had gone on to remark that he would be "good to have around in the event of trouble."

Jack remembered his comeback, that he wasn't looking to hire a bodyguard. He couldn't possibly have known then that the lanky, awkward youth with the hungry eyes would end up saving his life.

Again, he puzzled over why.

Just then, a doctor entered the waiting room. Jack shot to his feet, bracing himself for what they might be about to hear.

※

Samantha remained seated, her hands clasped tightly in her lap. The doctor was young, too thin, and had deep shadows under his eyes. A shock of light hair fell over one eye, and his examining coat was soiled in several places.

Samantha thought he looked exceedingly weary. But his eyes held both intelligence and compassion, and she felt reassured that his expression didn't appear too terribly grim.

The physician glanced from her to Jack, saying, "You're Mr. Sheridan's family?"

Jack looked at Samantha, and after only a slight hesitation, he replied, "Yes. We're the only family he has here in New York."

The doctor nodded. "I'm sure you're anxious about him. I wish I had better news for you, but I'm afraid his condition is very serious."

"But he's going to live?" Jack prompted. His hands were knotted into tight fists at his sides. His eyes still held a trace of the same anger Samantha had seen after the shooting.

The doctor took off his glasses and slipped them into the pocket of his examining coat. "I can't say just yet. The wound to his shoulder is bad enough, of course, but my main concern is the chest wound. We were able to get the bullets out, but he's lost a dangerous amount of blood." He hesitated. "I'm sorry. It's going to be a while before we know."

"How long?" Jack said tightly.

The doctor shrugged, but it wasn't a careless gesture, merely an indication of his uncertainty. "Perhaps in a few hours, though it might be longer. I'm going to have him watched very closely, you can be sure."

He looked at Samantha, then Jack. "Why don't you and your wife go on home and get some rest? There's nothing you can do here."

Samantha felt her face grow warm when Jack did nothing to correct the doctor's assumption.

"We'll see," Jack said shortly.

After the doctor left the room, Jack sat down beside her. "I'm going to stay," he said. "But if you'd rather not, I'll see that you get home."

Samantha shook her head. "No, I'll wait with you. I couldn't possibly rest, not knowing."

Jack nodded and put a hand to her arm. "Why don't we move over there, then?" he said, gesturing across the room to a wooden bench with two thin, worn cushions. "That looks a bit more comfortable than these chairs, and I expect it's going to be a long night."

42

A Place for Memories, A Time for Secrets

For back to the Past, though the thought brings woe,
My memory ever glides.

James Clarence Mangan

The sounds of the hospital in the middle of the night were achingly familiar to Jack. Footsteps in the corridor, sometimes rushing, sometimes subdued. Doctors and attendants speaking in hushed voices. A chilling cry from somewhere down the hall. The jarring clatter of utensils. Someone shouting. Someone weeping.

The memories came driving in on him with a vengeance. He had thought those nights he'd spent here with Martha had finally been relegated to a place of bad dreams—not quite forgotten, but no longer real enough to torment him. Now here he was again, and the memories were back, pummeling his mind and heart in a renewed assault on an old wound.

It was past two in the morning, and they had heard nothing about Sheridan for hours now. Numerous times, Jack had gone to the door of the ward to look in, but a screen—which he knew from experience often denoted dying—had been set in place. If he so much as tiptoed in to look past the screen the matron in attendance shook her head and frowned at him as if to discourage any further intrusion.

He drew in a long breath, then stood and stretched. He glanced at Samantha and saw that her eyes were closed, but he couldn't tell whether she was sleeping...or praying again.

Samantha, he had learned, did not call attention to her prayers. She simply sat very quietly, eyes closed, her lips moving only slightly as she—to use one of Rufus Carver's expressions—"communed with the Lord."

He stretched again and started toward the door.

"Jack?"

He turned back. "Sorry—did I wake you?"

She shook her head. The only light was from an oil lamp on a table near the door, but the signs of fatigue engraved upon her features were clearly visible. Her eyes were deeply shadowed, her skin uncommonly pale. Even in this state of exhaustion and mild disarray, however, to Jack's eyes she was still incredibly lovely.

"I wasn't sleeping," she assured him. "Do you know what time it is?"

"A little past two. Samantha, why don't you let me get a cab to take you home? You're exhausted."

"No more than you," she pointed out. "Besides, I want to stay. Cavan may need us when he wakes up."

If he wakes up. Jack kept the thought to himself.

"There is one thing, though," Samantha said. "Do you think you could somehow get word to Rufus to come? I'm sure he would, and I think Cavan would want him here. Besides, I'd feel better if I weren't the only one praying."

Jack frowned, puzzled by the request. "Of course Rufus would come. But I didn't realize he and the boy knew each other all that well."

"Cavan usually attends services at Rufus's church," Samantha explained.

Jack looked at her in surprise. "Sheridan goes to Rufus's church? But that's a Negro congregation!"

"Mostly, but not altogether." She smiled a little. "I attend there, too, as a matter of fact."

Jack studied her for a moment, then shook his head. "You never fail to surprise me, Mrs. Harte. But, yes, I'll get a message to Rufus somehow."

In the end he hailed a cab not far from the hospital entrance and paid the driver to bring Rufus to Bellevue as soon as possible. He looked at his watch. "There's an extra two dollars for you if you're back within the hour," he told the driver.

After begging a cup of water for himself and Samantha from one of the matrons, he returned to the waiting room. "There's a cab on the way," he said, handing her the water and lowering himself onto the bench beside her.

He was rewarded with a grateful smile and found himself wishing he could do something else for her. He did fancy Samantha's smile.

To help take their minds off Sheridan, Jack tried to make conversation. At first they spoke of mundane, inconsequential matters. Before long, however, Jack was surprised to find himself talking about things he had seldom, if ever, discussed with anyone else. Samantha had a way about her, he discovered, of drawing thoughts, and even feelings, from him that he would have normally found difficult, if not impossible, to verbalize.

More surprising still was that, to some extent, she responded in kind. Perhaps it was their mutual concern for Cavan Sheridan. A contributing factor might also have been the late-night quiet and the sense of somehow being cut off from reality. In any event, they talked for a long time, easily and openly, and Jack found himself more at ease with her than usual. He couldn't be certain, but he thought it might have been the same for her.

He learned that her father was Samuel Pilcher, a senior partner in one of the city's more distinguished investment firms. Her mother was apparently a moving force in New York's upper echelon of society.

Samantha also revealed that, while they weren't exactly estranged, there was "tension" between herself and her family.

That her parents were old family—moneyed and highly respectable—didn't surprise Jack. He had sensed it in Samantha almost from their first meeting.

What *did* surprise him was that he found himself telling her about *his* parents: the highly unrespectable, wild, rebel father who had managed to get himself hanged as a result of a night raid with one of Ireland's countless secret societies—and his mother, who had died giving birth to Brady. He told her about his sister, Rose, "a nun and the best of the lot of us," and about Brady—his art, and even the strain of rebelliousness and selfishness Jack found so worrisome in his younger brother.

Samantha told him about growing up as a pampered, somewhat spoiled daughter. When Jack made a skeptical protest, she assured him it was true. He also learned that, having benefited from a contingent of carefully selected tutors, she probably had a finer education than most of the men he knew.

When he commented to that effect, she merely gave a small laugh, saying, "All it means is that I know a great deal about many things of no importance and not nearly enough about real life."

On the other hand, she seemed genuinely impressed by his own erratic attempts to attain an education. Jack had actually attended night classes similar to those Samantha taught. Not when he was a boy—he'd been too busy working to feed himself and the younger ones then—but later. Most of what he'd learned, however, had come about through his own continuing efforts to educate himself.

It intrigued him to learn that she had her heart set on buying her own buggy, that indeed she had been saving for some time now for just that purpose—though she evidently still had a ways to go. He was surprised to realize how much it pained him to think of her scrimping and saving for something he could probably have purchased with the money he had in the pocket of his trousers at this very moment.

Finally, he even told her a little about Martha. He could talk about her now without much of the old hurt, could even smile a little at the good memories—and there were many. But if he had been hoping Samantha might reciprocate by speaking of her marriage, he was disappointed. In fact, she had grown silent, as if she no longer had anything to contribute to the conversation.

Acting on impulse—would he never learn?—Jack finally asked her about Bronson Harte. "I confess that I don't know how your late husband died. I don't believe I've ever heard you say."

She sat staring down at her hands for a long moment, making no reply. When she finally replied, she continued to keep her gaze carefully averted from his. "It was—very sudden."

"I see. How long has he been gone?"

"Nearly four years now."

Her voice had dropped to a near whisper. "You must have married very young," he said.

She shot a look at him. "Not really. But we were married only two years before—before he died."

Again Jack caught a sense of some undefinable tension in her, but before he could ask anything else she made what appeared to be a deliberate attempt to change the subject.

"Do you think we should check on Cavan again?" she said.

Jack knew she was genuinely concerned about Sheridan. All the same, he recognized evasiveness when he saw it, and Samantha was definitely being evasive. He had learned more about her tonight than he had in months, and he was reluctant to end the conversation.

"Why don't we wait a bit?" he replied. "The matron is starting to give me evil looks."

She nodded her assent, and after a moment of uncertainty, Jack said carefully, "Samantha? I can't help but notice—you're really not very comfortable talking about your husband, are you?"

The quick, fitful look that darted across her features confirmed Jack's instincts, but her reply still surprised him. "I—no, actually, I'm not. I'm afraid my marriage wasn't…as happy as yours apparently was."

Jack didn't miss the trembling of her hands or the way she had begun to press her arms against her midsection as if to hold herself together.

He wished he dared take her hand. "I'm sorry," he said softly.

"Yes…well, it's…over now."

Jack thought that was a strange way to put it. He said nothing, but the suspicion that had begun to form in his mind reasserted itself. When he thought of how concerned—how intense—she had been about the Shanahan woman and her problems, the peculiar silence she maintained in regard to her deceased husband, and most especially, the stricken look that came over her at the mention of his name, he could not help but wonder if the late Bronson Harte had really been the saint he was reputed to be.

He was seriously beginning to doubt it.

❧

Samantha saw something in Jack's eyes she had never seen in Bronson's—a tenderness, a gentleness she could not fathom. But there was something else there as well, some unsettling dark emotion she couldn't define.

Uneasily, she wondered if she had said too much, had somehow allowed him to catch a glimpse of the sordid truth that lay buried beneath her defenses. At times his dark eyes seemed to cut through the wall of her self-protection and see far more than she wanted him, or anyone else, to see.

She hated all this evasion—always skirting the truth, hiding the pain, pretending…always pretending.

It was more difficult, somehow, with Jack. He had asked for her friendship, and in spite of her initial skepticism and reservations about him, Samantha was surprised to realize that she *wanted* his friendship.

Had she been less weary, less depleted, she might have found the energy to rationalize her feelings. He was her employer, after all, and since it wasn't likely she would find a more attractive position anywhere in the city that paid as well or allowed her the flexibility in hours, wouldn't she be wise to cultivate his friendship?

No. It wasn't anything like that, and she knew it. Even if ensuring her position had been at the heart of all this, she had sensed nothing in Jack Kane's character to indicate that, by rejecting his friendship, she might be endangering her job. The truth was that she had come to *like* the man, was even attracted to him, and she might just as well confront the fact instead of denying it.

Perhaps a part of his appeal for her was his kindness. Despite all the rumors about his ruthlessness and callousness, Jack *had* been kind to her—even though she had given him every reason not to be. That kindness had been a balm to her wounded spirit.

Ever since leaving the fellowship, Samantha had lived a very isolated, solitary existence. She stayed busy enough—work was never a problem. But her days revolved around her work for the newspaper, her teaching, and her other responsibilities with Immigrant Aid. Any "social life"—even the term brought a rueful smile—consisted of suppers with Amelia and Rufus and an occasional potluck at the church. As for her former "friends" among Bronson's followers, they had begun to drift away soon after his death. When Samantha finally separated from the fellowship, they made no further effort to maintain contact.

Most of the time she was able to ignore her feelings of loneliness. But once in a while, the solitude of her apartment and the lack of companionship in her life seemed to close in on her, and she found herself longing for something more.

She was loath to admit that Jack Kane might represent that something more. But if he did, how could she consider even the most innocent of friendships with him when there would always be this veil of secrecy between them?

Dear God, must I live the rest of my life in the shadows? Will there ever come a time when I'll be able to forget the past and live a normal life, when I'll find the courage to trust again…even to love again?

"Samantha?"

Jack's voice, hushed but laced with concern, pierced her thoughts. Samantha glanced up to find him leaning toward her, his features knit in a frown.

Again Samantha felt torn between the instinctive caution his closeness sparked in her and whatever it was that invariably drew her to him in spite of that caution.

"I'm sorry," she said, forcing a smile. "I'm afraid my mind tends to wander sometimes." She was keenly aware of his searching gaze and could almost feel him choosing his words.

"He hurt you, didn't he?"

Samantha tensed, at first thinking she'd misunderstood him. "What?"

"Your husband. He hurt you. That's why it's so difficult for you to talk about him."

An alarm went off in Samantha. What had she said…what had he seen that could have given it away?

The humiliation flooding over her made her want to leap to her feet and run away. From Jack…from the hospital…from the pain. Somehow he had glimpsed her secret shame.

He knew…

So he'd been right. Jack knew it the instant her head snapped up. He saw her stiffen, saw the white-knuckled grip of her hands at her waist and the startled, almost frightened, look in her eyes.

"I don't know what you mean," she said, suddenly cool to the point of freezing him out.

"I think you do, Samantha," Jack said, as gently as possible. "And you don't have to sidestep with me. I've suspected for some time now."

She squared her shoulders and fixed her gaze on some nonexistent object across the room. "I don't know what you're talking about, but I hardly think it's any of your business, whatever it is."

This wasn't anger he was seeing in her, Jack sensed. It was an attempt to protect, to ward off. He had cut through too suddenly, too deeply, had laid open some sort of wound she'd believed to be concealed—and now she was scrambling to shield it.

He disliked himself for exposing her pain—whatever it was—at a time when she was so clearly vulnerable, but something had compelled him to voice his suspicions. Not for his sake, but for hers.

He could only hope she would forgive him.

"You can tell me about it, Samantha," he said quietly. "If you want to, that is. If not—I understand. But at least know that you don't have to pretend with me any longer."

She said nothing but merely sat there, straight-backed and unmoving, her lips pressed together as she deliberately avoided looking at him. Even now, despite the cloak of denial she had drawn about her, Jack could see the despair in her eyes, and the sight of it hit him like a blow. More than ever before, he wished he could hold her…hold her so closely he could somehow absorb her pain into himself so that she would feel nothing—nothing but his love for her.

His *love* for her. It was the first time he had allowed the word to identify his feelings for Samantha, even though he had feared for some time now the direction in which those feelings were headed.

So that was the way of it, then. He loved her. The admission astonished him.

It also terrified him.

To keep from touching her, he knotted his hands together. "I'm sorry if I've made you feel awkward, Samantha," he said, surprised at the hoarseness in his voice. "I thought if you realized that I knew, you might find it easier to…be with me, to be yourself with me. We don't have to mention this again, not ever, if you'd rather not."

Finally, she turned to look at him. Her eyes, woefully solemn now, searched his, and Jack felt himself measured as he had never been before.

"How did you know?" she whispered.

Jack shook his head. "I'm not sure. It was just…something in your eyes." He hesitated. "I was right, wasn't I?"

Slowly, she nodded. He saw her eyes fill with tears, and for a blinding instant of rage, he wanted to make Bronson Harte pay. "Do you want to tell me?" he prompted, dropping his voice to match her whispered tone.

She shook her head. "I can't. I've never…told anyone. Not even my family. I can't…"

Jack thought he would strangle at the look of anguish on her face. The idea of her carrying this alone made him want to weep for her. "Samantha…I'm sorry. So very sorry." No longer able to stop himself, he reached out a hand to her, waiting.

She stared at his hand, then lifted her gaze to meet his. And finally, as relief and hope and love rose up in Jack, she clasped his hand. She was trembling, and Jack wished he could impart a portion of his own strength to her. "It's all right, Samantha. Perhaps someday you'll be able to tell me," he said. "I have my secrets, too, you see. But I'd like to think that one day there will be no secrets between us, none at all. That's my hope."

He drew a steadying breath. "I want to promise you something," he said, his voice soft. She was watching him closely, and he squeezed her hand. "First, I'd like you to know that if there's anything—anything at all—of any value in me, it's my word. I don't break my word, Samantha. You can believe that. And I give you my word now that I will never…*never* hurt you. Do you understand? I will never hurt you in any way."

Her hand trembled in his. *So small, so fragile, that hand.* She was such a small, delicate woman. And yet what incredible strength must lie within her, to endure her painful secrets in silence.

Her eyes glistened with unshed tears. He wanted to kiss them away. "I will say it again, Samantha. I will never hurt you. And neither," he promised, "will anyone else. My word on it, I intend to see to it that no one ever hurts you again. Can you believe me?"

Oh, sweetheart, please, please believe me…I have never meant anything more in my life…

"Yes," she finally said, her voice soft, her eyes shining. "I believe you."

Jack had all he could do not to pull her into his arms, but he checked himself. And then the moment passed, abruptly shattered by the appearance of one of the matrons in the doorway.

"Mr. and Mrs. Kane?" she said brusquely. "Doctor says you should come now."

They looked at each other, and Jack saw his own alarm and dread mirrored in Samantha's eyes.

43

VIGIL AT BELLEVUE

*Now, no one is likely to die for a good person, though
someone might be willing to die for a person who is
especially good. But God showed his great love for us by sending
Christ to die for us while we were still sinners.*

ROMANS 5:7-8

Jack was standing at the foot of Cavan Sheridan's bed, watching Samantha dab the boy's forehead with a damp cloth, when Rufus Carver arrived.

Sheridan was still unconscious, though he would occasionally moan or move his head from side to side. His eyes were closed, his face drenched with perspiration, his skin pale and waxen. The thin scar that traced the side of his face had become an angry slash against his ashen pallor. Unless the doctor was mistaken—and Jack feared he was not—any hope for recovery was slim indeed.

After giving Jack and Samantha the disheartening news, Dr. Van Curen—the same doctor who had admitted Sheridan—had left the ward, promising to return soon. Jack wondered when the young physician managed to sleep. He had seen him going up and down the corridor most of the night, and he looked absolutely exhausted.

On the opposite side of the bed from Samantha stood a new matron. This one seemed less irascible and more interested in Sheridan's condition than in keeping things quiet and undisturbed. Which was probably a good thing, Jack thought, because Rufus was not given to speaking in whispers.

The moment the big, affable preacher walked into the room, Jack felt a sense of relief, taking his first deep breath in what seemed an interminable time. Rufus had a way of easing things for others. Jack had never quite understood what it was about his old friend that should account for this rare gift, but over the years he had seen Rufus make a difference in some rather remarkable ways in some very difficult situations.

Samantha turned as Rufus entered, and Jack saw that her relief matched his own.

"How is he?" Rufus said, brushing the dampness from his coat before giving Jack's shoulder a quick squeeze.

Jack shook his head. "Bad. They called us in a few minutes ago, said he was weakening."

Rufus looked at Cavan Sheridan, then at Jack. "Your message said he'd been shot."

Jack nodded. "It was supposed to have been me," he bit out, gripped by the same angry ache that had been gnawing at him all night. "Instead, Sheridan pushed himself in front of me. He was hit twice."

"Any idea who was responsible?"

Again Jack gave a shake of his head. "I couldn't see his face. Just a man with a gun."

Rufus studied him. "But you're sure he was after you, not the boy?"

"I was practically looking down the barrel when Sheridan shoved between us. He saved my life, no doubt about it."

No matter how he tried, Jack could not seem to get past this point, that someone had deliberately taken a bullet—*two* bullets—in his place. He still found it inconceivable, and yet he was alive because of Cavan Sheridan's selfless act.

As if he could read his thoughts, Rufus again put his hand to Jack's shoulder. "It was brave of the boy, no denying it. But this isn't your fault, Jack. Don't go tryin' to make it your fault."

They stood for a moment, watching Samantha as she bent over the unconscious Sheridan, clasping his hand. Her voice was so low Jack could only barely make out what she was saying. But clearly she believed Cavan Sheridan could hear every word.

"Cavan…listen to me; you mustn't give up. You have so much work to do yet, so many people to reach with your writing. And your sister—you have to find Terese, remember? You have to find her and bring her here, to be with you. You still want that, don't you? You have to fight. Please, Cavan…fight."

Jack's throat tightened, and he turned to Rufus. "He can't die, Rufus! The boy is too young! And he's a better man than I'll ever be, certainly. He doesn't deserve to die—not for the likes of me."

Rufus searched his eyes. "Your Savior died for the likes of you, Jack," he said, his voice uncharacteristically quiet. "He didn't deserve it either, but he did it all the same. You need to realize that Jesus has a hold on this boy, brother. I expect young Cavan here was only doing what the Lord moved him to do."

Jack was as exasperated with Rufus as he was shaken by his words. This was hardly the time to start preaching at him! But when Jack would have told him so, Rufus stepped away and went to stand beside Samantha.

Jack saw him give her a reassuring nod as they both stood watching the unconscious Cavan Sheridan. "Amelia wanted me to tell you she'd be standing in for the boy, too," Rufus said to Samantha. "She'll be praying right along with us. And it appears that we'd better start doing some mighty serious praying about now."

It stung a little, being excluded in such short order, but Jack understood. There certainly wouldn't have been any point in including him in what was clearly about to become one of Rufus's prayer meetings.

Again, it was as if Rufus could read his thoughts. "Wouldn't hurt for you to put in a word, too, Jack," he said without taking his eyes off Sheridan. "The Lord knows how much you care about this boy."

Jack looked at him, then at Sheridan. He *did* care about the lad, that was true enough. But there was little chance of any prayer he might utter rising higher than the ceiling. The Almighty had turned a deaf ear on his prayers for Martha, and that had been the one and only time in his life when he had virtually besieged the gates of heaven. If his soul had been so tarnished even back then that God ignored him, He would be a lot less likely to pay him any heed now.

But Rufus was watching him as if he expected some sort of effort on his part. "Come here, brother," he said quietly, reaching out to Jack. "At least stand with us beside the boy. That would please young Cavan, I expect."

Jack tried to swallow against his swollen throat. But even as he shook his head with the futility of it all, he took his first step toward Rufus and Samantha.

Caught completely off guard by the wave of emotion that swept through him, Jack watched as Rufus clasped the unconscious Cavan Sheridan's hand and smiled gently down upon the boy as he might have gazed upon a sleeping child.

And then he lifted his face heavenward—still holding Sheridan's hand—and began to pray, his features taking on an almost transfiguring intensity and strength. "Lord...Lord, this is your child lying here in need of your mercy and your healing hand. Cavan Sheridan, Lord—you know him by name, and you know his heart. You know it was that good and noble heart that put him in this situation in the first place. The bullets that brought this terrible thing on him were meant for someone else, but he took the pain willingly, in love for a brother.

"Now surely it must thrill your heart, Lord, to know that one of your earthly sons was willing to lay down his life for another, just as your only beloved Son was willing to pour out his life for all of us. Yes, Lord, it must surely thrill your heart..."

Jack thought his *own* heart would shatter from the pressure that had been building within him over the past few minutes. His mouth was as dry as cotton batting, and he felt about to strangle on the knot in his throat.

And yet at the same time he knew a strange, unfamiliar kind of exultation as he listened to his old friend and Samantha beseeching heaven for Cavan Sheridan's life. They had clasped hands, Rufus and Samantha, and while Rufus stood, shoulders straight, head tossed back, smiling upward as he sought divine mercy, Samantha stood quietly, eyes closed, lips barely moving, her words but a whisper.

But there was no doubt that they were both calling on the same power. And it was abundantly clear that they knew Him well and felt they had the right to address Him as a good and faithful friend.

"It's up to you, Lord," Rufus went on, "whether you take this boy home right now, tonight, or leave him here with us. That's not for us to decide, and we're purely glad we don't have that kind of fateful decision to make. But we're just asking if you might consider letting him stay. This is a good boy, Lord, who maybe can make a difference in this poor old troubled world, if you see fit to leave him here long enough.

"We trust your wisdom in this, Lord, as in all things. We trust your wisdom and your mercy, and oh, Lord, we surely do trust your Father-heart of love! Pour out that love, Lord, on Cavan Sheridan this very hour…and pour out your love on the one he risked his life for, your child, and our brother, Jack. Wrap your arms around them both, Lord, and hold them close, close to your heart…"

Jack drew in a ragged breath. This wasn't the first time Rufus had prayed in his presence, and if Jack knew him at all, he knew it wasn't the first time Rufus had prayed for *him*. Before tonight, he had always taken his friend's efforts on behalf of his soul with nothing more than a kind of grim humor and a blatant skepticism. Tonight, however, he found himself somewhat hard-pressed to understand how the Almighty could possibly ignore the earnest praying going on in this room.

It was an unnerving thought, to say the least.

When Rufus finally concluded, Jack was suddenly seized by the disconcerting feeling that, even though he had not closed his eyes throughout the entire litany—had not uttered a word, so far as he knew—*he* had been praying too, in spite of himself.

Bewildered, badly shaken, he stepped back a little. Rufus did the same, making room for Samantha to take up her former place close to Sheridan, where she resumed her soft, strangely maternal, soothing words for Cavan's ears alone.

❧

Cavan Sheridan was dreaming about home. He was there, back home in Ireland, with his parents, his sister, Honor, and Baby Mada. And yet there was little of the joy he would have anticipated—at least on his part—had such a thing ever come to pass. His family seemed contented enough, but the initial burst of happiness he had felt upon first sight of them was quickly fading, giving way to confusion.

They were all of them walking upon the shore, with the water splashing high upon the rocks. In his dream, Cavan *knew* he was dreaming, knew this was not real, although it was real enough that he tried to speak with each family member, even the baby.

Mostly, he was asking after Terese, her whereabouts, for he had not yet seen her. She was the only one absent, and he was growing anxious.

His family behaved in a most peculiar fashion. They spoke and laughed among themselves, but other than Baby Mada, who stared at Cavan with large, studying eyes, no one paid him the slightest heed. Cavan had thought they would be glad to see him after so long a time. Instead they virtually ignored him, even his questions about the missing Terese.

Because he knew he was caught up in a dream, he shouldn't have grown impatient with them. But he thought they might have shown a bit more sensitivity to his exhaustion, his weakness—and his need to gain some word of Terese before he could rest. Instead, they simply continued walking along the shore, not even bothering to wait for him when he fell behind.

Suddenly, he realized someone was calling out to him, and he turned, expecting to finally see Terese running up the shore to greet him. But there was no one.

The water was slamming harder and harder against the rocks now, driven by the strange wind that had blown up in the middle of the sea. Above, the sky had darkened to an ominous, dark pewter, the clouds hanging so low he could almost touch them.

His family had gone on ahead of him, not waiting, and Cavan could scarcely make them out. He could no longer keep up. His breathing was tortured, his chest pounding, and he was finding it difficult to walk, much less run, after the others.

Cavan...

He *had* heard someone calling his name. Again, he turned to look but could see nothing...nothing but a thin, dark mist where the clouds were now slipping down behind him.

Cavan...

The voice sounded nearer now...a woman's voice, sure, but not *Terese's* voice.

He turned once more to look after his parents and sisters, but they had disappeared into the distance, hidden by the clouds that now encompassed him from behind and before, hiding his family, the rocks, even the waves of the sea.

Finally, he began walking back the way he had come, away from his family, back along the shore, out of the clouds...out of the mist. Someone was holding his hand, and he allowed himself to be led as he followed the voice that continued to call his name...

❧

Over an hour later, Jack saw the boy stir slightly and moan. He tensed, fearful of the worst. But as he watched, Sheridan blinked, squeezed his eyes shut once more, then opened them again.

Jack put a fist to his mouth to suppress a gasp of relief. Samantha made a soft cry and turned to look at him and Rufus. The latter voiced an enthusiastic, "Praise God! Thank you, Lord!"

Sheridan was watching Samantha, who still had hold of his hand. She smiled at him and murmured something Jack couldn't make out. The boy seemed to be having trouble focusing his eyes, but he looked surprisingly alert, given the gravity of his condition.

"*Mr. Kane?*"

Jack flinched at the sound of his own name, the first words Sheridan uttered as he regained consciousness.

The matron was already rushing out to fetch the doctor, so Jack went to take her place across the bed from Samantha.

He knew as soon as he looked in Sheridan's eyes that the lad was going to be all right. He stood staring down at him, wondering at the way Cavan was searching his gaze. Finally, Sheridan gave a small nod, as if to reassure himself, and said, "'Tis safe you are, then."

It was the most natural thing ever for Jack to fall into the Irish cadence they held in common, even though his throat had tightened treacherously. "Aye, 'tis safe I am, lad. All thanks to you."

The boy's smile was wobbly as with a languid motion he turned his face toward Samantha. "It was you I heard."

Samantha's expression was questioning as she leaned slightly closer to him. "What, Cavan? What did you hear?"

"It was you who called me out of the dream," he said. "I heard you, Mrs. Harte…I heard you calling my name…"

His eyes fluttered a little, and seeing his weakness, Jack was reluctant to risk tiring him. But the question that had raked at him throughout the night would give him no peace. He had to know.

Bending over the boy, he studied his pale, lean face for a moment. "Why did you do it, Cavan Sheridan?" he said, his voice rough with emotion. "You could have been killed, you young pup! You almost were, you know. Why would you do such a fool thing?"

The lad made no reply right away, but instead lay looking up at Jack as if uncertain as to how to answer. When his response finally came, it was so soft that Jack had to lean still closer, straining to hear.

"To give you more time, sir."

"What's that?" Jack frowned, wondering if he'd heard him correctly.

"I had…to give you more time, don't you see? You need…more time. The Father knows you, knows your heart…but you don't know him…can't choose…unless you know…his love…"

Jack's breath seemed lodged in his throat. He tried to swallow but found he could not. He stayed as he was for a moment more, watching as Cavan Sheridan closed his eyes and drifted off, this time, obviously, to a more natural sleep.

Jack straightened and looked across the bed at Samantha, who merely gave a gentle lift of her eyebrows, as if to ask what he intended to do with the gift…the time…he had been given.

GIFTS OF GOLD AND GRACE

'Tis grace itself, this letting go of yesterday,
The relinquishing of old days and old ways
To make room for the gift of God's tomorrows.

CAVAN SHERIDAN, FROM *WAYSIDE NOTES*

NEW YORK CITY

On the following Monday, Samantha was visiting Cavan Sheridan, along with Rufus and Amelia, when Jack strode into the ward.

It was late afternoon, but the man certainly did not look as if he had spent the day at the office. Samantha couldn't stop a smile at his jaunty air and his light, almost dancing, step as he approached. He was his usual natty self—impeccably groomed, freshly barbered, and dressed to the nines in an elegantly tailored gray suit and a silk neckcloth in a shade of lustrous pearl.

He was carrying something—a rather thick letter, so it appeared.

As he walked up to the bed, his greeting took in everyone, but his smile seemed just for her.

"I hope you're getting good and tired of playing the slugabed, boyo," he cracked to Cavan Sheridan, who, although still obviously weak and in some discomfort, was propped up by a flock of pillows at his back. "I'll grant you only a few more days, and then it's back to work for you!"

As he spoke, he waved the letter he was carrying in Samantha's direction. "And for you as well, Mrs. Harte—we have company coming, you see."

Samantha wondered what on earth he was talking about, then realized—"You've heard from your brother!"

"Indeed. As it happened, the letter's been lying about the house since last Friday, but with all the fuss and confusion, I'd forgotten to read it until this morning. It seems we have a wee boy and girl coming across very soon now—and my troublesome brother even remembered to send along the copy for their story."

He stopped, studying Cavan Sheridan for a moment before going to stand alongside him. When he spoke again, he dropped his voice and put a hand to the boy's good shoulder. "And you must brace yourself, Sheridan, for the rest of the news in my brother's letter will surely astound you." He paused. "Your sister has been found, lad, and even as we speak, is more than likely on her way to America."

❦

Jack had the satisfaction of seeing Sheridan's eyes grow wide enough to pop as he delivered his news. For once, he thought wryly, the boy was actually speechless.

"Aye, it's true," Jack assured him. "Apparently, she traveled to Galway after the big storm, and that's where Brady came upon her. It seems he has worked things out so she and the children can travel together, with your sister looking after the youngsters."

"Terese…" The boy breathed her name like a prayer. His eyes suddenly filled, and for a fraction of a second Jack feared the news might have been too much for him. Perhaps he should have waited until the lad was stronger.

He *had* withheld a less joyous portion of the announcement. The bitter fact that the girl was with child as a result of an attack would have to wait until Sheridan was well enough to bear the whole story. For now, let him rejoice over the *good* news. The rest could come later.

The lad looked about to weep. Jack released him, fumbling in his pocket for a handkerchief, just in case.

"Is she…is she well, then, sir—Terese?"

Jack chose his words carefully. "It would seem from my brother's letter that your sister is quite healthy. The children, however, sound a bit frail."

He gestured again to the letter. "When you're feeling stronger, you can read it all for yourself. But for now, you must concentrate on getting well as soon as possible. I can't have my newest reporter working from his bed. It wouldn't do at all, don't you see? You are needed at the office, and the sooner the better."

"Sir?" The puzzled frown on the boy's face gave Jack more satisfaction still.

"Why, didn't you hear me, lad? It has occurred to me that you will prove far more valuable with a pad and pencil in your hands than sitting on a driver's bench. I'm putting you on the *Vanguard*'s payroll as soon as you're able to come back to work." Jack paused, then added, "And lest you think this has anything to do with your injury, it does not. I had already made the decision before you pulled that fool stunt on Friday night."

"Mr. Kane—what have you learned about the shooting? Have the police found the man yet?"

Jack shook his head. "No, but they're doing what they can. They've little to go on, of course, with the bounder disappearing as easily as he did, but they have some of their best men on it."

Jack had his own suspicions about the affair, but this was not the time to voice them. Even though a hired gun would hardly seem the sort of thing a man like Turner Julian would resort to, he couldn't afford to dismiss the possibility out of hand. But as he had told Avery Foxworth, there was no denying that he had made some enemies. The truth was, it could have been *anyone* behind that gun.

"Jack—*Mr. Kane*—?"

Jack turned to see Samantha blushing furiously at having used his given name in front of the others. He grinned at her discomfiture. *"Mrs. Harte?"* he said with deliberate emphasis.

Her eyes flared a little, but being Samantha, she regained her composure nicely. "Have you considered—what if he should try again?"

It had occurred to him, of course, and he supposed he had to allow for the possibility. But Jack thought it unlikely that a second attempt would come so soon after the recent failure. Still, her concern pleased him.

Rather than alarm her, however, he dismissed the question with a wave of his hand. "Well, I suppose we shall simply have to outfit Sheridan here with a suit of armor, now won't we?"

Jack laughed at her thoroughly outraged expression. "Don't fret yourself, Samantha. Despite what you may have read in the newspapers—" he grinned—"our police department is not without resources. Besides, I've already looked into the matter of a private investigator as well."

He turned back to Sheridan. "About your sister, lad: She'll be needing a place to stay once she arrives, and even though you won't be driving for me by then, I rather like the idea of having my bodyguard close by, all the same. So I thought we might partition the room above the stable and make a place for the two of you, for now at least. The room is large enough, and it will give you time to save a bit of money for something larger."

Sheridan shook his head, as if somewhat bemused by the offer. He pushed himself up as much as possible, extending a hand to Jack. "How can I ever thank you for all you've done, Mr. Kane?"

Jack's gaze flicked from the lad's hand to his bandaged shoulder and chest. "Well, now," he said, grasping Sheridan's hand in his, "it seems to me you have already made a right proper job of it."

❦

Before Jack escorted Samantha from the ward, Amelia surprised him by pressing a parcel into his hands. "What's this?" he said, looking down at the package wrapped in brown paper.

"Happy birthday, Jack," she said. "I bet you thought we'd forgotten all about it, didn't you, what with all the commotion?"

Jack looked at her, then laughed. "Actually," he admitted, "I'd forgotten it myself. So what is this, then?"

"Well, why don't you open it and find out?" she teased, linking arms with Rufus.

"I will indeed." Jack glanced from one to the other, then at Samantha. He felt somewhat awkward, for it was a rare occasion of any sort when he received a gift. But Amelia was clearly expecting him to open the package as they watched, so he began to tear at the string.

His fingers were clumsy as he worked to free the contents from the paper wrapping. For a moment he could do nothing but stare at the elegantly fashioned vest—obviously one of Amelia's own creations.

His throat tightened treacherously as he held the garment up for all to see. It was a resplendent effort, woven of carefully blended shades of deep crimson and burnished gold, finished with precise gold stitching. Jack found himself pleased beyond imagining.

"Amelia—I am…I don't know what to say!"

"Well, now, that's a first," Rufus said, ignoring his wife's punch in the ribs.

Samantha stepped closer to inspect the vest, smiling up at Jack as if she sensed his discomfort as well as his pleasure. "Oh, Amelia, this is absolutely lovely!"

"It is indeed, Amelia," Jack seconded. "I confess I have always envied Rufus his handsome vests. I can't thank you enough."

He went to her and kissed her lightly on the cheek. When he would have stepped back, however, Amelia stopped him with a little tug on his sleeve. "I've been working on this for a long time now, but after our talk last Friday, I was determined to get it finished for your birthday."

Jack frowned. "Last Friday?"

"Friday evening," she said. "In the sewing room. Remember what I told you about the 'cloth of heaven'?"

Jack nodded slowly, wondering what she was getting at.

"Well, I want you to promise me that every time you wear this vest, you'll think on that little talk we had—about what the Lord can make of your life if you'll just let him have his way. I want your word on it, Jack Kane."

"Do I have a choice?" Jack said dryly.

"You always have a choice, brother," Rufus put in. "It seems to me that Amelia, she's just doing her part to help you make the right one."

THE ATLANTIC, OFF THE COAST OF IRELAND

Terese Sheridan stood on the deck of the *Providence*, taking a last look at Ireland. She pulled her emerald cloak more tightly about her shoulders, trying not to think of the night Brady had bought it for her. At the same time, she attempted to shake off the melancholy that had engulfed her since early morning. She reminded herself how fortunate she was to be up here, on deck, where she could breathe in the fresh air, rather than suffering belowdecks. That was one thing she could thank Brady for, at least—by paying the extra passage money, he had spared her and the Madden children the rumored horrors of steerage.

She would thank him for nothing else, that much was certain. She glanced behind her, where wee Tully Madden was hobbling up and down the short distance of the deck to which Terese had confined him. She watched him for a moment, feeling a tug at her heart for the limp that slowed his little-boy gait. His cheerfulness seemed not to suffer, however; each time he caught Terese's eye, he favored her with a quick smile.

Tully's older sister, Shona, stood close to Terese's side. Terese could feel the girl's eyes on her but did not turn to look. Those large, haunted eyes with their sorrowful blue gaze discomfited Terese. The child seemed to be always staring at something, yet seeing nothing.

Despite her resolve to put the past behind her, her gaze—and her thoughts—returned to the fading coastline in the distance. For another moment, Terese allowed herself a brief memory of Inishmore and all that she was leaving behind: her home—the only home she had ever known—her mother, her da, her sisters…Brady…

Her heart wrenched at the thought of Brady, but it was a pain kindled by anger. She had promised herself she would never again think of him without remembering his betrayal, his rejection. She would get over him by despising him.

Only the thought of Jane Connolly brought any real sadness to her spirit. Poor Jane, trapped forever in her chair by the window, looking out upon a world of which she could have no real part. At the end, she had been kind, kinder than Terese would have had any right to expect. That last evening before her departure, Jane had added an extra week to Terese's wages.

And she had given her the ring.

Terese held out her hand and looked at the gold ring Jane had pressed upon her the night before she left. "'Twas made right here, in the Claddagh," Jane had told her. "It belonged to my mother, who passed it to me. My daughter wore it for a time, but she left it behind when she married and left the Claddagh. You wear it now, girl. Wear it to America, and remember Jane Connolly, who gave it to you. Remember me and the Claddagh—and remember Ireland. For Ireland is not only where you come from, Terese Sheridan—Ireland is what you *are*."

Terese lifted her hand to study the ring. The *Fede* ring—the "faith ring," Jane had called it—displayed two hands holding a heart surmounted by a crown. Cast in fine gold, its tradition was one of love and friendship, honor, loyalty, and the hope of future glory.

It was the only piece of jewelry Terese had ever owned, and she touched it now, turning it a bit so that the two hands and the heart were clearly visible.

Finally, she raised her eyes from the ring for one final look at her homeland. In that moment, she placed a hand over the child who grew within her and quietly gave voice to the longing of her heart.

"Please…merciful Savior…let my child be born to a better life in America…a life

of hope instead of hunger…and freedom instead of fear…A better life, Lord, please…a better life…"

Then she turned…turned her back on Ireland, on all her yesterdays. And as she turned her face to the west, to America, she lifted the hand bearing the Claddagh ring, lifted it in farewell to the old life…and in salute to the new.

Ashes and *Lace*

PART ONE

LIKE GOLD IN THE FIRE

*I go east, but he is not there. I go west, but I cannot find him. I do
not see him in the north, for he is hidden.
I turn to the south, but I cannot find him. But he knows where I am
going. And when he has tested me like gold
in a fire, he will pronounce me innocent.*

JOB 23:8-10

BETWEEN DESTINY AND DESPAIR

Roll forth, my song, like the rushing river
That sweeps along to the mighty sea.

JAMES CLARENCE MANGAN

❦

ABOARD THE *PROVIDENCE,* ON THE ATLANTIC, LATE SEPTEMBER, 1839

The bunk creaked as Terese Sheridan turned to look at the little girl beside her. Although it was still long before dawn, the child was awake, staring at Terese with those large, still eyes that seemed to hold a river of sorrow. At their feet the girl's younger brother slept, though fitfully.

Already the children had been marked by the voyage. The girl, Shona, had become frighteningly lethargic, showing no interest in anything except for her little brother, Tully. As for the boy, he had developed a cough that seemed to deepen with each passing day. And packed in as they were among countless others who carried all manner of sickness and ague, there was no telling what they might yet come down with.

Again Terese shifted, hoping to ease the ache in her back. The berths were little more than wooden shelves nailed to the wall, with nothing to cushion the constant, bruising impact as the ship rode the sea. There had been no thought that they would need to bring their own mattresses, and so they had come with only minimal bedding, this provided by the Orphan Friends Society. Their first day out, Terese had tried to soften the bunks by lining them with blankets, but the nights were too cold to lie uncovered, and so they now faced interminable weeks of the punishing bare berths.

By the time they had been at sea a week, some of the steerage passengers had taken to calling the *Providence* a "coffin ship." An apt description if ever there was one, Terese thought. It was like a dungeon, this stinking hole: cold and dark, the air foul with the stench of aging timbers, bodies crammed too tightly together, and human waste. In the dim, unventilated quarters, the sounds of light snoring or women weeping mingled with the moans of those who writhed on their bunks in the throes of sickness and the prayers of those still strong enough to storm heaven in search of deliverance.

And always there was the relentless, sickening pitch and roll of the ship.

It only made their cup more bitter still that they had never been meant to travel in steerage at all! Brady had thought to spare them that much at least, arranging, through the sponsorship of his brother's newspaper, for proper cabins in second class for Terese and the children.

By the end of their first day aboard ship, however, they had been herded off to steerage like cattle, the officer in charge viciously driving them below with a few other "filthy peasants" who had straggled on board after them.

Terese had screamed at him, had even tried to shove her way past him to plead their case with another officer, but the lout easily threw her off, strong-arming her and the children below, where they remained, virtual prisoners with the rest of the poor souls packed in around them.

Terese had existed in a state of barely contained fury ever since, daily blaming Brady for spurning her, for not being man enough to claim responsibility for the child she carried, for not going aboard with them to inspect their accommodations—indeed, she blamed Brady for every imaginable grievance, even for the disgusting food and vile water.

Unable to lie still any longer, she rose, stepped away from their bunks, and stared at the mass of bodies stretched out in all directions. A familiar feeling of confinement, of being caught in a trap and abandoned—cut off from everything and everyone except the underworld of this ship—threatened to overwhelm her. The dank hull of the ship seemed to close in on her, and the passengers sprawled wherever she looked made her want to scream at the futility of her situation.

She almost thought it would be easier to make her way up to the deck and fling herself into the sea than to endure this cursed existence another day. So wretched was she, so nearly defeated with disillusionment and despair, that she might have done just that had it not been for the babe she carried and the two young orphans dependent upon her.

Instead she forced herself to turn her back on the squalor all around her and, squeezing her eyes shut, hugged her arms to herself so fiercely that she shook with the very effort. She reminded herself once again that with every day that passed in this hellhole, she was putting the misery of her past in Ireland behind her.

Unexpectedly, the voice of Jane Connolly, the poor crippled woman whose brittle facade had concealed a surprisingly compassionate heart, rang through Terese's mind like the wail of the wind, and she lifted her hand to study the gold ring on her finger.

On the night before Terese's departure, Jane had not only added an extra week's

pay to Terese's wages but had astonished her with the gift of a solid gold *Fede* ring—
the faith ring of the Claddagh, once worn by Jane and then by her daughter.

But the gift had not been given without a chilling admonition...

"Wear it to America," Jane had said of the ring. *"Wear it...and remember me and
the Claddagh...Remember Ireland. For Ireland is not only where you come from, Terese
Sheridan—Ireland is what you are."*

Jane was wrong! Ireland was *not* what she was. Ireland was her past, a past as dark,
as cold and bitter, as the bowels of this accursed ship.

With her back still turned to the abominable reality of steerage, she reminded herself that Ireland was behind her, while America—her future—lay ahead. All she had
to do was survive this pit of perdition, and she would be free to begin a new life.

And survive it she would. Whatever it took.

If God allowed it...

The whisper in her spirit chilled the heat of her resolve like an icy waterfall. The
farther they put out to sea, the more difficult it became to hold on to her already
tenuous faith. She could almost feel it slipping away from her, like the waves in the
wake of the ship. There were times, usually in the dead of night when the sounds of
suffering all around her were heightened by the groaning and creaking of the old ship,
when she feared that God might have abandoned her altogether.

What if, because of her sin with Brady, God had turned his back on her for good?
What if there *were* no future for her and her child, only an unremarkable death in
this squalid hole before she even reached the harbor of New York?

The thought made her shudder, and in spite of her determination not to give in
to her circumstances, she was suddenly afraid. She began to tremble, her entire body
racked by one seizure of chills after another.

*Oh, please, Lord, I'll not be denying that I deserve your punishment, but my babe is
innocent of any wrongdoing, he is! Won't you please help me to survive this horror and
give my child something better?*

*Sweet Savior, at the end of this nightmare, let there be a new life waiting, a future
for the both of us, in America!*

I

A MOST RESPECTABLE MAN

It's the jewel that can't be got that is the most beautiful.

IRISH PROVERB

❧

NEW YORK CITY, EARLY NOVEMBER

Jack Kane sat in his office at the *Vanguard,* pondering, not for the first time, at what point his fascination with Samantha Harte had deepened to love—and exactly what he was going to do about it.

It was an autumn-apple-crisp Monday morning. The past week, typical of New York, had been wet and gray, but today seemed to promise at least a glimpse of late fall as depicted by the poets: brisk and clear and golden.

Jack's mood was almost light, if somewhat distracted. He had more than enough work to keep him busy the rest of the day, yet he seemed incapable of concentrating on anything but Samantha.

How had things come to such a pass?

He had scarcely touched the woman, after all, other than an occasional clasp of the hand. The one act toward her that might possibly have been construed as something more than merely a harmless, friendly gesture had occurred weeks ago, when he'd come treacherously close to kissing her: an impulsive move and one quickly halted when Samantha virtually recoiled from him. Ever since, Jack had almost religiously exerted his self-control when they were together.

A priest could not have been more restrained.

But hang it all, he was no priest, and for all his earlier intentions to be nothing more than her employer and her friend, he was more bedazzled by the woman than ever!

He had managed to maintain his self-imposed discipline not merely because he was determined to win her trust—although that was at the heart of it—but perhaps just as much because he feared he might frighten her off altogether. Although Samantha had told him hardly anything about her previous marriage, she had at least confirmed Jack's suspicion that she'd been mistreated. How badly, or what form the mistreatment had taken, he didn't know—perhaps never would—for Samantha was obviously either unwilling or unable to speak of it. In fact, she had seemed to indicate that she hadn't even confided in her parents.

On one level Jack longed for her confidence—he coveted her trust, if not her affection. Yet at times he felt something akin to relief that she had kept her silence, for he wasn't at all sure he could handle the truth.

He could not bear the thought of Samantha's being hurt; indeed, he cringed at the very idea. The few times he had allowed himself to wonder about the circumstances of her marriage to Bronson Harte, a treacherous kind of fury would invariably rise up in him. Perhaps he was better off not knowing the details.

He couldn't help but wonder if this might not be a form of cowardice, but then again, he had no doubt but that if Samantha *should* ever choose to unburden herself to him, he would be quick to listen and even grateful for her confidence.

The truth was that he desperately wanted Samantha to trust him, no matter what it took to achieve that trust.

He wanted her to trust him. He wanted her to need him.

And he wanted her to marry him.

Jack sighed and leaned back in his chair. He was in a bad way, no doubt about it.

He found himself wondering if his exemplary conduct was having any effect at all on Samantha. Was he only deluding himself that his campaign to win her over was actually working? He could never be quite sure what to make of the woman.

She had a way of looking at a man, Samantha did, that seemed to peel right past any and every layer of subterfuge while revealing nothing of her own emotions.

More than once Jack had been struck by the discomfiting suspicion that she was only too well aware of the effort required of him to play the gentleman. And while he might not go so far as to say she found his attempts amusing, on occasion she would regard him with a certain quirk of the eyebrow that made him wonder if she wasn't simply biding her time, expecting him at any moment to trip over his newly cultivated respectability.

He let out another long sigh of exasperation, but he couldn't quite suppress a smile at the thought that he was going to see Samantha today. Indeed, if all went well, he hoped to see her later this morning and again tonight.

His mood brightened considerably at that point, and he pushed away from the desk in anticipation. This could be a very important day in his life, and he didn't want to waste another minute before getting on with it.

Samantha had been expecting Tommy Ryder with the day's copy, so she wasn't surprised when someone rapped on the door a little after eleven.

Tommy was late, which meant that she would have to really push in order to have the proofing ready for the afternoon pickup. Even so, she felt no real annoyance, only a mild relief when the boy finally arrived.

Her smile quickly fled, however, when she opened the door to find not the youthful messenger from the *Vanguard* but the *owner* of the *Vanguard*.

"Jack!"

He stood there, tall and dark, filling the doorway like a lean black bear. Under one arm was tucked the day's copy; in his free hand, he held a small bouquet of fall flowers.

Samantha stared, her gaze going from his slightly smug smile to the bouquet. Flustered, she couldn't seem to find her voice.

Even now, after months in his employ and despite the odd—and often confusing—sort of friendship that had developed between them, Jack's presence still unnerved her.

To say the least.

His smile widened, as if he found Samantha's discomfiture highly gratifying. "It seems that I'm your messenger boy today," he said smoothly, extending the bouquet. "May I come in, Samantha?"

Samantha stared at the bouquet without making a move to accept it. "Oh—well, actually, I don't know that that would be a good idea."

She thought she had long since passed the time when Jack Kane—or any other man, for that matter—could make her stammer like a schoolgirl, but even as she struggled to regain her composure, Samantha felt her mind go to mush.

She reminded herself that she was *not* a schoolgirl—indeed would soon be turning thirty—and she could think of nothing less becoming to a mature woman than to suddenly start behaving like a mindless chit.

She supposed she *should* invite him in; despite the difficulties of their relationship, he was still her employer, after all. But if her landladies downstairs, the Misses Washington, should learn that she had allowed a man inside her apartment, even for only a moment, they would be scandalized.

She suddenly realized that Jack was watching her with a decidedly amused expression, as if he knew exactly what she was thinking.

"No doubt you're anxious about offending your delightful landladies," he said. "You needn't worry. I believe the dears actually find me rather charming."

Samantha stared at him.

"Oh, I met Miss Rena and her sister on the way in," he said, as if in answer to her unspoken question. "They were bringing in the flowers from the stoop—they seem to think we'll have frost tonight, you see—and I offered to help. I explained that my call is rather urgent and strictly business, and they were most understanding. And very helpful," he added, still smiling cheerfully.

"So, you see, Samantha, it's perfectly all right to have me in. We'll leave the door open, of course, but I assure you that both Miss Rena and Miss Lily have the utmost confidence in me. Apparently, I look every bit the gentleman to them."

He looked, Samantha thought worriedly, like a *pirate*. A pirate in a perfectly tailored suit, as it were, and with a white posy in his lapel.

But a pirate all the same.

Again Jack extended the bouquet, and this time Samantha practically yanked it out of his hand. "All right, then, I suppose you might as well come in."

"Why, thank you, Samantha," he said, making a quick little bow and then breezing by her. "I was hoping you'd ask."

2
A SMALL HINT OF REBELLION

Something there is in the virtuous heart
that rebels if a thing is unfair.

ANONYMOUS

❧

Inside, Samantha put the flowers in water, at the same time groping for something to say that didn't sound altogether banal. Jack had followed her to the kitchen and, after placing the copy on the table, stood leaning casually against the sink as he watched her arrange the bouquet.

When he reached across her to inspect a wan-looking blossom that looked out of place among the others, Samantha almost stumbled in her haste to step away. He lifted an eyebrow but said nothing as he moved to reposition the drooping flower with great care, gently plucking a leaf or two before bracing it between a couple of larger, healthier blooms.

He straightened and turned back to her with a smile. Only then did Samantha manage to drag her gaze away from his hands.

"The copy is late, you know," she said abruptly, cringing at the waspish tone of her own voice. "I'll have all I can do to be finished by two."

"Well then, why don't I just stay and help?" he said, making a move as if to shrug out of his suit coat.

"No!" Samantha blurted out, more sharply than she'd intended.

Again one dark brow lifted as he hesitated, half out of his coat.

"I mean—that's not necessary." Her words spilled out in a rush as she fumbled to conceal her discomfort. "It won't be all *that* late. Besides," she hurried to add, "I wouldn't want you to get news ink on your suit."

He studied her, his eyes glinting with something Samantha couldn't read. "If a little news ink bothered me, I'd be in a terrible fix, now wouldn't I? May I?" he said, not waiting for her reply before slipping the rest of the way out of his jacket and rolling up his shirtsleeves. "Do stop fretting yourself, Samantha. I'll just give you a hand with this and take it back to the office with me."

With that, he sat down at the table and started in on the top sheet of copy. "Besides, there are some things I've been wanting to discuss with you. That's the real reason I'm here, as it happens."

Samantha would have raised yet another objection, but the words lodged in her throat. It occurred to her that her small, cozy kitchen suddenly looked even smaller—cramped and almost suffocating—with Jack's long legs stretched out under her table and his dark head bent over the work at hand.

They worked without speaking for several minutes before Samantha broke the uncomfortable silence. "I should have thanked you for the flowers. They're very nice."

"You're welcome," he said, not looking up. After a brief pause, he said, "One of the reasons I wanted to see you was to ask a favor, if I might."

Samantha glanced up from the copy.

"I'm a bit concerned about Cavan's sister and the Madden tykes. You recall that they're due to arrive any day now?"

Samantha did remember, of course. As a part of her various job responsibilities, she had begun weeks ago to make the necessary arrangements for Terese Sheridan and the two orphaned children who were traveling with her.

Jack's newspaper, the *Vanguard,* had begun to publish a series of articles about the Irish immigrants arriving in the States in ever increasing numbers. Written by Cavan Sheridan, each article focused on a specific individual or family and the circumstances that had precipitated their immigration, as well as the difficulties that might await them when they arrived in America. Already the series had attracted considerable interest around the city, even throughout the state. As a result the *Vanguard's* subscriber list had begun to expand—and Cavan Sheridan had won his first byline.

Samantha had been only too pleased to be involved in this unprecedented project, a project that had actually been Cavan Sheridan's idea. In addition to the stories themselves, the paper had committed to financing the featured immigrants' passage and assisting in their resettlement. Samantha's duties included meeting the new arrivals at the harbor and then helping them with their living arrangements and employment possibilities while monitoring their situations as they adapted to their new country.

The fact that one of the first arrivals would be none other than Cavan's sister—his only surviving family member, in fact—merely added to the importance of the project for Samantha. Cavan was her "star" student from the night classes she taught among the immigrant settlements. From the beginning he had stood out as particularly gifted. He had a fine, quick mind and an aptitude for painting pictures with words that was unrivaled even by many of the city's more experienced newsmen.

The young Irish immigrant had actually been responsible for Samantha's position with the *Vanguard.* Initially employed as Jack's driver and stableman, Cavan had brought the proofreading job at the newspaper to Samantha's attention, at the same time bringing *Samantha* to Jack Kane's attention.

At first Samantha had resisted Jack's insistent efforts to hire her, largely because of his notorious reputation. By now, however, she had come to count her job with the *Vanguard* as one of the best things that could have happened to her. She enjoyed the proofreading, enjoyed even more the editorial assignments Jack had lately begun to send her way. And the additional responsibilities she would soon assume with the immigrant resettlement project only added to the job's appeal. As far as Samantha was concerned, she couldn't have custom designed a job with more advantages or one with fewer drawbacks.

Except, perhaps, for the man who had given her the job.

She glanced over at Jack, saw him watching her, and realized he was waiting for some sort sort of response from her.

"I'm sorry?"

"I asked if you'd mind keeping tabs on the harbor while I'm gone."

"Gone?"

He looked at her. "I'm leaving for Philadelphia Wednesday, remember?"

There was no accounting for the sudden but undeniable twist of disappointment that coiled through Samantha. He would be away for only a few days, after all, but for some reason she felt an almost painful emptiness at the prospect.

"I'd forgotten. Your meeting with Mr. Poe."

He nodded. "I'm to meet with him on Thursday and, depending on how that goes, possibly once or twice more before I come back." He paused, watching her. "I don't suppose you've changed your mind about coming with me."

Samantha felt the heat rise to her face. "You know I can't possibly do that. Please don't mention it again."

"It would be entirely proper," he said reasonably. "You'd be traveling as my assistant."

Samantha had the feeling he was deliberately baiting her. She was appalled by the fact that for an instant she had actually caught herself wishing she *could* go with him.

"I hardly think it would be seen as proper," she said, forcing herself not to rise to his bait. "And I'd rather not discuss it any further. Now, shouldn't we try to finish the proofing if you want it for today's edition?"

He feigned a sigh of disappointment before turning his attention back to the copy. "You concern yourself too much with what people think, Samantha."

She made no reply. Minutes later, she changed the subject to safer ground. "You've still had no word from the ship, I take it?" Samantha asked after a moment.

He shook his head. "The Sheridan girl is to send a message by one of the runners from the harbor as soon as they pass quarantine. So far there's been nothing. I assume the ship hasn't anchored yet, but I'd like to know for certain. You'll recall that Brady said the two children weren't in the best of health."

Samantha nodded. Shona and Tully Madden were two Irish orphans whom Jack's brother had submitted for sponsorship, at the same time arranging for Terese Sheridan to oversee their welfare during the crossing. Apparently, both of the children had been in rather poor health when the arrangements were made.

"Wouldn't there have been something in the arrival notices if the ship had put in?" she asked Jack.

He made a dismissing motion with one hand. "You can't count on those. They miss more than they list. It's occurred to me that they might end up in quarantine once they arrive. We'll need to keep check on them."

Samantha looked at him. "Oh, Jack, I'd hate to think of those children being held at Tompkinsville. It's such an awful place."

"'Tis that," he said, making a sour face. "In any event, you'll stay in touch with the harbor while I'm away?"

"Yes, of course. But shouldn't you ask Cavan instead of me? He's already been haunting the docks for days. I'm sure he's desperate to see his sister after all these years."

"He is," Jack agreed, "but he won't be back from Albany until the weekend or possibly Monday. Bill Worth is down with the grippe, so I sent Sheridan up to the governor's mansion in his place to find out what shenanigans Weed's been up to this month."

Samantha saw his expression turn even darker. Jack's dislike for Thurlow Weed and his Whig politics was no secret.

"I don't mean for you to go to the harbor alone, mind," he went on. "Until Sheridan gets back, one of the lads from the paper will drive you."

Samantha didn't argue. She had no desire to frequent New York Harbor by herself.

They finished the proofing within the next few minutes, and Jack leaned back in the chair, stretching his arms out in front of him. "You see—right on schedule," he said, watching Samantha. "Have supper with me tonight?"

Samantha glanced away for fear he would see how much she wanted to accept.

"Please," he put in quickly.

"Jack—"

"I missed lunch. We'll have an early meal. We can go to the club, if you like."

Over the past two months, Samantha had had supper with Jack on three or four occasions, each time at the Portico Club, an unpretentious midtown eating establishment, off the beaten track. No one there was likely to recognize either Jack or Samantha.

Samantha knew it was in deference to her reputation that Jack always suggested the club when he asked her to supper. While she was touched by his caution on her account, she resisted the idea that her reputation could be irrevocably damaged simply by dining out with a man society happened to deem "unacceptable."

It was actually Jack who continued to "protect" her from scandal. Left to herself,

Samantha would probably have ignored the gossipmongers and gone wherever she pleased with *whomever* she pleased. But he insisted that for her sake they be discreet, and she supposed his way was best. At least this way her mother—who was as sensitive to society's approval as Samantha was *not*—needn't be subjected to the sort of notoriety that seemed to hang over Jack like an ugly thundercloud.

For a long time now, Samantha had questioned the rumors that so relentlessly dogged Jack. There was no denying that he had a "past," as her mother was fond of pointing out. Nor did he seem inclined to conceal that fact from Samantha. He had actually made reference to his earlier gambling habit once or twice, for example, even admitting that he'd won most of the purchase price for the *Vanguard* in a marathon round of blackjack.

But at the same time, Samantha believed him when he said he no longer indulged in the vice. "I gambled because I was set on making a lot of money fast," he had once told her matter-of-factly. "When I discovered I had a streak of luck about me, I went for higher stakes. But once I had what I wanted, I quit. It was never that much fun, in truth. It was simply—" he shrugged—"a means to an end."

As for the rumors that he was a notorious womanizer, Samantha had no way of knowing how factual they were. She *did* know it was all but impossible to walk into a room with him without being aware of his effect on women. Even the gazes of the more "respectable" matrons invariably followed him. Jack was a startlingly tall man, uncommonly handsome, with a definite air of power—perhaps even a certain ruthlessness—that seemed to make the very air in the room crackle with excitement.

His conduct toward Samantha was unfailingly irreproachable. Oh, he never entirely lost the roguish air that clung to him like a playful shadow. And his manners might be slightly rough edged, his speech blunt and even harsh at times. But he was obviously determined to be the soul of propriety with her, and most of the time he carried it off quite well; indeed, his mien with her often bordered on old-world *courtly*. On occasion Samantha found herself hard-pressed to conceal a touch of amusement at the effort she speculated this sterling behavior might require of him.

Mostly, however, she was moved by his attempts to gain her approval, even though she suspected that if she were to press, he would cheerfully admit to being the reprobate he was rumored to be. He almost seemed to take an unaccountably grim sense of satisfaction in not contradicting his questionable reputation. In fact, it was this that kept Samantha from dismissing the gossip about him out of hand. In spite of the way he conducted himself with her—and in spite of an undeniable attraction for her—she had to admit that Jack could conceivably be the ruthless, cold-blooded infidel the rumors held him to be.

Her mother obviously believed, even seemed to relish, the worst of the stories, haranguing Samantha at every opportunity with comments to the effect that "that awful man you work for" was nothing more than an Irish thug whose success had been ill gotten and whose reputation was an absolute disgrace.

What if her mother was right?

Well, what if she was?

Whatever Jack might have been in the past, with *her* he had never been anything but a gentleman—kind, courteous, perhaps even overly protective of her. In most of the other areas of her life, Samantha had overcome the tendency to perform according to her mother's convention-bound expectations. Why shouldn't that hard-won independence extend to Jack?

Abruptly she turned to him. "I'd like very much to have supper with you tonight," she said before she could change her mind. "And why don't we try somewhere besides the club for a change?"

He stared at her for a long moment. Then he smiled, his dark eyes holding her captive as he caught her completely off guard with his reply.

"What I would really like, Samantha, is to have dinner with you at my home. I confess that for a long time now I've fancied the idea of seeing you at my table. I don't suppose you'd consider it?" He paused only an instant before adding, "It would be altogether proper, I promise you. My housekeeper would be there, as well as Mrs. Flynn, my cook. We wouldn't be alone. Not at all."

Samantha studied him, already questioning her impulsiveness yet intrigued in spite of the clamoring of her better judgment. This was the last thing she'd expected. And yet he suddenly looked so eager, so hopeful, she found herself loath to refuse.

"I...that hardly seems fair to your cook, to invite a guest on such short notice."

Jack waved off her concern. "Mrs. Flynn routinely cooks for half a dozen or more every time she fires up the stove. She cannot seem to help herself. I do my part, of course, to digest her bounty, but even a greedy Irishman has his fill sooner or later." He grinned at her. "I can't think of anything that would please her more than knowing she has a legitimate license to overdo. Besides—don't you ever get tired of dining alone? I know *I* do."

When Samantha continued to hesitate, he glanced around the kitchen, saying, "I've been in *your* home now, and I should like it very much if you would visit mine." He leaned forward, reaching across the table to lightly touch her hand. "You would honor me, Samantha."

There it was again, that unexpected, almost quaint touch of humility that seemed so out of keeping with the air of utter confidence he usually exhibited,

Apparently, this was her day for acting on impulse.

"I...all right. But I'd have to make it an early evening, you understand."

The light that suffused his features somehow seemed to make years drop away. He was suddenly animated, almost boyish, as if he had just been given a delightful gift.

"Aye...yes, well...that's grand then! I'll send Ransom around for you close on seven; how would that be? And of course he'll drive you home whenever you say."

Samantha smiled at his pleasure, at the same time trying hard to suppress her own.

3

SHADOWS OF THE HEART

I sat with one I love last night.

GEORGE DARLEY

Jack's house—if such a sprawling old mansion could actually be reduced to the word *house*—was both a surprise and a study in contrasts.

From the first moment she entered, Samantha was both intrigued and somewhat confused by the splashes of ostentation that she would have thought foreign to Jack's nature. Her initial sense of the house was a disturbingly oppressive feeling of *gloom*. Most of the furnishings were dark and massive and heavily ornate. Yet there were also touches of restrained elegance as well—simple, but classic and in excellent taste. She found herself wondering which extreme was more in keeping with Jack's character.

The enormous entrance hall was almost garish with its crimson silk damasks and gilded wall hangings. But the massive mahogany staircase was absolutely splendid, solid and unyielding yet exquisitely carved with a certain grace in its rise all the way to the third story. Its overpowering presence and stately strength somehow reminded Samantha of Jack.

The dining room was immense, its table nearly spanning the length of the entire room, flanked by tall chairs, a large sideboard, and a china cabinet that appeared more in keeping with a medieval castle than a house on Thirty-Fourth Street. The room was just barely saved from vulgarity by the collection of lustrous silver, delicate china, and crystal that graced the table, all in unembellished, tasteful patterns.

Being in Jack's home, eating at his table, fueled Samantha's curiosity about the deceased Martha Kane. What had she been like, Jack's tragic wife who, according to Amelia Carver, had died childless while still in her twenties, leaving Jack in bitter despair at her passing? Had she chosen the more tasteful objects in this cold, dreary room? Had it been Martha who embroidered the scrolled *K* on the white dinner napkins?

Did Jack still miss her, still grieve for her?

Samantha dismissed the questions by reminding herself that the answers were actually none of her business. Yet she couldn't quite shake the image of Jack sitting here, dark and silent and alone in this enormous, echoing room with only his memories to keep him company. The thought wrenched her heart with such unexpected force that she actually flinched, her fork clattering against the plate.

She looked up to find him watching her. "Ugly, isn't it?" he said, taking in the room with a quick sweep of his hand.

Flustered, Samantha glanced away. "No, no, of course not. You have a very impressive home."

"It's grotesque," he said, seemingly indifferent to the fact as he took a bite of cheese soufflé. "Most of this stuff was already here when I bought it. I always meant to make changes but never seemed to find the time. I often think about selling the place, moving into something a bit less—formidable." He flashed a quick smile. "I must say you brighten up the old horror with your presence."

Unnerved by the warmth of his gaze, Samantha again looked away from him, feigning interest in her dessert. "You didn't exaggerate about Mrs. Flynn's cooking. Everything was delicious."

The truth was that she had scarcely tasted the food at all. She had eaten most of the roast pork and baked apples without any real appreciation of flavor.

"I'll tell her you were pleased," Jack said dryly, as if he knew very well how little attention she had actually given to the meal.

Silence hung between them for a moment, until the housekeeper, Mrs. O'Meara—"Addy," Jack called her—came back into the room, one of several appearances she'd made throughout the evening.

"Didn't I tell you we'd be well chaperoned?" Jack said under his breath.

Samantha had to smile. The housekeeper's intention *had* been almost amusingly obvious as she continued to come and go, even after the final course of the meal had been served.

"Mrs. O'Meara would seem to take very good care of you," Samantha said after the woman had again left the room.

"Ha. 'Tis *you* the outrageous woman is looking after, you can be sure."

Samantha studied him. "You don't fool me, you know. The two of you badger each other terribly, but I can tell that you're actually quite fond of her."

His dark brows drew together in a mockery of a frown. "Yes, well, you so much as breathe a word of that to our Mrs. O'Meara, and my life will be pure misery from this night on."

"It strikes me that she already knows her position is safe."

He shook his head. "I don't know what I'd do without her, and that's the truth. But she'd be at an utter loss if I didn't give her a bit of grief on a daily basis."

Samantha laughed at his wry expression. "How long has she been with you?"

"Forever," he cracked, then added, "A long time, as it happens. In between ruling my life and running my household, she also helped to mother my brother and sister."

Samantha remembered that Jack's sister, Rose, was a nun in New Jersey, while his younger brother, Brady, was still in Ireland, working on the immigrant series.

"How long does your brother plan to stay in Ireland?" she asked him now.

He made a sour face. "I'm beginning to think he means to take up permanent residence there."

"And you don't like the idea?"

"Troublesome rascal that he is, I find that I miss him. And Rose as well. But there was no dissuading either of them once they set their heads to what they wanted."

Samantha saw something in his eyes at that instant—a flash of regret or even sadness—that tugged at her heart. Not for the first time, she wondered how much Jack actually enjoyed the wealth he'd accumulated, the power and influence he wielded.

What had motivated him to attain such heights? She knew he had emigrated from Ireland when he was still a boy. The rumors about his past claimed that he had launched his publishing empire by sweeping floors at a small print shop. Now he owned one of the country's most powerful newspapers, as well as two large, prestigious publishing houses. Yet he couldn't be much past forty, if that. His astonishing level of success had to have come in a relatively brief span of years. Either he had been incredibly fortunate in his dealings—or incredibly driven.

How much of his ambition had been for himself, she wondered, as opposed to a desire to provide a better life for his younger siblings?

Even the harshest of Jack's critics were inclined to allow him a certain grudging admiration. He had, after all, achieved a stunning level of success with nothing more than his wits, a cavalier kind of courage, a great deal of hard work, and—according to Jack himself—a considerable amount of good luck. Yet in spite of his prosperity and power, Samantha had never sensed any measurable degree of happiness or contentment in him. To the contrary, she was beginning to believe that his success had gained him little more than a self-imposed loneliness and a deep, barely concealed anger.

Almost from the first, she had sensed the quiet rage in him, the darkness that seemed to lie never far from the surface of his emotions—a darkness that could be explosive, Samantha suspected, even frightening. In fact, she couldn't quite shake the feeling that there was a side to Jack's nature that, once unleashed, could easily turn ugly. While she had never actually seen him lose control, had never been the recipient of his legendary temper or scathing sarcasm, she had heard more than she cared to about the verbal assaults that reputedly could be venomous, if not downright cruel.

Yet she found it difficult—nearly impossible—to reconcile the rumors with the man who had been so exceedingly kind to her. In spite of the undeniable attraction between them—and the tension resulting from that attraction—they had managed to become friends. Good friends, as it happened, and at a time when Samantha *needed* a friend. Jack's kindness to her, his consideration and encouragement, had been like a balm to her sorely wounded spirit.

Because of this, perhaps she tended to dismiss the sordid stories about him too easily. But she simply did not care as much about his past, about the man he might have been, as she did about the man he was with *her*—the man who had befriended her and who seemed so quick and willing to tolerate in her even what he could not hope to understand.

How, then, could she do less for him?

Besides, who knew better than she about the darkness of the human soul, the shadows lurking in the secret places too deeply hidden for the world to ever see? And who was she to judge Jack for what he was *rumored* to be when she had learned firsthand how appearances could deceive, how easily darkness could conceal itself behind a mask of goodness and light?

❦

He still could scarcely believe she was here. When he'd extended the invitation he had literally held his breath, anticipating her refusal. Then, when she astonished him by accepting, there was no describing the wave of unreasonable pleasure that had washed over him.

Watching her now, Jack was acutely mindful of the conflicting emotions Samantha set off in him. Her very presence seemed to turn him from a badly jaded forty-year-old man into an awkward, inarticulate schoolboy. Surely the pleasure he took from simply being with her bordered on foolishness, if not utter lunacy. Why, every time he was with the woman, he had to fight back a grin as idiotic as that of the village simpleton!

But even as he struggled to control this annoying streak of boyish eagerness, he was almost painfully aware of the same strange, uneasy sensation that invariably gripped him when he was with her: the feeling that by simply coming too close to her, he might somehow *tarnish* her.

She had a light about her, Samantha did, a soft light of loveliness and goodness of which she seemed entirely unaware. It was a quality that both endeared her to Jack and at the same time served to restrain him from acting on his growing desire for her.

With Samantha he felt as if he had been somehow openly tarred with every mean, reprehensible thing he had ever done, for her and all the world to see. At times his very skin seemed to crawl with the awareness of the dark that lurked within him, the mire that had attached itself to him, and he wished he could physically peel away the layers of contamination so that he might be more acceptable, more decent, more *worthy* of her.

❦

They moved to the study for coffee, and here Samantha found yet another marked contrast in decor. Immediately she was more comfortable with her surroundings, for there could be no mistaking Jack's influence. Spacious, but not so cavernous and oppressive as the dining room, the study seemed more a retreat. It was a peaceful room, she decided: restful, like a kind of sanctuary, with its green damask-covered walls, its fine, sturdy furniture of rosewood and leather, and the aged, honey-rich paneling.

Every wall but one held bookshelves crammed with volumes that appeared well used. On the single plain wall hung an assortment of opera and theater posters, many of which, Samantha noticed, had been signed by some of the leading performers of the day.

They sat by the fire, at opposite ends of a somewhat worn sofa, a small table in front of them. Jack watched her as he drained the last of his coffee. "You still haven't told me whether you think I should publish Poe," he said, setting his cup on the table.

Samantha gave him a quizzical look. "I'm hardly qualified to offer an opinion on whom you publish, Jack."

"In truth, Samantha, you're probably more qualified than I on that very subject. Now, tell me what you think. I've come to trust your instincts."

Samantha took a sip of her tea, trying to ignore the flush of pleasure his words stirred in her. "I thought you'd already decided to publish Mr. Poe's latest work."

He shrugged. "I may try to strike a deal with him. Once I'm certain I want to." He traced the line of his mustache for a moment. "I'd not be the one to argue Poe's genius. But genius or not, I find his work almost too—" He stopped, as if the word he wanted eluded him.

"Dark?" Samantha supplied.

He looked at her, nodding slowly. "Aye, there's that. I'd take him for a very sad fellow, even troubled. Have you read him?"

Samantha had, and although she appreciated Poe's formidable skill, for the most part she found his work too dreary for her liking. "I've read his poetry, mostly. And a few pieces of his shorter fiction."

"What about the novella?"

Samantha set her cup on the table, shaking her head. "I think even Mr. Poe must not have taken that particular effort too seriously. Frankly, I thought it a bit silly."

"Not one of his better efforts," Jack agreed. "He has a rather odd background, doesn't he? For a writer, that is. He was actually at West Point for a time, did you know that?"

"He was court-martialed at the Academy," Samantha pointed out. "And it's rumored that he brought it on himself deliberately, to spite his godfather, or some such foolishness."

Jack shot her a look of surprise. "How on earth would you know that?"

Samantha shrugged. "Mr. Poe's life hasn't exactly been a closed book."

Jack slanted a look of pained disbelief at her unintentional pun. "That was awful,

Samantha. So, then, what else do you know about him? Apart from the scandalous stuff, I mean. I've already heard that business about his marrying his thirteen-year-old cousin."

"Actually, she was almost fourteen, I believe." Samantha hesitated, reluctant to further the gossip she'd heard, yet understanding Jack's need to know as much as possible about a prospective writer. "It's said that he drinks. To excess, though for Poe that might not be all that much. Apparently, he's of a rather delicate constitution."

Jack turned, settling himself against the arm of the sofa as she went on.

"It's not that he drinks all the time," she explained. "In fact, he seems to have long periods of sobriety."

"Let us hope that this is one of them," Jack said dryly, crossing his arms over his chest.

Because of Jack's own past, Samantha was hesitant to mention the next piece of information. She chose her words carefully. "I've heard that he also gambles rather a lot. But either he's not very good at it or not very lucky." She paused. "So I've been told."

Jack leaned back as if he were starting to enjoy this. "Samantha, you never cease to amaze me. Where do you get your information, if you don't mind my asking?"

"My mother," Samantha said matter-of-factly. "She's a veritable treasure trove of gossip."

Jack grinned. "Perhaps I should offer *her* a job."

Samantha couldn't help but smile at the thought. The very mention of Jack's name was enough to strain Angela Pilcher's strait-laces to the breaking point. Her mother tended to relegate Jack to the same level as foreign sailors and opium eaters.

He poured himself another cup of coffee from the pot on the table. "Incidentally, I haven't forgotten the appointment with your Mrs. Shanahan and Avery Foxworth. We'll get that taken care of after I return." He paused. "I suppose you're still set on being there?"

Samantha nodded. "I think Maura will be more at ease if I'm with her."

"I expect you're right. But I'm still not sure why you want me there."

Samantha hesitated, then said carefully, "I hope you don't mind too much. But I suppose in this case it's *I* who would be more comfortable if *you* were there. I don't know Mr. Foxworth at all."

Jack arched an eyebrow. "Really? I was under the impression the two of you had met. He knows who *you* are."

"I can't think how," Samantha said, frowning.

Jack gave a thin smile. "Well, you may have forgotten, but Foxworth hasn't. In any event, he thinks you're exceptionally attractive. I gave him no argument on that score, of course."

Flustered, Samantha avoided his gaze while trying to think of a way to return the subject to Maura Shanahan. Back in the summer, the woman had shot and killed her husband, who had apparently been beating her and threatening the children.

Samantha had good reason to believe that Mrs. Shanahan had acted in self-defense and out of fear for her children.

One of those children was a little newsboy for whom Jack seemed to hold a particular fondness. To Samantha's surprise, he had not only supported her interest in the matter but had gone so far as to retain his own attorney for the court case.

"I know it's presumptuous of me," she said, "asking you to take time out for something like this, especially as busy as you are. Maura Shanahan is just another immigrant in trouble, after all—a common enough occurrence. But with the trial about to begin—"

"Samantha—" Jack leaned toward her, his eyes glinting with faint amusement. "You needn't apologize. I don't mind in the least. You seem to forget that I'm just 'another immigrant' myself." He moved a little closer to her and took her hand. "Besides, if it's important to you, it's important to me."

Samantha felt the heat rush to her face. "I don't want you to do this for *me*, Jack!" she blurted out, keenly aware of the warm strength of his hand covering hers.

He pulled back a little but didn't release her hand. "And don't I know that well enough?" he said with a long sigh. "It would be a terrible thing entirely if you should somehow feel beholden to me."

"It's not that—"

"It's exactly that," he said bluntly. "And we both know it. Our...'friendship'—" Samantha winced at the sardonic edge he gave the word—"would never survive your feeling obligated to me. Nor would I want you to feel put upon. But, woman, you do make it devilishly difficult sometimes for me to supply a bit of help."

"I'm sorry, Jack," Samantha said, meaning it. "I suppose I've been so intent on making my own way that I'm not always as gracious as I ought to be when a friend does me a favor."

He was watching her closely, an expression on his face that she couldn't quite identify. Whatever it was, it made her uncomfortable.

With his hand still holding hers securely, he closed the remaining distance between them on the sofa. "The thing is, Samantha," he said, his voice much lower than before, "I don't want to be your friend. I want to be your husband."

Samantha stared at him in total shock. The firelight flickered, dappling his face and softening his strong features. He was smiling a little, clearly aware that he had stunned her, yet obviously expecting a reply.

Samantha forced herself to meet his gaze. "You're joking, of course."

He gave a slight shake of his head and lifted his eyebrows. "You know I'm not, Samantha. I think you also know I'm in love with you and have been for some time."

Samantha glanced away. "Then I think you're just trying to rattle me," she said, trying hard for a lighter tone. "You do seem to enjoy doing that, I've noticed."

"Samantha, look at me," he said, increasing the pressure on her hand.

She heard the slight hoarseness in his voice. Somehow she managed to drag her gaze back to him, and when she did, she saw that he was not teasing her at all, that he was deadly serious. Her heart slammed against her ribs, and she couldn't seem to get her breath. "Jack, I don't know what you want me to say."

She was aware that she had edged as far away from him as she could and was now pressing against the arm of the sofa.

"I should think that would be fairly obvious. What I want you to say is *yes.*" The searching look he gave her seemed to arrow right to her soul. "Samantha," he said softly, "don't draw away from me. Not this time."

His grip on her hand tightened even more, and slowly, with great gentleness, he began to pull her toward him, bringing her as close...no, closer...than she had ever been to him before. She could see the unyielding line of his jaw, the faint silvering of his black hair, and the reflection of the fire in his dark eyes. She could actually feel his breath on her face, tinged with the faint scent of clove she had come to associate with him when he hadn't been smoking one of his cigars.

She thought that he would surely kiss her, but other than holding her hand, he made no move to touch her. He simply sat there, his eyes going over her face, then capturing and holding her gaze. "Marry me, Samantha."

A surge of panic shot through Samantha, but only for an instant. As she watched him, she could see nothing in his eyes to be afraid of. To the contrary, she sensed that the only threat to her at this moment was her melting heart.

"Jack, please don't do this—"

"Look at me and tell me you feel nothing for me but friendship."

It took everything she had to look away from him. In the end it was the intensity of his gaze, the sheer, almost overwhelming force of the look in his eyes—the *power* that virtually hummed from him—that enabled her to resist him. Jack was a man used to getting anything he wanted, she reminded herself as she tugged her hand free of his grasp. It wouldn't do to let him believe, even for a minute, that just because he wanted *her,* anything could come of it.

"Jack—*please!*"

The look of surprise that now went over his face only confirmed that he had not really expected her to resist him.

It occurred to Samantha, with some sense of irony, that the very aspects of Jack's personality that most likely enabled him to achieve whatever he fixed his sights on were the very traits that served to turn her away from him. If she wasn't exactly afraid of his strength, the force of his will, his driving self-confidence that made him believe he could bend any situation—perhaps any *person*—to his control, she was at least intimidated enough by it all to back away from him.

Mustering as much composure as she could, she stood. "I—should be going. It's after nine."

Jack studied her for a long, tense moment, then, almost as if he had read her thoughts, gave a reluctant nod. "If you must," he said, slowly getting to his feet.

"Don't take offense, Samantha. Please? I simply can't pretend any longer that all I want from you is friendship."

Samantha deliberately kept her gaze averted. "Just promise me we won't speak about this again. It's an impossible situation for me, Jack, it really is."

"Nothing," he said, his voice the low rumble she had come to recognize as an indication of his resolve, "is impossible, Samantha. Nothing." He stopped, and with one finger tipped her chin up to make her meet his eyes. "I won't raise the subject again for now. But eventually..." He shrugged, his meaning clear.

At the front door, she waited while he helped her with her coat. "Do you mind if I ride along while Ransom takes you home?"

"I—suppose not," Samantha said, aware of his hands lingering for perhaps a moment too long on her shoulders. "But it's not necessary."

He squeezed her shoulders lightly, then turned to shrug into his topcoat. "But I want to," he said. For a long moment, he stood looking down at her. "Samantha," he finally said, "thank you."

Samantha gave him a questioning look.

"For coming tonight," he explained. "It meant a great deal to me, your trusting me enough to come to my home."

Only then did it strike Samantha that she *did* trust Jack, in spite of all the very real reasons she probably *shouldn't*. Even now, after the discomfiting scene in the study, she found it impossible *not* to trust him, or at least his affection for her.

But at the moment he was standing much too close, and Mrs. O'Meara seemed to have disappeared. Samantha was keenly aware of his dark handsomeness, his almost black eyes searching hers. Her throat tightened, and she took an involuntary step back from him.

Nothing registered in his expression, no sign that he had noticed, other than a slight tightening of his jaw as he turned away from her to open the door. Outside, he took her arm on the way to the carriage, but it was purely a courteous gesture, impersonal and even perfunctory.

Samantha knew that she had hurt him, and for an instant she wanted to touch him, to take his arm and tell him she was sorry. Sorry she couldn't be what he wanted her to be, couldn't give him what he seemed to want from her. She almost wished that she dared tell him that she *did* care for him, perhaps cared too much—and that was why she couldn't possibly be anything more to him than a friend.

Instead, she allowed him to take her to the carriage. They ventured nothing more in the way of conversation than polite small talk for most of the drive home. When he had delivered her safely to her door, he merely gave her that quick little mocking bow that was his way, leaving her with an aching sense of disappointment—and an unaccountable feeling of loss.

❧

Jack would have flatly denied that he was sulking. But the truth was that all the way back to the house, he had to struggle to keep from doing just that. He recognized that part of his dark mood had to do with the fact that he was simply not accustomed to being rejected. The more common scenario had *him* doing the spurning, not the other way around.

But he had been rebuffed all right, and with enough firmness that his pride was still smarting. He had backed off the instant he'd seen her eyes go cold with that familiar closed look of withdrawal. It would have been a fatal mistake to press her, and he'd known it.

But what Samantha most likely did *not* know was that a challenge had never yet sent him packing. To the contrary, a bit of a struggle served merely to raise the stakes, so far as Jack was concerned.

His mood lightened somewhat as he pondered his next move. The first thing was to retrench and consider where he'd miscalculated. Samantha wasn't the type who simply wanted to be coaxed. When she said no, she meant just that. At the same time, he found it difficult to believe he'd been reading her wrong all this time. She was attracted to him, and he knew it; before tonight he would have said it was *more* than attraction.

Perhaps he'd been rash in springing the idea of marriage on her so abruptly, without a proper job of courting beforehand. But hang it all, he had *tried* to court the woman, hadn't he? Samantha didn't make it easy for a man, after all, with that wall she kept so squarely in place most of the time.

Well, and what about that wall? The thing to do was figure a way to break it down, wasn't that so? If his memory served him correctly, he'd tumbled more than a few walls in the past.

Granted, he knew more about breaking down business opponents than a woman's resistance, but it all called for strategy, didn't it? And even if he said so himself, he did know a little something about strategy.

Indeed.

4
WHAT KIND OF WELCOME?

*We came to the city in search of a dream, but the
high gate to hope was closed against us.*

<small>CAVAN SHERIDAN FROM</small> *WAYSIDE NOTES*

❦

STATEN ISLAND, NEW YORK, NOVEMBER

Terese Sheridan had spent her first two weeks in the United States in a quarantine hospital.

Tompkinsville, as it was called, sat on a hill across the river from New York City. Terese and a host of others from the *Providence* were taken there in a skiff and dumped on the beach like bags of rotten potatoes. The grounds were virtually littered with immigrants. Entire families huddled together: men with gaunt faces and angry expressions, women with frightened eyes, and restless, fretful children in raggedy clothing. All manner of languages could be heard, but mostly Irish or else English that was laced with a thick Irish accent. Some seemed to have set up camp as if they anticipated making their homes there.

Their arrival in America had been a nightmare from the beginning. Terese and both of the Madden children, Shona and Tully, caught cold the last week of the crossing. By the time they arrived in the harbor, their coughs sounded severe enough that after a hasty examination, the medical inspectors pronounced the three of them as "possibly consumptive" and ordered them to be quarantined for an indeterminate length of time.

Terese tried to protest, but the officials ignored her claims, refusing to even read the letter from Brady's brother, which clearly stated that she and the Madden children were under the sponsorship of the Kane newspaper—the *Vanguard*.

Subsequently she, Shona, and Tully were pressed back into the line. As they stumbled forward, Terese heard one of the men mutter an aside to his companion.

"Filthy Irish rabble! They wash up on the docks like starving rats with their dirt and disease and expect to be treated like royalty! I'd send them all back to their miserable pigsty island if it were up to me."

Furious, Terese would have turned and flown at him had she not glanced down over herself, then at the children. The sight of their shabby homespun clothes and her own faded dress and worn-out shoes stopped her where she stood. Even the fine emerald cloak Brady had given her back in Ireland was soiled and crushed from weeks aboard ship. She had made an attempt to tidy the children upon their arrival, but Tully's nose continually needed wiping, and there was a rip in the hem of Shona's dress. Shame coursed through her as she realized they looked no better than the rest of the woeful souls traveling with them. No wonder the Americans treated them with such contempt.

Now, close on two weeks later, they were still at Tompkinsville, and fear had begun to seep through her every waking hour. Not long after dawn, she sat on the sagging, lumpy cot that served as a bed, thinking about their situation and trying to figure a way out of it.

The humiliation of being confined to such a dismal place would have been bad enough if she had been ill. But she was *not* ill, and her resentment and frustration at the injustice of their predicament had begun to eat at her like acid.

She couldn't imagine how the people from the *Vanguard* would ever find them. They wouldn't go on trying forever, sure. How long would it take before they simply gave up, thinking them lost or perhaps assuming they had never sailed at all?

And then what would she do? How could she possibly manage on her own, with two frail children to drag along and Brady's child growing bigger in her belly every day?

No, *not* Brady's child, she corrected herself. She must not forget the story Brady had concocted for her, the tale he had already written to his brother. She must remember that so far as Jack Kane was concerned, her condition was the result of having been raped by an unknown attacker. Brady had insisted it was the only way, that his brother was sure to withhold any hope of assistance if he knew the truth.

So she and the Madden children had become a part of a much larger program, initiated by the Kane newspaper. A few carefully chosen individuals and families would be the subjects of an ongoing series published by the paper, and thereby provided the means to start a new life in America.

More than anything else under heaven, Terese wanted the opportunity for that new life, and so she would keep the bargain with Brady. She would stick to their story, no matter what.

Aye, well, little matter about the story if there was nary a one to hear it!

She had to find a way out of this place and get back to the harbor. She *must!* If need be, she would even take the children into the city in search of Jack Kane and his newspaper. But to stay here seemed an almost certain end to her plans—if not certain *death!*

She glanced at the youngsters who lay dozing on the next cot. The girl, Shona, was listless and wooden, almost as if she took no notice at all of her surroundings. But it was the boy who concerned Terese even more. His fever seemed never to abate. By now it was raging almost out of control, and his cough was so deep and hard it pained her to hear it.

This place—this *hospital*—was in truth little better than a prison. They were packed in among hundreds of other immigrants, many of whom seemed desperately ill. In fact, Terese lived in dread that she and the children would contract some sort of terrible disease from the other poor wretches before they could make their escape.

Just yesterday she had heard that there was typhus among them. In cold terror, she had squeezed a place for herself and the children in a corner across the room, but there was no real protection in such cramped quarters.

She had begun the voyage with no end of resentment at being saddled with the responsibility of two orphaned children, and strangers to her at that. At some point during the crossing, however, she had actually begun to feel a certain fondness for her young charges. The girl, Shona, was a sad little thing whose eyes were already old with untold sorrows. But her brother, Tully, was different. Fragile as he was and crippled from a severe case of frostbite, the small boy was invariably cheerful and tried to boost his older sister's spirits at every opportunity.

Her growing affection for the children only made their present circumstances that much more difficult. If she could have managed to remain indifferent to them, perhaps she might have been able to break free of this accursed place and strike out on her own. As it was, she felt trapped and frightened not only for herself, but for the two young ones as well.

At times she allowed herself the hope that surely someone from the newspaper would be searching for them by now and would show up any day to take them out of here. On the heels of this thought, however, came the stark reminder that a man as rich and important as Jack Kane would not likely go to much trouble for a trio of raggedy strangers.

Terese turned on her side, away from the children, her mind still groping for a solution to their plight. Her condition could no longer be concealed. Although she was still lean everywhere else, her swollen midsection blazoned the fact that she was with child. She felt awkward and extremely vulnerable.

And ugly.

In frustration, she ran a hand through her hair—what was left of it. She had been forced to submit to having her hair cropped upon their arrival at the quarantine center. To rid her of lice, the officials claimed.

Terese had protested, had even tried to break free and run once she learned their intention, fiercely protesting that she did not have lice. They had ignored her entirely, dragging her back to the chair and threatening her into submission.

"*All* the Irish have lice," the fish-eyed matron had sneered, giving Terese's hair such a vicious yank that she cried out. "Bugs breed in your filth. Now sit down and hush your impudence, or I'll have you *tied* down. You're in America now, and if you want to stay here, you'll obey the rules. You can be sent back, you know."

In the end, Terese had had no choice but to sit and be sheared like a sheep. Later that night she wept for the first time since leaving Ireland. While not exactly vain about her hair, she had not cut it for years, and it had grown long and thick with a heavy natural curl.

It would grow back, she reminded herself, dropping her hand away from her head. She wouldn't look like a poorly thatched roof forever.

But Terese could not forget the way she had felt, watching them lop off her hair and then sweep it up into a dustpan like a pile of dead leaves. It had been not only her hair that had been lost to her that day. They had taken something else from her, something that went much deeper than what Brady had often called her "shining glory."

Aye, her hair would eventually grow back, but in her heart of hearts, Terese could not help but wonder how long it would take to recover her self-respect.

5

A MEETING IN THE MARKETPLACE

A vulture preys upon our heart; Christ, have mercy!

RICHARD D'ALTON WILLIAMS

THE CLADDAGH, CO. GALWAY, WESTERN IRELAND

Roweena caught her breath at the sight of Brady Kane near the far end of the quay. He seemed intent on something at one of the other food stalls, and her first inclination was to gather her baskets and flee the marketplace before he saw her. But she needed to sell more of her brack and breads if she was going to take Evie to the auction later, as she'd promised. So instead of leaving, she simply turned her back, hoping Brady wouldn't notice her in the crowd.

It was a mild morning for November. The fog was already clearing, and the sun showed signs of breaking through the clouds soon. Roweena's spirits had been high until now. At the sight of Brady Kane, however, confusion and doubt had set in, combined with a niggling sense of guilt that threatened to steal her earlier cheerfulness.

She could all too easily imagine Gabriel's displeasure if he should happen to see her with the "troublesome Yank," as he was wont to call Brady. Although he hadn't strictly forbidden her and Evie to stay away from the American, there was no doubt but what he expected them to do just that.

After Terese Sheridan had left the Claddagh, her shame a secret known only to a few, Gabriel had explained about the affair with Brady Kane that had left Terese with child. Although his features had been set in a careful mask, there had been no mistaking the fact that he was deeply troubled about the situation.

Some thought Gabriel a hard man, but Roweena knew better. While he seldom showed his deepest feelings, he was nevertheless a man of sensitivity and great compassion. Roweena sensed that he carried a heavy burden for Terese Sheridan and for the American artist also, to whom he had opened the door of their home.

Her own heart still ached, not only for the island girl, who must have loved Brady Kane very much to surrender to him in sin—but for Brady as well. She found it difficult to reconcile the man who had behaved so dishonorably toward Terese Sheridan with the same lively, spirited artist who had been nothing but kindness itself to her and wee Evie.

Although Gabriel had made it clear enough that he did not trust the American, at the time Roweena had thought he was simply being overly protective, as was his way where she and Evie were concerned. For herself, she found it difficult to imagine Brady as anything but the fun-loving, good-natured soul he appeared to be: thoroughly American yet possessed of a genuine affection for Ireland—especially the Claddagh—and its people.

Unfortunately, his affection for Terese Sheridan had turned into something else, something deceitful and debasing.

After everything that had happened, Roweena no longer knew exactly how she felt about Brady. There was no mistaking *Gabriel's* feelings, however. Even now, months after the trouble, he remained unrelenting in his attitude, so much so that Roweena knew she would be going against his will simply by speaking with Brady Kane.

This, too, made her very sad, although she had encountered him no more than two or three times in recent months, and each time in the marketplace, surrounded by people. Even so, guilt suffused her after each meeting, for she knew that Gabriel would be sorely disillusioned—perhaps even angry—if he should happen to come upon the two of them together.

She had long sensed Gabriel's disapproval of the American's attentions to her. Yet for her part Roweena could not bring herself to believe that Brady Kane meant her any real mischief. There was something in the way he looked at her that was kind and even careful, something that hinted of a tenderness belying any casual motives or deviousness.

But she sensed there was no convincing Gabriel of this, and she had no heart to go against his wishes if she could help it. So how was she to manage the unavoidable encounter with Brady without incurring Gabriel's disapproval or causing Brady further indignity?

He had seemed genuinely hurt by Gabriel's scathing rejection and subsequent notice to stay away from their home. Apparently, Gabriel had even gone so far as to advise that perhaps Brady should avoid the Claddagh altogether.

The American artist's outrage had been fierce and explosive when he managed to catch Roweena long enough to tell her of Gabriel's pronouncement. "He's not your *father* after all!" he stormed. "Why do you allow him such control over you?"

What she could not make Brady understand was that while Gabriel was not a *father* to her—although in truth he was exactly that to Evie, indeed, the only father the child had ever known—he was much more than a guardian: he was also her closest and dearest friend. It seemed that any attempt she made to defend Gabriel only angered Brady even more.

She drew in a long breath and turned slightly to check his whereabouts. At that same instant, she realized that he had seen her and was now striding briskly in her direction. Quickly, Roweena turned and began to retrieve her things, intent on avoiding him if at all possible.

Something akin to sadness clenched her heart with the reminder that the time was almost certainly coming when she would not have to worry about running into Brady, for he would be going away. He had spoken often enough about traveling the country, making his pictures for his job back in America. He had never had any intention of staying in Galway, after all, and by his own admission, he had already lingered longer than he'd planned. Surely his work would soon be finished, and then he would leave.

But long after Brady Kane had left Galway, she would still be here. She and Evie and Gabriel.

Gabriel…how often had she secretly wished that he would look at her as Brady did, with gentleness and warm affection? But it was not to be. Even now, after all these years, it seemed that to Gabriel she would always be a child—a somewhat helpless child in need of a protector.

He had been faithful and diligent in his self-appointed role as her guardian from the time she *was* a child, and so perhaps it was only natural that in his eyes she had *remained* a child. It was not what she wanted from him—in truth, she didn't know exactly what she *did* want from Gabriel. Perhaps to have him look at her and see her as she really was, rather than as the lost, terrified wee girl he had taken under his care so long ago.

One thing she *did* know: She would give much if he would only lose the closed, guarded expression he invariably wore when he was with her.

At times Roweena almost envied Evie her childishness. With Evie, at least, it seemed that Gabriel could be lighthearted, even playful. But with herself he was all seriousness—kind and even tempered but never carefree, never really open or demonstrative.

Foolishness! How dare she hope for more than she already had! Hadn't Gabriel provided her with a good home, a shelter? Hadn't he taken care of her when she'd been unable to take care of herself? When others had thought her odd or even mad, Gabriel had found value in her. More than likely, he had saved her from certain destruction.

He had been brother and friend to her, as well as her teacher. It had been Gabriel who taught her to read, to figure, even how to speak, despite her inability to hear sounds. And always, he had tried to instill in her a sense of adequacy and self-worth.

Gabriel was a good man, a *godly* man. Of course, he would not conduct himself like other men—he was not *like* other men. He was…larger. Finer. And she had no right, no right at all, to be longing for anything more than he had already given her. Certainly she had no right to cheat him of the respect to which he was entitled. So if he preferred that she not keep company with Brady Kane, then she would not.

But obviously there was to be no escaping the American today. By the time she had gathered her baskets and prepared to leave, Brady had almost reached her, his dark gaze locked upon her as if to demand that she acknowledge him.

⚜

Brady's heartbeat quickened as he increased his stride, determined to make his way to Roweena before she could run from him. He had seen the look in her eyes, the sudden confusion and indecision as she watched him approach. He wouldn't have been surprised had she tossed her baskets aside and bolted down the quay.

Gabriel had really done a job with her. For months now, every time Brady had come upon her, she appeared half afraid of him, as if she thought he might attack her like a mad dog in the streets!

At the back of his mind, the thought occurred to him that it might not be Gabriel's doing that accounted for Roweena's behavior. Maybe the bad business with Terese had left her with so much contempt for him that she simply didn't want anything to do with him.

Roweena was hard to read, to say the least. Even before all the trouble, he had never quite known what to make of her—her excessive shyness, her furtive looks, her unmistakable devotion to Gabriel.

When it came right down to it, Brady didn't know what to make of his *own* behavior where Roweena was concerned.

He had never played the fool for a woman before. There had never been any need. Women liked him, and he'd always found it easy to attract those who caught his interest.

Roweena was attracted to him, too—he was sure of it. In spite of her shyness, those enormous gray eyes of hers held something besides indifference, or he'd be a monkey on the moon.

But getting her to *act* on that attraction was another matter entirely. Between Gabriel's heavy-handed meddling and Roweena's own reserve, he was beginning to despair of ever managing more than a hasty exchange in the middle of a crowd.

For the first time he could remember, Brady found himself wanting more than a casual fling, more than just the excitement of a brief affair. He wanted to *know* this girl, wanted more than a few stolen hours of passion with her. Without understanding why, he found himself wanting to know everything about her: what accounted for the frightened look that sometimes darted across her face, what went on in her silent world, what her dreams were, what made her happy.

She evoked something in him that no other girl had ever tapped. Sometimes he was almost overcome with the desire to draw that fragile form into his arms, to protect her, to take care of her.

He was struck by the nasty reminder that Roweena hardly needed *him* to take care of her, not with the mighty Gabriel breathing over her shoulder with fire in his eye.

But Gabriel wasn't here now. And even at this distance, Brady could see Roweena watching him as if there were no one else around. For one breathless moment, he felt as if he would drown in those eyes, and he knew an insane need to somehow capture her so she couldn't run away from him ever again.

He was closing in on her, looking neither left nor right, when he slammed into an old woman trying to hoist a sack of potatoes onto her back. Brady hit her hard enough that the potatoes went flying, bumping over the cobbles and scattering everywhere.

Impatient, Brady muttered an apology and shoved past the woman more roughly than he might have at another time.

To his surprise, the old biddy caught the hem of his coat, stopping him. She was a good head shorter than Brady and probably didn't weigh ninety pounds, potatoes and all, but she went at him like a harpy, haranguing him in the Irish, stabbing a gnarled finger in his face with every word. People were staring now, and Brady felt his face heat with anger.

"I *said* I was sorry!" he snarled, bending to help scoop up some of her precious potatoes. After a moment, he left the rest to the sour-tempered old woman and took off at a half run, still intent on catching up with Roweena.

───◆───

At the edge of the marketplace, Gabriel watched the whole thing. He had been about to go and help Roweena carry her baskets home when he saw the altercation between Brady Kane and Maire Fahy. He continued to watch as the American hurried up to Roweena and took her by the arm.

Blood rushed to Gabriel's head, and he took a step in their direction, then stopped. Roweena would not thank him for playing the watchdog in her behalf.

In truth, he had not come to the market to spy on her but to purchase some fabric and ribbon for both Roweena and Eveleen, so they could sew new dresses for the festival. Happening upon her and the American had been pure coincidence.

He was close enough to see Roweena's expression change as Kane stood speaking to her. At first she had appeared uncertain, as if she might have wanted to run from him. Now, however, she was smiling a little.

Whether the encounter had been accidental or not, she looked as if she were pleased to see the persistent American, Gabriel observed, trying to ignore the ache in his throat.

Aye, Kane had her attention now. She was watching his lips in an effort to understand his words.

The temptation to confront them was like a pressing shove at his back. But what end would it serve? What could he do? Accuse them of deception? Chastise Roweena for disobeying his wishes? She was twenty-seven years now, a woman grown. She was no child to be scolded; Kane, no schoolboy to be bullied. He had no right to issue demands to either of them, though he had admittedly done just that with the American rogue.

With Roweena, he had simply informed her of his wishes, asking her to voluntarily abide by them. But he had no taste for trying to force her to comply. She would be hurt. She would not understand.

He wasn't certain *he* understood. Oh, Kane's shabby treatment of the Sheridan girl and the shirking of his responsibility were reason enough to want him well away from Roweena. But there was more to his own hostility than that unfortunate affair, Gabriel knew.

From the beginning, there had been something about the American artist that had set him on edge. He had never quite trusted the young wag. Even though he hadn't actually disliked Kane, at least not at first, he had invariably felt an uneasiness about him.

Watching him with Roweena now, he felt it again. Was it merely a measure of reasonable caution—the fear that he would ensnare Roweena, in all her innocence, with his sweet talk and attentions? Kane was young and handsome, after all—the kind who seemed to have no trouble charming women. And there was Roweena, infinitely lovely and completely innocent—good through and through. But oh, so vulnerable, so easy to deceive.

Another possibility asserted itself on Gabriel's mind—a vile thought, and one he had shrunk from until now. How much of his distrust and growing dislike for the American was born of his own barely controlled jealousy?

Jealousy?

It was an ugly thing to face, but there it was. He had loved her forever, cherished her as he might have a beloved sister when she was but a frightened child under his protection and throughout the years of her growing up.

But somewhere along those years his love had begun to change, had taken on a different complexion, a depth he'd felt bound to conceal, lest he drive her away from him.

He had no illusions about what he was to her. Roweena loved him in her own way, he knew. But as a guardian, a surrogate brother, perhaps, who had virtually raised her from a wee wane to womanhood. Her feelings for him were true and strong, feelings of trust and devotion and certainly affection. But hardly the affection of a woman who loves a man.

No doubt she would be shamed if she were ever to learn that his devotion to her was anything more than the brotherly concern she believed it to be. She might turn against him. She might even leave him.

And how would she manage then, on her own? How would she survive, alone in her silent world?

With a heavy sigh, Gabriel watched the two a moment more, the bitter admission of his jealousy a hot, tearing blade ripping through all his preconceived motives and noble intentions. Perhaps it was time he admitted the truth and stopped trying to dance around it, even if the truth made him nearly ill with self-disgust.

All that aside, he wasn't yet convinced that jealousy alone accounted for his growing aversion toward Kane. There was something more, something maddeningly elusive, and he knew it would give him no peace until he discovered its nature.

He resolved to set about doing just that without further delay. He meant to find out exactly who Brady Kane really was and what he was doing in Galway.

After another moment and one last, hard look at the couple in the marketplace, he turned and walked away.

6

UNEASY LIES THE HEART

The best lack all conviction, while the worst
are full of passionate intensity.

W. B. YEATS

❧

Disgruntled by Roweena's resistance, Brady left the marketplace in a huff. The fact that she wouldn't so much as take a walk with him foiled any hopes he might have had of breaking down her defenses.

Given half a chance, he was certain he could bring her around and make her see that he wasn't the dragon Gabriel had undoubtedly made him out to be. But first he had to figure out a way to get her out from under the big fisherman's hawk eye for more than a few minutes.

By the time he left the Claddagh and headed back into the city, he was in a thorough sulk. The day had lost its appeal. He had no interest in doing anything or going anywhere.

The idea of being trounced by a deaf girl and a surly fisherman who fancied himself some sort of feudal overlord grated on him more than he liked to admit. It occurred to him, though not for long, that the smart thing to do would be to simply give it up. Forget about Roweena, get out of Galway, and get on with the work he was supposed to be doing for Jack.

No doubt that was what he *ought* to do, instead of mooning around like a lovesick schoolboy over a girl he'd never so much as kissed...never so much as held *hands* with!

Never before had he been in such a state.

He tried to tell himself it was simply the thrill of the chase, that he wasn't all *that* infatuated with her. Hadn't he always been more interested in the girls who played hard to get?

But Roweena wasn't playing games—he doubted very much that she would even know *how*—and he despised himself for even thinking of her in such a way. The truth was that he had really come to care about her. Even though he'd scarcely seen her for weeks, every effort to put her out of his mind invariably failed. He had feelings for her he couldn't begin to understand, feelings he found almost frightening. But clearly, she was having no part of him—whether purely by her own choice or because of the cantankerous Gabriel, there was no telling.

By the time he reached his apartment building, he was fuming: at Gabriel, for the man's insufferable heavy-handedness; at Roweena, too, for allowing Gabriel to dictate her life as he did; but most of all at himself, for playing such a fool over Terese that he might have spoiled any chance he could have had with Roweena.

He stamped up the steps, the thought of Terese fueling his anger. It seemed to him that he'd taken all the blame for that to-do, even though he wasn't convinced that Terese had been entirely innocent. In fact, now that enough time had elapsed for him to gain some perspective, Brady wondered if the girl hadn't planned to deliberately entrap him.

She hadn't exactly made any secret of the fact that she expected some sort of commitment from him once they'd been intimate. A commitment that he had been unwilling to give. When he made it clear that he had no intention of taking her with him on his travels—much less on his return to the States—well, perhaps she'd thought a baby would change his mind.

He no longer saw her as an innocent, instead was beginning to believe that she might have set out to deliberately seduce him for her own purposes. And a big part of Terese's purposes, he had always known, was to get to America.

Ah, well, she was gone and that was that. And they would both be all right, so long as she didn't do anything to arouse Jack's suspicions. Brady had sworn her to secrecy, and he didn't think there was any real need to worry about her slipping up. Terese was too clever to be careless. Still, he'd feel better when he knew for certain that Jack had bought their story.

Only then would he really breathe easy again.

With that thought, he put Terese behind him for once and for all, poured himself a drink, and turned to the need at hand, that of deciding what *he* was going to do. He knew he ought to be leaving Galway soon; it was getting more and more difficult to justify his extended stay to Jack. But every time he thought about leaving, Roweena came to mind, and he found himself delaying once again.

He knew he *had* to leave before much longer. Jack wasn't going to keep up his wages indefinitely, not without getting something for his money. If he began to suspect that Brady was lying to him, he wasn't past cutting him off cold, with no warning.

No one bamboozled Jack Kane, not even his brother. A few had tried—and paid a treacherously high price for it.

No, he would have to make a move soon, and to that end he needed to be deciding where to go. Up to Westport, perhaps, and then Sligo. But instead of getting out his maps and drawing up an itinerary, he plopped down on the bed with his drink, giving in to an increasingly familiar pall of inertia.

More and more these days he found himself feeling like a shipwrecked sailor stranded on an island that was quickly being eroded by the sea. He knew he had to get off the island or eventually drown, but because he couldn't see anything in any direction except more water, he simply continued to sit where he was, watching the waves move in on him.

Up until now Brady had seldom had any problem making decisions. In fact, Jack had often accused him of making them *too* easily, too casually, and it was true that he didn't always trouble himself much about the consequences of his actions. Once he decided on a thing, he simply did it.

Lately, though, he seemed to haggle over every little thing, changing his mind, then changing it again. Something as basic as choosing the subject for a sketch could bring him to a total halt for hours, until he got so frustrated he would discard the entire idea.

He didn't know what was going on, but he *did* know he'd better be doing something about it or he was going to ruin himself with Jack.

For the moment, however, he would just have a quick snooze, then get up and go to work. First thing, he'd decide on his next stopover, then set a date to leave.

Soon, he told himself again. It would have to be very soon.

Brady's last thought as he drained the glass of whiskey and finally drifted off to sleep was of stumbling backward in a futile attempt to escape a towering, fast-encroaching wall of water.

~❧~

Gabriel waited until the table had been cleared, the dishes put away in the cupboard, before sending Evie out to play and indicating to Roweena that he wished to speak with her.

He noticed that she kept her eyes averted as she sat down at the table across from him. He touched her hand once to get her attention, and she looked up, watching his lips closely as he began. "I saw you with Brady Kane at the market."

A faint stain blotted her cheeks, and she glanced away for a second or two before looking back at him and nodding.

"'Tis not a good idea, Roweena. He is trouble, that one, don't you understand?"

As always, she focused her full attention on his lips until he had finished speaking, then seemed to consider her reply with care.

"He came up to me," she finally answered, signing with her fingers but speaking the words as well, as Gabriel insisted that she do. Her voice was halting, the words coming slowly but remarkably clearly, given her deafness. "What was I to do?"

He had always found her voice pleasant to the ear. Others no doubt thought it somewhat strange, since she spoke with the lack of inflection common to those who could not hear. Perhaps it was because he had worked so hard and so long with her, teaching her to speak. It had been a laborious, often frustrating process for them both—but a vastly rewarding one as well. She did not seem so locked out of his world once she could form words, and he no longer felt at such a disadvantage in trying to communicate with her.

At this moment, however, he almost dreaded what he might hear from her. He realized that she was studying him with an expression that hinted of anxiety, and he found himself suddenly impatient with her for being so careful with him.

"I'm not angry," he said, reassuring her. "I simply don't want you hurt, don't you see? I don't trust Brady Kane, and you shouldn't either."

He was surprised to see the look of sadness that crossed her delicate features. For a moment he thought she was about to weep.

Instead, she nodded as if to say she agreed, then lifted her gaze to his. "Please don't...worry, Gabriel," she said. "Perhaps I'm not as...foolish as you think."

Dismayed, Gabriel reached to take her hand, then stopped himself. "I have never thought you foolish, Roweena," he said, holding her gaze. "I mean only to protect you."

Again she nodded, looking down.

"Roweena?" Gabriel leaned across the table and tipped her chin with one finger to get her attention. She looked up, but he was unable to read her expression. "Do you care for this man?"

She frowned as if she didn't understand.

"Do you have—*feelings*—for him?" He heard the thickness of his own voice, felt apprehension spring up in him like a bitter weed when she deliberately looked away without making any response to his question.

His mouth dry, Gabriel again reached to turn her face toward his. "He is not the sort of man who can be trusted. You must see that."

He felt himself shrink under the searching gaze she turned on him.

"You always say we are not to...judge others, that we...must try to see them as...the Savior sees them. With tolerance...and forgiveness."

Her words seemed an indictment of sorts, and Gabriel found himself at a loss. "That's so," he said gruffly, fumbling for the words to explain himself. "But there will always be those who take advantage. I'm not suggesting that you judge Kane, simply that you be cautious."

Her dark gray eyes never left his. "But...you are judging him, Gabriel. Are you not?"

He tensed still more. "Kane brought much trouble on the Sheridan girl with his lack of restraint. And he continues to sneak his way past me to you. That would seem to speak of a nature that cannot be trusted. I will ask you again to stay away from him. For your own good."

Her mouth tightened, and for a moment Gabriel thought she was going to argue with him. But at last her features softened, and she gave a small nod of assent. "I will...try," she said. "But what am I...to do when he happens upon me in the marketplace? Would you have me run away then, like a mindless child?"

Now it was Gabriel who turned away without an answer, even though he silently admitted to himself that indeed, that was exactly what he would have her do.

If only it could be that simple.

7

BETWEEN FRIENDS

Two are better than one...

ECCLESIASTES 4:9, NIV

❧

That same evening Gabriel made a rare visit to an out-of-the-way tavern in Galway City. Although he wasn't one to frequent such a place, the man he was looking for did.

He had no way of knowing whether Ulick was anywhere in the area, but he could leave word with Phelim Lynch, the owner, that he was looking for him. As soon as he entered, however, he spied the wild shock of silver hair and the drooping mustache of his old friend.

Ulick was sitting at the far end of the room in front of a cold fireplace with two other weathered seamen. The room was dim and uncrowded. It smelled of dampness and ale and cooked fish. Only a few men were seated at tables, their faces solemn as they huddled over their pints.

Ulick looked up and, seeing Gabriel, gave a one-sided grin. At the same time, he made a sharp jerk of the head as if to order his companions away. By the time Gabriel reached the table, the other two men had scraped their chairs back and, with nothing more than a brief nod in his direction, ambled off to a table near the bar.

Ulick motioned Gabriel to one of the recently vacated chairs. "Your gob would sour new milk, Gabriel Vaughan. Have Lynch fetch you a jar to lighten your load."

"'Tis your poison, not mine, Ulick. I came to talk, not drink."

"Sit down then, you great oaf. As you know, I take pleasure in both."

They spoke in the Irish, in low tones: two men who had known each other too many years to count and whose conversation needed no embellishment.

"So then, Gabriel, what is on your mind? It would appear to be heavy, whatever the nature."

Gabriel took the chair across from him, and Ulick waved the aproned owner away.

"You have some time, do you, Ulick?"

"I have nothing else," the other said, watching Gabriel closely. In contrast to the brown, leathered face, Ulick's eyes appeared so pale they might have been glazed with ice. "You have a reason for asking after my time, I expect."

Gabriel gave a nod and got right to it. "I'm wanting some information on a man. He claims to have been born here, in the city, and I'm curious about his people—who they might have been, if he's telling the truth. I thought that if anyone would know, you would, or, if not, you could find out."

Ulick turned his glass around in his hand. "Who is this man?"

"Brady Kane," said Gabriel.

Ulick lifted heavy brows. "The American who does the drawings? He was born here?"

"So he says." Gabriel paused. "I wouldn't stake much on his word, though."

Ulick nodded. "I heard he brought trouble on one of the island girls."

"He did that." Gabriel's mouth tightened.

"And then he packed her off to America."

"There is quite a story in that. I didn't get the whole truth, I expect, but what the Sheridan girl told Jane Connolly was that Kane had connections of some sort with a big newspaper in New York. Supposedly this newspaper was paying passage for some orphaned children to go across and offered to pay the girl's way as well, if she would tend to the orphans during the voyage. That's all I know about it, but I suspect there's more."

Ulick quirked one corner of his mouth, and the heavy mustache lifted. "The Yank's connections must be good ones. You think the story was put-up?"

Gabriel shrugged. "I don't know, and what's done is done, so that part of it isn't my concern." He stopped, uncertain as to how much he wanted to tell his old friend.

Ulick set his glass on the table and waited.

"'Tis Roweena I'm thinking of," Gabriel finally offered. "Kane won't leave her alone, though I've done everything but threaten him to warn him off."

"Then he is a fool as well as a rake," said Ulick with a laugh. "Few men would want to bump heads with you, had they their wits about them."

"The coals of my temper have cooled considerably, man," Gabriel said, his tone gruff. "I, too, was a fool in my youth."

"Ah, and isn't every man?"

"As for Kane," Gabriel went on, "the boy is not an easy one to dislike. All the same, I've never trusted him. And less now, after the bad business with the Sheridan girl. I don't want him anywhere near Roweena."

Ulick's expression turned thoughtful, and he nodded, slowly. "What is it, then, Gabriel? What are you thinking, that you might learn something to discourage him for once and all?"

In truth Gabriel didn't know what, exactly, he was hoping for. "Kane keeps his silence about himself. Too much so, it seems to me. He tells little, other than that he lives in New York City, and he has an older brother. Supposedly, he earns his keep by making drawings for newspapers in the States. He claims to be in Ireland on some sort of 'special assignment.' I expect he told the Sheridan girl more, but if that's the case, she kept it to herself." Gabriel leaned across the table a little. "I don't know quite what I'm looking for, but I intend to keep him away from Roweena by any means I can find. I'm wondering if there isn't a reason for his telling so little about himself. You know the city better than any man and can find what I want faster than I could. Will you help me?"

Ulick traced his heavy mustache with one finger. His expression was dubious. "It seems to me you might accomplish more by simply knocking the laddie about some. If you've not the taste for it, I know a pair of lads who would do the job. A good thrashing ought to get the Yank's attention, wouldn't you think? Perhaps even persuade him to leave Galway altogether."

The suggestion turned Gabriel's stomach, and he shook his head. "That's not my way, Ulick. For now, all I want is information."

Ulick gave a shrug. "As you say, then. So this Kane—do we know if that's his real name?"

"There's no telling. But I've no reason to think otherwise."

Ulick shifted his bony frame in the chair a little and cupped the back of his neck with one hand. "All right, then. We'll start where we are. *Kane...MacCathain* or *O Cein,* that would be...let's see, now..."

Ulick went on muttering to himself for a moment, then glanced up. "Has he by any chance mentioned when he went across? How old he might have been when he left Galway?"

"No, I told you, he has little to say about himself."

They went on that way for a few more minutes, Ulick throwing out possibilities and more or less thinking aloud, with Gabriel unable to provide any real assistance.

Finally, Gabriel stood. "I must get back. Come to the house or send a message anytime. I'll be waiting."

Ulick seemed to scarcely notice his leaving, so engrossed was he in the puzzle Gabriel had presented him. "I'll be going over to Dublin soon for a few days, to visit the boy and his wife," he said after a moment. "Not for long, though. You'll hear from me, sooner or later."

Hoping it would be sooner rather than later, Gabriel turned and left the tavern.

8
ENCOUNTER WITH DARKNESS

Know thou the secret of a spirit
Bow'd from its wild pride into shame.
O yearning heart! I did inherit
Thy withering portion with the fame.

EDGAR ALLAN POE

PHILADELPHIA

Jack made no attempt to conceal his study of the man seated across the table from him. With some effort, however, he had managed to conceal his impatience with the self-important Mr. Poe, suppressing the inclination to suggest that the morose, albeit esteemed, writer grow up and cease his whining.

He had met Edgar Poe only once before, nearly two years ago while Poe was still staying in New York. He seemed to have changed little. Jack knew he was no more than thirty, though the writer had a haggard, discontented look about him that made him seem much older. Poe was a small man, a somber, delicate sort, with an unusually broad forehead and uncommonly sorrowful eyes. It occurred to Jack that Poe looked every bit the tortured genius he was rumored to be.

He also looked not altogether well. Poe's complexion had an unhealthy pallor, emphasized by the man's apparent proclivity for black: black frock coat, black cravat, black gloves. Poe's hair was also dark, his gray eyes intense; taken together with his attire, the appearance of the man was strangely spectral.

They had met at the oyster house over an hour ago, and so far the writer had done little more than pick at his food, elaborate on his misfortunes, and undermine with a blistering tongue a number of his literary contemporaries—including Washington Irving, a personal favorite of Jack's.

"Overrated," Poe commented now, summarizing his poor opinion of Irving. "Greatly overrated."

Jack said nothing. It had already occurred to him that Poe's arrogant dismissal of his peers might be born of envy, perhaps even resentment. His own sales weren't all that impressive; Poe was notorious for his financial woes and had, in fact, faced jail on more than one occasion for his bad debts.

Jack reminded himself that he had not come all the way to Philadelphia to let himself be provoked by a troublesome writer. Poe had distinctly expressed interest in publishing with the *Vanguard* or one of Jack's other publishing interests, such as Perriman and Ware. Poe's work was well-enough regarded that Jack had thought he ought to at least explore the possibilities.

So far this evening, however, Poe had exhibited little interest in a professional relationship with *any* of the Kane publishing enterprises. To the contrary, he seemed bent on conducting himself like some sort of a literary lion being pursued by a runny-nosed newsboy.

Jack was used to being patronized by the aristocrats in the literary community. Although he had become fairly adept at concealing his feelings, there had been a time when some of the more supercilious among the elite had managed to make him feel like a clumsy Irish peasant, out of his class and over his head.

These days, however, it took more than a pretentious author to put him at a disadvantage. His years in publishing had taught him that many of the brightest stars of the literary galaxy, no matter how eminent or highborn they might be, actually lived in dire financial straits. Indeed, some, like the notable Edgar Poe, seemed to exist in near poverty much of the time. So while the blue bloods might raise their eyebrows at his Irish commonness, they almost never turned up their noses at the smell of his money. He'd warrant that in that regard Poe was no different from the rest.

By the time dessert was served, he had grown impatient with the man's posturing; in fact, he wasn't at all sure he even wanted to bother with him.

With no further delay, he came to the point. "Well, Mr. Poe, let me just explain what I'm looking for, and you can give me a yes or a no as to whether you're interested."

Ignoring Poe's somewhat huffy frown, Jack scooped up the last bite of his sugar-cream pie before going on. "I'm looking for material I can serialize in the *Vanguard,* preferably over a period of weeks. An adventure story, perhaps—something on the high seas, for example, with plenty of action and lots of excitement. Something to keep people buying the papers."

Poe regarded Jack as if he had suddenly sprouted a horn in the middle of his forehead. "You're not serious, of course."

"I am entirely serious."

Poe lifted a pale hand to finger his cravat. "I don't write...*serial fiction,* Mr. Kane. I assumed you were familiar with my work."

"Oh, I'm well acquainted with your work, Edgar—you don't mind if I call you 'Edgar'?—but tell me, how does your work *sell?*"

"I beg your pardon?" Poe's mouth twisted downward, as though he had caught a hint of a bad odor.

"Your work," Jack said. "Does it sell well for you?"

Poe's features seemed to constrict. The fingers on the cravat trembled slightly. "I don't write simply for profit, Mr. Kane."

Jack saw the unsteadiness of the white hand, the uncertainty in Poe's mournful eyes. "Be that as it may, Edgar, I am obliged to *publish* for profit. So, you see, I'm wondering if you wouldn't like to try your hand at something different, perhaps a large adventure story, as I mentioned earlier. Something with a hero in jeopardy, a defenseless lady, and a great deal of excitement. *And—*" Jack deliberately emphasized his words—"*a happy ending.* In other words, a story that would have subscribers eager for the next edition. I'm willing to pay very generously for that kind of story if you can give it to me."

Poe was still looking at him with something akin to distaste, but Jack thought he detected a glimmer of growing interest as well.

"As I said, I'll pay well for the right material," he pressed. "Are you interested?"

It was Jack's observation that Poe was *very* interested, all right, but was unwilling to admit to it. His impatience with the man grew.

Poe crossed his arms, hugging them to himself, as he fastened his eyes on something just above Jack's head. For his part, Jack took the opportunity to study the writer even more closely. For the first time, he noticed that, despite Poe's distinct impression of breeding and Byronic airs, the man had a certain indefinable seediness that didn't quite square with the image he obviously meant to project. There was a strange sense of interior *decay* about Edgar Poe that Jack found unsettling, to say the least.

"I find myself wondering if I should be insulted by your offer, Mr. Kane."

Jack shrugged. "It's not actually an offer, merely an idea. But I'm curious as to why you'd be insulted. As I recall, you contacted *me.* I'm simply trying to figure a way this might work for both of us and make you a bit of money in the process."

Poe's eyes flashed. "I do not hire myself out to the highest bidder, sir. I have a certain reputation to maintain in the literary world, as you must be aware."

Jack placed his fork carefully on his plate and leaned back in his chair, looking Poe directly in the eye. "I can't think your reputation would be impaired by getting your work out to a larger audience, Edgar. Certainly it wouldn't hurt your bank account."

"Really, Mr. Kane—"

"Why don't you call me 'Jack,' Edgar?"

"I'm not accustomed to discussing my bank account—*Mr. Kane.*"

"Sorry, Edgar, I meant no offense." With some effort, Jack kept his tone casual. "I confess that *I'm* not accustomed to dealing with men who are insulted by the subject of money. Most of them find the idea of getting paid for their labors fairly appealing. Especially," he added with a considerably harder edge in his voice, "those with families to support."

Poe started to rise from his chair. Jack watched him in silence. By now he was relatively certain he was wasting his time and even more convinced he wanted nothing to do with this man. Poe seemed unable to let go of his insufferable pride, and Jack had neither the patience nor the inclination to coddle him to a decision that would salve his ego.

Besides, something in the man put him off, genius be hanged. He thought Poe might be a little mad; he was almost certainly more than a little foolish.

But Poe had apparently changed his mind about leaving. Looking everywhere but at Jack, he slowly lowered himself back into the chair and sat examining his dessert plate.

Jack decided to make one—and only one—last attempt to get past the man's pride. "Though it may surprise you, Edgar—coming from a peasant like myself—I think I can appreciate your commitment to quality in your work." At Poe's skeptical glance, Jack gave a rueful smile. "Oh, the *Vanguard* prints its share of sensationalism, of course, along with the usual tripe—got to keep that segment of the population satisfied so we can pay the bills. But I make it a point to offer something better as well—not just through the paper but by way of my publishing houses. That's why I'm here."

He paused, again sensing more than a grudging flicker of interest from the other. "Let me be perfectly frank, Edgar. I've read your stuff"—he saw Poe's mouth tighten—"your *work,*" he amended, "and I think you're a man capable of writing what I'd like to publish. You're more clever by far than most of the writers I've worked with, and despite your somewhat grisly choice of subject matter, you do spin a grand tale."

Jack paused, ignoring the other's surly expression. "The thing is, Edgar, I happen to think you could pen just as fine a story using a less morbid tone than is your custom. Something...brighter, perhaps. More acceptable to the *Vanguard's* readers than what you usually write. No less gripping, of course, but possibly less...depressing. More wholesome, is what I'm getting at."

Poe shook his head. "Considering your reputation, Mr. Kane, I find your request somewhat puzzling. You hardly strike me as the kind of man given to the sort of pedestrian drivel the religious element so admires."

Jack inwardly bristled. There was something about having his reputation called into question by a man like Poe that set his teeth to grinding. But he managed to give a casual shrug, saying nothing.

"I do not subscribe to the sort of artificial prattle you seem to want," Poe went on, his tone less pedantic now, even somewhat rambling. "I don't believe in...happy endings, Mr. Kane. Therefore, I do not write them."

Jack leaned his elbows on the table, steepling his fingers and regarding Poe with growing annoyance. "I'm not personally acquainted with too many happy endings myself, Edgar, but that doesn't mean they don't exist—or *can't* exist, at least in a story. And I'm certainly not suggesting that you write—*drivel*—for my readers. Quite frankly, I respect them more than that. But I see nothing artificial about stories that contain at least a touch of hope to mitigate the despair. A bit of light to relieve the darkness, if you will."

He sat watching the somber Poe for a moment. "Forgive the observation, Edgar, but I can't help thinking that you're quite a young man to take such a dismal view of life."

"What has age to do with anything?" Poe said, lifting a languid hand.

"Perhaps nothing. But aside from age, you're a bright, gifted fellow with a lovely young wife, a home, a fine education—and the means of earning a highly respectable income from doing something you apparently enjoy. As for myself, I admit to being the worst of cynics. But I can't help wondering what would account for your preoccupation with such dreary, macabre subjects."

Poe looked at him as if considering how to reply. Then, without warning, he launched into a bitter tale of misfortune that should have moved Jack—and ordinarily would have, had the man not been so obviously engulfed in self-pity.

He already knew about the "premature loss" of Poe's actor parents, his alienation from his foster father, his ongoing problems with poor health and indebtedness. But so far as his poor health and even poorer finances were concerned, a great deal of Poe's difficulties in both areas seemed to be the products of his own excesses.

By the conclusion of Poe's diatribe, Jack's patience was at an end. All he could think of was getting away. He felt an almost desperate need for fresh air and light; at the same time, he wondered why he found the man across from him so oppressive.

At one time or another over the years he had had dealings with some thoroughly unsavory characters, a number of which were almost certainly as odd as Edgar Poe and a sight less gentlemanly in their conduct. He had trafficked with felons and traded with fools, rubbed elbows with thieves, and risked his own skin countless times in New York's most abysmal slums—including the vile Five Points—just to ferret out the facts for a story. By now he had surely encountered the very dregs of humanity and should have been inured to just about any manner of corruption.

Given all that—not to mention that he wasn't exactly the salt of the earth himself—why did the decadence he sensed in Edgar Poe strike him as so particularly offensive, even as the man himself seemed to hold an eerie kind of fascination?

In that instant Jack's eyes met Poe's, and what he saw there shook him like a blast of winter wind. It was as if something in that dark and haunted gaze threatened to draw him in and trap him in a vacuum from which there was no outlet. In some bizarre way that set him to trembling, he recognized looking out at him something that appeared treacherously familiar, yet terrifyingly alien.

At that moment he realized that the darkness he sensed in Poe might well be but a reflection of the darkness that inhabited his own spirit.

Thoroughly chilled, Jack decided that this meeting was at an end.

And so was his interest in publishing the "tormented genius."

He would leave Philadelphia tomorrow. He suddenly found himself not only excessively eager to be away from Edgar Poe but more eager still to be with Samantha. He craved the light of her, the sweet...*goodness* of her. Perhaps he could figure out a way to see her again before the meeting with Foxworth next week.

He had every intention of renewing his proposal in the near future—the *very* near future. This time, he would be more convincing.

And more resistant to any attempt on her part to turn him down again.

His decision made, he brought the interview to a close as speedily as possible without being unnecessarily rude. He couldn't be sure, of course, but it seemed to him that Poe was every bit as anxious to part company as he was.

It was as if, he thought grimly, like had recognized like and could not abide the resemblance.

9

IN THE HARBOR

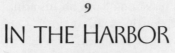

November's wind is a lonely song.

ANONYMOUS

NEW YORK CITY

Cavan Sheridan's reservations about bringing Samantha to the harbor could not have been more evident. Even now, after nearly an hour on the docks, he was obviously still wishing he had come alone, his strained expression clearly signifying that a lady had no place in such surroundings. But Samantha's new duties required that she meet any immigrants traveling under the *Vanguard*'s sponsorship, and she felt it particularly important that she present herself to their first arrivals—especially since Terese Sheridan, Cavan's sister—was one of them.

Cavan returned from Albany on Saturday morning, sooner than expected, and had arrived on Samantha's doorstep that same afternoon, explaining—with obvious reluctance—that "Mr. Kane had left instructions" for him to escort Samantha to the harbor if and when she wanted to go.

So far, their excursion had proved futile. Inquiries of harbor officials had yielded only the disturbing news that the *Providence* had actually docked over two weeks ago. Yet, there had been no message to this effect from any of Jack's sources, no word from Terese Sheridan and the Madden children. Consequently, there was no way of knowing their whereabouts.

As they stood looking around, trying to decide what to do next, Samantha pulled her heavy coat more tightly about her. It was bitter cold on the docks. A stinging drizzle had settled over the day, and a harsh wind was blowing off the water. Despite the inclement weather and their lack of success, however, she was glad she hadn't let Cavan come alone. He was obviously shaken and apprehensive about his sister's well-being.

On impulse, she lay a reassuring hand on his arm. "Try not to worry, Cavan. We'll find them. We'll keep looking until we do."

He managed only the lamest of smiles. "'Tis just that we don't know where to begin."

"You said Jack—Mr. Kane—had employed someone on the docks to send word when the ship put in, a Mr. Hoey?"

Her voice was almost drowned in the pandemonium of their surroundings: the loud clamor of men shouting in foreign tongues, mothers and children wailing, dockworkers clanging metal against metal as they loaded and unloaded cargo—all was noise and mass confusion.

But both of them heard the familiar voice behind them clearly enough.

"You might have at least brought along an umbrella, Sheridan."

Samantha and Cavan spun around at the same time to find Jack standing directly behind them, a faint smile belying the rebuke in his tone.

"Jack!" Samantha blurted out his given name before she thought, but Cavan Sheridan seemed not to notice the familiarity. "I thought you weren't coming back until Monday."

She found herself hard pressed to conceal her pleasure at the sight of him. He stood watching her, one dark eyebrow crooked, the familiar quirk of a smile on his face in response to her surprise. As always, he wore no hat, indeed had not even bothered to open the umbrella he carried, and so his head and shoulders were slick with rain.

With a flourish, he now opened the umbrella and held it over Samantha.

The way he was looking at her, as if he had been away for months and was virtually starved for the sight of her, made her heart turn over.

"What—why did you cut your trip short?" she said, struggling to regain her composure, at the same time trying to ignore the way his black eyes continued to hold her gaze.

"I found myself impatient to get back," he said quietly, still watching her.

His close scrutiny and the warmth of his tone disarmed Samantha's attempt to formulate a cool response. At the same time, the memory of his proposal only a few nights past struck her unexpectedly, threatening to snap the already frazzled thread of her self-control.

Fortunately, Jack turned his attention to Cavan Sheridan for a moment. "I saw your report from Albany. Fine job."

Cavan flushed noticeably under his employer's approval. "Thank you, sir. I hope it's all right that I came back sooner than we'd planned. Nothing much seemed to be going on, so there didn't seem any point in staying."

Jack waved off his explanation. "That's fine, though I may be sending you off again soon."

Cavan frowned, and Samantha sensed that he would be reluctant to go anywhere until his sister had been found. "Where might that be, sir?"

"Connecticut," said Jack.

For a moment Cavan's face registered only bewilderment. "I…ah…don't believe I know where that is, sir."

"Well, you may be finding out soon enough. There's been some sort of slave mutiny on a Spanish ship. For some reason, the Navy seized the entire vessel and towed it to Connecticut. Sounds as if there's going to be quite a fuss. The abolitionists have gotten involved somehow, and who knows what's going to come of it? I don't have any of the details yet, but could be we'll want in on the story. But we'll talk about that later. What of your sister and the little ones? Any word?"

"Apparently, their ship put in two weeks ago," Cavan replied.

"Two *weeks* ago?" Jack cut a glance to Samantha.

She nodded. "We haven't been able to find out anything about Cavan's sister or the Madden children. None of the officials we talked with were any help. We were just about to look for the other gentleman you told us about—Mr. Hoey."

"Hoey's no gentleman," Jack said absently, turning to glance around. "But he usually knows most everything going on about the harbor. That's why I use him now and then."

A few feet away, a boy with a filthy face and wearing a coat two sizes too large was perched on his haunches, fishing a string through the cracks of the wharf. Jack got the boy's attention with a sharp whistle, then palmed a coin from his pocket and held it up.

The youth, who looked to be no more than eight or nine years old, dropped his string and came running.

"You know Hoey, lad?" Jack asked him.

The boy nodded, his eyes locked on the coin in Jack's hand.

"Fetch him for me, then, and this is yours."

The child stretched a hand for the coin, but Jack held it out of reach.

"Ah, no—first you bring Hoey to me. And be quick about it, mind! If I have to wait too long, you'll not get a cent."

The boy took off at a run, the tops of his oversized boots flapping about his thin legs. Jack turned back to Samantha and Cavan. "Hoey's a runner—one of the older boyos," he said, his expression dark with distaste. "A real master of the trade, Hoey is."

Jack's look of contempt mirrored Samantha's own feelings. She knew about the runners who infested the docks, a low breed who earned their subsistence by fleecing unsuspecting immigrants right off the boat, many of them the runners' own countrymen. These unscrupulous creatures would actually board the ships, virtually overwhelming the bewildered immigrants, hawking their services either through ingratiating spiels, or, more often, sheer intimidation. Under the ruse of arranging "decent lodgings at reasonable rates," the runners would quickly manage to seize an entire family's baggage and belongings before leading them off the ship and out of the harbor.

Almost without exception, runners worked for unprincipled men who owned some of the most disgraceful tenements and boarding houses in New York. Once he had maneuvered a band of immigrants off the docks, a runner would proceed to one of his employer's tenement buildings, where the new arrivals would be packed into dark, filthy rooms with other victims of their deceit and charged exorbitant rates for quarters scarcely fit for animals.

Jack gestured that they should move back a ways, under the shelter of a warehouse overhang. "You shouldn't have come out today," he said, raking a hand through his wet hair as he turned to Samantha. "'Tis a wretched day entirely."

"I'm not as frail as all that," Samantha said. "Tell us about your visit with Mr. Poe."

His shrug and sour face said it all. "As you see, I wasn't inclined to spend a great deal of time with the man."

"What happened?"

Jack shrugged. "Let's just say that Mr. Poe and I seem to have decidedly different viewpoints on the publishing process."

"I see," Samantha said after a second or two.

He gave a wry smile. "But you still want to know all about him."

In fact, she did. She had come to realize that Jack's perceptions of human nature could be chillingly insightful, if at times almost brutally cynical; she was learning more and more to trust his judgment. Still, even though some of Poe's work repelled her, and the more lurid stories about the man appalled her, she could not help but be curious.

"I promise a thorough recounting over supper," he said.

Samantha looked at him.

Still smiling, he darted a quick glance from her to Cavan, then went on, making it clear that both of them were included in the invitation. "I thought I'd take the two of you to Guiliardo's, if you're free. It would seem to be perfect weather for something a bit spicy."

Samantha knew she should say no; she'd been seeing far too much of Jack lately. But she had seen the way Cavan's eyes brightened at the idea, and no doubt he could use some cheering up after the disappointment of the day.

Besides, the truth was that *she* wanted to go. It would be an opportunity to hear about the meeting with Edgar Poe, without any concern that Jack might raise the troubling subject of marriage again. Cavan's presence would guarantee an impersonal atmosphere.

As for Cavan, he hesitated only a moment, as if to gauge Jack's sincerity. "Perhaps I should be getting on back—"

Samantha was relieved when Jack waved off his uncertainty. "Nonsense. Mrs. Harte wants to hear about my meeting with Poe, and I want a briefing on your trip to Albany. You'll have supper with us." He stopped, inclined his head toward Samantha, and said, "That is, if you're free?"

Just for an instant, caution renewed its war with an unsettling desire in Samantha to be with him. As seemed to happen more and more frequently these days, caution lost the battle.

"Yes, that would be nice," she said. "And, of course, you'll come, Cavan. We know all about your passion for Italian food."

Cavan gave a weak smile, but it was obvious that he was still distracted by concern for his sister—as well he might be.

Samantha turned back to Jack. "Can you think of anywhere else we should look?"

She stopped as a rumpled, wizened little man in a tattered sweater and a stovepipe hat trotted up to them, the raggedy child Jack had sent off a few moments before at his side.

This would be Hoey, she presumed.

The man doffed his hat and bowed so low he almost chinned himself on the planking. "At your service, Mr. Kane!"

Jack tossed a coin to the boy who had fetched the runner before turning to the strange little man. "I seem to recall that you were going to send word the day the *Providence* dropped anchor."

The man nodded vigorously.

"The ship put in two weeks ago, you little monkey! Why wasn't I told?"

The runner gaped. "Two weeks ago? Why, I didn't know, sir!"

Jack nailed him with a black scowl that made Samantha cringe. "You were to keep a sharp eye out for certain passengers I described; isn't that so?"

"Indeed, Mr. Kane! But as luck would have it, I was sick for a time, don't you see."

Jack waved off the man's attempt to explain. "Hah! Sick, is it? I know you, Hoey; more than likely you've been in your cups since the day I gave you the money."

The wiry runner seemed excessively nervous under this cross-examination but again made an effort to defend himself. "Now, Mr. Kane, sir, I'm not a drinking man, and that's the truth! The ship must have put in while I was indisposed. Sure, you can't blame a man for a bad stomach, now can you?"

For the first time, Samantha got a glimpse of Jack's legendary temper. With one hand, he gripped the lapels of Hoey's coat, practically lifting the bantam runner off his feet. "'Tis not a smart idea to take my money and not give me what I paid for, Hoey! And now that I think of it, I believe we have had this discussion before."

"I'm on it right now, Mr. Kane, I swear to you! I'll have the information you want yet today, I will! No later than tomorrow for certain!"

When Jack still didn't release him, Hoey's eyes bugged until Samantha felt almost sorry for him. Jack was twice again the size of the little runner, after all. And why had he paid the man in the first place if he didn't trust him?

"Jack."

If he heard her, he pretended not to, though he did finally release the frightened Hoey. "I'll expect to see you at the *Vanguard* first thing in the morning, and no later. You'd best be there well ahead of me, mind, and with the information I want. Understand?"

Hoey nodded so violently he nearly lost his ridiculous hat. "But, sir—Mr. Kane?"

Jack's eyes narrowed.

"It—it occurs to me," the little man stammered, "that these passengers you're expecting—if they weren't met when they put in and you've had no word of them, they might be at Tompkinsville—the quarantine hospital."

Jack seemed to consider the idea, then gave a nod. "It's possible." He jabbed a finger in the air at the runner. "You hotfoot it over there yet today, d'you hear? Ask after a girl named *Terese Sheridan*. As I told you, she'll be traveling with two youngsters by the name of *Madden*. See what you can find out."

Hoey shifted from one foot to the other, obviously eager to get away. "I'll go right now, Mr. Kane! This very minute. And I'll keep on the situation until I find them."

"First thing tomorrow, Hoey, don't be forgetting it."

"First thing tomorrow it is, Mr. Kane! You can count on me, don't you know?"

Jack gave him a murderous look, and the man went scurrying down the dock.

Samantha watched him go, then turned to Jack. "Why don't we just go to Tompkinsville ourselves?"

Still scowling, he turned toward her. "I'd hardly be taking you to that miserable pesthouse, Samantha. Besides, let the little soaker earn his money."

"I imagine I've been in worse places than Tompkinsville," she said mildly.

"Not with me, you haven't," he snapped, his tone and the look in his eyes making it clear the subject was closed.

"Is it a bad place, this Tompkinsville?" Cavan said, speaking for the first time since Hoey had come on the scene.

Jack exchanged a look with Samantha. "It's a kind of hospital," he said, "a place where they detain immigrants who are ill when they come into the country.

"Brady did say the Madden children weren't all that well," Jack continued, in an attempt to spare Cavan further alarm. "It could be that they've been taken to the quarantine center for a time. Just until they're found fit."

"Please don't worry, Cavan," Samantha put in. "We'll find them." But even as she spoke, her mind went to some of the more harrowing stories she had heard about quarantine facilities. There had been frequent attempts on the part of some of the city's politicians and concerned citizens to have the place razed on the premise that it was a health hazard.

For the most part, Samantha thought the concern about quarantine stations was probably justified. Some of the tales about such places were the stuff of nightmares. Silently, she hoped Cavan's sister and the children had somehow managed to find their way to a decent lodging house rather than being held at Tompkinsville.

From what she knew of quarantine hospitals, Jack's reference to Tompkinsville as a "pesthouse" might actually be too kind.

A BITTER HOPE

There is always hope for those who will dare and suffer.

JAMES CLARENCE MANGAN

Terese stood at the top of the hill behind the quarantine hospital, her eyes averted from the trenches where numberless dead had been buried—one of the most recent being wee Tully Madden. The child had died in the night, finally surrendering to weeks of fever and a cough that would have devastated a man grown.

Terese had watched the tyke die, her own insides wrenching at the sound of the death rattles in his throat—a dreadful sound and one she remembered all too well from the time when her own mother and sisters lay dying. She swallowed, biting down hard on the acid taste of a grief she did not want to feel, telling herself she could not afford to expend what strength remained to her on the death of a child she had hardly known. And yet she *did* grieve for the sunny-faced little boy who had deserved so much better than a painful death in a mean, cruel place among strangers who had not even noted his existence.

She glanced over at the boy's sister. Shona had not uttered a word since her brother's death. Even after the attendants took away the small, wasted body for burial, the girl had remained speechless, weeping silently for her brother. Now her pale features registered no emotion at all.

Terese feared for her. The girl had been frail when they started the voyage, and by now she was little more than a shadow. But it was her mind that concerned Terese most. Throughout the crossing, Shona had spent entire hours without speaking, staring straight ahead with a vacant gaze as if she had no real awareness of her surroundings.

Ever since their arrival at the quarantine hospital, she had withdrawn deeper and deeper into herself; at times she hardly seemed to be breathing, so quiet, so listless had she become. Only her little brother had managed to rouse her from her peculiar soporific state now and again.

But with Tully gone, Terese could not think what would become of the girl. For that matter, she didn't know what was to become of either of them unless she could somehow manage to find a way out of this abysmal death trap.

But perhaps she *had* found a way. While standing at the grave site, a plan had begun to form in her mind, a plan that might just mean escape from this miserable island. It would mean stealing, and Terese had vowed never again to resort to such an act—especially in light of the fact that only months ago she'd very nearly landed in a Galway *gaol* for stealing a basket of bread.

But which was the greater sin, she wondered, stealing a piece of paper or ignoring a chance to save a child's life—and perhaps her own in the process?

She shifted her poke—the sack that held her meager belongings—and glanced down at Shona. The girl stood clutching her own small satchel close to her chest, her eyes glazed in the familiar numb expression. Although she appeared to be studying the trenches of fresh graves before them, Terese questioned whether she actually saw anything at all.

After a moment Terese turned from Shona to watch a throng of people descending the hill. These were passengers from another ship, the fortunate ones who, having passed a final medical inspection, had just received their tickets to freedom. As they hurried along, many waved their precious papers of escape—the papers that would allow them to leave the quarantine center and enter the city. At the same time, an even larger group—new arrivals—were making their way *up* the hill.

Terese's mind raced, her mouth going dry as her gaze locked on a woman and a young, ginger-haired girl trying to jostle their way through the band of immigrants hurrying down the hill. With one hand, the woman gripped the girl's arm, while in her free hand she held the same papers of release as most of the others.

The two looked to be having a difficult time threading their way through the crowd. Terese's gaze traced a line from the papers in the woman's hand out toward the docks. She hesitated only a moment before grasping Shona's hand in hers, anchoring the girl at her side.

"Come on," she said, her voice low as she began to move toward the crowd. "Hurry!"

The ground was mud-slicked from the cold rain that had fallen the night before, but Terese took the hill at a near run, stumbling more than once in her haste as she pulled the wooden Shona along beside her.

When they reached the others, Terese wedged herself and the girl into their midst with little effort, snaking through the crowd until she was directly behind the two she had singled out. The woman was bone thin and shabby, clad in little more than rags; the girl was even more wraithlike than Shona. Heart pounding, Terese swallowed hard, then in one swift, lightning move kicked out, smacking the woman in the backs of the legs with enough force to throw her off balance.

The woman cried out, her feet flying out from under her, the passes sailing out of her hand as she fell. The others around them either didn't notice or didn't care, going on down the hill as Terese, dropping Shona's hand, made a pretense of stopping to help the woman.

In the press of the crowd, she almost went down herself but somehow managed to scoop up the passes with one hand while pulling the woman to her feet with the other. She grabbed for Shona then, pushing herself and the girl quickly forward, squeezing their way through the others until they were almost at the front of the crowd and well on their way to the docks.

By the time the frenzied wailing rose far behind them, they were boarding the ferry for Manhattan, passes in hand.

❧

With a silent, trembling Shona clinging to her skirt, Terese stood at the edge of the South Street port, looking out toward the ragged streets of New York. Her face stung, slashed by the frigid wind and driving rain. She was beginning to wonder if she would ever be warm again.

The scene in front of her was almost enough to drive her back to the quarantine station. The streets teemed with people, all of them hurrying and shouting, many in languages she had never heard before today. She saw peddlers pushing carts filled with rags, and other dark-faced men in tattered clothing hawking hot chestnuts, apples, and other delicacies. The spicy smell of food drifted out on the wind, and her stomach clenched in a fierce stab of hunger.

As she watched, arrivals from the docks meshed with the bustling crowds in the streets, some chattering loudly, excited; others scurried along, shoulders hunched against the elements, looking as apprehensive as Terese felt. The churning in her stomach was as much fear as hunger, and she fought down a surge of nausea. Panic pressed in on her as she considered the situation in which she had thrust herself and the girl at her side.

Here she stood, in a strange city in a foreign land, without so much as a familiar face or a recognizable landmark. She had no way of knowing what had happened to the newspaper people who were to have met them, no idea where to look for them, where to go…what to do.

Her attention was caught just then by two suspicious-looking creatures coming toward them. Brady had warned her about the runners, the unscrupulous leeches who preyed upon arriving passengers in an attempt to bilk them of their money and any other belongings. Instinct told Terese that the two heading their way might well be of this class of brutes.

One seemed little more than a boy, with a cheeky grin, a shiny coat, and an exaggerated swagger. The other was older and badly in need of a shave and probably a wash, from the looks of him. Both were eyeing Terese in a calculating way as they approached. The older man did not seem all that interested, no doubt because he saw no fine luggage or other signs of prosperity. The younger of the two, however, continued to appraise the length of her with eyes that made Terese think of a fish gutter.

"Can we help you and the wee miss?" The younger spoke first, his voice unctuous, his eyes still clinging to Terese's form, which in truth had filled out some with the child she was carrying. "Perhaps you're in need of directions or decent rooms to let?"

The two planted themselves in front of Terese in such a way that she suddenly felt trapped.

"Not at all," she said, forcing a note of confidence into her voice. "We are waiting for our friends, so you need not concern yourselves."

The two glanced at each other, and this time it was the older man who spoke. "Ah, so 'tis Irish you are then?" He cracked a gaping grin, and Terese could almost smell the rotten breath that surely emanated from that toothless cavern. "We are Irishmen ourselves and bound to look out for our own. Come along with us now, and we'll take you to safe lodgings where you can stay as long as need be."

Terese was aware that the two were closing in on them still more. Suddenly angry, she bared her teeth and made a slashing motion with one hand. "Didn't I say we're meeting friends? Now let us pass, if you please!"

The young one thrust his face only an inch or so from hers. "Ah, now, you needn't pretend with us. We're here to help you and your little sister, don't you know? We'll see you safely to the city and a proper place to stay. Here, now, let us help with your belongings," he insisted, making as if to relieve Terese of her sack.

"You'll be taking us nowhere at all!" she hissed at him, lunging sideways with Shona firmly in tow.

The younger of the two bounders was quick and blocked Terese's move, his maddening smile still in place even as a definite threat glinted in his eyes. "A comely lass like yourself alone on the city streets is an invitation to trouble itself! Be a clever girl now and come along with us. We know a fine boarding house where you and the wee lass can have a good meal and a warm bed for a reasonable rate."

"Are you deaf as well as ugly?" Terese shot back. "We're being met, I tell you! We are in no need of your *assistance!*"

With that, she surprised him by stamping on his foot, then hauling herself and Shona off at a fierce run.

The cobbles were slippery from the rain, and Shona was weak, stumbling and faltering as she went. But Terese was determined to put as much distance as possible between themselves and their pursuers. She kept going, her chest pounding as much from anger as exertion as she dragged Shona down the street beside her.

They didn't stop until they reached a narrow alley. When Terese looked back, she was relieved to see no sign of the runners. Apparently they had decided that two poor, hungry-looking girls were not worth their efforts.

With their backs to the entrance of the alley, they stood watching the mass of pedestrians pushing past. Finally, because she did not know what else to do, Terese took a tight grip on Shona's hand, and, with the girl snug at her side, slipped in among the crowd.

She had no thought of where they were going, no idea as to what to do next. She knew only the need to get away from the docks, to make her way into the city that beckoned.

They trudged down the street, so close to those hurrying by that they could overhear a jumble of conversations in different languages all at once.

Yet in spite of the host of strangers on all sides and the child clinging tightly to her hand, Terese had never felt more alone in her life.

II

A FUTILE SEARCH

*They brought her to the city
and she faded slowly there.*

RICHARD D'ALTON WILLIAMS

NEW YORK CITY

It was Sunday morning before Terese and Shona finally reached the forbidding brick building that housed the *Vanguard*.

They had spent the night huddled in the doorway of an abandoned warehouse. Once again Terese was more than thankful for the emerald cloak Brady had bought her back in Ireland, for its folds were generous enough to keep the chill from both herself and the girl. The overhang of the building warded off the worst of the rain and kept them fairly snug.

Even so, it had been a long, uneasy night. For the most part, the few people who passed by ignored the two desolate girls in their crude shelter. In the deepest hours of the night the city seemed to pulsate with strange sounds and even stranger inhabitants. Terese felt as if she hadn't been asleep at all, though in truth she had managed to doze some off and on.

She had awakened long before dawn with a fierce gnawing in her belly and a sick taste clinging to her mouth. By now they were both famished. They hadn't eaten since the day before at the quarantine center, a breakfast of thin gruel that wasn't enough to satisfy even a puny child like Shona.

They might have found the newspaper building the day before had they not gotten themselves lost numerous times. The directions gleaned from strangers had varied widely enough so that each route they followed led them to a different place. Finally, with darkness and a heavy rain settling thickly over the city, Terese had given up the search and sought shelter for the night.

This morning, with the help of a jolly pushcart vendor's directions, given in broken but understandable English, they had found the *Vanguard* building at last.

But the doors were locked, and from all appearances the building was empty.

Dismay swept over Terese as she remembered that this was Sunday. Of course no one would be working, even at such a big, important enterprise as the *Vanguard*.

For a long time, she stood staring at the building. Rain water had pooled in the cobbles of the street, and her *pampootas*—her homemade shoes—were worn so thin she might as well have been barefoot. But Terese was scarcely mindful of her wet feet. The only thing she could think of was the seemingly hopeless situation into which she had plunged them by her foolhardy act of stealing the passes and fleeing the hospital for the city. Now they truly had no place to go, no shelter from the bitter cold and rain.

But if they *hadn't* left the quarantine center, she reminded herself, they probably would not have survived another week.

Aye, but at least at Tompkinsville there had been a roof over their heads.

It was still raining when she led Shona around to the back of the building, in hopes of discovering an unlocked door. A few sodden sheets of newspaper were strewn randomly on the ground, as if the wind had blown them off the wagon parked nearby. A few feet away, two young boys were hunched over a barrel where something was burning. A thin ribbon of smoke snaked upward from the barrel.

The two boys eyed Terese and Shona with suspicion, and it occurred to Terese that she and Shona must look a fright by now. They were probably dirty, and their clothing was soaked from head to toe. But as she took in the boys' shabby apparel and pinched faces, she decided that these two would probably pay little heed to another's tattered apparel.

She tried to smile but felt it come more as a grimace. "Please, could we share your fire for a moment?" she said, grateful—not for the first time—that she had learned the English as her da and Cavan had insisted.

Neither boy made a reply, but finally the taller of the two—who looked to be eight or nine at most—gave a jerk of his head as if to indicate assent. He was a proud-looking little fellow, his worn cap set at a jaunty tilt atop a mop of red hair.

With Shona in tow, Terese wasted no time in joining the boys at the barrel. Whatever they were burning stunk of something vile, but Terese was too thankful for the warmth to mind the smell. "Would there happen to be anyone about this morning, do you suppose?" she asked, nodding to the building.

The boy with the cap looked at her, and Terese was caught off guard by the utter lack of childishness in his features. He might have been a tiny man, so hard were his eyes, so tight his mouth.

"'Tis Sunday," he said with a hint of a sneer.

"Aye, it is that," Terese shot back, irritated by his insolence. "But the two of you are here."

"We sleep over there," said the smaller of the two, pointing across the street where another brick building stood, this one with a stairway crawling up its side. "Under the steps."

"'Sides," the older boy put in, "we've sold out of our Sundays."

Terese looked at him. His speech wasn't quite as thick with the Irish as her own, but not far from it. "Sundays?"

"The Sunday *papers,*" said the boy, looking at her as if she hadn't all her wits.

"You work here?" she said, hope quickening in her.

Again the redheaded boy watched her as if she were a fool. "Not *here.* We're *newsboys,* don't you know?"

"Newsboys?" For some reason, Terese seemed to be having a difficult time concentrating. Her head ached, and her hands and feet felt strangely numb, disembodied. Her own speech sounded slurred to her, and the boy with the red hair was staring at her as if he found her peculiar entirely.

"We sell newspapers," he said in a snide tone, as if he were trying to communicate with an eejit. "We work mostly for Black Jack himself."

"Black Jack?"

"What are you, then, just off the boat?" cracked the boy. "Black Jack Kane, of course. Him who owns the *Vanguard.* Mr. Kane, he don't let out his papers to just any boy. He picks and chooses those he knows he can trust." His chin went up a notch higher. "Like me and Whitey here. We got a better deal than most, don't you see? Most places, they make you pay for your papers right up front, no matter what. If you ain't got the money, you get no papers. But Mr. Kane, now, once he learns he can trust a boy, he'll dole out the papers for a few days without makin' us pay, if we're short."

Terese was only vaguely aware of the boy's spiel. She wasn't interested in his newspapers. All she cared about was finding Jack Kane.

"Your Mr. Kane—could you be directing us to his house, then?"

The two boys gaped as if she'd taken leave of her senses altogether. "Sure and you're daft, if you're thinking you can just march up to Black Jack's *house!*"

"Sure and I will be doing exactly that," Terese snapped, suddenly impatient with his cheek, "once you give me the directions!"

Both boys snickered. Again it was the older of the two who spoke. "Even if I knew where himself lived—which I don't—but if I did, and say I was to tell you where that is, wouldn't the coppers run you off the street? Old Black Jack, they say he lives in a fine big mansion somewheres uptown. You ain't likely to be finding much of a welcome there, I expect."

Terese was so numb from weakness that her ears were ringing. "Mr. Kane is expecting us!" she grated. "And you can keep a civil tongue."

The boy reached to give her a shove. "And *you* can find your own fire!"

Just then the back door of the building swung open to reveal a big, angry-looking baldheaded man. He poked his head out, then stepped the rest of the way into the street. "What're you boys up to now, hangin' around here on a Sunday mornin'? That you, Snipe?"

"Me and Whitey, that's right, Mr. Wall. We ain't up to nothing. Just warmin' ourselves up a bit, is all."

"Well, you can just be warming yourselves somewhere else! You know the rules—there's to be no pottering about once you've finished with your papers. Now get on with the both of you!"

The older boy cast a sly look at Terese. "Well, but wasn't we tryin' to help these girls, Mr. Wall? They're wanting Mr. Kane's home address. They claim that he's *expecting* them, don't you see?"

The bull of a man turned to glare at Terese. She felt Shona pull behind her, clinging to her skirt.

"What's this?" he snarled, his gaze raking Terese with undisguised contempt. "What the divil are you up to, girl?"

Nausea scalded Terese's throat. She could scarcely force a reply. "Please, sir," she choked out. "I need to find Mr. Kane. I need to find him right away."

The man shot her a look of outrage mingled with suspicion. "And what sort of business would the likes of you be havin' with Mr. Kane?"

The building behind the man had begun to sway, and Terese felt the street tilt crazily beneath her feet. "He's expecting us, and that's the truth."

"Oh, indeed?" The big man sneered, and planted his hands on his hips. "Expecting you, is he? Well, ain't that strange now, seein' as how he only left his office but a short time ago? Seems odd, don't it, that he wouldn't have waited, if he was *expecting* you?"

Terese groped for something to steady herself, found nothing, and staggered toward him. "He was here? We missed him?"

"He was. And he didn't say nothin' about two raggedy girls either."

Terese moistened her lips, struggling to get the words out. "If you'd just be telling me where to find him…"

"I'll be telling you nothing of the kind, you foolish girl! Whatever your game is, you'd best look elsewhere. Why, Black Jack Kane no doubt has scrawny little girls like you for supper!"

He made a move toward her, and Terese stumbled backward. For an instant, the man's hard features seemed to gentle. Then he began to spin crazily right in front of her, his mouth moving with words no longer audible as a storm of darkness hurtled toward him, sucking him up and out of sight before swallowing Terese along with him.

※

Madog Wall—predictably dubbed "Mad Dog" by his cohorts—thought of himself as a hard man: hardfisted, hardheaded, and hard hearted.

No one was likely to disagree with him. He had earned his reputation as a formidable fighter by brawling on the docks before coming to work for Jack Kane, and he could still trounce a man twenty years his junior if the situation called for it. His stamina was legendary. No man had ever seen him swagged, and though he seldom engaged an opponent, everyone knew Madog Wall would never back down from a challenge.

What was *not* so widely known—indeed it was not known at all—was that although Madog coveted the reputation he had earned for himself and maintained it with deliberate effort, he nevertheless had his soft spots. His loyalty to Jack Kane, for example, was so fierce as to be blind, if not obsessive. Then, too, he harbored an almost maudlin weakness for the helpless— especially injured animals and abandoned or orphaned children.

When he saw the older girl's eyes roll back in her head, Madog lunged to catch her before she dropped to the street. At the same time, he caught a glimpse of the little one at her side, the thin face crumpled in bewilderment and fear.

As he caught the older of the two in his arms, her fancy cloak parted and Madog saw that she was in the family way. Was she the mother of the smaller lass as well? Surely not—she looked little more than a child herself!

The girl was unconscious entirely, limp as a rag doll in his arms. The little one had begun to wail—an odd, thin sound like that of a sick kitten—and tug at the older girl's hand as if she feared that she were dead.

Madog's wits failed him for a moment. Clearly, the two lasses were either ill or starving—possibly both. The little one was so thin her flesh appeared like paper drawn over her bones. And the unconscious girl in his arms, though she seemed not so frail, looked as though she might be bad sick. Her cheeks were flaming, and he could feel the heat of her even through that heavy cloak. And her with child!

A thought struck him, and he gave the girl a sharp look. But, no, surely Jack Kane would not be responsible for her *condition!*

Ah, no, of course not! There was little likelihood of the boss's consorting with a peasant girl.

So what sort of deviousness was she up to, then?

There was no thought of allowing her to get next to Mr. Kane, of course. If by some unimaginable chance the boss had actually been looking for these two, well, then, he would have stuck around until they showed up, wouldn't he?

What to do with them, then? They were none of his affair, these two shabby strangers.

He looked at the little girl and saw that she was shaking. Was she that cold, then, or simply afraid?

She looked directly at him, her gaze never wavering. Something in Madog softened in spite of himself. There was no call to be cruel to a wee one like this, after all.

As he stood looking around, it occurred to him that the mission over on Pearl Street would almost certainly take them in. That Dr. Leslie, who ran both the women's dwelling and the house for the men a few doors down, was a good enough sort. It was said that he never turned a needy soul away.

Madog's gaze came to rest on one of the newspaper wagons pulled close to the door, then flicked to the wee girl who still stood watching him, a fist pressed against her mouth.

Finally, Madog heaved an exasperated sigh and jerked his head toward the wagon. "Come on then," he told the little one, hoisting the other girl more securely in his arms. "Let's get the both of you to shelter."

12

FACES IN THE CROWD

A man has often cut a rod to beat himself.

IRISH PROVERB

The choir had already begun their opening hymn when Samantha stepped inside the sanctuary. She had shed her coat in the closet at the entrance, but her shoes were dripping, her feet and hands chilled. She tried to ignore thoughts of a head cold as she slipped into a pew next to Cavan Sheridan, who smiled and motioned for the two youngest Carver children next to him to move down and make more room.

Rufus's oldest boy, Gideon, had come for Samantha in the church wagon, already packed with children from outlying neighborhoods. But the wagon leaked badly, offering little protection to its occupants, and Samantha was almost as wet as if she'd walked part of the way.

As she settled into the pew, Samantha promised herself—again—that from now on she would put aside even more from her wages until she could afford her own buggy. Jack was actually paying her quite handsomely; she should be able to save an extra dollar or two a week without any great sacrifice.

She glanced at Cavan Sheridan again, saw that his pleasant features showed definite signs of strain. Dark smudges under his eyes plainly indicated that his concern for his sister had kept him up most of the night. Samantha wished she could think of some reassurance to offer him, but what was there to say? They could only hope that Jack's informant—Hoey—would turn up some word before much longer.

She smiled at Rufus's and Amelia's two youngest, on Cavan's right. The taller of the two, Ezra, was whispering something to his brother, Tommy. Both stopped long enough to give Samantha a sheepish grin when she caught their eye.

The church smelled of rainwater and mildew and was, as usual, far too cold for the sake of comfort. The small woodstoves in the front and back never quite managed to chase away the chill in the drafty old building. Rufus sometimes joked that he kept it that way on purpose to make it more difficult for certain members to doze off.

But the choir was warming things up now with their lively rendition of a spiritual. Heads were nodding and shoulders swaying, and Rufus looked animated and eager to begin as the song ended and he approached the pulpit to greet his flock.

The Mercer Street Tabernacle had been Samantha's church home for over two years, ever since she'd gotten to know Rufus Carver, the preacher, and his wife, Amelia. She no longer felt the need to explain to anyone why she had chosen to join a mostly black congregation. It wasn't altogether due to the friendship that had sprung up between her and Amelia Carver as they worked together in the slum settlements, although in the beginning that might have accounted for a part of her interest. The fact was that in this place Samantha had found a genuine working out of the gospel of Christ, as well as the kind of unconditional acceptance of herself as a person, that she had never known within the cold stone walls of her former uptown congregation.

The little clapboard building on Mercer Street was not only a shelter, a haven to its people, but it was also a happy place, the kind of place where people *wanted* to be.

The friendliness and goodwill of the congregation, the soulful, stirring music, and Rufus's lively Bible preaching worked together to create an atmosphere that was both cheerful and worshipful. It seemed to Samantha that God must be very much in attendance here, and surely he enjoyed every minute of his time among them.

Not all the members were Negro, as it happened. Over the years, several of those who, like Samantha, taught and worked in the settlements—and others, like Cavan Sheridan—had found themselves drawn to the Mercer Street congregation. On any given Sunday morning, one could look out over the crowded pews, as Samantha was doing now, and see an increasing number of light-skinned faces among the regular members.

The one face Samantha wished she might find in their midst, however, was never there, nor, if she were to be honest with herself, was it likely that it ever *would* be.

But she could still hope. She could still pray. A mocking thought insinuated itself at the edges of her mind: that she was almost certainly praying for the impossible. Yet that scornful whisper could not completely drown out the quieter, gentler voice deep within her spirit reminding her that the God she loved and trusted was Lord of all things, even the impossible.

And so she had not as yet given up her heart's plea, had never completely ceased searching for that one special face—Jack's face—among the crowd.

❧

For years now it had been Jack Kane's habit to work off his tensions or an occasional foul mood with a lengthy, brisk walk. When his mind was cluttered or his emotions in a jumble, he would simply start out walking and not stop until decisions were made or problems solved—or until he had at least managed to clear his head and lighten his mood a bit.

The weather had never been a deterrent. In fact, he actually found something rather cleansing, even invigorating, about a good walk in a driving rain or a winter snowstorm.

This morning was no exception. He had left the house in an almost desperate rush to get away from the pandemonium of his own thoughts. Addy's barbed remarks about his "heathen" ways—in other words, his neglect of the Sunday morning mass—had only thrown coals on the fire of his exasperation.

His hovering housekeeper meant well, and for the most part Jack tolerated her impertinence in areas where no one else would have dared to go. But this morning the woman had come very near to exhausting his patience.

In truth, this morning he seemed to *have* no patience.

After his walk he had taken the buggy as far as the office, where he'd waited in vain for Hoey to turn up with information on the missing Sheridan girl and the two orphans. When the little weasel hadn't shown, Jack had finally gone storming out of the building.

As much as he tried to blame Addy's meddling or Hoey's failure to show up for his black mood, he knew he was dissembling. He had risen from his bed before dawn feeling sour and edgy, and as the morning went on his disposition had only darkened.

His bad temper almost certainly had more to do with the events of the previous day than the morning's irritations. He had come back to New York eager to see Samantha, hopeful of spending the entire evening with her. Well, he had seen her all right, but not in the manner he would have chosen. They had spent most of the afternoon prowling about the harbor in the rain with Cavan Sheridan, trying to find news of the boy's sister, who seemed to have disappeared almost as soon as the ship put in.

At supper both Samantha and Sheridan had been too distracted to do more than peck at their meals while they fired questions at Jack about the possible whereabouts of the missing travelers. And to his great disappointment, there had been virtually no time alone with Samantha later on. To cap it off, when they called it a day, he'd come home to find that infernal letter waiting for him.

It was the first of its kind since last summer, during the time when Cavan Sheridan had taken a bullet in Jack's place—a bullet which had very nearly cost the boy his life. Before then there had been other threats—random ones mostly and seemingly unconnected—which Jack had discarded as the meaningless ravings of a lunatic or some hothead with an ax to grind. Even now he still wasn't convinced that any of the earlier letters had been related to the attempt on his life.

But this latest one was different. Written in a hand that would suggest a certain measure of literacy, it gave the sense of being carefully composed, its threat ever so much more chilling because of the lack of choleric raving that had been common to its predecessors. There had been such a cold precision about the whole thing, such a complete lack of emotion throughout, that Jack had found himself more troubled by it than by any of the others.

Supposedly the motive for the anonymous writer's umbrage had to do with the *Vanguard's* current series of articles dealing with immigration—a series under Cavan Sheridan's byline, focusing on the individual stories of immigrants whose passage and resettlement were being sponsored by the newspaper. Certainly there was no denying the undercurrent of racism that ran through the writer's invective. There was also an obvious attempt to apply a tone of outrage against Jack's encouragement of immigration, "an odious practice that would eventually pollute the city and the entire nation with undesirables."

Yet despite the pervading bluster of bigotry throughout, Jack sensed there might be something else at work, something more *personal* behind the words. More disturbing still, however, was the fact that the malice was directed not only toward Jack himself but against the entire newspaper, along with Cavan Sheridan and anyone else who happened to be associated with the immigration project.

Quite possibly, it was the kind of grievance that could even extend to Samantha. She was a part of the resettlement program, after all.

The thought that he might have unknowingly placed Sheridan and even Samantha in jeopardy had kept Jack awake much of the night. No doubt it was also responsible for the knot of dread and hot anger building inside him now as he tramped the streets of the city in the rain.

He pulled the collar of his topcoat tighter against the cold sting of the rain, a wave of chilling isolation settling over him as he picked up his pace even more. The feeling of being cut off from everyone else was nothing new to him. He often felt himself to be a stranger in an entire city of strangers. Entire settlements existed side by side, so close that their cooking odors and the stench of their refuse often intermingled. And yet no one really knew anyone else. Each community lived within its own environment, its own boundaries. People came and went and sometimes intermarried but more often than not mated within the colony. Neighborhoods sprang up and died, but those who moved on often relocated only to build a new community in which the old traditions and customs—and insularity—were reestablished.

And so it went. And all the while no one really knew more than a few others outside his own small circle of existence.

Jack's sense of New York was not so much that of an enormous, sprawling city but of many *hidden* cities, a number of which were still unknown to him and perhaps always would be. Although as a newspaperman he was probably less confined to place, less limited by boundaries, than other men, he often felt as if there were vast communities of which he knew virtually nothing.

He had spent a quarter of a century in this city, had come to love it with a strange ferocity, loved it for its weaknesses as well as its strengths. New York was a city of great power and little patience. A place teeming with grandeur and riddled with squalor. A domain that glittered with opulence and reeked with decadence. A city of sinners and saints, barons and beggars, mystics and monsters.

And always it was a city of secrets.

In a little over two decades, Jack had managed to carve out his own small monarchy in this place, had established a dominion of sorts over the publishing business while gaining for himself, if not respect, at least the stature—and notoriety—inherent with that kind of success. He had friends, and he had enemies—and he liked to think he knew one from the other.

But did he? He was no longer quite so sure. Was it possible that somewhere among these secretive, violent streets an enemy lurked—perhaps one with a familiar face but with the soul of a stranger—who harbored a hatred intense enough to destroy not only him but everything and everyone he cared about?

Over the years he had fought and defeated many an adversary.

But they had been rivals he recognized, opponents he knew well enough to anticipate. This was different. A faceless foe would be harder to trounce.

That being the case then, what he must do was learn the identity of his nemesis. At the same time, he had to warn Samantha and Cavan Sheridan.

He felt a sudden, almost feverish urgency to reach them. He knew where to find them, of course. At this hour on a Sunday morning, there was only one place they were likely to be.

As soon as he realized the direction in which he was headed, Jack was struck by a grim sense of irony. Both Samantha and Sheridan had been anything but subtle in their attempts to lure him to Sunday morning services at Rufus's church. Sheridan in particular was positively blatant in his efforts to see Jack "saved," whereas Samantha was more likely to drop a light-handed invitation every now and then.

Jack's response—routine by now—to their tactics was an offhand allusion to the effect that, short of an act of Providence, they should not pitch their hopes too high on his behalf.

Now, as he approached the Mercer Street Tabernacle, his insides still humming with a sense of urgency to reach the two of them, Jack couldn't stop a thought of that "act of Providence" to which he'd so casually referred.

It occurred to him to simply wait outside until the service was dismissed, lest they get the wrong idea.

He had not quite reached the entrance doors when the sky opened in earnest and sent the rain pouring down in a fury. Jack stopped and looked up, scowling at the surprising force of the downpour.

After another moment and a wry mutter of resignation, he hurried up the front steps and made for the door.

13

A SHELTER FROM THE STORM

Whence came you, pallid wanderer, so destitute and lorn,
With step so weak and faltering, and face so wan and worn?

ANONYMOUS: *A LAMENT FROM THE NATION*

Terese felt herself surfacing through dark waters, floating back to awareness. She was cold, so cold her entire body was shaking in a frenzy. In spite of the trembling, her limbs felt leaden and useless, and a weight seemed to be pressing down on her chest, her breath coming in labored gasps.

Had the rain stopped? No…she was inside, in a place she had never seen before… lying on a cot or a bed…and she was ill…hurting…

She turned her head, and the mere effort sent a fierce pain shooting up the back of her skull. She blinked, trying to focus—and looked directly into the eyes of a lean-faced man who was stooped down on one leg beside her, watching her closely.

Terese shrunk back.

"Don't be afraid," the man said in a quiet voice. "You're quite safe. No one's going to hurt you."

He brushed a shock of sandy-colored hair away from his eyes and tucked the blanket more closely about Terese's shoulders.

"What…" Terese's voice sounded muddy to her ears, thick and unnatural. Her head felt the same way. She couldn't think of the words she needed to form a simple question.

The stranger smiled at her. "It seems you fainted," he said in the same quiet voice.

Fainted? Had she ever fainted before?

She couldn't remember. She remembered only a big man with a shining dome of a head and a gruff voice. And the rain…the cold, relentless rain…

"You were out for quite some time," said the man with the light hair. "How do you feel?"

Terese's mind was still scrambled. She found it impossible to think. Trying to ignore the pain in her head, she turned to look around her surroundings. The room was large, like a big meetinghouse of some sort, and furnished with only single cots such as her own—perhaps twenty or more—and some small tables. Most of the cots were empty, but here and there a woman or child lay sleeping or staring at the ceiling.

"Where am I?"

"You're at the Grace Mission house. Mr. Wall brought you and the little girl here in a wagon, after you fainted. My name is David Leslie. I'm a doctor."

Terese stared at him.

She had never met a doctor before. She studied him, trying to take his measure. He did seem kindly natured, and he had a strong, open face that somehow invited trust. But she no longer trusted any man, doctor or no.

She glanced toward the foot of the cot and saw Shona standing there. The girl's features were drawn taut. She looked terribly frightened.

"Shona…"

"Ah, so that's her name. She wouldn't tell us. Is she your sister?"

Terese shook her head. "I've…been looking after her, is all."

After a slight hesitation, the doctor went on. "Well, she's all right, I think. She has something of a cold, but nothing serious. Someone will keep an eye on her until you're up and about."

He looked to be a fairly young man, Terese realized, and his dark blue eyes, though intense, appeared kind. But when he reached to put a hand to her forehead, she drew back.

He made a slight motion with his hand, shaking his head. "I'm not going to hurt you. Just lie still a moment, won't you?"

His hand on her brow was warm. Somehow it seemed to leave a chill when he took it away. Terese watched as he reached inside a small black case and withdrew a bottle, then poured something into a spoon.

"I want you to take this," he said, putting the spoon to her lips. "It won't taste very good, I'm afraid, but it will help you."

He put a hand behind Terese's head, helping her to sit up. A wave of sick weakness slammed into her with the effort, and she barely managed to swallow the vile-tasting liquid.

The doctor quickly eased her back onto the cot.

For a moment the floor seemed to tilt beneath her, and Terese thought she would pass out again. But she fought the nausea bubbling in her throat, knotting her fists and pulling in a deep breath, then another.

"What is this place?" she finally asked him.

He smiled again as he closed the black case. "Think of it as a shelter from the storm," he said. "A place to stay until you have somewhere else to go. You'll find it clean and warm—well, as warm as one could hope for from such a drafty old house."

He had an odd way of speaking: hesitantly, as if he might be somewhat unsure of himself, and his words came clipped and short, with a slight roll and a lift of his voice at the end. Even when he wasn't asking a question, it sounded as if he were.

He stood, and Terese saw that he was a fairly tall man, but slender and deep eyed. He had a way of leaning slightly forward that gave his shoulders a bit of a stoop.

She was so cold! She thought she would surely freeze to death. And it hurt so much to breathe! "What's…wrong with me?" she choked out.

He stood looking down at her. "You're very ill. I'm afraid you have pneumonia."

Pneumonia? Pneumonia was a death disease! It had taken the lives of her mother and her sisters.

"Am I going to die, then?" she asked him, fear churning in her stomach.

He frowned. "Not if I can help it," he said firmly. "Tell me, how far along are you in your pregnancy?"

Terese felt her face flame at this strange man's bluntness about her condition. She couldn't bring herself to look at him when she replied. "Six months—perhaps close on seven." She caught a breath. "Is—will the babe be sick too?"

"Not necessarily. And I'd caution you not to worry about that right now. Let's concentrate on getting you well, so you can take care of your baby." He studied her for a moment. "You're Irish, isn't that right?"

Terese nodded.

"And am I right in assuming that you haven't been here—in New York—very long?"

How long *had* it been? A week? Two? A month? Terese couldn't remember. Her head felt heavy and cluttered, like broken pieces of pottery about to fall free. He was asking her something else, and her mind fumbled to grasp what he was saying. But so consumed was she by the pain in her chest and the nausea driving through her in waves that she couldn't think of anything but how utterly wretched she was.

She felt herself turning hot as a furnace. Dizziness whirled around her, and she could scarcely make out the doctor's words as he went on. He seemed to be apologizing for his questions, for tiring her. "I'll let you rest for now," he said.

He went on to add something more, but his words were swept away by the sudden storm of hot, angry pain and sickness that came roaring in on her. His voice, then his face faded as Terese felt the churning black water close over her.

❦

David Leslie watched in dismay as the girl again spiraled down into a state of semiconsciousness. Even as he fumbled for the smelling salts in his case, he knew they would do no good. She was too deeply under, too tightly trapped in the delirium-clouded stupor of a raging fever.

He also knew the chances of losing her were great. Both lungs were afflicted. Her temperature was dangerously high, and she was obviously malnourished as well. From the looks of her and the little girl, neither had enjoyed an adequate meal for days, perhaps longer.

Her condition was all too familiar to him. Among the hundreds of immigrants he had seen at the men's and women's mission houses over the past few months, pneumonia was a common ailment, though certainly not the only one. Bronchitis, measles, scarlet fever, and the deadly typhus seemed to ride the backs of these foreign immigrants—especially the indigent Irish—like leeches.

He had saved a number of those he'd cared for—by God's grace and the benefit of his Edinburgh medical training—but he had lost almost as many. Pneumonia was especially treacherous for those poor travelers who came across on the "coffin ships." Trapped in the dank, cold bowels of steerage, with an utter lack of fresh air, proper food, and the means of keeping themselves dry and warm, they more often than not arrived dangerously ill—if they arrived at all. The Irish seemed particularly victimized by the unconscionable ship owners, who often packed in three or four times as many persons as should have been allowed, then fed them nothing more than slop and foul water for weeks on end.

David pulled up a stool by the girl's bed and again took her pulse, which was entirely too fast. Listening to her chest, he found almost no healthy sounds, but instead the whistling and the dreaded rattle that meant the pneumonia was advancing to the final, almost always mortal, stages.

He watched her for a moment. Her breathing was rapid and labored, her skin flushed an angry crimson.

"What's her name?" he said, turning to the young girl at the foot of the bed.

The child stared at him. She had said nothing since they arrived at the mission. David was beginning to wonder if she could speak at all when she finally murmured a single word.

"T'reece."

"*Terese,* is it?"

The girl nodded.

"What about her last name?"

The child looked at him, then shook her head.

The poor thing was clearly frightened half out of her wits. No telling what she had been through by now. David smiled at her, hoping to put her at ease. "And your name is *Shona,* isn't that right?"

She looked at him with those sunken, woefully solemn eyes, then again gave a hesitant nod of her head.

"Well, I expect you know *your* last name, Shona, now don't you?" David said lightly.

"Madden," she said softly after a moment.

"Ah. Well, Shona Madden, I'm going to go downstairs and fetch one of the ladies to help me. I'd like you to just come round and sit close by until I come back. All right?"

The child was obedient, he'd say that for her. Like a little martinet, she walked around the cot and sat down on the stool, her eyes fixed on the girl named *Terese.*

David took a last look at his patient as well. Despite the fact that she was in the throes of a devastating illness, wasted by fever and malnutrition—and swollen with child—she was difficult *not* to look at. At her worst—for he couldn't imagine her being in a much worse condition—she was striking; at her best she must be absolutely magnificent. Even cropped and tangled, that russet hair was lovely. And when she'd first opened those shadowed, smoke-blue eyes, David had experienced a catch in his throat that caught him completely unawares. She was too thin by far, of course, disheveled, and frighteningly ill. But somehow none of that took away from her uncommon loveliness.

As he went downstairs, he found himself wondering again about the lack of a husband. She was wearing a ring—an unusual object cast in heavy gold. But it didn't appear to be a wedding band. Had her man perished during the voyage? Even the strongest weren't exempt from the ravages of an Atlantic crossing.

There had been no time to learn anything about her, really. And he suspected the child would be of no help, since apparently she didn't even know the other's last name.

Always, he wondered about their stories, these immigrants who risked so much to come to America. Sometimes they told him of whatever it was that had compelled them to break all ties with their past and begin new lives in a strange land.

Sometimes they failed to survive long enough to tell him anything.

His own parents had made this same life-changing decision; perhaps that fact accounted for his ongoing curiosity about other immigrants. In the case of Annice and Duncan Leslie, faith had been the motivating factor. David's father had heard a "clear call of God" to America when David and his brother, William, were still boys. Duncan Leslie's first congregation had been a dying church in Boston, which, by the time Duncan received a "new call" a few years later, had virtually doubled in membership.

Although his parents had long since retired and gone back to their home country to live, David had returned to Scotland only twice, to take his medical education in Edinburgh and to visit his parents on a later occasion. America was David's home, and he loved it: its sprawling expanse, its energy, its excitement, its people—especially the people, with their never-ending, fascinating diversity.

His own "call of God" had not been quite so clear as that of his father's, at least not in the beginning. He had known only that he was called to some sort of ministry and had for a time assumed that ministry would take place behind a pulpit. Only when he returned from Edinburgh and began to do some charity work in the tenement sections of the city did he finally catch God's vision for his life's work. Since then he had established four mission houses—two of which he still supervised on a daily basis—and trained two "Timothies" of his own, sending them out to launch similar missions, one near the harbor and the other in the notorious Five Points slum.

During the years that he labored as both physician and pastor, he came to realize that he was no more one than the other. His patients had become his church, a church without walls. They had also become his family. He had no real home of his own. Home was whichever mission house he happened to lodge in on any given night. With his parents back in Scotland and his brother, William, teaching in a New England college, there was no reason, after all, to maintain a home.

He could easily have slipped into a solitary, empty life, had it not been for his patients and others who passed through the mission houses. Most of the time, though, David would have said his life was anything but empty. He seldom indulged in introspection, and when loneliness crept in on him, he usually managed to deflect it by busying himself even more.

So far as he was concerned, God had granted him a full life, one blessed by a work he loved to do and a faith that had thus far sustained him through all manner of change and challenge. As he now approached his midthirties, however, the occasional thought of a home and family edged its way into his thoughts. Sometimes a particular event—such as coming upon the lovely but unfortunate young expectant mother upstairs—would evoke a yearning for something more than what he had.

Other times it was the bleak prospect of returning to an empty room late at night, with no one waiting to care whether he returned or not.

He hoped these longings didn't mark him in the Lord's eyes as an ingrate. At those times when loneliness crept in on him without warning he would remind himself that Christ, too, had lived a solitary life.

But wasn't it possible that even Christ had sometimes been lonely?

The thought came unbidden, catching David by surprise, and he found himself wondering if the Lord might not suffer similar pangs of loneliness and disappointment when his own creation, the children he loved beyond all understanding, drifted through their days with only halfhearted attempts to seek his presence, his fellowship—when they sought him at all.

The possibility caused David to take time out from his efforts and stop to offer a heartfelt prayer of loving thanks to his Savior, the one friend who *did* share that empty room late at night.

14

TEARING DOWN THE WALLS

The Pharisee's cant goes up for peace,
But the cries of his victims never cease.

JOHN BOYLE O'REILLY

Samantha was so astonished to glance over and see Jack—very wet, slightly disheveled, and obviously disgruntled—slipping into the pew beside her that she could do nothing but stare at him, speechless. Jack countered with a narrow-eyed, somewhat challenging look, as if daring her to show even the slightest hint of satisfaction at his appearance.

"Jack! What are you doing—"

Heads turned at her loud whisper, and Samantha felt her face flame.

"You invited me, remember?" he muttered a little too loudly. Again, people turned to look, including Cavan Sheridan—who broke into a wide smile at the sight of Jack—as did the Carver children and the widowed Sadie Brown at the other end of the pew.

"I—well…yes, I did," Samantha finally managed to choke out as he settled himself into the cramped space beside her. "I'm so glad…you could make it."

She tried to move down to allow him more room, but the pew was packed to capacity.

"You're drenched," she whispered.

One dark brow lifted a fraction. "It's raining," he said, straight-faced. His gaze flicked over her. "As you've obviously discovered for yourself."

Samantha put a hand to her still damp hair, and his eyes followed her movement.

"I need to talk with you and Sheridan immediately after the service," he whispered, leaning closer. "It's important."

"Has something happened? Did you find Cavan's sister and the children?"

He shook his head. "Not yet. But there's something you need to know. Both of you."

At that point, an elderly black lady directly in front of them turned to scowl. Again, Samantha's face burned. But Jack merely shot the woman an engaging smile, at the same time giving Samantha a slight nudge with his elbow.

Rufus was just stepping up to the scarred wooden pulpit. The instant he spied Jack, his face broke into a wide, gleeful grin. For a moment Samantha thought he was going to delay the sermon and come barreling out into the congregation!

Instead, he delayed only another second or two, then launched into the morning message.

"Brethren!" he thundered. Every head snapped to attention, including Jack's. "This morning the Lord has laid it on my heart to speak to you about tearing down the *walls* of this church!"

Predictably, several people in the congregation glanced at the interior walls, then cast questioning looks at their large, usually jovial preacher.

"That's what I said, brethren. We need to tear down these walls!" Rufus made a wide, sweeping motion with one arm to encompass their surroundings. "Tear them down and take this church out of this old building!"

It took Samantha only a few seconds to realize where Rufus was going with his curious opening. She was pleased to note that, beside her, Jack seemed to be all ears.

Always direct, Rufus leaned over the pulpit and began to scan the faces of his congregation, as if to make eye contact with each of them, one by one.

"The Lord, he's made it clear that we've been sittin' in our pews long enough. It's time to quit hidin' behind these walls. We need to get out there in the world and find out what's been goin' on all this time we've been hunkerin' down in our warm, comfortable church building."

Samantha suppressed a smile. The slight lift of Jack's shoulders told her that they—and others—were likely thinking along the same lines: The wooden pews were anything but comfortable, and even with both stoves firing full blast, the building was never really warm.

But Rufus seemed not to notice his congregation's amusement. He was clearly a man with a message. "It strikes me, brethren, that we've been playin' church so long, we might just have forgotten what the real world out there is like. Well, today the Lord says it's about time we go find out!"

◆

It wasn't that Jack had never heard Rufus speak before. He'd had occasion, if infrequently, to observe his old friend's ability to hold an audience and would thus have speculated that no sermon of Rufus Carver's would ever be boring.

What he hadn't expected was to find his interest so immediately and wholly captured by the subject of this particular message. At first he'd been intrigued to realize that the thrust of the sermon apparently had to do with one of his own personal grievances against the "institutional church"—be it the Roman Church of his boyhood or an uptown society congregation. It had long been Jack's observation that most of the churchgoing crowd, at least those with whom he'd come in contact over the years, knew next to nothing about the "real world"—and cared even less.

When he realized where Rufus was heading, he could have no more shut him out than he could have ignored Samantha's disquieting presence beside him. Never mind that he felt much like the proverbial black sheep in the midst of the flock. In spite of his general feeling of not belonging, he settled back, frankly curious to hear what Rufus had to say.

And it seemed that Rufus had quite a lot to say.

"I want you to understand that I'm not just preaching to *you,* brethren. I'm preaching to *myself* here, too. Because all of us, myself included, have been guilty of bein' so busy with *church* work of late that I fear we might just have lost sight of the *Lord's* work. We've been havin' such a good time with our suppers and our socials, been so wrapped up in our prayer meetings and our board meetings and our Sunday-after-service meetings that we haven't taken the time for meeting with the people—the folks who need what you and me already got. The *Lord!* People like the tax collectors and the trash collectors, the publicans and the prostitutes, the gamblers and the guttersnipes, and the godforsaken souls dyin' in the streets because we've been too *busy* to take the love of Jesus to them!"

Jack stared at the massive black man whom he had long counted as his closest friend as if he'd never seen him before. Rufus had just issued the same indictment on the camp who called themselves *Christians* that Jack himself had harbored for years now.

With the exception of a few—Rufus, obviously, for one, and certainly Samantha, for another—it seemed to him that many of the churchgoers who professed to be "imitators of Christ" gave rather poor imitations indeed.

From the little he knew about him—and it *was* little, he conceded—the man called Jesus hadn't just sat around singing hymns and looking pious and generally doing nothing. Jack wasn't exactly sure what he *did* do, for his education in spiritual matters was sorely lacking if not bordering on nonexistent. But according to those who claimed to know, Jesus had been a lot more than mere talk.

Rufus's voice abruptly jerked him out of his reflection. Startled, Jack felt as if his friend had been reading his mind as he went on with his sermon.

"Too often we act like we might catch some fearsome disease, were we to go among the *heathens* out there. But from what I can tell, the Lord, he didn't seem to be the least bit concerned about that. He made it his business to get to know all kinds of folks. He went to their houses. He sat down at the supper table with them."

Jack grinned at the thought of Rufus's fondness for a good meal.

Rufus was just getting warmed up, it seemed. "Jesus, he got to know people. Who they were, what their troubles were, what they needed—and more times than not, he pitched in with some help...*before* he started preaching to them!

"The Lord, he was smart enough to know that people wouldn't pay much attention to what he had to say if they were hungry or sick or down-and-out. He knew they weren't goin' to care about what a fellow had to say unless they saw that that fellow cared about *them*.

"And something else, brethren—I don't know about *your* Scriptures, but I don't recall *my* Bible sayin' a whole lot about the Lord criticizing folks, much less *condemning* them. Fact is, the only ones I recollect the Lord ever condemning were the *Pharisees.*" Rufus paused, drew in an expansive breath, then broke into a big, broad smile as he added, "You know. The *religious* people. Like *us*.

"And I sure don't recollect his *ignoring* folks! He paid *attention* to people, the Lord did!"

Jack studied his old friend. He had often taunted Rufus—good-naturedly—that he could have been a rich man if he had chosen politics instead of a pulpit. But he had never realized before today just how accurate that observation probably was.

No matter how much he needled Rufus, however, he never doubted the conviction of his friend's heart. Rufus was exactly where he was meant to be, doing what he was meant to do—what he wanted to do.

In truth Jack knew beyond the shadow of a doubt that the big, jovial son of a slave, who now stood leaning on his pulpit and smiling on his people, was above all else a true man of God.

Indeed, if ever he had known such a man—a man of God—Rufus Carver was that man.

He hadn't the faintest notion what had set Rufus off this morning. Apparently, he'd had one of his "words from the Lord" and felt constrained to share it. As for himself, he had to admit that he felt a certain satisfaction in knowing that Rufus didn't necessarily equate *religious* with *Christlike*.

Jack would concede that his own contempt for the mealymouthed hypocrites who could quote the Scriptures at length but saw nothing whatsoever wrong with tearing children away from their parents and selling them on an auction block might be somewhat excessive. As was, no doubt, his disgust for those who saw no disparity between warming the pews every Sunday and charging impoverished immigrants obscene rent monies for rooms unfit for pigs the rest of the week.

Pharisees, Rufus had called them.

Jack's censure would have undoubtedly been a lot less charitable.

But what had captured his interest so thoroughly today wasn't the realization that he and Rufus apparently saw eye-to-eye in this regard. He was more intrigued by the portrait Rufus had drawn of a Christ who wasn't above rubbing shoulders with the infidels of his day.

Jack supposed his reaction to this bit of enlightenment might have something to do with the fact that he was an infidel himself.

In any event, this was a different view of the Christ he remembered from his mother and his brief experience with the church of his childhood. That Christ had been a suffering Savior, who, to Jack's childlike imagination, had seemed somewhat pale and wan, beleaguered and victimized by his accusers, then mercilessly nailed to a tree, where he died in agony. That Christ had been beyond his comprehension.

Another view, again almost entirely based on his boyhood recollection and to some extent the teachings of a few particularly tyrannical nuns, had been that of a stern rule maker, a kind of divine disciplinarian. Fiercely stubborn and independent even then, Jack had responded as he was wont to do with authority in general: with deep-seated rebellion and even a certain measure of animosity.

Perhaps if Martha had lived longer, he might have come to know *her* Christ better. Certainly the Jesus Martha had worshiped had been a more approachable Christ, albeit a compassionate, long-suffering one. But they had had so little time, he and Martha, and back then he had lived in a virtual frenzy, establishing the paper and amassing his fortune. Work had become his god. And after Martha's death, work had also become his salvation.

The Christ Rufus had spoken of this morning was unfamiliar to Jack, but he was not without appeal. This Jesus would seem to be a more *manly* Christ, someone who wasn't afraid to get his hands dirty, who valued Everyman and perhaps even enjoyed going into the midst of a crowd and getting to know them while making himself known to them.

He considered Rufus's frequent references to the fact that Jesus had been a great one for sitting down to supper with the worst of the worst. Now, Jack could say for a certainty that most of the Christians he had known would never dream of jeopardizing their reputations by having supper with Black Jack Kane. Yet from what Rufus claimed, Jesus had sat down at the table with some very shady types. Obviously, he hadn't been one to mind what other people said.

He thought about Samantha, about the night she had graced his table with her presence, how surprised—and delighted—he had been that she would dare to risk her reputation in such a way. For him.

The memory warmed his heart all over again.

And Rufus and Amelia—how many meals had he shared with them over the years? Countless times he had sat at their table and known himself to be the object of their affection and goodwill.

Yes, Jack decided, he thought he could almost believe in, even admire, a Christ such as the one Rufus had described.

The thought startled him, and he was almost relieved when Rufus again yanked him out of his musings, so foreign to his nature, with a rousing declaration that was surely meant to challenge the entire congregation:

"You are good people, brethren! Truly good people. But I think the Lord is telling us today that we're in danger of thinking ourselves *too* good, too *holy* to be of any earthly *good!* Seems to me we need to roll up our sleeves like the Lord did and commence to knock down the walls of this church building. We need to be taking our religion out there where it belongs—into the streets of the city, to the people! *Amen,* brethren?"

Jack actually jumped when the entire congregation issued forth a resounding communal *"Amen!"* He realized with great surprise that for a minute there, he'd been close to adding one of his own.

❧

Samantha was keenly aware that Rufus had captured Jack's full attention. She had known almost the exact moment when he honed in on the morning message with the same intensity he seemed to bring to everything that engaged his interest. It was evident in the way he sat, unmoving except for an occasional flexing of his shoulders, his arms crossed over his chest, his gaze locked on Rufus in absolute concentration.

She made an effort to suppress the ripple of excitement coursing through her, warning herself not to make too much of this. Jack had already indicated that his coming here today had nothing to do with the worship service.

Still, she found it impossible not to be encouraged, at least a little, by his unmistakable attention to Rufus's words, enough so that she closed her eyes for a moment and breathed a silent but fervent prayer for him. God knew Jack's motives for coming, after all, and, if he chose, could use those motives to his own ends.

Please, Lord…

15

A DIVIDED HEART

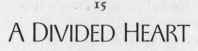

Dread has followed longing,
And our hearts are torn.

W. B. YEATS

❧

GALWAY, WESTERN IRELAND

Outside, the evening was bitterly cold, but inside Brady Kane's rooms, a fire had just been lit.

He couldn't believe he had missed something so obvious. Why, it had been right under his nose all the time! Big Brother Jack would have ragged him for not seeing the solution long before now. And he would have been right.

"You'll catch more flies with honey than vinegar, boyo," Jack would say.

He slugged down another shot of whiskey, a slow smile forming as he studied the roughly drawn portrait in front of him. Yes, it was really quite simple. Why had it taken him so long?

Since it seemed that the only way to Roweena was through Gabriel, it stood to reason that somehow the big fisherman must be made to serve as a door instead of a wall.

With an energy he hadn't felt for weeks, he began to tinker with the sketch of Roweena. One of many others by now, this one was exceptional, if he did say so himself, especially considering that he was working from memory, without a live model.

But then Roweena's image was so clearly engraved upon his mind—upon his heart—that he carried her with him, wherever he went. She haunted him, surrounded him...at times even seemed to obsess him. So excruciatingly clear was his vision of her that he thought he could have captured that exquisite face on canvas blindfolded.

He had drawn her as he'd last seen her, standing in the marketplace, the morning wind whipping her dark hair into a cloud about her face and wrapping her skirt around her bare legs. He reached out and with one finger gently traced her profile, smudging the line of her mouth and delicate jaw a little as he did so.

He took another drink, glancing down at the glass in his hand for a moment. It occurred to him that he was drinking too much of late. He supposed he ought to ease off a little.

Until lately, he had never had a particular fondness for the drink. On the other hand, he'd never shared Jack's disgust for it. To his way of thinking, the stuff was neither poison nor elixir but merely something to enjoy or not, as one chose.

Jack, however, called it the "poison of our people" and would have nothing to do with it. But then Jack tended to dismiss—or condemn—anything that didn't quite square with his own set of tightly held paradigms.

Brady was aware that he drank even more when he was alone; of late, that was often the case. Some claimed it was the solitary drinker who ended up in trouble, enslaved by his habit. Perhaps he'd best be a bit more careful. Just in case. He had never had much use for those ne'er-do-well weaklings who tossed their self-respect down along with the whiskey. He had no intention of becoming one of them.

Besides, he was going to need all his wits about him. There was a plan to be made, and he would have to be clearheaded entirely to devise it. Gabriel was no fool, not by anyone's measuring rod; it would take some doing to win him over.

He took a last, reluctant look at his now empty glass, then deliberately set it and the bottle—not quite empty—well away from his reach.

❧

Gabriel looked up with a faint smile at the sound of the child's laughter. Across the room, Roweena was soaping Eveleen's hair while the wee wane pulled foolish faces at her.

Roweena, too, was laughing now and mimicking her smaller charge. Once she bent her dark head over the child and hugged her in a spontaneous gesture of affection. Her embrace was returned by an immediate, hard clasp about the neck that splattered soap and water over them both.

Gabriel watched them for another moment from his chair beside the fire. They were like blood, those two; no sisters could be closer. Roweena cared for the child and hovered over her with a fierce protectiveness. As for the little one, she delighted in the attention. She also, for one so young, displayed an uncanny sensitivity toward Roweena's fragile emotions.

As he studied them, Gabriel thought he would be a fool to crave more from life than the contentment of times like this: a quiet night, a cozy cabin and cheerful fire, the reassuring sounds of the girls' laughter and play. He valued a peaceful hearth as much as any man and had no need for idle luxuries about him. Instead he had long sought, like the apostle Paul, to be content in any circumstance.

'Twas a treacherous thing, the tendency to wish for more than one had, and well he knew it. Yet of late, to his dismay, he would find his imagination wandering down forbidden paths, dreaming like a callow youth of things that could never be—pretending, if only for a few shadowed moments, that Roweena was his wife and the child their own.

It was at this place he now found his traitorous thoughts, and only by an act of deliberate will did he manage not to pursue his folly. He got up suddenly, so suddenly the chair scraped the floor with a loud screech, causing the child to whirl around in surprise. Roweena, too, upon seeing Evie's wide-eyed stare, turned to look.

An unexpected dart of annoyance stabbed at Gabriel. He gave a wave of his hand and started for the door. "It would seem," he said gruffly, "that if a man is to have some peace he must seek it outdoors. I will take some air until the two of you have tired of your foolery."

He slammed the door behind him with uncommon force, wincing at his own churlishness. Outside, the chill night wind slapped at him. He trudged off down the path, feeling the great fool, for, sure, wasn't his vexation in truth directed at himself and not at the two girls? He could only hope that Roweena would consign his odd behavior to nothing more than a fit of sour stomach or ill temper and not the surliness of a middle-aged man caught up in the futility of a secret, unrequited love.

The thought only served to darken his already black mood, and he went lumbering down the street like an injured bear.

The Claddagh was deep in darkness at this time of night. Most residents had retired at an early hour, and few dwellings showed any signs of light from within. But Gabriel, wide awake with his turbulent thoughts, trudged on through the cobbled streets, scarcely aware of the black night and the bitter cold.

From his own house at the eastern edge of the village, he had walked into the heart of the settlement, where a number of mud-walled, thatched-roof cottages converged. Gabriel stopped, his gaze scanning the small, primitive colony that had been his home for nearly two decades. There was little that could be seen. Here and there a dim stream of lamplight from one of the houses relieved the dark. But for the most part, he was surrounded by shadows and a deep, familiar stillness.

To some, no doubt, the remoteness and solitude of the Claddagh, especially at night, might be unnerving. To Gabriel, however, it had always been a place of peace. For Roweena, especially, it had offered a haven from a less kind world, where those who were different were often viewed with suspicion and even distaste. Here in the Claddagh, however, a deaf girl was not perceived as savage or mad—or accursed—but simply as "special." Here, among these simple folk, she had been accepted and made a part of the normal, daily life of the village, which was what Gabriel had sought for her when he first brought her here as a frightened child.

Roweena's mother had been little more than a child herself when a British soldier, drunk and ablaze with lust, had brutally taken her innocence. A few years later, Roweena, by then an achingly lovely but lonely child, was rescued from the same convent fire that killed her mother, who had sheltered among the nuns since her attack. Gabriel's deeply devout but elderly parents took the child in, but when they too passed away within months of each other, Gabriel assumed guardianship of the little deaf girl.

He had brought Roweena to the Claddagh to find peace from the ignorant fear and malice that might otherwise have destroyed her. And peace is what they had found—for Roweena, at least. During recent years, however, Gabriel had found his own peace more difficult to come by. His fierce sense of protectiveness for Roweena, his resolve to do what was best for her, seemed more and more often in conflict with his growing love for her, until of late he sometimes felt as if his very heart were being torn asunder.

More than once the desperation of his love had driven him to the very edge of declaring himself. But always he stopped, either out of fear that such a confession would repulse her, even drive her away from him, or, worse, that she might actually feign affection for him out of some misplaced sense of obligation. He simply could not bring himself to face either possibility. But recently he seemed to live with an encroaching sense of dread, a sick awareness that he was nearing a time when he would no longer be able to hide his true feelings. He felt trapped, much like a fox cornered on a great precipice, with a pack of slavering hounds at his back and the prospect of a bottomless fall if he jumped.

If Roweena were to learn the true nature of his love for her and be repelled by it—as she almost certainly would be—what would he do? Walk out of her life? And what would *she* do then? How would she manage in her silent, sheltered world, inexperienced and untrained as she was in any sort of skill required to sustain herself, not to mention her sometimes irrational fears, her excessive shyness and lack of knowledge of the world's hard ways?

If, on the other hand, he did nothing—if he should somehow manage to keep his secret—he might not die of it, but he would almost certainly grow more and more restless and contentious under the strain.

Either way she would surely come to resent him and finally despise him.

With a heavy sigh, Gabriel looked up. The night sky, thick and unyielding, without stars or moonlight to relieve it, seemed to mirror his spirit. He raked a hand through his hair, then dropped it to his side.

"What am I to do, Lord? What is your will in this? I can no longer see your way in any of it."

His whispered, anguished plea was met by silence, and he wondered if he had offended his God with his self-pitying reflections. Or did his love and desire for Roweena contain elements of an unholy lust he refused to confront?

"I am only a man, Lord, not a saint. I know my thoughts, my needs, are sometimes impure. But is my love for her such a bad thing? How can that be, when I cherish her so completely and wish nothing for her but good? I want to do the right thing for Roweena, but I live in dread of doing *anything* lest I make the wrong choice. I cannot imagine a life without her—and yet I would rather lose her entirely than bring harm to her. What shall I do, Lord? What am I to do?"

Wait...

Gabriel expelled a shaky breath. "But do I wait in silence, Lord? Or do I unburden my heart to her and take what comes? Ah, Lord, you know the state I'm in! I am like a blind man who does not dare to move this way or that, for fear of falling to my doom!"

Dismayed, Gabriel pressed both hands to his temples. Was that what this was about? His weak, demanding flesh? Did it all come down to an older man's foolish desire for a younger woman? Had he been lying to himself all along, deceiving himself into believing that his love for Roweena was pure, that it transcended mere lust or the body's demands for fulfillment?

Was he really such a hypocrite?

Gabriel hugged his arms to himself, for one of the few times in his life feeling small and weak and utterly inadequate. The black sky seemed to descend and crowd in on him, engulfing him in a cloying, oppressive darkness.

He squeezed his eyes shut against the stifling sensation. Slowly, then, it began to dawn on him—a truth that he thought he had learned long ago. It seemed he had forgotten the need to surrender. Everything. In his own hands, his dreams, his needs, his wants, his highest hopes were but poor things of the flesh and easily tarnished or misused. In God's hands, they became holy.

He opened his eyes, the words echoing through him like a carillon. *Surrender. Surrender everything.*

His eyes filled with quick tears. "Aye, Lord...it seems I needed reminding, even now. Forty years I am, and yet I still forget. 'Tis your will, not mine, that I'm to seek. Always your will, Lord. No matter the cost."

For a considerable time, he stood there in silence, the bleakness lifting from his spirit, the night bathing him now in serenity rather than dread. Finally, he stirred and turned back toward the way he had come, leaving behind him, at least for now, his earlier feelings of loneliness and confusion as he started for home.

16

A Plan Conceived in Darkness

What lies within the dark of the heart,
What whispers the words of deceit?

Anonymous

Brady had been awake all night, plotting. Even now, with the hour bordering on midday, he felt no need for sleep. He had spent the hours into late morning at the small table in his sitting room, sometimes getting up and pacing the floor, his mind and body pulsating almost feverishly with excitement and expectation.

It would work. He was sure of it. Once before he had ingratiated himself with Gabriel by coming to the aid of Roweena and Evie. Of course, that event had been totally fortuitous; he had simply encountered the two girls the night of the devastating windstorm back in January and helped them to reach safety. Even though Gabriel's acceptance of him had always seemed somewhat grudging, he had, for the most part, made Brady feel welcome in his home.

Until the situation with Terese.

Now he saw an opportunity to win Gabriel over again. If he played things right, the big fisherman would not only grant him his earlier acceptance, but perhaps even his approval—thereby removing the barrier to Roweena.

During the night, he had formulated a plan to achieve his goal. He had tried to anticipate everything. There must be no carelessness, no idle mistake—nothing left to chance.

Finding just the right help to see it through, however, might take some doing. It would take two men, just to be safe. He didn't know all that many fellows around Galway, especially the sort he'd need. But he knew the kind of place where he was likely to find them, and tonight he would go looking.

He went to the window and looked out on the street below, where a beggar in shabby clothes squatted, staring up at a priest who had stopped to converse. Two men in broad Connemara hats passed by without a glance at the priest or the beggar. Several women, probably on their way to market, hurried by, talking among themselves.

For a moment a faint stirring of uneasiness nudged Brady. Admittedly, the plan wasn't without risk. If anything should go wrong, there would be the devil to pay. But nothing *would* go wrong. He'd make absolutely certain the fellows he hired understood that they had to carry out the plan exactly as he instructed. It was simple, really. All they had to do was visit the house on a Thursday evening, when the girls were alone, with Gabriel gone to the meeting hall for whatever it was he did there on Thursday nights.

There would be enough time, probably more than enough. Brady had watched the house for nearly a month running, hoping—in vain—for an opportunity to be alone with Roweena. Gabriel was always gone for exactly an hour and fifteen minutes—seldom more, never less.

On two consecutive Thursdays, Brady had gone to the door and tried to coax Roweena into talking with him. Both times she had appeared badly flustered, almost frightened, so much so that she'd practically slammed the door in his face.

Even so, he continued to watch. He knew that Evie would come outside a few minutes before six to empty the basin, that she would dawdle in the yard for a bit—not long—mostly staring up at the evening sky or simply standing, unmoving, as if listening for the call of a night bird.

Brady felt certain that once he managed to carry out the first part of his plan, the second part could proceed without a hitch. To that end, he must make every attempt to convince Gabriel that he was properly penitent for his behavior with Terese, that he deeply regretted his actions and was making a genuine effort to redeem himself.

He hadn't deceived himself into thinking this would be easy. No matter; he would scrape and grovel if that's what it took. It wouldn't do to go ahead with the rest of the plan until he'd won Gabriel over. He *had* to soften him up before going any farther. His instincts told him it would be a vast mistake not to lay the necessary groundwork first.

This decided, it was all he could do not to rub his hands together in glee as he anticipated the all-important first step, which he intended to take this very afternoon.

❦

Clearly, he was the last person Gabriel had expected to find when he opened the door. The big fisherman's eyes went as cold as ice chips as he took one look at Brady. Without blinking, he moved to close the door.

Brady caught only a glimpse of Roweena and Evie behind him, both wide eyed as they watched from beside the hearth.

He pretended not to notice and instead turned his full attention on Gabriel.

"Gabriel. I—would you just step outside for a moment? This won't take long."

Gabriel's craggy features remained rigid. Without speaking, he continued to chill Brady with that same relentless stare.

"Please, Gabriel? It's important."

Brady was careful to keep his eyes off Roweena, his expression properly solemn. Gabriel studied him for another long moment through narrowed eyes, as if to gauge his intent. Finally, with a quick, backward glance, he stepped outside, closing the door firmly behind him.

Brady gave a deep sigh. "Thank you. I was hoping you'd see me."

No response.

Brady met the frigid blue eyes with a steady gaze of his own. As he faced the towering, black-bearded fisherman, it occurred to him—not for the first time—that Gabriel almost seemed to step out of another time. All the giant needed was a kilt and a pike and he would have resembled for all the world one of the ancient warrior chieftains from whom every man in Ireland seemed to claim descent.

But it wouldn't do to let that ice-pick stare intimidate him or, even worse, provoke so much as a hint of defiance.

Brady reminded himself to adopt the proper note of remorse as he commenced his speech. "I have something that needs saying," he began. "I don't quite know how to go about this, but it's important to me that you understand."

The jaw lifted a fraction, but the cold stare never wavered.

"I've come to apologize," Brady said quietly, casting his own gaze downward. "For everything."

At the continued lack of response, he looked up to find the big fisherman still watching him with a poker-faced expression.

"I'm aware that you think poorly of me," Brady went on. "And rightly so. I've behaved in a—a despicable manner. But whether you realize it or not, Gabriel, your opinion matters to me. I had even thought we were friends once. I'd like to somehow regain your approval."

He could detect no sign of softening in the other, but he was determined to go on with this. "I just—wanted to tell you that I'm sorry."

Gabriel's gaze, still void of emotion, flicked over him. "You owe me no apology. 'Twasn't me you wronged."

The man's coolness was beginning to wear on Brady, and he had to force himself not to show at least some irritation. "True enough. Nevertheless, I lost your respect, and I deeply regret it." He paused, keeping his expression grave. "Well…that's all I came to say, that I'm sorry. I'll be going."

He actually turned to walk away before Gabriel could speak.

"What is it you want from me, man?"

Brady turned back, hopeful now. "If possible, your forgiveness. Nothing more."

Gabriel's close scrutiny was unnerving, to say the least. "As I said, you did me no wrong."

Brady fumbled for the right response. He knew he could spoil it all by going overboard; Gabriel was no fool. On the other hand, he thought he had at least managed to crack the big fisherman's defenses, and he was reluctant not to press the advantage.

"Perhaps not directly. But the fact remains that you trusted me, and I abused that trust." Brady paused for effect, even managed to make his voice catch a little as he went on. "Gabriel…I *am* ashamed of my actions with Terese. And while there's no reason you should believe me just yet, I want you to know I've changed. I've—done some growing up."

He met Gabriel's eyes with a look that he hoped was entirely open and without guile.

If the big fisherman had been moved in any way by Brady's speech, he gave no indication of it. The silence that hung between them was long and thick until, finally, Gabriel made a slight nod. "You have had your say, and you've been heard. I bear you no ill will."

It wasn't all Brady had hoped for, but he would have to be satisfied with it for now. It was a start. He returned the nod and extended his hand. "That's that, then. I'll be on my way."

Gabriel hesitated long enough to make the moment awkward before accepting the handshake. Brady forced himself to leave without further delay, but he was keenly aware of the fisherman's measuring gaze until he reached the end of the yard and turned for home.

❦

Gabriel watched him until he was out of sight.

He was both puzzled and vaguely disturbed by Kane's unexpected behavior. The young American's words had seemed sincere enough, and he had not belabored the proffered apology. But had the regret been genuine? And why bring this sudden avowal of penitence to *him?* Why indeed?

It was not up to him to judge Brady Kane, although Roweena had accused him of doing just that. In spite of his personal reservations about Kane, he could at least hope that the young rogue was truly contrite, that he did indeed regret his contemptible behavior and meant to change his ways. There was no reason *not* to believe him, after all, though his previous conduct might make it a bit of a struggle.

Was it merely a disagreeable streak of cynicism in himself that made him suspicious of Kane's remorse?

There had been nothing concrete, nothing specific, in the American's professed self-reproach to make Gabriel doubt him. And yet doubt him he did. Those dark eyes, always so deep, so difficult to read, had seemed more shuttered than usual today. Try as he would, Gabriel had been unable to take Kane at his word. Nor could he dismiss the sense of uneasiness that still lingered, long after the lad had disappeared from view.

He knew that once he went back inside, the girls would expect an explanation as to what had transpired between himself and Kane. He made up his mind to offer only a cursory one. Unless and until he was satisfied that the American was indeed a changed man he would say nothing—absolutely nothing—that might serve to warm Roweena toward him even more. For whatever reason, he was uncomfortable with her believing that Brady Kane had undergone some sort of transformation.

He would reserve his opinion until this surprising—and, to his way of thinking, still highly questionable—change had been proven.

If it ever was.

17

ROGUES' GATHERING

One rogue knows another.

IRISH SAYING

❦

GALWAY, WESTERN IRELAND

Brady found the men he wanted with surprising ease. He'd been discreet; it took only a few careful questions of one of the local tavern owners and a brief show of money.

By Monday night he found himself sitting down at a table in the Brown Sail, a pub he seldom frequented but knew of from its rough reputation. Across from him sat a duo who almost certainly had helped to establish that reputation.

The one called Biller was small and whip thin, with a beak of a nose and narrow, pale eyes that never quite met Brady's gaze. He seemed to be charged with energy. He was also openly hostile.

The second man, while not exactly cordial, wasn't as surly as his cohort. Oddly enough, however, Brady felt more uneasy around him than the other. Robuck was the only name he offered. He had red hair, thick and heavy, and he had obviously not seen a barber's chair in recent weeks. His face, broad and flat featured, was nearly as florid as his hair. The man was solid and wide, a burly sort. In New York he would probably have been called a thug.

Unlike his companion, Robuck had no problem looking Brady in the eye. In fact, his heavy-lidded gaze held such a mocking glint that Brady found himself looking away.

Neither was the sort he'd want to pal around with, that much was certain. But for his purposes, they would suit. Besides, his dealings with the two would be short-lived.

"There can be no mistakes. No rough stuff." Brady kept his voice low but firm.

"So you've said," Robuck came back at him. "And why would we get rough? A wee girl, isn't it?"

"That's right. I just want to be sure you understand. You put a mark on her in any way, and you'll never see the rest of the money. Not a cent of it."

Biller scowled even more darkly at that, but Robuck merely flicked Brady an amused look. "Ah, now, there's no need to be getting riled, man. We heard you clear enough, and we'll do the job just as you want it done. No questions asked. And no roughness. But I'm thinking, seeing as how the task would seem to require such careful handling and all, we might need a bit more in payment than you're offering."

Brady flared. "I'm offering you plenty, and you know it."

Robuck's sneer returned. "Well now, that might be so, mister. But you're obviously a particular man, wanting things done just right. And quietly, as well. That sounds to me as if it's a very important matter to you, this thing you're asking of us. That being the case, then—another fifty. In your American money, of course."

Brady fumed, but they had him. He was paying not only for a hole-and-corner piece of work but for caution.

He was also paying for their silence.

"All right. Another fifty. But not until after the job's done and I'm satisfied. Take it or leave it."

"Oh, we'll take it," Roebuck said casually. "Now—as to when you'll be wanting the deed done?"

Brady expelled a long breath and proceeded to tie up the deal.

❦

Gabriel knew it was too soon for word from Ulick, but each day he grew more impatient to hear if his old friend had learned anything about the American. Kane's behavior—the sudden apology, the uncharacteristic self-effacement, and the alleged desire to set things right with Gabriel—puzzled him.

There was something in the lad that made Gabriel almost wish that he had been wrong about him, that he could indeed trust this unexpected transformation. Yet the fact was that he did *not* trust it, had in truth never trusted Brady Kane—and still didn't. In spite of his suspicion—or perhaps because of it—he found himself increasingly curious about the American and each day now hoped for a visit or a message from Ulick.

This day, however, was nearly over. There would be no news tonight. After listening for a moment for the sound of Roweena's and Evie's slumber behind the curtain and offering up, as he always did, a quiet prayer for them, he went to his own bed.

He slept fitfully, waking often and abruptly, as if jolted from sleep by some unfamiliar sound or troubling dream. Once he heard an outcry from Roweena, followed by the predictable drowsy murmur from Eveleen. This was no unusual occurrence; since childhood Roweena had often cried out or even wept in her sleep. Always, the wee wane woke just enough to reassure her until they both fell off to sleep again.

But no matter how many times Gabriel had heard those night cries, they pierced his heart. He ached to think that Roweena had endured something that years later still troubled her peace of mind, even in her sleep. And every time it happened, he never failed to wish that he could go to her, hold her, and comfort her until her haunted dreams disappeared.

The thought that she might always suffer so filled him with an infinite sadness.

The thought that he could never be close enough to her to console her made him sadder still.

PART TWO

TOO CLOSE TO THE FLAME

Take no part in the worthless deeds of evil and darkness.

EPHESIANS 5:11, NLT

18

LOOKING PAST THE VEIL

Pulse of my heart,
What gloom is thine?

From Walsh's Irish Popular Songs

NEW YORK CITY

By Tuesday afternoon there had still been no news about Sheridan's sister and the children. At that point, Jack decided to get the police involved.

He sent word to Ed Boyle, a sergeant at the first precinct, including in his message any information that might help with a search. It could easily take days, Jack knew, if not longer, to turn up anything. If the city would ever stop dithering around and set up a harbor police patrol it could make all the difference in this kind of situation. As it was, he could only hope that the already overworked Boyle and a couple of his best men would be willing to look into the situation as a personal favor. Boyle owed him more than one, as it happened.

In the meantime he was doing his best to keep Sheridan busy. Jack had sent the boy on a story right after lunch—a murder at one of the dime museums in the Bowery. Although that wasn't exactly news in New York, Sheridan must have found enough to occupy him, since he hadn't yet returned to the office.

The lad was understandably downhearted. What should have been a happy reunion with the sister he hadn't seen for years had turned into a nightmare.

There was no way of knowing the girl's whereabouts or the circumstances of her disappearance. Jack's apprehension for Terese Sheridan and the orphaned tykes traveling with her deepened daily. The more time that passed with their not being found, the less likely it was that they *would* be found.

There was also the reality that because the Sheridan girl and the two children were the first immigrants to be brought over under the *Vanguard's* experimental resettlement program, it was vital to the project itself that everything go well. If the initial effort turned out to be a failure, it might well doom the entire venture.

He gave a long sigh, pulled away from his desk, and stretched. Beyond impressing upon Ed Boyle the importance of finding the missing immigrants as quickly as possible, he couldn't think of what else to do. For now, it was time to leave the office and pick up Samantha. They were scheduled to meet with Avery Foxworth and Maura Shanahan at the jail within the hour.

With Sheridan off on assignment, Jack decided not to drive himself but to take a cab instead. It was another wretched day—would this miserable cold rain never end?—and he didn't much take to the idea of driving when he could ride snug inside a cab with Samantha.

He took time to check his appearance in the closet mirror, running a hand through his hair and frowning at the dark shadow of beard already in evidence. Well, there was no help for it now. It had been a hectic day, with no time for anything but work. In truth, Samantha had seen him looking worse by now, but he still wished he'd managed to spruce up a bit.

Shrugging into his topcoat, he took the steps at a clip, whistling as he went. As always, the prospect of seeing Samantha had made him somewhat rattlebrained. He couldn't remember when he'd felt such conflict in his emotions. One minute he was cross as a bear, the next as sappy as a schoolboy. He certainly hoped his foolishness didn't stick out on him the way he felt it must. He never quite knew what was going to strike him next.

If nothing else, love certainly made a man one great mass of contradictions.

Perhaps she would have supper with him. Unless, of course, she happened to be in one of her "distant" moods, as he thought of those times when she seemed to withdraw from him for no apparent reason.

Ah, well, perhaps he could change her mind with a bit of Irish charm.

Though he wasn't aware of that particular ploy ever working with her before.

❦

The meeting with Avery Foxworth, Jack's attorney, and Maura Shanahan took place in the "visiting room" of the jail.

In truth, the room was little more than a storage area, and a cold one at that. Samantha sat at a table beside Mrs. Shanahan, with Jack and Avery Foxworth directly across from them.

Jack had asked Foxworth to handle the Shanahan case as a favor to Samantha, who had taken a personal interest in the woman. He knew Avery found Samantha's involvement curious, her work among the immigrants notwithstanding. Few women of Samantha's station would care one way or the other about a hapless Irish immigrant woman in trouble with the law.

Maura Shanahan had shot her husband to death a few months past. According to her story, the man had abused her for years. On the day in question, he had allegedly beaten her with a gun, threatening to go after the children as well. Samantha was convinced that Mrs. Shanahan had simply snapped after years of horrific abuse and, in a state of terror, acted to defend herself and her children.

Jack was inclined to agree and had brought Avery Foxworth in to defend the woman. As it happened, Avery had suggested to Jack that he might be able to make some sort of a deal with the prosecutor, given the history of abuse. Jack had opted to say nothing to Samantha about this just yet, however, for fear of raising her hopes in vain.

The speculative looks his attorney had been giving Samantha since the start of the meeting clearly indicated that he was more than a little curious about her interest in the Shanahan woman's predicament. As for himself, Jack thought he knew what lay behind Samantha's determination to help Maura Shanahan.

After some months of getting to know Samantha, becoming friends with her— and falling headlong in love with her—he had no doubt but that she'd been caught up in this particular case because of her own history. By her own guarded admission, her deceased husband, the highly esteemed clergyman Bronson Harte, had beaten *her*.

Samantha never talked about her husband. But Jack was convinced it was Bronson Harte who was responsible for the pain that darkened those magnificent eyes and the closely guarded restraint she wore like a suit of armor. On the one occasion when he had confronted her about her marriage, she broke her silence only enough to confirm his suspicions. At the same time she made it perfectly clear there would be no further discussion of the subject.

More than once, the perverse thought had struck Jack that perhaps it was just as well Harte was dead. Otherwise, he might have been tempted to add murder to his already lengthy list of sins.

When he first admitted to himself that he was in love with Samantha, the idea had terrified him. He had loved only one other woman besides his mother and sister, and he had lost Martha to cancer after only a few years.

A succession of meaningless flings had followed—all brief, all unsatisfying. His lack of commitment had not been altogether deliberate. He had always found it next to impossible to trust anyone other than himself. The very idea of revealing his innermost heart to another human being evoked something akin to panic in him. Even Martha had accused him of being "shuttered," of closing certain parts of himself off from her and others.

After Martha's death, he simply couldn't seem to muster the interest in or the initiative for a new relationship. Instead he continued to drive himself harder and harder, reaching higher and higher, until eventually he knew no other way to live. For years now he had kept himself so busy there was little time for anything other than work. He had allowed no closeness, no intimacy, no real friendships with anyone, save Rufus.

Rufus was fond of saying he had seen the best in Jack and couldn't ignore it. But

Jack thought the truth was that Rufus had seen the *beast* in him and *did* somehow ignore it.

He valued his friendship with Rufus Carver beyond telling, but there had been no inclination to extend anything remotely like it to anyone else.

Until Samantha. She had swept into his life with her quiet grace and haunted eyes before he knew what hit him, and he hadn't been the same man since.

He was mad for her. He wanted to take care of her, protect her, be with her. He wanted to lavish everything he had on her.

He wanted to marry her.

Jack flinched, then actually glanced around to make sure the others hadn't noticed.

He needn't have worried. Samantha's attention was concentrated on Avery Foxworth, who was outlining the legal options of the case. As for Avery, he couldn't seem to drag his gaze away from Samantha, even as he spoke.

A jolt of something primitive arced through Jack at a blistering speed. Shaken, he took a minute to recognize the feeling for what it was.

Jealousy.

It was an unfamiliar emotion to Jack. Indeed, he couldn't remember having ever experienced it before today. With Martha, there had been no occasion. Their courtship had been brief and uncomplicated; their marriage, the same. And although his reputation as a womanizer still dogged him—a reputation he found amusing for its very exaggeration—the truth was that no woman since Martha had meant enough to him to provoke anything as intense as jealousy.

Until now.

Unsettled, he glanced from Avery to Samantha, who seemed to be engrossed in the attorney's every word. Occasionally, she turned to give Maura Shanahan an encouraging smile, but for the most part her attention belonged to Foxworth.

In that moment, Jack couldn't help seeing her as Avery Foxworth undoubtedly saw her. Even with her glistening chestnut hair confined to that stuffy little bun at the nape of her neck, and in spite of the fact that she was dressed as always in an unadorned—but exquisitely cut—suit, Samantha was a stunning woman. Her presence seemed to cast a soft glow even on the dingy visiting room.

Any man would be taken with her. Why should Avery be the exception?

Feeling increasingly edgy and out of sorts, Jack started to pull a cigar from his pocket, but stopped in deference to Samantha, who claimed to abhor the smell. He turned his attention back to his attorney. Although he had retained Avery Foxworth years ago, he still didn't know all that much about the man. Like himself, Avery kept his own counsel, seldom revealing anything of a personal nature. Their relationship over the years had been strictly business, by mutual consent.

The man was a study in contradictions, the total opposite of his partner in the firm, Charlie McCann. Charlie was colorful, jolly, and unabashedly vulgar, whereas everything about Avery fairly shouted *breeding*.

Avery was British, and although removed from his native land for more than twenty years now, he had retained a slight accent, which Jack half suspected might be a deliberate affectation. Where Charlie was large and lumbering, Avery was slender and fine boned. Jack had never seen the man looking anything less than impeccably barbered and attired, while Charlie McCann was a tailor's nightmare.

The one thing the two partners held in common was that they were both, Jack was convinced, thoroughly corrupt—Charlie blatantly so, whereas Avery was careful to maintain the veneer of a gentleman—and one of integrity.

Jack almost grinned at the thought. Avery Foxworth was probably one of the shrewdest, most resourceful men Jack had ever done business with. He was also quite possibly the most ruthless. As to integrity—an alley cat probably had more.

At the moment, he was more curious about what sort of impression Avery might make on a woman.

More to the point, a woman like Samantha.

Not a tall man—Jack probably topped him by several inches—Avery somehow *looked* tall and struck a sense of importance and power that didn't seem in the least practiced, though Jack suspected it was exactly that. He was probably in his late forties, only a few years older than Jack himself. If he was graying—and he most certainly should be by now, Jack thought peevishly—it was well camouflaged by the natural, sand-colored shade of his hair. He had a long, lean face. His eyes were an indefinable shade of gray, like cold slate, with an unnervingly intense gaze.

There was no denying the fact that he was a "well set-up man," as the Irish would put it, and while not exactly handsome, Jack grudgingly conceded that Avery Foxworth would probably hold a certain appeal for women.

Apparently, he was also eligible. There was a daughter somewhere, but to the best of his recollection, Jack had never heard tell of a wife.

He looked at Samantha, and the thought struck him that both she and Avery Foxworth bore that elusive air of refinement that someone like himself could never hope to attain; one was born to it, he supposed. Indeed, his attorney's enviable elegance only served to remind Jack of his own somewhat ungainly height and the callouses—and news ink—embedded in his hands. He had the long arms of a plowboy, the near swarthy skin of a Galway sailor, and while his own tailor was the finest in Manhattan, he had never quite lost the memory of the threadbare pants and run-down shoes he had once worn.

In truth, although he was obscenely rich, at times he still felt wretchedly poor.

And always, he felt thoroughly, blazingly *Irish*.

More irritable than ever, Jack reminded himself that he had come here today as a favor to Samantha, to lend a bit of moral support, as it were, not to wallow in his own shortcomings. Samantha seemed to think his presence might influence Avery to make a more vigorous defense on behalf of the Shanahan woman, and the very idea that Samantha would look to him for help of any sort went a long way in relieving his self-doubts. At least for the moment.

Of course, he knew Avery Foxworth too well to think he could influence him one way or the other, but if Samantha wanted him here, he was only too happy to oblige.

Given the way the conversation was going, he thought Samantha could rest her concern about Maura Shanahan. Avery clearly had a plan in mind.

"I've given you a rather detailed account of what *could* happen, Mrs. Shanahan," Avery was saying, "but it's by no means what I think is *going* to happen."

His well-modulated voice held an uncharacteristic warmth, Jack noted.

For Samantha's benefit?

"In my opinion," the attorney went on, addressing his words to Maura Shanahan but still watching Samantha, "I can bring an end to this unfortunate situation rather quickly. If you'll just sign this paper, Mrs. Shanahan, I'll take care of things from here. I've arranged a private meeting with the prosecutor, and I'm fairly certain that when he reads your statement and hears my assessment, he'll dismiss your case without a trial."

He handed the paper to Maura Shanahan without a glance, his gaze still locked on Samantha.

Jack knew a sudden, unreasonable desire to take a swing at him.

Again he told himself that Avery was surely not the first man to be smitten by Samantha's loveliness.

Indeed.

For the moment, he dragged his attention away from Samantha to Maura Shanahan, who sat staring at the paper in her hand with an absolutely dismal expression. Finally, she looked up. "I'm sorry, sir, I don't...I can't—"

Obviously, she couldn't read. Samantha moved to save the woman from further embarrassment. Gently, she took the paper from her, saying, "Here, Maura, this light is terrible. Perhaps Mr. Foxworth wouldn't mind explaining what it says."

She looked at Avery, who gave her a faint, knowing smile and nodded. "Of course. Briefly, Mrs. Shanahan, this is a chronicle of the circumstances leading up to the day of the shooting, as well as the events of the day itself. It gives an account of the long-term mistreatment you suffered at your husband's hand, both physical and emotional. It also details his threats and actions during the hours before you...shot him."

He leaned back, linked his well-manicured hands over his handsome waistcoat, and continued. "Clearly, you felt yourself and your children to be in grave danger of physical harm. He was threatening you. You were terrified, and you reacted. It was self-defense, pure and simple. I believe we'll have you back home in no time, without the delay and aggravation of a trial. For now, though, I'll need your signature."

Without looking at him, Maura Shanahan murmured, "I cannot write, sir."

Jack saw Samantha's eyes cloud with compassion as she touched the other woman's hand. "That doesn't matter, Maura. All you need to do is make a mark. I'll help you."

Her expression was dubious as she looked across the table at Avery. "I don't mean to question your judgment, Mr. Foxworth, but are you quite sure about there not being a trial? It would seem almost—too easy."

Avery Foxworth leaned forward, folded his hands on the table in front of him, and gave Samantha a look of steady earnestness. "I wouldn't mislead you, Mrs. Harte. I'm almost certain we'll avoid a trial. In the first place, Mrs. Shanahan's husband sounds as if he were a low sort all 'round."

Maura Shanahan seemed to wince at his words, but Avery appeared not to notice.

"If the shooting happened as she says," he went on, "I'm quite sure the prosecutor will conclude that the man got no more than he deserved and will then summarily dismiss the case."

Jack was surprised at the strength of the Shanahan woman's response. Her face tinted with emotion, she leaned toward Avery and burst out, "Why, it *did* happen the way I said! Don't you believe me, then?"

Avery Foxworth's eyebrows lifted a fraction. "It doesn't matter in the least whether *I* believe you or not, Mrs. Shanahan. My job is to make certain the prosecutor believes you. And I assure you, he will."

"But will he *care?*"

Samantha's voice was low and none too steady. Jack looked at her, saw the set line of her mouth, the tautness of her features.

"I'm not sure I understand, Mrs. Harte." Avery Foxworth's tone warmed considerably when he addressed Samantha.

"Are you quite sure the prosecutor will appreciate Maura's circumstances, that she *had* to act to defend herself and her children?"

The attorney smiled a little. "I'm afraid I can't vouch for the humanitarian instincts of the prosecutor, Mrs. Harte. But I *can* tell you not to concern yourself with the outcome of all this. It's a *fait accompli.*"

As Jack watched, Samantha studied Avery Foxworth as if she were taking his measure and was none too certain she liked what she saw.

"Maura *is* telling the truth, Mr. Foxworth," she said firmly. "Her husband beat her for years. Viciously. The day she shot him, he was threatening to kill not only her but the children as well."

"I'm not questioning Mrs. Shanahan's story." Avery gave her a conciliatory smile. "If I gave that impression, I apologize. I'm simply trying to explain that what will count in the long run isn't so much whether the authorities believe her or are sympathetic to her but rather that they're aware of the caliber of her husband. The man was obviously a bully, so it's not as if we're dealing with any great loss. Once the prosecutor understands as much, he's not likely to initiate the expense and fuss of a trial."

Again Jack saw a cloud of anger darken the Shanahan woman's face, as if she resented this condemnation of her late husband. But it was Samantha's response to Avery's somewhat glib dismissal that took him aback.

For an instant he thought she was going to rise from her chair. Instead she gripped her hands on top of the table so tightly her knuckles went white as she faced Avery Foxworth. Her face was pale, her voice noticeably strained. "So whether or not a woman is to be believed—or exonerated—depends on the mettle of her husband? If he's a drunken boor, then her chances with the courts improve, but if he's a man of good reputation, the law might not be quite so sympathetic to her plight, is that it? Even if his offense is just as heinous?"

Avery Foxworth's gaze was speculative as he replied. "That might be oversimplifying somewhat, but yes, it's probably a fair assessment of how things work."

As Jack watched, Samantha drew in a long, none-too-steady breath. He didn't miss the slight trembling of her chin and the sudden flush of color to her face that told him she was probably aware she might be overreacting and already regretted it.

He wanted to go to her, but, of course, he could not. He could do nothing but sit there and agonize for her, for the old, clearly unhealed pain that Avery Foxworth's rather callous summation must have evoked in her.

—❦—

If Samantha hadn't realized her mistake right away, that she had reacted too strongly to Avery Foxworth's words, Jack's pained expression would have told her as much. She was aware, too, of the attorney's close scrutiny.

She felt the heat of embarrassment stain her neck and rise upward. Quickly, she fixed her gaze on her knotted hands atop the table.

Jack came to her rescue after only a second or two. "I think Mrs. Harte's concern in the matter is the same as mine, Avery. You really are convinced this won't go to trial?"

Samantha could have kissed his hand in gratitude for the way he managed to divert Avery Foxworth's attention away from her so smoothly.

At the attorney's nod of confirmation, Jack turned to Samantha with a faint smile. "I think you can rest easy, Mrs. Harte," he said, his tone one of careful formality. "As I may have told you, Avery—Mr. Foxworth—has represented me and the *Vanguard* for some years, and I can assure you that when he makes a judgment about some legal matter, he is almost always right on the money. After hearing what he's had to say this afternoon, I feel certain there won't be a trial. So if you'll just make your mark on that paper, Mrs. Shanahan—"

He gave an almost imperceptible nod to Samantha, indicating that she should help Maura, then turned back to Avery Foxworth. "Mrs. Harte and I have another appointment yet today, so we need to be getting along. You'll contact us once you have final word?"

Samantha looked at him in surprise. He hadn't said anything to her about another appointment.

The two men shook hands as she showed Maura where to make her mark. Jack seemed altogether oblivious to Avery Foxworth's inquisitive glances in Samantha's direction, but Samantha was sure he noticed. For her part, she had been uncomfortably aware of the attorney's studying, appraising looks throughout the entire meeting. She had also observed the way his expression occasionally altered when he looked at Jack, though she was fairly certain Jack didn't notice. She wasn't quite sure what she was seeing in the attorney's gaze, but she almost thought it might be resentment. Once she even thought she'd caught a glimpse of overt dislike.

But to be fair, her impression of Foxworth might well have been colored by a few of his seemingly insensitive remarks.

In any event, she found herself suddenly anxious to leave and was only too grateful for that "other appointment" Jack had referred to, whatever it was.

19

An Unexpected Proposal

I had a thought for no one's but your ears.

W. B. Yeats

❧

Outside, the gloom of early evening was drawing over the streets. It would be dark soon, and the raw wind and rain hinted of a bitter night ahead. The smell of the sea and the ever present stench of garbage mingled with the damp air to hang heavy over the streets.

Their cab was to return between six and six-thirty, but there was no sign of it yet. Even at this time of day, Broadway was still busy. The hooves of horses clopped over the wet streets, impatient drivers shouting or cursing the traffic, cracking the reins as they tried to push ahead of slow wagons or pedestrians pooling into the streets.

After Avery Foxworth had pulled away in his carriage, Samantha turned to Jack. "Thank you for trying to cover my blunder back there. I don't know what…came over me."

The softness and depth of understanding in his eyes as he looked down at her stabbed at Samantha's heart. "Don't fret yourself about it," he said gently. "I doubt that anyone noticed but me."

Samantha wasn't so sure, but she still felt embarrassed about the incident and had no intention of dwelling on it. Instead she changed the subject. "What was that about another appointment?"

The cab pulled up just then, and Jack took her arm as they began to walk. "It was just a way to get us out of there," he said, gesturing to the driver that he would help Samantha in himself. "Besides, I rather hoped we *might* have another appointment. For supper."

Samantha started to protest—they had been together entirely too much recently—but Jack pretended not to notice. Inside the cab, he caught her at a loss by sliding into the seat beside her, instead of sitting across from her as he usually did. Ignoring her scrutiny, he draped the lap robe about her, then rapped on the roof to signal the driver before turning back to her.

Unsettled by his closeness, Samantha edged toward the door as much as possible. She avoided his gaze as she clenched her hands in her lap and stared straight ahead. "Do you really think Mr. Foxworth can convince the prosecutor not to go to trial?"

"Avery can be a very persuasive fellow," Jack said. "I think it's safe to assume there won't be a trial."

"I do hope you're right."

Out of the corner of her eye, Samantha saw that he was still watching her. She felt the need to keep talking, to avoid that intense dark gaze. "Have you spoken to the police yet about that anonymous letter?"

Ever since Jack had told her of the recent threatening note, Samantha couldn't help but speculate as to whether it had been written by the same madman as the unknown assailant who had shot Cavan Sheridan—an unintended target—a few months past.

The thought of how close Cavan—and Jack—had come to tragedy that night still froze her blood. Either of them might have been killed. As it was, Cavan had taken the bullet in Jack's place, but now it seemed that Jack was still in danger.

"There's been no time for that," Jack said in reply to her question about the police. "Besides," he went on with a shrug, "it's not as if they can do anything about it."

Samantha stared at him. "Jack, you can't afford to take this lightly! Someone is threatening you! You've already had one attempt on your life. Now this. You thought it important enough to warn Cavan and me," she reminded him. "Please promise me you'll not ignore this."

He eased his shoulders a little and passed a hand over the back of his neck. "I'm hardly ignoring it, Samantha. But I'll admit I don't quite know what to do about it. Except—" he turned toward her again—"it *has* occurred to me that perhaps I should keep my distance from you for a time, given the nature of the threat."

Samantha tried to ignore the sick wrench of dismay his words evoked. It startled her—and troubled her more than a little—to realize how much she didn't *want* him to "keep his distance."

"Obviously, I'm not doing so well in that regard," he said wryly. "No doubt you've noticed that I can't seem to stay away from you."

Samantha couldn't look at him, instead made a pretense of smoothing the glove on her right hand. He had thrown her emotions into a turmoil. She was puzzled by his behavior, puzzled even more by her reaction to it. She thought she'd caught a glimpse of some sort of change in him this evening, at least in regard to his treatment of her. Not that she wasn't used to these unexpected shifts in character. The gentlemanly conduct Jack was usually so careful to maintain with her sometimes reverted to a lighter, almost roguish—and blatantly flirtatious—guise.

Although she continued to discourage it, Samantha had reached the point where it no longer annoyed her—or flustered her—as it once had. This was just Jack...being Jack. She had come to suspect that the role of a rake he sometimes affected might be little more than a kind of protective veneer—that at the same time he seemed to be playing bold, he was actually withdrawing, instinctively arming himself against any genuine closeness or the threat of a serious relationship.

She sighed inaudibly. There were so many contrasting facets to Jack, she never quite knew what to expect. He could be droll or somber, carefree or intense. She was told he could be an impatient taskmaster, harsh and demanding. But according to Rufus and Amelia, he was also a model of friendship and something of a phi-lanthropist. He had a relentless sense of humor, yet often seemed given to dark fits of melancholy. He loved flowers and the opera, and she had never seen him in a suit that wasn't impeccably tailored. Yet, on occasion he seemed altogether oblivious to the fact that he reeked of cigar smoke and his shirtfront was stained with news ink.

Jack had an iron reserve, she knew, a hardness about him that almost certainly would have warded off anyone who dared to come too close. He was distrustful, occasionally arrogant—at least on the surface—and openly contemptuous of society in general, New York's elite in particular.

He almost always had the last word, and it was more often than not a sharp-edged one. Samantha suspected he had a defense for any occasion, and even after months of working for him and spending more time with him than was wise, she was never quite sure when she was seeing the "real" Jack.

But it was at those rare times when he seemed to drop all the masks, like now, that she found him the most unsettling. These were the times when he seemed almost vulnerable, and in that very vulnerability, he somehow became more of a threat to her emotions.

In any event, something was definitely different about him this evening. And whatever it was, it was sending up warning signals at a dizzying rate.

"Samantha?" His voice was soft, and when Samantha turned to look at him, he was watching her with the same tenderness, the same softness she had seen in his gaze earlier.

Her throat tightened, but she couldn't seem to look away from him.

"Are you in a hurry for supper?"

"Jack, I really don't think—"

"I thought we'd drive around a bit first," he interrupted.

She knew she ought to go home. She had work waiting: papers to grade before her next night class, an article to proof before tomorrow's edition, and a number of other tasks that lately kept getting brushed aside.

"A drive would be nice, but—"

"Good," he said, his pleased expression clearly indicating the matter was settled. Samantha didn't know whether to be annoyed with him or with herself.

After another second or two, he took her hand on top of the lap robe. Surprised, she almost pulled away—but didn't. For a time, they rode along in silence. Samantha wondered that she no longer felt threatened, as she once had, when Jack touched her. To the contrary, she found his touch strangely comforting, the strong clasp of his hand almost reassuring. Yet she would have thought that in light of his recent proposal—and her rejection—she would have felt distinctly ill at ease in such an intimate setting.

Darkness drew in on them now, and in the shadowed interior of the cab Samantha felt the strain and tension of the past few hours begin to drain away. When Jack again turned toward her, this time with a studying look, she was able to meet his eyes and even smile at him. "What?"

"I've always been somewhat intrigued with how comfortable you apparently are with silence," he said, his tone thoughtful. "That's unusual, you know. Most people seem to think they have to blather incessantly, as if they always have to be amusing."

"I don't amuse you?" Samantha teased lightly.

Something glinted in his eyes, then banked. "I would hardly describe your effect on me as amusing, Samantha."

Still puzzled by his odd behavior, Samantha frowned and turned a little to study him more closely. "Jack? Is something wrong?"

He didn't reply for a moment. When he did, Samantha was completely caught off guard. "What exactly do I mean to you, Samantha?"

She stared at him, her mouth suddenly going dry. "I—don't understand."

"I think you do."

His expression was unreadable. "Samantha—am I wrong in thinking that you have feelings for me? That you care for me?"

Samantha saw that he was deadly serious. Her heart slammed against her ribs, and she couldn't seem to get her breath. "I don't...I can't—"

She broke off, instinctively edging away from him a little.

"Tell me the truth, Samantha. Do you care for me at all?"

Samantha's gaze went to his hand on hers. Even through their gloves, she could feel the warmth of his touch. "Of course I do. You've—been a wonderful friend to me."

His clasp on her hand tightened, and his tone turned unexpectedly hard. "Don't do that, Samantha. Don't dissemble. I'm not talking about friendship, and we both know it. I'm not going to hold you to anything or expect anything of you—I give you my word. But I think you feel something more for me than friendship, and I need to hear you admit it."

Somehow he was clasping both of her hands now. He sat there, watching her, dwarfing her with his dark, powerful frame, and Samantha felt as if his eyes were searing layer after layer away from her soul.

She drew in a ragged breath. "I don't know...how I feel. Not really."

"Then will you permit me to say what I need to say," he asked quietly, "before it burns a hole in my heart?"

Samantha's head roared with warning, but something in his eyes told her that with or without her consent, he intended to speak.

She saw the rigidity of his shoulders relax, but he retained his firm grasp on her hands. "Just—let me speak my piece, if you will, before you answer me."

His jaw tightened, and although Samantha again felt a panicky urge to stop him, she hesitated too long.

"You already know that I'm in love with you," he began, holding her gaze. "I suppose if you hold the more common opinion of me, you might question whether or not I even know what it means to be in love. But I assure you, Samantha, I do."

Samantha's pulse began to hammer as he went on.

"I expect I've employed every known device to *not* love you," he said with a self-mocking smile. "But the fact is that I find myself in a hopeless state entirely."

"Jack, please—"

He shook his head to quell her interruption. "Let me finish. Please. I know you must think I have a colossal nerve. If I offend you, Samantha, I'm truly sorry. But I can't stop now. I have to finish this.

"Samantha—I've asked you once to marry me. And I confess that I had high hopes—unfounded, as it happened—that you would say yes."

His words were coming faster now, as if he felt compelled to say everything at once to allow her no chance to interrupt. "Well, I'm asking you again, Samantha. And this time I'm going to predicate everything else by saying what we both already know—that admittedly, I'm no great prize. To the contrary, you might just have reason aplenty to laugh in my face—or slap it—for my even *thinking* you might marry me."

Now Samantha *did* try to stop him, but again he cut her off. His words continued to spill out in a rush. In the darkness of the cab, Samantha's head was swimming, her ears thundering, and for a moment she had an insane urge to leap from the cab into the street. She hadn't expected this, not again, at least not so soon. Indeed, after she'd turned him down the first time, Jack being Jack, she thought his pride would have stopped him from raising the subject of marriage ever again.

Samantha thought she would strangle. Shaken, she had to stop him before he went any further, but she couldn't seem to get the words past the swollen knot in her throat. In fact, she couldn't seem to do *anything* but sit and stare at him as if she had suddenly been struck dumb.

❦

This wasn't going the way he'd intended, Jack realized with a swell of agitation. Samantha was staring at him in what could have been either utter incredulity—or abject misery.

He had set out to deliberately make himself vulnerable, to appear less confident, less in control. He had already decided he would grovel, if necessary—though the thought made him grind his teeth—if that would help him win her trust and make the idea of marriage more appealing to her. Or at least less loathsome.

Obviously, he had been wrong. He seemed to have succeeded only in making himself appear pathetic and perhaps making an already awkward situation for her even more impossible.

He swallowed down his impatience with himself. He had to think. He'd been careless with both attempts to convince her to marry him; he saw that now. In short, he had assumed too much. Even if his instincts had been right, and she really did care for him, why had he been foolish enough to think a woman like Samantha—the very epitome of virtue and respectability—would willingly subject herself to marriage with a middle-aged Irishman with a sordid past and the presumption of a fool?

Small wonder she looked as if she might jump screaming from the cab at any instant.

He had made a blunder, and he knew it, blurting out his feelings like an adolescent and presenting himself as an importunate bumbler. He stared down at their entwined hands, watching with increasing annoyance at himself as she slowly withdrew from his grasp. He fiercely wished he could somehow retract everything that had happened during the last few minutes, but what was done was done.

Once again, it seemed, he would have to change courses. Fast.

Not looking at her, he uttered a short, dry laugh. "Well, perhaps the third time will be the proverbial charm."

He was surprised to feel a light touch on his sleeve. His head snapped up to find her watching him with those magnificent, shining eyes that never failed to make him go weak.

"Jack, I'm sorry."

He heard the distress in her voice and could have kicked himself for putting her in such an untenable position. But at the same time his hopes rose when he saw the way she was looking at him. "I apologize, Samantha. The last thing I wanted was to offend you—"

"Offend—" She seemed genuinely bewildered. "Oh no—no, you haven't offended me, Jack!" She gave him a tremulous smile, and he could almost feel the effort it took for her to manage even that. "Stunned me, perhaps, but not offended me."

Jack studied her. "I can't help the way I feel about you, Samantha. Believe me, I never expected this. I meant only to be your friend."

She shook her head, averting her eyes. "I never thought of anything like this either. Perhaps if I'd only realized sooner—"

She let her words drift off, unfinished.

Jack pulled at his fingers, cracking his knuckles. He suddenly felt coarse and common—a feeling he would have thought long forgotten, but one that occasionally tore at him when he least expected it. A feeling that never came without an accompanying wave of self-disgust.

"Well," he managed to say with a lame attempt at a smile, "there's no help for it now. It seems to me that the entire city must know how I feel. I can't look at you without gaping like a lovesick schoolboy."

She turned back to him, her expression one of dismay. "Oh, Jack! I'm sorry. But I thought you understood."

Jack groped to recover his control of the situation, which he felt rapidly spinning away from him. "Samantha, let me be altogether honest with you. I have no illusions about myself. I've never tried to deny what I am, and I've never tried to lie to you. I'm bitterly aware that you could have your choice from all number of respectable fellows—the veritable cream of society, I'm sure—who would be far more in keeping with your background and station."

He took a breath, then hurried on. "But for all I lack in that regard, I believe I could more than compensate in terms of—well, to be blunt, Samantha, I can give you just about anything you'd ever want! And it would be my greatest pleasure to do just that! Isn't that worth anything at all to you?" He paused, "Isn't it?"

To Jack's dismay, he saw that she was trembling, a look of extreme distress settling over her features. "Oh, Jack! Please try to understand! This isn't about you or the kind of man you are—and it certainly isn't about what you can or can't give me! This is about *me!*"

Jack stared at her in bewilderment. She looked absolutely miserable, and for the first time since he'd launched tonight's campaign, he began to realize that he might have done a terrible thing. Clearly, he had put her in an utterly wretched position. She looked as if she were about to weep.

"I was wrong to do this," he said, trying to ignore the painful tightness in his chest. "Somehow I thought—"

"I can't possibly marry you, Jack," she interrupted, almost as if she hadn't heard him. "Don't you see—I can't marry *anyone!*" She stopped, and the look of raw anguish that lashed her features hit Jack like a hammer blow. "That doesn't mean I don't love you—"

She stopped, her hand going to her mouth, her eyes widening as if she were stunned by her own words.

For an instant, Jack felt a surge of hope, and he reached for her again.

But she drew back, shaking her head. "I can't allow myself to…love you. I *can't!* Not after—Bronson."

Jack stared at her, understanding finally dawning as he saw the torment in her eyes. "Samantha—I would never—*never*—hurt you! Whatever happened between you and Harte, you can't think it would be like that with me. Surely you know me better than that by now!"

Jack was totally unprepared for the blast of bitterness that met his words. "I thought I knew Bronson Harte, too! But I couldn't have been more wrong!"

She fairly hurled the words at him. "You don't know what it was like for me! You couldn't possibly *imagine* what it was like! No, I can't believe you would ever hurt me. But then I never dreamed that *Bronson* would hurt me either."

She stopped, her voice breaking as she added, "As it was, he would more than likely have *killed* me—if he hadn't killed himself first!"

20

SAMANTHA'S SECRET

Too long a sacrifice
Can make a stone of the heart.

W. B. YEATS

They sat staring at each other in what was clearly mutual astonishment. Jack saw that she had been taken as unawares by her extraordinary disclosure as he had been, hearing it.

"Harte committed suicide?" he said softly.

Samantha nodded. He saw her bite her lip, obviously struggling to keep her emotions in check.

"I'm sorry, Samantha. I didn't know."

Pain, sharply drawn, constricted her features and made her appear suddenly older. "No one knew," she said, her voice little more than a whisper as she looked away.

She had knotted her hands into fists, and Jack longed to cover them with his own. But he hesitated, not certain she would welcome any attempt to comfort her.

"How?" he finally said.

"Bronson had suffered from a heart condition for years." Her words sounded strangled. As she spoke, she began to clasp and unclasp her hands in a strange, awkward rhythm. "He took quite a lot of medicine. The note he left for me indicated that he'd deliberately taken a massive overdose with the express aim of ending his life."

Finally, she looked at him, and her stricken expression tore at Jack's heart. He wanted to take her into his arms and hold her. He wanted to heal her.

Instead, he sat unmoving, feeling utterly, miserably helpless. "You said no one ever knew. What about his doctor?"

She shook her head. "Ethan Carter—Bronson's physician—was also a close friend. If he suspected anything, he kept it to himself. He continually tried to convince Bronson to retire, to live a more sedentary existence, but Bronson ignored him." She glanced down at her hands and for a moment ceased wringing them. "In fact, during the last few months of his life he seemed to push himself even more relentlessly. When he died, the assumption was made that his heart had finally given out, and it probably would have, had he continued on as he had been. But it wasn't exertion that killed him."

She drew in a long, ragged breath, as if the disclosure had completely drained her of all her strength.

Jack studied her, sensed the effort she was making to keep from falling apart. "Why didn't you tell anyone, Samantha?"

She raised her eyes to his.

"Why the secrecy?" he said gently.

Her eyes flickered with what might have been painful memories. "At first, I suppose I meant to protect his reputation, his…name. Bronson was held in high esteem by a great many people. And there were his parents to consider. They were good people, and getting on in years—they're both gone now—and Bronson was their only son. The truth would have devastated them. Losing him was a terrible blow in itself, but at least they were able to find comfort in…the kind of life he'd led, the good he'd done."

Jack felt an unreasonable stab of anger that she would go to such lengths to protect the memory of a man who had caused her such incredible anguish. Apparently, she sensed his resentment, for she shook her head slightly as if to ward off any objection he might make.

"Bronson *did* accomplish quite a lot of good, Jack. There are countless numbers of people who might never have found faith without his preaching, his writings—his attention to their needs." Her voice trembled as she added, "I've never understood how he could be such a saint to so many and yet be…as he was with me."

She wiped a hand across her eyes and slumped back against the seat. Her tortured look broke Jack's heart, and he wondered how she could have ever kept silent for so long a time about something that must have caused her such despair.

"I don't mean to rationalize or try to justify what he did to me," she said, averting her gaze. "It was a nightmare. But I finally came to realize that in the last few years of Bronson's life he was almost certainly—mad. The fact that he made me a victim of his madness was simply because I was the one closest to him, I suppose."

Her expression was one of acute misery, and Jack felt chilled by the thought of what she must have endured at Harte's hands. Again he longed to pull her to him and try to ward off the pain, the agonizing memories. But she was hugging her arms to herself now, her eyes glazed with a numb expression, her entire bearing one of stony self-control. He sensed it would be a huge mistake to try to encroach upon that rigid restraint, and so he forced himself to do nothing but wait—and listen.

"I was very young when I married him," she went on in a quiet voice. "Too young, no doubt, and too naive to recognize the warning signs. I was so—overwhelmed by Bronson, so in awe of him, that I was completely blind to the *darkness* in him. For a long time, he actually convinced me that it was…*my* fault, that I had somehow driven him to—"

She broke off, her face, her fragile composure, crumpling.

Fury at Bronson Harte clashed with a monumental sorrow for Samantha's pain, and Jack could no longer *not* touch her. Gently, he covered her hand with his, relieved when she didn't pull away. After a few seconds, she straightened and seemed to regain at least a remnant of calm.

It occurred to him that Samantha was more than likely the bravest—and unquestionably the most unselfish person—he had ever known, but the torment in her eyes at this moment tore him apart.

"Your parents—surely you told them?" he said, his voice raw with his own heartache for what she must have gone through. "Your mother?"

She visibly shuddered at the suggestion, and he gripped her hand a little more tightly.

"I could never have made my mother understand my marriage! Believe me when I say that it would have only made matters worse. Besides, I realize now that I wasn't merely protecting Bronson's good name or his family. The truth is, I was protecting *myself* as well."

Jack looked at her in disbelief.

"It's true," she insisted. "For months after his death, I was convinced that I'd failed him somehow. I couldn't shake the thought that there must have been something I could have done, some way I could have prevented my own husband's self-destruction. I blamed myself, and I suppose I thought everyone else would blame me, too, if they were to learn that Bronson had committed suicide."

Jack lifted one dubious eyebrow, and she hurried on, seemingly intent on explaining. "You must understand that everyone who knew Bronson admired him deeply, even *revered* him. He drew people to him, won their affection—and held it—by the sheer force of his personality. I can't really explain what it was in him—but he had a kind of power over people that was almost…frightening. I simply couldn't face the disappointment or the disapproval of his friends and followers. By the time I came to realize that there was really nothing I could have done, that perhaps I had been wrong to keep his suicide a secret—well, by then it was too late. I had been silent too long."

She paused, and Jack saw her shoulders sag slightly—a weary gesture that spoke more of dejection than fatigue. "Besides," she added in a near whisper, "I'm not at all sure anyone would have believed me."

The thought of what it must have cost her to live with such an abominable secret set off an ache in Jack that made him almost ill.

"What a remarkable woman you are, Samantha," he said quietly.

His praise seemed to embarrass her. She shook her head, turning away. "There was nothing noble in what I did, Jack. I was protecting myself as much as Bronson's memory."

Jack realized that she truly had no sense of her own courage, her innate decency.

Not only that, but he wasn't convinced but that even now she still didn't blame herself, at least a little, for whatever Harte had done to her. Perhaps even for his suicide.

More incredible still, he was sure he had glimpsed, if only for an instant, a genuine sorrow for the loss of the man who had in all likelihood brutalized her throughout their marriage. She was *sorry* for him, sorry at least for the tragedy he had made of his life!

Shaken, Jack wondered how he could have ever hoped to win such a woman.

She had spoken of the "darkness" in Bronson Harte, triggering the unsettling awareness—not for the first time—of the darkness in *himself*. Indeed, he never felt that darkness more keenly than when he was with Samantha. One brief hour with her could somehow tilt the axis of his existence and set him to searching his soul, albeit unwillingly.

The faint, indefinable light that seemed to glow within her somehow brought the shadows in himself roaring to the surface. It was a singularly unpleasant, bewildering experience, much like that of a nocturnal animal who crawls out of the depths of a dark cave in search of the sun, only to find upon exit that the brightness brings such pain he must close his eyes against the very light he came seeking.

And yet he needed her. Needed whatever it was in her that spoke of something better, something finer than anything to which he could ever hope to aspire. He needed her goodness, her gentleness, her honesty.

He thought perhaps he needed her to survive.

Jack suddenly realized that she was watching him, her features strained and showing signs of fatigue even in the weak glow from the cab's lanterns. He glanced down at the slender hand enfolded in his, then met her gaze and held it. "I wonder... do you think you could ever trust me, Samantha?"

Her brows knit in a frown of confusion. "What kind of question is that?"

"The kind leading up to yet another proposal," Jack replied.

"Jack, *don't*—"

He lifted a hand to forestall any protest. "Wait. Hear me out. I think you love me, Samantha. If that's true, then perhaps I can eventually gain your trust. And if you can trust me—well, then, perhaps you'd consider marrying me."

"Didn't you hear anything I said?" she countered, her voice rising in pitch. "This isn't about you—"

"It *is* about me, Samantha," Jack broke in, tightening his clasp on her hand when she tried to pull away. "Of course, I heard what you said, and every word of it was like a knife to my heart. I can scarcely bring myself to imagine your going through such torment. Samantha—I would give everything I own if I could somehow wipe those years completely out of your memory, as if none of it ever happened."

She stared at him in what appeared to be confusion, but her hand had relaxed somewhat in his.

"That's a fiddler's dream, I know. Only a fool would think you can simply forget the past and go on as if it never happened. It *did* happen, and to my grief I expect you will wear the scars for a long, long time. But here's the thing, Samantha, and please let me finish: We *both* have a past we'd like to forget, yours through none of your own doing; mine—well, to my shame, mine *was* largely my own doing."

Her gaze never left his face as Jack went on, choosing his words with as much care as if he were on trial for his very life. In a way, perhaps he was. Surely he had never felt so desperate a need to convince anyone of anything as he did at this moment.

"What I'm trying to say, and making a royal muddle of it, is that I think we might be able to help each other, Samantha, even heal each other. In time."

She was studying him with an unnerving intensity. Once she seemed about to speak but stopped, as if she'd thought better of it.

By now Jack was gripping both her hands, as much to steady himself as to keep her from withdrawing from him.

"Samantha, I confess to you that at sometime in my past, I may have done every despicable thing you've heard me accused of. But this much I can promise you: I will never, ever hurt you. I will never lay a hand on you in anger. I will never touch you—unless I touch you with love. My word on it, Samantha."

He watched her, searching for some slight crumbling of resistance, uncertain as to whether or not he detected any. "Let me try to explain something, *macushla,*" he said softly.

She blinked at the endearment that had rolled off his tongue so easily, without thought. But when she made no move to pull away from him, Jack continued. "Samantha, hard as it may be for you to trust my word, I vow to you that if you'll give me the chance, I'll spend the rest of my life trying to be the kind of man you can respect. And trust. With all my faults, I promise you that I can be—I *will* be—a good husband to you."

Jack saw her tense and begin to shake her head. Yet he sensed that her earlier resolve had weakened, if only a little, so he kept a firm grasp on her hands. He *had* to get through to her. He had tried everything he could think of: He had attempted to charm her into wanting him; he had tried to make himself so vulnerable in her eyes that she would feel no threat whatsoever from him, no fear of him; he had even tried to win her on the basis of his wealth—what he could give her. And nothing—*nothing*—had moved her.

Now he would try to make her *believe* in him. Somehow, he had to convince her that she could trust him.

"Samantha?" he said quietly.

Her eyes stripped past every defense Jack had ever built for himself, and again a surge of hope rose in him. "Marry me, Samantha," he said, making no attempt to control the urgency, the desperation, behind his plea. He was beyond pride now, beyond any pretense of caution. "I don't care if you don't love me the way I love you. I can live for a long time on the hope that your love for me will grow. We can make a good life together, Samantha. I'll build you the house you want—you don't have to live in that ugly old horror of mine. We'll make a home, have a family—"

She uttered a low sound, much like a moan, stopping him cold. The stricken look she turned on him hit Jack like a blow.

"I can't have children," she said, her voice breaking.

Stunned, Jack stared at her. Almost instantly, he saw her withdraw from him, heard the door to her heart slam shut.

Jack struggled to conceal his shock, the wave of disappointment that came hurtling through him with her grim announcement. He knew that how he responded in this moment might well cost him any hope he'd ever had of winning her.

"All right," he said, somehow managing to keep his voice even as he looked directly into her eyes. "You can't have children. I didn't know that, Samantha. But it needn't make a difference. It *doesn't* make a difference. Not to me."

It was as if she didn't hear him. "I was carrying his child at the last," she said, the words little more than a broken whisper. "Not long before he—killed himself, he beat me so viciously, the baby died." She caught a breath that was more a sob. "After that, there was—I can't have children. Not ever."

Jack felt a boiling, savage hatred slam through him, and it was everything he could do not to explode with rage at what had been done to her. It seemed a monstrous twist of fate that he could not somehow make Bronson Harte pay for the evil he had inflicted on Samantha.

"Oh, Samantha, I'm sorry. I'm so sorry," he said lamely.

She looked at him. "So you see, I have nothing I can give you. You say it doesn't matter, but eventually it would. A man like you, you ought to have children. You need a wife who can give you more than I can. You should have a son to carry on your name, the newspaper—"

She broke off, her face a mask of bleak resignation.

Jack had not wept since Martha's death, and even then the tears had come sparingly, as if being ripped from him. But at this moment he had everything he could do not to give in to a fit of weeping.

He steadied himself, caught her by the shoulders and forced her to meet his gaze. "Samantha, you couldn't be more wrong! All right, I would have liked to have had children. And, yes, it was a disappointment to us, to Martha and me, when we didn't. But this is the truth, Samantha, and you *must* believe me: I can live without children. But I don't think I can live any sort of life from now on without *you!*"

He pulled her closer, and she allowed it, but he was careful to hold her gently. "You have spoiled me for ever going on as I was before I met you. I can't go back to that life, Samantha. Please, don't make me."

Suddenly she was weeping, the tears tracing a slow path down her cheeks. Racked by the sight of her pain, Jack gathered her into his arms, wrapping her in a careful embrace. "I'm sorry," he said, feeling as if he would strangle on his own words, tasting the salt of her tears as he pressed his lips to her wet cheeks. "I am so terribly, terribly sorry for what he did to you. Please, Samantha...*please*...give me a chance to heal you with my love."

Jack held her to him while the tortured sobs shook her slender body. He thought her pain would tear him apart. After a long time, he felt her shudder, then grow quiet in his arms.

"You haven't answered me, Samantha," he whispered.

She looked up, her gaze still clouded with tears.

"Will you marry me?"

She closed her eyes. "You don't understand," she choked out. "I'm...*afraid*. I don't know...I don't think...that I can ever be a wife to any man again! But it's not just that—"

"What, then?"

"Jack—you say we can heal each other. But we can't. Not really. No matter how much we might *want* to, we can't. Only God can bring that kind of healing."

He studied her. "And has he brought it to you?" he said bluntly.

She seemed to frame her answer with great care. "Not entirely. But in part, yes, he has. He's done something for me that I could never have done for myself, something I could never do for you." She stopped, then added quietly, "But *he* could."

Jack wasn't sure what kind of a reply she expected from him. This had always been an issue between them, this matter of her faith and his inability to share it. But he wouldn't deceive her, wouldn't try to make her believe a lie. All he could do was attempt to understand.

"What do you mean, Samantha?" he asked her. "What, exactly, has God done for you?"

He had seen her pain, after all, seen it for himself, had witnessed the torturous memories that still haunted her. What sort of healing was that?

"He's given me peace," she said quietly.

Jack studied her. "I don't always see peace when I look in your eyes, Samantha. I see suffering."

She flinched visibly. "God's healing doesn't always come quickly, or all at once. But it comes, Jack. If you open your heart to it...to him...it comes. I expect what you're seeing are the scars. Not the wounds themselves, but the scars they left on my spirit. Eventually—"

She looked away, and he saw her throat work as she stopped, swallowed hard, then went on. "Eventually I hope even the scars will disappear."

Again Jack puzzled over a way to overcome this barrier between them. But this was one place where he could offer her nothing. Whatever hope he might have held for some sort of divine healing or true peace had burned to ashes long ago, if indeed he had ever known such a hope at all. Yet there was no denying that something about Samantha—something indefinable, but the very essence of everything she was—set off a yearning in him for *something more,* something he instinctively knew he could never buy or win on his own.

"I confess that I don't understand what you're talking about," he said. "But I believe life with someone you love has to be immeasurably better than life alone. I love you, and

I want to be with you." He tightened his embrace, but only a little. "And I'm willing to try to learn to be—the man you need me to be in order to make that happen.

"Samantha—I won't give up. I'm going to keep right on trying to convince you to marry me. No matter *what* it takes. No matter how *long* it takes."

She started to protest, but he stopped her, pressing a finger to her lips and shaking his head. "I'm only asking you to think about what I've said tonight. Don't be too quick to give me a decision. Not this time."

She gave him a troubled look but made no more argument. Finally, Jack bent his head to search her gaze, and what he saw there gave him the courage to cup her face between his hands and gently kiss her on the forehead, then, even more gently, on her lips. Her eyes were closed, and there was a softness about her mouth that wrenched his heart. He touched her cheek, gently. She opened her eyes.

"Samantha," he said, "we'll make it work. Somehow. We will, I promise you."

They rode the rest of the way in silence, the only sound the clopping of the horses on the wet streets and the steady rain falling on the roof of the cab. Jack was content to simply hold her hand and breathe in her closeness.

❧

Hours after Jack had left her outside the door to her apartment, Samantha sat on the side of the bed, staring at the floor, twisting her hands in her lap. This was not the way a woman should feel after having just received a proposal of marriage from the man she loved.

That she *did* love Jack was no longer in question. She had known it for a long time, no matter how fiercely she might have tried to deny it to herself.

Nor could she refuse to face what she had only suspected up until now, that Jack cared for her, too, and cared deeply. He had said he loved her, and after tonight she would have found it difficult to question his sincerity; she had seen it in his eyes every time he looked at her, even with the awareness that she would come to him damaged and wounded—and barren.

Shouldn't she be feeling elation instead of this aching despair of the soul?

She had wept until she was too spent to weep any longer. The scene in the cab had apparently uncapped an old but still extant reservoir of pain, propelling it full force to breach her hard-won wall of self-defense. Tonight for the first time she realized how desperately she had needed to purge herself of the truth about her marriage and Bronson's suicide. Yet now that she had done so, guilt and regret had come gnawing at her like angry scavengers.

The enormity of what had transpired this night still shook her to the core. A confession of love, a proposal of marriage, and the fall of the stronghold where her darkest secrets lay buried had left her emotions in turmoil. Her head was pounding, as much from the chaos of emotion as from exhaustion. She knew she needed nothing so much as a full night's rest, knew just as certainly there would be no such peace for her tonight.

Somehow she mustered the initiative to drop to her knees beside the bed and attempt to pray. For a long time, words failed her. She could manage nothing more than to hide herself in the presence of God and let his peace settle over her, his comfort quiet her.

But gradually, as she felt the first faint stirring of renewal in her spirit, she was able to form at least a faltering entreaty, a plea for guidance. When her petitions were met by only silence, she reached to the night table for her Bible and began to pray through some of the dearly familiar verses that over the years had strengthened and sustained her when her entire world seemed to be crumbling.

Samantha knew that even if she were to eventually overcome her resistance—her *fear*—to the idea of marriage again, she could not lightly dismiss the Scriptural admonition to not be "unequally yoked with unbelievers." By his own admission, Jack professed only a "limited" faith of any sort and apparently had lived most of his life as an unbeliever. How could she even consider a proposal from him?

The Scriptures spoke of an unbelieving husband's being sanctified by a believing wife, but this was different. She would be going into a relationship as a believer, knowing from the beginning that Jack didn't share her faith. Samantha had seen firsthand the consequences of willful disregard of this particular counsel, had seen too many Christian husbands or wives whose spiritual beliefs had been either shaken or completely decimated, if not by the immoral lifestyle of an unbelieving partner, then by the lack of shared commitments and values. How could she consider embracing a life with someone who had no interest in the very things that were most important to her?

But she *loved* him! "Oh, Lord…how can I simply ignore my feelings? How do I dismiss the fact that I love him…and he loves me?"

Pray for him…and trust me…

Startled by the clarity of the whisper in her spirit, Samantha caught her breath. It occurred to her that she wasn't quite sure *how* to pray for Jack.

"He doesn't know you, Lord, although sometimes I think he believes in you. But by his own admission, he's lived a life that must be anathema to you. Surely you don't want me to love a man like Jack. And yet I do! Dear Lord, help me; you know I love him…"

And so do I, child…So do I. Trust me with your beloved. Pray for him, and trust me.

Thoroughly shaken, Samantha squeezed her eyes closed as if to shut out her surroundings, forcing herself to see nothing, know nothing, but the silence. Scarcely breathing, fervently yearning for still more than she had been given, she waited, clinging to the One who had never failed her. And finally, little by little, she felt the darkness in her spirit give way to light. From the deepest recesses of her being came an all-encompassing calm, a singing peace that flowed and filled her until she could no longer keep silent.

And finally she was able to pray. She prayed for an indeterminate time, prayed for the man who called himself an infidel, the man who only tonight had vowed his love and protection to her. She prayed for the divine pursuit of Jack's soul, the redeeming grace offered by a suffering Savior. She prayed for deliverance for the man she loved. And she prayed for the courage to love him rightly and to entrust him to the only One who could heal him and make him whole.

❦

Uptown on Thirty-Fourth Street, Jack Kane paced the floor in his bedroom. The room was shadowed, its only light the dying fire and an oil lamp on the bedside table. The house was quiet and cold, the streets below deserted.

Earlier he had donned his smoking jacket in the expectation of relaxing by the fire, perhaps reading for a time before going to bed. Such optimism had been foolish, he admitted sourly to himself. For hours, thoughts of Samantha had filled his mind like swarming bees. He had thought of nothing else, had done nothing else since arriving home except to walk the floor and think. Think about Samantha.

She had come close to admitting that she loved him tonight. His heart rose to his throat every time he recalled that admission, inadvertent though it had been.

And he had kissed her, there was that. And even though she hadn't actually kissed him back, neither had she resisted him.

Best not to dwell on that, he told himself firmly. Still, he couldn't quite stop the thought of how she had looked at him after he released her, not with the revulsion he had half dreaded, but with her magnificent eyes still shining from the tears that had filled them earlier, and a softness he hadn't seen in them before—at least not for him.

Unwillingly, he also remembered the utter despair that had clouded her features when she told him of the beating that had killed her unborn child, the terrible anguish in her voice when she revealed the bitter truth that she was now barren because of that same beating.

Jack knotted his fists at his sides and went to stand at the window. The night had cleared, the rain finally giving way to a sky studded with random stars and a bright half-moon. He stood looking out, staring into the night, seeing nothing but Samantha's lovely but tormented features. It was incredible to him that he had come to love her so fiercely when she in turn had done everything possible to discourage him. Even the wrenching awareness that marriage with her would never include children, that it would more than likely always see her haunted by the tragedy of her past, wasn't enough to turn him away from her.

Indeed, he couldn't imagine *anything* that could turn him away from her. Except perhaps Samantha herself. If she simply would not have him, if she refused to even consider making a life with him—well, then, what could he do?

There had to be something. Some way to finally make her his. There *had* to be!

He looked up to the pale wisps of cloud passing over the moon. For a long, still moment he watched the sky. Finally, he brought one clenched fist to his mouth, pressing it against his lips so hard he tasted blood. And then for the first time in years, he addressed an unknown Deity he wasn't even sure he believed in—but one in whom Samantha most definitely *did* believe—with an utterance of desperation that began in the very depths of his spirit.

"If you're as real as she believes you are," he grated out, "if you're really out there and as all-powerful as she seems to think you are, then show me how to help her. How to heal her. Let me, somehow, make up for all the pain she's suffered. Show me how to be the kind of a man she deserves, the kind of a man she can love. Not for me, mind—but for her. Just—do it for her."

Feeling suddenly self-conscious in spite of the fact that there wasn't another soul within earshot, Jack shoved his hands in the pockets of his jacket and started to walk away from the window. But then he stopped and turned back, his gaze again lifting upward as he added, "I do love her, you know. More than I ever thought I could love anything or anyone, and that's the truth. I'll take care of her, I promise you. I'll cherish her. And I'll never hurt her, or let anyone else hurt her, not ever again. My word on it."

21

DAVID'S SEARCH

I stood beside the couch in tears
Where pale and calm she slept,
And though I've gazed on death for years,
I blush not that I wept.

RICHARD D'ALTON WILLIAMS

David Leslie had never agonized over a patient as he agonized now over the suffering young woman named Terese.

He had been excruciatingly close to losing her more than once, but each time she had surprised him by clinging to life with a tenacity he wouldn't have thought possible in one so weak, so dangerously ill. He could actually *see* her fighting to defeat the specter of death that seemed to hover in the room.

David had witnessed similar struggles at other bedsides, and his experience had led him to wonder if it wasn't only the most rugged, valiant spirits who battled so fiercely. So great was the ordeal taking place in this room that he now found himself laboring along with his patient, as if by his own efforts he could somehow facilitate hers.

It had been over a week since Madog Wall had brought her to the mission, and so far there had been no improvement; if anything, her condition had worsened. Most of the time, she drifted in and out of consciousness, and for the past three days, she hadn't been coherent for more than a couple of minutes at a time. David knew she couldn't possibly last much longer if she didn't turn for the better soon.

He fretted that there must be someone he ought to notify, but he had no idea where to look. He hadn't been able to get anything out of the little girl, Shona, and as for Terese, although she had muttered the same word two or three times in the throes of her delirium, David wasn't sure what she was saying or even if it was a name at all. It sounded like "Gaven," but when he questioned Shona, she merely shook her head, obviously as much in the dark as he.

He *did* know that he had become too involved emotionally. Against everything he had been taught—and even against his own instincts—he had allowed himself to make a kind of *attachment* to this young woman that was neither professional nor practical.

It wasn't only that he was spending too much time at her bedside. He was also sacrificing the few precious hours at night when he might have been taking his own much-needed rest to dig into every medical text he could find, in hopes of discovering something he might have missed, some new treatment he didn't know about.

The truth was that he had come to care too much. He knew better. He was aware of the pitfalls of becoming emotionally involved with a patient, had actually known physicians who had suffered the consequences of ignoring this counsel. He'd never thought it would happen to him. Certainly not with a perfect stranger, one swollen with child, and one with whom he had scarcely exchanged a reasonable conversation.

But it had happened before he'd realized, and now he wasn't quite sure how to extricate himself, how to step back and regain some semblance of emotional distance. And yet he knew he must.

Even if she survived—and the thought that she might not wrenched his heart— there was more than likely a husband waiting somewhere, worrying about her, wondering what had happened to her. David knew his own part in this ought to be limited to treating her condition and trying to learn anything he could that might lead to that husband, or at least to a member of her family.

The thing was, he didn't even know where to start. He supposed he could always go and speak with Madog Wall, see if the man could think of anything at all that might help. But he was fairly certain it would be a waste of time. Wall claimed he had never seen either Terese or Shona before the day he brought them to the mission.

A soft moan from his patient jarred David back to his surroundings. He put a hand to Terese's forehead, and the heat from her skin nearly scorched him.

On the other side of the bed, Shona sat, silent and intense, watching David. He forced a smile but could see she wasn't fooled. The child had something almost painfully *un*childlike about her that was disconcerting to say the least.

But then, from what David had seen of the immigrants from Ireland, most of them, children included, had experienced the kind of adversity and tragedy that tended to age one quickly—if one survived at all. The little girl across the bed had probably endured more affliction in her few years than most adults could even imagine. There was no telling what she…and Terese…might have gone through up till now.

And, sad to say, he seemed incapable of making things any better for them.

❧

When David finally found time later in the day to pay a visit to the *Vanguard,* he found Madog Wall lying on his back, working on the underside of one of the newspaper wagons. The big man hauled himself up, wiping his grease-smeared hands down the sides of his trousers as he mumbled a greeting.

It would have been easy to feel threatened by the big, lumbering Irishman's size and battered features. But David had come in contact with Wall on other occasions and by now knew that he wasn't the mean-spirited thug he appeared at first glance. Mostly he saw in Madog Wall a rather shy giant who thought slowly and spoke haltingly, but almost certainly wasn't vicious or cruel. Wall *was* said to be fiercely protective of his employer, the notorious Black Jack Kane, but David didn't necessarily think that was a character flaw.

Today, however, he was surprised to sense a certain evasiveness in the man as he inquired about Terese and Shona. Madog seemed almost defensive, insisting that he knew nothing—"nothing a'tall"—about the girls.

"Didn't I already tell you everything I know, Doc?" he said, still rubbing his large hands against his thighs. "They showed up on a Sunday morning, they did, lookin' half starved and poorly. When the older one fainted away, I brought them to the mission house. I didn't know what else to do, don't you see?"

"You did the right thing, Madog," David assured him. "I'm simply trying to find out if by any chance they have relatives or friends here in the city. Terese—the older of the two—is seriously ill. I was hoping she might have said something to you, anything at all, that might help me to locate a family member." He paused, studying Wall for a moment. "You're quite sure there was nothing?"

The other frowned and looked away. "It's as I said, Doc, I don't know nothin' else. The older girl, she passed out almost as soon as they showed up."

Still, David couldn't shake the feeling that Wall was concealing something. Perhaps it was only because he'd had his hopes disappointed. There seemed no reason for the man to dissemble, after all.

"Well, then—if you're sure—" He gave a nod, turned, and started to go.

"Doc?"

David turned back. Wall seemed to be squirming where he stood. His small eyes went over David's face as if he were trying to gauge whether or not he ought to say more.

"What is it, Madog? Did you think of something?"

The big man shoved his hands down into his pockets. He pursed his lips together, watching David. After a frustratingly long time, he finally replied. "Well, there was one thing—and mind, I'm that certain the girl wasn't tellin' the truth—but she did keep goin' on about how Mr. Kane was 'expecting' them."

David frowned. "Mr. Kane? *Jack* Kane?"

Wall nodded, his mouth twisting with disapproval. "I didn't pay her any heed, of course. Sure, and Mr. Kane wouldn't be acquainted with two poor immigrant girls such as them, now would he?"

David stared at him. "Did you tell Mr. Kane about this, Madog?"

Wall shook his head. "He wasn't here at the time, and there didn't seem to be no need to bother him with it. Then after a day or so I just forgot." His expression changed to a troubled frown. "Now that you come askin', though, I wonder if I did wrong."

Wall was clearly seeking for reassurance, but David's mind had begun to race. "Tell me exactly what the girl said, Madog. Try to remember everything."

Wall took his hands out of his pockets and wiped one over his bald head. "Well, let me think now. She was set on finding out Mr. Kane's home address. Said he was *expecting* them—her and the little lass. Is she all right, by the way, Doc—the little girl?"

David gave a nod. "She's fine. Go on, Madog. Please. What else do you remember?"

Wall shrugged. "Just that she was set on seeing Mr. Kane. *Right away,* she kept saying. She was a pushy one, she was."

"Anything else? Think carefully, Madog."

Wall shook his head. "No, sir. That's all there was." He cast another uneasy look at David. "Should I have mentioned it to Mr. Kane, do you think, Doc?"

"Well...yes, actually, Madog. I believe you should have told Mr. Kane. It might be important."

"But I'm that sure Mr. Kane wouldn't have had nothing to do with that girl's... condition, Doc! She isn't the sort he'd traffic with. Mr. Kane is an *important man.*"

David was beginning to feel some pique at Wall's adulation of his employer, whose reputation couldn't have been much more deplorable. He reminded himself that Wall was obviously rather slow-witted and slavishly loyal. There was no call to be impatient with the man.

"Well, what's done is done," he said. "The important thing is that you tell Mr. Kane now. You need to tell him exactly what you've told me without delay."

Wall's face underwent an immediate transformation. David supposed it spoke leagues about the infamous Jack Kane if a man like Madog Wall could be intimidated by the mere thought of his displeasure.

Almost in the same instant, however, the thick features seemed to relax. "Can't do that, Doc. Mr. Kane is away."

"Away? For how long?"

Wall shrugged. "A day or two more, I expect. He and that young Mr. Sheridan went up to Albany to some sort of a big political conference and a—a *banquet.* Whatever that might be," he added.

The thought went through David's mind that a day or two might be too late. "Is there anyone else who might have information about this, Madog? Someone who works with Mr. Kane, perhaps?"

Wall frowned, rubbing a hand over his chin. "Well, there's Mrs. Harte, of course."

"Mrs. Harte?"

"Aye, Mrs. Harte—the lady who sometimes works for Mr. Kane. Real nice lady, Mrs. Harte. Mr. Kane seems to admire her a lot." Wall gave a knowing smile—not a leer, but more a pleased expression, for his employer's good judgment. "Now that I think of it, seems to me she's been helping Mr. Kane and young Mr. Sheridan with some kind of a newspaper story about the people coming across."

A thought struck David. "You don't mean Mrs. *Samantha* Harte, by any chance, do you?"

"That's her. Do you know Mrs. Harte, then, Doc? Isn't she a fine lady?"

David gave a distracted nod. He had met Samantha Harte several times, actually, most often in response to a summons for medical attention for one of the immigrant families in the area. She had also visited the mission with some of the other members of Immigrant Aid. He had found the young widow to be a gracious, compassionate woman whose efforts on behalf of New York's immigrants were seemingly tireless.

From what he knew of her, he needn't hesitate to enlist her help, whether Jack Kane was involved or not.

"Madog, do you by any chance know how I can reach Mrs. Harte?"

"I don't, Doc." The big man seemed to consider the question for another moment, then brightened. "I know. We can ask Tommy Ryder. He delivers copy to Mrs. Harte most every day for her work. Tommy will know just where to find her." Wall stopped, darting a glance away from David. "Are you goin' to let Mr. Kane know what I done, Doc? Not tellin' him about those two girls, I mean?"

David studied the big Irishman. He sensed it wasn't so much fear he was seeing behind Madog's anxiety as a reluctance to disappoint the man he apparently truckled to. Obviously, Madog Wall coveted his employer's trust and good opinion.

"Wouldn't you rather explain things yourself?" David asked kindly. "I'm sure Mr. Kane would understand."

Wall passed a hand over the top of his head. "To tell you the truth, Doc, I was hopin' that maybe you'd ask Mrs. Harte to explain for me. Seems as though the boss takes things better from her. She has a way about her, she does. Do you think you could ask her for me?"

David smiled and nodded. "I'll be glad to speak to Mrs. Harte for you, Madog."

A fleeting image of Samantha Harte went across his mind, and he found it interesting to think that such a small, reserved woman might have tamed the great Black Bear, as Kane was sometimes called.

"Ah—Madog? About Tommy Ryder?" he prompted, now exceedingly eager to get on with his search.

22

CHILDREN OF LONELINESS

*Where does the search for love begin and the soul's
long road of loneliness end?*

CAVAN SHERIDAN, FROM *WAYSIDE NOTES*

❧

Samantha was so surprised to find David Leslie at her front door that for a moment she could do nothing but stand and stare at him. She scarcely knew the man, having met him but a few times and then for only brief intervals.

Vaguely it registered that he felt the awkwardness of the situation, too. "Mrs. Harte? Do you by chance remember me? David Leslie?"

His smile was apologetic and perhaps somewhat strained. "I'm awfully sorry for intruding like this. I know it's rude, but it's rather important that I speak with you. Could you spare me a moment?"

At a loss, Samantha very nearly forgot her manners. When she finally thought to invite him in, he declined her offer of tea, instead stood just inside the door, glancing around. "I know this is an imposition, but I've reason to think you might be able to help me with information about one of my patients at Grace Mission."

Puzzled, Samantha indicated that he should take a chair, but he gave a quick smile and shook his head. "I don't want to take much of your time. It's kind of you to see me at all."

He paused, removed his gloves, and began tapping them against the palm of one hand. "I have a seriously ill patient, you see—pneumonia—a young Irish woman, who was brought to the mission several days ago, along with a little girl. Both immigrants. The older of the two is in a bad way, I'm afraid."

Still wondering why he had come to her, Samantha said, "Have you contacted Immigrant Aid, Doctor? I don't usually assist with the mission residents. I'm a teacher, primarily."

"Yes, I understand that. But this is an unusual case. Madog Wall brought this

young woman and the child to the mission after the woman collapsed in front of the
Vanguard building. Before that, she apparently made some reference to Mr. Kane, to
the effect that he should be notified of their arrival in New York, that he was in fact
expecting her and the little girl."

Samantha frowned, unable to grasp what he was getting at. "Mr. Kane? What
does he have to do with this?"

"I'm sorry—I suppose I'm not making this very clear, am I? It seems that Mr.
Kane is out of town—"

Samantha nodded, and he went on. "Well, Madog—Mr. Wall—indicated
that in his absence you might be able to help, that you might know something about
the matter."

Samantha's confusion deepened. "I really don't see how—"

She stopped, bewilderment suddenly giving way to a flare of excitement. "This
young woman—you said there was a little girl with her?"

He nodded.

"What about a boy? Was there also a little boy? He'd be the child's brother."

The doctor frowned and shook his head. "No, just the two, the little girl and the
young woman who's so seriously ill. In truth, she's little more than a girl herself." He
paused. "Although she's expecting a child."

Samantha's heart slammed against her rib cage. It couldn't possibly be coincidence! "What's her name?" she asked, holding her breath. "The young woman?"

"*Terese,*" said the doctor. "I'm afraid I don't know her last name. The child calls
herself *Shona.* Shona Madden."

The blood rushed to Samantha's head. "And they're at the mission? Grace Mission?"

Again he nodded.

"I wonder—would you take me to them?"

David Leslie had obviously not been expecting this. "Why…yes. Yes, of course.
But—now?"

Samantha had already started for the closet to get her coat. "Yes, please, if you
would. I'll explain on the way."

❧

Although David Leslie had tried to prepare her, Samantha was still shocked by
Terese Sheridan's condition. The girl was quite literally wasted, her features gaunt,
her skin dry and flaming with fever. In spite of her swollen pregnancy, there didn't
look to be an extra ounce of flesh on her.

She was obviously delirious, moaning unintelligibly and thrashing about on the
bed as David Leslie tried to soothe her. Samantha could see what the doctor had
meant when he'd described her as "seriously ill."

She saw something else as well. Watching David Leslie, there was little doubt
that he had formed an emotional attachment to his patient. He couldn't seem to

drag his eyes away from the stricken young woman, even as he replied to Samantha's questions.

The girl *was* lovely. Despite her grave condition, there was no mistaking her comeliness. Her strong, arresting features had been ravaged by disease and, probably, the extreme privation so common to the Irish immigrants. But in a better time she must have been positively striking.

Samantha was almost relieved that Cavan wasn't here to see his sister's condition. She could just imagine what it would do to him to see her in such a state.

After another moment, she turned her attention to the child who sat on the other side of Terese Sheridan's bed. She'd been aware of that bright, intense gaze ever since her arrival at the mission and several times had ventured a smile of reassurance. Invariably, however, she received only a solemn, blue-eyed gaze that seemed to hold an entire lifetime of sorrow.

Samantha sensed that this child had had no reason to smile for a very long time, if ever. The thought brought her an immeasurable sadness.

She went around the bed to the little girl, who watched her with the guarded stare of a stray kitten. "You must be Shona," she said gently, waiting for some acknowledgment from the child.

When none came, she tried again. "I'm Samantha, Shona. I want you to know how sorry I am that no one was at the harbor to meet you. There was some confusion, and we didn't know you'd arrived. We should have been there." She paused. "Your brother, Shona? Didn't he come with you?"

The little girl's lip trembled. "He died. Tully died at the hospital." The look of bewilderment and pain in the child's eyes cut through Samantha like a scream of grief.

David Leslie had been watching them. "What hospital is that, Shona?" he asked gently.

The girl hesitated, her gaze going to Terese. "She said it was called 'Tompkinsville.'"

Samantha sucked in a quick breath. So they had been caught up in that terrible place after all! "Oh, Shona, I'm so sorry! I know all this has been awful for you. But we're going to help you now, I promise."

The girl turned slowly back to face Samantha, and that small, thin face with the haunted eyes again tore at her heart. This child, who could not be more than nine or ten years old, surely, wore a look of wretchedness and defeat that made Samantha want to gather her into her arms and comfort her. Yet she sensed the gesture would be rebuffed. This was a child who almost certainly would not dare to trust such a show of emotion.

So she simply stood there, hurting for Shona Madden and Terese Sheridan, at the same time painfully aware of her own helplessness and inadequacy. After another moment, she shrugged out of her coat and turned to David Leslie. "What can I do to help?"

He looked at her with something akin to relief. "Would you mind staying for a while? I need to tend to some of the other patients."

Samantha loosened the cuffs of her shirtwaist and briskly rolled up her sleeves. "Of course, I'll stay. But I'd like to get a message to Mr. Kane as soon as possible." She nodded to Terese Sheridan. "He and her brother are in Albany."

David Leslie looked at her. "So she *does* have family here! I was hoping there would be someone."

Samantha dipped a cloth in the basin by the bed. "Not only does she have her brother, who's going to be absolutely thrilled to find her, but she's also under the sponsorship of the *Vanguard*. That's where I come in." She glanced at the little girl who seemed to be watching her every move. "And she has her friend, Shona, of course. I know how much that must mean to her."

David Leslie gave a wan smile, and Samantha noticed again how tired he looked. It was obvious that Terese Sheridan had a highly dedicated doctor looking after her. That, along with the love and concern of her brother, and the resources of Jack's newspaper as well, would make it seem that she had a great deal in her favor.

But as she turned back to the suffering girl on the bed, she wondered if anything would really make a difference.

❦

Samantha was aware of Shona's close scrutiny throughout the evening as she tended to Terese Sheridan. The child scarcely moved, except once to go downstairs to eat, and even then one of the women volunteers had to coax her.

She returned in scarcely no time, sitting down on the same bedside chair to resume her vigil. Other than shifting her gaze from Terese to Samantha periodically, she remained quiet and unmoving. If Samantha attempted to draw her into a conversation, she would make an almost inaudible reply, then again fall silent.

Samantha ached for the child's misery. With her entire family lost to her, she was apparently all alone except for Terese Sheridan. She seemed such a forlorn little thing, with those sorrowful eyes and solemn demeanor. Samantha wished she could think of something to brighten those pinched features, but she felt at a loss to manage more than a consoling smile every now and then. This was a very sad little girl, badly in need of affection and attention. But the only person left to whom she was likely to turn now lay hovering between life and death, according to David Leslie.

Samantha felt Shona watching her. For a moment their eyes met, and she realized that in addition to the sadness brimming in the child's gaze, there was also a sharp glint of fear lurking there.

She knew a moment of dismay and even anger, that any child should have to feel so abandoned and so utterly alone. Without warning, her thoughts went to Jack. From what she knew, he couldn't have been all that much older than Shona Madden when he arrived in New York, still a boy, with the sole responsibility of a younger sister and a baby brother.

As hard as it was to picture Jack ever being frightened of *anything*, it occurred to her now that he must have been terrified. Cast onto the shores of a foreign country, in a strange city, with no one to meet him, no one to turn to for help—how could he *not* have been frightened?

Her heart softened even more toward him as she tried to picture that unyielding chin and hard-set mouth, the restless dark eyes and strong, always busy hands on the person of a bewildered fourteen-year-old boy. A boy with no parents, no home, no friends or family waiting for him—only a sprawling, noisy city teeming with hidden dangers and unknown terrors.

She wondered how much of that boy still lingered in the man—a man who could go cold and stonyhearted in an instant, whose rage unleashed was the stuff of outrageous gossip and whose very name had become synonymous with power and notoriety.

How much of what Jack had become had begun with that frightened, lonely boy who had entered the city with nothing but the clothes on his back and the will of a titan?

She could have wept for them both, for the little girl sitting across from her and for the man she sometimes thought she really didn't know at all. Who could say which of the two had actually suffered most?

She looked back at Shona Madden, who had taken Terese's hand between both her own and was rubbing it gently, over and over again in a kind of insistent rhythm, as if to will her return to consciousness.

Again Samantha knew a fierce urge to reassure the girl, to tell her she was no longer alone and that everything was going to be all right very soon now.

To her sorrow, she didn't think the girl would believe it. In truth, she wasn't sure she believed it herself. And so she kept silent as she went on trying to cool the raging fever of the girl who lay delirious, seemingly losing the battle for her life, while the child with the pain-filled eyes willed her to survive.

23

LONG NIGHT'S VIGIL

Have mercy, Heaven, on feeble clay—
Hear Thy stricken people pray.

RICHARD D'ALTON WILLIAMS

It was after nine o'clock the next night before Jack and Cavan arrived at Grace Mission. Samantha was still there. She hadn't left Terese Sheridan's bedside except to eat in the mission kitchen and take a brief rest the night before. The child, Shona, had slept only sporadically; for the most part she, too, remained seated by the bed, watching over the older girl with a steady, solemn intensity.

Samantha knew she must appear altogether disheveled by now, but for once she didn't care how she might look to Jack. Her only thought was one of overwhelming relief when he and Cavan Sheridan walked in.

Nor did it occur to her to be in the least surprised that Jack would accompany his young reporter on so personal a quest. She never questioned but what he would come, once word of Terese Sheridan's condition reached him. Not only did he hold Cavan in high regard, but Samantha suspected that he had also developed a kind of protective, big-brotherly affection for him. At times she wondered if Cavan Sheridan hadn't in some way helped to ease the absence of Jack's younger brother, Brady.

She rose at the sight of them, catching her breath at the anguished expression on Cavan's face the moment he saw his sister. Jack must have noticed, too, for he grasped the boy's shoulder as they approached the bed.

Samantha couldn't begin to imagine what must be going through Cavan's mind as he gazed down on his sister—his only surviving family member—for the first time in years. Like Jack, he had left Ireland years ago, when he was still a boy, so Terese would have been only a child at the time. Indeed, she was scarcely more than a child now, despite the fact that she was carrying a baby of her own.

Jack gave her a long look, releasing Cavan's shoulder as they came to stand on the other side of the bed from Samantha and Shona. "How is she?" Jack asked, his expression skeptical after another glance at Terese.

Trying not to alarm Cavan, Samantha chose her words carefully. "There's been… no change as yet. She's still very ill."

Jack searched her gaze for a moment, then stood watching as Cavan dropped to his knees beside the bed.

Samantha could have wept for the stricken look on his face as he knelt there, staring at his sister, who lay as still as death itself, except for her harsh, labored breathing.

Cavan's eyes held utter torment as he covered his sister's hand with both of his. His gaze traveled the length of her form, lingering only a second or two on the swollen mound of her abdomen beneath the bed linens. Samantha saw him shudder, then bring Terese's hand to his lips.

His voice sounded hoarse and strangled as he murmured to her. "Oh, *alannah, alannah,* I should never have left you behind. What have I done to you?"

Again Jack reached to grasp his shoulder. Samantha was surprised at the strained expression that settled over him all of a sudden. He had the look of a man who had suffered a great blow. His usually dusky complexion was strangely pale, and as he stood gazing down on Terese Sheridan, he was perspiring as though the room weren't almost uncomfortably chill. As she watched, his gaze swept the dormitory room like that of a man seeking escape. Yet he remained with Cavan, one large hand gripping the other's shoulder.

As for Cavan, he seemed unaware of anyone else in the room as he bent even closer to his sister, tears streaming down his cheeks. He went on crooning to her, now in the strange tongue Samantha had come to recognize as Gaelic. Across the bed her eyes met Jack's, and he gave a small nod of his head to indicate they should leave the two alone.

❦

The corridor outside the room was dimly lit, the building hushed with the stillness of night except for an occasional outcry from one of the women in the dormitory.

For a moment Jack stood staring back into the room, and Samantha thought he seemed vastly relieved to have left it. Finally, he turned to her. "You said David Leslie is taking care of the girl?"

Samantha nodded. "Do you know him?"

"Only by reputation. He's said to be a fine doctor."

"Oh, he is, I'm sure! But…I wonder just how much he can do. She's *very* ill, Jack."

"Aye, so it would seem. We came none too soon, I'm thinking." He paused. "I wonder if she shouldn't be moved to the hospital."

Samantha expelled a long breath. She was only now beginning to feel the signs of a dragging fatigue and a kind of numb inability to think clearly. "I don't know if

it would make any difference, but I suppose we could ask. Doctor Leslie said he'd
be back around ten."

She looked up to see him watching her, his dark eyes sharp with concern. "You
look exhausted," he said bluntly. "How long have you been here?"

Samantha evaded his question. "I'm all right. I thought I should stay, at least
until Cavan got here."

"Well, he's here now. I'm going to take you home."

"No, not yet," Samantha told him firmly. "Didn't you see his face? He shouldn't
be alone…if something happens. I believe I'll stay awhile longer."

Impatience sparked in Jack's eyes but quickly subsided. "If you must," he said.
"I'll stay for a bit, too, then. I'd like to see what the doctor has to say."

Samantha was too tired…and too grateful for his presence…to argue. The truth
was that she *wanted* him to stay. She felt the need for the strength and steadiness he
seemed to impart simply by being in a room. And at the moment, she feared they
were going to need all that and more as the night wore on.

Yet at the same time she puzzled over the strange mood that had come over him.
He seemed restless—even agitated—as though something more than sadness for
Cavan and Terese Sheridan were gnawing at him. Now that she thought of it, he had
been peculiar since he first walked into the room.

"Jack—is there something wrong?"

He shook his head in reply, not quite meeting her gaze. "No, nothing's wrong.
I'm a bit tired is all."

Samantha could almost see the shutters slam closed over those dark eyes. She
supposed it was possible that her own turbulent emotions and exhaustion were simply
playing tricks on her, but she didn't think so. Still, there was no point in thinking
he would explain. She had seen the hard set to his mouth, heard the edge in his tone
that plainly spoke of barriers that would not be breached.

At least not until she was willing to risk more of her own heart, her *self*, than she
had ventured so far.

❦

Back inside the dormitory, Jack could feel Samantha watching him. He stood
leaning against the wall nearest the door, while she stood beside Sheridan at his sister's
bedside. He hadn't meant to be short with her, but there was no explaining what had
come over him at the sight of the Sheridan girl.

He didn't understand it himself; he certainly hadn't *expected* it. But one look at
her, lying there, so tragically young, so dangerously ill—so obscenely *violated*—had
sent a wall of bitter memories crashing over him like an avalanche.

She didn't look a bit like his mother, this girl. She wasn't dark or delicate, instead
appeared tall and almost lanky. Her hair was a copper blaze, where his mother's had
been black as jet. And she was younger, this unfortunate lass—quite a bit younger
than his mother had been…at the last.

He supposed it was her pitiful condition: the illness, the delirium, the pregnancy, the utter *tragedy* of what had happened to her. The savage assault and its bitter consequences.

No, Samantha couldn't possibly understand, couldn't begin to comprehend how the sight of the poor girl on the bed had ripped through him like a reaper's scythe, tearing through years of grief and a suppressed rage that even he knew to be irrational. He had no way, no words, of making her understand why the sight of a victimized girl he had never seen before tonight should suddenly threaten to undo him.

But she had seen the change in him, Samantha had, and was troubled by it.

Her eyes had been filled with questions, questions he couldn't answer. He couldn't explain this, not even to Samantha. No one knew the secret that ate at him. No one. Not even Rose or Brady.

Especially not Brady. After all, it was because of Brady he had bottled up the pain and kept his silence all these years, even though there had been times when his insides virtually *screamed* to tell someone the truth.

He glanced around the room, his attention caught by the child who had been sitting beside the Sheridan girl's bed all this time. The little Madden tyke, Samantha had explained. The hollow-eyed wee girl had lost everything —parents, home, brother—and now it seemed she was in danger of losing the one familiar face left to her, the one person who at least knew her and perhaps could relate to her.

His thoughts went to Rose, his own younger sister. She must have been about the same age as the little Madden girl when he'd brought her and Brady across. No doubt she had been just as frightened, too, although at least she had had a big brother to turn to.

His mouth twisted in remembrance. *A big brother indeed!* He had been all of fourteen and as terrified as his younger sister and baby brother—Brady—had been, though he had steeled himself to conceal his fear from them. With nothing but the clothes on their backs and a pittance in his pocket, he had led them out of the harbor into a veritable nightmare.

New York. A city teeming with strangers who spoke in unknown languages. Dogs and pigs running rampant in the streets, rooting through heaps of rotting garbage and waste. Painted women crooking their fingers at him despite his youth and the two wee wanes clutching at him. Filthy street urchins diving in and out among the bustling crowds, shoving and shrieking and begging.

The stink of the sprawling city had seemed like the stench of hell itself, and the angry voices and jostling bodies pressing in on them might have been a legion of demons, so terrifying had they appeared to them that day. Jack had wanted nothing so much as to turn and run, to bolt back onto the ship with his siblings and head home.

But of course by then there had *been* no home.

Somehow they had survived, at first on the squalid streets, then later in the sordid warrens of the Five Points—ah, now *there* was a place that could easily be construed as a demon's den.

He knew what was said about him, now that those ugly years were all in the past: that he'd built an empire with nothing but Irish brass and the devil's luck. In truth, he had built it all from a boiling well of rage and an equally fierce resolve to never again be at the mercy of another human being.

But somewhere inside him, buried so deep he had thought never to confront it again, there had always been the memory of what had driven him here in the first place…and a sense of dread he had never admitted to another soul.

And tonight it had taken but a brief glimpse of another's misery to newly ignite his own.

He looked at Samantha and found her watching him. Quickly, he glanced away, but not before he had seen the questions…and the hurt in her eyes. And suddenly, for the first time in a *long* time, he found himself wanting—*needing*—to unburden himself, as much to break down any remaining barriers between him and Samantha as to purge himself, at least once, of the dark secret that had driven him out of Ireland, only to ride his soul for all the intervening years with the relentless ferocity of a bloodthirsty vulture.

But this wasn't the time—and certainly not the place. The people in this room had their own pain, their own dark agonies, to deal with. He had come to help, if he could, not to add to their misery. They already had more than enough of their own.

He hesitated for only an instant, then pushed himself away from the wall and started toward the lonely looking little girl beside the bed.

24

A MEETING IN THE MISSION HOUSE

There should be more than trials and tears
For those of young and tender years.

ANONYMOUS

Samantha watched with growing curiosity as Jack went to stand beside Shona. From all appearances, he was managing to carry on a conversation of sorts with the little girl, although the tone of his voice was so low that from the opposite side of the bed one couldn't make out more than a few words of what they were saying.

The child's face was lifted toward Jack, her countenance just as solemn and intent as ever, though perhaps slightly more animated than before. Jack, on the other hand, was smiling: a different kind of smile for him, one with not even a hint of cynicism, no sardonic twist of the mouth, no mocking glint in the eye. There was a gentleness about him now, a softness in his eyes rarely seen.

It occurred to Samantha, with a twinge of guilt, that she really ought to be reassuring Cavan rather than trying to eavesdrop on Jack and the little Madden girl. But Cavan seemed to have withdrawn to a private place occupied only by himself and his sister, and Samantha almost felt that to speak to him at this time would be to intrude. He and Terese had been separated for years, after all, and in spite of the grim circumstances, this had to be an extremely momentous occasion for them…and one not necessarily meant to be shared.

Besides, she couldn't help but be intrigued by the scene on the other side of the bed. So she moved away a little, and Jack, seeing her, gave her a smile and gestured that she should come around the bed and join him and his new friend.

❧

She was a sober little thing, the Madden tyke, but then she had reason to be, given all that she had likely endured in her few brief years. The child was so gossamer thin that Jack fancied she would snap like a butterfly's wing under the slightest amount of pressure.

He recalled Brady's writing that the girl was ten years old, but she might have been two or three years younger, so small and fragile was she. She had a cloud of flaxen hair, so fine it might have been spun silk, and the biggest, most sorrowful blue eyes Jack had ever seen, eyes that seemed enormous in that thin little face. For some incomprehensible reason he suddenly found himself wondering if those eyes had ever lighted with a childish delight instead of the fear and the unhappiness that now looked out at him.

What would it take, he thought, to coax a smile from such a child as this, a child who looked as if she might never have known what it *was* to smile?

❧

"You've met Shona, of course?" Jack said to Samantha as she came to stand beside him. "She's ten years old, it seems, and comes from Limerick."

Samantha smiled at the girl, who ducked her head down as if confused by all this attention. She would have been quite a lovely child had she not been so thin and pale as to appear unhealthy. Even in her malnourished state, with her fair hair in tangles and her face all sharp planes, there was a winsomeness about her that tugged at Samantha's heart.

She was surprised to realize that the child had apparently evoked a similar response in Jack. She looked from one to the other. Jack had stooped over to reduce the distance between himself and the little girl, who was watching him closely with something akin to awe—and perhaps a measure of fearfulness as well. It occurred to Samantha that to one so small, Jack must appear a veritable giant, and a somewhat dark, forbidding one as well.

"Do you understand who we are, lass?" he asked the child, his tone as quiet and as solemn as Shona's countenance.

Shona stared up at him, studying him as if bewildered by his attention. "Mr. Kane."

Jack nodded. "That's exactly right, just as I told you. And this is Mrs. Harte, my...good friend and one of the editors from the newspaper." He paused. "Do you know what that is, Shona—a newspaper?"

The child shook her head, her gaze never leaving Jack's face.

Interesting, Samantha thought, that Jack had realized right away that a child like Shona would very likely have no conception of something as common as a newspaper. Not many would have even thought of such a thing, herself included.

"Well then, we shall have to bring you a copy when we come again," said Jack cheerfully. "A newspaper is a little like a book, you see—though with not as many pages. People read it to learn what's going on about the city and perhaps find stories of particular interest to them. The name of my newspaper is the *Vanguard,* by the way."

He motioned toward Cavan. "The lad there with your friend, Terese, is her brother, Cavan. They haven't seen each other for a number of years, did you know that?"

Shona glanced across the bed to watch Cavan and Terese for a moment but made no reply.

The exchange went on like that for several minutes, almost entirely between Jack and the child, with Samantha merely looking on and nodding her agreement every now and then as called for.

She supposed she should have found it curious, how Jack seemed to have managed to win over the girl—if not her trust, exactly, at least her interest—in such a short time. Yet watching the two, his rapport with the child seemed so easy, so natural, that anyone who didn't know better would have assumed he was an old hand at dealing with children, that he almost certainly had a family of his own.

Samantha knew, of course, that he had raised his younger brother and sister almost entirely single-handedly; that might account for the ease with which he communicated with the Madden child. Still, she couldn't help but remember how quick he had been to insist that he could accept a marriage without children, once he'd learned that she was barren.

As she stood there, watching him with the forlorn little girl, a sudden wave of sadness rose in her. The painful realization of what she would be cheating him of, should she ever agree to his proposal, nearly doubled her over, and she had to struggle to keep from bolting from the room.

But in the same instant she told herself she was fretting over nothing, because she *wouldn't* agree to his proposal; she couldn't even *consider* it.

"Samantha?"

She looked up to find him watching her with a question in his eyes. Samantha shook her head a little to clear it. "I'm sorry?"

"I was telling Shona that perhaps one day soon she could come and have supper with us. Would that be all right with you?"

Samantha looked from one to the other, barely managing a smile. "Yes, of course. I'd...like that very much."

She deliberately avoided looking at Jack. "Perhaps I could have you both to my place for a meal," she said with forced enthusiasm. "We'll have to make plans."

Jack seemed to be caught off guard as much as Samantha by the child's reply. "Thank you very much, but I'd want to wait until Terese is well enough to come, too, please."

Samantha didn't know what to say and looked to Jack for help. He straightened, taking his time to answer. "I'm sure your friend, Terese, wouldn't mind if you came just once without her," he said carefully. "Later, we'll all of us celebrate your arrival in proper fashion."

Samantha turned to look at Cavan, who had risen to his feet and now stood staring down at his sister. She despised herself for giving in to the pessimism that had been lurking at the edges of her mind all evening, but at this moment it was difficult to believe that Terese Sheridan…or Cavan either…would be likely to have cause for celebration in the near future.

Unwilling to give in to her own dismal thoughts, she walked quickly around the bed and took Cavan by the hand. "Would you like me to pray with you?" she asked him. His eyes filled as he nodded, and Samantha squeezed his hand. She wished she could do more, but at this point she believed the most important thing she could do for Cavan or Terese Sheridan was to pray, and pray unceasingly.

As she and Cavan knelt beside the bed, she saw that Shona had followed their lead and was kneeling, hands folded, looking up at Jack as if she clearly expected him to join them.

He looked at the child, then at Samantha, but merely stood aside, his jaw set in a stubborn line, his gaze carefully averted from Terese Sheridan.

❧

By the time David returned to check on Terese, it was after ten. He stopped just inside the room, surprised by the contingent surrounding her bed. Samantha Harte and a young man were kneeling, obviously praying, as was Shona, while a startlingly tall, dark-haired man in a well-tailored overcoat stood watching them.

The man locked eyes with David for an instant, then returned his attention to Samantha Harte, still deep in prayer. Although David suspected that the young man kneeling beside Terese's bed might be her brother, he couldn't think who the other man might be. After another moment, he bowed his own head and added a fervent request to that of the others.

Afterward, Samantha Harte introduced him to Terese Sheridan's brother, a likable young fellow who was obviously devastated by what had happened to his sister. David wished there were something he could say to alleviate Cavan Sheridan's fears, but under the circumstances false reassurance would be worse than nothing at all.

The dark, imposing man he'd noticed on entering turned out to be Jack Kane— *the* Jack Kane. Upon their introduction, David had all he could do to conceal his surprise. From everything he had heard about the publishing giant, he would hardly have expected Kane to show up here on behalf of an immigrant Irish girl. Of course, Kane was thoroughly Irish himself, and it was his newspaper that was funding a number of immigrant resettlements. Even so, it seemed more than a little peculiar to find him making a personal call at a mission house.

For that matter, Jack Kane himself wasn't at all what David might have expected. Oh, it was easy to sense a certain…hardness in the man, a self-confidence, perhaps, even a kind of arrogance, not to mention the unmistakable aura of power that seemed to vibrate in the very air around him. There was no mistaking the fact that this was a man accustomed to having his own way; he wore authority like an outer garment. Yet there was an openness about Kane when he shook David's hand and looked him square in the eye that seemed to instantly draw him in and include him as an equal.

It soon became apparent to David as well that Jack Kane's concern for Terese was wholly genuine, if unexpected.

"I was wondering what you would think," Kane inclined his head toward Terese, "of moving her to the hospital."

"I've considered that, and frankly, I think it might be treacherous to move her just now," David replied. "Besides, in my opinion, nothing can be done for her at the hospital that isn't being done right here."

David found it necessary to actually look up to Kane—an uncommon occurrence for him, since he was nearly six feet himself. It seemed to him that Kane's expression projected no hint of condescension nor any suggestion that David might be inadequate. To the contrary, he felt the man was merely exploring all the possibilities for helping Terese—which, of course, was what David himself wanted, too.

Kane studied him for a moment, then nodded. "You're reputed to be an excellent doctor. Do you agree with that?"

David lifted an eyebrow but had to smile a little at Kane's directness. "Of course," he said dryly. "How else would I have attained such a lucrative practice?"

It was Jack Kane's turn to quirk an eyebrow.

"Yes, Mr. Kane," David went on, "as it happens, I do consider myself a good doctor."

Again Kane gave that short, expedient nod. "Yet you work almost entirely with the poor."

David glanced at Samantha Harte, who stood watching the two of them. "It's where God put me," he said matter-of-factly. "I expect Mrs. Harte would understand what I mean."

David felt himself being measured under Jack Kane's scrutiny and had to make an effort not to squirm a little. The man was almost disturbingly *intense*.

"Here's the thing, Dr. Leslie," Kane said brusquely. "If you say she shouldn't be moved, I'll accept that. But I expect you to do everything you can for the girl. If there's any question of money, you've only to ask. I—my newspaper—will be paying her expenses, for however long it's necessary. I'd like her to have the very best of care, whatever it takes."

David bristled a little at his tone. "I give all my patients the best care I can manage," he said shortly.

"No doubt you do," Kane said in the same clipped tones. "I'm simply asking you to make Miss Sheridan a special case."

David studied the man, but Kane's expression was now unreadable. Whatever warmth he might have imagined he'd seen earlier had given way to a shuttered, flinty stare. Only slightly annoyed, David decided that this was simply Jack Kane being...Jack Kane.

What Kane couldn't know, of course, was that Terese Sheridan had already become a "special case" to David. A very special one indeed.

Samantha could see nothing in David Leslie's face that gave reason for encouragement, no sign of any change for the better in Terese. Her heart ached for Cavan, who hovered nearby, watching the doctor closely, almost fearfully.

Finally, Dr. Leslie asked them to step out of the room so he could examine Terese. Shona made no move to go, as though the decision had already been made for her to stay.

Cavan followed Samantha and Jack out of the room with obvious reluctance. In the hallway, he turned to Samantha. "Mrs. Harte? Is there a chance, do you think?"

Samantha delayed her reply. The truth was that she held little optimism for Terese Sheridan's recovery. Yet Cavan was obviously pleading for some remnant of hope, no matter how slim, and she couldn't quite bring herself to disappoint him.

She felt Jack's hand on her shoulder as if to steady her. "Cavan...I don't know what to think," she ventured. "Terese's condition is...critical, as you know. It seems to me that all we can do for her right now is to keep praying."

"Aye," Cavan said dully, his expression bleak. "I know she's in a bad way, all right." He stopped, and in that instant something like anger flared in his eyes. "'Tis a hard thing to grasp, why God would allow such a bitter blow to fall to her. So much suffering, and her so young. There's no telling all that she's gone through, and now this—"

He stopped, turning abruptly to walk off as if he could not get away quickly enough.

Instinctively, Samantha reached out to him, but Jack stayed her hand. "Let him go, Samantha. He might do well to be alone for a time. Besides, you can't help him. No one can help with a grief so great."

Samantha turned to look at him. Something in his tone of voice—a kind of weary knowing, a sad but certain conviction—caused her to study him carefully.

She saw in his face a look of raw anguish, and she was struck by the inexplicable sensation that, for a very long time now, Jack had burned with some sort of agonizing pain that the tragic incident with Terese Sheridan had somehow rekindled.

"Jack? What's wrong?"

He didn't answer, instead looked away, as if staring off into a great distance. The past, Samantha wondered. Was he remembering whatever had happened to cause him such despair?

"Jack?" she prompted gently. "Can't you tell me?"

He turned back to her, searching her eyes, the pain in his still unabated. "Do you really want to know, Samantha?"

"Yes, of course I do."

"Why?"

"Because you seem so sad," she said directly. Unable to stop herself, she put a hand to his face.

He caught her hand and held it to his cheek. "The only time I am sad these days," he said softly, "is when I'm away from you."

For an uneasy moment, Samantha thought he was about to revert to his more typical role of the seductive rogue. It was a role she found increasingly difficult to reconcile with the great gentleness of which she knew him to be capable, and the kindness and genuine compassion he could display when least expected.

For the most part, Samantha had learned to look past the masks he was given to donning. The man behind those masks, after all, was the man she had come to know…and love.

The thought froze in her mind. There it was again, that unbidden admission of her feelings for Jack, feelings that both thrilled and terrified her. Heart hammering, she tried desperately to cage the thought, but she might as well have given actual voice to the words, might as well have *shouted* them down the corridor, so clearly and insistently did they continue to echo in her heart.

In any event, she must have been wrong about his intentions, at least for the moment. Although his dark gaze was piercing and almost intimate, it seemed to hold nothing but a surprising tenderness and the same searching question that had been there before.

Slowly, then, he released her hand. "Perhaps I *will* tell you, *mavourneen.*" His voice was a low rumble in the hushed hallway. "But not here, not tonight. There is already enough darkness afoot in this place. I'll not be dredging up still more. For now, why don't you go back inside while I go and see about the boy?"

Samantha studied him for another moment, but she sensed he was right. Their responsibility here tonight was to Cavan and his sister, not to each other.

God willing, there would be another time and place to learn just what lay behind the pool of sorrow in his eyes.

25

THROUGH THE EYES OF THE BEHOLDER

The Lord sees not as man sees; man looks on the outward appearance,
but the Lord looks on the heart.

1 SAMUEL 16:7

THE CLADDAGH, IRELAND, LATE NOVEMBER

The afternoon was cold and dreary, with a soft rain that showed no signs of abating soon. Brady had covered his parcels well with three thicknesses of canvas, but even so, by the time he reached the Claddagh, the weight felt damp under his arm.

He half ran up the path to Gabriel's house, stopping at the door to pull in a couple of deep, fortifying breaths before knocking. As he'd expected, it was Gabriel who answered. The big fisherman showed no sign of pleasure at the sight of Brady. That, too, was to be expected.

From the look on Gabriel's face, Brady knew he would have to talk fast, and so he plunged right into his discourse. "I apologize for dropping by unannounced like this, Gabriel, but I'll be leaving soon, you see, and wanted you to have these before I go."

He shifted the paintings to both hands, holding them out to Gabriel. The big fisherman glanced from Brady to the paintings, then back at Brady. The bright blue eyes remained cold, the craggy features implacable.

"They're portraits," Brady explained, pushing them at Gabriel with such persistence it would have been awkward for him *not* to take them. Even so, the other made no move toward acceptance.

"They're portraits," Brady said again. "One of each of you—Roweena, Evie, and yourself. I did them some time ago, with the intention of making them Christmas gifts. Since I've decided to leave before then, I thought I'd go ahead and bring them by. Won't you take a look at them?"

Gabriel Vaughan's face, Brady reflected, would have foiled Michelangelo. The man might have been chiseled from granite, so resolute and unyielding was that bearded countenance. With the pronounced aquiline nose and the deep blue eyes so piercing they could have shattered an iceberg, the big fisherman never failed to remind Brady of one of the ancient clan chieftains—a *warrior* chieftain, at that.

At the moment, he had all he could do not to squirm under Gabriel's narrow-eyed scrutiny. He could see the play of emotions flitting across the giant's features: surprise, skepticism, suspicion, and finally what appeared to be a reluctant desire to accept the proffered gifts.

"Step in, then," said Gabriel after a noticeable hesitation. There was no mistaking the grudging tone in his invitation.

Brady would have liked nothing better than to accept, but to do so would mean going against the casual air he hoped to convey.

"I'd really like to, Gabriel, but I have an appointment. I just wanted to drop these off while I had the chance."

That said, he finally managed to press the paintings into the other's hands. "I hope you like them."

Gabriel studied him. "You say you'll be leaving soon?"

Brady nodded, giving a quick, somewhat rueful smile. "Afraid so. I still have a lot of territory to cover."

"When will you go?"

"Oh, not for a couple of weeks yet. But I'm going to be pretty busy in the meantime. I still have some things to finish up in the city before I leave. I'm going to head north, to Westport, then on to Sligo."

Gabriel nodded, regarding him thoughtfully for a moment. "You might as well come in and say your good-byes, then. Since you'll be leaving soon." He paused. "If you want."

Brady pretended to hesitate. "Well, all right. Perhaps for just a moment. I do have to be on my way soon, though."

He saw Roweena the instant he walked inside the cottage. She was stirring something in the large black pot hanging inside the hearth. She gave no smile, merely a furtive, quick glance and a nod before turning back to her work.

Evie, however, came trundling across the room in a rush. "What's this, Brady Kane? What have you brought us? And where have you been?"

As always, she piped his name in her childish singsong voice as if it were but one word: *Bradykane.* Brady smiled at her and gestured toward the paintings, which Gabriel was laying out on the table.

"Here, Gabriel, let me help you with those," he said, pulling the canvas wrappings off the one on top, which was the portrait of Evie.

He held it up to the child, and she slapped both hands to her cheeks, her eyes going wide, her mouth pursing in a circle of surprise and delight. "'Tis *myself!*" she cried, bobbing up and down. "You made a painting of *me,* Brady Kane!"

"It is you, indeed," Brady said, laughing at her antics. "Mischievous imp that you are."

The next portrait was of Roweena. Brady held it up for their admiration—in his own estimation, this was his finest work to date—but Roweena hung back, clearly feeling awkward and badly flustered. Color stained her cheeks as she finally approached, and she kept looking from the painting to Gabriel—but never at Brady.

"Ohhh, Roweena!" cried Evie. "See how beautiful you are! Didn't I tell you? Didn't I?"

Roweena only blushed even more furiously as Gabriel shushed the child. Brady discreetly refrained from making any observations about the portraits, especially Roweena's. But in truth he thought he *had* managed to capture her delicate beauty, her fragile grace, as well as the high spirits that sometimes flared in those magnificent eyes when least expected.

Now he uncovered the painting of Gabriel. The big man was clearly discomfited by what was, Brady felt with no small amount of pride, an impressive likeness, if not entirely realistic. The force of the man, the strength and power so evident in every move he made, had somehow come through. But even Brady recognized the fact that something was either askew or lacking; his rendering of the stubborn black hair, the proud nose, the flashing eyes, the rugged jaw—although technically true to form—failed to capture the elusive essence of the giant.

There was something about Gabriel Vaughan that simply could not be contained by a piece of canvas. Perhaps that accounted for the puzzlement in Roweena's eyes—and in Evie's, too, to some extent—as they studied the portrait of Gabriel. Both of them kept stealing glances at Gabriel as though trying to identify just what was different from the man in the painting.

For the most part, Brady's stay was gratifying. Although Roweena never looked at him directly or said a word to him, Brady sensed that she was pleased by the portrait, if self-conscious about all the attention that accompanied it. He also suspected that the mere fact of Gabriel's allowing him entrance had given her some satisfaction.

As for Evie, the child didn't quit chirping about her "par-tret" the entire time Brady was there. And Gabriel, although obviously at a loss about his own likeness, did seem taken by the girls' portraits, from which he could not seem to tear his eyes away.

All the way back to the city, Brady could scarcely contain his elation. No mistake about it, his plan was working just as he'd hoped.

Soon now—very soon—he could play his trump card.

❦

By evening, only Evie seemed to have lost interest in the portraits. She had propped her likeness against the corner wall of the kitchen and gone outside to empty the washbasin. She would not return for several minutes, Roweena knew—not until she had "followed the first stars," as she liked to say, and dawdled a bit in the yard.

In the meantime, Roweena sat at the table where the *faideog* flickered in the draught. The wick was nearly too short for the tray of oil and would soon have to be replaced. From time to time she stole a glance at Gabriel's portrait, dappled in the glow of the firelight. Ignoring his protests, she had positioned his likeness on top of the dresser, where it could be seen from any place in the room.

As to her own image, she would have tucked it away behind the curtain if Gabriel had not insisted that it remain where he had placed it, resting against the hearth wall. She watched him for a moment, sitting in his chair beside the fire, seemingly lost in thought entirely and oblivious to her presence in the room.

Just as well, for she would not have him notice how his portrait drew her gaze. It was not merely the fascination his strong, rugged features held for her, although in truth she had always found Gabriel pleasing to look on—unobserved, of course. But what most commanded her interest in the painting was the obvious difference in how she saw Gabriel as compared to how *Brady Kane* apparently saw him.

For the life of her, she couldn't fathom how Brady could be so blind to Gabriel's true appearance. No matter how closely she searched, she could find no trace of the kindness, the wisdom, the dry humor, the *gentleness,* so much a part of Gabriel's nature. There was no light in the eyes, no tenderness about the mouth—no softening whatsoever of the rough-hewn countenance she knew by heart.

The face in the portrait was more that of a hard, unyielding man, perhaps even a sour-tempered man. A man who had never known a sunset or a song, who had never rescued a baby bird from the bushes, never tended to a child's scraped knee or carried that same child, laughing, on his sturdy shoulders.

Ah, no, the man with the cold, relentless visage in the painting wasn't Gabriel. Not *her* Gabriel.

Her Gabriel...

Roweena caught her breath at the effrontery of her own thoughts. How had such irrational musings gained a foothold on her mind?

She had no right to think of Gabriel in such a way, had no right to think of him in *any* way other than in the role in which he had placed himself—the role of her guardian. Clearly, that was how he saw himself in relation to her, and so must she.

Even so, she could not comprehend Brady Kane's apparent inability to see Gabriel as he really was.

This much she knew: Gabriel might not be to her all she would wish. But she *knew* him, knew his heart, his spirit—knew the good things, the noble things that made him the man he was.

Brady Kane had rendered only a shell of the man she knew, and she somehow resented him for it almost as if he had stolen something from Gabriel.

❦

Gabriel could not seem to drag his gaze away from the portrait of Roweena, now bathed in the flickering glow from the hearth fire. It was inconceivable to him how Brady Kane could have captured her likeness with such clarity and perfection. He seemed to have missed not the smallest detail, not the slightest aspect of her loveliness. Even the tiny imperfections—the slight rise at the bridge of her nose, the almost imperceptible way one corner of her mouth would lift higher than the other when she smiled, the small birthmark just below her left ear which time had nearly faded to nothing—had been caught by the American's considerable skill and depicted with uncanny accuracy. Kane had missed nothing, it seemed. So lifelike, so compelling was his portrait of Roweena that it almost seemed to breathe under one's scrutiny.

But it wasn't the realism of the portrait that confounded Gabriel. What had set his mind to spinning had little to do with the exceptional ability of the artist or even the stunning, true-to-life resemblance of the painting to Roweena. It was something much more elusive, something another might have missed.

But Gabriel had practically raised her from a child, had cared for her over the years, day after day. Living in such close proximity for so long a time, it would have been impossible *not* to know her, and know her well—know her by *heart,* as it were. And what he saw in the portrait, the distinction that not for the first time now made his heart hammer and his blood pound in his head, was the unmistakable *desire,* the passion, with which the painting had been rendered.

Gabriel had no knowledge of art, not even an inkling of all that must have gone into the creation of such a work. He knew nothing of what must be, he was certain, an emotionally and physically challenging endeavor, perhaps even, for some, a kind of spiritual experience. So how, then, was it that he knew, and knew with a heavy certainty, that this portrait of the one he held more dear than anyone else in the world had been painted by a man who burned with an unholy desire for her, an obsessive—possibly even a *dangerous*—need for her?

There were those among the Old Ones in the village who had long held that he possessed the gift of discernment. It had been pointed out to him over the years, and while he had never admitted as much to another, he accepted the reality that indeed he *did* seem to possess a strong—sometimes so strong as to be a burden—sense of what was of the darkness as opposed to what was of the light, of that which was good and that which was evil, and, at times, even the needs and passions of those with whom he came in contact.

He had not coveted the gift, in fact on more than one occasion had even bemoaned it. But it had been a long time since he had attempted to *deny* it. He simply tried as much as possible not to dwell on it, not to make much of it, but rather to keep close communion with his Lord, to walk in the light of his presence, to obey his teachings, and to listen closely to the whisper of his Spirit. If God had indeed gifted him with this ability to discern, to sense the truth, then he felt the need to always be sensitive to the responsibility that must surely be a part of it.

Tonight he had no question in his mind but that the emotion kindled in him by the portrait of Roweena was more than a man's natural response to a lifeless work of paint and canvas. Her likeness had been rendered as through a veil of sensuality, a cloud of compulsion and dark desire.

He knew now that Brady Kane burned with an obsession...and the obsession was Roweena.

Somehow, it was all connected, he sensed: the dark motives behind the paintings, Kane's sudden show of remorse, and, most recently, his casual gesture of friendship.

The realization made him almost physically ill and strangely frightened, though he could not as yet clearly identify the source of his fear.

Again came the near-desperate urgency to hear from Ulick. He didn't even know what he hoped to learn, but more and more he felt a wild clambering inside him to learn *something*.

Soon his troubled reflection took the form of a silent, insistent prayer, to the effect that if there was indeed something—anything—he needed to know about Kane, it would soon be revealed. In time to ward off any possible harm to Roweena.

26

UNEASY DREAMS, UNHOLY PLANS

All omens monstrous and appalling
Affright my guilty mind.

JAMES CLARENCE MANGAN

Brady Kane was trapped in a fog, a fog that reeked with the stench of fear and decay. Shadows, dark and terrifying in their distortion, darted in and out, looming at him, writhing about him and clutching at him like a band of unholy dervishes. The foul miasma of the fog seeped into his nostrils, his mouth, the very pores of his body.

Somewhere nearby, though he couldn't see her, he heard Roweena, screaming as if the terrors of hell itself held her captive. In a frenzy, he lashed out with both arms, trying to beat off the deadly shadows surrounding him, fighting desperately to free himself so he could rescue Roweena. But the more he struggled, the more the fog and the shadows sucked him in.

There was nothing around him, above or below him, but darkness—a blackness deeper than night itself, an impenetrable, wet gloom that cloyed at him, tossing him about like a piece of driftwood in a sea storm. He was blinded by the darkness, totally trapped by his own helplessness, while the fog swept him farther and farther away from Roweena.

Her terror-stricken screams were growing fainter now. Brady reached out, thrashing wildly in search of an opening, a hole in the barrier of fog that kept him from her.

He tried to call out to her, but the fog choked off his shouts, turning them to weak, ineffectual bleats.

All he could hear of Roweena now was a strangled, broken weeping, like that of a child frightened beyond all reason. He exerted every ounce of strength available to him in one enormous strike against the fog, only to find himself pitching forward into a deep, spiraling fall.

Roweena's voice faded to nothing as he hurtled headlong through the darkness.

❦

Brady came awake with a cry, gasping for breath, thrashing his arms. His heart was beating against his rib cage in a savage fit, as if it would explode right out of his chest. He was drenched in perspiration, the bedclothes tossed into a tangled heap.

Light flooded over him, and he blinked and shook his head, looking around the room in bewilderment.

Finally, awareness dawned, and he sank back onto the pillow with relief.

It had been only a dream...only a nightmare...

It was morning. There was no fog, there were no evil shadows, and Roweena was not screaming in the distance.

From the light pouring into the room, he thought it must be nearly noon. His head began to clear, slowly at first, until he remembered what day it was. The sudden recognition was like downing a full pot of strong black coffee all at once.

Thursday. Tonight was the night.

He lay unmoving, his heart still racing, his breath coming in ragged gasps. His head felt like a blacksmith's anvil, and his mouth was as foul as a pigpen. He'd practically drunk himself into a stupor the night before, finally stumbling into bed a couple of hours before dawn.

In spite of his good intentions, he had been drinking for two days almost without letup. He wasn't sure why. Some of it had to do with today's affair, of course. He was tense, had been all week.

He hadn't been able to work for days now, and that in turn caused him even more tension. At this point, he was so far behind in his assignments for Jack, he'd be lucky if he didn't get a furious summons home.

Added to that was the fact that he was running out of funds. The initial payment to Biller and Robuck had set him back a pretty penny. If he didn't post a story and a new recommendation as to some immigrants for Jack to sponsor soon, he was going to land himself in a real fix.

No wonder he needed a drink now and then to steady his nerves.

Now and then?

He ignored the uneasiness lurking at the edge of his mind. This was no time for self-examination. Besides, once today was over with, he'd be able to concentrate again. Get back to work. Redeem himself with Jack, knock off the drinking, and get some much-needed work done. It was just the anticipation of tonight that had him rattled, that was all.

As he lay looking around his rented room, arms locked behind his head, he felt the beginning of the need for a drink to start the day, even though he was still slightly high from the night before. Only the chill of the room and the sickening pounding of his head kept him from getting up to retrieve the bottle on the desk.

He swallowed down the vile taste in his mouth and stretched a little. He ought to get up, have some breakfast, get himself together. But he was still shaken by the nightmare, still disoriented.

He refused to give a stupid dream any credence. It had just been the liquor and maybe some anxiety about tonight, nothing else.

He wouldn't think about it. Better to think about Roweena instead. Just for a minute or two.

After tonight, he was pretty sure he wouldn't have to resort to dreaming about her. If everything went as planned—and why wouldn't it?—then he'd be able to see her out in the open whenever he wanted.

With Gabriel's blessing.

He smiled, then winced as his lips cracked from the dryness. He needed to clean himself up a bit. Get a haircut and a shave. Have his landlady press some clothes. Needed to look presentable tonight, even though he'd get roughed up a little in the fray.

Not much, of course. He'd warned those two uglies to have a care when he appeared on the scene. He didn't want any broken bones for his trouble. In fact, he didn't want any more pain than absolutely necessary. They were to push him around just enough to make things believable, no more.

He wished he didn't feel so uneasy about those two. Especially Robuck. They were both bad business, but something about Robuck literally gave him the creeps.

Well, what did he expect? It wasn't exactly a job for missionaries. Besides, he'd seen the way their eyes bugged when he quoted the price. Money was everything with their kind. They would do the deed, he'd pay them off, and that would be the last he'd ever see of them. And good riddance.

This was worth a few risks, after all.

Roweena was worth a *lot* of risks.

He let his mind wander, imagining what it would be like with her once Gabriel took the cuffs off and they had a chance to be together.

Roweena was a total innocent. She had never been with a man; he was sure of it. No way a man would have ever gotten past Gabriel.

His mouth twisted at the sudden, unbidden image of the big fisherman, beefy arms crossed over that massive chest of his, standing guard with a scowl.

But not for much longer, he reminded himself. It would all be different after tonight.

He was going to be good to her. He really was. He would court her in grand fashion, make her head swim, make her wild for him. He'd gain her trust, win her over entirely. And eventually…soon…she'd be warm and willing in his arms.

This time, though, it was going to be different. *Roweena* was different, a different kind of girl. She was everything he could ever want. He had never felt this way about a woman. Never.

This time, he wanted more than just another quick fling. He was going to change, change for Roweena. He'd be different with her. She was so good, so innocent—so trusting. He would be the kind of man she'd look up to. She'd be crazy in love with him, and he would cherish her. Even Gabriel would approve.

Eventually...who could say? He might even marry her.

He wasn't so sure he'd ever go back to the States, at least to stay. He was Irish now, thoroughly Irish. And Ireland was where he belonged.

There was still Jack to be dealt with, of course. He had to figure a way to keep big brother from disowning him until he could support himself. He might want to live in Ireland, but he had no intention of living *poor*.

Ah, well—he could handle Jack. Hadn't he always?

For now, he needed to get on with the day. This was the day that was going to change everything.

He pushed himself up, slung his feet over the side of the bed, grabbing his head with both hands when the pain slammed down on him. His eyes went to the bottle on the desk, and he decided to have just one quick drink. Just one. To settle his stomach, ease the headache.

After all, he had to be in top shape for the day ahead.

In another minute, he got to his feet and headed for the desk.

27

AN ILL WIND OVER THE CLADDAGH

How sad to see eyes clouded, dim…
Eyes meant by God to mirror Him.

ANONYMOUS

Gabriel took the streets at a brisk clip, his coat buttoned all the way up, the scarf Roweena had knitted him drawn snugly about his throat.

Early in the evening, a raw wind had blown up, cutting across Galway and the Claddagh with a wintry chill. The sea tossed and heaved like a bad-tempered behemoth roused too soon from its nap. In deference to the weather, the village lanes were nearly deserted. The Claddagh's fishermen were huddled by the hearth fire tonight, their children shut safely indoors against the wind. Gabriel himself had issued a caution to Eveleen not to get her "feathers blown off" by dawdling in the yard, as was her custom this time of day.

No one had yet forgotten the Big Wind that had caught all Ireland by surprise January past, nor was it likely that anyone would forget it for a long time to come. Memories of animals and entire houses blown out to sea by the savage storm were still all too vivid in the minds of mothers and fathers, daughters and sons. Loved ones had been lost, homes destroyed, lives devastated. Ever since, each time a strong wind stirred the thatch on a roof, all Galway looked to the sky with apprehension.

Gabriel's haste was not born of fear, however. He had endured enough winds in his time to recognize tonight's as nothing more than an ordinary blow that would subside without wreaking any real damage. What had him pounding the cobbles in such haste at this hour was the message from Ulick, delivered late in the afternoon. Immediately after reading his friend's hastily scrawled note, he sent word to the other men that he would not join with them to pray this night, as was his custom, that instead he had another obligation to see to.

He was to meet Ulick at the house of his cousin, near the priory. Gabriel didn't question why his friend simply didn't come to his home. Those who knew Gabriel Vaughan best also knew that he was adamant about keeping men's business removed from his personal life. Because of Roweena and the child, he exercised every caution; he had never allowed much tramping in and out of his house, even by those with whom he had a long-standing friendship.

The thought of Roweena and Eveleen alone at the house made him pick up his stride still more. They were used to his Thursday night absences for prayer meeting, and tonight he had left the house even earlier than was his habit. But for some reason, he was exceedingly anxious to get the meeting with Ulick over and done with—not only because he was eager to hear whatever information the man might have for him, but also because he was uneasy about leaving Roweena and the child alone.

Perhaps the wind had unnerved him more than he'd realized. He looked up at the sky, totally bereft of moon and stars. It seemed that the wind had already died. The dark streets had fallen silent, with an unnatural stillness hanging over the entire Claddagh. An unaccountable shudder seized Gabriel as he turned onto the lane that led to his destination. He felt chilled through, but not as a result of the night air. It was more the unexpected calm that had spooked him, he realized.

Like most fishermen, he had experienced firsthand the strange, singular quiet that often preceded a storm. As he trudged up to the front door of the small, mud-walled cottage where Ulick was waiting, he caught himself holding his breath, as though bracing himself before yet another blast of December wind could come shrieking down upon his head.

Ulick threw open the door only a second or two after Gabriel knocked. The mouth beneath the drooping mustache was set in a thin, hard line, and the uncommonly pale eyes met Gabriel's with a look that seemed to hold something more akin to dread than welcome.

In that moment, Gabriel feared that he was about to be caught up in more than one storm this night.

❧

Clive Robuck shifted his bulk and stepped back a little deeper into the shadows, accidentally tromping Biller's foot.

An oath from the smaller man brought an indifferent shrug from Robuck. "Get yourself some proper boots, why don't you?"

"I'll be getting myself a hot water bottle and a roaring fire after this night, I can tell you," Biller groused.

"Aye, and for me a warm-blooded woman as well. This infernal weather has me near frozen. I wish the little chit would come out so we could get on with it."

"'Tis still early," Biller reminded him. "I can't help but wonder why Vaughan left before his usual time. You don't think there's something wrong?"

Robuck turned to eye him. "You worry too much. You'd worry yourself witless if you had any to begin with."

"Seems to me there's a fair measure to worry about with such a stunt as this," Biller muttered.

"Are you cracked, man? We couldn't have found a softer job! We scare a wee girl for a bit and let the man who's paying us come to the rescue. Nothing could be easier, it seems to me."

Still scowling, Biller continued to dig a crater in the mud with his toe. "Unless something goes wrong."

"What could go wrong?" Robuck snapped, out of patience with his cohort. "Any *gawm* could pull this one off. Even you." Without turning away, he spat on the ground, then added, "Quit your bellyaching. You saw for yourself, the big man is gone—just as Kane said he would be. What does it matter if he left a bit early? The girl will show any time now, and when she does, we'll get this—"

Biller fastened a hand on his arm and jerked his head in the direction of Vaughan's house. Robuck turned to see a dark-haired tyke trundle out the door, a basin in hand. She stopped just long enough to clumsily pull the door shut with her other hand, then went around to the side of the house, where she tossed the contents of the basin onto the ground.

As Kane had predicted, the chit clearly meant to dawdle awhile in the yard. For a moment, she stood unmoving, looking idly about at her surroundings. After a time, she tucked the empty basin under her arm and did a few skips and a couple of hops around a piece of bare shrubbery growing near the house. She stopped long enough to pull her bulky sweater more tightly around her, then headed toward the back of the house, all the while staring up at the sky as she went.

Robuck lifted a hand to Biller to signal that they would move in a moment. On instinct, he pulled his pistol out of his back pocket.

"What are you doing?" Biller hissed behind him. "The American said no weapons! And we agreed!"

Robuck whipped around. "Shut your gob!" he ordered in a harsh whisper. "You want to give us up?" He palmed the gun and aimed it square in Biller's face. "This isn't a weapon. 'Tis insurance, is all. Weren't you just the one fretting that something might go wrong? This is to make sure nothing does. Now come on before she—"

They stopped, turning to look as the door was flung open with a bang and another girl—no, a woman, this one—stuck her head out and called, "Evie! Eveleen—come inside now!"

Robuck thought her voice peculiar, as if she had a sore throat or was perhaps hoarse from a cold.

She couldn't see the little one from the doorway, of course. And the mischievous tyke stood unmoving, her shoulders hunched, one hand over her mouth as if she were enjoying her fun altogether.

Robuck looked from the wee girl to the woman, who now stepped outside the door and once again called to the child. She waited only a moment before ducking back inside, then returning with a lantern in hand.

In the lantern's faint glow, Robuck could see that she had a full mane of dark hair and, though slender, was a fine, well set-up woman. Something stirred inside him as he watched her look about the front yard, then start toward the side of the house.

"What's this?" Biller rasped behind him. "Kane made no mention of anyone besides the child!"

"This," Robuck whispered, taking a step forward and gesturing that Biller should follow, "is clearly more than we bargained for. Indeed, I'm thinking this job comes with a bit of a bonus."

"Wait! We're not to move until Kane is in place. That was the plan."

But Robuck was already moving. Gun still in hand, he went at a crouch, as quickly and quietly as a mountain cat.

"Kane be skunked. I have my own plans," he said under his breath, heading for the house.

※

Brady went at a run, his heart banging against his chest wall. He stumbled once on a loose cobble, righted himself, and hurried on. He'd meant to be in place well before now, to make certain that Gabriel had indeed left the house and that the two thugs had actually showed up. At the last minute, however, he'd delayed just long enough for a quick drink, to fortify himself.

He should have left earlier...shouldn't have stopped...

He tried to reassure himself as he rounded the corner. He still had time, after all. In fact, he was exactly on time.

The wind had blown up again after a brief break, stinging his face as he ran. But he picked up his pace still more as he spotted the old oak tree directly across the road from Gabriel's cottage. He'd chosen the tree as his "station"; from there he could see both the front and the side of the house, as well as Robuck and Biller when they made their move.

His chest was burning, and the pounding in his head matched the slamming of his heart as he reached the oak tree. He stopped, gasping for breath, looking around.

He saw Roweena first, holding a lantern, then Evie, hunched down at the side of the house. He snapped his gaze right and spotted both Robuck and Biller.

Everything seemed to happen at once. Without warning, his carefully scripted plans spun out of control, and he was left reeling.

He had never considered the possibility that Roweena might come outside, too. Not once in all the times he had watched the house to study their routine had she ventured outdoors with Evie.

Until tonight.

Suddenly, Robuck and Biller started to move, going at a crouch but going fast. Brady knew he had to think, had to do something.

Instead he froze. His mind was as leaden as his feet. Even as he watched the two take off—Roweena turning and starting for the side of the house, calling Evie as she went—he realized that Evie was oblivious to it all, at least in that moment. He watched the men split, with the bullish Robuck heading for Roweena while the smaller Biller lunged at Evie. Even knowing what was about to happen, Brady couldn't move, couldn't stop his mind from spinning.

He didn't dare break in on them yet—he would ruin everything. He would have to explain himself to Roweena, and then she'd know that he was behind it all. Everything would be spoiled.

But what if things got out of hand and Roweena got hurt? Could he trust Robuck not to get rough?

Trust him? Of course, he couldn't trust him! He hadn't trusted him from the beginning. The perpetual sneer on his face, the hooded, calculating set of his eyes, his obvious contempt, had set Brady on edge the moment they met.

But that was to be expected. He was just another roughneck. That didn't mean the two wouldn't carry off the job as planned. Roweena complicated things by showing up as she had, but Robuck could keep her at arm's length long enough for Brady to make his stand.

He wouldn't dare hurt her. To him and Biller, this was nothing but another job. A work for hire. The only thing they'd even questioned him about was the money, and he'd agreed to their price. They wouldn't do anything to risk the rest of their payment.

And he wouldn't delay his part. No, he'd actually move it up a little. He'd wait only a few minutes, just long enough for his "rescue" to have the desired effect.

For an instant, the irrational desire for some sort of weapon seized Brady. Maybe he should have brought something along, just in case. A gun.

But he'd never used a gun in his life. Besides, he didn't need a weapon. Robuck and Biller wouldn't have weapons. He'd been dead clear about that.

He reminded himself that the two toughs he'd hired were just that—common thugs. Not killers.

Everything had been orchestrated, right down to the last detail. They would do their part as planned, and he would do his.

Brady's hands were shaking, his entire body trembling so violently that pain shot through him like a volley of grapeshot. He steeled himself, trying to stay calm. But the throbbing in his skull sent a surge of nausea exploding up in him, and try as he would, he could not rid himself of the panic that jolted through him at the sight of the two men—men he had hired—heading directly for Roweena and Evie.

28

A DARKNESS IN HEAVEN

What that fate may be hereafter
Is to us a thing unknown.

"A Southern" from the Samuel B. Oldham Collection

At the corner of the house, Roweena stood for a moment, looking about. It was a dark night entirely, with no lights of heaven overhead. The wind that had died earlier had renewed itself over the past few minutes, and she pulled her thin shawl more closely about her shoulders.

She lifted the lantern a little higher as she started around the side of the house, stopping the instant she saw Evie, hunched down, laughing as if her sides would split.

The child *did* test her patience at times. "What…are you doing? Don't you know… you frightened me?" she scolded.

Evie straightened, her smile still in place but somewhat more tentative now, as if she saw that Roweena was in no mood for her foolishness.

"I was only having fun with you," she said, speaking slowly so that Roweena could make out her words in the dim light from the lantern. "I was playing hidey-seek."

"There is no fun…in being thoughtless!" Roweena snapped. She knew she was being shrewish—perhaps she was making too much of little—but in truth she *had* been frightened. There were no stars for the child to "follow" this night, and with Gabriel away she didn't like her roaming about in the darkness for any length of time.

Evie's puckish features pulled into a fierce pout, and she stood scuffing the toe of her shoe without looking at Roweena.

The child invariably melted most of her attempts at sternness, but Roweena tried to keep a firm tone. "Inside with you now, do you hear? Gabriel will not be pleased to learn of your little joke."

Evie finally looked up and started toward her, and Roweena lifted the lantern to illumine her steps. When the child suddenly stopped in midstride, Roweena renewed her warning. "Eveleen, if you don't come with me right now, you will not play outside again for another week!"

Evie's gaze lighted on Roweena for only an instant before deflecting to something behind her. Suddenly, the child's eyes grew wide, and her mouth pursed in a circle of surprise.

"Evie?"

Without warning, a look of fear spread over the girl's features, sending a crawling sensation along Roweena's spine.

She felt the blood drain from her head. A gust of wind lashed at her face, whipping her hair over her eyes, nearly obscuring her vision. Her pulse racing, she started to turn to see what had spooked Evie so. But at the same moment, the dark form of a man leaped out of the shadows and grabbed Evie.

Roweena cried out and lunged forward, but before she could reach Evie, a heavy arm came around her own neck, another around her waist, trapping her.

Panic and the foul scent of body odor and stale tobacco induced a surge of nausea that lodged in her throat and threatened to strangle her. She gagged for breath and tried to scream, but the thick arm pressing against her windpipe choked off her air and smothered her voice.

Stunned, Roweena felt herself hauled back against a large, solid body. She stumbled, trying to twist free, only to be seized in an even more vicious, bruising grip.

In a blinding blaze of horror, she saw Evie struggling to break free of a small, wiry man with a kerchief over the bottom half of his face. Even though her ears were deaf, Roweena could hear in her mind the child's terrified screams.

At the sight of Evie in such a state, her own fear gave way to a fury so intense that something inside Roweena snapped. She flailed her arms like a wild thing, striking out, meeting nothing but air, trying to wrench herself free as her futile attempt to scream was once again choked off and the arm about her waist tightened to the point that she thought she would be sick.

Then the night itself exploded into madness.

❧

Brady stood, frozen in rising panic and confusion. It was happening too fast. Everything was going wrong. Evie screaming, then silenced by Biller's hand over her mouth. Roweena struggling, thrashing and pounding her feet like a wild woman in an insane dance of terror.

And Robuck—holding her, shouting and swearing at her, spewing vile obscenities that seemed to contaminate the very air around her, even though Roweena wouldn't be able to hear a word he was saying.

Brady's own insides were screaming, and for an instant he thought he had cried aloud, then realized his protests were only in his head.

His ears thundered as his pulse sped out of control. His mind began to spin, groping for reason, scrambling to think of what to do.

The scene erupted before him like a nightmare exploding into reality. A raging wave of guilt and self-revulsion crashed over him as he stood watching the horror he had unleashed.

He was trapped between desperation and indecision, shocked into near paralysis by the catastrophe he himself had set in motion.

❦

Gabriel made his way through the narrow lanes of the Claddagh with a blind eye to almost everything around him.

The wind that had seemed so ineffectual only minutes ago now carried a slicing edge that slashed his face and an angry roar that filled his head.

The vague sense of apprehension that had been rising in him all evening was now a shaking, hammering dread, driving him home in a fever, pressing him on despite the feeling that he was dragging a ball and chain around his ankles.

Ulick's words virtually shrieked inside his skull with every step he took, and he could not take the darkened streets quickly enough. In the moments since he had left Ulick, his earlier uneasiness about leaving Roweena and Evie alone had spiraled into a taut coil of tension.

Perhaps he was merely being foolish or reacting to the wildness of the night; Ulick's startling revelation had left him badly shaken, after all. But whatever the reason, whatever the anxiety squeezing at him, he had to get home, and as quickly as he possibly could.

He was almost running now, the blood thundering in his head, his heart pounding from the exertion.

The only thought his mind would hold was what he had learned from Ulick this night. Of everything he might have expected to hear, never in a lifetime would he have expected what he *did* hear.

But thank the gracious Lord that he *had* heard it, before disaster could strike.

Unbelievable—*incredible*—that something which had happened so long ago, so far away in the past, could still reach out across the years and touch today, that one night of savagery could possibly alter the lives and even the destinies of two or more generations.

They had to be told, but how he dreaded the telling. Yet it would be a dangerous folly entirely to keep such a secret from the two of them.

But *was* it a secret? Roweena, of course, knew that she was the result of a brutal attack on her mother. Gabriel had told her what he knew, once she was old enough to understand. Then, too, she actually remembered bits and pieces of the past: the convent where she and her mother—badly deranged by then—had lived when she was only a wee girl. The fire that had destroyed the convent and killed her mother.

The years she had lived with Gabriel's parents, then later his uncle—until finally Gabriel himself had assumed her guardianship.

But what about Brady Kane? Was it possible he had never been told? Or, if he knew, did he simply not grasp the significance, not realize what it might mean to him? And to Roweena?

An unbidden thought of the portraits Kane had painted struck Gabriel, and he stopped for an instant where he was. He remembered how the likeness of Roweena had disturbed him, the sense of something...sick, even obsessive, behind the artistry. Had he really seen what he thought he had, or had the *wrongness* of the portrait merely been a kind of warning?

Sick at heart, anguished in spirit, but more anxious than ever to reach home, Gabriel finally broke into a full run, his heavy boots slapping and pounding the cobbled streets that only minutes before had been silent.

29

ENCOUNTER WITH EVIL

Men of the same soil placed in hostile array,
Prepared to encounter in deadly affray.

ROBERT YOUNG

Roweena fought against the man's effort to turn her about, to make her face him. Perhaps a part of her thought, irrationally, that to see him face-to-face would only make him more real—more dreadful. But her strength was as nothing compared to his.

He turned her easily, roughly. He was a big man—not tall, but thickset with massive shoulders and a barrel chest. His hair was a dull shade of red, worn long and heavy. Like the other, he wore a kerchief covering his mouth, but even as she watched, he lifted a hand to tug it down, letting it fall around his neck, as if he *wanted* her to see his face.

His eyes were the worst: close set and hooded, they held the flint of a mean spirit and the coldness of one who would inflict pain without so much as a second thought.

Only a deliberate act of will empowered her not to scream in his face as he lifted his free hand and passed it back and forth in front of Roweena, bringing it so close he almost touched her.

He had a gun.

Unwilling to let him see her fear, Roweena tried to avert her gaze. But he pressed the cold barrel of the gun under her chin to tilt her face, forcing her to look directly at him.

He was speaking to her. Roweena had all she could do to concentrate on the cruel line of his mouth, to try and read what he was saying. For some reason, she did not want him to know about her deafness, for fear he would somehow use it as an advantage. His words came too fast, though, and she managed to make out only fragments of his speech.

"...careful...you do. Me and you...inside...have ourselves...fun...Behave your-self...neither you nor her...get hurt..."

No...oh, dear Lord, no...not that...not the evil thing that had been done to her mother...please...blessed Savior...not that...

He looked past her, to the other man holding Evie. Again Roweena tried to read his lips.

"...shut that brat up! And keep...out here until...won't take long..."

Roweena managed to half turn to see Evie draw her leg back and kick her captor on the shin, hard. In retaliation, the man hauled her up against him, holding her like a rag doll. Flailing her arms, twisting and kicking, she intensified her fierce, but futile, attempt to escape his clutches.

Roweena saw that she was calling out for Gabriel almost with every breath until the man slapped a hand over her mouth. Wide eyed, she held out her arms to Row-eena in supplication.

Roweena could bear no more. She squeezed her eyes shut, only to be yanked roughly about to face the redheaded man again. This time he pressed the gun up against the side of her head. His eyes held fire, his mouth twisted into an ugly scowl as he harangued her with obscenities, then, "...I'll blow...brains out and hers as well if you don't do as..."

No, not Evie...she could not let them hurt Eveleen...

"Please—make him let her go!" she begged him. "She's...little more than a babe! Please!"

She had no way of knowing if he answered, for he merely pushed her around and began shoving her toward the house. Roweena's legs threatened to give way beneath her, but she forced herself to go on, hoping that by doing what he wanted she might be able to protect Evie. And yet she knew that her sanity—perhaps her life and Evie's life as well—depended on her *not* going inside the house. At least out here there was a chance that someone would hear...someone would see...

Even with the thought, she knew her hopes were in vain. Everyone was inside on a night like this, and the wind would no doubt swallow all their pleas for help.

She choked down her panic, digging deep inside herself for some semblance of calm. She sensed that her captor was an angry, impatient man. If she fell to pieces entirely, there was no telling what he might do.

Gabriel...where was Gabriel? Shouldn't he be back by now?

Her mind began a desperate litany as she stumbled and her captor shoved her on, the gun prodding her in the back. *Oh, God, have mercy on us...Christ, have mercy on us...Mercy, please, Lord, have mercy...*

❧

Reason deserted Brady when he saw Robuck put a gun to Roweena's head, then begin to push her toward the house.

But there wasn't supposed to be a gun! They had agreed—there would be no weapons! And he couldn't let him take her inside the house! She'd be trapped there with Robuck!

His stomach wrenched.

What have I done?

At that moment, Evie let go a volley of blood-chilling shrieks. He saw that Biller had picked her up like a sack of flour in one arm and was trying to silence her with his other hand.

A storm exploded in Brady's mind and propelled him into action. He shot forward, sprinting across the road, shouting until he thought his lungs would burst as he went. He twisted his ankle on a protruding stone, stumbled, gasping with the pain, but kept on going, driving into the yard and storming toward Robuck and Roweena.

Robuck whirled around, one burly arm wedged under Roweena's throat, the gun barrel pressed against her temple as he used her to shield himself.

"That's far enough! Back off, or I'll plug her!"

Brady stopped, fury scalding him, pouring through him, nearly blinding him and filling his ears with a deafening roar. "Let her go, Robuck! Let her go *now*! What do you think you're doing?"

Robuck's lips curled back over his teeth in a feral grin. "Whatever I want, Yank. Whatever I want. You going to stop me—you and your...'no weapons'?"

Brady's mind raced. Roweena was facing him, her eyes wild with fear. Out of the corner of his eye, he saw Biller set Evie to her feet, not releasing her but trapping her by the neck of her sweater.

Brady couldn't think. Roweena could read his lips, but even if she were too terrified to make out what he was saying, Evie would hear. She would know he'd had a part in this. A big part.

Somehow he had to salvage his plan, without either Roweena or Evie getting hurt. But how?

"Let her go," he said, his voice a low threat. "You can't get away with this."

Robuck continued to sneer. "I already have. Get lost, Yank. Come back in a few minutes, when I've finished with her. Then you can 'rescue' the both of them!"

He gave an ugly laugh, then jerked Roweena around and, as if Brady presented not the slightest threat, turned his back on him and renewed their trek toward the house.

Suddenly Brady's *plan* no longer seemed important. It didn't matter whether Roweena knew what he had done. The only thing that counted was saving her. And Evie.

His head cleared, and he felt almost weightless as he launched himself at Robuck's back like an arrow shot from a bow.

But Biller shouted a warning, and the big man turned just in time, yanking Roweena around with him. With one beefy arm locked around her throat and the gun leveled at her head, he stood, legs outspread, his entire bearing a challenge.

"She's dead if you don't back off, Kane! You know I mean it!"

Brady saw the wildness in his eyes, the tears of terror in Roweena's. He took a step backward, then another, and as he did, Robuck's sneer broadened.

"That's better, Yank" he said, waving the gun toward Brady. "Now then, you get yourself right over there, where Biller can keep an eye on you until I've finished my business with the lassie here."

Brady wasn't sure what happened next. Roweena must have thought Robuck was distracted to the point that she could free herself, because she gave a violent wrench, crying out with the effort, pitching herself forward. But Robuck apparently had the strength of a bull and yanked her back by the neck. She collided against him with such force that she screamed in pain.

At the same instant, out of the corner of his eye Brady saw Evie shrug free of her sweater, leaving Biller holding it by the neck, empty. The child took off running, shrieking as she went, but suddenly stopped dead, directly between Brady and Robuck.

She whirled around toward Brady, then toward Robuck and Roweena, clearly uncertain as to what to do.

Brady saw the danger and called out to her, waving her off. "No, Evie! Go back! Go back!"

She gaped at him, then again turned to look at Roweena. She stood there as if transfixed, staring at Robuck who now raised the gun and with an oath aimed it directly at her.

"Robuck!" Brady shouted, waving his hands. "No! You hurt her—you *touch* her and the deal is off, you hear me? No deal!"

Robuck looked at him, narrowing his eyes as if calculating his options.

"No deal," Brady repeated again, his voice low and threatening. "And so help me, I'll see you hang."

Still the big man eyed him, seemingly unmoved, showing no sign of taking the gun off Evie. Roweena was staring at Brady with an expression of total shock and something else…something terrible, something so wounding that it pierced him through, cutting right into his very soul.

Finally, Robuck looked back at Evie and waved the gun toward Brady. "Over there with your pal, chit. And stay put, or I'll hurt this beauty in ways you've never heard tell of."

Still Evie hesitated, whipping around first to Brady, then to Roweena, who shouted at her to run. For some reason, this seemed to infuriate Robuck. He slapped Roweena, hard.

At that point Brady went mad.

❖

Gabriel had just slid in behind the elm tree on the rise back of the house when he saw Roweena try to twist free of her captor, only to be hauled back against him.

He knotted his fists, struggling against a near mindless fury as she cried out in pain. At the same moment, wee Evie *did* manage to break free.

Gabriel held his breath as the child ran to the ground between Roweena and Brady Kane and stood, looking from first one to the other, as if trying to decide which way to run.

He took it all in: Kane's uncertainty and indecision. The girls' terror. The small wraith of a man now standing off to the side, looking as if he'd rather be anywhere else than where he was.

As he listened to the exchange between Brady Kane and the man with the gun, he realized that Kane had apparently orchestrated this whole thing.

But *why?*

He clenched his hands so hard that his nails dug blood from his palms. His ears drummed, and his stomach twisted with sick fear as he stood in the darkness, waiting for the right moment.

Suddenly Roweena screamed at Evie, and the child took off running toward Kane. At the same time, the man with the gun slapped Roweena in the face.

The last shred of Gabriel's self-control snapped, and rage rose up in him like a deranged monster unbound.

He pushed away from the tree and went roaring down the yard, heading straight for Roweena and the man with the gun.

❦

The sight of Gabriel hurling himself across the yard, rushing toward them, elicited a cry of almost delirious relief from Roweena. At the same instant, she saw Brady Kane break into a run, right behind Gabriel, while the smaller man who had held Evie captive took off running into the night.

But her relief was short lived. The man with the gun suddenly pushed her away. She staggered, swaying on her feet, as she saw him sweep the pistol toward Gabriel.

In that instant, Roweena realized what was about to happen.

She never hesitated but lunged forward, bolting madly toward Gabriel, her feet scarcely touching the ground in a desperate attempt to reach him before the bullet did.

❦

"Roweena—no!" Gabriel saw her fly toward him and called out to her as he ran, hoping to block her from the path of the gunman's bullet. At the same time, Brady Kane, running toward them, shouted a warning.

But Roweena kept running, fairly leaping over the ground toward Gabriel, throwing herself in front of him as the gunshot exploded and shattered the night into pieces of despair.

❦

At first Brady didn't even realize that the screams being ripped from someone's throat were his own. He saw Roweena fling herself wildly at Gabriel, saw the look of a love in torment fade from her face as Gabriel caught her in his arms and lowered her to the ground, saw the crimson stain blossom quickly over her shoulder and down one side of her chest—and all the while he kept on screaming.

The raw anguish in the giant's face hit him like a blow. For a moment he stood numbly, watching Gabriel cradle Roweena against him. Then Gabriel looked at him, and Brady saw the dreadful *knowing* in his eyes.

When the racking clarity of what had happened finally registered, he swung around toward Robuck and, heedless of the gun the man held trained on him, charged him like a bear gone mad with blood lust.

A shot rang out, and he felt a blast of pain tear through his shoulder. But he threw himself at Robuck, pounding him with his fists, cursing him—and himself—with all the fury that been unleashed by the sight of Roweena lying limply in Gabriel's arms.

They grappled for the gun, and another white hot slam of pain ripped through Brady, this time in his side. Nausea swept through him, and the night rushed in on him as he felt himself thrown off Robuck and slammed onto the ground, on his back.

He caught one brief glimpse of Gabriel hurling himself at Robuck, hammering a mighty fist at the man's head, and saw the gun go flying out of Robuck's hand as the man fell to his knees, then facedown in the mud.

<hr />

Brady thought he must have drifted in and out of consciousness for a time, but for how long he had no way of knowing. He glanced over at Robuck. The man was still lying in the mud. Apparently, he was unconscious, not dead, for Gabriel was trussing his hands and feet behind him.

Biller was nowhere in sight.

There were others milling about now, a few men, mostly women. Probably neighbors who had finally heard the commotion and ventured out. They spoke in hushed tones, standing back, watching.

Brady lifted a hand to Gabriel, groaning at the pain that scalded his side with the effort.

"Roweena…"

For a moment, Gabriel stood staring down at Brady in silence. Finally, he gave a terse reply. "She's alive," he said. "Evie is with her. I will see to your wounds in a bit, but not until after I take care of Roweena."

"But she'll be all right?"

Gabriel didn't answer, merely stood looking down at Brady in stony silence.

"Get her a doctor, Gabriel," Brady urged, reaching up for the big man's sleeve, but missing it when the pain again shot through him with a vengeance. "I'll pay. Whatever it costs. She needs a doctor."

"I *am* a doctor," the big fisherman said dully. Slowly, he shrugged out of his coat and knelt to one knee to cover Brady with it. Brady shrunk inwardly from the terrible sorrow in the big fisherman's eyes.

"What have you done here tonight, Brady Kane? And why have you done it?"

Brady couldn't bring himself to look at him. "I…didn't think…No one was supposed to get hurt…I only meant to bolster your opinion of me. It was all put-up."

He could feel Gabriel's eyes boring into him. "Why, man? Why would you do such a thing?"

"For Roweena," Brady said, shame flooding him like a fever as he turned his gaze back to Gabriel. "But it all went wrong. Roweena wasn't even supposed to come outside. Only Evie. I thought, by pretending to save Evie…I could get in your good graces and you'd not fight Roweena's seeing me…I never thought…I never wanted anyone to get hurt."

Brady stopped to catch his breath. The sky overhead was beginning to spin, and he felt sick, so sick…

"It's you she loves, Gabriel…did you know? Roweena…she loves you…I saw it in her face when she was running toward you,…and I knew I had done it all…for nothing. I almost got her killed…for nothing…She meant to die for you…"

For a long, terrible moment, Gabriel looked at him. Dazed, weakness sucking him in, Brady saw the other's anger and surprise fade, to be replaced by a patent look of contempt.

"You poor, pathetic fool," Gabriel finally said, an inexplicable note of sadness edging his words and making Brady cringe. "So you didn't know."

"Know what?" Brady muttered, feeling the ground beneath him start to whirl, along with the sky.

"You need to be told, I suppose, though I should not have to be the one to tell you."

Gabriel's voice sounded farther and farther away, as if he were retreating into a dark, winding tunnel. "Roweena and you—" he said, "there is every possibility that you had the same father."

Brady struggled to keep his eyes open. "You're mad," he said, attempting a weak laugh but failing.

"I'm not mad. Roweena's mother was violated by a drunken British soldier. Revenge for a raid by one of those infernal secret societies Ireland is forever spawning. There were three women tortured and raped that same night. All Galway women." Gabriel paused. "Your mother was one of them."

"You *are* mad," Brady mumbled. "My father was Sean Kane."

Gabriel shook his head. "No. Sean Kane was your brother's sire. And your sister's. But not yours. Your father was one of a band of soldiers—an Englishman."

Brady pushed at him, as if by pushing him out of his sight he could also drive Gabriel's words out of his hearing. "I don't believe you…"

"'Tis the truth," Gabriel said, getting to his feet. "But I will waste no more time with you for now. I must get back to Roweena." He paused, staring down at Brady. "When you are strong enough, you write to your brother in America, Jack Kane. *John* Kane—*Sean,* in the Irish. Named after *his* father, so it seems. You write and ask him to tell you the rest of the story. Just know for now that Roweena may well be your half sister. There is no way of knowing for certain she is *not.*"

That said, Gabriel walked away.

A long, keening wail ripped from Brady's throat. Then he turned his face into the mud and retched.

Ashes and *Lace*

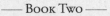

PART THREE

On an Altar of Ashes

We went through fire and flood. But you brought

us to a place of great abundance.

Psalm 66:12

30

A SUBTLE THREAT

Wherefore do ye pause
Before the rich man's dwelling? Will your woes
Avail to move his pity, or to touch
One chord of feeling in his hardened heart?

ELIZABETH WILLOUGHBY VARIAN

NEW YORK CITY, DECEMBER

The plan had begun to take shape in the back of Jack's mind the night before. So suddenly had it come—and so clearly could he imagine its success—that by the time he left his office late in the afternoon on Monday, he decided to go directly to Grace Mission and speak with Terese Sheridan.

During previous meetings, he had sensed a number of contradictions in the girl, and he knew that any doubts or uncertainties she might have would only work to his benefit. If a vague uneasiness tended to plague him on the way to the mission house, he told himself it wasn't because he meant to take advantage; to the contrary, he would be doing her a great favor. Not only would his plan considerably ease the way for her, but at the same time he would be able to give Samantha something he believed she wanted more than almost anything else.

If he was right, then he was convinced that she would finally agree to marry him.

He had not realized that Samantha could be so exasperatingly stubborn. Without fail, every time he had raised the subject of marriage over the past month, *she* had raised the subject of their differences—most particularly the fact that Jack didn't share her faith—almost always followed by a mention of her inability to give him a child.

No matter how adamantly he insisted that he would do whatever he could about their religious differences, and that a childless marriage was far preferable—at least to him—than no marriage at all, she remained unconvinced.

Yet Jack no longer questioned her feelings for him. The few times—and they *were* few—that she'd allowed him to embrace her, he had sensed an unmistakable depth of emotion, even passion, in her response, although she clearly tried to suppress it.

But hang it all, she wasn't fooling him, and the frustration of knowing that she did in fact care for him but was unwilling to do anything about it was driving him over the edge.

He was desperate to make her see things his way, to find something that would turn the battle to his advantage.

Now that he thought he had found just the thing, he was almost in a fever to get on with it.

❦

It seemed to Terese that she woke up a few minutes at a time, day by day, until the vast sea of sickness finally lay behind her.

In the days that followed the first step of her healing, she couldn't seem to keep her eyes open. She slept night and day. When she did rouse, it was like waking from one dream only to enter another. Her surroundings were veiled, her mind a fog-obscured maze. She couldn't manage to hold onto a logical thought more than a few seconds or remember what happened from one hour to the next.

Yet now, more than three weeks later, she could still recall her first glimpse of Cavan on the night that had marked the turning point in her recovery.

She hadn't known him at first—indeed, hadn't even remembered where she was or how she got there. It had seemed to require a monumental effort just to force her eyes open, and when she did, she'd been startled by the sight of a figure sitting in the shadows, close beside her bed. But at her quick intake of breath, he had moved to clasp her hands in his, calling her by name and whispering, over and over again, "Glory be to God…He has spared you, little sister!"

He had wept the first time Terese called him by name, and she had also wept, out of her weakness, but more from the incredulity of being reunited at last with her brother, the only family left to her.

In the days that came after, she often awakened to find him sitting beside her bed, holding her hand tightly, as if he feared that he might lose her again. Little by little the years between them began to fall away as her memories of the brother she had not seen for so long a time faded into the reality of the man he had become. A *good* man, she sensed, a man of gentleness and integrity.

They talked much, but never once did he question her about the babe or show shame for her condition. As for Terese, she avoided as much as possible any mention of his job, for the thought of his connection with Jack Kane, Brady's brother, never failed to trouble her.

Mostly they filled in the blank spaces of their years of separation, sharing their mutual grief for the father who had died not long after coming across and the mother and sisters who had perished in the heartless poverty and hunger of an island winter. As Terese grew stronger, they sometimes talked for hours, almost always speaking in the Irish, unless others were in attendance—as was often the case.

There was Shona, of course. Little solemn-faced Shona, whose quiet presence was as dependable as the sunrise. It seemed the only time the child left Terese's side was at mealtimes and during evening vespers.

And Mrs. Harte—*Samantha,* as she insisted Terese call her—was the loveliest and, as both Terese and Cavan agreed, surely the *kindest* lady one could hope to meet, with a smile that seemed to warm the entire sickroom and great dark eyes where flecks of light sometimes danced, but where more often than not a hint of old sorrows seemed to brim.

She was a real *lady,* Samantha Harte was: delicate and slender with thick, glossy hair neatly wrapped in a twist at the back of her neck, skin the color of fresh cream, and soft hands with delicately manicured nails. So quietly did she move that her skirts gave hardly a rustle, and always, she seemed to smell like flowers.

Yet, on the very next day after Terese regained consciousness this elegant lady with the fine manners and educated speech had rolled up the sleeves to her dainty shirtwaist and bathed Terese as gently as if she were a wee babe. She had even washed her hair and put a ribbon in it. And all the while she had continued to speak in that soft and gentle voice, telling Terese that she was "lovely," that her cropped hair was "magnificent," and that everyone was "thankful and relieved" that God had granted her so great a healing.

As the days passed, Samantha Harte had continued to come, sometimes tending to Terese's most personal needs, but also offering her a kind of womanly companionship unknown to Terese before now. She even read aloud to her, mostly from the Holy Scriptures. One in particular had caught Terese's attention and had quickly become her favorite, so much so that she would ask Samantha to read it over and over again, relishing the way it sounded in her new friend's refined way of speaking:

"For I know the plans I have for you, says the Lord, plans for welfare and not for evil, to give you a future and a hope."

She would smile then, Samantha would, and assure Terese that God did indeed have a plan for her, and that it was for good, and she must keep her hope. Terese wanted to believe her, but at times she couldn't help but question whether such a promise was truly meant for her. She was beginning to wonder if, because of her sins, God hadn't given up any plans he might have had for her and turned his back on her altogether.

She appreciated the way Samantha spoke of the babe: as if it were a *good* thing, not a burden to be borne or a problem to be solved. The baby was a *gift,* Samantha would say, an image that more and more appealed to Terese. As far as she was concerned, the child she carried was the only good thing to come out of her relationship with Brady, other than the passage to America.

She liked it best when Samantha came alone, but on occasion Jack Kane accompanied her. Terese felt awkward entirely around Brady's older brother. He was a formidable man, even frightening. He reminded Terese of a dark and dangerous mountain cat with his unfathomable gaze that seemed to bore right through her soul and the hard mouth that could no doubt say cruel things when provoked.

Part of the reason she felt so miserably uncomfortable with him, of course, was the lie Brady had propagated about the baby's being the issue of an "unknown attacker." But now that she had actually met him, Terese thought she better understood Brady's reluctance to incur his brother's displeasure.

Other than an unmistakable similarity in appearance, the two obviously shared little in common. Jack Kane would be no dreamer, no lighthearted jester or careless rogue who indulged himself in soft living. Brady's brother was clearly a hard man. Even when he smiled, those granitelike features gentled not a bit.

Terese wished he would just stay away, but being her *benefactor*—the word was bitter on her tongue—she supposed he had every right to come as often as he wished.

The one visitor she *did* look forward to each day, even more than Samantha Harte, was Dr. Leslie. If evening arrived without a sign of him, Terese would grow restless and disappointed. But when he finally walked into the room, her dark mood would instantly flee at the sight of his slightly crooked smile and soft but decidedly warm greeting.

She had never known a man as kind and seemingly good-natured as the lean-faced physician who, according to Samantha, had cared for Terese "tirelessly." Something in his gentle treatment of her, his infinite courtesy toward her—and that somewhat shy, heart-squeezing smile that always seemed especially for her—evoked an unfamiliar longing in Terese. It was a desire to be different—*better*—than what she was.

Yet even as she yearned to be a *lady*—someone like Samantha Harte, for example, worthy of a man's respect and admiration—she knew a terrible, aching shame that made her want to hide herself from David Leslie's gaze. No doubt he would despise her if he knew the truth.

As for Jack Kane, he would probably toss her out into the street if he were ever to learn that the child she carried was the result of a clandestine affair with his younger brother.

Given the churning state of her emotions, it was small wonder that her head began to swim in confusion when the two men directly responsible for her turmoil walked into the room together.

"Ah, Terese. How are you this evening?" Dr. Leslie reached her first, smiling as he took her hand and, as he always did upon entering the room, proceeded to check her pulse.

Jack Kane stood behind him at a slight distance. He neither smiled nor frowned but merely stood watching, his eyes shuttered, his expression inscrutable.

"A bit stronger," Terese answered honestly. "I sat in the chair by the window for quite a long time this afternoon. And I was actually hungry for supper."

"Excellent! Well, then, tomorrow, if you feel up to it, we'll let you begin walking in the corridor instead of just tiptoeing about your room."

Terese had been moved into a room by herself nearly two weeks past. According to Samantha, the change of rooms had been at the specific request of Jack Kane, who insisted Terese would rest better in quieter surroundings. Although Dr. Leslie had agreed, Terese couldn't help but wonder if the move hadn't been precipitated more by Kane's obvious discomfort with the dormitory, where the other women often moaned or wept aloud in their distress.

The doctor released Terese's hand and straightened. "And where is your faithful shadow this evening?"

"Shona? She went down to vespers."

"That's where I'm headed as well. Terese, Mr. Kane would like to speak with you if you're up to it."

Terese looked from the doctor to Jack Kane, whose quick smile wasn't reflected in his eyes. "I won't stay long," he offered in that deep, strangely quiet voice that still held more than a hint of his Irishness. "A few minutes, no more."

"Yes...of course," Terese managed, trying not to sound as grudging as she felt.

"Very well, then," said David Leslie. "I'll leave the two of you to your visit."

He turned to go, promising to look in on her later. Terese had all she could do not to call him back. Jack Kane's dark presence unsettled her when others were in the room; the prospect of being alone with him for any length of time unnerved her entirely.

Kane stepped closer to the bed. "May I?" he said, pulling up a chair and sitting down before Terese could answer.

"I won't tax you with small talk, Terese," Kane said. "I just want to say that I'm sorry for your troubles. All this has been very difficult for you, I know, but Dr. Leslie assures me that you're making good progress these days."

"Aye...yes, I'm...feeling much better now."

The cat seemed to have taken her wits along with her tongue. Unsettled by his close scrutiny, Terese glanced away.

"I'm glad to hear it," Kane said in the same flat tone of voice that made Terese think he wasn't glad at all, that indeed, he didn't much care one way or the other how she was doing.

"Mrs. Harte visits you often, does she?"

Terese turned back to him. "Almost every day. She's been kindness itself."

"Yes, she's a remarkable lady, isn't she? And of course you'll want to heed any suggestions she might have for you. She'll be instrumental in helping you to get settled." He paused. "Your brother hasn't been the same since you arrived, by the way. We seldom see him without a smile on his face these days."

Kane also cracked a smile, which quickly fled.

Terese was beginning to wonder why, exactly, he had come. Certainly he didn't *want* to be here; he looked almost as if he couldn't wait to take his leave.

"I'd like to ask you about *my* brother," said Kane.

Terese's heart slammed against her chest. "Your brother?"

He nodded. "Brady. I haven't wanted to disturb you with this, but since you say you're feeling stronger, I thought you wouldn't mind if we had a chat."

"No—I mean, that's fine, sir."

"Brady made the arrangements for your passage, isn't that so?"

Terese gave a nod, not trusting her voice. Her mind raced in alarm. Had he somehow learned the truth about her and Brady—about the baby?

"The thing is, I haven't heard from him in some time, you see, and I thought perhaps you'd at least be able to tell me how he was when you last saw him, before you came across."

Only slightly relieved, Terese caught a breath to steady herself. "Oh…well, he seemed quite…fit to me, sir."

Kane was still watching her as he framed his next question. "Did you know Brady well?"

Terese's pulse accelerated again. *Careful,* she warned herself. *Be careful…*

"Oh…no, hardly at all. Though he was…a great help to me—and the children."

The room was close, and Kane moved to unbutton his topcoat and take off his gloves. "Yes. I was sorry to hear about the little Madden boy, by the way. Too bad, that." He hesitated, then went on. "So then—I don't suppose you'd have any idea why my brother has been so out of touch of late? In truth, I'm somewhat concerned about him. Not that he was ever the great communicator."

Terese felt suddenly cold, so cold she had to steel herself against the chattering of her teeth. "I can't imagine, sir. I'm sure you'll be hearing from him soon. He's probably just…busy."

Kane's eyes were so dark—almost black—they seemed to hold no light at all. It was impossible to even begin to sense his thoughts. Moreover, the man seemed to almost never blink, giving his gaze even more intensity.

"Well—let's hope you're right." He paused. "I trust he took good care of you—and the children?"

Terese's mouth had gone dry. "Sir?" She cringed as she heard her voice crack.

"Brady—I hope he saw to everything you needed for the passage."

"Oh…aye, he did." Terese could not resist adding, "Though I expect he made payment for more than we got."

Kane frowned. "How's that?"

"As I understood it, your brother—he took what your newspaper sent and paid for second-class passage for the three of us. But we were put in steerage."

A dark crimson flush spread over Kane's features. "You traveled in steerage?"

"Yes, sir. But I don't mean to sound ungrateful."

His mouth twisted downward. "You needn't apologize. I know all about steerage, as it happens. I came over that way myself. A wretched experience entirely."

Terese found it impossible to imagine this big, brooding man, in his fancy attire and daunting air of confidence, trapped in steerage like any ordinary peasant.

Kane brushed a hand down the side of his face, and his expression seemed to clear a little. "I regret that you had to go through that. I can't think how it happened. Didn't my brother see you onto the ship?"

Terese hesitated. She mustn't tell him, of course, that his precious brother couldn't be rid of her soon enough, once the arrangements were made.

She had to be that careful of what she said. She didn't want Kane asking too many questions.

Even so, her response nearly stuck in her throat. "He...your brother said he had other business to attend to. A lady from the orphan home—where Shona and her brother had been staying—saw us to the ship. But she wasn't allowed on board with us."

"I see." Kane's mouth was a thin, unyielding line. "Well, there's no undoing it now. Nevertheless, I'm sorry it happened."

He didn't *look* sorry, Terese thought. He looked almost as if he had no feelings at all. She also noticed that he was no longer meeting her eyes but seemed to be considering how to phrase his next words as he lightly slapped one glove against the palm of his hand.

"So then—what are your plans for the child?"

"My...plans?" Terese was startled by his directness. Men didn't refer to a woman's delicate condition unless they were family—and even then, only if it were absolutely necessary; it was unheard of.

But perhaps Jack Kane considered himself above the proprieties. Perhaps he figured he could say and do whatever he pleased.

"You'll not be keeping it, surely." His tone made this no question, but a statement of fact.

Suddenly furious with the man's presumption—never mind that he was her *benefactor*—Terese pushed herself up from the pillows. "I will indeed be keeping my child!"

He never so much as blinked but merely crossed his arms over his chest, still not quite meeting her gaze. "And how, exactly, will you manage?"

"Why, I intend to work! I'll not be asking for charity once I'm well again."

He raised an eyebrow. "That's very commendable, I'm sure, but perhaps not altogether practical. What sort of a position do you expect to find with a babe in arms?"

He sat there, so large and intimidating—so confident in himself and his money and his...control over her—that Terese knew a sudden stab of fear. The truth was that at this moment, at least, Jack Kane *did* have control over her, even had the power to keep her—and the babe—from going hungry.

And he knew it, perhaps was even flaunting it.

Then she remembered Cavan, and relief came rushing over her. "I don't know just yet what sort of work I'll be finding, sir. But as soon as I'm able, I'll be looking for a position. Until then, I expect Cavan will take care of me and the babe. He's already assured me that he would look after us."

Kane traced his dark mustache with a finger and nodded. "Cavan's a fine young man. And of course, he'll not see you go without. In fact, he'd likely assume full responsibility for you and the child." He stopped. "If you were to allow it."

Now he did look directly at Terese, his eyes narrowing as he did so. "But perhaps you can see that you'd be making things impossibly difficult for both you and your brother if you were to burden him in such a way. Cavan is scarcely more than a boy himself. It doesn't seem quite fair to put so great an obligation on the shoulders of one so young."

Silent for a moment, Kane continued to slap a glove against his hand. When he again spoke, his tone was thoughtful, even mild. "You might want to consider the fact that Cavan is only beginning his own career. And though he's a talented lad, he has a long road to travel before he'll be making the kind of wage it takes to support an entire family. I have every intention of helping him to further his education and gain as much experience as possible, but he'll need to apply himself. I'm afraid your brother will have little time for anything but work in the next few years if he's to be as successful as he hopes to be—and as successful as I think he *can* be."

Terese stared at him in dismay, too confused and uncertain to form a reply. She hadn't thought of being a burden to Cavan. In truth, she hadn't thought much about the future at all. She had been too ill, too overcome by her circumstances to do much more than simply exist from day to day.

Consequently, Jack Kane seemed to think she was nothing more than a useless, idle girl who would need to be dependent on someone else for an indefinite time. She groped for something that might convince him otherwise, convince him that she could be—*would* be—responsible. Self-sufficient.

But he gave her no chance for argument, instead rose to his feet. "We needn't speak of this right now," he said, buttoning up his finely tailored overcoat and slipping on his gloves. His tone was almost friendly as he added, "I promised Dr. Leslie I wouldn't stay long, after all. For the most part, I simply wanted to drop by and make certain you have everything you need. We'll talk again soon. When you've had more time to think."

With that, he gave a quick nod and turned to go, leaving Terese more confused and troubled than ever.

She had expected to dislike Jack Kane, given Brady's interminable grousing about his brother. She had not, however, expected to be *frightened* of him, indeed hadn't thought of feeling *anything* toward Kane other than a grudging acceptance of his help in getting out of Ireland and making it possible for her to start over here in the States.

But she *was* frightened. Kane's voice had been quiet, his manner smooth and even solicitous at times. Nonetheless, the man had threatened her; she was sure of it.

But threatened *what?* What could a man like Jack Kane possibly want from her so much that he would employ threats to obtain it?

Shaken, Terese began to tremble, only a little at first, then more violently. She was no match for such a man, and she knew it. Her mind went to Cavan. There had been something in Kane's tone when he spoke of Cavan—something veiled, something too subtle to decipher—but it had been there all the same.

Her stomach gave a sudden wrench at the reminder that Kane was Cavan's *employer.* And Cavan, although he admitted to not being blind to Kane's shortcomings, fiercely admired the man. More than that, however, he loved his job. The job that Jack Kane had made possible for him.

She wouldn't dare mention to Cavan what had just transpired. He might get angry, do something foolish and spoil his standing with Kane, even lose his position. No, no matter how badly she wanted to tell him, she would have to keep her silence.

Samantha. Samantha would know what to do.

But almost as quickly as she considered it, Terese dismissed the possibility. There was something in Samantha's eyes when she looked at Jack Kane, something in her tone of voice when she spoke about him, that left little doubt as to her feelings for him. Terese had seen it more than once and puzzled over it, wondering how a woman as fine and good as Samantha Harte could be taken with the likes of Jack Kane.

But that she *was* taken with him, Terese had no doubt.

Come to think of it, Kane's grim features seemed to soften when he was with Samantha. He became—less forbidding. Perhaps he fancied *her,* too. Perhaps they even had an understanding.

No, she couldn't tell Samantha either. It seemed she couldn't tell anyone.

Throughout the rest of the evening, Terese went back and forth with her suspicions, struggling to convince herself that she was wrong, that she was being foolish and had only imagined any covert threat in Jack Kane's demeanor.

But her alarm only grew, so much so that by the time David Leslie returned from vespers she was too distracted and tense to enjoy his company.

***

If Jack felt a nagging uneasiness, even a measure of self-disgust, after his visit with Terese Sheridan, he quickly brushed it aside as he rode home. He was too gripped by his plan, too stirred by the possibilities and what they might mean to his relationship with Samantha to allow any misplaced sense of guilt to spoil his mood.

Clearly, the girl had been shaken. If nothing else, he had set her to thinking. And his instincts told him that Terese Sheridan was smart enough and enough of a survivor to reason things out to her own benefit.

Also, it was evident that she cared deeply for her brother. She wasn't likely to do anything that might go against Cavan.

He would give her a few days—three or four at the most—then pay her another call. This time he would put his offer on the table.

Unless he had misjudged the girl entirely, by then she would have seen the logic in his idea and would be ready, even eager, to accept.

Only once before he reached home did he fully consider the enormity of what he was about to set in motion. He actually had to bite down hard on the sudden surge of guilt and self-reproach that rose up in him, bringing with it the temptation to abandon the idea altogether. But the thought of Samantha and what he held in his power to give her was all he needed to suppress any doubts he might have had.

Samantha was worth any price he had to pay, certainly worth more than Terese Sheridan's foolish notion of raising a child on her own.

31

BEFORE THE STORM

I it is who shall depart,
Though I leave with heavy heart.

GEORGE SIGERSON

By the time Samantha and Jack left Maura Shanahan's flat, evening had drawn around the city, wrapping it in the deep, gray iron of a lowering sky and a bitterly cold wind that held the threat of snow.

Their breath misted the air inside the cab, and Samantha tugged the fur lap robe more snugly about her. It had been a good day, she thought with satisfaction as the cab neared her apartment. Earlier in the afternoon, Jack had sent a message with the news that the case against Maura Shanahan had been dropped, and would Samantha like to be at the jail when she was released? They would then see the woman safely home.

After leaving Maura—still slightly dazed by her good fortune but vastly relieved to be reunited with her children—Samantha had spent most of the ride back trying to thank Jack for his intervention. Although he pretended to dismiss her effusive gratitude as excessive and unnecessary, Samantha was convinced she was right: Maura Shanahan would never have gained her freedom if Jack hadn't taken a personal interest in her case. Instead, she might well have been swallowed up in a justice system that was at best unpredictable and often corrupt.

He had gone out of his way to help a woman he scarcely knew, and if Samantha wasn't mistaken, he had done it, not so much for Maura Shanahan, but for *her*—because of her own personal desire to help the unfortunate woman. Admittedly, Jack seemed to have a genuine fondness for Maura's son, Willie, whom he insisted was one of his "spunkiest" newsboys. But there was no denying the fact that he'd first become involved in the Shanahan case primarily because of Samantha. How, then, could she *not* be grateful?

"I think perhaps I may start calling you 'Sir Jack,'" she said teasingly.

He lifted an eyebrow. "Well, now, I've been called many things, Samantha, but certainly that's a new one. To what do I owe such a radically inappropriate moniker?"

"It seems that you've been spending rather a lot of your time lately rescuing damsels in distress."

"Ah, I see. A knight in tarnished armor."

"I'm not so sure about that."

"Badly tarnished, Samantha. Take my word for it."

Samantha studied him, thinking he did indeed wear a kind of "armor" much of the time. His way, she had learned, of keeping others at a safe distance.

"I can't help but wonder," she said, "why you are so intent on making yourself out to be such a blackguard."

One corner of his mouth quirked, but his expression was without humor. "Just living up to my reputation, Samantha. I have a certain image to protect, you know."

"Not with me, you don't. And I'm not sure I give much credence to your so-called reputation anyway. I'm beginning to think you may just perpetuate the myth so people won't know that you're actually a very decent man."

He gave a small whoop of amusement. "Now there's an original thought! I declare, Samantha, you ought to try your hand at writing. With your imagination, you'd trounce my other reporters."

"Oh, do stop it, Jack!" she scolded him. "You don't fool me anymore. Just look what you've done for Maura Shanahan. Going to the trouble of hiring your own attorney for her, accompanying me to the jail and the meetings with Avery Foxworth—even driving her home after she was released today. And what about Terese Sheridan?" she went on. "Your protection of that poor girl hardly qualifies you as a scoundrel. Not to mention little Shona Madden. The child thinks you're ten feet tall!"

He didn't smile as she'd expected, instead sat tapping his fingers on the handle of the door. "That woebegone wee tyke would no doubt adore anyone who happened to throw a crumb of attention her way. Samantha—"

He stopped, his expression turning even more solemn as he faced her. "Samantha, I only wish you were right. I wish I *were* a better man than I appear to be, better than I'm presumed to be. I'd like nothing more than to be the kind of man you might *wish* me to be. But the truth is, I'm not, and you mustn't delude yourself into thinking otherwise."

He waved off her attempted objection. "Don't try to paint me as something other than what I am, Samantha. We both know I'm on my best behavior with you because I'm set on making you my wife. And I meant what I told you the night I first asked you to marry me: I'll devote myself to winning your trust and to being a good husband. But I'll not attempt to deceive you nor allow you to deceive yourself."

Samantha sensed that this declaration was absolutely sincere. And doubtless she ought to heed it, word for word. But it wasn't quite that easy, given the fact that she had come to love Jack Kane—loved him in spite of his questionable past, in spite of his less than admirable qualities, and in spite of his harsh opinion of himself. It was too late to go back, now that she knew—and loved—not the facade he presented to the world, the man he was presumed to be, but rather the heart he had opened to her, the man he was.

"Samantha?"

She tried not to look at him, for he would surely see more in her eyes than she wanted him to. But he was not to be put off. With one hand, he gently but firmly turned her about to face him. "Do you understand what I'm saying?"

Something flickered in his eyes, and Samantha saw again that he was altogether serious and, moreover, that he was determined to make her accept this uncompromising depiction of himself.

"You won't permit me to even give you the benefit of the doubt?" she said, trying for a lighter tone.

His eyes searched hers, and for a moment Samantha thought there was something more he wanted to say to her. But then he blinked, and his features cleared.

"Not a bit of it," he said, matching her tone. "Though if you're inclined to show me a measure of mercy now and then, I wouldn't be too proud to accept it."

He released her, and a heavy silence hung between them for several minutes, with nothing to be heard except the jangle of harness and the clop of the horse's hooves on the street.

"Here we are," he said, rousing Samantha from her thoughts as they pulled up in front of her apartment building. "I don't suppose you're going to invite me in," he said.

"You know very well I won't, so why do you always ask?"

"My image, remember?" He grinned at her, a return to his earlier sardonic humor. "Outrageous womanizer that I am, I have certain standards to maintain."

"Yes, well, not with me, you don't."

"Very well," he said. He gave a long, dramatic sigh—known as an "Irish sigh," according to Jack, because "didn't we perfect the art?"

His gaze went over her face with such a depth of tenderness and unmistakable longing that Samantha thought he would surely kiss her. Instead, he merely lifted her hand and brushed his lips over her gloved fingers.

Samantha didn't know whether she was relieved or disappointed. Perhaps a little of both.

He left her at the door, again lifting her hand to his lips before making his quick little bow and returning to the cab.

Samantha stood and watched the cab until it disappeared into the night. Was he right? Was he really the awful man he made himself out to be, the infidel others rumored him to be? Was she merely blinded by her love for him, too foolish, too stubborn to get away from him while she still could?

Oh, Lord, she prayed silently, *you told me I should pray for him and trust you...and I have...but nothing's changed—no matter how much I pray, nothing seems to change—including my feelings for him. What am I to do, Lord? What am I to do?*

She stood there for a long time, praying for Jack and about what she was to do, but the night—and her spirit—refused to give up the silence. Finally, chilled and heavyhearted, she went inside.

For the first time since their arrival, Terese had been able to talk Shona into playing with some of the other children at the mission house. She stood watching them now, a small circle of little girls, all as thin as Shona and just as shabbily dressed, moving the wooden pieces of a puzzle around the floor of the hallway downstairs.

Even in play, Terese observed, the girl's face was solemn and intent, as if set firmly on some grave purpose. But she was a generous and good-natured child, if unnaturally quiet, and seemed to be getting on well with the others.

When the front door opened, the children scarcely noticed. But Terese felt her heart give a small leap as David Leslie walked in.

His doctor's bag in hand, his sand-colored hair ruffled by the wind, he smiled at Terese and came directly to her. "I can't tell you how glad I am to see you and Shona downstairs!"

Terese felt her face flush at the way he was looking at her—as if he truly *was* glad to see her. Quickly, she reminded herself that he was her doctor, after all. It was only natural he would be gratified to see any improvement.

Yet at times she sensed it was more than that, that his interest in her perhaps went beyond that of a physician for his patient. Why that would be so, however, eluded her. By now she was heavy with the child; she could not possibly be attractive to him or any other man. Still, the way his eyes seemed to brighten when he looked at her, and the way he could not seem to drag his gaze away from her, made her wonder.

More than once of late, she had caught herself wishing she could have met him at another time...before Brady, before the foolish, sinful dallying that had brought her to her present state.

Her hand instinctively went to her abdomen. But David Leslie seemed not to notice. He brushed a stray strand of hair away from his forehead, still smiling at her. "It's good to see Shona with the other children. I've tried to coax her to join them, but with no success. You're very good with her."

"She only agreed because I promised to watch," Terese told him. "She's terribly shy and unsure of herself."

"And reluctant to leave you as well, I've noticed. But she looks content enough for now. Why don't we go to the kitchen and see if there's any coffee left from supper? I'm chilled through."

Without waiting for a reply, he went to Shona, leaned down and said something to her, gesturing toward the hallway, then came back to Terese. "We have permission to excuse ourselves," he said, pressing her arm to turn her toward the doorway.

In the kitchen, they sat across from each other at the table—a large, badly scraped, makeshift affair around which the matrons and volunteers took their meals. David Leslie insisted that Terese have a glass of milk while he drank his coffee. "Only milk for you until the baby is born, young lady," he said with mock sternness.

Terese made no reply. He seldom mentioned her condition, hardly ever referred to the baby itself, and when he did she felt a wretched sense of shame and embarrassment course through her.

"Terese?"

She looked up to find him watching her.

"I know it's probably difficult for you, but I think perhaps we ought to talk about the baby. Have you thought about what you'll want to do after the child is born?"

Terese tried to take a drink of the milk he had set out in front of her, but it stuck in her throat. She set the glass down, avoiding his gaze. "I...don't know as yet what I'm going to do."

"I understand," he said gently. "You've been too ill to make any kind of decision. But keep in mind that you're not alone in this. Since you and Shona are both under the *Vanguard*'s sponsorship, it's not as if you're without means, you know. Samantha Harte will do everything possible to assist you."

His mention of the *Vanguard* sent a chill down Terese's spine. She could still see Jack Kane's face as it had been when *he* asked her about her plans.

"Mr. Kane doesn't think I should keep the baby," she said bluntly, lifting her face to watch his reaction.

He stared at her, his brows knitting in a frown. "What?"

"Mr. Kane," Terese repeated, unable to keep the anger out of her voice. "He made it perfectly clear he doesn't think I'm fit to care for a child."

David Leslie's lean features tightened still more. "Did he say that?"

Terese shrugged. "Not in so many words, he didn't. But he made his meaning clear enough all the same." She paused, the anger and apprehension Kane had evoked in her still all too real. "Do you agree with him? Do *you* think I ought to give away my baby?"

David Leslie studied her in silence. When he finally replied, his tone was quiet but firm. "What you do about the baby is your decision, Terese, no one else's. Certainly, given the circumstances, no one would fault you if you decided *not* to keep the child. But I must say, I've had the impression all along that you want to keep it."

"I *do!*" she cried. "I wouldn't be giving it up for anything!" She leaned forward, her hand brushing against the glass of milk. "But Mr. Kane—"

David Leslie reached to steady the glass, then covered her hand with his own. "No one is going to make you do anything you don't want to do, Terese. I'm sure Jack Kane didn't mean to insinuate that you should give up your own child. After all, he's committed the resources of his newspaper to helping you resettle. You must have misunderstood him."

Terese glanced at his hand covering hers, and he quickly released it.

She had *not* misunderstood Jack Kane. The more she thought about the encounter, the more certain she was that for whatever reason, the man had been telling her not to keep the baby.

"...Kane would have no reason to care one way or the other, after all," David Leslie was saying.

He went on, but Terese no longer heard him. A sudden jolt of fear sent the blood rushing to her head at a dizzying speed. There was the puzzle, right enough: Why *should* Jack Kane care what an unmarried Irish immigrant girl decided to do with a child that he doubtless assumed to be unwanted entirely?

More to the point, if Kane thought her unfit to care for the child of an unknown attacker—what would he do if he knew the baby had been sired by his own brother? If he was this dead set on her giving up the child when he knew nothing of its father, then dear Lord have mercy, he would probably take it from her himself if he knew it was of his own bloodline!

Terese almost strangled on the thought. It was as if someone had looped a noose around her neck and suddenly tightened it.

David Leslie was watching her, she realized, his expression questioning. "Excuse me," she mumbled, drawing away from the table. "I mustn't leave Shona alone any longer."

In her haste to get away from the doctor's searching gaze, she nearly knocked over her chair as she got clumsily to her feet and fled the room.

~

David stood, watching her go, dismayed that he must have somehow upset her still more when he had only meant to reassure her. For a moment he had actually thought she was about to faint, so quickly had she paled and begun to tremble.

He called out to her once, but if she heard him, she pretended not to. She made her way to the door, swaying a little when she reached it, then steadying herself with one hand on the frame before starting off down the hall.

Obviously, this business with Kane had unsettled her more than he'd realized, though probably for no just reason. Kane surely couldn't have meant to frighten her.

But she *was* frightened, that much was clear. What in the world could the man have said to unnerve her so completely?

One thing was certain: She would have been at a grossly unfair disadvantage with him. Kane *was* rather formidable, after all. He could easily overwhelm someone in Terese's tenuous position.

On the other hand, he did not think that Terese Sheridan would be easily cowed. To the contrary, one of the things that had first drawn him to her was the strength he had sensed in her, the seemingly indomitable will that, even in the worst of her delirium, had often surfaced and blazed, if only for a brief moment.

No, he decided, even taken unawares, Terese would somehow manage to dig in and stand her ground if the situation required it.

In any event, David resented Kane's apparent lack of sensitivity, even if his intentions had been totally without malice. Besides, he couldn't be absolutely certain that Kane had meant Terese no ill will. Jack Kane was legendary for his ruthlessness; if the rumors were not overblown, he had destroyed more than one businessman who dared to go against him. Look at that series of articles he'd done some time back about the prominent citizens who doubled as the landlords of brothels and gambling dens all over the city. Kane had pulled no punches, had actually named names and cited their abhorrent practices one by one.

Even though David had silently applauded the articles, the act itself could be pointed to as an example of Kane's cold-bloodedness.

Whatever the man's intentions, David thought he would probably raise the issue of his interest in Terese's unborn child next time they met. She was his patient, after all, and still recovering. He had the right to inquire into whatever might have occurred to unsettle her so.

But even as he tried to convince himself, David knew his concern was something more than a natural desire to protect a patient. For a moment there he had been absolutely furious with Jack Kane at the mere thought that he might have somehow, even inadvertently, intimidated Terese.

He swallowed against an unfamiliar tightness in his throat, wondering not for the first time what he was to do about these increasingly disturbing feelings for his lovely young patient. The entire situation was unthinkable. He was a good deal older than she, for one thing; even though she was in the advanced stages of her pregnancy, she was little more than a girl. He had learned that she was from a radically different culture, a primitive, remote place—one of the Aran Islands. More than likely only a handful of people in the States had ever heard of. In addition, she was only now recovering from a precarious illness and still had a long way to go before she fully regained her health.

The rest of it was that she probably had no interest in him whatsoever except as her physician.

David raked a hand through his hair in frustration—frustration with himself and with the situation as a whole. If he were to be completely honest, he would simply admit the fact that he was a fool and stay well away from Terese Sheridan.

Very well, he was a fool. But as for staying away from Terese—he already knew he would do no such thing.

What he *would* do, however, was to try to think of a way to help her gain a measure of independence rather quickly. He admired her for wanting to keep her baby, indeed would have been disappointed if she had *not* wanted to keep it. If for some reason Jack Kane *did* mean to see that she gave it up because of her precarious circumstances, then the best thing *he* could do for her was to find a way by which she could support herself and the child.

As it happened, by the time he reached his office under the stairway, an idea had already begun to form.

32

SUSPECTED ENEMIES

There is something here I do not get,
Some menace that I do not comprehend.

VALENTIN IREMONGER

A winter storm greeted New Yorkers just before noon Thursday and didn't pass until it had deposited several inches of snow on the city. A vicious wind blustered most of the day, whipping snow in the eyes of the horses as they ploughed through the streets with their various vehicles and forcing pedestrians to hunch their shoulders and bow their heads against its fury.

By late afternoon the snow was still falling. City streets were treacherous, and merchants and office managers began to close shop and send their people home.

At Grace Mission, Terese Sheridan sat in a chair by the window, watching the wind-driven snow spiral around the iron fence that ringed the building. The sky was the color of gunmetal, but the ground was totally white, its brightness relieving much of the gloom that ordinarily settled over the city this time of day.

Shona was perched on the bed, cutting out snowflakes from a page of newspaper, an activity learned from one of the other children. From time to time she glanced up, as if alert to Terese's glum mood.

Terese pretended not to notice. She was too preoccupied, too embroiled in her own worries to reassure the child.

At another time she might have enjoyed watching the curtain of snow whipping about the grounds. Earlier, when the storm first settled in, the children had scurried up and down the corridor, darting from one window to another to watch the drama taking place outside. Even Shona had seemed excited at first, later settling into a kind of quiet contentment as she occupied herself.

Perhaps it was natural to experience a sense of serenity and well-being while watching the wintry world from a safe, warm place inside. But for Terese, the wail of the wind and the sight of the heavy, congested sky emptying itself onto the city only served to darken her spirits still more.

If Samantha had come, Terese thought, perhaps this black mood would have passed by now. And, in fact, she *had* promised to come by today with new books for both Terese and Shona. But, of course, no one would venture out in weather such as this if it wasn't necessary, so the afternoon promised to drag on with no surcease from the monotony.

The attacks of dread that had seized Terese since the encounter with Jack Kane had become more frequent over the past two days. No matter how much she tried to suppress her fears, she couldn't seem to bury them altogether. She worried over the health of the child in light of her long, drawn-out illness and the brutal ship crossing. She worried over how long it might take her to recover from the birthing itself. She worried over the money she would need to make some sort of a home for herself and the child.

And she worried about Shona, for she had already decided she would not let the child go to strangers if she could help it. There was no telling what it would do to the girl to be ripped away from the one familiar person in her life, and this after losing her parents and brother, all in such a short time.

Terese had lived with dread so long that it seemed she couldn't remember a time when her chest didn't ache with it. But it was worse now than ever. Before, she had had only herself to fend for, and she had always been strong and able to manage, even in the harshest of circumstances.

But now she had the added responsibility of a baby. She drew a weary sigh as yet another blast of wind-driven snow lashed the side of the house. What would it be like, she wondered, to be Samantha Harte or Jack Kane, to be permanently secure in the knowledge that you had a roof over your head and food in the larder and adequate means to care for yourself and your family? Did their kind have any inkling of what it was like to live in fear of hunger or the cold, always at the mercy of another's whim or act of charity…when the very meaning of existence could be summed up in one word: *survival?*

Perhaps one of the reasons she so admired David Leslie was the way he seemed to devote himself to making survival possible for others less fortunate, obviously sacrificing his own comforts in the process.

Terese stared out into the storm, shivering, not so much from the cold as from the thought that she could just as easily be on the other side of the window, trudging through the snow in search of a place to sleep where she and her unborn babe would not freeze to death. At least here, thanks to David Leslie, she could count on a clean bed and enough to eat.

Which was more than she'd been able to count on most of her seventeen years.

The babe gave a strong kick just then, and Terese pressed a hand against her stomach. "It will be better for you," she murmured. "It *will*. Somehow, some way, I'll see to it that you don't have to scratch and scrape just to survive, I promise you."

When an ugly whisper insinuated itself at the corner of her mind as to how, exactly, she expected to keep such a rash promise, Terese brushed it aside.

She *would* keep it, no matter what it took. In her heart of hearts, she was determined to find a way.

———

"Turner Julian has finally made good on his threat, Jack. He's bringing suit against you. Along with three of the other businessmen he claims you 'defamed.' They're filing a joint suit."

Avery Foxworth tapped his fingers on the arm of the chair, watching Jack closely.

They had met at the *Vanguard* for a change, rather than at the attorney's office; considering the weather, Jack was just as glad.

He shrugged and made a dismissing gesture with his hand. "Julian is the instigator, I take it?"

Foxworth nodded.

"Besides my scalp, how much does he want?"

"Half a million."

Jack whistled softly. "The man does carry a fierce grudge, now doesn't he?"

"I warned you, Jack. Julian has been verbally filleting you ever since the exposé you published on the brothels—your...'Harlots and Hypocrites' piece." Foxworth wrinkled his nose as if he'd caught a whiff of a particularly vile odor. "I told you that you were asking for trouble when you ran it."

The exposé Avery Foxworth was referring to was an entire series Jack had done some time back on crime in general and prostitution in particular—and on those who helped to perpetuate the vice running rampant in the city. It was hardly a secret among the newspapermen—and the police force—that quite a few of the city's bawdy houses and gambling dens, not to mention some of the most abominable tenement buildings in New York, were owned by certain wealthy, "upstanding" citizens.

One of those citizens was the society physician, Turner Julian—a man Jack knew to be a consummate bigot, a hypocrite of the first rank, and, as a doctor, little more than a charlatan. In his editorials accompanying the exposé, Jack had applied a number of scathing epithets to Julian—"Fifth Avenue medicine man," for one—as well as an entire slate of allegations, which he had carefully documented. In addition, the series itself listed specific "business establishments" and other properties—some of which were virtual death traps—owned by Julian and his cronies under the cover of a middleman.

Admittedly, there was more to it on Jack's part than some sort of high-minded desire to expose the crooked shenanigans of Turner Julian and his kind. What Avery Foxworth didn't know—nor did anyone else, for that matter, except for Rufus Carver—was that to this day Jack was convinced that Turner Julian was directly responsible for the worst of Martha's suffering and final humiliation during the last days of her life, before the cancer finally claimed her.

Julian had made no secret of his contempt for the Irish, had shown Martha not a shred of mercy as the vicious disease ravaged her body and stripped her dignity from her day by day. When Jack persisted in trying to get the condescending physician to do something to ease her pain, Julian had dismissed him with unthinkable callousness, telling him that if he "wanted miracles, then call a priest."

The next day, however, the insufferable physician had gone on to perform—and totally botch—a hasty surgical procedure that caused Martha more agony than ever. When Jack realized what had happened, he went after Julian like a madman. If Rufus hadn't pulled him off the terrified doctor, Jack would probably have murdered the man in the middle of the hospital hallway.

He had bided his time in the intervening years, determined that he would not only expose Julian for the quack he was but for his shady business practices as well. Finally, after accumulating all the evidence he needed, he published everything he had in the *Vanguard*.

Since then, he'd heard from various sources that Julian's practice had suffered considerably in the wake of the exposé. Of course, Julian was old money—as was his wife—so financial ruin was never a real consideration. No doubt what galled the man most was the besmirching of his precious family name and the aspersions cast on his competence.

"Tell me again exactly what sort of proof you have." Avery Foxworth's prodding yanked Jack back to his surroundings.

"I have more than enough," Jack assured him. "Signed statements from some of the newsboys who also work as bagmen for Julian's 'managers,' and others from a couple of his former landlords. Copies of the deeds Julian holds—the man wasn't clever enough to reassign them. And, as I believe I told you before, I also have a sworn account from a former prostitute who used to work in one of his brothels and whom Julian himself patronized on several visits—before he beat her almost to death." Jack paused. "She was fourteen at the time."

Again Foxworth made a face of distaste. "The…young lady in question—did she give a statement to the police at the time?"

Jack twisted his mouth. "She was little more than a child—and a prostitute, Avery. Of course she didn't go to the police."

"But she talked to you?"

Jack shrugged. "Money will buy almost anything, as you undoubtedly know. Even the truth." He studied his attorney. "You seem annoyed, Avery. Anything in particular?"

Foxworth pursed his lips. "You don't seem to be taking this quite as seriously as I think you ought to."

"Now there you're wrong, Avery. I take being sued very seriously. Very seriously, indeed. But I don't see how Julian can hurt me. I'm not fool enough to go public with a fire-baiting story unless I have the means to put out the blaze. My own character may be a bit questionable, but I wouldn't risk the integrity of the paper."

Avery seemed to consider that for a moment. "No, I'm sure you wouldn't. Well, I trust you have all your documentation under lock and key, because we're likely to need it before this is over and done with."

Jack nodded, jerking his head toward the safe behind his desk. "It's all there. Don't fret yourself."

Foxworth stood, slipping on his fine leather gloves and smoothing them one finger at a time. "Very well, then. I believe I'll be getting along while the streets are still passable. It's getting nasty out there."

Jack got to his feet and came around the desk. "Thanks for coming by, Avery," he said, shaking his attorney's hand. "You'll be in touch?"

Foxworth gave a nod. "I'm going to prepare some sort of informal reply to the suit first thing. Just a letter, you understand, expressing the proper indignation and perhaps a veiled threat or two. It will get us nowhere, of course, but I want to go through those papers you have before we do anything else." He paused. "I don't suppose I could take them with me?"

Jack thought about it but didn't like the idea. "No offense, Avery, but I'd feel better keeping everything here for now."

"Never trust an Englishman, eh, Jack?"

Jack merely smiled as he opened the door to the hallway. "I never trust *any* man, Avery."

Foxworth left, shaking his head as he went.

Jack went to the window that looked out on the street and stood watching for a moment. He was tempted to change his mind about going to the mission house yet this afternoon. From the looks of it, the snow wasn't going to stop anytime soon.

But his plan had been burning a hole in his gullet for three days, and he was simply too impatient to put it off any longer. Besides, he had already sent Cavan Sheridan up to Albany, just as a precaution. This storm ought to keep the lad there over the weekend, at least. If the girl should get too wrought up, she might be tempted to confide in her brother, and Jack didn't want to have to deal with the both of them at once. He was fairly certain he could bring Cavan around without any great difficulty, but one problem at a time for now.

It was almost two-thirty. He would go to Grace Mission yet this afternoon, then come back and work for another two or three hours.

No point hoping to see Samantha tonight, after all; she wouldn't be venturing out in this kind of storm. He might as well finish the piece on the Harrison–Tyler ticket and get started on tomorrow's editorial.

Outside, he found Madog Wall shoveling off the stoop. The man tipped his hat to Jack and made way for him.

"You're not drivin' yourself home, are you, Mr. Kane?"

Jack pulled his topcoat collar a little higher around his throat. "Not yet, Madog.

I thought I'd take the paper wagon over to Pearl Street. I figure it will get me there and back with less trouble than the carriage."

Madog looked appalled. "But, Mr. Kane—the way this is comin' down, you'll be soaked clear through by the time you get there! And half froze, to boot."

"Nonsense!" Jack waved off the man's concern and headed for the wagon. Given half a chance, Madog would fuss over him like a nervous granny. "A little snow isn't going to hurt me. I rather like the stuff. But I'll have your cap if you don't mind."

The burly Irishman looked altogether bewildered. "Sir?"

"Your cap, man! Lend me your cap if you're so worried about my staying warm!"

Madog stared at him as if he'd taken leave of his senses, but, always obedient, grabbed the cap off his head and tossed it to Jack. "'Tis good and clean, sir. Practically new, it is."

Jack laughed at him as he perched the wool cap on his head and hiked himself up on the bench of the wagon. "You're a good man, Madog!"

He clucked his tongue a couple of times, and the sturdy gray started off through the snow.

33

A PROCESSION OF VISITORS

Hope, like the gleaming taper's light,
Adorns and cheers our way.

OLIVER GOLDSMITH

By the time Samantha reached Grace Mission, she realized she might have made a mistake by venturing out into the storm. But she had said she would come today and hated not to keep her word. Besides, she had new books for Terese, as well as a lovely doll for Shona, made by one of the ladies at church.

The cab she had taken was small and far too light for such a heavy snowfall. Twice on the way they had gotten stuck, another time nearly tipping over when they rounded a corner. Samantha didn't relish the thought of the return trip in the same vehicle, but she might not be able to hire anything else. Given the way the snow was coming down, she had no intention of staying more than a few minutes, so she asked the driver to wait for her outside the mission.

The street was nearly deserted and desolate in the storm, the afternoon almost as dark as late evening. Snow sliced her skin, and the wind brought tears to her eyes as she hurried up to the front door.

Inside, it was more cheerful. Some of the children, no doubt aided by the volunteer workers, had made paper snowflakes and other winter decorations, hanging them from the banisters. A fire blazed in the grate in the front room, and from the direction of the kitchen came the sound of voices and pans rattling.

As Samantha started up the stairway, she heard the familiar sounds coming from the "sickroom"—the dormitory that housed the women and children who were seriously ill. The faint moans and cries never failed to tear at her heart, and ordinarily she would have gone there first, before visiting Terese and Shona. There was little she could do except to walk among the beds, inquiring after each patient or clasping a hand to offer reassurance. Sometimes she would hold one of the infants or toddlers for a while so that its mother could take a much-needed rest. Sometimes she could do nothing at all but pray for them.

Today, however, she went directly to Terese's room. She found Shona perched on the bed, making cutouts, while Terese sat by the window, watching the snow. Their obvious pleasure when she walked into the room warmed Samantha's heart, and now she was glad she'd made the effort to come.

She explained that she could stay only a few minutes. "I've left a cab waiting for me because of the storm. But I wanted to at least come by and give you these."

She gave Shona the doll and was rewarded to see the child's entire countenance light up with delight. After only a moment's hesitation, she received a hug from the girl, who then sat holding the doll in her arms as if it were the most precious, wondrous thing she had ever seen.

"What will you name her?" asked Samantha, smiling.

Shona looked up, seeming to consider the question with great care. "Her name is 'Samantha,'" she said solemnly.

Samantha blinked quickly, for an instant overcome with emotion. "Well," she finally managed, "I have never had a doll named after me, Shona. Thank you."

Terese's eyes also brightened when Samantha handed her the parcel of books. Included were a copy of Dickens' *Pickwick Papers* and a collection of Mr. Irving's regional stories. The books actually came from Samantha's own small library, but she chose to keep this information to herself.

Samantha had been surprised at how well Terese could read. So many of the immigrants she worked with—the Irish in particular—were either illiterate when they arrived or at best had only a rudimentary grasp of the English language; many from the more remote regions in western Ireland spoke only Gaelic. But both Cavan and Terese had been extremely fortunate in that their father, schooled in the basics by a Catholic priest, seemed to have passed on a love of reading to his children.

Shona was another matter. The child had obviously received very little in the way of education, a situation Samantha hoped to eventually remedy.

Watching Terese, Samantha sensed that in spite of her pleasure at the new books the girl seemed distracted, perhaps even troubled. There was a tension about her that hinted of some concern.

"Terese? Are you not feeling well?"

The girl looked at Samantha, then quickly glanced away. "No, I'm fine," she said, the reply coming perhaps a little too quickly.

Samantha didn't want to pry, but she couldn't shake the feeling that there was definitely something wrong. "You're quite sure?" she prompted gently.

The smile Terese gave seemed a little forced. "'Tis the snow, perhaps. It makes me feel a bit...edgy somehow."

Samantha studied her. "You *do* know, don't you, Terese, that if you ever have a problem, I'm here to help. I hope you wouldn't hesitate to ask."

The girl smiled again, this time more naturally. "You're very kind to us, Samantha. But please don't fret yourself about me. I'm perfectly fine. Truly, I am."

Samantha was hesitant to leave so soon but knew she must. "Well, then, I should go, I suppose. The storm is getting worse by the minute. Oh—I almost forgot. Cavan wanted me to tell you that he had to go out of town but will be back in a day or two. Mr. Kane sent him to Albany—that's the state capital—to gather some information for the paper."

Terese frowned. "Cavan went away in such a storm? Will he be all right?"

"Oh yes, he'll be fine! You mustn't worry about him. He's already there by now, and I'm sure if the storm gets too bad he'll simply stay over until the worst has passed."

Terese didn't look altogether convinced, but she said nothing more.

Still reluctant to go, Samantha drew on her gloves with deliberate slowness. Finally, after another hug from Shona and an extended good-bye to the two of them, she left.

The blast of icy snow and wind that greeted her as she stepped outside made her suddenly anxious to get home and stay there.

⬥

David Leslie seldom found himself at a loss for words with a patient.

But then, Terese Sheridan was no ordinary patient.

He hesitated at the door to her room, feeling as ill at ease as a callow school-boy—not altogether because of what he was about to suggest but more because he knew how disappointed he would be if Terese turned him down.

But then why would she, he reasoned? This could easily be—indeed, would certainly appear to be—at least a partial solution to her concern about how she was going to support herself and her baby.

Ever since their conversation of the day before, David had been mulling over a number of possibilities as to how he could help her. He thought he might have finally settled on an idea that would relieve her mind somewhat about the future.

And what might it mean to *his* future, a sly voice whispered at the back of his mind. He could hardly pretend this was entirely for Terese, now could he?

By now David was thoroughly annoyed with himself for his own ambivalence. At the worst, she wouldn't be interested. He could still offer.

He drew in one long steadying breath, cleared his throat, and walked into the room.

⬥

Snow swirled like thick fog all about Jack. Madog had been right; he *would* be wet clear through by the time he reached the mission. His topcoat was already soaked.

This was no ordinary snowstorm; that much was certain. It was more of a blizzard. He had thought he was prepared for the worst, but he was beginning to wonder if he might have been a bit of a fool for hopping onto an open wagon in such a storm. The wind was ploughing up the street, shrieking like a banshee, hurling the snow full force as it came. Jack wouldn't have been all that surprised to find himself lifted off the wagon and tossed into the street.

He kept his head down, his shoulders hunched, but there was no real protection for his stinging skin or burning eyes. He caught a breath, sucking in a blast of snow and choking on it. Everything was white, the very air a heavy curtain of ice and snow blowing wildly in the wind.

He considered turning back, but he was over halfway there by now. Besides, by tomorrow the streets might be well nigh impassable.

The decision made, he swept his woolen neck muffler up over the bottom half of his face as a kind of mask and kept going.

❦

Terese looked up when David entered, and he was unreasonably pleased at the way her eyes lighted when she saw him.

He had half expected to find Shona with her, perhaps had even been *hoping* she would be here, to give him an excuse for delay.

"Dr. Leslie," she said quietly.

David stopped just inside the room, transfixed for the moment by the sight of her. Even in the dusky room, with only the gray light from the window framing her, her hair was a cloud of fire. Cropped as it was, it still curled softly around her face. She was dressed in a faded hand-me-down garment donated by one of the church benevolent societies. Even in this, and noticeably swollen with child, she somehow managed to strike a bearing of uncommon loveliness.

And she *was* lovely. This pregnant, seventeen-year-old girl with the haunted eyes and the slightly cynical smile literally took his breath away. He was in love with her, no doubt about it: hopelessly, helplessly in love for the first time in his life.

Almost thirty-five years old and he had suddenly turned into an awkward, lovesick fool. David sighed. Was there anything more pathetic, he wondered, than a wretchedly shy bachelor in love for the first time?

"Would it be terribly difficult," he said, walking the rest of the way into the room, "for you to call me 'David'?"

Terese looked surprised but then smiled. "Not so terribly difficult, I suppose... *David.*"

He savored the sound of his name on her lips. "That's better. So—how are you feeling?"

"Stout," she said dryly. "A bit like a bloated whale." The next instant she blushed, as if she had only then realized that her response might be indelicate.

David laughed, hoping to relieve her embarrassment. "I assure you, you don't in the least resemble one. Where is your shadow, by the way?"

"Shona? She went downstairs to show off her new doll, I expect. Samantha brought it for her."

"I'm surprised Samantha would venture out on such a day. But no doubt you're glad she did."

She nodded, and he pulled up a chair directly in front of her. "I had an idea I wanted to discuss with you," he said. "Are you up to a chat?"

Again she gave a nod, watching him.

"Terese, I know you're concerned about the future," he began somewhat awkwardly. "About how you're going to manage with a new baby to care for."

She frowned, a guarded look rising in her eyes.

"I've been thinking about you—your situation, that is—ever since we talked yesterday. And I believe I may have a solution. One that could benefit both of us." David paused, then decided to just get on with it. "I'm wondering if you might consider staying on here—after the baby is born I mean—as an employee?"

She stared at him, clearly bewildered. "I don't understand."

David undertook to explain. "Like most of the missions in the city, we depend almost entirely on volunteer assistance, and we've been fortunate in that respect. The churches and some of the immigrant societies have been wonderful in helping us as much as they can. But as it happens, we've grown too large to continue without at least a few full-time employees." He stopped. "I—was thinking that perhaps you might be interested in a position with us."

Her mouth dropped open a little. "A position? What sort of position?"

"I'm in rather urgent need of someone to help care for the children, you see. They don't get nearly enough attention, as you may have noticed. You're awfully good with them, Terese—I've watched you from time to time. The children take to you."

"Why...I like them, too, sure, but how much help could I be—"

"Oh, I don't mean right away," he hurried to assure her. "Naturally, you can't take on anything of the sort until after the baby comes. But I was hoping that, later, you might consider a job here."

She was still frowning, but David thought she also seemed interested.

"But surely that wouldn't be a real job—taking care of the children," she said.

He laughed a little. "Actually, it would probably take a great deal more time and effort than you might expect. But even if it didn't, I could use your help in other areas. Didn't you tell me you'd done housework and even a bit of nursing for a woman back in Ireland?"

She nodded slowly. "Aye. Jane Connolly. She was in a bad way, Jane was. I kept house for her and helped tend to her personal needs as well."

David laced his fingers together on one knee. "That kind of experience would be awfully helpful to me. Would you be willing to do the same sort of thing here at the mission? I realize it would be menial work, but it's important work, all the same."

Her chin lifted a little. "I'm not above doing for others, if that's what you mean."

David smiled at her. "No, I didn't think you would be. Now I'll be perfectly honest, Terese: The salary wouldn't be all that generous. I'm trying to build a staff here and at three other mission houses in the city, so there's not a great deal of money available. But you would have a small wage, plus a room of your own for you and the baby—and your meals, of course."

He could definitely see a glint of excitement in her eyes now. "You're serious about this, then?" She leaned forward a little. "You'd do this for me?"

"No, Terese, I'd actually be doing it for *me*," David emphasized. "I'm rather desperate for help."

She studied him with an intensity that made David squirm a little.

"But why *me?*" she asked. "No doubt you could get another woman right away, someone who's not going to be—indisposed—for a time. Why would you wait for me?"

He should have known she was too sharp-witted to simply grab at the idea without questioning his motives. He expelled a long breath, holding her gaze, although he could feel a bit of a flush creeping up his face. "I might just as well be honest with you, I suppose. I *do* need the help—that's no exaggeration. But the rest of it is that I…ah…I really don't want you to leave."

Her eyebrows lifted slightly.

David's palms suddenly felt clammy, and he knotted his hands into fists on top of his knees. "I'm not very good at this sort of thing, Terese. Haven't had much practice, you see. What I'm getting at is that I…ah…find you attractive, and I like…being with you."

He gave a helpless shrug. "I'm not saying this very well, am I?"

She was looking at him with unconcealed disbelief. "You think me…*attractive?*"

Had he not been so ill at ease—or so intent on convincing her—David might have laughed at her incredulity. "Only a blind man wouldn't find you attractive, Terese. But it's much more than that. I—*like* you. Very much, actually. And I don't want you to go away."

She straightened a little, her hands gripping the arms of the chair. She sat in silence for a time, seeming to consider his idea. "Shona? Would she be staying, too?"

"Oh—well, of course, she can stay as long as need be. I suppose later Samantha Harte will try to locate a family who will take her in—even adopt her—if Shona is agreeable. But until then, naturally she can stay right here with you."

He could almost see her uncertainty warring with a growing interest in his proposition.

"You don't have to decide now," David offered. "I just thought…it might relieve your mind a bit to know you have a job waiting—if you want it."

A shadow of something touched her face. A sinking feeling struck David. Perhaps he had put her in an untenable position by admitting his attraction to her, and she simply didn't know how to reject him without spoiling her chances for the job.

He rose, suddenly anxious to get out of the room before she turned him down altogether. "I should be going," he said, his words spilling out in a rush. "I haven't finished my rounds yet. As I said, I don't need an answer from you right away. Just...take your time. And, Terese—"

She looked up, her expression unreadable.

"I want you to understand," he said awkwardly. "The job is in no way connected to my...interest in you. I mean, I wouldn't want you to think that you'd have to suffer my...attentions...just because you took the position. If it happens that you don't return my feelings, that wouldn't affect your employment in any way, I assure you."

He turned, then, almost stumbling in his haste to flee the room before she could reply.

❦

Terese watched him go, her emotions rioting in his wake. She was stunned by what had just occurred. The offer of a job would have been wonder enough—it was like a gift from heaven—but that a man of David Leslie's stature would take a fancy to her, and in her condition at that, was nothing short of astounding!

Bitterly, she reminded herself that he knew virtually nothing about her, indeed believed her to be an innocent girl victimized by an unknown assailant. No doubt if he knew the truth about her—and the baby—he would change his tune entirely.

But in the meantime he had thrown her a lifeline, had given her a means of escape from a situation that only hours ago seemed utterly hopeless.

Now if the great Jack Kane came sniffing around with his prying questions and subtle threats, she need not cower. She had the promise, not only of a job, but a roof over her head and safekeeping for her baby.

As for the other—David's interest in her—she need not deal with that now. It was enough that he had offered her a position—and with no strings attached.

He was a good man, a kind man, and she was drawn to him, no denying it. But she must not for one minute allow herself to believe that anything could ever come of it. He would not want her if he knew the truth, and she would not deceive him, if ever it came to that.

She had had quite enough of deceit. If she ever managed to extricate herself from the web of lies and deception that she and Brady had initiated by their own actions, she would never tolerate anything less than the truth again, not in herself or in another.

But for now she would take comfort in the knowledge that perhaps God had not deserted her after all. She had begun to fear she might have imagined his forgiveness. From the day she had dropped to her knees in the middle of a mean, squalid street in Galway City and begged in desperation for his mercy, she had tried to hold fast to the belief that there was hope for her and her child, after all, in spite of her sin. But during the nightmare voyage across the ocean and all that came after, she had found it difficult, nearly impossible, to hold on to that hope.

Now she somehow felt as though her hope had been renewed. For the first time in months, the burden of fear dropped away, and relief washed over her like a fountain of goodness.

"Perhaps God has not forgotten us after all," she murmured, touching her abdomen where the babe rested within her. "Perhaps he truly *has* given us a future and a hope."

❧

Jack pulled the wagon as close as he could get to the curb, which because of the drifting snow wasn't very close at all. Tugging Madog's cap down over his ears, he turned his coat collar up about his throat, then leaped off the wagon bench and hitched the gray to the post in front.

Inside, he glanced into the front room, pleased to see the little Madden girl playing with a group of the other children. As much as he enjoyed the child, today he wanted Terese Sheridan alone.

He took the steps two at a time. At the door to her room, he stopped. She was sitting in a chair by the window. She looked to be asleep, and Jack hesitated, but only for a moment before pulling the cap from his head and walking into the room, not bothering to knock.

❧

Terese had dozed after David left, but she roused the instant Jack Kane stepped inside the room.

He had caught her off guard, and for a moment she was somewhat disoriented. The light squeezing in through the window was gray and weak, casting the room in shadows. But she could see Kane clearly enough, and at the sight of him a wave of black fear swept through her.

Clad in an obviously expensive topcoat with a white posy in the lapel, he looked every bit the city gentleman. But Terese was not fooled: Jack Kane was no gentleman. Brady's brother, by Brady's own definition, was a shark.

His dark features were set in a hard, unyielding look. He raked a hand through his hair, never taking his eyes off her as he walked the rest of the way into the room.

Every muscle in Terese tensed. But then she remembered that, thanks to David Leslie, she need not fear this man. She straightened, lifted her chin and braced herself for whatever was to come.

34

EYE OF THE STORM

The winter is cold, the wind is risen.

From COLLOQUY OF THE ANCIENTS, The Fenian Cycle

"Terese," Jack said with a quick nod. "How are you keeping today?"

"Very well, thank you." The unmistakable note of caution in her voice was reflected in her eyes.

Without waiting to be asked, Jack crossed the room and took the chair opposite her, close to the window. "Quite a storm we're having," he said, gesturing toward the window.

She made no pretense at casual conversation, nor did she attempt to conceal her suspicion as she sat watching him.

"You'll want to know that Cavan is out of town for a day or so," Jack offered conversationally. "He's in Albany, on assignment. I expect he'll be back in a couple of days, if he doesn't get snowbound."

"Aye, Samantha told me."

Jack frowned. "Samantha was here?"

She nodded. "She left a short while ago. Half an hour, perhaps. She was anxious to get home because of the storm."

"She came by cab, I suppose?"

"She did, yes."

Jack was as irritated as he was surprised at the thought of Samantha traipsing about in such beastly weather. She could be the most *headstrong* woman at times.

His attention returned to the Sheridan girl. He hadn't missed the fact that she'd referred to Samantha by her given name, rather than "Mrs. Harte." He supposed that shouldn't surprise him. Samantha wasn't one to stand on formalities, and she'd spent a great deal of time with Terese Sheridan—and with Shona as well—over the past few weeks. He had already observed that a kind of unlikely friendship had developed.

Samantha did have a deucedly soft heart when it came to those less fortunate, and she seemed particularly drawn to Terese Sheridan. That being the case, he should probably take care not to antagonize the girl too much; he wouldn't want to give her a means of unduly influencing Samantha against him.

As she might be tempted to do. Especially after today.

Watching the girl, he caught the same sense of something he had glimpsed before: a strength of will not usually seen in one so young. There were times when her countenance took on a look of challenge, a defiance that brought to mind the words *Irish proud,* as he tended to think of it—the often irrational obstinacy and hardheaded willfulness that he sometimes thought must characterize a major part of the Irish race, and that unchecked often proved to be their undoing. Brady displayed it in strong doses. And if truth be told, he himself had been afflicted with a goodly measure of it as well.

He was dealing with a girl, or rather a proud young woman, who might not be so easily brought to heel if she were not almost entirely dependent—at least for now—on his support. A part of Jack could not help but admire her spirit, even the way she was glaring at him at the moment in spite of her ashen appearance and the profound effort it was undoubtedly taking to reveal no sign of unease in his presence.

He had not come to match wills or wits, however. In the long run, if the girl were even half as clever as he suspected her to be, she would concede. What choice did she have, after all?

He did not like himself very much at this moment, indeed felt slightly ashamed of the way he meant to take advantage. But this was for Samantha, he reminded himself.

And ultimately, for Terese Sheridan as well. He couldn't imagine what she must be thinking, to believe that she could support herself and a child, given her present circumstances. On her own, she was utterly destitute, still severely weakened by her extended illness, and entirely without resources, aside from whatever the *Vanguard* chose to provide and the small stipend her brother could perhaps manage. She had no income, no position, and perhaps an extended lying-in period ahead of her yet. What could she hope to offer a child but more of the same poverty from which she herself was trying to escape?

Originally he had planned to allow young Cavan and his sister to live above the stable in back of his house. He had even gone so far as to partition it and make an extra room. But that was before he decided to pursue his present plan, to gain custody of the child. Of course, if the Sheridan girl cooperated, the rooms would still be available to her and her brother if they were interested.

He still believed that, although Terese might not see it his way until a long time hence, he was actually offering her the opportunity to make a new beginning without the encumbrance of a child. Eventually, she would realize what he had done for her and even be grateful to him. Until then, however, he would have to suffer her resentment and what was almost sure to be a great deal of anger.

He realized he'd been woolgathering then and looked across at her to find her watching him with a wary, inquisitive expression.

"We talked the other day about your plans for the future," Jack said. "I thought we might continue the conversation, if you're up to it."

He saw her tense even more. The hands on the arms of the chair were white knuckled by now, and her features, always sharp, grew taut and almost unpleasant.

She didn't care for him; that much was clear, Jack thought with a touch of grim amusement. But then, why should she? Certainly, he had given her no reason to feel much of anything toward him except distrust and dislike.

But he would give the girl credit: she didn't blanch, didn't flinch, didn't even blink under his scrutiny. If he unsettled her at all, she wasn't about to give him the satisfaction of seeing it.

Ah, well, the Irish always did like a worthy opponent. "Have you thought any more about the possibility of giving the child up for adoption?" he said with no further preliminaries.

She paled. "No! As I told you, I will be keeping my baby."

"And I will ask you again, how do you plan to manage?" Jack said mildly.

Her eyes blazed and she threw her answer back in his face with an ill-concealed note of triumph. "I have a job, as it happens. A job with room and board."

Caught off guard, Jack studied her for any sign of dissembling. His deliberately moderate tone was in direct contrast to her obvious agitation as he replied. "I see. Well, now—you seem to have accomplished a great deal in three days. May I inquire as to the nature of this—position?"

She smiled at him, a catlike smile that was both sly and defiant at the same time. "Dr. Leslie has offered me a job with the mission. I'm to have a room for myself and the baby, as well as wages."

Jack had not for a minute anticipated this, but he was careful not to react. "Good of him, I must say. But what happened to your idea of letting your brother take responsibility for you and the child?"

Anger sparked in her eyes. "*I* will take responsibility for *myself*—and for my child!" She paused, shooting Jack a look of transparent dislike. "As you were so quick to point out to me, Cavan should not be burdened at this stage of his own career. Now I won't have to depend on him. Or anyone else."

Jack was having a difficult time keeping his own anger under control. He wasn't sure whom he was most aggravated with—the Sheridan girl or David Leslie. He detested being caught unawares, being put at a disadvantage—especially by a seventeen-year-old immigrant girl.

He had come here prepared to be fair, even generous, thinking he knew exactly the strings to pull that would disarm Terese Sheridan and put her on the defensive. Now he apparently would have to rethink his strategy.

So be it. He was convinced that in spite of her obvious satisfaction with herself, she could still be turned easily enough.

As he'd told Avery Foxworth earlier, money would buy just about anything.

❧

Samantha was dismayed to see how the street conditions had worsened since she'd first left home little more than an hour ago. Now she was stuck in the cab, sandwiched between a freight wagon in front and a carriage behind. They had been sitting here for several minutes. The horse was pawing the ground and snorting from the cold, while Samantha's breath steamed the air inside the cab. They had covered only two blocks from the mission when they came to a stop, but it seemed as if it had taken forever to gain even that.

She was cold and growing more and more restless, but there was absolutely nothing she could do except to sit and shiver, waiting. All around them, other drivers and passengers were either out of their vehicles, checking to see what the delay was, or shouting impatient barbs at one another.

When they finally began to move again, Samantha breathed a long sigh. She couldn't reach home soon enough. But her relief was short lived. As they rounded the corner onto Beckman, the wheels skidded, throwing the cab into a skid. One wheel must have hit a deep rut, causing the cab to careen. It swayed, shuddered, and then pitched sideways.

Samantha cried out as she was thrown hard against the side of the cab, wrenching her shoulder. It took her a moment to realize that she wasn't actually hurt, merely stunned.

There was silence for a few seconds; then she heard the loud whinnying of the horse and voices approaching. The nervous driver hurried around to help her out.

Outside, Samantha found the horse still standing, but the cab seemed lodged with one wheel embedded in a treacherous rut and the other severely bent. Clearly, she would be going no farther in this vehicle.

Some of the people in the crowd expressed concern for her, but after Samantha assured them that she was all right, they began to dissipate.

She stood in the middle of Beckman Street, which was hopelessly rutted and dangerously icy, trying to decide what to do. She decided it would be foolish to try her luck with yet another cab, and the chances of getting one of the rare conversion sleighs or a cutter were probably next to nothing in this part of town. She considered her situation for another moment. Fortunately, she had worn a pair of sturdy boots and her warmest coat and gloves. She wasn't all that far from the mission; the most practical thing would be to return.

If David Leslie was there, perhaps he could manage to see that she got home somehow. If not—then she supposed she would have to spend the night there.

Her decision made, she brushed herself off, secured her hat, and started walking in the direction from which she had come.

❧

She would not let him see so much as a hint of fear in her—she would *not!*

Terese sat waiting for Jack Kane's next remark; clearly, he had not finished his business with her yet. She cautioned herself against feeling too much satisfaction at this point, even though his surprise upon learning about her job offer had been obvious. She knew little about Brady's powerful older brother, but she had seen enough to know that Jack Kane was not a man who appreciated being outfoxed. She must be careful. It would be foolish entirely to deliberately antagonize this man, no matter how her blood boiled at his insufferable bullying.

So she continued to watch him carefully, determined to stay calm and coolheaded in anticipation of yet another barrage of unpleasant questioning.

It wasn't long in coming.

"No doubt the good doctor's proposition seems like an excellent solution to your future," Kane said in a tone that sounded almost friendly. "A job, a place to stay—a place with which you're already familiar—and a small wage for pocket money. I'm right in assuming it would be a *small* wage, am I not?"

Terese made no reply but simply gripped the arms of the chair a little more tightly.

"But I would suggest that you think about this at some length, girl. What about later? Will you be satisfied to stay here indefinitely, working for a pittance, never striking out on your own, never being more than a drudge—and raising your child in the midst of sickness and despair? Is that all you want for yourself—for the child?"

Terese clenched her teeth, determined not to let him shake her. "It would not be forever," she said tightly. "Just for a time, until I decide what I want to do." She paused, choosing her words carefully. "I should think you would approve. Sure, it must be an expensive venture, bringing so many to America and paying for our keep indefinitely. Wouldn't you prefer that we earn our own way instead of being dependent on you and your newspaper?"

He regarded her with a look that made Terese go cold inside. Those black eyes of his gave no hint of what he might be thinking, but his hard mouth had thinned until it was little more than a slash.

"Despite what you may have been led to believe by my brother," he said slowly, his tone still smooth and unperturbed, "I have no intention of supporting you or anyone else 'indefinitely.' As a matter of fact, should you fail to cooperate, to keep up your part of the arrangement, I can always arrange to have you sent back to Ireland."

Terese's heart slammed hard against her chest. At the same time the babe kicked, as if the womb itself had been shaken by Kane's threat.

"Why are you doing this?" she choked out. "Why are you so—set against me?"

He stood, his lean frame looming tall and dark in the dreary room. "I'm not against you, Terese. To the contrary, I'm trying to help you. But since you're so determined not to *accept* my help, it occurs to me that I should approach this as I would any other business matter, one in which we can both benefit."

He began to tap his gloves lightly against the palm of one hand. "The simple fact is that you have something I want," he said quietly, his eyes glinting like black fire. "And I have the means to make your life either considerably easier or—much more difficult." With that he turned away, leaving Terese to stare at his back.

Her throat burned as if she had swallowed acid. "What—could I possibly have that a man like you would want?" she asked him warily.

He had been looking out the window, but now he turned and gave her a cold, unpleasant smile. "I think you already know the answer to that, Terese," he said, his voice a low rumble in the stillness of the room. "I want your child, of course. And I'm willing to pay you a handsome price for it."

❧

She looked up into his face, her own countenance going ghastly white. *"Why?"*

Jack debated about what, exactly, to tell her, then decided it might work to his advantage to simply tell her the truth. "For Samantha," he said quietly. "She can't have children of her own, you see. I want to marry her, but she feels that she would be—cheating me, because she can't give me a child. I don't care about that, but she *does*. And, to put it bluntly, Terese, I happen to believe that at this particular time in your life, you wouldn't be nearly as good a mother as Samantha."

A flush of anger suffused her features, but Jack went on, giving her no chance to interrupt. "You're young, girl. Some would say *too* young to shoulder the responsibility a child brings. Be that as it may, you have your entire life ahead of you—you'll have plenty of time to bear all the children you want. Right now, this baby that you're carrying will be more burden to you than blessing. But it can make all the difference in the world to Samantha."

"And to you," she said with an ugly twist of her mouth.

Jack nodded. "Exactly." He drew in a long breath. "Terese, you can't fight me. As I see it, you really don't have a choice. If you go against me, you'll regret it. If you cooperate, I'll see that you—and Cavan—are well taken care of for years to come. Be reasonable, girl. You like Samantha. You know she'd be a good mother. Do this for her, and you'll have my gratitude."

"And if I don't?"

Jack lifted his brows. "Do you really want me to answer that?"

Jack saw the sudden blaze of fury in her eyes, only to be replaced almost instantly by fear, and at that moment he disliked himself more than he had for a very long time.

He was deliberately baiting and intimidating a vulnerable young girl, a girl who had already suffered a brutal assault, who carried a *child* because of that assault, a girl who had left her own country to begin anew in a strange city in a strange land—with the help of the newspaper he owned. He was the one individual committed to helping her—and instead he was manipulating her.

Suddenly, something stopped him, riveting him as he stood staring at her. He remembered the night he had seen Terese Sheridan for the first time, how it had affected him. He had nearly gone weak at the excruciating memories she had evoked in him with her critical illness, her weakness, the seeming hopelessness of her situation.

That night there had been no sign of the dauntless will, the inner strength, the fiery spirit that by now he had come to recognize in the girl. He had not yet encountered the brashness that dared to challenge him, the stubbornness that, at least in one more mature and more experienced, might well have presented a fair match for his own bullheaded resolve. He had not yet caught a glimpse of her fundamental *toughness*. But he saw it now, and he thought he saw something else as well, something that didn't quite add up: This girl was no ordinary *victim*. He had known his share of victims—those who had suffered bitter, sometimes devastating abuse or trauma. And while many eventually overcame the worst of the effects, it had been Jack's experience that it almost always took years—as was most definitely the case with Samantha, who still showed evidence of her ill treatment. And in some cases, like his own mother's, healing never came at all.

When his mother was brutalized, it had destroyed her health—and nearly her mind as well. Jack had been old enough at the time to be only too aware of her suffering; she had never been the same after her agonizing experience. Ever after, she had lived in a kind of invisible cage, frightened of living, often uncertain, and always watching…watching everyone and everything. Jack was fairly certain that she never again experienced so much as one night of unbroken sleep. In her nightmares, she suffered the attack over and over again until the day she died giving birth to Brady.

The girl who sat glaring up at him was no doubt frightened, but her fear seemed more to fuel her determination than to cower her. She feared, not him, exactly, but more the threat he represented. And she was willing to fight him. This girl was not weak, not fainthearted, in mind or in spirit. In short, she simply gave little sign—other than the pregnancy itself—that she had been beaten or violated. Terese Sheridan, he sensed, was not so much a victim as a survivor.

His every instinct suddenly engaged and went on the alert. *What if she hadn't been assaulted at all?* What if she were lying about some clandestine affair, using the *Vanguard*'s resettlement program to flee her past and improve her circumstances? Or what if she had been promiscuous and gotten herself trapped by her own indiscretion? She didn't seem the type, but then there was often no telling the "type."

At the back of Jack's mind, he recognized that his present line of thinking might be nothing more than an attempt to rationalize his own heartless behavior, and again he felt an uncomfortable dart of self-disgust. Nevertheless, he decided to test his suspicions.

"Forgive my bluntness, Terese," he said. "But I confess I might have made the assumption that you wouldn't mind giving up the child all that much, considering the experience that brought about your condition in the first place. Perhaps I even thought you'd be relieved." He paused, ignoring her attempted protest. "It isn't such a rare thing, after all, for an unwanted infant to be put up for adoption."

"But my child is *not* unwanted!" she shot back at him, half rising from the chair. "And you're not talking about adoption. You're trying to buy my baby!"

Jack took his time in answering, raking her with a speculative gaze. He deliberately remained standing, keeping the advantage. "I suppose you might see it that way," he finally said. "But I tend to think of it more as giving you your freedom."

"I don't *want* to be free of my own child!"

Jack continued to feel his way. "Yes, I'm beginning to understand that. And I must say that while your…commitment to your attacker's child might be admirable, it's also passing strange. I should think you'd find it very difficult, if not impossible, to feel any sort of affection for a child that was forced upon you through such a heinous experience—and one over which you had no control."

He waited, watching her closely. For the first time he thought he detected some confusion in her and perhaps a measure of uncertainty.

He saw her swallow with noticeable effort. "'Tis not the child's fault, what was done to me," she said, her eyes averted.

"Of course it wasn't," Jack agreed amicably. "But the fault was not yours, either. And yet you seem to feel obligated."

He let the words hang, unfinished, not quite a question, yet not quite a statement either.

"'Tis not obligated I feel," she said after a noticeable hesitation. "The child is a part of me, after all."

"How did it happen, Terese?" he said quietly.

She looked up at him, her eyes slightly wild. "Please don't—ask me to talk about it," she stammered out, quickly lowering her gaze to her lap. "I can't possibly."

"I see. Because it's still too painful?"

"Yes, of course it's painful!" she said, her words shooting out like bullets. "Besides," she added, her voice lower and slightly unsteady, "it's not—seemly, to speak of such things with you, a man I scarcely know. I—don't want to speak of it at all, not ever again!"

Jack said nothing, deliberately waiting. When she refused to look at him, he stepped a little closer to her. "This…unspeakable act that was perpetrated on you—where did it happen?"

She looked up. "What?"

"Where did the attack occur? Where were you?"

"I—in Galway," she stammered. "Galway City."

She was rattled, Jack could tell. He sensed it was time to press. Hard.

"At night?"

"Night—yes, it was at night." She frowned at him. "Didn't I say I don't want to speak of it?"

"What were you doing alone in the city at night?"

She was clearly confounded by the way he was baiting her. "I—I had an errand. I was doing an errand for Jane Connolly. My employer."

"An errand you couldn't attend to during the day?"

"If I could have seen to it by day, wouldn't I have done so?"

"Did you know the man?"

She stared at him, not answering.

"The man who assaulted you," Jack said roughly. "Did you know him?"

"N-no, I did *not* know him! And I will not discuss this any further with you! It—shames me!"

Jack jumped on that. "But why should it shame you, when you were entirely innocent? You *were* innocent," Jack said, pausing. "Weren't you?"

She glared at him with all the scalding hostility he suspected she was capable of and something else, something Jack had seen in the eyes of other adversaries whom he had outmaneuvered: the quick fury at being found out, followed by panic and a desperate attempt to maintain the lie.

"What are you saying?" Her words were little more than a harsh whisper, and Jack suspected that the insolence in her tone was nothing more than an attempt to shield herself.

Jack no longer gambled, not at the gaming table. But the old instincts that had once made him such a formidable opponent remained keen. He was responding to those instincts now, convinced that Terese Sheridan's anger and indignation rang patently false.

The girl was lying through her teeth or he would be a salmon marching.

❧

As Samantha approached Grace Mission, she saw the newspaper wagon parked in front of David Leslie's chaise and drew a sigh of relief.

She tried to walk faster, but the depth of the snow made if virtually impossible to hurry. She hadn't thought of Jack stopping by to visit Terese on a day like this, but she was grateful he had. Apparently he had decided the newspaper wagon would be more sensible than a carriage. A wise decision, she thought, considering her experience with the cab.

His being here meant that she would almost certainly have a ride back to her apartment. And the thought of driving through a snowstorm in an open wagon was still more appealing than being stranded away from home overnight.

The heavy snow sucked at her feet, rendering her boots nearly useless as she trudged the rest of the way up the street. In her haste, she stumbled and nearly fell when she turned onto the walk leading to the mission building. Righting herself, she conceded that at one time she might have tried to pretend that her eagerness had nothing to do with seeing Jack, that she was simply anxious to get out of the storm. But in truth she *was* eager to see him; these days, that seemed to be the case more often than not.

She was also exceedingly pleased that he had ventured out in the middle of a snowstorm to visit Terese Sheridan. No doubt he would minimize any mention of it, but to Samantha it was one more example of the kindness she knew to be a part—albeit a well-concealed part, much of the time—of his nature.

She was almost at the front door before she realized she was smiling like a school-girl.

———❧———

Jack was angry now, too, his temper suddenly stoked by the thought that he had, for a time, almost fallen for her scheme. But now that he knew she was no different from any of the others—most of them far older and a great deal more shrewd—who at one time or another had tried to dupe him, the last shred of sympathy for the girl drained away and he dropped all pretense of consideration for her feelings.

"You know exactly what I'm saying." He slung the words at her with blistering contempt. "You had yourself a tawdry little affair and then didn't quite know how to deal with the consequences, wasn't that it? You've been lying all along, haven't you? You thought you'd play me for the great fool: wangling free passage to the States for yourself, taking advantage of a program meant for those genuinely deserving of it—and then what would it have been, eh? Living on the *Vanguard*'s dole as long as you could pull it off, you and your—"

She hauled herself to her feet, the chair scraping the floor with a loud screech. Her eyes blazed with a poisonous rage, and she actually raised a hand as if to strike him.

But Jack merely gave her a cold look and launched his final volley with deliberate scorn. "No doubt it was easy enough to hoodwink my brother into buying your story. It never did take much for one like you to wrap Brady around her little finger. He always was a fool for a cheap skirt, especially if she could work him for a bit of sympathy in the process."

A sound like that of an animal in torment ripped from her throat. The cords in her neck stood out as if she were strangling, and her features, admittedly striking even in the advanced stages of her pregnancy, now contorted with hatred, taking on a dark, ugly flush of crimson.

She raised both arms as if to dive at him, and for a moment Jack thought she actually would attack him.

"'Twas your good-for-nothing, deceitful brother who got me into this fix, I'll have you know!"

35

TRUTH AND BETRAYAL

And I hardened my heart
For fear of my ruin...
I hardened my heart,
And my love I quenched.

PADRAIC PEARSE

Jack reared back as if she had struck him. Indeed, she *did* lunge for him, but he caught her wrists between his big hands, easily trapping her.

A thunderous pounding worked its way up his skull as he stared down at her, holding her captive. "What are you talking about?"

She twisted and bent backwards, trying to loosen his hold on her, but Jack had her in a merciless grip, and she couldn't shake him. Shock mingled with fright in her eyes, and he saw that she was as appalled by her outburst as he was. The look of utter horror on her face sent a cold blade of dread twisting through him, a warning that what was to come would be nothing he wanted to hear.

But surely this was more of her lies!

"Tell me!" Jack shouted at her. "And I'll have the truth this time, you little slut!"

The fear in her eyes suddenly faded, and she was now one furious pyre of hatred. She bared her teeth like a wildcat and screamed at him. "I'm no slut, but if I am, 'tis your brother you can thank for it! *He* sired the child I carry!"

"I don't believe you!"

"Believe me or don't believe me, but it's the *truth* I'm telling you! That's what you wanted, wasn't it? The truth?"

"You were attacked—*raped!* Brady told me the whole ugly story in his letter."

"Brady *made up* the whole ugly story, man, don't you see? He got me with child by leading me to believe I *meant* something to him, playing me for the foolish green girl I was, and then after using me, he sent me packing. To *you!* But not until after he put up the lie he knew would get me here!"

She disgorged the words as if she were spewing poison at him, her face a crimson, enraged mask of pure fury. "'Twas your precious *brother* who gave the lie, not me! I only did what he told me to do, in order to keep my child! Your darling Brady would have had the babe cut from my womb entirely, but I couldn't bring myself to do it! I could not do away with my own child even if its father *is* a worthless dog!"

A murderous, black rage rose up in Jack. His ears roared with it, his head swam with it. He began to shake, violently, like a man with the palsy. Fury possessed him, like a great dark beast unleashed from a pit somewhere deep inside him.

He wanted to strike her, to slap her face until her neck snapped, to inflict on her the depth of pain she had settled on him. The same malevolent force that had overtaken him so completely in the past that had almost driven him to violence now surfaced in him again, and he knew that the last shred of self-control was all but lost to him.

He looked at her, then grasped her shoulders and gave her a vicious shove, tossing her away from him with a force that knocked her backwards into the chair. She shrieked at him and would have scrambled to her feet, but Jack raised a warning hand to her, and she sank back against the chair, the anger rapidly fading from her eyes, giving way to a rising fear.

"Don't...say...another word!" he warned her.

"It's the truth and I can see you know it!" she countered in an unexpected blast of defiance.

"Shut up, you little baggage! Shut up!"

The room seemed to echo with their shouting, that and the sound of his own harsh breathing. Jack knotted his fists at his side until pain darted up both arms, but it was nothing compared to the pain of betrayal that threatened to unman him. *Brady's betrayal.*

She looked up into his face, and she was as still as death except for the tears beginning to pool in her eyes. And Jack knew, knew beyond all doubting, that the girl had spoken the truth. And yet he could not seem to take it in.

He saw that she was shivering, whether from the cold of the room or fear of him, he didn't know or care. He had no pity in him for her now, no shame for his treatment of her. He was still caught in the grip of a darkness that felt as if he would explode with it, and there was no room for anything but the wild, savage fury that threatened to take his mind, his sanity.

"Why?" he choked out. "If you're telling the truth—and mind, I will find out if you're not—if it's so, then why the deceit?"

She hugged her arms to herself, rubbing her shoulders as if they ached. "He— Brady—said it was the only way. That you would—disown him and throw me out into the streets if you knew the truth." She glared at him as if she had no doubt whatsoever that Brady had been right.

Jack studied her, still struggling for some semblance of control. "He refused to marry you? He wanted you to get rid of the child instead?"

"He used me!" she fairly hissed the words at him. "He pretended to care for me, but all the time he was only trifling with me! And myself fool enough to believe I mattered to him!"

Something occurred to Jack, and he hurled the charge at her. "You thought to trap him with the child, didn't you? You *let* it happen, thinking to hold him."

To his surprise, she seemed to falter. As he watched, some of the defiance faded from her eyes. "At first, I may have meant to do just that," she said, her voice trembling but quieter now. "I wanted to get away so desperately, don't you see, that I admit I would have done most anything! But later—" She stopped, squeezing her eyes shut for a moment. Then she opened them and went on. "Later, I came to care for him, and I truly thought he—"

She broke off, shaking her head as if dazed. Her eyes were dark with despair, and she began to sob, her shoulders heaving. But Jack scarcely saw.

"I will have the child," he said with a bleak, hard coldness. "You know that, don't you? Perhaps my spineless brother didn't want it, and you, my girl, most assuredly cannot afford it. But if you have finally spoken the truth, then the child you carry is of my blood."

He stopped, yanking the chair in which he had earlier sat roughly off the floor, then slamming it down with a shattering blow. *"And make no mistake, I will have it!"*

Without another word then, he turned and charged blindly from the room, leaving the sound of her anguished weeping behind him.

❦

Samantha heard the voices the minute she stepped inside. Bewildered at first, she stood in the entryway, looking around.

When she realized where the sound was coming from, she approached the stairway, then hesitated. Her heart seemed to skip a beat when she recognized Jack's voice, raised in what was plainly a fit of anger.

Then she heard Terese scream. She was screaming at Jack. In that moment, Samantha knew something terrible had happened.

Heart pounding, she grasped the banister and started up the steps, stopping dead when a heavy thud shook the floor above her. Samantha heard Jack shout something, followed by the sound of Terese weeping.

She gathered her skirts and took the steps at a run, halting at the top when she saw Jack come lurching out of Terese's room, his dark features distorted and forbidding with unmistakable rage.

He stopped in the hallway at the sight of her, close enough to Samantha that she could see the searing blaze of fury in his eyes. A shock of black hair had fallen over his brow, and his face was an angry crimson. He stood there, legs astride, his black topcoat hanging open, his eyes wild, his face a dark thunderhead.

For the first time, Samantha was afraid of him.

He closed the distance between them in two wide steps, coming to stand directly in front of her. "Did you know about this?" he grated out in a tone Samantha had never heard from him before. *"Did you?"*

"Know about what? Jack—what's wrong?" Instinctively, Samantha reached a tentative hand to his arm. He shook her off with a violence that stunned her and left her trembling.

At that moment, David Leslie came up the stairway, taking the steps two at a time.

He hesitated at the top when he saw Samantha and Jack. "Samantha?" He looked from one to the other. "What's happened?"

Jack ignored him, his eyes boring into Samantha. "I asked you if you knew," he said again with the same raw bitterness in his voice.

"Knew *what?* Jack—"

Suddenly, he uttered a low sound in his throat and shoved his way past her. When David Leslie would have stopped him at the top of the steps, Jack hurled him aside with such force Samantha thought the young physician would surely go hurtling down the stairway.

She cried out Jack's name, but he was already barreling down the steps.

David Leslie turned toward her, his dazed expression mirroring Samantha's own state of shock and bewilderment. At that instant, a long, chilling wail shattered their inertia and sent them rushing toward Terese's room.

36

DARKNESS AND DECEPTION

Why is it effects are greater than their causes…
And the most deceived be she who least suspects?

OLIVER ST. JOHN GOGARTY

It took well over an hour for Samantha and David Leslie to get the entire story of what had transpired between Jack and Terese. A large part of that time was spent simply trying to calm Terese enough that she could tell them *anything*.

She seemed caught in the grip of near hysteria when they reached her. Indeed, Samantha feared that the girl might have suffered a kind of emotional breakdown. Although David seemed inclined to reserve his opinion, Samantha could tell that he, too, was deeply concerned.

Because of the baby, he didn't administer a sedative, but instead relied merely on smelling salts and a cold cloth. And prayer.

Samantha quickly learned that David Leslie was one physician who relied as much—perhaps even more—on divine power as he did on his own medical skills, exceptional as they seemed to be. He bade Samantha to pray as he worked over Terese, and clearly he was praying, too. In truth, Samantha sensed he had not ceased praying since they entered Terese's room.

At first, much of the girl's account had been almost unintelligible, even irrational. But after David finally got her to bed, applied the salts, and soothed her with a continuous stream of reassurances, she began to make herself understood. Even so, her disjointed, fragmented story seemed almost unimaginable.

What Samantha did manage to glean left her reeling in confusion and disbelief. Much of it made no sense, but as she stood at the foot of the bed, watching David with Terese and listening to the girl's ranting, she slowly, little by little, began to fit the pieces together.

Whatever had transpired between Terese and Jack had obviously been ugly, even violent, and had left Terese convinced that he meant to take her baby away from her, once it was born. If she was to be believed, Jack had made a number of particularly vile accusations during the heated exchange, had even threatened her.

As much as Samantha wanted not to believe what she was hearing, she had seen Jack's face for herself. The man who had come charging out of Terese's bedroom had been enraged, capable of anything.

Incredibly, it seemed that Terese had not been assaulted after all—there had been no rape. Jack's brother had evidently fathered the child during the course of an affair, and together the two of them—Brady and Terese—had woven a web of deceit that had fooled everyone, including Jack.

But now that he knew the truth, he was threatening to take the child.

Again Samantha found herself hard pressed to credit Jack with such unthinkable cruelty. And yet…there were the old stories, the rumors of his ruthless business dealings, his relentless and often merciless pursuit of anything he wanted. The men he had ruined. The corruption that shadowed him. And always, his vicious, fearful temper.

Samantha could not forget the look in his eyes: the wildness, the explosive rage she had seen there when he confronted her on the landing. By now, she was more than bewildered and shocked by Terese's account: She was heartsick and terrified that everything the girl had told them might be true.

Without warning, Terese suddenly pulled Samantha back to her surroundings, pushing herself up from the pillows and, her eyes still glazed but more lucid now, calling out to her. Samantha hurried around to the side of the bed and took her hand. For a moment, she feared the girl was going to lapse into yet another fit of mindless weeping. Instead, she seized Samantha's hand and began to repeat the same thing over and over again, like a frenzied litany: *"He's going to take my baby, Samantha! He's going to take my baby away from me!"*

When Samantha tried to reassure her, Terese lifted herself even more, grasping Samantha's arm and pleading, "Help me, Samantha! Please! You have to stop him!"

Overcome by pity for the girl and her own feelings of helplessness, Samantha again attempted to comfort her. "Terese, I'm sure Jack didn't mean anything he said—he wouldn't—"

Terese clutched at Samantha's arm. "No, Samantha, you don't understand! You didn't hear him. He wants the babe for *you!* He *told* me so. He told me how you—can't have children. He means for you to have my baby! He says you'll marry him then. Oh, Samantha, please—don't let him do this! Don't let him take my baby!"

Samantha stood staring at Terese Sheridan. So great was her shock, so brutal the pain that knifed through her, that she thought her heart would surely shatter to pieces.

At the same time, a terrible anger began to surface in her. "Jack…actually said that? That he wants the baby for *me?"*

Terese nodded. She was weeping again. "And when he found out about Brady and me—it only made things worse! He was furious! He was like a crazy man!"

Terese's hand tightened still more on Samantha's arm. "You can reason with him, Samantha," she said, her voice lower but her eyes still burning with desperation. "I'm nothing to Jack Kane! He doesn't care what happens to me. But he *does* care about you, Samantha! Please—don't let him do this!"

The weight centered in Samantha's chest grew even heavier. She patted Terese's hand absently, all the while feeling as if she would be sick at any moment. She glanced at David Leslie, saw him watching her with something akin to pity.

"It will be all right, Terese," she managed to say, her voice sounding distant and strangled in her ears. "Just…you rest now. I'll…take care of this. No one is going to take your baby from you."

Then she turned to David Leslie. "David—your buggy…may I use it, please?"

He gave her a blank look. "My buggy?"

Samantha nodded.

"Well…of course, you can use it, but, Samantha, you can't take a buggy out alone in this storm!" He stopped, glanced at Terese, and added uncertainly, "I don't think I ought to leave—"

"No, of course, you mustn't leave. I can drive myself. Really," she insisted at his dubious look. "I drove my mother's buggy all the time when I was still at home. I'm quite capable."

"But it's already dark, Samantha! It's far too treacherous. At least, wait until tomorrow—"

"David—please. I'll walk if I must, but I have to do this. I have to see Jack tonight."

He studied her, then, with obvious reluctance, gave a nod of assent. "I wish you wouldn't, but—please, Samantha, be careful."

But Samantha was already halfway across the room, stopping only long enough to gather her coat and hat from the chair.

❦

Jack sat hunched over his desk, the dim light from the oil lamp on his desk casting shadows over the blank piece of paper in front of him. He was making no pretense of working. He could think of nothing else, indeed had thought of nothing else since leaving Grace Mission, but Brady's betrayal.

He had no doubt but that Terese Sheridan had finally spoken the truth. He had known it the instant the words left her mouth, in spite of his initial attempt to deny it. He hated admitting it, even to himself, but he knew that Brady was just irresponsible and selfish enough to be guilty of the girl's accusations. It both infuriated him and sickened him that his brother had not been man enough to admit to his own child, had instead allowed the girl he had wronged—scarcely more than a child herself—to not only shoulder the entire burden alone, but to live a lie in the process.

Not that the Sheridan girl was innocent. Apparently, she had been a willing enough participant in the affair itself. But as for the rest of it, he tended to believe her insistence that Brady had spun the lie, and she had simply gone along with it, not knowing what else to do by then.

Jack shook his head. "Blood tells," 'twas often said, and perhaps it was truer than anyone thought. Perhaps his younger brother was merely displaying the same craven willfulness of the British soldier who had sired him. For whatever the man had been who forced himself on their mother—and God only knew how many other women that hellish night—he had above all else been an ignoble, spineless brute. Was it possible for such a thing to be passed down from one generation to another?

He expelled a harsh, ragged sigh. Perhaps he had been wrong all these years, to keep the truth from Brady. He wondered now if it would have made any conceivable difference, had he told him everything from the beginning.

He had thought to give the boy an untroubled mind, to protect him from the painful truth about the vicious assault on their mother—the assault of which Brady was the fruit. Had he erred, then, in concealing the fact that his brother was not, after all, the son of Sean Kane, an allegedly fearless—or would that be *foolish?*—rebel leader, that he was in fact the seed of a drunken soldier of the Crown, bent on revenge? Revenge for a night raid led by Sean Kane and some of his cohorts. A raid for which their mother, God rest her soul—and others—had paid a terrible, obscene price.

Would the truth somehow have made Brady stronger, more careful of his actions and their consequences? Or, as Jack had feared, would it have made him even wilder and more reckless than he was?

If he were altogether honest, he would have to concede that Brady's parentage was not the only unpleasantness from which he had shielded the boy over the years. Indeed, he was beginning to think he might have shielded his brother from too much, too long.

When Brady got into trouble with the nuns at school, Jack had invariably intervened, playing on their sympathy for the "poor, motherless boy," whose only home life consisted of a too-busy older brother and a housekeeper. And those times when Brady's gambling debts soared above what his monthly stipend could cover, Jack had never permitted the thugs to take it out of his hide, but instead bailed him out, the only punishment a stern lecture—which was promptly forgotten—and some menial jobs about the house, which were likewise either forgotten or ignored.

There had been a girl or two as well—summarily condemned by Jack as fortune hunters before he paid them off and sent them packing.

Not so different a scenario as what he had thought to enact with Terese Sheridan, he thought guiltily.

He had been holding a cigar between his fingers, unlighted and forgotten, and now he crushed it in his hand and tossed it onto the floor. After a moment, he propped his elbows on top of the desk and put his head between his hands, squeezing his temples in an attempt to blunt the brain-splitting headache that had begun on the frenzied drive back to the office.

The pain in his head, however, was nothing as compared to the immense black pain in his soul. He felt as if the center of his being had been bayoneted, brutally ripped through.

He would have thought he had known despair before tonight, but the raw, gaping hole that now opened somewhere inside him was as agonizing as any desolation he had ever suffered. He felt as if it might well tear him asunder before the night was done.

And Brady's deceit was only a part of it. Jack could still see the stark lines of terror engraved upon the Sheridan girl's face, and the awful thing of it was that for a moment he had actually reveled in her fear of him.

But the worst had been Samantha: the way she had looked at him, the unmistakable horror in her eyes that, at least at that moment, had not even moved him.

By now the Sheridan girl would have told Samantha everything. No longer would she doubt the unsavory stories, the rumors that dogged him; from this night on, she would believe them and even worse.

And she would be justified entirely. Oh, he had improved his behavior some over the years, modified his dealings to some extent, even played at being respectable. After meeting Samantha, he had taken his efforts even more seriously. But had he ever actually believed he could change?

Perhaps for a time. A very *brief* time. No doubt that accounted for his rash promise to Samantha that he would attempt to be the kind of man she deserved, the kind of man she wanted him to be. A man she could trust.

But while he might have been able to fool Samantha, he had never once managed to deceive himself. Inside, tenuously concealed, lurking just behind the facade he had erected, was the same man he had always been, the man he was reputed to be.

Samantha knew by now that his promises were false. Unreliable. Worthless.

His heart was as black and as cold as the pit itself. For a moment his mind raced back to the evening in Philadelphia when he had met with Edgar Poe. He remembered the decadence he had sensed about the man, the abhorrent *darkness,* and how shaken he had been when he realized that perhaps the reason Poe evoked such a conflict of feelings in him—feelings that ranged all the way from a reluctant sort of fascination to a chilling kind of dread—was the fear that the same darkness resided in *himself.* So eager had he been to get away from the man, to return to Samantha—the brightness and the goodness of her—that he had been almost rude.

His light had been Samantha, and she was lost to him. Now there was no light left to him, only darkness.

The old black melancholy draped itself over him like a shroud. At the back of his mind, he was aware that he was sinking quickly into a disgusting state of mawkishness. Only his fierce aversion to self-pity kept him from sliding the rest of the way down into the loathsome swamp of Irish despondency.

At least he could do the humane thing for Terese Sheridan. He would go back to the mission tomorrow and put the girl's fears to rest. There was no reason to terrorize her any longer. Without Samantha, why would he want someone else's child—even his brother's?

No, Terese could keep her baby, and the *Vanguard* would keep the resettlement agreement intact. After all, the girl had been duped by a master, he thought bitterly. Brady was nothing if not the consummate confidence man.

He would make sure she and the child were taken care of; that much, at least he could do. There would be Cavan to deal with, of course. The lad knew nothing as yet. Once his sister had bent his ear, no doubt he would leave the *Vanguard*'s employ. But he was a good enough reporter and writer to land a job on any other newspaper in the city—with or without a reference from Jack, though he would surely give him a sterling one if need be.

It occurred to Jack that he would miss Cavan Sheridan, and he was saddened by the realization. Strange entirely, the things one recognized when it was too late.

As for Brady...Jack glanced down at the blank paper in front of him, then reached for a fresh cigar. After lighting it, he took up his pen and began to compose a letter to his brother. It struck him that he didn't even have a current address. He supposed he would simply post it to the one in Galway in hopes the young fool had at least taken measures to have his mail forwarded, wherever he was.

Jack had once thought that, should he ever decide to tell the boy the truth about his brutal beginnings, he would tell him face-to-face and be prepared to help him deal with the shock. But he was now convinced he had waited too long as it was, had protected Brady to a fault, perhaps had even inadvertently encouraged his lack of character. He would write him this very night with the whole story and let him take the blow on his own, to deal with it however he could.

He would, of course, tell him he knew about the affair with Terese, the baby, and the lie Brady had fostered. He would also make it clear that from now on Brady would have to earn his keep—and he meant exactly that: He would earn it, whether from the *Vanguard*'s payroll or somewhere else. He would do the job, or there would be no pay.

He would also suggest that, as long as he was being paid by the *Vanguard*, Brady would apply a portion of his salary to his child's support.

But Jack knew even as he wrote that he could not bring himself to do the one thing Brady apparently feared: He could not completely reject his brother. He was still Brady, the boy he had raised more as a son. And the bitter truth was that Brady's deception, painful as it was, somehow seemed no worse than his own.

37

I WOULD GIVE YOU THE WORLD...

This heart, fill'd with fondness,
Is wounded and weary.

FROM WALSH'S *IRISH POPULAR SONGS*, 1847

Half an hour later, Jack finished the letter, sealed it in an envelope, and stuffed it inside his waistcoat pocket for posting.

He stood, easing his shoulders and wishing he had a powder for the pain in his skull. He walked over to look out the window, but there wasn't much to be seen. It was still snowing, though the wind seemed to have died some. The street was all but deserted, except for Whitey and Snipe. The two newsboys typically slept under the steps of the bindery across the street but at the moment stood warming themselves at one of the trash barrels.

Jack shoved his hands down in his pockets, watching the two. When the weather was as brutal as it was tonight, he sometimes allowed a few of the lads to sleep in the hallway downstairs or in the horse barn, which they seemed to prefer.

The city teemed with homeless children—a fair number of whom were newsboys. They slept wherever they could, ate whatever they could beg or steal usually, and some even grew up to be respectable. But to New York's shame, many died from exposure or hunger before they had the chance to grow up at all.

He turned and looked around his office, small and cluttered and dark, and decided he would spend the night here, on the sagging sofa across the room. He already knew that sleep wasn't likely to come tonight, so why brave the snowstorm to reach home?

He went back to his desk and put out his cigar. He moved to snuff out the lamp but decided first to call down to the newsboys and tell them to come inside if they wanted. Just then he heard footsteps on the stairway. He stopped where he was, frowning. There was no one here this time of night, except for Madog Wall, and the big Irishman would not be so light footed on the stairway. The presses were shut down for the night, the workers gone.

One of the newsboys? Not likely. They knew they weren't allowed past the door unless Jack offered.

As a precaution, his hand went to the top right drawer of the desk, where he kept his gun.

The drawer was locked. He glanced across the room at the door. It was closed, but through the frosted window at the top he could make out the vague shape of someone standing outside. Quickly, his eyes still on the door, he fished in his pocket for his keys, then quietly unlocked the desk drawer and withdrew the pistol.

He stood waiting, the gun leveled directly at the door as it opened.

＊

Samantha was almost certain that, in the heat of his rage, Jack would come here, rather than going home—not only because he'd been driving the newspaper wagon, but because, if she were not badly mistaken, the *Vanguard* was more home to Jack than the sprawling mansion on Thirty-Fourth Street. This was where he spent most of his days and, by his own admission, a good many of his nights.

She had been to Jack's office only once before, and then in broad daylight. The building seemed eerily quiet and dark this time of night, but a dim light could be seen through the frosted glass of his office door.

She hesitated, her hand gripping the doorknob, realizing now that it had probably been the worst kind of foolishness to come here. Because of the snow, it had taken her more than twice as long as it should have just to get here, and she'd held her breath most of the way, praying the buggy wouldn't hang up or overturn.

It occurred to her that she didn't even know what she intended to say to him. Nevertheless, she was here, so finally, with a shuddering breath, she turned the doorknob and prepared to face him.

The door creaked open, and she stepped inside to find him standing behind his desk, pointing a gun directly at her.

The office was dim and gloomy and reeked of cigar smoke. The light flickered in the draft, casting Jack in shadows, making him appear more a dark and menacing stranger than the man she knew.

Or the man she had thought *she knew...*

Samantha was too stunned to speak, much less cry out. She could do nothing but stand and stare at Jack and the gun in his hand.

"*Samantha!*"

In an instant, he lowered the gun and came round the desk. "What are you *doing* here?" He virtually shouted at her, making it more an accusation than a question.

Samantha opened her mouth to speak, but the gun was still in his hand, albeit lowered to his side, and her mind seemed unable to get past the sight of it.

As if he had read her thoughts, Jack glanced from her to the gun in his hand, then turned and went back to the desk, shoving the pistol inside a drawer.

"Sorry about the gun," he said. "I couldn't think who might be in the building this time of night."

Samantha made no reply. He came around the desk again, not taking his eyes off her. This time when he spoke his voice had returned to its earlier sharpness. "I hope you didn't come here alone."

Before Samantha could answer, he said, "You *did*, didn't you? What on earth possessed you?" He looked thoroughly put out with her, which for some reason did nothing but anger Samantha.

She found it incredible that he would have the presumption to show impatience with her after what he had done. "Don't concern yourself with how I got here," she countered. She heard the chill in her voice and realized that it was merely a weak reflection of the cold fury she felt toward him at the moment.

"Samantha—"

He had come to a stop a few feet away from her, and he stood now, hands clenched into fists at his sides, looking at her. Samantha was momentarily caught off guard by how utterly drained and exhausted he appeared.

Something tugged at her heart, but she forced herself to ignore it. "I came here because I have to know one thing," she said, cringing at the tremor in her voice.

He took a step toward her, repeating her name, but Samantha quickly raised a hand to stop him. "Just tell me if it's true: Did you threaten to take Terese's baby away from her?" She paused. "And did you really tell her you wanted the baby for me? *Did* you?"

His eyes searched hers, and for a moment Samantha could see him hesitate, as if he might be trying to arrange his thoughts exactly right.

"The truth, Jack," she said, raising her voice. "There's been quite enough lying."

She saw him expel a long breath, but he didn't try to avoid her gaze. "I'd not be the one to argue that. All right, then, Samantha: Aye, it's true. I did tell the girl I meant to have the child, and that I wanted it…for you."

Samantha tried to swallow, nearly choking on the dry knot in her throat. "How *could* you? That girl is supposed to be under your protection! You're committed to helping her, and instead you *terrorize* her! And then try to excuse your unforgivable behavior by claiming you did it for me!"

"But it *was* for you, Samantha, and that's the truth."

Samantha heard the sudden thickening of his Irish accent as he visibly grew more agitated.

"Surely you can believe that much, at least. Why else would I want the child?"

"Don't you *dare* to use me as an excuse for your bullying!" Samantha hurled the words at him with enough force that he actually blanched as if she'd struck him.

She almost faltered, surprised at the intensity of her own anger. But she couldn't stop what she had begun. "Did you ever once think to question how I might feel about such an insane idea?" she railed on. "But, no, of course, you wouldn't. *You* decided what was best for me, and that was that, wasn't it? You just naturally assumed that I would consent to whatever you decided. Because you're Jack Kane! It doesn't matter how cruel or obscene your behavior happens to be; if you want a thing done, then that's the start and finish of it! Jack Kane takes what he wants, no matter who gets hurt or destroyed in the process. That's just how it is with you, isn't it, Jack?" She stopped to catch a breath. "Well, *isn't* it?"

He stood there, saying nothing, his hands now unclenched and hanging limply at his sides, his face dark—not with anger, Samantha sensed, but with pain.

But his pain didn't move her. Not now. She wouldn't allow it.

"Why?" She choked out. "Why would you do such a terrible thing to that girl? To me?"

A hint of the old mocking smile curved his lips when he answered her. "As you said, Samantha, there was something I wanted. I simply did what needed to be done in order to get it. Aye, you're right: That's my way. Always has been. And what I wanted this time was you. As my wife. So I set about to make it happen."

Samantha gaped at him in utter astonishment. "You couldn't possibly believe I would marry you after you did such a deplorable thing to Terese."

He merely lifted one dark eyebrow.

Samantha felt ill. "You did," she said slowly, her voice trembling. "You actually thought you could...buy me! With a child."

A cold vise closed around Samantha's heart as she stared at him in horrified disbelief. "I can't believe you did this," she said brokenly. "I thought...I knew you—"

"And didn't I try on more than one occasion to convince you that you *didn't* know me, Samantha?" His voice cracked like a whip in the quiet of the room. "Didn't I try to warn you I wasn't the man you seemed bent on making me out to be? *Didn't* I?"

He had, of course. And she had blindly tried her best to ignore him, to see him as she wanted him to be instead of how he really was.

She should have listened to him...She should have believed him...

Slowly, he walked toward her, stopping directly in front of her, only inches away. His eyes burned into Samantha, but he made no move to touch her. She saw that he looked ravaged and drawn. But she closed her heart against him. She *had* to.

When he spoke again, his voice had gentled. "Whether you believe me or not, Samantha, I regret what I did. My actions were despicable; that's true. For whatever it's worth, I will tell you that I have every intention of making amends to the Sheridan girl—however I can."

He paused, his shoulders slumping slightly. "Something tells me, however, that there's nothing I can do to make amends to *you,* and for that I am sorrier than you can possibly know."

Samantha looked away before she could allow herself to soften toward him. "I simply do not understand...how you could do such a thing. I never would have believed it of you, Jack. Never."

"Samantha? Samantha, look at me."

She did and instantly regretted it. Her mind insisted that he had betrayed whatever trust she had begun to hold for him, that he had done a terrible thing, and she must bury any feelings she might have ever felt for him. But her heart reminded her that he was still Jack, still the man from whom she had known great kindness and gentleness and...affection. He was still Jack—the man she loved. And something in her spirit made her hesitate to turn completely away from him.

So she faced him, waiting.

As he began to speak, his fingers kneaded the lapel of his coat. Samantha could not help but notice that his hand wasn't all that steady.

"'Tis not likely I can make you understand, Samantha. In truth, I'm not at all sure I understand myself. But I do know this much, wrong as I may have been: I wanted to give you something, Samantha, something to make up for what had been taken from you, so that you wouldn't mind so much...your childlessness."

When Samantha would have interrupted, he lifted a hand to stop her. "You seemed so intent on not marrying me—for two reasons: the fact that you couldn't give me a child, and also because—as you put it—I could not share your faith. Well, it seemed to me that there was little I could do about the faith. But there *was* something I could do about a child. And so—" he gave a light shrug—"I set about doing it."

Something seemed to open in Samantha, just enough that she could glimpse the truth behind Jack's words. *Oh, God, he really did do it for me, didn't he? But it was still wrong, Lord...so very wrong!*

Samantha felt her heart squeezed nearly beyond endurance as Jack went on. "You're absolutely right to be furious with me. I should never—*never*—have presumed to do such a thing and expect that somehow you would sanction it. I must have been a little mad to even conceive of it."

His voice had grown hoarse, deeper, the brogue even thicker. "Samantha...will you try to believe this much, if nothing else: I...love you, as I have never loved another woman."

As if anticipating her protest, he again raised a hand to silence her. "Even Martha, though I did love her well. Quite frankly, *mavourneen,* I would have done almost anything to make you mine."

Watching him, Samantha could see the difficulty with which he swallowed, as if trying to choke down the bitterness of his own words. "Instead, I've turned you away. And for that, I will never forgive myself."

He gave a lame attempt at a laugh. "What a fool I've been. I set out to be the kind of man you could love—and only managed to prove to you that I'm not."

O, Lord, what am I to do about this man? What?

Samantha blinked back the unshed tears that had begun to scald her eyes while he spoke. "You're right," she said softly, her own voice now thick with emotion. "You *have* been a fool. You didn't have to do anything to make me love you, Jack! I already *did* love you!"

As she watched, he squeezed his eyes shut for an instant. When he opened them, he took a step toward her, then stopped. *"Did,* Samantha? And what about now?"

Samantha saw the agony in his eyes, saw his need, his unspoken plea. *Oh, God— what do I do?*

She knew that she could do nothing less than tell him the truth.

"I do love you, Jack," she said simply. "I wish I didn't. But, God help me, I do."

He reached for her, but Samantha lifted her arms as a shield. "No—don't. Please."

He held out his hands to her, turned palms-up in a gesture of supplication. "At least say you can forgive me, Samantha."

Could she? How could she *not?* Christ forgave, didn't he, had forgiven her and so many others, would forgive Jack as well if he would only ask. How could she dare to withhold her forgiveness from the man she loved more than anyone or anything in the world?

She supposed she could view what he had done as a measure of his love for her. But it was still wrong. Terribly wrong. And so horribly unfair to Terese.

"I...don't know. You'll have to give me time, Jack."

"Woman," he said, his voice raw, his gaze steady upon her, "I would give you anything you asked of me. I would give you the very *world,* if I could. Don't you know that by now?"

His words struck Samantha like a blow. She realized then that she *did* know it, *had* known it for some time. And she also knew in that moment that whether she could trust anything else about Jack or not, she could trust the fact that he loved her.

But somehow, it wasn't enough.

She looked at him, saw his eyes, bruised by fatigue, his features, world-weary and dispirited. She wanted to touch him, to reach out to him and comfort him.

She wanted to *change* him, and she knew she was on dangerous ground. No one was going to change Jack. She could not hope for such a thing. Nor could he change himself. Only God held it in his power to change a heart, to heal a soul.

Please, God...I know you love him enough to help him...Please, somehow...make him the man you want him to be...the man he seems to believe he never can *be. Not for my sake, Lord, but for his good...and for your glory...change him.*

He was watching her with an expression of such tenderness...and such sadness... that Samantha thought he would break her heart.

"Samantha, I can't—"

He broke off as the quiet of the room was shattered by a long, screeching wail.

They both froze in stunned confusion. Samantha saw Jack tense, a frown crossing his face.

"Jack?"

He closed the distance between them in one long stride, grasping her arm and pulling her to his side as the blood-chilling screech again pierced the night.

He spun around, dragging her with him toward the door.

"Jack, what is it?"

"The *Vanguard*'s fire whistle," he said, his eyes reflecting Samantha's bewilderment and sudden surge of fear.

38

IN THE CRUCIBLE

*When you walk through fire you shall not be burned,
and the flame shall not consume you.*

Isaiah 43:2

❧

Before they even reached the door, he heard Madog Wall come roaring up the steps. *"Mr. Kane! Fire! There's a fire in the pressroom!"*

The moment they reached the open door, Jack smelled it—the acrid, scorching odor his cigar smoke must have earlier masked.

He and Samantha almost collided with Madog at the top of the stairway.

"How bad?" Jack saw the fear in Samantha's eyes, the spark of panic in Madog Wall's, and deliberately kept his voice calm and all business.

" 'Tis bad, Mr. Kane! Blowin' up fast, it is. You and Mrs. Harte have to get out of here! Now!"

Jack's mind went into a spin. He glanced from Madog to Samantha, then handed her off to him. "Take Mrs. Harte out. You see her safely outside, and don't come back into the building! I have to see what I can do."

"Oh, Jack—no! You have to come with us!" Samantha cried out.

Already the smell of smoke had sharpened. Jack tightened his grip on her arm. "I won't be long. I have to see if there's any way I can save the presses, Samantha! Go on now—go with Madog! I need to know you're safe outside!"

To his amazement, she pulled back, clutching at his arm. "No, I'm not leaving you in here alone!"

Jack looked at her, then glanced over her head to Madog with a look the big Irishman quickly grasped. As Jack freed himself from Samantha, he set her carefully but firmly back, away from him and into Madog's sturdy arms.

"Is there anyone else in the building?" Jack shouted as Madog led Samantha to the top of the stairway.

"No one but yourself, sir, so look lively! Will the fire station hear the whistle, do you think?"

"We can hope. More likely one of the fire spotters will sound the alarm. As soon as you get outside, start pumping. Use the buckets from the horse barn." Jack stopped, then added, "And yell for help!"

Jack watched them go partway, Madog holding on to Samantha, trying his best to reassure her as they went. "It will be all right now, Mrs. Harte. Mr. Kane, he'll be out directly. For now, though, it's for me to get you out of the building."

Back inside his office, Jack fumbled with the combination on the safe until the door sprang open. His hand was shaking a little as he retrieved the envelopes that held the evidence for the exposé, along with a couple of other packets he couldn't afford to lose.

The odor of smoke was much stronger now, and he knew he had to get to the pressroom without waiting any longer. With a last glance around the office, he started for the door, stopping only long enough to grab his coat off the sofa, where he'd tossed it earlier.

He sprinted down the steps, throwing on his coat and shoving the documents from the safe in his pockets as he went. At the bottom he veered right and took off at a run down the narrow hallway that led to the pressroom. He could see small clouds of smoke floating under the door and out into the hall.

He was almost there when a roar sounded from inside the room and the door exploded open, unleashing a roaring burst of flame and churning smoke. Jack could actually feel the heat. He stopped, stunned by the force of the treacherous blaze. His eyes were already tearing, and his chest burned from the thick fumes of the smoke.

For a moment he could think of nothing but the new steam press—his pride above every other piece of equipment in the pressroom. Then his mind went to all the flammable materials stored inside that room, and he realized the entire building was surely doomed.

Dense smoke and flames were pouring out the door into the hall. There was no way he could get into the room, and if he didn't move fast, the flames would overtake the hall as well, trapping him.

He would not allow himself to think of what the fire would take from him. One thing he was determined it would *not* take was his life.

He turned then and, with the flames beginning to snake along the floor behind him, raced down the hall toward the outside door. His chest was burning as if the fire had exploded inside *him,* and the bitter, black taste of smoke filled his mouth. As he charged out the door and into the street, his eyes sought and found Samantha, watching Madog ply the pump. Jack leaped over a frozen pool of ice and came to stand in front of them.

Samantha's eyes went over him as if to make certain he was all right. There was something else there, too, but Jack had no notion of what. He couldn't think of anything except the *Vanguard*'s going up in smoke, although he realized his hopes

n't entirely dead when he caught himself listening for the sound of the fire
.gon.

Madog paused long enough to give Jack a quick glance. "Thanks be you're all
right, sir!" he said, then resumed his pumping.

Jack wiped a hand over his forehead and, glancing at it, saw that it was black
with smoke.

"Is it bad, sir?" said Madog.

Jack stood staring at the building. "It's bad," he said quietly.

The words were no more out of his mouth than he felt Samantha tug at his arm.
"Jack! Look! Up there!"

Jack glanced at her, then turned to look where she was pointing. His blood chilled
at the sight of a small face framed in the upstairs window of his office. A closer look
revealed a boy, gesturing wildly. Although they couldn't hear the child's screams
through the closed window, there was no mistaking that he was crying for help.

Madog had dropped the pump handle and now stood staring up at the window.
"Merciful Lord, 'tis Whitey!" he cried out.

The little newsboy whose only home was under the steps at the bindery.

"What's he *doing* up there?" Jack groaned.

Madog stood, shaking his head. "Snipe is probably in there somewheres, too.
You don't see one without the other. I'll bet the two rascals let themselves in to get
out of the snow."

Jack had never known the boys to come inside without permission, but perhaps
the storm had made them bold.

He tried to think, but his mind seemed frozen on the sight in his office window.
He couldn't stop the image of the way the fire had blasted through the door of the
pressroom and gone rolling down the hall. By now the blaze had surely cut off the
landing of the stairway.

The boy was probably trapped.

❖

Samantha looked from the terrified child in the upstairs window to Jack. His
face was set in a hard mask, his eyes narrowed as he scanned the *Vanguard* building.
She could almost see his mind working, considering the options—of which there
seemed to be none.

"Could he jump, do you think?" asked Madog Wall.

Jack hesitated, then shook his head. "Even if he managed to break the window,
we'd never catch him. We've nothing to stop his fall."

Suddenly there came the sound of several explosions. Samantha screamed as
windows shattered and smoke began to billow through to the outside.

She felt Jack's arm go around her as he started to drag her backwards. "Madog,
get her away from here!" he shouted, thrusting her toward Madog Wall. "The two
of you, go over to the bindery!"

Indecision crossed the big Irishman's face. "Please, sir, I'll be going after the boy! You stay with Mrs. Harte!"

"No!" Jack roared at him. "No offense, man, but I can move faster! You see to Mrs. Harte—I'm going back in!"

Samantha reached out, grasping his arm. "Jack! No, you can't!"

He turned to look at her, his gaze softening for an instant before he turned back to Madog Wall. "Pour that bucket of water over me, man! Be quick!"

Madog didn't hesitate but picked up the bucket he had just filled and doused Jack with its contents.

Samantha shivered at the sight of his head and topcoat drenched in the bitter cold.

Suddenly in the distance they heard the sound of bells clanging furiously.

"There they come, sir!" shouted Madog. "The fire wagons are coming! There's help for the lad now!"

Others from surrounding buildings had begun to gather as well: newsboys and factory workers who had heard the commotion. Samantha felt a quick surge of hope for the first time since they'd seen the child in the window.

Jack stood, listening to the fire bells, then shook his head. "They'll never get here in time! I'm going after him! Now get away from here—both of you!"

He paused, his eyes hard on Madog Wall. "You're a good man, Madog, and I'd trust you with my life. But right now I'm trusting you with *Mrs. Harte's* life, and hers means a great deal more to me than my own. I don't want you to leave her side, not for a minute, no matter what happens. You understand? If that fire begins to move, you take her and get her a safe distance away. I want your word on it!"

Madog hesitated but after a second or two nodded his head in agreement. "Aye, sir. You have my word."

Again Samantha tried to stop Jack, but he pulled free and went tearing up the walk to the building.

She saw him come to a halt at the entrance door, glance inside, then step back to look up at the second story. She followed the direction of his gaze and saw that the boy was no longer at the window.

At that same instant, the window where the child had been standing only moments before suddenly exploded, shattering glass and blowing debris high into the night sky. Sparks and cinders sprayed the darkness like fireworks.

For the first time, Samantha realized the snow had stopped.

But not the wind.

For a moment she and Madog Wall stood staring in horror at the burning building. Then the big Irishman swept her to his side and propelled her across the street.

From their watching place at the side of the bindery, Samantha saw Jack disappear inside the *Vanguard* building.

She cried his name softly to herself and began to pray.

When Jack saw no trace of the newsboy in the window, he took a tentative step inside the building, then another. He might as well have stepped into a nightmare.

Heat like that of a furnace smacked him full in the face. The stairway was engulfed in flames, the hall leading to the pressroom completely cut off by a curtain of smoke and fire. To his right, the hallway was still clear, but he knew it wouldn't be long before the blaze spread the length of the building.

Already the heavy dark smoke was searing his lungs and scalding his eyes. He was trying to decide which way to move when a scream sounded above him. He looked up and saw the newsboy standing at the top of the stairway. The lad's eyes were wild with terror, his incessant screams nearly choked off by the smoke and roaring flames.

"Mr. Kane! Help me, Mr. Kane!"

Jack saw that the blaze would catch the boy up at any second and waved him away. *"Get away from the stairway, boy! Move back!"*

At first the lad made no attempt to move but simply stayed where he was, screaming his head off.

Again Jack shouted up at him. *"Whitey! Get away from the steps! That way—"* he flung out his arm motioning the boy to the hallway on his right. *"Go to the back of the building, boy! I'll meet you there!"* A thought struck him. *"Whitey—is Snipe in the building, too? Where is he?"*

The boy stared at him, then shook his head. "He—Snipe was in the pressroom."

Jack knew with a sinking feeling that there was no getting the other boy out, not if he was in the pressroom.

"All right, son—you go on now! As fast as you can, you hear!"

Relief flooded him when he saw the boy finally break and run. Taking time only to swab his handkerchief against his wet coat and cover his mouth with it, Jack leaped around the flaming wall and took off down the hallway.

At the back of the building, he saw that although the smoke was thick and heavy, already coiling around the ceiling and windows, the old iron steps that wound up to the second floor were still clear.

He took the steps two at a time, his boots clanging loudly on the metal. At the top, however, there was no sign of the boy.

"Whitey!" He started off down the hall, shouting the boy's name as he went, then came to a dead stop. Between him and the top of the main stairway, which by now was a blazing pyre, the hall that he had prayed would be clear was instead blocked by a veritable barricade of smoke and flames.

Jack looked up and realized that the pocket of fire must have been kindled by the flames snaking along the ceiling and partway down the door frame, reaching the crates and boxes stacked high outside the archives room.

His gaze traveled downward. To his horror he saw the prone figure of the little newsboy lying on the opposite side of the wall of fire separating them.

❧

Across the street at the bindery, Samantha and Madog Wall stood watching the inferno that had been the *Vanguard*. Samantha refused to let herself dwell on the enormity of the loss this would be to Jack. She could do nothing for now except to pray God's protection around him and the little newsboy.

The thought of her last few minutes with Jack in his office, the harsh words, the painful scene between them, struck her like a heavy fist, and she nearly doubled over with the memory.

Oh, Lord, to think that only moments ago I was asking you to change him! Now, all I can think of, all I can pray for, is that you'll save him! Lord, put a wall around him and the child—a barrier between them and the flames! Carry them through the fire, Father! Just…lift them up in your arms and carry them through the fire!

Lord, you know how much I love him! Right or wrong, I can't seem to help myself, even after everything that's happened. Please, Father, in your mercy and in your love, please save Jack! Save him for me…and save him for you! Even if we can never be together, please get him safely out of that building! Please!

She gasped aloud in relief as two fire wagons, bells clanging, finally rounded the corner and pulled to a stop in the middle of the street.

"Thanks be," muttered Madog. "And about time, too."

Their relief was short lived. At the chilling sound of glass shattering, Samantha looked up to see that the whole building now appeared to be ablaze, with smoke and flames pouring from the windows and rising from the roof.

Beside her, Madog Wall added what might have been a fervent petition to her own earlier prayers when he said, in a choked voice, "Lord, have mercy! Only you can save them now!"

With tears stinging her eyes, Samantha again took up her desperate plea in Jack's behalf, now praying the promises of God for him and the child he had gone to rescue.

❧

Jack's chest threatened to explode along with the windows as he dropped to his belly and began to crawl closer to the blazing pocket between him and the unconscious child.

"Hold on, son!" he muttered to himself as he stopped, poised on all fours while he tried to gauge the best way around the fire. There looked to be a fraction more room on the outside wall, but if he went that way and the window blew, he was sure to be caught in a storm of fire and glass.

He opted for the side nearest the wall and started in that direction, again keeping as close to the floor as possible. Even in the space of a few seconds, the flames had fanned out, coming toward him at an incredible speed. In no time the boy would be past reaching.

He was fighting for breath now, his lungs raw and burning from swallowing too much smoke.

He stopped at the very edge of the fire and saw there was scarcely an inch of floor space that wasn't aflame. He knew what he had to do, and he also knew that he was going to get burned, he and the boy both. But his one chance to get Whitey out of the building was to keep low and move far enough into the fire that he could make a grab for the boy and yank him back to himself, quickly enough that neither of them got caught up in the blaze.

Head down, he paused to steel himself before inching any farther. Flames lapped out at him, and for a minute he lost his nerve. He couldn't imagine anything much worse than death by fire. If he turned back now, he could still save himself.

Through the veil of smoke he saw the boy flinch slightly, saw the small, fair head twist a little to the side, and knew he was still alive.

He couldn't just leave him. But he was more frightened than he'd ever been in his life. Still he hesitated, staring into the hellish wall of fire that separated him from the boy.

Suddenly, without warning, it was as if somebody had crawled alongside him and whispered a warning. In that instant he knew he couldn't do what he had to do on his knees. He would have to use his long legs for more than slugging about the city for once and jump—far and high.

He hauled himself upright. The handkerchief he had pressed against his mouth was useless now, dry and smoky. He tossed it aside and stood staring into the fire.

"He will cover you with his pinions, and under his wings you will find refuge..."

Jack looked around, startled. Now where did that come from? It was Scripture, he knew that much, having heard Martha refer to it during the last days of her agony. What, then—a memory?

He let out a long puff of breath, flexing his legs and knotting his fists. In spite of the blistering heat, he suddenly felt cold and began to shake.

But only for an instant. He felt his shoulders clasped by strong, steadying hands as another whisper sounded. From behind him? Or in his head?

"When you walk through fire you shall not be burned, and the flame shall not consume you..."

He turned to look. There was nothing behind him but smoke, thick and oily, nothing in front of him but a wall of fire.

"...the flame shall not consume you..."

Jack took in as much smoke-filled air as he dared and leaped through the fire, sweeping the boy up in his arms and hurling himself and the child into—and out of—the flames, then on down the hall to the back stairway.

He knew. He didn't know how, he didn't know why, but he *knew.* He knew his escape had had nothing to do with *him. Nothing.*

He ran, and with every step, inside his head he was chanting one word, a word that was both plea and prayer: *God!*

God!

God!

And in his soul he knew that in losing everything...he had gained even more.

He made it outside with the boy in his arms, then collapsed in the snow.

39

SECOND CHANCES

The Cross is the hiding place of the hopeless and brokenhearted,
The meeting place for all those
who seek a second chance.

CAVAN SHERIDAN, FROM *WAYSIDE NOTES*

❦

THE CLADDAGH, CO. GALWAY, WESTERN IRELAND, CHRISTMAS EVE

Roweena uncovered the spiced beef, pressed in between two plates, where she had left it to set overnight. After marinating for over a week and simmering most of yesterday, Gabriel's favorite Christmas dish now filled the entire cottage with its piquant aroma. They would enjoy it tonight, cold, along with potato cakes, which were ready to bake, and her own special barm brack, already cooling on the table. Today, as was their custom on every Christmas Eve, they had fasted, but tonight they would break the fast with the late supper she had spent most of the day preparing.

She straightened, watching as Evie added some additional ivy and bay leaves to the mantel above the fireplace. The child was fairly dancing by now with excitement, and Roweena was grateful that Eveleen, at least, seemed determined to display a measure of the season's cheer.

The days leading up to Christmas had been a solemn time this year. Right up to today, there had been no real sign of merriment or festivity, except for wee Evie's brightness and anticipation of the hours to come.

Of all the things that might account for Gabriel's quietness and restraint these days, Roweena hoped that worry for her was not one of them. She was recovering nicely, after all, thanks to his expert care and healing skills. By now her wound required nothing more than a small bandage and a quick examination each day. She had not regained much use of her arm as yet, but Gabriel said that was only a matter of time and proper exercise.

It was not unusual for Gabriel to be somewhat contemplative during the season of Christmas, of course. It had always been a time of reflection for him, a time of much prayer and meditation. Each year during Christmas week, it was his custom to go off by himself for a bit each day, to be alone with the Lord and the Scriptures. Even afterward, he would often seem quiet and somewhat distracted throughout the evening.

This year, however, his times away from the cottage had been more frequent and longer in duration, his moments of preoccupation more often than not marked by deep-creased frowns and eyes clouded with what appeared to be a faint sadness, even a kind of brooding.

He had performed the yearly pre-Christmas tasks as usual: making repairs and patching the cottage, discarding any dross that had gathered inside and out over the preceding months, cleaning the outbuildings and applying whitewash where needed. He had even helped Roweena and Evie scour the furniture with sand, scrub the hearth, and clean the fireplace.

Yesterday he had gone to the *Margadth Mor*—the Big Market—to "bring home the Christmas," just as he always did. In fact, Roweena thought he must have emptied his pockets in the process, for he had returned bearing a fine, plump goose and a more than ample supply of dried fruits, spices, and tea.

Evie had practically swooned at the sight of the delicacies. But when Roweena commented, "Sure, and you've brought home a feast for the kings," Gabriel had merely smiled somewhat absently and gone to sit by the fire.

Any departure from custom had been so slight as to be negligible—except for his uncommonly grave demeanor. Roweena could not help but wonder just how much of his behavior had to do with Brady Kane. She suspected that Brady's betrayal still troubled him greatly, as it did her.

But for herself, it wasn't the actual betrayal she found most painful—although, sure, Brady had done a shocking, terrible thing. What she could not seem to put out of her mind was the stunning revelation that she and Brady might actually be half brother and sister.

There was no way of knowing for certain, of course. According to Gabriel, there had been many soldiers drunk on the whiskey and mad with the blood lust that horrible night. But even the possibility that the same man might have fathered both herself and Brady, no matter how incredible it might seem, could not be ignored.

When she remembered the feelings Brady had once stirred in her at the beginning, when they had first met, a wave of sick shame invariably washed over her. Those feelings had always been confusing and troubling to her, and in truth they had weakened and died long before she'd ever learned of the possible blood tie between herself and Brady. Even so, Roweena still bitterly regretted the fascination he had once held for her.

Every time she looked at Gabriel, she wondered how she could have ever misplaced, even for a moment, her affections. Once she faced the truth about her feelings for *him,* there had been no emotion left for Brady, except a kind of sad fondness, the same sort of hopeless affection she might have felt for a wayward friend.

Or brother.

It was Gabriel she loved. It would *always* be Gabriel, despite the fact that he could not see her as anything but a defenseless child.

In any event, she was concerned about his unusual behavior and decided that when he returned later today she would speak with him about it.

❧

For weeks, Gabriel had heard the rumors about Brady Kane but had steeled himself not to listen, not to care. Whatever happened to the deceitful young American, he had only himself to thank, with his profligate ways, his scheming, and his lies.

It was said in the marketplace and elsewhere that the Yank was drinking himself to death, that in fact Kane lay drunk most every day and night. Gabriel hardened his heart to the stories. If the young fool was indeed intent on killing himself with the drink, then let him have at it.

He was resolved not to feel anything for the boy, not to care even a little about what happened to him. Kane had dug his own hole; let him lie in it.

For a time he had almost succeeded. What man could not harden his heart, after all, if he set his head to doing so?

But it seemed the Spirit had a different idea. At first the nudging was gentle, more a whisper. But when he remained obdurate, the holy whisper became a shout; in the dead of night, at the break of day, when he worked, when he walked, he felt the urging upon his heart until he could no longer ignore what his God would apparently have him to do.

And so he had gone to the city. He had gone grudgingly at first, on the pretense of tending to the boy's wound, which was, in fact, festering badly and in desperate need of attention. Brady was already far more ill than he would have been had he had proper medical care on an ongoing basis. That fact alone had pricked Gabriel's conscience rather sharply.

The rumors about Kane's drinking had not been exaggerated. Each time Gabriel stopped by, he found the American in his cups. It soon became clear that the lad was never sober. His physical condition had deteriorated badly. He had lost a great deal of weight in a very short time, and his skin was tinged with the unhealthy, puffy appearance of the malnourished drunkard.

At first he fought Gabriel, trying to ward him off with a volley of abusive language and self-pitying protests. But finally, seeing that Gabriel would not be turned away, he took to whining about his pain, his wastrel ways, his brother's deception—all the while fueling a poisonous, self-centered hatred.

He seemed particularly fond of insisting that he was hopeless. Forsaken. Lost.

"No man is truly lost unless he chooses to be," Gabriel would counter.

Kane's reaction was to turn suddenly hostile, even angry.

Late one afternoon, Gabriel entered the flat—never locked—and knew an instant of alarm when he thought the boy had died. Sprawled across the bed, clad only in his underclothing, Kane gave no indication that he still breathed.

When Gabriel tried to rouse him, there was no response whatsoever, although by now he knew the lad was still alive. He glanced around the cluttered bedroom and saw several whiskey bottles scattered about, all empty. At first, he was merely disgusted, then angry. He shook Kane hard, not really caring if he hurt him. At last, however, he realized that this was no ordinary drunken sleep: Brady Kane was unconscious.

He flew into action, tugging him over to the pump and splashing cold water over his head. Other than a slight moan, there was still no response.

Gabriel charged out of the flat, taking the steps two at a time, frightening Meg Hannafin, the landlady, nearly out of her wits when he charged into her front room, demanding, "Hot tea or coffee at once!"

For almost two hours he forced strong tea down Brady's throat, doused him with cold water, chafed his arms and legs to get his blood moving, and walked him back and forth through the flat until finally he roused him out of his stupor. Kane awoke in a foul temper and sick with a thunderous headache—but for all that, he was alive.

The next day, Gabriel hired Murtagh Molloy to move in with Kane temporarily. The lad's indignant shouts of protest had bounced off the buildings in Galway City for two days. He stopped raving only because he finally lost his voice.

Big Murt, as he was called, was even larger than Gabriel. Molloy was, in fact, huge, a veritable colossus who never failed to make Gabriel think of a rampaging Norseman. But the man fell into the role of both warden and steward with surprising ease. Of course, considering what he was paying him, Gabriel thought Molloy should perhaps do the wash and feed the geese as part of the bargain.

First thing, the two of them set about clearing every bottle of the drink out of the flat. Within the hour, they had the place as whiskey-free as a nun's prayer closet. And dry it remained. They also took care to remove the young American's clothing, all but his night wear, as well as his room key.

Gabriel put out the word that any man selling the Yank whiskey would answer to both himself and Big Murt. At the same time.

It took nearly three weeks. Kane shouted, he cursed, he pounded the walls until they shook; other times, he cried and took on like a motherless babe. But at last he was sober and reasonably stable.

And with a little help from Big Murt and Gabriel, he had remained so.

But it was time now for the lad to make it on his own, and Gabriel could not help but be concerned for what might happen.

He had gone to Kane's flat again this afternoon with the thought of trying to talk some common sense into that thick head and perhaps even convince him to go back home to his brother.

He found the lad at the desk, head in his hands, staring at what appeared to be a fairly lengthy letter spread out in front of him. Kane looked up when Gabriel entered, but only for an instant before turning back to the vellum sheets on top of the desk.

Gabriel looked at Murtaugh and jerked his head toward the door. The big man gave a nod and stepped outside.

Gabriel waited, and finally, after a long enough time to make the silence awkward if not downright rude, Kane acknowledged his presence. "Making our daily rounds to check on the prisoner, are we?"

Gabriel ignored the jibe. Some days the lad took refuge in sarcasm. Other days he was almost civil. "Good day to you, too, young sir," he said, going to sit down, uninvited, on the only other chair in the room, a lumpy affair by the window.

Once seated, he studied Kane and saw with some concern that the American's eyes were red rimmed, his countenance patently haggard. More troubling still was the noticeable trembling of his hands.

"Not bad news, I hope?" Gabriel ventured, inclining his head to the letter at Kane's fingertips.

The lad's smile was bitter. "Oh, indeed not! It seems that for reasons of his own, my esteemed big brother has finally decided to tell me the charming story of my ever-so-humble beginnings."

His words fairly dripped acid, but Gabriel could hear the pain behind the anger.

"I see."

Kane's eyes were slightly wild as he continued in the same cutting tone. "Yes, apparently Jack's had a recent attack of conscience—a surprise, that, since I was unaware that he even possessed such a burdensome thing—and decided to come clean with the whole ugly truth. I can scarcely wait to write back and tell him that you stole his thunder."

Gabriel remained silent. He found himself hurting for the young American. Why, he wondered, had the brother waited until now? How much better it would have been to tell the lad face-to-face, not in a letter when they were an ocean apart.

"He kept the secret for my own good, of course," Kane said, his voice even harder now. "You have to understand, Gabriel, that my brother is always doing something for my own good. Jack always knows best. About everything."

"Well—at least he has told you the truth, finally," Gabriel said, knowing the words to be rather lame. Given the young American's state of mind, he was hesitant to ask the next question but wanted to know. "And…does he mention the Sheridan girl? Did she arrive safely, then?"

As he watched, Brady Kane seemed to shudder. When he spoke, his voice had dropped considerably. "She had a difficult time of it, apparently. But she's all right now." He passed a hand down the side of his face. "Jack knows everything," he said. "About me and Terese. About the lie. He knows the baby is mine."

Gabriel frowned. "What lie is that?" What sort of a story had the young fool concocted, he wondered?

Brady looked at him, seemed about to answer, then apparently thought better of it. "Nothing. It's nothing. I don't want to talk about Jack," he said firmly. "Or Terese. And I especially do not want to talk about my illustrious *pedigree,* if you don't mind! Whether you realize it or not, it's no easy thing to find out that not only was your father not the man you believed him to be, but worse yet, he was an *Englishman.* And a rapist to boot."

Gabriel shrugged. "There are good Englishmen and bad. The same could be said of the Irish. But in truth I know a little of what you mean, being a foundling myself."

Kane turned toward him, his eyes widening in surprise. "You?"

"Aye. I never knew the identity of my natural parents. I was set out in a basket at the door to Lynch's Castle on a summer's night. Fortunately for me, I was taken in and adopted by an aging couple who treated me as their own." He looked at the troubled young man across from him, studying him for a moment. "Is your brother a bad man, then?"

Kane glanced away, then shook his head. "No, not a bad man. Just—a stiff-necked one."

"Nevertheless, I'm sure he thought he was doing right by you, lad. Don't be too hard on him."

Gabriel stirred himself back to the reason he had come. "So, now—how are you feeling, lad?" Gabriel asked.

Brady scowled at him. "Do me a favor, would you, Gabriel? Stop being so blasted nice to me! I know you hate my guts, so stop pretending you don't! What has all this been about, anyway? A matter of your Christian duty?"

"In the first place, Brady Kane, I don't hate you at all," Gabriel said mildly. "'Tis only you, hating yourself, that would seem to be the problem. And as for my Christian duty, aye, that's a part of it, no doubt, but not the whole."

Kane curled his lip. "No preaching today, Gabriel. I'm not up for it."

Gabriel crossed his arms over his chest. "Perhaps you'd rather talk about what you plan to do next. Will you be going back to the States?"

Brady laughed—an ugly sound. "I haven't the faintest notion what I'm going to do next, but I'm most assuredly not going back to the States. I don't know that I ever will. Jack made one thing perfectly clear, however."

He feigned a stern frown and a harsh tone that Gabriel assumed was meant as mimicry of his brother. "I will earn my own keep from this time forth. From now on, there will be no monthly wage unless I *earn* it."

"That would seem fair enough," Gabriel replied. "'Tis how it is with most men, after all."

"Yes, well, in that event, perhaps I can convince you to give me back my clothes and my wallet," Kane shot back sarcastically. "I can hardly go about the business of earning my own keep until then."

Gabriel studied him. The face, a handsome one when it was not contorted in anger or bitterness, was leaner than it had been when they'd first met. And there had been lines added, he noticed now, lines that gave at least the appearance of maturity. The lad no longer looked like a boy—which indeed he wasn't—but a man. A man who had lived hard and perhaps foolishly, but a man all the same.

"I did what I did to save your life, you know. There was no meanness in it," Gabriel said, hoping it was the truth.

To his surprise, Kane gave him no argument. Instead, he sat quietly, regarding Gabriel with a curious expression. "And perhaps you *did* save my life. Even I know I would have destroyed myself if I'd kept to the same road. But if you don't mind my asking, man, why did you do it? Why did you bother?"

"I thought you were worth saving," Gabriel said simply. "As did the Lord, I'm sure."

"I said no sermons, Gabriel." Kane stopped, glancing away for a moment. When he turned back, his expression had cleared some. The anger and bitterness were no longer evident. In their place was a look that might have been genuine curiosity. "You've gone out of your way to help me, and you took a great deal of abuse from me in the process. Yet you didn't have to do *anything* for me. So why did you?"

Why, indeed? Gabriel wondered. He had asked himself the same question many times. With no real answer, except for one.

"I merely saved your hide, boy, to buy you time for the Lord to save your soul."

"Am I supposed to understand that?"

Gabriel shrugged. "It would be to your benefit to try, I expect."

Brady waved a hand as if to dismiss the subject. "No more talk of saving me, Gabriel. We both know I'm hopeless."

"I know nothing of the kind. 'Tis as I told you, no man is hopeless unless he chooses to be."

"Better stop it, Gabriel," Kane said with a sly look. "Your harping at me only makes me thirsty for a drink."

"Far better that it make you thirsty for a cup of God's grace."

Kane looked at him. "You told me yourself that you're a doctor, but I declare, Gabriel, you do sound a whole lot more like a priest."

Gabriel smiled a little. "'Tis true that I'm a doctor. But I am no priest."

Brady studied him with a quizzical expression. "You really are a doctor, then? But you have no practice."

Gabriel gave a shrug. "My practice is the Claddagh. I care for many people there. Whoever needs me. I simply do not refer to myself as a physician. 'Tis not a title that gives worth to a man, only the good he does."

"Did you *ever* have a practice?"

"I was a doctor on the mission field for a time. I made the choice not to return."

"Because of Roweena." It was a statement, not a question.

Gabriel narrowed his eyes.

"Oh, come on, man! You're in love with her, and don't deny it! But why did you feel it necessary to give up your career?"

Gabriel hesitated, then saw no reason to answer. "It was a choice I made. Roweena was but a child then, and she needed a guardian. She had lost everyone in her world, you see. I could not take a frightened child to the mission field, and I could not bring myself to leave her behind. She had no one. So I stayed."

Gabriel got to his feet. "I should be going. But there is something I would ask you first. 'Tis one of the reasons I came." He paused. "I thought perhaps you might want to join us for Christmas dinner tomorrow."

40

WISE MEN AND KINGS

The Lord has sought out a man after his own heart.

1 SAMUEL 13:14, NLT

❧

From the look of utter astonishment on Brady Kane's face, Gabriel might just as well have asked him to charge into a sea of fire blindfolded.

"You can't be serious!"

"I am entirely serious," Gabriel assured him. "I'll admit that I'm speaking on impulse, without asking Roweena first. But I know her well enough to know she will not mind. To the contrary, she will probably be pleased. She has been fretful for some time now about the state of your health and your heart. And in case you've wondered, she bears you no ill will for what you did."

It was true. They had talked, the two of them, and he had not been surprised to realize that Roweena's only thought for the American was one of concern for him—and even a kind of sadness that he would stoop to such dishonorable behavior.

Even so, there was something here that needed saying, and he commenced to do so. "Your dangerous and foolish scheme might have ended in a terrible tragedy, which you have no doubt realized by now. As it was, your betrayal caused Roweena much pain, in addition to the physical injury she sustained. Nor was wee Eveleen unscathed by your treachery. The child was terrified. She had nightmares for weeks afterward."

Kane's expression was one of abject misery, but when he started to speak, Gabriel stopped him. "To their credit, neither bears you any grudge. Roweena's heart is a forgiving one, as is the child's."

Kane shook his head, as if to clear it. "I—don't know what to say."

"Well, whatever you might want to say, it would be best said to Roweena and the child, I'm thinking. We will set an extra place. If you decide to come, you will be made welcome."

He turned as if to go, then stopped. "There was one other thing—"

Kane, his expression still somewhat stunned, gave a distracted nod.

Gabriel was suddenly uncertain as to whether he should even ask. But he had to know. He had to.

"The night...you were shot. You said something—"

Again he stopped, unable to get the words out.

Kane was watching him, one eyebrow raised in a question.

"You said...that Roweena—that you saw her love for me in her face. You said that she loved me, that she meant to die for me—"

Again Kane nodded, his gaze raking Gabriel's face. "You honestly didn't know, then? You had no idea?"

"No." Gabriel looked away. "And I can scarce believe it, despite what you seem to think—"

"Gabriel," Kane said softly, "I know what I saw. And you'd see it, too, if you would only open your eyes. Roweena is no child for you to watch over. She is a woman, and make no mistake, man, she's in love with you."

Gabriel finally managed to expel the breath he'd been holding. He looked at Brady Kane, half expecting to see a sneer. Instead he saw something that could have almost been taken for a kind of affection.

"I must go," he said again, now somewhat embarrassed and anxious to get away. "You think about tomorrow. It will be awkward for you at first—for all of us, no doubt—but it will be all right. If you want to come, that is."

"Gabriel—"

Gabriel turned back to him, waiting.

"I suppose I should thank you. For everything."

Gabriel could not stop a smile. "That would seem to be in order."

"But I still don't pretend to understand why you did it," Kane said. "Roweena... Evie...they could have been killed. You as well. Because of me. You could have had me prosecuted! Yet you didn't. I don't see how you...how *any* of you...can possibly forgive what I did. And I certainly don't understand why you went out of your way to help me. No one would have blamed you if you had just let me die."

"I expect the Lord God would have made things sorely miserable for me if I had done that. I don't know what to tell you, lad. There is no disputing the fact that you are a thickheaded, self-indulgent, reckless young fool."

He saw Kane wince, but there was no easy way to say this. "I'll not deny that at first I tended to you somewhat grudgingly. I wasn't at all convinced that you were worth my efforts. In truth, I believe I was more inclined to snap your neck than lend you a hand. But for some reason known only to him, God had other ideas, and he pressed me until I simply had to obey. Now that is the only answer I can give you, whether you understand it or not. I expect God merely used me to keep you from destroying yourself, so he might yet have his way in your life."

Brady shook his head. "Gabriel, Gabriel—you are a study! Why would you even think the Almighty would want anything to do with the likes of me? I'm sure he prefers to deal with a better class of fellow than myself, and who would blame him?"

Gabriel tried to think, tried to pray at the same time. *Lord, there must be some way to penetrate that thick skull and that cynical heart. Show me, for I am at my wit's end with this boy.*

Something occurred to him, and he leaned against the door frame, considering. "There was a man," he finally said, "who, if truth were told, more than likely could have matched you sin for sin, Brady Kane. Indeed, in many ways, I would say there is much resemblance between the natural man in each of you. Like you, he was a man of the arts: a singer, a writer of songs, a fine musician. He was also a sensual, passionate man, at times to his own destruction.

"This man, he probably didn't miss much when it came to mucking up his life. He lied when it was expedient. At times he manipulated, at least when it was in his best interests. He even feigned madness," Gabriel went on, with a slight shake of his head, "in order to extricate himself from a nasty piece of business. He was also a murderer. He slaughtered men by the thousands and ten thousands. Perhaps worst of all, he sent one of his own men—a good man, it would seem—to his death…just so he could seduce the man's wife."

"Even *I'm* not that bad," Brady muttered, cracking a sardonic smile.

Gabriel didn't answer his smile. "He did all that and other terrible things as well, this man. And yet, the Lord God, didn't he call him 'a man after my own heart' in spite of his sinfulness? He loved this man. He treasured him. He prospered him, even made him a king. And through this man—this philandering, scheming, often devious, bloodstained man—God established the lineage of his only beloved Son, Jesus the Christ."

Gabriel stopped. "Perhaps you've heard of him? He was David, son of Jesse. Writer of the Psalms. King of Israel. And in many ways, a man like you, Brady Kane. Only wiser."

He stopped, aware of the other's now unwavering attention. "David, don't you see, was wise enough to know that no matter how far he ran or how grievously he sinned, he could not escape the love of his Father God. He was human, and so he sinned. But he was loved with a divine love, and so he was forgiven. And always, *always,* he was wise enough to accept his God's forgiveness and begin anew."

Gabriel looked at the young American long and hard. "That is the mark of a real man, I'm thinking. A man of strength and wisdom will not spurn his Creator's love and forgiveness. He will not lightly reject the divine opportunity to begin anew. And if you would once take the time to read that copy of the Scriptures I left lying on your desk some weeks ago," Gabriel said, inclining his head toward the desk where Kane sat, "you would find instance after instance of other men who gained such wisdom only after reaching the point where all seemed lost and hopeless."

He turned then and opened the door, but Brady Kane's voice stopped him before he could step outside.

"Gabriel?"

He turned back. The American was standing now, a faint, wry smile softening his features. "So long as we're speaking of wisdom, I have to submit that a true man of wisdom would surely recognize the love of a woman when he is faced with it day in and day out."

Gabriel stared at him, not knowing whether to berate him for his Yankee insolence or salute him for his boldness, given the tenuous state of their relationship. He did neither, instead merely lifted a hand in farewell, saying, "'Tis Christmas Eve, Brady Kane. I wish God's peace on you."

Then he left for home.

After Gabriel had gone, Brady stood staring at the closed door for a long time. He felt as edgy as a cornered cat, and he wanted a drink in the worst way. Yet he knew that if he weakened and somehow found the means to acquire a bottle, there would be no help for him this time. Gabriel had done more than any other man would have done. He wasn't likely to find another savior next time around.

Besides, he hated the thought that he couldn't lick this on his own. He had always prized his independence—or at least what independence Jack had allowed him. What did it say about him if he let himself become enslaved to something as crude as a bottle of whiskey?

He began to pace the room, thinking. Thinking about Gabriel Vaughan, who had never known his birth parents but apparently hadn't let it influence his life. He thought about Jack, who had tried his best to keep him from learning the truth about *their* parents. Yet even in the face of his still raw bitterness and shock, he knew that Jack had only meant to shield him.

Finally, he thought about a man named David, who seemed to have broken all the rules and yet had apparently been given more than his share of "second chances."

Was that what Gabriel had been trying to do for him, Brady wondered? Give him a second chance?

He stopped in the middle of the room, clenching his fists. He still felt as if every nerve ending in his body was screaming in protest at his hard-won sobriety. But that was one thing he *wouldn't* think about. He didn't dare.

Just then, his hulk of a jailer—"Big Murt"—let himself back into the flat. He was carrying a piece of Brady's luggage, and, without so much as blinking, walked up to Brady and set it down at his feet.

"Gabriel told me I should give you back your belongings now," he said. At the same time, he handed Brady the key to the flat. After a moment, he smiled, saying, "Well, then, I expect I will be on my way now. Best of luck to you, Brady Kane."

The only sound in the flat seemed to be that of Brady's hammering heartbeat as he stood contemplating his sudden solitude. The key in his hand felt as if it were burning his skin. He looked from it to the door, then turned, crossed the room to the desk, and placed the key on top of it.

After a moment, he sat down and, with slow and precise movements, folded Jack's letter and returned it to the envelope, tucking it inside the desk drawer for now. He would think about his brother later.

Along with a lot of other things.

For a moment, he sat staring at his hands, which were trembling slightly. Finally, he stirred, and, picking up the small, worn Bible lying where Gabriel had placed it, began to thumb through its pages.

41

CHRISTMAS EVE IN THE CLADDAGH

I follow a star
Burning deep in the blue,
A sign on the hills
Lit for me and for you.

JOSEPH CAMPBELL

❦

That evening they lit the three-branched candle, to commemorate the Holy Trinity. Later they would also light the large Christmas candle, which would burn through the night to show the Christ child that he was welcome in this house.

They took their time over their food, and when they had finally finished, Gabriel pulled away from the table, smiling contentedly. "I'm thinking 'tis a good thing altogether that we do not indulge ourselves like this more than once a year," he said, pulling back a bit from the table and thumping his stomach. "Else I would no longer be able to squeeze through my own doorway."

Roweena returned his smile, thinking that she could not remember a time when Gabriel had weighed a pound more or less than he did today.

He had returned late, too late for any discussion before the supper. But to Roweena's relief, he had seemed more himself this evening, teasing Eveleen and offering frequent and high praise for the food.

As he had at the beginning of the meal, Gabriel now led them in a prayer, this time an evening blessing. He kept his head up, to make certain Roweena could read his lips:

"In thanks we came to this table, sweet Lord and Savior…In thanks we rise and ask your angels round our hearth, your spirit in our heart, your blessing on the heads of all who love and serve you in this house."

Roweena rose immediately to remove the dishes, but to her surprise, Gabriel lifted a hand to stop her. "Let it wait for a time, and I will help you later."

Roweena scarcely knew what to do. She never allowed Gabriel's help in the preparation of a meal or in tidying up afterward. It simply was not done.

As she stood there, watching him in confusion, he turned to Evie. "I would speak with Roweena alone now, lass. Why don't you go along and ready yourself for bed?"

The child thrust out her chin, but he forestalled any attempted protest. "Later, you may share a last cup of tea with us, and we shall look for the Christmas star. But only if I hear no grumbling in the meantime."

Wee Evie looked at him, seemed to consider her options, then smiled. "Aye, but may I ask you first, Gabriel—"

He gave a nod, his expression tolerant and indicating that he already knew what was to come.

"Do you think," said the child, "that the animals will kneel at midnight? To worship Baby Jesus?"

Roweena smiled at the tender look that crossed Gabriel's rugged face. Evie had asked this same question every Christmas Eve since she could string words together— at least three years now. And every year, Gabriel could be depended upon to give the same answer.

"Why, I do not know, child," he said, taking Evie onto his lap. "Though some say such a thing does happen. 'Tis a secret, is it not? But what I *do* know, and this is no secret, is that one day the world itself shall kneel before the Christ and confess him King."

Satisfied, Evie locked her arms around his neck and kissed him soundly on his bearded cheek, then hopped down and scurried off to the back of the cottage, disappearing behind the curtain.

For just a moment, Roweena's heart swelled with love for the two of them. Then she realized that she was still standing, doing nothing, and habit again urged her to clear the table. She actually reached for a platter, but Gabriel caught her hand in restraint. "Sit down, lass. I want to talk with you."

Confused by his behavior, Roweena sank down onto the chair directly across from him, waiting. She wanted to speak with him, too, after all, so perhaps this would be her opportunity. But she would have been more comfortable waiting until her work was finished.

Gabriel sat watching her for a moment before he spoke. Her faint smile looked a bit uncertain, and her hands were clenched on top of the table as if she didn't quite know what to do with them. With some amusement, he realized the reason for her discomfort and, giving her a teasing smile, said, "This table will not quake beneath a few dishes left unwashed, lass."

She returned his smile with a sheepish one of her own.

"First, tell me how it goes with your shoulder today," he said. "Has it troubled you much?"

"Not a bit. Though won't I be glad when my arm is no longer so useless?"

"Once you increase the exercises, you'll see a marked improvement," he reassured her.

He dragged his gaze away from her slender hands for a moment to study his own but remembered to lift his face before he spoke again, so she could read his words. "Roweena—if I have seemed somewhat—preoccupied of late, I wanted you to know that it's nothing to be concerned about. In any event, I thought perhaps I should explain."

She leaned forward a little, obviously intent on what he was about to tell her. So she had been worried after all. He should have told her sooner; he knew that now. But he hadn't been at all sure how she would react, and he didn't want to trouble her, as the injury to her shoulder…and the one to her heart…had not yet healed.

"First, I would like to ask you something," he continued. " 'Tis about Brady Kane, though if you would prefer that we not speak of him, I'll understand."

She tilted her head in a puzzled expression. "I don't mind…talking about Brady. I seldom think about the…trouble he brought upon us. In my heart, I still feel sadness, but I have forgiven him. But what is it, Gabriel? Has something happened?"

Gabriel chose his words with great care, determined not to distress her. "I thought, at least for a time, that perhaps you had…feelings for him. I even asked you as much, if you recall."

A sudden flush spread over her face, and she quickly looked away. Fearing that he had embarrassed her, Gabriel again touched her hand to get her attention. When she looked at him, he went on, as reassuringly as possible. " 'Tis all right, lass, if that's the case. There was no way you could have known—about the other. The two of you are young, after all, and Brady Kane is a well-favored young man. And you, Roweena, you are a lovely young woman. It was a natural thing entirely if you were taken with him, and him with you. But now that you know—that there could be the same blood between you, well, you mustn't reproach yourself for anything you may have felt before you knew. Tell me you aren't, lass."

She looked at him, then shook her head. "No…not so much now. At first I felt…ashamed, you know? But in truth, my…feelings for Brady were so short lived and so fleeting that these days when I think of him at all, I usually try to think of him—I hope you don't mind my saying this, Gabriel—but I try to think of him as my…brother." She stopped, then added, "And it seems he could be."

Gabriel studied her, not for the first time greatly touched by the gentleness of her spirit, her forgiving nature—her honesty. He squeezed her hand a little. "Well…that's fine, then. So long as you have peace with it all. He is doing well now, by the way. I thought you'd want to know."

She brightened a little. "You've seen him?"

He told her then what had transpired in the preceding weeks, told her everything, leaving out only the coarser details. Her gaze scarcely left his face during the entire account.

Only when he had finished did Gabriel realize that he was still holding her hand. He made no move, however, to release it until he saw that tears had pooled in her eyes. Dismay clenched his heart, and he immediately got up and went around the table and sat down next to her on the bench.

"Oh, lass, don't, now! Don't cry. He will be all right. I have surrendered Brady Kane to the Lord's hands, and so must you. It's for God to take care of him now."

Awkwardly, he patted her shoulder. He was surprised by her reply when it came.

"But, Gabriel, I'm not weeping...for Brady Kane! I'm weeping because you are such...a kind, good man! To think that all this time...I have been worried for you, thinking that you were off somewhere...because you were troubled...and instead you were busy taking care of a man...who betrayed your trust!"

Gabriel could not seem to manage a proper response to that, indeed could not seem to do anything except continue the ineffectual patting of her shoulder. "Well, now...it will all work out in the end. I'm sure."

"Oh, it will, Gabriel! I know it will, thanks be to God—and thanks to *you.*"

It struck him then that there would likely be no better time than this, while they were close...and alone...to speak his heart. Gently, he took her by the shoulders and set her just far enough away from him that she could read his lips...and he could see her eyes. "Roweena—there is something else I would ask you."

She was looking at him in absolute trust, and Gabriel knew a sudden moment of utter panic. What if he was wrong? What if Brady Kane had been wrong? What if he somehow destroyed the bond between them, the good and pure affection that had grown throughout the years? Did he really want to risk that?

"Gabriel?"

At her quiet prompt, he searched her eyes, hoping desperately for a glimpse of whatever it was that Brady Kane had claimed to see. But her gaze on him was, as always, warm and trusting, and fond, too, there was that. But love?

And then Gabriel realized that he did not exactly know what love looked like in a woman's eyes.

"I—in truth, I am almost fearful of asking you—what I had intended to ask," he stammered.

Her delicate brows knit in a frown. "But you can ask me anything, Gabriel. What is it?"

He took so deep a breath he almost strangled on it. He seemed to have lost both his wits and his speech, all at the same time. "Roweena—what about your feelings for *me*, lass? Have you ever thought...what I mean to say is, how do you...think of me?" He felt a fierce rush of color spread over his face and could have trounced himself for being such a great *gommel.*

He dragged his gaze back to her and saw that her cheeks, too, were flushed with color. But where he was cringing, she was smiling.

"Oh, Gabriel...are you sure you really want me to answer that?"

His hands on her shoulders were trembling like those of a palsied old fool! He hadn't the courage to look at her, instead fastened his gaze on the candle in the middle of the table. "If you'd rather not, Roweena, I understand."

Oh, Lord, give me the courage to hear the truth, for I know her well enough to know she will not speak anything less. Unless—out of some misplaced sense of obligation, she might try to say what she thinks I want her to say. No, not that, please, God, I would rather she despise me than be...grateful...to me...

"Gabriel?"

He glanced back at her, almost fearfully. Her enormous gray eyes seemed to have caught the firelight as she studied him. Then she moved toward him, catching him entirely unawares as she lay her head against his chest.

Gabriel hesitated, then slowly slipped his arms around her in an awkward, uncertain embrace. He was fighting for every breath, it seemed, and lost the battle entirely when she said, her words muffled against his chest so that he had to strain to hear, "I think of you with love, Gabriel. 'Tis the only way I've *ever* thought of you, the only way I know *how* to think of you."

The knot in Gabriel's throat increased by half. He cupped the back of her head and tipped her face up toward his. "What are you saying, then, lass?"

"What are you *wanting* me to say, Gabriel?"

He gave everything over, then: his pride, his common sense...his heart. "I expect I am wanting to hear you say that you...could love me, Roweena. As a woman loves a man. That you could love me in that way, at least a little."

"And what if I...love you more than everything, Gabriel Vaughan? What if I always have?"

He squeezed his eyes shut for an instant, then opened them. "Is that the truth, lass?"

She smiled at him, and he could see the firelight flickering in her eyes, and he saw something else as well, and wondered how it was that he had not seen it before this moment, for it was as bright and shining as a star. He saw her love for him.

He traced the sweet line of her cheek with his fingertips, marveling at the sheer perfection God had made of her face. "As for me," he choked out, "it seems I have loved you forever. I have loved you since you were a wee lass, holding on to my hand and trying to match my wide steps. I have loved you as a brother and as a friend. But, oh, *mo chridh, mo chridh,* if it pleases you, I would love you from this time forth as a husband and a lover."

She eased back from him, only a little. "Are you asking me to marry you, Gabriel?"

"Indeed, I am, lass," he said, finally managing to cross the vast ocean of uncertainty and go where his heart had long wanted to be.

The firelight in her eyes began to dance the instant before she came into his arms again in a rush of softness and sweetness. "Then I am saying yes," she murmured against his heart, leaving Gabriel slightly startled...and infinitely thankful.

He might have held her forever, just as they were, had not wee Eveleen peeped out from behind the curtain, dark eyes snapping with impatience. "Gabriel? *Now* can we go looking for the star?"

Holding Roweena with one arm, he opened the other to the child, who immediately came bolting across the room to complete their circle. "Aye, *alannah,*" he said. "The three of us, we will go searching for the star together."

42

OUT OF THE ASHES

Out of the ashes of broken trust,
The rubble of failure and dreams burned to dust,
Out of the ruins of human deceit,
The pain of betrayal, the shame of defeat,
God sifts the gold from this worthless debris,
Lifting the good only his eyes can see,
Then turns the wheel of his sovereign design
And changes the dross of life to the divine.

BJ HOFF

NEW YORK CITY

It was Christmas morning, and Wall Street was almost entirely deserted. The light snow that had fallen the night before glistened beneath a light glaze of ice. There was no wind, leaving the city blanketed in a white stillness.

Jack Kane stood in front of the ruins of the building that only days before had housed the *Vanguard,* formerly one of the largest, most influential newspapers in the state.

His newspaper. His dream. His greatest success.

His life.

Or so he had once thought.

He smiled grimly to himself, partly to relieve the pain, but more because, no matter what else he felt, there was no mistaking the irony of it all. What had taken him nearly two decades to build had been reduced to a heap of bricks and ashes in one night by a couple of homeless newsboys. Sadly, one of those boys had died in the very fire he helped to ignite.

Had Whitey, the younger of the two, not lived to tell the tale, Jack might never have known the ones responsible. But Whitey *did* live and was only too eager to name the man who had paid him and his now deceased cohort, Snipe Jenkins, to set the blaze. The reason for Whitey's eagerness, of course, was Jack's promise, in exchange for the information, to do what he could to keep the boy out of the lockup.

The man who had set the two little miscreants to their dirty work was already gone. Avery Foxworth had hotfooted it out of the city before the police—or Jack— could get to him. Most likely he was on his way back to where he'd come from.

It still made Jack's blood boil that his former attorney would not have to pay the piper for his treachery. But it was done, and if he were altogether honest he supposed that throwing Foxworth's black hide into a cell wouldn't have helped much, if at all, to ease the hurt. So let the British have him then, and good riddance.

But Turner Julian and his corrupt pals who had hired Foxworth to double-cross Jack—well, now, that might be another story entirely. Granted, one frightened newsboy's word wasn't much. But it was a start.

Had they really thought he would quit if they burned him out? He doubted it. More than likely their main intent hadn't been so much to ruin him—surely they knew he would be heavily insured—but more to destroy whatever evidence he held against them, to foil any chances he might have against their lawsuit in the courts. By razing his building, they would also slow him down considerably, just in case he tried to retaliate in print.

Well, they might have accomplished that much at least. But they wouldn't stop him. There would be no end to any of this until he saw Julian and the others behind bars. He still had the evidence of their dubious dealings in prostitution and other questionable "business" practices. And he would have Whitey's testimony. If that wasn't enough—then somehow he would just have to find more.

Meanwhile, the documents they had sought to destroy in the fire were now safely stored in his desk at home.

But that was for another day. Today was Christmas, and he still had gifts to deliver. He was going to Grace Mission later in the morning, no matter how unpleasant it might turn out to be.

That it *would* be unpleasant he didn't doubt.

Still, he had taken the first step to making peace with Terese Sheridan days before. In truth, the girl had been decent enough about it—more so than Jack had a right to expect. Once she realized he was in earnest and meant to bully her no longer, that in fact he was even hoping to help her and the child, financially or otherwise, she had accepted his apologies, albeit somewhat coldly.

True to form, she had gone on to let him know that since she had a *position* now, she would not be needing his help. Nevertheless, Jack intended to find a way around her stubbornness. That baby she was carrying shared his blood, after all.

As for her brother—it would be a very long time, if ever, Jack suspected, before Cavan would be able to even tolerate the sight of him, much less grant him the grace of forgiveness. Jack understood, but even so, the loss of the boy's respect and admiration grieved him more than he would have anticipated. But as Rufus had reminded him, there were always bitter consequences to a man's sins.

The most bitter of all, of course, was the loss of Samantha. Not that she had ever been his to lose. Everything he had tried in order to win her had failed, even before the night of the fire. But what he had tried to do to Terese Sheridan had finally and irrevocably marked the end of any relationship they might have had—even their friendship.

He still thought about trying to see her at some point, though not in hopes of redeeming himself with her—he knew when he was defeated, after all. If he couldn't convince her to marry him when he could have still offered her...*everything*...he certainly had no chance whatsoever now. But he wanted at least to tell her how sorry he was, how deeply he regretted what he had done.

He had made no attempt in that direction, however, at least not yet. He still needed time: time to try to make some sense of what had happened to him inside that burning building two weeks ago. What had happened—and what it meant.

All he really knew for certain at this point was that he was different. He had come out of that fire changed in a way he would have never thought possible.

Rufus had tried to help him sort through it during the days that followed, was still helping him, one step at a time. God bless the man, he had accepted Jack's story at face value, never once questioning its veracity or its plausibility. Of course, Rufus being Rufus, he had practically been beside himself with joy for Jack and what he emotionally referred to as "finally, the answer to ten years of storming heaven for the most hardheaded man in the city!"

Jack wasn't sure he would ever find the courage to face Samantha, no matter how much time passed. He had no reason to hope she would even agree to see him, much less believe anything he told her. Worse still, there was always the possibility she would think it just another scheme on his part to wear her down and convince her to marry him.

Unable to bear the pain that the thought of Samantha still brought to him, he shoved his hands down inside his pockets and took a last look at the remains of what had once been the most important thing in the world to him.

On impulse, he walked around the rubble to see if he might spot anything worthwhile, anything that might still be usable. He was stooped over, sifting through the ashes surrounding a ruined piece of metal from one of the old presses, when the sound of a buggy coming to a stop made him turn and look toward the street.

What he saw brought him to his feet, heart pounding.

Samantha, in David Leslie's buggy, was pulling up in front of the building—the little that was left of the building, that was. Too stunned to move, Jack stood watching as she stepped out of the buggy and began to walk toward him.

She had never looked lovelier, her face rosy from the cold and framed in the black velvet hood of her cape. A touch of lace could be seen at her neck, above the fastenings of her wrap, and as she picked her way carefully toward him, he caught a glimpse of highly polished black boots.

The sight of her struck him like a blow, taking his breath.

She slowed her pace when she saw him watching her, as if she might be reluctant to reach him. But she didn't stop until she came to stand in front of him, only inches away.

"Samantha." He heard the strangled sound of his own voice, as if the cold air had snatched the word up and blown it out across the debris of the building.

"Hello, Jack."

He was somewhat surprised that she would meet his gaze so directly. When he thought about seeing her again, he almost always figured she would turn away from him—if not *run* away from him.

Instead, she stood there, searching his face as if she were looking for something.

Jack forced himself to meet her gaze, making no attempt to conceal his feelings as he did so.

❦

She had not seen him since the night of the fire, and as she faced him, Samantha was shocked to see how he had seemed to age in so brief a time. She was almost certain there had not been so much silver along his temples before, nor had his deep-set eyes ever looked so shadowed. Those were new lines bracketing his mouth, and his face looked even leaner than she remembered.

The softness in his eyes was new, also, as was the utter lack of defiance, and even the old, bristling arrogance seemed to have disappeared. But it was more than that. Even though he definitely looked rather the worse for wear, he seemed to have acquired a kind of…stillness about him that had never been there before.

He glanced at the street, at the buggy parked there, and his mouth quirked a little. "Have you stolen the good doctor's buggy for good, then, Samantha?"

Samantha smiled. "No, but he does tend to be excessively generous with it. I promised not to take advantage of his good nature any more after today. It's just that I…wanted to see you, to tell you how sorry I am about—everything." She inclined her head toward the ruins behind him, her heart aching for all he had lost.

She was relieved to see that he didn't seem nearly as devastated—or as angry—as she would have expected him to be. "How are you, Jack?" she finally asked, somewhat lamely.

"Well enough."

"Have you thought about what you're going to do? About the paper?"

He glanced over his shoulder, then back to her.

"Rebuild, of course. Right here."

She almost smiled at the decisiveness that was so much a part of his nature. "Yes, I thought you would."

"I'm glad you came, Samantha. I've—wanted to see you. Just hadn't worked up the courage as yet."

His faint smile was somewhat shaky, Samantha thought.

Suddenly, she couldn't remember anything she'd come here to say. Only that she had to see him, had to see for herself that he was all right. It was Christmas, after all, and he had lost so much.

More than anything else, however, she had to see for herself if it was true, what Rufus had told her.

And it was. She saw it in his eyes now, and for the first time in a long time, the stone lying heavy on her heart began to lift.

"You said you wanted to see me," she ventured. "Was there—something special?"

❦

Jack wished he could simply blurt out the truth: *Because I'm dying without you in my life! Because I need you more than I need anything else in the world! Because I love you beyond all telling!*

Instead, he merely stood there gaping at her like a colossal fool. "I wanted to tell you how sorry I am—for what I did," he finally managed. "For all of it."

She was looking at him with a peculiar expression. "Actually, you *did* tell me. The night of the fire."

"Yes, well, there's—something else, something that happened later, that I wanted you to know." He pulled in a deep breath, and the cold air burned his lungs.

"I do know."

Jack stared at her. "You know—what?"

"I've talked with Rufus," she said, not quite meeting his gaze. "He told me...everything. I hope you don't mind. He thought you might want me to know, but he wasn't sure you'd tell me; he was afraid you might be too—"

"Hardheaded?" Jack offered.

"I believe that was the word he used, yes," she said, turning back to him with a faint smile. She stood there, as if she wanted to say more but wasn't sure she ought to.

"Well, for once, Rufus is wrong. I would have told you—if I'd thought you'd see me, that is—but I wanted to wait until I'd thought it through more carefully. I had to know it was—real."

"And?"

"Well—I don't pretend to understand it, not all of it. But it seems to me that it's real." Jack paused. "And I'm fairly certain you had a hand in it."

She gave him a questioning look, but something told Jack she knew exactly what he was talking about.

"That night, when I was still inside the building, you were praying for me the entire time. Weren't you?"

Her look was guarded, but he could see the flare of curiosity in her eyes as she nodded. "How did you know?"

Jack thought about how to answer her, decided there *was* no answer. Not really. "I didn't, at least not then. Not until later. What I *did* know was that I didn't get myself or the boy out of that building on my own. I was—well, Rufus says I was *delivered* out of the fire."

"And what do you think?" she asked softly.

He cracked a ghost of a smile. "Did you ever try to argue with Rufus?"

She returned his smile. He had been so hungry for one of her smiles, Jack realized now. Starved for it.

"Actually, no," she said. "I don't believe I would want to match wits with Rufus."

"Then you take my meaning. Besides, I could no more deny it than explain it. Rufus is right: I was delivered out of that fire. Something—no, *Someone*—literally picked me up, the boy and myself, and carried us out of that building. That's what I believe happened, and I'd be the poor fool altogether if I were to try to convince myself that anyone other than the Almighty himself could pull off such a feat."

She was studying him with such intensity that Jack felt as if his very soul had been laid bare to her scrutiny. But somehow that didn't bother him now, not as it might have before. He wanted no more secrets in his life, especially where Samantha was concerned.

Samantha couldn't stop herself from searching those dark, disturbing eyes. But for the first time since she'd known Jack, the gaze she had more often than not found unfathomable—shuttered tightly against her and the rest of the world—now looked back at her with an unwavering directness that stole her breath.

There was a kind of freedom in that look she had never sensed before today. It was almost as if the man behind that gaze had been imprisoned and was now unbound.

Oh, my Lord…it's what I prayed for, isn't it? It's what I've begged you for all this time!

She realized she had missed whatever he said. "I'm sorry?"

"I wasn't burned. There isn't a mark on me or the boy." His words came faster now and fired with a kind of passion she could see reflected in his eyes. "I *heard* him promise me that I wouldn't be burned. And I wasn't. It was as if the fire never even touched me. But it *did*. There was no way it could *not* have touched me."

Samantha had all she could do to look at him. She was strangling to keep from bursting into tears.

Thank you, Lord! Oh, my wonderful, all-powerful Lord—thank you!

"Samantha?"

She looked at him, still fighting back her tears.

"Do you believe me?"

"Oh, Jack! Of course, I believe you!" It was all she could do not to close the brief distance that lay between them and take his hand, touch his face. She wanted… needed…to touch him.

She saw him drag in a deep, ragged breath. He closed his eyes for just an instant, then opened them. "Samantha—I promised myself I wouldn't do this. I have absolutely no right—but now that I see you, I have to ask. Samantha, is there—can there ever be any chance—for us?"

A raw, tearing pain knifed through Samantha's heart at the thought of walking away from him now. He *had* changed, she didn't doubt it for a moment. So strongly could she sense the Lord's working in his life that she no longer feared she might be in opposition to God's Word by marrying him.

Jack had changed.

But had *she?*

"You're afraid," he said quietly, never taking his eyes off her. "Of what, Samantha? The past? Because of what happened with Harte? Or are you afraid of me, afraid to trust me?"

The tenderness in his eyes was almost Samantha's undoing. Only now did she become aware of how close together they were standing.

When had he moved? Or was it *she* who had moved?

She shook her head. "I'm not sure. Both, I suppose."

"Do you know what I think, sweetheart?" he said, his voice low and slightly hoarse as he took her by the shoulders.

Samantha refused to meet his eyes.

"It strikes me," he went on without waiting for her to answer, "that a God who can carry a man and a child through a burning building and bring them out completely untouched can most likely take away any scars the past might have seared upon your spirit." He stopped, then added, "And in the process, perhaps he might even help you find a way to trust a hardheaded but somewhat wiser Irishman. What do you think?"

His hands tightened on her shoulders as he gently pulled her closer to him. "Samantha?"

He tipped her chin to make her look at him, and when she did, when she drank in the strong features and the depth of feeling in his eyes, she realized with a sudden, startling clarity that he was right. She had to trust the God who had saved Jack from the fire—and saved him from eternal death—to now enable her to trust *Jack*.

Her throat seemed swollen shut. She could only manage a small nod as he pulled her into his arms. He held her, his chin resting on top of her head for a moment, neither of them saying a word.

"Jack?" she said, finally stirring.

He dipped his head to look into her eyes.

"The last time you asked me to marry you, you told me not to give you an answer just then, to wait."

Something glinted in his eyes as he watched her, waiting.

"I'd like to give you my answer now, if that's all right."

His arms tightened around her, and Samantha lifted her face for his kiss.

"Is that your answer?" he said afterward, smiling into her eyes.

"Well—first I have a request."

He looked at her.

"I think I understand now what you were trying to do—about Terese's baby," Samantha said carefully.

A quick flash of pain and remorse crossed his face. "Samantha—"

She put a finger to his lips to silence him. "No, wait. I know now that you did what you did out of love for me. As wrong as it was, I understand what was behind it. And I forgive you."

He expelled a long breath. "Thank you, sweetheart."

"But I was wondering—"

His dark brows lifted.

"I never wanted Terese's baby—"

"Ah, I know that, Samantha. It was foolishness entirely on my part—"

Again she touched his lips. "I want Shona."

He blinked, and Samantha went on. "If you really want to give me a child, Jack, I would like it very much if Shona could be that child."

His eyes narrowed a little as he regarded her with just a trace of his old speculative scrutiny—and the hint of a smile. "Shona, is it?"

"Don't you see? She has no one else but Terese. And with the baby coming, it might be difficult for Terese to give Shona as much attention as she needs."

He seemed to consider the idea. "That's true. Of course, the lass would be needing *two* parents, it seems to me, not just a mother."

"Yes," Samantha said softly. "That's what I had in mind."

Somewhere across the city, Christmas bells began to ring with the ancient glad tidings and great joy...and the promise of peace for all who believed.

Epilogue

*Be very careful never to forget what you have seen the Lord do for
you. Do not let these things escape from your mind
as long as you live! And be sure to pass them on to
your children and grandchildren.*

Deuteronomy 4:9, nlt

Samantha and Jack were married in May of 1840. Shortly after their wedding trip, they adopted Shona Madden. In the years that followed, they adopted two other children, both Irish immigrants who had been orphaned: Donal, adopted at age four, and Molly, adopted at six months.

Jack rebuilt the *Vanguard,* which eventually became one of the largest and most influential newspapers in the country. He and Samantha labored throughout their marriage to found several immigrant aid societies. They also established two city orphanages.

Until his death, Jack Kane pioneered a number of reforms for the immigrants flooding America in the 1800s. The questionable reputation that once shadowed him eventually faded into the past, and he became known instead as a man of great faith and compassion, as well as one of true vision for the role of the Irish in America's future.

To celebrate their fifteenth wedding anniversary, Jack and Samantha journeyed to Ireland, where he was reunited with his brother, Brady.

Gabriel and Roweena became man and wife during the summer of 1840. In addition to Eveleen, whom they raised as their own daughter, they became the parents of four children: three sons, Matthew, Brian, and Connor; and one daughter, Aisling. Throughout most of the years of their marriage, they opened their home and their hearts to children who had nowhere else to go.

Terese Sheridan married David Leslie a year after giving birth to her son, Kieran, whom David later adopted. In time they allowed Jack Kane to share in Kieran's life as his uncle, along with Terese's brother, Cavan. They also had a daughter named Nessa, after Terese's mother.

Terese worked alongside David in the mission houses of New York City and continued her efforts even after David went to be with his Lord.

Brady Kane never returned to the United States but spent his life in Ireland. He became an artist of some renown, recognized especially for his landscapes of rural Ireland, Galway in particular. For most of his life, he struggled between a hard-won faith and a tendency toward alcoholism. He never married, nor did he ever meet the son he fathered with Terese Sheridan. He remained friends with Gabriel and Roweena Vaughan until his death at the age of forty-nine.

Cavan Sheridan rose to prominence as a reporter and a journalist, eventually reconciling with his friend and employer, Jack Kane, for whom he established a nationwide news service. In addition to his *Wayside Notes,* he also published several other books of poetry and essays with the Kane publishing houses. At the age of twenty-nine, he married Selia Ryan, a young Irish immigrant from County Clare, who bore him eight daughters and one son.

The descendants of the Kanes, the Vaughans, and the Leslies carried on the faith of their parents, passing down God's Word and his love to succeeding generations on both sides of the Atlantic.

BJ Hoff's bestselling historical novels first appeared in the CBA market more than twenty years ago and include such popular series as An Emerald Ballad, The American Anthem, and her most recent, The Mountain Song Legacy. BJ's critically acclaimed novels reflect her efforts to make stories set in the past relevant to the present, and continue to cross the boundaries of religion, language, and culture to capture a worldwide reading audience.

A former church music director and music teacher, BJ and her husband make their home in Lancaster, Ohio, where they share a love of music, books, and time spent with their family.

Be sure and visit BJ's website: **www.bjhoff.com**

Coming soon...

Bestselling author BJ Hoff promises to delight her many faithful readers with her compelling new series, The Riverhaven Years. With the first book, *Rachel's Secret,* Hoff introduces a new community of unforgettable characters and adds the elements readers have come to expect from her novels: a tender love story, the faith journeys of people we grow to know and love, and enough suspense to keep the pages turning quickly.

When the wounded Irish American riverboat captain, Jeremiah Gant, bursts into the rural Amish setting of Riverhaven, he brings chaos and conflict to the community—especially for young widow Rachel Brenneman. The unwelcome "outsider" needs a safe place to recuperate before continuing his secret role as an Underground Railroad conductor. Neither he nor Rachel is prepared for the forbidden love that threatens to endanger a man's mission, a woman's heart, and a way of life for an entire people.

Available October 2008

To learn more about books by BJ Hoff
or to read sample chapters, log on to our website:

www.harvesthousepublishers.com

HARVEST HOUSE PUBLISHERS

EUGENE, OREGON